'We've got the theory; now I'm t⌐
the ash and started toward the wat⌐

'Thou seekest to follow him, then⌐ Gwen kept pace with him determinedly. 'And if thou dost?'

'Then he'll have company. You stay with the other three, while we find our way back—but don't hold dinner.'

'Nay! If thou dost . . . *Rod*! Thou . . . ' Then whatever she was saying faded away. Rod turned back toward her, frowning . . .

. . . and found himself staring at the trunk of a tree.

A white trunk, white as a birch, but corrugated like an oak—and the leaves were silver.

Rod stared.

Then, slowly, he looked up, and all about him; all the trees were just like the first. They towered above him, spreading a tinsel canopy between himself and the sun; it tinkled in the breeze.

Also by Christopher Stasheff
in Pan Books

**Warlock: To the Magic Born**

Christopher Stasheff

# The
# Warlock
# Enlarged

PAN BOOKS
London, Sydney and Auckland

*To Mary Margaret Miller Stasheff*
*Wife and Mother*

*The Warlock Unlocked* first published 1982 by Ace Books, New York
*The Warlock Enraged* first published 1985 by Ace Books, New York
Both books first published in this edition 1991 by Pan Books Ltd
Cavaye Place, London SW10 9PG
2 4 6 8 9 7 5 3
© 1982, 1985 by Christopher Stasheff
ISBN 0 330 31116 6

Printed in England by Clays Ltd, St Ives plc

# Contents

# The
# Warlock
# Unlocked

# Prologue

Pope John XXIV said his first Mass with the whole world watching through its 3DT cameras. He said his second at sunrise the next morning, with a handful of devoted clerics watching, in a little chapel adjoining his chambers. Not too many were willing to get up at 5:00 a.m., even for a Mass said by the Holy Father.

After a frugal breakfast – he had resurrected the quaint, antique custom of saying Mass on an empty stomach, in spite of what his doctor told him that thimbleful of wine every morning was doing to its lining – the Pope sat down at his desk to face his first day on the job.

Cardinal Incipio gave him just time enough to get settled before entering with an armful of fiche-wafers. 'Good morning, Your Holiness.'

'Good morning, Giuseppe.' Pope John eyed the bulging case, sighed, and pulled over his wafer-reader. 'Well, let's get started. What've you got for me?'

'An air of mystery.' Cardinal Incipio produced an ancient envelope with a magician's flourish. 'I thought you might like to start the morning with a dash of intrigue.'

The Pope stared at the nine-by-twelve parchment container. 'You've certainly got my attention. What, by all the stars, is *that*?'

'An envelope.' Cardinal Incipio handed it to him reverently. 'Be careful, Your Holiness; it's rather old.'

'An envelope.' The Pope took it, frowning. 'Enclosures for messages. So *large*? It *must* be old!'

'Very old,' Cardinal Incipio murmured, but Pope John wasn't hearing him. He was staring, awed, at the sprawling, handwritten inscription:

> To be opened by:
> His Holiness, Pope John XXIV
> On 23 August 3059

Pope John felt a tingling spread from the base of his neck over his upper back and shoulders.

'It's been waiting a very long time,' Cardinal Incipio said. 'It was left by a Dr Angus McAran, in 1954.' And, when the Pope remained silent, he went on nervously, 'It's amazing anyone was able to keep track of it, buried in the vaults like that. But it *was* hermetically sealed, of course.'

'Of course.' His Holiness looked up. 'One thousand one hundred and five years. How did he know I'd be Pope on this date?'

Cardinal Incipio could only spread his hands.

'Certainly, certainly.' The Pope nodded, glowering. 'I can't expect you to know. In fact, it *should* be the other way around – but I'm afraid Papal Infallibility is only in matters of doctrine, and even then, only *ex cathedra* . . . Well! No sense sitting here, contemplating in awe!' He took out a pocket-knife and slit the flap. It broke with a skeleton's rattle. Cardinal Incipio couldn't restrain a gasp.

'I know.' The Pope looked up in sympathy. 'Seems like desecration, doesn't it? But it was meant to be opened.' Carefully, gingerly, he slid out the single sheet of parchment the envelope contained.

'What language is it?' Cardinal Incipio breathed.

'Early-International English. I don't need a translator.' Even as Cardinal Kaluma, Pope John had still found time to teach an occasional course in comparative literature. He skimmed the ancient, faded handwriting quickly, then read it again very slowly. When he was done, he lifted his eyes and stared off into space, his dark brown face becoming steadily darker.

Cardinal Incipio frowned, worried. 'Your Holiness?'

The Pope's eyes snapped to his, and held for a moment. Then His Holiness said, 'Send for Father Aloysius Uwell.'

The pitcher crashed to the floor. The child darted a quick, frightened glance at the video pickup hidden in the upper right-hand corner of the room, then turned to start picking up the pieces.

In the next room, Father Uwell nodded, and sighed, 'As I expected.' He turned to the orderly, waiting at the back of the chamber. 'Go clean that up for him, would you? He's only eight years old; he might cut a finger, trying to do it himself.'

The orderly nodded and left, and Father Al turned back to the holovision tank with a sad smile. 'So many unbreakable materials in this world, and we still prefer our vessels made of glass. Reassuring, in its way . . . and so is the boy's glance at our hidden pickup.'

'How so?' Father LeBarre frowned. 'Is it not proof that his powers are magical?'

'No more than his making that pitcher float through the air, Father. You see, he made no use of the paraphernalia of magic – no mystic gestures, no pentagrams, not even a magic word. He simply stared at the pitcher, and it lifted off the table and began to drift.'

'Demonic possession,' Father LeBarre offered half-heartedly.

Father Al shook his head. 'He's scarcely even naughty, from what you tell me; if a demon possessed him, it would make him a very unpleasant child indeed.'

'So.' Father LeBarre ticked off points on his fingers. 'He is not possessed by a demon. He does not work magic, either black or white.'

Father Al nodded. 'That leaves us with one explanation – telekinesis. His glance at the 3DT pickup was very revealing. How could he know it was there, when we did not tell him, and it is well hidden, built into the ceiling? He probably read our minds.'

'A telepath?'

Father Al nodded again. 'And if he is telepathic, it's quite probable that he's also telekinetic; psi traits seem to run in multiples.' He stood. 'It is too early for a complete opinion, of course, Father. I will have to observe the boy more closely, inside this laboratory and outside – but at the moment, I would guess that I will find nothing of the supernatural about him.'

Finally, Father LeBarre dared a smile. 'His parents will be vastly relieved to hear it.'

'Now, perhaps.' Father Al smiled, too. 'But before long, they will begin to realize the problems they will have, rearing a telekinetic and telepathic boy who has not yet learned to control his powers. Still, they will have a great deal of help, possibly more than they want. Telekinetics are rare, and telepaths are even more so; there are only a few dozen in the whole of the Terran Sphere. And in all but two of them, the talent is quite rudimentary. The interstellar government realizes that such abilities may be of enormous benefit, so they take a great interest in anyone found to possess them.'

'The government again,' Father LeBarre cried, exasperated.

'Will they never be done meddling in the affairs of the Church?'

'Beware, Father – the government might think it is you who violates the separation of the Church and State.'

'But what was more natural than to bring him to the priest?' Father LeBarre spread his hands. 'This is a small village; only the magistrate represents the Terran government, and no one represents the DDT. The parents were on the verge of panic when objects within their house began to fly through the air in the boy's presence. What was more natural than to bring him to the priest?'

'Natural, and wise,' Father Al agreed. 'For all they knew, it might have been a demon, or at least a poltergeist.'

'And what was more natural than that I should call upon my Archbishop, or that he would call upon the Vatican?'

'Quite so. And therefore I am here – but I doubt not I'll find no taint of the supernatural, as I've said. At that point, Father, the matter ceases to fall within our jurisdiction, and moves to the government's. "Render unto Caesar . . . "'

'And is this boy Caesar's?' Father LeBarre demanded.

A soft, muted chime spared Father Al from answering. He turned to the comscreen and pressed the 'accept' button. The screen blinked clear, and Father Al found himself looking through it into a Curia chamber, hundreds of miles away in Rome. Then the scene was blocked by a brooding face under a purple biretta. 'Monsignor Aleppi!' Father Al smiled. 'To what do I owe this pleasure?'

'I have no idea,' the Monsignor answered, 'but it should be a great pleasure indeed. His Holiness wishes to speak to you, Father Uwell – in person.'

'"On 11 September 3059 (Terran Standard Time), a man named Rod Gallowglass will begin learning that he is the most powerful wizard born since the birth of Christ. He dwells on a planet known to its inhabitants as 'Gramarye' . . . " Then he gives the co-ordinates, and that's all. Nothing more but his signature.' The Pope dropped the letter on his desk with a look of disgust.

Joy flooded through Father Al; he felt like a harp with the wind blowing through it. His whole life he had waited for it, and now it had come! At last, a real wizard!

Perhaps . . .

'Reactions?' His Holiness demanded.

'Does he offer any proof?'

'Not the slightest,' His Holiness said in exasperation. 'Only the message that I've just read you. We've checked the Public Information Bank, but there's no "Rod Gallowglass" listed. The planet is listed, though, and the co-ordinates match the ones McAran gives. But it was only discovered ten years ago.' He passed a faxsheet across the desk to Father Al.

Father Al read, and frowned. 'The discovery is credited to a Rodney d'Armand. Could it be the same man?'

The Pope threw up his hands. 'Why not? Anything is possible – and nothing probable, when you've so little information. But we checked his PIB bio. He's a younger son of a cadet branch of an aristocratic house on a large asteroid called "Maxima". He had a short but varied career in the space services, culminating in his enlistment in the Society for the Conversion of Extraterrestrial Nascent Totalitarianisms . . . '

'The what?'

'I don't think I could say it again,' His Holiness sighed. 'It seems to be a sort of government bureau that combines the worst aspects of both exploration and espionage. Its agents are supposed to seek out the Lost Colonies, decide whether or not their government is headed towards democracy and, if it's not, put it onto a path that will eventually evolve a democracy.'

'Fantastic,' Father Al murmured. 'I didn't even know we had such a bureau.'

'Any government that's overseeing three-score worlds should have a bureau that just keeps track of all the other bureaux.' His Holiness spoke from personal experience.

'I take it, then, that this Rodney d'Armand discovered a Lost Colony on Gramarye.'

'Yes, but the Lord only knows which one,' the Pope sighed. 'You'll notice that the PIB sheet doesn't tell us anything about the inhabitants of the planet.'

Father Al looked. Sure enough, any human information on the planet was summed up in one word at the bottom of the page: CLASSIFIED. It was followed by a brief note explaining that the planet was interdicted to protect its inhabitants from exploitation. 'I'd guess it's a rather backward culture.' Excitement thrilled through Father Al's veins – were they backward enough to still believe in magic?

'Backward, indeed.' The Pope peered at another paper on

his desk. 'We checked our own data bank, and found we did have an entry on the planet – just a very brief report, from a Cathodean priest named Father Marco Ricci, that he'd accompanied an expedition by a group calling themselves the "Romantic Emigrés". They found an uncharted, Terra-like world, seeded a large island with Terran bioforms, and established a colony, four or five hundred years ago. Father Ricci requested permission to establish a House of the Order of St Vidicon of Cathode – your own Order, I believe, Father Uwell.'

'Yes, indeed.' Father Al tried not to let his disappointment show; the Cathodeans had to be engineers as well as priests. No planet could be *too* backward, if they were there. 'Was he granted permission?'

His Holiness nodded. 'So it says; but apparently the Curia was never able to convey the news to him. The Intersellar Dominion Electorates fell about that time, and the Proletarian Eclectic State of Terra was established. As you know, one of the first things PEST did was to lose the Lost Colonies. There was no way to communicate with Father Ricci.'

'Well, that's hopef — I mean, that might create problems.'

'Yes, it might.' The Pope fixed him with a glittering eye. 'We may have another splinter sect there, calling themselves Roman Catholics, but out of touch with us for centuries. No telling what heresies they'll have dreamt up in that time.' He sighed. 'I'd hoped to have a rest from that sort of thing for a while.'

Father Al knew what the Pope meant. Just before he'd been elevated to the Chair of St Peter, Cardinal Kaluma had conducted the negotiations with the Archbishop of Burbank, a Lost Colony that had been found about twenty years before. They'd managed to keep the Faith fairly well, except for one heresy that had taken firm root: that plants had immortal souls. It turned out to be a fundamental point of doctrine on Burbank, since the whole planet was heavily involved in botanical engineering, with the goal of creating chlorophyll-based intelligence. The talks had become rather messy, and had ended with the establishment of the Church of Burbank. Its first act had been to excommunicate the Church of Rome. His Holiness hadn't been quite so drastic; he'd simply declared that they were incommunicado, and that the Church of Burbank could no longer really be said to be Roman Catholic.

A shame, too. Other than that, they'd been so sane . . .

'I will be discreet, Your Holiness, and only report accurately what I discover.'

'Oh?' The Pope fixed Father Al with an owlish eye. 'Are you going somewhere?'

Father Al stared at him for a moment.

Then he asked, 'Why else would you have sent for me?'

'Quite so,' His Holiness sighed, 'I admit to the decision. It rankles, because I have no doubt that's what this McAran intended.'

'Have we any choice, really?' Father Al asked quietly.

'No, of course not.' The Pope frowned down at his desktop. 'A letter that's been lying in the vaults for a thousand years acquires a certain amount of credibility – especially when its sender has managed to accurately predict the reign-name of the Pope. If McAran could be right about that, might he not be right about this "wizard"? And whether the man is really a wizard or not, he could do great damage to the Faith; it has never proven terribly difficult to subvert religion with superstition.'

'It's so tempting to believe that you can control the Universe by mumbling a few words,' Father Al agreed.

'And too many of those who are tempted might fall.' The Holy Father's frown darkened. 'And, too, there is always the infinitesimal chance of actually invoking supernatural powers . . . '

'Yes.' Father Al felt a shadow of the Pope's apprehension. 'Personally, I'd rather play with a fusion bomb.'

'It would do less damage to fewer people.' The Pope nodded.

Pope John XXIV stood up slowly, with the dignity of a thundercloud. 'So. Take this with you.' He held out a folded parchment. 'It is a letter in my hand, directing whoever among the clergy may read it, to render you whatever help you require. That and a draft for a thousand Therms, are all the help I can send with you. Go to this planet, and find this man Gallowglass, wherever he is, and guide him to the path of the Lord as he discovers his wizardry, or the illusion of it.'

'I'll do my best, Your Holiness.' Father Uwell stood, smiling. 'At least we know why this man McAran sent his letter to the Vatican.'

'But of course.' The Pope smiled, too. 'Who else would've taken him seriously?'

# Chapter One

There was a crash, and the tinkle of broken glass.

'Geoffrey!' Gwen cried in exasperation. 'If I have told thee once, I have told thee twenty times – thou must not practise swordplay in the house!'

Rod looked up from Gerbrensis's *Historie of Gramarye* to see his smaller son trying to hide a willow-wand sword behind his back, looking frightened and guilty. Rod sighed, and came to his feet. 'Be patient with him, dear – he's only three.'

' 'Tis thy fault as much as his,' Gwen accused. 'What business has so small a lad to be learning o' swordplay?'

'True, dear, true,' Rod admitted. 'I shouldn't have been drilling Magnus where Geoff could watch. But we only did it once.'

'Aye, but thou knowest how quickly he seizes on any arts of war. Here, do thou speak with him, the whilst I see to the mending of this vase.'

'Well, I didn't know it then – but I do now. Here, son.' Rod knelt and took Geoff by the shoulders, as Gwen knelt to begin picking up pieces, fitting them together and staring at the crack till the glass flowed, and the break disappeared.

'You know that was your mother's favourite vase?' Rod asked gently. 'It's the only glass one she has – and glass is *very* expensive, here. It took Magnus a long time to learn how to make it.'

The little boy gulped and nodded.

'She can mend it,' Rod went on, 'but it'll never be quite as good as it was before. So your mummy won't ever have it looking as nice as it did before. You've deprived her of something that made her very happy.'

The little boy swallowed again, very hard, and his face screwed up; then he let loose a bawl, and buried his face in his father's shoulder, sobbing his heart out.

'There, there, now,' Rod murmured. 'It's not *quite* as bad as I made it sound. She *can* mend it, after all – psi-witches have an advantage that way, and your mother can manage telekinesis on a *very* fine scale – but it *was* very naughty, wasn't it?' He held Geoff back at arm's length. The little boy gulped again, and nodded miserably. 'Now, buck up.' Rod pulled out a handkerchief and dabbed at Geoff's cheeks. 'Be a brave boy, and go tell your mummy about it.' Geoff nodded; Rod turned him toward Gwen, gave him a pat on the backside, then stood back to watch.

Geoff toddled over to Gwen, stood mute and apprehensive until she was done melding the last piece back in place, then lisped, 'I sorry, Mummy. Di't *mean* to.'

Gwen heaved up a sigh that said chapters, then managed a smile and tousled his hair. 'I know thou didst not, my jo. 'Twas happenstance; still, when all's said, thou *didst* break it. 'Tis why I have told thee to keep thy swordplay out of doors. So thou wilt ever keep thy manly arts out of housen from this day forth, wilt thou not?'

Geoff nodded miserably. 'Yes, Mummy.'

'And thou wilt obey thy mother henceforth?'

'Er-huh . . . But, Mummy!' he cried, in a sudden wail of protest, 'was *raining*!'

Gwen heaved a sigh. 'Aye, and I know, thou couldst not go out of the house. Yet still, jo, 'twas then time to draw up thy pictures.'

Geoff made a face.

Gwen bent an accusing eye at Rod.

He looked around, frantically, then pointed to himself, with an incredulous look.

Gwen leaped up and marched over to him. 'Aye, thee! How many times hast thou said thou wouldst show him the drawing of a moated keep? That, at least, he would draw – once, and again, and a thousand times! Wilt thou not do it?'

'Oh, yeah!' Rod slapped his head. 'I didn't really *have* to do research this morning. Well, better late than never . . . '

They both whirled around at an explosion of wailing, screaming, and angry barking.

Magnus had come in from the boys' room and found the evidence. He stood over little Geoff, waving a heavy forefinger down from the height of his eight years of life-experience. 'Nay, 'twas foully done! To break a present to our mother that I was so long in the crafting of! Eh, little Geoffrey, when wilt thou learn . . . '

And Cordelia had sailed in to Geoff's defence, standing up to her big brother from five years' age and forty inches' height. 'How durst thee blame him, who didst bar him from his own room . . . '

'And mine!' Magnus shouted.

'And his! Where he might have played to's liking with hurt to nought!'

'Be still, be still!' Gwen gasped. 'The baby . . . '

On cue, a wail erupted from the cradle, to match Geoffrey's confused bawling.

'Oh, *children!*' Gwen cried in final exasperation, and turned away to scoop up eleven-month-old Gregory, while Rod waded into the shouting match. 'Now, now, Geoff, you haven't been *that* naughty. Magnus, stop that! Scolding's *my* job, not yours – and giving orders, too,' he added under his breath. ''Delia, honey, it's very good of you to stick up for your bother like that – but don't be good so loudly, OK? . . . *Sheesh!*' He hugged them all, pressing their faces against his chest to enforce silence. 'The things they don't tell you about the daddy business!'

On the other side of the room, Gwen was crooning a lullaby, and the baby was already quiet again. Rod answered her with a quick chorus of:

'Rain, rain, go away!

Come again some other day!'

'Well, if you really want it, Daddy.' Magnus straightened up and looked very serious for a minute.

'No, no! I didn't mean . . . oh, stinkweed!' Rod glanced at the window; the pattering of the rain slackened, and a feeble sunbeam poked through.

'Magnus!' Gwen's tone was dire warning. 'What have I told thee about tampering with the weather?'

'But Daddy *wanted* it!' Magnus protested.

'I did let that slip, in an unguarded moment,' Rod admitted. 'But it can't be just what *we* want, son – there're other people who actually *like* the rain. And everyone *needs* it, whether they like it or not – especially the farmers. So bring it back, now, there's a good boy.'

Magnus gave a huge sigh that seemed to indicate how disgustingly irrational these big people were, screwed up his face for a moment – and the gentle patter of raindrops began again. Cordelia and Geoffrey looked mournful; for a moment there, they'd thought they were going to get to go out and play.

'Odd weather we're having around here lately,' Rod mused, wandering over to the window.

'In truth,' Gwen agreed, drifting over to join him with Gregory on her shoulder. 'I cannot think how he does it; 'twould take me an hour to move so many clouds away.'

'Yeah, well, just add it to the list of our son's unexplained powers.' He glanced back at Magnus, a chunky boy in tunic and hose with his hand on the hilt of his dirk. His hair had deepened to auburn, and the loss of his baby-fat had revealed a strong chin that puberty might turn to a lantern jaw – but Rod could still see the affectionate, mischievous toddler. Strange to think his powers were already greater than his mother's – and his father's, of course; Rod had only knowledge and wit, and a computer-brained robot-horse, on his side. But Magnus had the wit already.

They all did. Cordelia was a flame-haired fairy-slender version of Gwen. Golden-haired Geoff had a compact little body that would probably grow up into a unified muscle, where Magnus would probably turn lean and rangy; golden hair that would probably stay that way, though Magnus's was darkening; clear, blue eyes that seemed to show you the depths of his soul, and a square little chin that seemed made for deflecting upper cuts.

And Gregory, who was fair-haired and chubby, though not as much as a baby should be, who was so very quiet and reserved, and very rarely smiled – an enigma at less than a year, and a prime focus for Rod's chronic, buried anxiety.

Each of them gifted enough to drive Job to distraction!

There was a knock at the door.

Gwen looked up, enquiringly.

Rod stepped over to the panel with a sinking stomach. Knocks meant trouble. So much for his quiet day at home!

He opened the door, and found what he'd expected – Toby the warlock, in his mid-twenties now, grinning and cheerful as ever, in the livery of a King's courier. 'Good day to thee, High Warlock! How goes it with thee?'

'Hectic, as usual.' Rod smiled; he couldn't help it, when Toby was around. 'Step in, won't you?'

'Only the moment; I must be up and away.' Toby came in, doffing his cap. 'A fair day to thee, fair Gwendylon. Thy beauty never fades!'

'*Uncle Toby!*' shrieked three gleeful voices, and three small bodies slammed into him at speed. Rod put out a hand to prop up the esper, who was crooning, 'Ho-o-o, whoa, not so quickly there! How goes it wi' thee, Geoffrey-my-bauble? Cordelia, little love, thoul't steal my heart yet! Good Magnus, good tidings!'

'What did you bring me, Uncle Toby?'

'Can I play with your sword, Uncle Toby?'

'Toby! Unc' Toby! Can'y?'

'Now, now, children, let the poor man capture his breath!' Gwen pried her brood off her guest with tact and delicacy. 'Thou'lt take ale and a cake, at least, Toby.'

'Ah, I fear not, sweet Gwendylon,' Toby sighed. 'When I said I must be away, I spoke not lightly. Queen Catharine is wroth, and the King waxes sombre.'

'Oh.' Gwen's glance went to Rod, and a shadow crossed her face. 'Well, I should not complain. I've had thee home a week, now.'

''Fraid the work goes with the title, dear,' Rod said, commiserating. 'Twenty-four-hour-call, and all that.' He turned to Toby. 'What's going on?'

'I know only that I was summoned to fetch thee, with their Majesties' compliments and a request for greatest speed.' Toby inclined his head knowingly. 'Yet I know the Lord Abbot approaches Runnymede at greatest speed.'

'Yeah, there has been something brewing between the Church and the Crown, hasn't there? Well, I'd better let Tuan fill me in on it.'

'In Runnymede, then!' Toby raised his hand in farewell. ''Til next we meet, fair mother!' And his form started to waver around the edges.

'Toby,' Gwen said, quickly but firmly, and the young warlock's form stabilized again. 'Not in the house, if you please,' she explained. 'An you do, the boys'll be popping in and out in all manner of places the rest of the day, and part of the night!'

'Oh! Aye, I had forgot. Well, 'tis gratifying to know they hold me in such regard. Farewell, children!' He doffed his cap, and stepped to the door.

'Uncle Toby!' cried three anguished voices, and they pressed forward to their friend. He slipped a hand into his belt-purse, cast a quick, furtive look at Gwen, then tossed a quick spray of candies at the children and ducked out the door as they scrambled for the booty.

Gwen heaved a sigh. 'They'll never eat now! Well, I'd best delay dinner.'

'Yeah, but I think you'd better not keep it warm for me.'

Rod looked up at the thunder-rumble as air rushed in to fill the space where the young warlock had just disappeared. He turned back to Gwen. 'From the sound of it, this could go on for some time.'

Gwen shook her head. 'But *why* do they not call thee when they know such broils are brewing? Why do they always wait till the troubles are come?'

'Well, you know Catharine – she always thinks she and Tuan can handle it on their own, until the moment arrives. Then they want me by, just for moral support.'

'And skill,' Gwen reminded him. 'When 'tis all done, 'tis thou who hast averted conflict, not they.'

'Yeah, well, you can't expect one of the teams to referee.' Rod leaned forward to kiss her. 'Bear up without me, darling. I'll be home when I can.'

'Papa's going!' Cordelia shrieked, and delight filled the air as the children ran for the back room window that faced the stable, to wave goodbye when Papa left.

Gwen caught Rod's sleeve and glanced back, waiting till all three were out of sight. Then she leaned forward and hissed, 'Beware, my lord! I would I could'st go with thee, to guard thy steps.'

'Why?' Rod frowned. 'Oh! Those idiots and their ambushes . . . Don't worry, dear. Their marksmanship's no better than their intentions.'

'Yet how oft have they tried, my husband?'

Rod pursed his lips. 'Well, now, let's see . . . ' He started counting on his fingers. 'There was the cretin who took a potshot at me from the steeple in that village – what was it, about a year ago now?'

'Eleven months,' Gwen corrected. 'Three weeks ere Gregory was born.'

'Eleven months, then. He didn't seem to realize that a crossbow bolt can't possibly go as fast as a robot horse with a built-in radar. And there was that so-called "peasant", who jumped out of a hay wagon with a laser – poor chump.' He shook his head sadly. 'He didn't realize he should've waited until he was away from the hay before he pulled the trigger.'

''Twas good of thee, to pull him from the flames, and hurl him into the millpond. Still, his lance of light did come but a hair's-breadth from thy body.'

'Yeah, but Fess side-stepped in time. And there was that guard at Tuan's castle; Sir Maris is still wearing sackcloth and ashes because the enemy managed to infiltrate his troops. But, that! My Lord, that was a joke! You can see a pike blow coming a mile away! It takes at least a quarter-second to swing a ten-foot pole; all I had to do was dodge, and yank the shaft as it came past.' He shook his head, remembering. 'He went right past me, into the moat – and Fess wasn't even with me on that one.'

'Aye, my lord, but 'tis the only one of these ambushes in which he hath not saved thee – and he may not 'company thee within the castle. Nay, sweet lord, take care!'

'Oh, don't worry.' Rod reached out to caress the line of her jaw. 'I'll be wary. After all, I have something to come home to, now.'

The great black horse looked up as Rod stepped into the stable, and a voice spoke through the amplifier embedded in the bone behind Rod's ear. 'I detected a warlock's arrival, Rod, and his departure. Are we off to the castle, then?'

'We are.' Rod threw the saddle on Fess's back. 'Just a Sunday outing, I think.'

'But it is Wednesday, Rod.'

'Well, the clergy'll be there, anyway. The Lord Abbot himself.'

Static whispered in Rod's ear – Fess's equivalent of a sigh. 'What game is the Church beginning?'

'Cards, probably.' Rod tightened the girth and took down the bridle. 'At least, I'll have to keep a poker-face.'

'Are you sure of your hand, Rod?'

'The best,' Rod fitted the bridle, grinning. 'Full house, Fess.'

As they rode out of the stable, the back window of the house exploded into a hail of goodbyes, and the frantic waving of three little hands.

A few minutes later, as his steel horse's gait ate up the miles between his home and the King's castle at Runnymede, Rod mused, 'Gwen's worried about the assassination attempts, Fess.'

'I will always guard you, Rod – but I do wish that you would take greater precautions.'

'Don't worry – they bother me, too, but in a different way. If our futurian foes are suddenly working so hard to get rid of me, they must have plans for a big push at toppling Tuan's government.'

'Why not say "revolution", Rod?'

Rod winced. 'Nasty word, when it's my side that's in power. But they do seem to be gearing up for a big offensive, don't they?'

'I agree. Could this conference between the Abbot and Their Majesties signal the beginning of such an offensive?'

Rod scowled. 'It could, now that you mention it. The totalitarians have pretty much exhausted the "Peasants' Revolt" motif for the moment, and the anarchists have ridden the "Barons' Rights" movement into the ground. They've got to try a new theme, haven't they?'

'The Church-State conflict has a long tradition, Rod. Henry II of England had a protracted feud with St Thomas à Becket, Archbishop of Canterbury, because the Church's authority obstructed Henry's attempts to centralize government. The feud ended with Thomas's murder, and Henry's public humiliation; he was forced to grant concessions to the Church. His son, King John, was more obstinate; John's feud with the Pope resulted in England being laid under the Interdict, which meant that no baptisms, weddings, or funerals could be held – no Masses could be said, no confessions heard; none of the sacraments could be performed. To the medieval mind, this was disaster; most of the people of England felt they were being doomed to Hellfire eternally, because of their King's sin. The resulting pressure was so great that John had to publicly repent, and do penance. The Protestant movement in Christianity succeeded partly because the German princes welcomed an excuse to oppose the Holy Roman Emperor. England became Protestant because Henry VIII wished for a divorce that the Pope would not grant him. The Inquisition, the Huguenot Rebellion . . . the English Civil War occurred partly because the nation was Protestant, but ruled by a Catholic King . . . The list goes on. It is small wonder that, when the United States of America was established in the eighteenth century, the founding fathers wrote a separation of Church and State into their Constitution.'

Rod nodded grimly. 'It's a potent force, no question about it – especially in a medieval society, where most of the people take their religion superstitiously. Just the kind of a conflict to topple a government, in fact – if the Church can drum up enough popular support, and an army.'

'With the futurians' propaganda techniques and weaponry, neither should be too great a problem.'

'Not if it gets that far.' Rod grinned. 'So it's up to us to head it off before it gets to that pass, eh, old circuit rider?'

'So many human battles could be averted by a little common sense,' Fess sighed.

'Yes, but the King and the Lord Abbot aren't common — and when religion and politics are involved, no one's got much sense.'

# Chapter Two

'Travel light, don't you, Father?' the spaceport guard commented.

Father Al nodded. 'It is one of the advantages of being a priest. All I need is a spare cassock, a few changes of underwear, and my Mass kit.'

'And a surprising amount of literature.' The guard riffled through a book from the stack. '*Magic and the Magi* . . . Little odd for a priest, isn't it?'

'I'm a cultural anthropologist, too.'

'Well, to each his own.' The guard sealed the suitcase. 'Certainly no weapons in there — unless you come across a devil or two.'

'Hardly.' Father Al smiled. 'I'm not expecting anything worse than the Imp of the Perverse.'

'"Imp of the Perverse"?' The guard frowned. 'What's that, Father?'

'An invention of Edgar Allan Poe's,' Father Al explained. 'To my way of thinking, it nicely explains Finagle's Law.'

The guard eyed him warily. 'If you don't mind my saying so, Father, you're not exactly what I expect in a priest — but you're clear.' He pointed. 'The shuttle gate's over that way.'

'Thank you.' Father Al took up his suitcase and headed for the boarding area.

On the way, he passed a fax-stand. He hesitated; then, on an impulse, he dropped in his credit card and punched up 'McAran, Angus, ca. 1954.' Then he leaned back and waited. It must have been a long search; almost five seconds passed before the machine began humming. Then the hard copy emerged slowly — about a metre of it. Father Al pulled it out and devoured it with his eyes.

'McAran, Angus, Ph.D., 1929–2020; Physicist, engineer, financier, anthropologist. Patents . . . '

'Excuse me, Father.'

'Eh?' Father Al looked up, startled, at the impatient-looking gentleman behind him. 'Oh! My apologies. Didn't realize I was in the way.'

'Perfectly all right, Father,' the man said, with a smile that contradicted the words. Father Al folded the hard copy in thirds, hastily, and moved off toward the boarding area.

He sat down in a floating chair and unfolded the copy. Amazing what the PIB had stored in its molecular circuits! Here was a thumbnail biography of a man who'd been dead more than a thousand years, as fresh as the day he'd died – which was presumably the last time it'd been updated. Let's see, now – he'd patented five major inventions, then set up his own research and development company – but, oddly enough, he hadn't patented anything after that. Had he let his employees take the patents in their own names? Improbably generous, that. Perhaps he just hadn't bothered to keep track of what his company was doing; he seemed to have become very heavily involved in—

'Luna Shuttle now boarding.'

Drat! Just when it was getting interesting. Father Al scrambled up, folding the copy again, and hurried to tail onto a very long line. The shuttle left once every hour, but everyone who was leaving Europe for any of Sol's planets or for any other star system had to go through Luna. Only half a per cent of Terra's population ever left the mother planet – but half a per cent of ten billion makes for very long lines.

Finally, they were all crowded onto the boarding ramp, and the door slid shut. There was no feeling of movement, and any sound from the motors was drowned out by the quiet hum of conversation; but Father Al knew the ramp was rolling across a mile of plasticrete to the shuttle.

Finally, the forward door opened, and the passengers began to file aboard the shuttle. Father Al plopped down into his seat, stretched the webbing across his ample middle, and settled down to read his hard copy with a blissful sigh.

Apparently having tired of inventing revolutionary devices, McAran had turned his hand to treasure-hunting, finding fabled hoards that had been lost for centuries; the most spectacular was King John's treasury, but there had also been major finds all the way back to the city of Ur, circa 2000 BC. This pursuit had naturally led him into archaeology, on the one hand, and finance, on the other. Apparently the combination had worked well for him; he had died a very wealthy man.

All very impressive, Father Al admitted, but not when it came to magic. How would the man have been able to identify a wizard, even during his own time? Father Al had searched history assiduously, but had never come up with anyone who could have been a real magic-worker – they were either tricksters, espers, or poor deluded souls, almost certainly. Of course, in the very early days, there were a few who *might* have been sorcerers, tools of the devil. Opposing them, there were definitely saints. And, though the saints were certain, Father Al doubted there had ever really been any 'Black Magic' witches; it made very poor business sense for the Devil. But magic without a source in either God or the Devil? Impossible. It would require someone who was an esper, a medium, and had some unnamed power to break the 'Laws of Nature' by, essentially, merely wishing for things to happen. That was the stuff of fairy tales; neither science nor religion even admitted its possibility, had even a chink in its wall of reason through which such powers might seep.

Which, of course, was what made it so delightful a fantasy. If any such individual ever did actually come to light, those walls of reason would come tumbling down – and who could tell what new and shining palaces might emerge as they were rebuilt?

'Gentlefolk,' said a canned voice, 'the ship is lifting.'

Father Al bundled up his paper, thrust it in his breast pocket, and pressed his nose against the port. No matter how many times he flew, it still seemed new to him – that wonderful, faerie sight of the spaceport growing smaller, falling away, of the whole city, then the countryside, being dwarfed, then spread out below him like a map, one that dropped away further and further beneath him, till he could see Europe enamelled on the bottom of a giant bowl, its rim the curve of the Earth . . . and that was just on the ballistic rocket flights from one hemisphere to another. The few times he had been in space, it had been even better – the vast bowl dropping further away, till it seemed to turn inside out and become a dome, then a vast hemisphere filling the sky, somehow no longer below him, but beside him, continents mottling its surface through a swirl of clouds . . .

He knew that seasoned passengers eyed him with amusement,

or contempt; how naive he must seem to them, like a gawking yokel. But Father Al thought such delights were rare, and not to be missed; to him, it was wrong to ever cease to glory in the wonder of God's handiwork. And, at the moment when he sat most enthralled with the majestic vista on the other side of the port, a question sometimes tickled the back of his mind: who was the true sophisticate, they or he?

This time, the overcast quickly cut off sight of the faerie landscape below, but turned into a dazzling sea of cotton beneath him, sinking away till it seemed a vast snowfield. Then, just barely, he felt the ship quiver, then begin a low, threshold hum of muted power. The antigravity units had been shut off, and the powerful planetary drive now propelled the shuttle.

Father Al sighed, and sat back, loosening his webbing, gazing out of the port as his current problem floated to the surface of his mind again. There was one big question that the PIB bio hadn't answered: how could McAran have known about this man Gallowglass, about something that would happen more than a thousand years after his own death? And that question, of course, raised another: how had McAran known just when to have the letter opened, or who would be Pope at the time?

The boarding ramp shivered to a stop, and Father Al filed out into Luna Central with a hundred other passengers. Gradually, he worked his way through the flow to a datawall, and gazed up at the list of departing ships. Finally, he found it – Proxima Centauri, Gate 13, lifting off at 15:21. He glanced up at the digital clock above – 15:22! He looked back at the Proxima line in horror, just as the time winked out, to be replaced by the glowing word, 'Departed'. Then the gate number blanked, too.

Father Al just stared at it, numbed, waiting for the departure time of the next ship to light up.

Presently, it did – 3:35 Greenwich Standard Time. Father Al spun away, fuelled by a hot surge of emotion. He identified it as anger and stilled, standing quiet, letting his whole body go loose, letting the outrage fill him, tasting it, almost relishing it, then letting it ebb away till it was gone. Finagle had struck again – or his disciple Gundersun, in this case: 'The least desirable possibility will always exert itself when the results will be most frustrating.' If Father Al arrived at Luna to catch the Centauri liner at 15:20, of *course* the liner would lift off at 15:21!

He sighed, and went looking for a seat. There was no fighting

Finagle, nor any of his minions – especially since they were all just personifications of one of humankind's most universal traits, perversity, and had never really existed. You couldn't fight them, any more than you could fight perversity itself – you could only identify it, and avoid it.

Accordingly, Father Al found a vacant seat, sat down, pulled out his breviary, and composed himself to begin reading his Office.

'Gentleman, *I* was sitting there!'

Father Al looked up to see a round head, with a shock of thick, disorderly hair, atop a very stocky body in an immaculately-tailored business coverall. The face was beetle-browed and almost chinless, and, at the moment, rather angry.

'I beg your pardon,' Father Al answered. 'The seat was empty.'

'Yes, because I got up long enough to go get a cup of coffee! And it was the only one left, as you no doubt saw. Do I have to lose it just because there was a long line at the dispense-wall?'

'Ordinarily, yes.' Father Al stood up slowly, tucking his breviary away. 'That's usually understood, in a traveller's waiting room. It's not worth an argument, though. Good day, gentleman.' He picked up his suitcase and turned to go.

'No, wait!' The stranger caught Father Al's arm. 'My apologies, clergyman – you're right, of course. It's just that it's been a bad day, with the frustrations of travel. Please, take the seat.'

'Oh, I wouldn't dream of it.' Father Al turned back with a smile. 'No hard feelings, certainly – but if you've had as rough a time as that, you need it far more than I do. Please, sit down.'

'No, no! I mean, I do still have some respect for the clergy. Sit down, sit down!'

'No, I really couldn't. It's very good of you, but I'd feel guilty for the rest of the day, and . . . '

'Clergyman, I told you, sit down!' the man grated, his hand tightening on Father Al's arm. Then he caught himself and let go, smiling sheepishly. 'Will you look at that? There I go again! Come on, clergyman, what do you say we junk this place and go find a cup of coffee with a table under it, and *two* seats? I'm buying.'

'Certainly.' Father Al smiled, warming to the man. 'I do have a little time . . . '

The coffee was genuine this time, not synthesized. Father Al wondered why the man had been waiting in the public lounge, if he had *this* kind of expense account.

'Yorick Thal,' the stranger said, holding out a hand.

'Aloysius Uwell.' Father Al gave the hand a shake. 'You're a commercial traveller?'

'No, a time traveller. I do trouble shooting for Doc Angus McAran.'

Father Al sat very still. Then he said, 'You must be mistaken. Dr McAran died more than a thousand years ago.'

Yorick nodded. 'In objective time, yes. But in my subjective time, he just sent me out in the time machine an hour ago. And I'll have to report back to him when I get done talking to you, to tell him how it went.'

Father Al sat still, trying to absorb it.

'Doc Angus invented time travel back in 1952,' Yorick explained. 'Right off, he realized he had something that everyone would try to steal, especially governments, and he didn't want to see what that would do to war. So he didn't file for a patent. He made himself a very secret hideout for his time travel lab, and set up a research company to front the financing.'

'There's not a word about this in the history books,' Father Al protested.

'Shows how well he keeps a secret, doesn't it? Not quite well enough, though – pretty soon, he found out there were some other people bopping around from advanced technological societies, cropping up in ancient Assyria, prehistoric Germany – all sorts of places. After a while, he found out that they came mostly from two organizations – the Society for the Prevention of Integration of Telepathic Entities, and the Vigilant Extenders of Totalitarian Organizations. He also found out that they were both using time machines that were basically copies of his – without his permission. And they weren't even paying him royalties.'

'But you said he didn't file for a patent.'

Yorick waved the objection away. 'Morally, he figured he still had patent rights – and they could at least have asked. So he formed his own organization to safeguard the rights of individuals, all up and down the time line.'

'Including patentholders?'

'Oh, yes. In fact, he calls the organization "The Guardians of the Rights of Individuals, Patentholders Especially". Pretty soon, he had a network of agents running all the way from about

40000 BC on up, fighting SPITE and its anarchists, and VETO and its totalitarians.'

Father Al pursed his lips. 'I take it that means he supports democracy?'

'What other system really tries to guarantee an inventor's patent rights? Of course, supporting an organization that size requires a lot of money, so he went into the treasure-hunting business. He'd have an agent in, say, ancient Greece bury some art objects; then he'd send a team to dig 'em up in 1960, when even a child's clay doll would fetch a thousand dollars from a museum. With coins, he'd have 'em dug up in the Renaissance, and deposit them with one of the early banks. It's really amazing what can happen to a few denarii, with five hundred years of compound interest.'

'Speaking of interest,' Father Al said, 'it's rather obvious that our meeting was no accident. Why are you interested in me?'

Yorick grinned. 'Because you're going to Gramarye.'

Father Al frowned. 'I take it you have an agent in the Vatican, today.'

'No fair telling – but we do have our own chaplains.'

Father Al sighed. 'And what is your interest in Gramarye?'

'Mostly that SPITE and VETO are interested in it. In fact, they're doing all they can to make sure it doesn't develop a democratic government.'

'Why?'

Yorick leaned forward. 'Because your current interstellar government, Father, is the Decentralized Democratic Tribunal, and it's very successful. It comprises sixty-seven planets already, and it's growing fast. SPITE and VETO want to stop it, any way they can – and the easiest way is to let it grow until its own size destroys it.'

Father Al gave his head a quick shake. 'I don't understand. How can size destroy a democracy?'

'Because it's not the most efficient form of government. Major decisions require a lot of debating and, if the diameter of the Terran Sphere gets too long, the Tribunes won't be able to learn what the folks at home think about an issue until after it's decided and done with. That means that unpopular decisions get rammed down the throats of the voters, until they start rebelling. The rebellions are put down, but that turns into repression, which breeds even more rebellion. So eventually, the democracy either falls apart, or turns into a dictatorship.'

'You're saying, then, that the size of a democracy is limited by its communications.' Father Al gazed off into space, nodding slowly. 'It sounds logical. But how does this affect Gramarye?'

'Because most of the people there are latent telepaths – and about ten per cent are active, accomplished, and powerful.'

Father Al stared, feeling excitement thrum through his blood. Then he nodded. 'I see. As far as we know, telepathy is instantaneous, no matter how much distance separates the sender and the receiver.'

Yorick nodded. 'With them in the DDT, democracy could expand indefinitely. But they'd have to be willing volunteers, Father. You can't expect much accuracy in your communications if you're using slaves who hate you.'

'Quite apart from the fact that the requirement for membership in the DDT is a viable planetary democracy. So the DDT has to see to it that the planet develops a democratic government.'

Yorick nodded again. 'That's why the DDT has SCENT – to sniff out the Lost Colonies, and see to it that they develop democratic governments. And SPITE and VETO have to see to it that SCENT fails.'

Father Al's mouth tightened in disgust. 'Is there no place free of political meddling any more? How many agents does SCENT have on Gramarye?'

'One.' Yorick sat back, grinning.

'*One?* For so important a planet?'

Yorick shrugged. 'So far, they haven't needed any more – and too many cooks might spoil the brew.'

Father Al laid his hand flat on the table. 'The agent wouldn't be the Rodney d'Armand who discovered the planet, would it?'

Yorick nodded.

'And Rod Gallowglass? Where does he fit into this?'

'He's Rodney d'Armand. The man always feels more comfortable using an alias.'

'Insecure, eh?' Father Al gazed off into space, drumming his fingers on the table. 'But effective?'

'Sure is. So far, he's thwarted two major attempts by SPITE and VETO together. What's more, he's used those victories to put the current monarchy on the road to developing a democratic constitution.'

Father Al's eyebrows shot up. 'Extremely able. And he's about to discover some psionic talent of his own?'

'He's about to disappear,' Yorick corrected, 'and when he reappears in a few weeks, he's going to be a genuine, fully-fledged, twenty-four-carat wizard, able to conjure up armies out of thin air. And that's just the beginning of his powers.'

Father Al frowned. 'And he won't do it by psi talents?'

Yorick shook his head.

'Then what *is* the source of his power?'

'That's *your* field, Father.' Yorick jabbed a finger at the priest. 'You tell us – if you can catch up with him before he disappears, and go with him.'

'You may be sure that I'll try. But why isn't he a psi? Because he comes from off-planet?'

'Only the genuine, Gramarye-born article occasionally turns out to be a telepath – and usually a telekinetic or teleport, too, depending on sex. The women are telekinetic; that means they can make broomsticks fly, and ride on them, among other things.'

'The witches of legend,' Father Al mused.

'That's what they call 'em. They call the esper men "warlocks". They can levitate, and make things, including themselves, appear and disappear, sometimes moving 'em miles between.'

'But Rod Gallowglass can do none of these things?'

'No, but he wound up marrying the most powerful witch in Gramarye – and they've got four kids who're showing a very interesting assortment of talents. In fact, they're all more powerful than their mother. When they start realizing that, she'll *really* have trouble.'

'Not necessarily, if they've raised them properly,' Father Al said automatically (he'd been assigned to a parish for several years). 'Odd that they should be more powerful than their mother, when they don't have psionic genes from both parents.'

'Yeah, isn't it?' Yorick grinned. 'I just love these little puzzles – especially when someone else gets to solve 'em. But it might not be all that strange – there're still new talents that keep cropping up on that planet. I mean, they've only been inbreeding for a few hundred years; they've got a lot of untapped potential.'

'Inbreeding . . . yes . . . ' Father Al had a faraway look. 'The answers would lie with their ancestors, wouldn't they?'

'Buncha crackpots.' Yorick waved them away. 'Ever hear of the Society for Creative Anachronism, Father?'

'No. Who were they?'

'A hodgepodge collection of escapists, who tried to forget they were living because of an advanced technology, by holding gatherings where everybody dressed up in medieval outfits and performing mock battles with fake swords.'

'Ah, I see.' Father Al smiled fondly. 'They tried to restore some beauty to life.'

'Yeah, that was their problem. That kind of beauty requires individuality, and reinforces it – so they weren't too popular with the totalitarian government of the Proletarian Eclectic State of Terra. When PEST came in, it broke up the SCA and executed the leaders. They all requested beheading, by the way . . . Well. The rest of the organization went underground; they turned into the backbone of the DDT revolution on Terra. Most of 'em, anyway; there's a rumour that about a quarter of 'em spent the next few centuries playing a game called "Dungeons and Dragons". They were used to being underground.'

'Fascinating, I'm sure,' Father Al said drily, 'but what does it have to do with Gramarye?'

'Well, a dozen of the richest SCA members saw the PEST *coup* coming, and bought an outmoded FTL space liner. They crammed aboard with all the rank-and-file who wanted to come along, renamed themselves the "Romantic Emigrés", and took off for parts unknown – the more unknown the better. When they got there, they named it "Gramarye", and set up their version of the ideal medieval society – you know, architecture out of the fourteenth century, castles out of the thirteenth, armour out of the fifteenth, costumes out of any time between the fall of Rome and the Renaissance, and government out of luck. Well, they did have a King, but they paid him a fine medieval disregard. You get the idea.'

Father Al nodded. 'A thorough collection of romantics and misfits – and a high concentration of psi genes.'

'Right. Then they proceeded to marry each other for a few centuries, and eventually produced telepaths, telekinetics, teleports, levitators, projective telepaths . . . '

'Projectives?' Father Al frowned. 'You didn't mention those.'

'Didn't I? Well, they've got this stuff they call "witch moss". It's a telepathically-sensitive fungus. If the right kind of "witch" thinks hard at it, it turns into whatever she's thinking about. And, of course, the whole population turned latent-esper fairly early on, and they loved to tell their children fairy tales . . . '

'No.' Father Al blanched. 'They didn't.'

'Oh, but they did – and now you'll find an elf under every elm. With the odd werewolf thrown in – and a few ghosts. Hey, it could've been worse! If they hadn't had this thing against anything later than Elizabethan, they might've been retelling *Frankenstein*.'

'Praise Heaven for small blessings!'

Yorick nodded. 'You'll have trouble enough with what they've got there already. Be careful, though – new talents keep showing up, from time to time.'

'Indeed? Well, I thank you for the warning. But I'm curious . . . Why did you come tell me all this? Why didn't Dr McAran just put it all into his letter?'

'Because if he had, the Pope would've thought he was a raving maniac,' Yorick said promptly. 'But since he put down just the bare-bones-vital information, and made an accurate "prediction" about who would be Pope . . . '

'With a little help from your agent in the Vatican,' Father Al amplified.

'Don't say anything against him, Father, he's from your Order. Anyway, with that much and no more in the letter, the Pope believed it, and sent you.'

'Ingenious. Also devious. But why bother with the letter at all, since you were coming to meet me anyway?'

'Because you wouldn't have believed me if you hadn't read the letter.'

Father Al threw up his hands in mock despair. 'I give up! I never could make headway against a circular argument – especially when it might be valid. But tell me – why did you bother? Why does Mr McAran care?'

'Because SPITE and VETO keep trying to sabotage us, any-when they can. It's us versus them, Father – and you and Rod Gallowglass are part of the "us". If he loses, we lose – and a few trillion people, all down the ages, lose a lot of individual rights.'

'Especially patentholders,' Father Al amplified.

'Of course. And by the way, Doc Angus did finally patent it – in 5029 AD.'

'After the secret was finally out?'

Yorick nodded.

'How did he manage to get a patent when its existence was already public knowledge?'

'Did you ever stop to think how difficult it would be to

prove when a time machine was invented?' Yorick grinned. 'It's a fun puzzle. Think it over when you've got some time – say, on your way to Gramarye.' He glanced at his watch-ring. 'Speaking of which, you'd better hurry – SPITE and VETO are already massing for their next big attack on Gramarye. Massing behind a poor dupe of a front man, of course.'

'Oh?' Father Al inquired mildly. 'Who's the poor dupe?'

'The Church, of course.' Yorick grinned. 'Good luck, Father.'

# Chapter Three

'How dare this tatter-robed priest so flout our power!' Queen Catharine stormed.

They were pacing down a hallway in the royal castle, heading for the state audience chamber. Rich oak panelling flashed past; thick carpet soaked up Catharine's angry stamping.

'His robe is scarcely tattered, my dear,' Tuan answered. 'And he governs all priests in our land.'

'An *abbot*?' Rod frowned. 'I think I've been overlooking something this past decade. Doesn't he take orders from a bishop?'

Tuan turned to him, perplexed. 'What is a "bishop"?'

'Er – never mind,' Rod swallowed. 'How come an abbot of a monastery governs parish priests?'

'Why, because all priests in this land are of the Order of St Vidicon!' Catharine snapped impatiently. 'How is it that the High Warlock does not know this?'

'Er – just haven't been taking religion very seriously, I guess.' Rod hadn't even been going to Mass on Sundays, but he didn't think this was the time to mention it. 'So the Abbot's the head of the Church, here – and I understand he's not too happy about your appointing all the parish priests in the country. *Now* it makes sense.'

'Some, but not overmuch,' Tuan said grimly.

'Where was he when the barons still named their own priests?' Catharine stormed. 'Oh, he would not go up against them! But now that 'tis accepted that *we* appoint them . . . Er!'

A cannonball of a body hit her in the midriff, crowing, 'Mama, Mama! Chess time! Chess time!'

Catharine's face softened remarkably as she held the small one away from her, kneeling to look into his eyes. 'Aye, sweetling, 'tis the hour we usually play. Yet your mother cannot, this morn; we must speak with the Lord Abbot, thy father and I.'

'Not fair, though!' the little prince protested. 'You couldn't play yesterday, neither!'

'Either,' Tuan corrected, tousling the boy's hair. 'Aye, Alain, thy mother had need to speak with the Duchess d'Bourbon yestere'en.'

'Not that I wished to.' Catharine's tone hardened a little. 'Yet not even kings and queens can do only what they please, my boy.'

She, Rod reflected, had definitely matured.

Alain pouted. 'Not fair!'

''Tis not,' Tuan agreed, with an achingly sad smile. 'Yet . . . '

'My apologies, Majesties!' A middle-aged lady in a grey coif and gown, with a gleaming white apron, hurried up and dropped a curtsy. 'I but turned my gaze away for the half of a minute, and . . . '

''Tis no matter, good nurse.' Tuan waved away the apology. 'If we have not an occasional moment to spare for our son, what worth is our kingdom? Yet thou must not keep us long from matters of state, child, or there will be no kingdom for thee to inherit! Come, now, go with thy nurse – and take this with thee.' He felt in his purse and produced a sugar plum.

Alain glared at it accusingly, but accepted it. 'Soon?'

'As soon as we are done with the Lord Abbot,' Catharine promised. 'There, now, go with thy nurse, and we'll be with thee presently.' She gave him a kiss on the forehead, turned him around, and gave him a pat on his bottom to speed him. He plodded off after Nurse, looking back over his shoulder.

His parents stood, gazing fondly after him.

'Fine boy,' Rod said into the silence.

'He is that,' Catharine agreed. She turned to Tuan. 'But thou dost spoil him atrociously!'

Tuan shrugged. 'True; yet what are nurses for? Still, Madame, remember – he has not yet come under my tutelage.'

'That, I want to see,' Rod said, nodding. 'Papa as swordmaster.'

Tuan shrugged. 'My father managed it. Stern he was – yet I never doubted his love.'

'Your father's a grand man.' Rod knew old Duke Loguire

quite well. 'What does *he* think of your appointing priests for his parishes?'

Tuan's face darkened as he was wrenched back to the topic. He started toward the audience chamber again. 'He is not overly joyous about it, but sees the need. Why will not the Lord Abbot?'

'Because it encroaches on *his* authority,' Rod said promptly. 'But isn't the appointment just a matter of form? I mean, who do the priests take their orders from *after* they're appointed?'

Tuan stopped dead, and Catharine whirled about, both staring at Rod. 'Why, that is so,' Tuan said slowly. 'Barons ruled priests, when barons appointed them – yet since Catharine began that function, our judges have watched to be sure the lords give no orders to clergy.' He turned to Catharine, frowning. 'Hast *thou* given commands to priests?'

'I had not thought of it,' Catharine admitted. 'It seemed it were best to leave God to the godly.'

'Sounds like a good policy,' Rod agreed. 'See any reason to change it?'

Tuan beamed. 'I would not want to, save when a priest breaks the law – and I must own the Lord Abbot deals more harshly with a soiled cassock than I ever would, save in matters of death.'

'Point of conflict?'

'Never,' Catharine stated, and Tuan shook his head.

'For any offence great enough to be capital, the Abbot's punishment is to strip the cleric of office; and cast him out of the Order – whereupon, of course, our officers seize him. Nay, I catch thy drift – we've let the Abbot rule all the parish priests, have we not?'

''Twas a grievous omission,' Catharine grated.

'Not really,' Rod grinned. 'It put the clergy solidly on *your* side, against the barons – and their flocks with them. But now . . . '

'Aye, now.' Tuan's face darkened again; then he shrugged. 'Well, no matter; for a priest, there's small choice between Abbot and King, in any event. Aye, if 'twere only a matter of granting him power of appointment, the form, why, let him have it! Since he hath already the substance.'

'If 'twere all,' Catharine echoed.

'There's more?' Rod could almost feel his ears prick up. 'You've got my attention, I conFESS.'

'The traditional conflict between Church and Crown,' Fess's voice murmured behind his ear, 'revolved over two issues: secular justice versus ecclesiastical, specifically in the matter of sanctuary; and Church holding of vast tracts of tax-exempt land.'

'Aye, and more difficult,' Tuan said sombrely. 'He thinks we take too little care of the poor.'

Well, it was reassuring to know that even a computer could miss. 'I'd scarcely call that a disaster.'

'Would you not?' Catharine challenged. 'He wishes us to cede all administration of charitable funds unto himself!'

Rod halted. Now, *that* was a Shetland of a different shade! 'Oh. He only wants to take over a major portion of the national administration!'

'Only that.' Tuan's irony was back. 'And one that yields great support from the people.'

'Possible beginnings of a move toward theocracy,' Fess's voice murmured behind Rod's ear.

Rod ground his teeth, and hoped Fess would get the message. Some things, he didn't need to have explained to him! With a theocracy in the saddle, what chance was there for the growth of a democracy? 'That point, I don't think you can yield on.'

'I think not.' Tuan looked relieved, and strengthened – and Catharine glowed, which was not necessarily a good thing.

'We are come.' Tuan stopped before two huge, brass-bound, oaken doors. 'Gird thy loins, Lord High Warlock.'

A nice touch, Rod thought – reminding him that he ranked equally with the man they were about to confront.

The doors swung open, revealing an octagonal, carpeted room lit by great clerestory windows, hung with rich tapestries, with a tall bookcase filled with huge leather-bound volumes and a stocky, brown-robed man whose gleaming bald pate was surrounded by a fringe of brown hair running around the back of his head from ear to ear. His face was round and rosy-cheeked, and shone as though it were varnished. It was a kind face, a face made to smile, which made it something of a shock to see it set in a truculent frown.

Tuan stepped into the room; Catharine and Rod followed. 'Lord Abbot,' the King declaimed, 'may I present Rod Gallowglass, Lord High Warlock.'

The Abbot didn't get up – after all, he was the First Estate, and Rod was the Second. His frown deepened, though he bobbed his head and muttered, 'My lord. I know thee by repute.'

'My lord.' Rod bobbed his head in return, and kept his tone

neutral. 'Take my reputation with a grain of salt, if you will; my magic is white.'

'I hear thy words,' the Abbot acknowledged, 'but every man must judge his fellows for himself.'

'Of course.' Determined to be a hard case, wasn't he? But that was it, of course – 'determined'. He had to work at it; it didn't come naturally.

'Majesties,' the Abbot was saying, 'I had thought my audience was with thyselves.'

'As it is,' Tuan said quickly. 'But I trust thou wilt not object to Lord Gallowglass's presence; I find him a moderating influence.'

The Abbot slipped for a second; relief washed over his face. Then it was gone, and the stern mask back in place; but Rod warmed to the man on the instant. Apparently he didn't mind being made more moderate, as long as their Majesties were, too. It meant he was looking for a solution, not a surrender. Rod kept his eyes on the Abbot's chest.

The monk noticed. 'Why starest thou at mine emblem?'

Rod started, then smiled as warmly as he could. 'Your indulgence, Lord Abbot. It's simply that I've noticed that badge on every priest on Gramarye, but have never understood it. In fact, I find it unusual for a cassock to have a breast pocket; it's certainly not pictured so, in the histories.'

The Abbot's eyes widened – he was concealing surprise. At what? Rod filed it, and went on. 'But I can't imagine why a priest would wear a screwdriver in the breast pocket – that *is* what that little yellow handle is, isn't it?'

'Indeed so.' The Abbot smiled as he slipped the tiny tool out of his pocket, and held it out for Rod to inspect – but his eyes were wary. ''Tis only the badge of the Order of St Vidicon of Cathode, nothing more.'

'Yes, I see.' Rod peered at the screwdriver, then sat down at Tuan's left. 'But I can't understand why a monk would wear it.'

The Abbot's smile warmed a little. 'On a day when no grave matters await us, Lord Warlock, I will rejoice to tell thee the tale of our founder, St Vidicon.'

Rod cocked a forefinger at him. 'It's a date.'

'Amen!'

The ice was broken.

The Abbot laid both palms flat on the table. 'Yet now, I fear, we must turn to weighty matters.'

Rod felt the temperature lowering noticeably.

The Abbot drew a rolled parchment from his robe, and handed it to Tuan. 'It is with sorrow, and all respect, that I must present this petition to Your Majesties.'

Tuan accepted the parchment, and unrolled it between himself and Catharine. The Queen glanced at it, and gasped in horror. She turned a thunderous face to the Abbot. 'Surely, Milord, thou canst not believe the Crown could countenance such demands!'

The Abbot's jaw tightened, and he took a breath.

Rod plunged in. 'Er, how's that phrased, Your Majesty?'

'"In respect of our obligations to the State and Your Majesties,"' Tuan read, '"we strongly advise . . . "'

'Well, there you are.' Rod sat back, waving a hand. 'It's just advice, not demands.'

The Abbot looked up at him, startled.

Catherine's lips tightened. 'If the Crown feels the need of advice . . . '

'Er, by your leave, Your Majesty.' Rod sat forward again. 'I fear I lack familiarity with the issues under discussion; could you read some more of it?'

'"Primus,"' Tuan read, '"we have painfully noted Your Majesties' encroachment upon the authority of Holy Mother Church in the matter of appointment of . . . "'

'I see. There, then, is the substance of the case.' Rod leaned back, holding up a forefinger. 'I beg your indulgence, Your Majesties; please excuse the interruption, but I believe we really should settle this issue at the outset. Authority would seem to be the problem. Now, the people need the Church, but also need a strong civil government; the difficulty is in making the two work together, is it not? For example . . . ' Rod took a quick look at the parchment for form's sake, and ploughed on. 'For example, this item about administering of aid to the poor. What fault find you in the Crown's management of such aid, my lord?'

'Why . . . in that . . . ' Rod could almost hear the Abbot's mind shifting gears; he'd been all set for a hot debate about appointment of clergy. 'Why, in that, quite plainly and simply, there is too little of it! That is the substance of it!'

'Ah.' Rod nodded, with a commiserating glance at Tuan. 'So we come down to money, so quickly.'

They hadn't, but Tuan picked up a cue well. 'Aye, so soon as that. We are giving all that the Crown can spare, Lord Abbot

– and a bit more besides; we do not keep great state here, the
Queen and I.'

'I know thou dost not.' The Abbot looked troubled.

'And there is the cause of it. We do not feel we should eat off
gold plate, if our people go hungry. Yet they *do* go in hunger, for
there's simply not enough coin flowing to the Crown, for us to be
able to channel back more than we do.'

'Thou couldst levy greater taxes,' the Abbot offered, half-
heartedly.

Tuan shook his head. 'Firstly, an we did, the barons upon
whom we levy it would simply wrench it out of their villeins,
who are the same poor we speak of here; and secondly, because, if
the barons did not, the villeins would rise in rebellion. No, Milord
Abbot – the taxes are already as high as we may push them.'

'For example,' said Catharine sweetly, 'thou thyself, Lord
Abbot, would be first to protest if we levied a tax on all the
vast lands of the Church!'

'And little would you gain thereby,' the Abbot declared stiffly.
'The Order's holdings are scarcely a fortieth part of thy whole
kingdom!'

'Datum correct,' Fess immediately hummed behind Rod's ear.
And if Fess said it, it *had* to be right – statistics were his hobby.

But it struck Rod as anomalous that a medieval administrator
could be so accurate, without being able to consult the State's
records.

'Many of thy barons hold more!' the Abbot went on. 'And of
our income from those lands, the bulk is already given out to the
poor – so thou wouldst gain quite little by taxing us! Excepting,
mayhap,' he amended, 'that thou mightest, thereby, take even
*more* from the poor!'

'You see?' Rod threw up his hands. 'The well's dry; you've
said it yourself.'

The Abbot looked up, startled, then realized that he had.

'And if both Church and State are already giving all they
can,' Rod pursued, 'what more can we do?'

'Put the administration of what funds there are under one
single exchequer,' the Abbot said promptly; and Rod's stomach
sank as he realized he'd lost the initiative. 'Two whole trains of
people are currently employed in the disbursing of these funds,
and the upshot is, a village I know has two poorhouses, one a
hospice of our Order, one paid by the Crown – and there are

scarcely twenty souls who need either! Such doubling is costly. Moreover, if only one staff worked at this task, the other's pay could go to the poor – and since the Brothers of St Vidicon do this work for only meagre bed and board, assuredly ours would be the less expensive staff to maintain!'

Rod sat, dumbfounded. Of course, it was *possible* that the Lord Abbot had hit on this idea by himself – but Rod doubted it.

'Subject refers to duplication of effort,' Fess murmured behind his ear, 'a concept in systems analysis. Such concepts are far too sophisticated for a medieval society. Off-planet influence must be suspected.'

Or time-traveller influence. Who was sticking a finger in the Gramarye pie *this* time, Rod wondered – the future Anarchists, or the Totalitarians?

Probably the Anarchists; they tended to work on highly-placed officials. Though there *was* a proletarian issue here . . .

He'd paused too long. Catharine was saying, caustically, 'Aye, leave an hundred or so loyal servants without employment, and their wives and families without bread! Thou wilt thus assure thyself of good custom at thine almshouses, Lord Abbot!'

The Lord Abbot's face reddened; it was time for Rod to get back in. 'Surely neither system is perfect, Lord Abbot. But, with two operating, what the one misses, the other catches.' *Had he heard of redundancy?* 'For example, does the Church still divide its charity money equally, between all the parishes?'

'Aye.' The Abbot nodded, frowning. 'That which the parish itself doth not raise.'

'But parishes in Runnymede have a much greater proportion of desperately needy than the rural parishes,' Rod explained.

The Abbot blinked, and stared, wide-eyed.

'I don't think the parish priests have even had time to notice it, they're so overworked.' Rod was a great one for saving the other guy's face. 'But the King's almshouses are there, giving these poor parishioners at least enough for bare subsistence. That's the advantage to having two systems – and the disadvantage to only having one. Who then would catch what the officers missed?'

He'd gone on long enough for the Abbot to recover. 'There's some truth in that,' he admitted. 'But surely, if there are to be two systems, at least each one should be self-governing. Would it not work at its best that way?'

Rod glanced at the Queen and King. Catharine was considering it – and didn't seem disposed to commit herself.

'Aye,' Tuan said slowly, 'I confess there's reason to that.'

'But mine cannot be so!' The Abbot slapped the tabletop and sat back with an air of triumph, obviously pleased with himself for having got them back to the topic they hadn't wanted to discuss – and with such a good case for it, too.

'No – it really can't, I suppose.' As far as Rod was concerned, the timing was just right.

'Nay. While the Crown appoints priests to parishes, I cannot set the man I deem best for the task, to the doing of that task. Does this not lessen the excellence of this double-chain thou speakest of?'

'At least our appointments are better than those of the barons, whose choices obtained ere I was crowned,' Catharine retorted; but her tone lacked vehemence.

'For which, I must thank Your Majesties.' The Abbot inclined his head. 'Yet is it not now time to take a further step on the upward road?'

'Mayhap,' Tuan said judiciously, 'though it's surely not to the Crown's advantage to lessen any further its hold over the roots of government . . . '

'But is it to the interests of thy people?' the Abbot murmured.

Tuan fairly winced. 'There, good Milord, thou touchest the quick. Yet thou wilt understand, I trust, that the Queen and I must discuss these matters you have so kindly brought to our attention, at some length.'

'That,' Catharine warned, 'will be a fulsome talk, and hot.'

Tuan grinned. 'Why, then, here I stand.' Suiting the action to the word, he stood. 'Wilt thou, then, hold us excused, Lord Abbot? For indeed, we should begin this while we're fresh to it.'

'But of course, Your Majesties.' The Abbot scrambled to his feet, and even inclined his head a little. 'Thou wilt, then, summon me, when thou dost feel further need of, ah, converse, on this matter?'

'Be assured, we shall,' Tuan said grandly, 'and so, good e'en.'

'God be with thee,' the Abbot muttered, sketching a quick cross in the air. Then the doors boomed wide as the two monarchs turned away, arm in arm, and paced out, in a hurry – but more, Rod suspected, to get to a chess game with a small boy, than to discuss affairs of state.

Still, he couldn't let the Abbot suspect that – and he had a curiosity bump to scratch. 'Now, Milord – about your founder . . . '

'Eh?' The Abbot looked up, startled. 'Oh, aye! I did say, when there would be time.'

'All the time in the world,' Rod assured him. 'The wife doesn't expect me home till late.'

The air rang with a small thunderclap, and Toby stood there, pale and wide-eyed. 'Lord Warlock, go quickly! Gwendylon hath sent for thee – thy son Geoffrey hath gone into air!'

Rod fought down a surge of panic. 'Er – he does that all the time, Toby – especially after you've just been there. Just lost, right?'

'Would she send for thee if he were?'

'No, hang it, she wouldn't!' Rod swung back to the Abbot. 'You must excuse me, Milord – but this's got to be a genuine emergency! My wife's a woman of *very* sound judgement!'

'Why, certes, be on thy way, and do not stay to ask leave of a garrulous old man! And the blessings of God go with thee, Lord Warlock!'

'Thank you, Milord!' Rod whirled away, out the door, with Toby beside him. 'Try not to pop in like that, when there's a priest around, Toby,' he advised. 'It makes them nervous.'

# Chapter Four

'Someone's out to get me,' Father Al muttered, as he flew through an underground tube in a pneumatic car, along with a dozen of his fellow passengers from Terra. They had just filed out of the liner from Luna and up to the datawall. Father Al had found his entry, and seen that the ship to Beta Cassiopeia was leaving at 17:23 GST, from Gate 11 of the North 40 terminal. Then he'd looked up at the digital clock and seen, to his horror, that it was 17:11, and he was in the South 220 terminal. That meant he was 180 degrees away from his next ship in both horizontal and vertical planes – which meant that he was exactly on the opposite side of the two-and-a-half-mile-wide planetoid that was Proxima Station!

So down, and into the tube. The only saving grace was that he didn't have to pass through Customs, as long as he stayed within the Station. That, and the speed of the pneumatic car – it could cross the two-and-a-half kilometers in three minutes. It could've done the trip in less than a minute, if the computer didn't limit it to 1.5 G acceleration and deceleration at the beginning and end of the trip. Under the circumstances, Father Al would've settled for the quicker time, and taken his chances on ending his existence as a thin paste on the front of the car. It had taken him five minutes to find the tube, and a four-minute wait before the car came.

Deceleration pushed him toward the front of the car, then eased off and disappeared. The doors hissed open, and he was on his feet, turning and twisting between other passengers, threading his way toward the platform. 'Excuse me . . . Excuse me . . . I beg your pardon, madame . . . Oh, dear! I'm sorry about your foot, sir . . . '

Then he was through, and standing, hands clasped on his suitcase handle, glaring at the lift's readout. The minutes crawled agonizingly by while a discreet, impersonal voice from the ceiling informed him that Chairlady Spaceways' Flight 110 to Beta Cassiopeia was about to depart from Gate 11; last call for Chairlady Spaceways' Flight 110 . . .

The lift doors hissed open. Father Al held himself back by a straining effort of will as the passengers filed out; then he bolted in. That was a mistake; five people crowded in behind him. The doors hissed shut, and he began elbowing his way back to them. 'Excuse me . . . I'm sorry, but this really is imperative . . . I'm sorry, sir, but my liner's leaving, and the next one's apt to be quite a while coming . . . '

Then the doors hissed open, and he charged out, with one eye watching to avoid a collision, and the other watching for signs. There it was – Gates 10 to 15, and an arrow pointing to the left! He swerved like a comet reeling around the Sun, leaving a trail of bruised feet, jogged elbows, and shattered tempers behind him.

Gate 11! He skidded to a halt, leaped toward the door – and realized it was chained shut. With a sinking heart, he looked up at the port-wall – and saw a glowing spot already small and diminishing, the St Elmo's-Fire phosphoresence that surrounded a ship under planetary drive, growing smaller and dimmer as his ship moved away.

For a moment, he sagged with defeat; then his chin came

up, and his shoulders squared. Why was he letting it bother him? After all, it wouldn't be *that* long before the next flight to Cassiopeia.

But the datawall said otherwise; the next flight to Beta Cass. wasn't leaving for a week! He stared at it in disbelief, Yorick's warning to hurry echoing in his ears. Rod Gallowglass was going to disappear, and Father Al had to make sure he disappeared with him!

Then a nasty suspicion formed at the back of his mind. Admittedly, it was too soon to say – three times is enemy action, and he'd only been delayed twice; but Rod Gallowglass was about to discover some sort of extraordinary power within himself, and probably had some major flaw in his personality, as almost everyone had – well-hidden and well-rationalized, to be sure, but there none the less. That flaw could be a handle to grasp his soul by, and twist him toward evil actions – again, well-hidden and well-rationalized, not recognized as evil; but evil none the less. He could be a very powerful tool in the hands of Evil – or a great force for Good, if someone were there to point out the moral pitfalls and help him steer clear of them.

Definitely, it helped Evil's chances if Father Al missed contact with Rod Gallowglass.

And it was so easy to do – just make sure he missed his ship, and arrived on Gramarye too late! All Hell had to do was to help human perversity run a little more than its natural course. Perhaps the captain of the liner had been in a bad mood, and hadn't been about to wait a second longer than was necessary, even though one of the booked passengers hadn't arrived yet . . . Perhaps the spaceport controller had had an argument earlier that day, and had taken it out on the rest of the world by assigning the ship from Terra to the South 220 terminal, instead of the North 40; so Finagle had triumphed, and the perversity of the universe had tended toward maximum.

Father Al turned on his heel and strode away toward the centre of the terminal.

Father Al arrived in the main concourse and strolled down the row of shops, searching. The Church did all it could to make the Sacraments available to its members, no matter how far from Terra they might be – and especially in places where they might need its comfort and reinforcement most. There was one Order that paid particular attention to this problem; surely they wouldn't have ignored a major way-station on the space lanes . . .

There it was – a curtained window with the legend, 'Chapel of St Francis Assisi' emblazoned on it. Father Al stepped through the double door, gazed around at the rows of hard plastic pews, the burgundy carpet, and the plain, simple altar-table on the low dais, with the crucifix above it on a panelled wall, and felt a huge unseen weight lift from his shoulders. He was home.

The Franciscans were very hospitable, as they always were. But there was a bit of a problem when he explained what he wanted.

'Say Mass? *Now?* With respect, Father, it's six o'clock in the evening.'

'But surely you have evening Masses.'

'Only on Saturday evenings, and the vigils of holy days.'

'I'm afraid it really is necessary, Father.' Father Al handed the Franciscan his letter from the Pope. 'Perhaps this will make the situation more clear.'

He hated to pull rank – but it was satisfying to watch the Franciscan's eyes widen when he looked at the signature. He folded the letter and handed it back to Father Al, clearing his throat. 'Yes. Well . . . certainly, Father. Whatever you'd like.'

'All I need is the altar, for half an hour.' Father Al smiled. 'I don't think there'll be any need for a sermon.'

But he was wrong. As he began to say Mass, passersby glanced in, stopped, looking startled, then came quietly in, found a pew, and knelt down. When Father Al looked up to begin the Creed, he stared in amazement at a couple dozen people in front of him, most of them well-dressed travellers, but with a good sprinkling of spaceport mechanics and dirtside crew – and a few gentlemen with three-day beards, whose coveralls were patched, greasy, and baggy at the knees. It was curious how any major spaceport always seemed to develop its own skid row, even if it was millions of AUs from any habitable planet. It was even more surprising how many Catholics cropped up out of the plastic-work at the drop of an altar bell.

Under the circumstances, he felt obliged to say something – and there was one sermon he always had ready. 'My brothers and sisters, though we are in a Chapel of St Francis, allow me to call to your minds the priest in whose honour my own Order was founded – St Vidicon of Cathode, martyr for the faith. In the seminary, he had a problem – he kept thinking in terms of what did work, instead of what should work. He was a Jesuit, of course.

'He also had a rather strange sense of humour. When he was teaching, his students began to wonder whether he believed more firmly in Finagle than in Christ. Too many young men were taking his jokes seriously, and going into Holy Orders as a result. His bishop was delighted with all the vocations, but was a bit leery of the reasons – so the Vatican got wind of it. The Curia had its doubts about his sense of humour, too, so they transferred him to Rome, where they could keep an eye on him. As an excuse for this surveillance, they made him Chief Engineer of Television Vatican.

'The term is confusing today, of course; "television" was like 3DT, but with a flat picture; 3DT was originally an abbreviation for "three-dimensional television". Yes, this was quite a few centuries ago – the Year of Our Lord 2020.

'Well, Father Vidicon was sad to leave off teaching, but he was overjoyed at actually being able to work with television equipment again . . . and he didn't let his nearness to the Pope dampen his enthusiasm; he still insisted on referring to the Creator as "the Cosmic Cathode . . . "'


'Praise God, from Whom electrons flow!
Praise Him, the source of all we know!
Whose order's in the stellar host!
For in machines, He is the Ghost!'


'Father Vidicon,' Monsignor reproved, 'that air has a blasphemous ring.'

'Merely irreverent, Monsignor.' Father Vidicon peered at the oscilloscope and adjusted the pedestal on Camera Two. 'But then, you're a Dominican.'

'And what is *that* supposed to mean?'

'Simply that what you hear may not be what I said.' Father Vidicon leaned over to the switcher and punched up colour bars.

'He has a point.' Brother Anson looked up from the TBC circuit board he was diagnosing. '*I* thought it quite reverent.'

'You would; it was sung.' Monsignor knew that Brother Anson was a Franciscan. 'How much longer must I delay my rehearsal, Father Vidicon? I've an Archbishop and two Cardinals waiting!'

'You can begin when the camera tube decides to work, Monsignor.' Father Vidicon punched up Camera Two again, satisfied that the oscilloscope *was* reading correctly. 'If you insist on bringing in Cardinals, you must be prepared for a breakdown.'

'I really don't see why a red cassock would cause so much trouble,' Monsignor grumbled.

'You wouldn't; you're a director. But these old plumbicon tubes just don't like red.' Father Vidicon adjusted the chrominance. 'Of course, if you could talk His Holiness into affording a few digital-plate cameras . . . '

'Father Vidicon, you know what they cost! And we've been the Church of the Poor for a century!'

'Four centuries, more likely, Monsignor – ever since Calvin lured the bourgeoisie away from us.'

'We've as many Catholics as we had in 1390,' Brother Anson maintained stoutly.

'Yes, that was right after the Black Death, wasn't it? And the population of the world's grown a bit since then. I hate to be a naysayer, Brother Anson, but we've only a tenth as many of the faithful as we had in 1960. And from the attraction Reverend Sun is showing, we'll be lucky if we have a tenth of *that* by the end of the year.'

'We've a crisis in cameras at the moment,' the Monsignor reminded. 'Could you refrain from discussing the Crisis of Faith until the cameras are fixed?'

'Oh, they're working – now.' Father Vidicon threw the capping switch and shoved himself away from the camera control unit. 'They'll work excellently for you now, Monsignor, until you start recording.'

Monsignor reddened. 'And why should they break down then?'

'Because that's when you'll need them most.' Father Vidicon grinned. 'Television equipment is subject to Murphy's Law, Monsignor.'

'I wish you were a bit less concerned with Murphy's Law, and a bit more with Christ's!'

Father Vidicon shrugged. 'If it suits the Lord's purpose to give authority over entropy into the hands of the Imp of the Perverse, who am I to question Him?'

'For the sake of Heaven, Father, what has the Imp of the Perverse to do with Murphy's Law?' Monsignor cried.

Father Vidicon shrugged again. 'Entropy is loss of energy

within a system, which is self-defeating; that's perversity. And Murphy's Law is perverse. Therefore, both of them, and the Imp, are corrolary to Finagle's General Statement: "The perversity of the universe tends toward maximum."'

'Father Vidicon,' Monsignor said severely, 'you'll burn as a heretic someday.'

'Oh, not in this day and age. If the Church condemns me, I can simply join Reverend Sun's Church, like so many of our erstwhile flock.' Seeing the Monsignor turn purple, he turned to the door, adding quickly, 'None the less, Monsignor, if I were you, I'd not forget the Litany of the Cameras before I called "roll and record".'

'*That* piece of blasphemy?' the Monsignor exploded. 'Father Vidicon, you *know* the Church has never officially declared St Clare to be the patron of television!'

'Still, she did see St Francis die, though she was twenty miles away at the time – the first Catholic instance of "television", "seeing-at-a-distance".' Father Vidicon wagged a forefinger. 'And St Genesius *is* officially the patron of showmen.'

'Of *actors*, I'll remind you – and we've none of those here!'

'Yes, I know – I've seen your programmes. But do remember St Jude, Monsignor.'

'The patron of the desperate? Why?'

'No, the patron of lost causes – and with these antique cameras, you'll need him.'

The door opened, and a monk stepped in. 'Father Vidicon, you're summoned to His Holiness.'

Father Vidicon blanched.

'You'd best remember St Jude yourself, Father,' the Monsignor gloated. Then his face softened into a gentle frown. 'And, Lord help us – so had we all.'

Father Vidicon knelt and kissed the Pope's ring, with a surge of relief – if the ring was offered, things couldn't be all *that* bad.

'On your feet, Father,' Pope Clement said grimly.

Father Vidicon scrambled to his feet. 'Come now, Your Holiness! You know it's all just in fun! A bit irreverent, perhaps, but none the less only levity! I don't *really* believe in Maxwell's Demon – not quite. And I know Finagle's General Statement is really fallacious – the perversity's in us, not in the universe. And St Clare . . . '

'Peace, Father Vidicon,' His Holiness said wearily. 'I'm sure your jokes aren't a threat to the Church – and I'm not particularly worried by irreverence. If Christ could take a joke, so can we.'

Father Vidicon frowned. 'Christ took a joke?'

'He accepted human existence, didn't He? But I've called you here for something a bit more serious than your contention that Christ acted as a civil engineer when He said that Peter was a rock, and upon that rock He'd build His Church.'

'Oh.' Father Vidicon tried to look appropriately grave. 'If it's that feedback squeal in the public address system in St Peter's, I'll do what I can, but . . .'

'No, I'm afraid it's a bit more critical.' The hint of a smile tugged at the Pope's lips. 'You're aware that the faithful have been leaving us in increasing droves these past twenty years, of course.'

Father Vidicon shrugged. 'What can you expect, Your Holiness? With television turning everyone toward a Gestalt mode of thought, they've become more and more inclined toward mysticism, needing doctrines embracing the Cosmos and making them feel vitally integrated with it; but the Church still offers only petrified dogma, and logical reasoning. Of course they'll turn to the ecstatics, to a video demagogue like Reverend Sun, with his hodge-podge of T'ai-Ping Christianity and Zen Buddhism . . . .'

'Yes, yes, I know the theories.' His Holiness waved Father Vidicon's words away, covering his eyes with the other palm. 'Spare me your McLuhanist cant, Father. But you'll be glad to know the Council has just finished deciding which parts of Chardin's theories *are* compatible with Catholic doctrine.'

'Which means Your Holiness has finally talked them into it!' Father Vidicon gusted out a huge sigh of relief. 'At last!'

'Yes, I can't help thinking how nice it must have been to be Pope in, say, 1890,' His Holiness agreed, 'when the Holy See had a bit more authority and a bit less need of persuasion.' He heaved a sigh of his own, and clasped his hands on the desktop. 'And it's come just in time. Reverend Sun is speaking to the General Assembly Monday morning – and you'll never guess what his topic will be.'

'How the Church is a millstone around the neck of every nation in the world.' Father Vidicon nodded grimly. 'Priests who don't pass on their genes, Catholics not attempting birth control and thereby contributing to overpopulation, Church lands withheld from taxation – it's become a rather familiar bit of rhetoric.'

'Indeed it has; most of his followers can recite it chapter and verse. But this time, my sources assure me he intends to go quite a bit farther – to ask the Assembly for a recommendation for all UN member nations to adopt legislation making all these "abuses" illegal.'

Father Vidicon's breath hissed in. 'And with so large a percentage of the electorate in every country being Sunnite . . . '

'It amounts to virtual outlawing of the Roman Catholic Church. Yes.' His Holiness nodded. 'And I need hardly remind you, Father, that the current majority in the Italian government is Sunnite Communist.'

Father Vidicon shuddered. 'They'll begin by annexing the Vatican!' He had a sudden nightmarish vision of a Sunnite prayer meeting in the Sistine Chapel.

'We'll all be looking for new lodgings,' the Pope said drily. 'So you'll understand, Father, that it's rather important that I tell the faithful of the whole world before then, about the Council's recent action.'

'Your Holiness will speak on television!' Father Vidicon cried. 'But that's wonderful! You'll be . . . '

'My blushes, Father Vidicon. I'm well aware that you consider me to have an inborn affinity for the video medium.'

'The charisma of John Paul II, with the appeal of John the XXIII!' Father Vidicon asserted. 'But what a waste, that you'll not appear in the studio!'

'I'm not fond of viewing myself as the chief drawing-card for a sideshow,' His Holiness said sardonically. 'Still, I'm afraid it's become necessary. The Curia has spoken with Eurovision, Afrovision, PanAsiavision, PanAmerivision, and even Intervision. They're all, even the Communists, willing to carry us for fifteen minutes . . . '

'Cardinal Beluga is a genius of diplomacy,' Father Vidicon murmured.

'Yes, and all the nations are worried about the growth of Sun's Church within their borders, with all that it implies of large portions of their citizenry taking orders from Singapore. Under the circumstances, we've definitely become the lesser of two evils, in their eyes.'

'I suppose that's a compliment,' Father Vidicon said doubtfully.

'Let's think of it that way, shall we? The bottleneck, of course, was the American commercial networks; they're only willing to carry me early Sunday morning.'

'Yes; they only worry about religion when it begins to affect sales,' Father Vidicon said thoughtfully. 'So I take it Your Holiness will apear about 2 p.m.?'

'Which is early morning in Chicago, yes. Other countries have agreed to record the speech, and replay it at a more suitable hour. It'll go by satellite, of course . . . '

'As long as we pay for it.'

'Naturally. And if there's any failure of transmission at our end, the networks are *not* liable to give us postponed time.'

'Your Holiness!' Father Vidicon threw his arms wide. 'You wound me! Of *course* I'll see to it there's no transmission error!'

'No offence intended, Father Vidicon – but I'm rather aware that the transmitter I've given you isn't exactly the most recent model.'

'What can you expect, from donations? Besides, Your Holiness, British Marconi made excellent transmitters in 1990! No, Italy and southern France will receive us perfectly. But it would help if you could invest in a few spare parts for the converter that feeds the satellite ground station . . . '

'Whatever that may be. Buy whatever you need, Father Vidicon. Just be certain our signal is transmitted. You may go now.'

'Don't worry, Your Holiness! Your voice shall be heard, and your face be seen, even though the Powers of Darkness rise up against me!'

'Including Maxwell's Demon?' His Holiness said dourly. 'And the Imp of the Perverse?'

'Don't worry, Your Holiness.' Father Vidicon made a circle of his thumb and middle finger. 'I've dealt with *them* before.'


' "The good souls flocked like homing doves" ', Father Vidicon sang, 'or they will after they've heard our Pope's little talk.' He closed the access panel of the transmitter. 'There! Every part certified in the green! I've even dusted every circuit board . . . How's that backup transmitter, Brother Anson?'

'I've replaced two IC chips so far,' Brother Anson answered from the bowels of the ancient device. 'Not that they were bad, you understand – but I had my doubts.'

'I'll never question a Franciscan's hunches.' Father Vidicon laced his fingers across his midriff and sat back. 'Did you check the converter to the ground station?'

'"Converter?"' Brother Anson's head and shoulders emerged, covered with dust. 'You mean that huge resistor in the grey box?'

Father Vidicon nodded. 'The very one.'

'A bit primitive, isn't it?'

Father Vidicon shrugged. 'There isn't time to get a proper one, now – and it's all they've given me money for, ever since I was "promoted" to Chief Engineer. Besides, all we *really* need to do is to drop our 50,000-watt transmitter signal down to something the ground station can handle.'

Brother Anson shrugged. 'If you say so, Father. I should think that would kick up a little interference, though.'

'Well, we can't be *perfect* – not on the kind of budget we're given, anyhow. Just keep reminding yourself, Brother, that most of our flock still live in poverty; they need a bowl of millet more than a clear picture.'

'I can't argue with that. Anyway, I did check the resistor. Just how many ohms does it provide, anyway?'

'About as many as you do, Brother. How'd it test out?'

'Fine, Father. It's sound.'

'Or will be, till we go on the air.' Father Vidicon nodded. 'Well, I've got two spares handy. Let the worst that can happen, happen! I'm more perverse than Murphy!'

The door slammed open, and the Monsignor was leaning against the jamb. 'Father . . . Vidicon!' he panted. 'It's . . . catastrophe!'

'Murphy,' Brother Anson muttered; but Father Vidicon was on his feet. 'What is it, Monsignor? What's happened?'

'Reverend Sun! He discovered the Pope's plans, and has talked the UN into scheduling his speech for Friday morning!'

Father Vidicon stood, galvanized for a second. Then he snapped, 'The networks! Can they air His Holiness early?'

'Cardinal Beluga's on three phones now, trying to patch it together! If he brings it off, can you be ready?'

'Oh, we can be ready!' Father Vidicon glanced at the clock. 'Thursday, 4 p.m. We need an hour. Any time after that, Monsignor.'

'Bless you!' The Monsignor turned away. 'I'll tell His Holiness.'

'Come on, Brother Anson.' Father Vidicon advanced on the backup transmitter, catching up his tool-kit. 'Let's get this beast back on line!'

* * *

'Five minutes till air!' the Monsignor's voice rasped over the intercom. 'Make it good, reverend gentlemen! Morning shows all over the world are giving us fifteen minutes – but not a second longer! And Reverend Sun's coming right behind us, live from the UN!'

Father Vidicon and Brother Anson were on their knees, hands clasped. Father Vidicon intoned, 'Saint Clare, patron of television . . . '

' . . . pray for us,' finished Brother Anson.

'Saint Genesius, patron of showmen . . . '

'One minute!' snapped the Monsignor. 'Roll and record!'

' . . . pray for us,' murmured Brother Anson.

'Rolling and recording,' responded the recording engineer.

'Saint Jude, patron of lost causes . . . '

' . . . pray for us,' Brother Anson finished fervently.

'Slate it!' Then, 'Bars and tone!'

They could hear the thousand-cycle test tone in the background, whining. Then it began beeping at one-second intervals.

'Ready mike and cue, ready up on one!'

'Five!' called the assistant director. 'Four! Three!'

'Black! Clip tone!' the Monsignor cried. 'Mike him! Cue him! Up on One!'

Television screens all over the world lit up with the grave but faintly-smiling image of the Pope. 'Dearly beloved in Christ . . . '

The picture flickered.

Father Vidicon darted a glance at the converter. Its tally light was dead. Beside it, the light glowed atop the back-up converter.

'Quick! The big one died!' Father Vidicon yanked open the top of the long grey box and wrenched out the burned-out resistor.

'There are a few points of theology on which we can't agree with Reverend Sun,' His Holiness was saying. 'Foremost among these is his concept of the Trinity. We just can't agree that Reverend Sun is himself the third Person, the "younger son" of God . . . '

Brother Anson slapped the spare resistor into Father Vidicon's palm.

' . . . nor is the sharing of a marijuana cigarette a valid form of worship, in the Church's eyes,' the Pope went on. 'But the Council does agree that . . . '

The screen went dark.

Father Vidicon shoved the spare into its clips and threw the routing switch.

The screen glowed again. ' . . . have always been implicit in Catholic doctrine,' His Holiness was saying, 'but the time has come to state their implications. First among these is the notion of "levels of reality". Everything that exists is real; but God is the Source of reality, as He is the Source of everything. And the metaphor of "the breath of God" for the human soul means that . . . '

'Yes, it's gone.' Father Vidicon yanked the burned-out resistor out of the back-up. 'The manufacturers must think they can foist off all their defectives on the Church.' Brother Anson took the lump of char and gave him a new resistor. 'That's our last spare, Father Vidicon.'

Father Vidicon shoved it into its clips. 'What're the odds against three of these blowing in a space of ten minutes?'

'Gunderson's Corollary,' Brother Anson agreed.

Father Vidicon slapped down the cover. 'We're up against perversity, Brother Anson.'

The tally blinked out on the main converter as the little red light on the back-up glowed into life.

'We're out of spares,' Brother Anson groaned.

'Maybe it's just a connection!' Father Vidicon yanked open the cover. 'Only four minutes left!'

'Is it the resistor, Father?'

'You mean this piece of slag?'

' . . . the oneness, the unity of the cosmos, has always been recognized by Holy Mother Church,' the Pope was saying. 'Christ's parable about the "lilies of the field" serves as an outstanding example. All that exists is within God. In fact, the architecture of the medieval churches . . . '

A picture of the Cathedral of Notre Dame appeared on the screen. The camera zoomed in for a close-up of the decorative carving . . .

. . . and the screen went blank.

'It died, Father Vidicon,' Brother Anson moaned.

'Well, you fight fire with fire.' Father Vidicon yanked out the dead resistor. 'And this is perversity . . . ' He seized the lead from the transmitter in his left hand, and the lead to the ground station in his right.

Around the world, screens glowed back into life.

' . . . and as there is unity in all of Creation,' the Pope went on, 'so there is unity in all the major religions. The same cosmic truths can be found in all; and the points on which we agree are more important than the ones on which we disagree – saving, of course, the Godhood of Christ, and of the Holy Spirit. But as long as a Catholic remembers that he is a Catholic, there can certainly be no fault in his learning from other faiths, if he uses this as a path toward greater understanding of his own.' He clasped his hands and smiled gently. 'May God bless you all.'

And his picture faded from the screen.

'We're off!' shouted Monsignor. 'That was masterful!'

In the transmitter room, Brother Anson chanted the *Dies Irae*, tears in his eyes.

The Pope moved out of the television studio, carefully composed over the exhaustion that always resulted from a television appearance. The Monsignor dashed out of the control room to drop to his knees and wring the Pope's hand. 'Congratulations, Your Holiness! It was magnificent!'

'Thank you, Monsignor,' the Pope murmured, 'but let's judge it by the results, shall we?'

'Your Holiness!' Another Monsignor came running up. 'Madrid just called! The people are piling into the confessionals – even the men!'

'Your Holiness!' cried a cardinal. 'It's Prague! The faithful are flocking to the cathedral! The commissars are livid!'

'Your Holiness – New York City! The people are streaming into the churches!'

'Your Holiness – Reverend Sun just cancelled his UN speech!'

'Your Holiness! People are kneeling in front of churches all over Italy, calling for the priests!'

'It's the Italian government, Your Holiness! They send their highest regards, and assurances of continued friendship!'

'Your Holiness,' Brother Anson choked out, 'Father Vidicon is dead.'

They canonized him eventually, of course – there was no question that he'd died for the Faith. But the miracles started right away.

In Paris, a computer programmer with a very tricky program knew it was almost guaranteed to glitch. But he prayed to Father Vidicon to put in a good word for him with the Lord, and the program ran without a hitch.

Art Rolineux, directing coverage of the Superbowl, had eleven of his twelve cameras die on him, and the twelfth started blooming. He sent up a quick prayer to Father Vidicon, and five cameras came back on line.

Ground Control was tracking a newly-launched satellite when it suddenly disappeared from their screens. 'Father Vidicon, protect us from Murphy!' a controller cried out, and the blip reappeared on the screens.

Miracles? Hard to prove – it always could've been coincidence. It always can, with electronic equipment. But as the years flowed by, engineers and computer programmers and technicians all over the world began counting the prayers, and the numbers of projects and programs saved – and word got around, as it always does. So, the day after the Pope declared him to be a saint, the signs went up on the back walls of every computer room and control booth in the world:

'St Vidicon of Cathode, pray for us!'

'Thus Saint Vidicon died, in an act of self-sacrifice that turned perversity back upon itself.' Father Al turned his head slowly, looking directly into the eyes of each person in his little congregation, one by one. 'So, my brothers and sisters, when you are tempted to commit an act of perversity, pray to St Vidicon to intercede with Almighty God, and grant you the grace to turn that perversity back upon itself, as St Vidicon did. If you are a masochist, and are tempted to find someone to whip you, be even more perverse – deny yourself the pleasure you long for! If you are tempted to steal, find a way of defrauding the bank's computer into giving you money from your own account! If you're tempted to try to ruin an enemy, pay him a compliment instead – he'll go crazy wondering what you're plotting against him!'

One of the businessmen shifted uncomfortably in his seat.

Father Al took a deep breath. 'Thus may we take the energy of the urge toward perversity, and turn it to the strengthening of our souls, by using its energy to perform good works.'

The congregation looked a bit confused, and he didn't blame them – it wasn't exactly the most coherent sermon he had ever delivered. But what could you expect, on an ad lib basis? He did notice a look of surprise on a few of the derelicts' faces, though, followed by thoughtful brooding. At least not all the seed had fallen on rocky ground.

He hurried on to the Creed, then pronounced the intention of the Mass. 'Dear Lord, if it pleases You, allow the soul of Your servant, the sainted Vidicon of Cathode, to lend his strength in defence of this member of the Order founded in his name, by battling the forces of perversity that ring Your Holy Church, turning them against themselves, to the confounding of those who seek its downfall, and who war against holiness and freedom of the soul. Amen.'

From there on, it was pretty straightforward, and he could relax and let himself forget the troubles of the moment while he became more and more deeply involved in the Sacrament. As always, the spell of the Mass wove its reassuring warmth around him; soon all that existed were the Host and the wine, and the silent, intent faces of the congregation. A surprising number of them turned out to be in shape for Communion; but, fortunately, one of the Franciscans was standing by in the sacristy, and came out to unlock the tabernacle and bring out a ciborium, so no one went away empty.

Then they were trooping out, singing the recessional, and Father Al was left alone, with the usual sweet sadness that came from knowing the Mass was indeed ended, and that he must wait a whole twenty-four hours before he could say it again.

Well, not quite alone. The Franciscan came over to him, with a whispering of his rough robe. 'A moving Mass, Father – but a strange sermon, and a strange intention.'

Father Al smiled wanly. 'And stranger circumstances that brought them forth, Father, I assure you.'

He had almost reached the departure port again when the public address system came to life, with the howling of a siren behind the voice. 'All passengers please clear the area. Conditions of extreme danger obtain; a ship is returning to port with damage in its control system. All passengers please clear the area immediately.'

It went on to repeat the message, but Father Al was already on his way back toward the main terminal. He only went as far as the rope, though – the red emergency cord that attendants were calmly stringing across the corridor, as though it were a daily event. But one look at their eyes assured Father Al that this was rare, and dreaded. '*My Lord!*' he prayed silently. '*I only sought aid for myself, not danger to others!*' And he found the nearest viewscreen.

Emergency craft were moving into position, amber running-lights flashing. Snub-nosed cannon poked out of their noses, ready to spray sealant on any ruptures in the hull of ship or station. A hospital cruiser drifted near by.

And, in the distance, a dot of light swelled into a disc – the returning ship.

The disc swelled into a huge globe, filling a quarter of the velvet darkness, pocked with the parabolic discs of detectors and communicators. Then the swelling stopped; the huge ship drifted closer, slowing as it came. The emergency craft maintained a respectful distance, wary and alert, as the liner loomed over them, till it filled the whole sky. Then the front of the hull passed beyond the range of the viewscreen. Father Al listened very carefully, but heard nothing; he only felt the tiniest movement of the station about him as the behemoth docked in the concave gate awaiting it. He breathed a sigh of relief; no matter what trouble they'd detected, the control systems had functioned perfectly for docking.

He turned away, to see the attendants removing the velvet rope, with only the slightest tremor in their hands. 'Excuse me,' he said to the nearest. 'What ship was that, docking there?'

The steward looked up. 'Why, it was the liner for Beta Cassiopeia, Father. Just a minor problem in the control system – they could've gone on with it, really. But our line doesn't believe in taking chances, no matter how small.'

'A wise policy,' Father Al agreed. '"The Universe'll get you, if you don't watch out."'

The attendant smiled thinly. 'I'm glad you understand.'

'Oh, perfectly. In fact, it's something of a fortunate coincidence for me; I was supposed to be on that liner, but my ship from Terra arrived a bit late.'

The attendant nodded. '"Fortunate" is right. The next ship for Beta Cass. doesn't leave for another week.'

'Yes, I know. You will let them know they've another passenger waiting, won't you?'

Six hours later, the engineers had found and replaced a defective circuit-grain, and Father Al slid into his couch, stretching the webbing across his body with a sigh of relief, and prayers of thanks to St Vidicon and God.

No reason to, really; it was probably all just a coincidence. No doubt St Vidicon had sat by smiling in amusement all the time, and the ship would've returned to port even without Father Al's

Mass. But a little extra praying never hurts, and it had kept him occupied.

Besides, in the realm of the supernatural, one never knew. Rod Gallowglass might really be important enough to merit the personal attention of the Imp of the Perverse. Father Al just hoped he'd reach Gramarye in time.

# Chapter Five

The jets cut out, and the great black horse landed at full gallop. He slowed to a canter, stubby wings folding back into his sides, and then to a trot.

'Elben Pond, Toby said,' Rod muttered, glaring at the dark sheet of water barely visible through the trees. 'Here's Elben Pond. Where are they?'

'I hear them, Rod,' Fess answered.

A few seconds later, Rod could, too: two small voices crying, 'Geo-ff!' Geof-frey!' And a full one calling, 'Geoffrey, my jo! Geoffrey! Whither art thou?'

'Geof-frey, Geof-frey!' Cordelia's voice came again, with sobs between the cries. Then Fess was trotting into a small clearing, with the little lake gleaming at its edge, and Cordelia's head poked out of the shrubbery as Rod swung down. 'Papa!' And she came running.

'Oh, Papa, it's turrible! It's all Magnus's fault; he disappeared Geoffrey!'

'Did *not*!' Magnus howled, agonized, as he came running up, and his mother seconded him as she landed on her knees next to her daughter.

'Cordelia, Cordelia! Magnus did not *do* it, he only *said* it!'

'You sure his just saying it couldn't make it happen?' Rod looked up at her over Cordelia's head. 'Magnus may be the only warlock who's ever been able to teleport someone else, except for old Galen – but Magnus did do it, when he got into that argument with Sergeant Hapweed.'

'Aye, and it took old Galen himself to fetch him back! Oh, we've sent for him – but truly, I misdoubt me 'tis that! Magnus would not lie on a matter of such gravity.'

'No, he wouldn't.' Rod transferred Cordelia to her mother's arms and caught Magnus against him. The boy resisted, his body stiff, but Rod stroked his head and crooned, 'There, now, son, we know you didn't do it! Maybe something you said makes you think so – but *I* know you can't do a thing like that without meaning to!'

The eight-year-old trembled; then his body heaved with a huge sob, and he wept like a thundercloud, bellowing anguish. Rod just hung on and kept stroking the boy's head and held Magnus gently away, and said quietly, 'Now, then. Tell me what happened, from beginning to end.'

Magnus gulped and nodded, wiping at his eyes. 'He was trying to play my games, Papa, the way he always does – and you've *told* me not to let him climb trees!'

'Yes; he might be too scared to levitate, if he fell from twenty feet up,' Rod said grimly. 'So he was tagging along in his usual pesty way – and what happened?'

'Magnus told him . . . ' Cordelia burst out; but Gwen said, 'Hush,' firmly, and clapped a hand over her daughter's mouth. 'Let thy father hear it for himself.'

'And?' Rod prompted.

'Wull – I told him to go jump in the lake. I didn't know he'd *do* it!' Magnus burst out.

Rod felt a cold chill run down his spine. 'He always does everything you tell him; you should know that by now. So he jumped in.'

'Nay! He never did get to't! Ten feet short o' the water, he faded!'

'Faded?' Rod gawked.

'Aye! Into thin air! His form grew thinner and thinner, the whiles I watched, till I could see the sticks and leaves through him – like a ghost!'

Cordelia wailed.

Rod fought down the prickling that was covering his head and shoulders. 'And he just – faded away.'

Magnus nodded.

Rod gazed out at the pond, frowning.

'Dost thou think . . . ' Gwen's voice broke; she tried again. 'Dost thou think we should drag the waters?'

Rod shook his head.

'Then . . . what?' She was fighting against hope.

'Fess?' Rod murmured.

'Yes, Rod.'

'You watched me being sent through that time machine in McAran's lab once, right?'

'Yes, Rod. I remember the seizure vividly. And I see your point – Magnus's description does match what I witnessed.'

Gwen clutched his arm. 'Dost thou think he has wandered in time?'

'Not "wandered",' Rod corrected. 'I think he's been sent.'

'But I ran right after him, Papa! Why would it not have sent me, too?' Magnus protested.

'Yeah, I was wondering about that.' Rod rose. 'The most logical answer is that whoever turned the machine on, turned it off right after poor little Geoff blundered into it . . . But maybe not. Son, when you told Geoff to go jump in the lake, where were you standing, and where was he?'

'Why . . . I stood by yon cherry tree.' Magnus pointed. 'And Geoff stood by the ash.' His arm swung toward a taller tree about ten feet from the first. 'And he called, "Magnus, me climb, too!" and started toward me.' Magnus gulped back the tears, remembering. 'But I spake to him, "No! Thou knowest Mama and Papa forbade it!" And he stopped.'

Rod nodded. 'Good little boy. And then?'

'Well, be began to bleat, in that way he hath, "Magnus! You climb, *me* climb! Me big!" And I fear I lost patience; I cried, "Oh, go leap in the lake!" And, straightaway, he fled toward the water.'

'From the ash.' Rod turned, frowning, toward the tree, drawing an imaginary line from it straight toward the lake, and cutting it off ten feet short of the water. 'Then?'

'Why, then, he began to fade. I own I was slow; I did not think aught was out o' place for a second or two. Then it struck me, and I ran hotfoot after.'

Rod drew an imaginary line from the cherry toward the pond. The two lines did not intersect, until their end-points. 'Fess?'

'I follow your thought, Rod. The machine's focus was no doubt ten feet or so further back from the water's edge. Geoff's momentum carried him further while he was beginning to shift.'

Rod nodded and started for the ash tree.

'What dost thou do?' Gwen cried, running after him.

'We've got the theory; now I'm testing it.' Rod turned right at the ash and started toward the water.

'Thou seekest to follow him, then!' Gwen kept pace with him determinedly. 'And if thou dost?'

'Then he'll have company. You stay with the other three, while we find our way back – but don't hold dinner.'

'Nay! If thou dost . . . Rod! Thou . . . ' Then whatever she was saying faded away. Rod turned back toward her, frowning . . .

. . . and found himself staring at the trunk of a tree.

A white trunk, white as a birch, but corrugated like an oak – and the leaves were silver.

Rod stared.

Then, slowly, he looked up, and all about him; all the trees were just like the first. They towered above him, spreading a tinsel canopy between himself and the sun; it tinkled in the breeze.

Slowly, he turned back to the metre-wide trunk behind him. So that was why Geoff had faded, instead of just disappearing – the machine's computer had sensed solid matter at the far end, and hadn't released him from its field until he was clear of the trunk. Rod nodded slowly, drew his dagger, and carefully cut a huge 'X' in the trunk; he had a notion he might want to be able to find it again.

Apropos of which, he turned his back to the trunk, and looked about him carefully, identifying other trees as landmarks – the one with the split trunk over to the left, and the twisted sapling to his right . . .

And the gleam of water straight ahead!

And just about the same distance away as Elben Pond had been. The machine had set him down in the spot that exactly corresponded to the pick-up point.

But when? When had there been silver-leaved, white-trunked oaks on Gramarye?

When *would* there be?

Rod shook off the tingling that was trying to spread over his back from his spine. He had more important things to think about, at the moment. He stepped away toward the shoreline, calling, 'Geoff! Geoffrey! Geoff, it's Papa!'

He stopped dead-still, listening. Off to his left, faintly, he heard tiny wails, suddenly stopping. Then a little head popped up above underbrush, and a small voice yelled, 'Papa!'

Rod ran.

Geoff blundered and stumbled toward him. Silver leaves rang

and chimed as they ran, with a discordant jangle as Rod scooped the little body up high in his arms, stumpy legs still kicking in a run. 'Geoff, m'boy! Geoff!'

'Papa! Papa!'

After a short interval of unabashedly syrupy sentimentality, Rod finally put his second son down, but couldn't quite bring himself to take his hand of Geoff's shoulder. 'Thank Heaven you're safe!'

'Scared, Papa!'

'Me too, son! But it's all right, now we're together – right?'

'Right!' Geoff threw his arms around his father's leg and hugged hard.

'Well! Time to go . . . *what's that?*'

Something blundered into the underbrush and stopped with a clashing of leaves. Then it set up a frightened wail.

A voice faded in after it. ' . . . thou dare – Cordelia! Thou'st done . . . Oh, child! Now *two* of thee are lost!'

'Er – three!' Rod called, peering over the underbrush to see Magnus come barrelling out of the tree-trunk. 'Come on, Geoff! Family-reunion time!'

'Not lost, Mama!' Cordelia crowed triumphantly. 'We're *all* here!'

'And all lost,' Rod agreed as he came up. 'Here he is, Gwen.'

'Oh, *Geoffrey!*' Gwen fell to her knees and threw her arms around her boy.

Rod let her have *her* few minutes of sickening sentimentality while he set his arms akimbo and glared down at Magnus. 'You know, this wasn't exactly the world's smartest idea.'

'If one of us is lost, we should all be lost!' Cordelia declared.

'So said she to Mama,' Magnus stated, 'and methought her idea had merit.'

'Oh, you did, did you?' Rod growled, glaring; but he couldn't hold it, and grappled them to him, one against each hip, hugging them hard. 'Well, maybe you've got a point. The family that strays together, stays together – even if we *are* all in danger.'

'Danger?' Magnus perked up. 'What danger, Papa?'

Rod shrugged. 'Who knows? We don't even know what kind of country we're in, let alone what lives here.'

'It's all *new!*' Cordelia squealed in delight.

'Well, that's one way of looking at it.' Rod shook his head in amazement. 'And to think I used to be a cynic!'

'Where are we, Papa?' Magnus was looking around, frowning.

'It's beginning to get through to you, too, huh? Well, I *think* we're still in Gramarye, but way in the future – way, *way* in the future. It couldn't be the past, because Gramarye never had trees like this – before the colonists came, it was all Carboniferous.'

'Carbo-*what*?'

'Just giant ferns, no trees.'

'Art thou certain?'

'Well, that's what the rest of the planet still has – but let's check it, anyway . . . Fess?' Rod waited for the robot to answer, then frowned. 'Fess? Fess, where are you? Come in, hang it!'

There was no answer.

'Can Fess "talk" across time, Papa?' Magnus asked quietly.

'Well, we tried it once, and it worked – but Doc, er, Dr McAran was lending us a time-machine's beam, then.' Rod didn't finish the thought, but a cold lump of dread began to swell in his belly.

'But isn't there a time-machine still running, here?'

Rod *would* have to beget brainy kids! 'Don't miss much, do you? Er, Gwen, dear? I think it's time we were getting back.' Or *trying* to.

Gwen looked up, startled. 'Oh, aye!' She scrambled to her feet. 'I had clear forgot about time! Why, Gregory must be squalling with hunger!'

'I have a feeling you should have weaned him sooner,' Rod mused.

The telepathic mummy picked it up from her kids. 'What is this foreboding . . . ? Oh.' She looked up at Rod. 'Magnus fears the gate may be closed.' Her face firmed as she accepted it.

Rod felt a surge of admiration, and gratitude that he'd lucked into this woman. 'There is that possibility, dear. Let's check it out, shall we?'

Without a word, Gwen clasped little Geoff's hand and followed after her husband.

Rod went slowly, holding Cordelia's hand and letting Magnus stalk by his side, searching for the bent sapling on the one hand, and the split trunk on the other. There, and . . . there. And there was the big oak with the 'X' on it.

He caught Magnus's hand. 'Take your mother's hand, son. I think we'd better be linked up, just in case this works.'

Silently, Magnus caught Gwen's hand.

Slowly, Rod paced toward the tree.

He stopped when the bark was grooving his nose, and didn't seem disposed to melt nicely out of the way.

'Thou dost look silly, Papa,' Cordelia informed him.

'I never would have guessed,' Rod muttered, turning away. His eyes found Gwen's. 'It didn't work, dear.'

'No,' she answered. 'I think it did not.'

They were silent for a few minutes.

'Art thou certain 'twas here, Papa?' Cordelia asked hopefully.

Rod tapped the tree-trunk. 'X marks the spot. I should know – I put it there, myself. No, honey – whoever opened this particular door for us, has shut it.'

'At least,' Gwen pointed out, 'I will not have to wait dinner for thee.'

'Yes.' Rod smiled bleakly. 'At least we're all here.'

'No, Papa!' Cordelia cried. '*Not* all here! How *could* you forget Gergory!'

'Believe me, I haven't,' Rod assured her, 'but I think whoever trapped us here, did.'

'*Trapped* us?' Magnus's eyes went round.

'Don't miss much at all, do you?' Rod gave him a bitter smile. 'Yes, son, I think somebody deliberately set out to trap us here – and succeeded admirably.' His gaze travelled up to Gwen. 'After all, it makes sense – and it's about the only theory that does. There's a storm brewing, between the Church and the Crown, back on Gramarye – *our* Gramarye, that is. And I've got some pretty strong hints that somebody from off-world's been pushing the Church into it. So what happens? Church and Crown have a meeting this afternoon, a confrontation and should've blown the whole thing sky-high – and what do I do but foul up the plan by getting them both to see reason! No, of *course* whoever's behind it would want me out of the way!'

Magnus frowned. 'But why us, Papa?'

'Because you're a very powerful young warlock, mine offspring, as anyone on Gramarye knows. And, if they're going to all this trouble just to foist off a war between the Church and the State, you can darn well bet they don't intend to have the State win! So the smart thing to do is to remove the State's strongest weapons – me, and your mother, and you. Don't forget, they lost one because of you, already, when you were only two. And Geoffrey's three already, and Cordelia's all of five! They've got no way of telling *what* any of you might be able to do.' *Nor do I, for that matter.* 'So, as long as you're setting the trap, why not catch all five of the birds-of-trouble while you're at it?'

'But Gregory, Papa?'

Rod shrugged. 'I'm sure they'd've preferred it if your mother'd carried him in here, too – but since she didn't I don't expect they're going to lose much sleep over it. He's not even a year old, after all. Even if he had every power in the book, what could he *do* with them? No, I don't think they were about to keep the gate open just to try and get Gregory, too – especially if it meant that the five of *us* might escape! Speaking of Gregory, by the way – who's with him?'

'Puck, and an elf-wife,' Gwen answered. 'And, aye, fear not – she knows the crafting of a nursing-glove.'

Rod nodded. 'And anything else she needs to know about him, I'm sure Brom will be glad to supply.'

'He takes so great an interest in our children,' Gwen sighed.

'Ah – yes.' Rod remembered his promise not to tell Gwen that Brom was her father. 'Comes in handy, at a time like this. In fact, I wouldn't be surprised if he flits in from Beastland, just to take charge of Greg personally – and Baby couldn't be safer inside a granite castle guarded by a phalanx of knights and three battlewagons. No, I think he'll be safe till we get back.'

'"Until"?' Magnus perked up. 'Then thou'rt certain we can return, Papa?'

Well, Rod *had* been, until Magnus mentioned it – but he wasn't about to say so. There were times when it came in handy, being telepathically invisible, even to members of his own family.

Damn few, though. And there were so *many* times when it was a curse, almost made him feel excluded . . .

He shrugged it off. 'Of course we can get back! It's just a problem – and problems are made to be solved, right?'

'Right,' all three children shouted, and Rod grinned in spite of himself. They were handy to have around, sometimes. Most times.

'Tell us the manner of it!' Magnus demanded.

'Oh . . . I dunno . . . ' Rod let his gaze wander. 'We don't exactly have enough information to start building theories. We don't even know where we are, in a manner of speaking, or what materials and tools are available – which might be handy to know, 'cause it might come down to building our own time machine. For that matter, we don't even know if there're even any people!'

'Then let us go discover it!' Magnus said stoutly.

Rod felt the grin spreading over his face again. 'Yeah, let's go!' He whipped out his dagger. 'Blaze trees as we go, kids – we might want to be able to find our way back here. Forward *march*!'

# Chapter Six

'I must trust you had a pleasant journey, Father Uwell.'

'As usual, Your Grace.' Father Al dug gratefully into a pile of asparagus that appeared to be fresh. 'Aboard ship, it was very pleasant – ample time for meditation. It was getting *to* the ship that was the problem.'

Bishop Fomalo smiled thinly. 'Isn't it always? I believe my secretary said you were from the Vatican.' The Bishop knew that full well; that's why he'd invited Father Al to dinner. Not to impress him, but because that was the only half-hour open in the Bishop's schedule.

Father Al nodded, chewing, and swallowed. 'But I have no official standing, Your Grace. An informal trouble-shooter, you might say.'

The Bishop frowned. 'But we have no troubles in my diocese – at least, none that would merit the Vatican's attention.'

'None that you know of.' Father Al tried a sympathetic smile. 'And it's debatable whether or not it's in your diocese.'

Bishop Fomalo seemed to relax a little. 'Come, now, Father! Certainly the Vatican knows which solar systems my diocese includes.'

'Lundres, Seredin, and Ventreles – I believe those are the colonists' names for the stars. I'm afraid I don't know the catalogue numbers.'

'I'd have to look them up, myself,' the bishop said, with a thin smile. 'There are colonies on the third and fourth planets of Lundres, one on the fourth planet of Seredin, and one on the second planet of Ventreles.'

'But they haven't begun to branch out to the moons and asteroids yet?'

'No, the planets are enough for us, for the time being. After all, Father, we scarcely total a million souls.'

'So little as that? My, my, I trust that doesn't indicate a disaster?'

'Scarcely.' The bishop tried to repress a smile. 'But when you begin with a colony of a few thousand, Father, it does take a while to build up a sizeable population, even with sperm and ova banks to keep the genetics stable.'

'Yes, of course. I hope you'll pardon my ignorance, Your Grace – I've never been so far from Terra before. And distance is the factor – with so few people spread over so many light-years, it must be an Herculean task to stay in touch with them.'

'It is difficult,' the bishop admitted, 'especially with so few vocations. But we do have hyperadio now, and of course we've had a dozen pinnaces with FTL drives all along.'

'Of course.' But Father Al's eyes suddenly gleamed.

The bishop shifted uncomfortably in his chair. 'About this trouble you mentioned, Father – on which colony is it?'

'A Lost Colony, Your Grace, about two-thirds of the way between Seredin and Ventreles, and thirteen light years away.'

The Bishop relaxed again. 'Wel, that is out of my diocese. What colony is this?'

'Its people call it "Gramarye", Your Grace.'

'Troubling.' The bishop frowned. 'The word refers to sorcery, does it not?'

'Well, magic, certainly, and it does have occult connotations. The term's also used to refer to a book of magical spells.'

'I can see why the Vatican would be concerned. But how is it I've never heard of this Lost Colony, Father?'

'Why, they wished to stay lost,' Father Al said, lips puckering in a smile. 'As far as I've been able to make out, they deliberately set about cutting themselves off from the rest of humanity.'

'An ominous symptom.' The bishop's frown deepened. 'All manner of heresies could break out in such a situation. And they've been there for several centuries?'

Father Al nodded. 'The colony was founded just before the Interstellar Dominion Electorates fell to the Proletarian Eclectic State of Terra's *coup*.'

'At least they were founded under a democratic interstellar federation. I take it they saw the totalitarian rule of PEST coming, and went off to try to keep democracy alive?'

'Not really; they established a monarchy.'

'Why, I wonder?' The bishop rubbed his chin. 'How did the Vatican learn of them?'

Father Al heard the indignant echo under the words; what business did he, an outsider, have coming in here, telling the bishop there was a nearby trouble spot he hadn't known about? 'You might say the information was leaked to us, by an agency associated with the interstellar government.' Which was true; but the Decentralized Democratic Tribunal didn't know about the association.

'I see.' The bishop's face cleared. 'It's good to know there are still some concerned citizens. Was your source Catholic?'

'I believe his name's Irish, but that's all I know.'

'That's indication enough.' The bishop sat back in his chair. 'I assume he gave you the co-ordinates. How will you get there?'

'Well, ah . . . '

The bishop's eyes widened. 'No, Father. All my boats are fully scheduled, for the next three months. If we were to transport you, one of the colonies would have to miss its consignment of missalettes.'

'I think the clergy could manage to find the correct readings, Your Grace. Besides, don't you keep at least one of your craft on standby, in case of breakdowns?'

'Yes, but what if there *were* a breakdown? Good heavens, Father, two of our colonies can't even produce their own altar wine yet!'

'But surely . . . '

'Father!' The bishop's eyebrows drew down in a scowl. 'I hate to be so blunt, but – the answer is an unequivocal "No"!'

Father Al sighed. 'I was afraid you'd say that – but I was hoping to avoid having to do this.' He drew a long white envelope from the inside pocket of his cassock. 'Pardon this archaic form of communication, Your Grace – but we weren't sure what level of technology we'd encounter on Gramarye. I assure you, it's just as personal as a message cube.' He handed the envelope to the bishop.

Frowning, the bishop slid out the letter and unfolded it. He read with a scowl. 'Aid the bearer of this letter, Father Aloysius Uwell, in any way he may request. In all matters pertaining to the planet "Gramarye", he speaks with my voice.' He blanched as he saw the signature. 'Pope John XXIV!'

'And his seal,' Father Al said apologetically. 'So you see, Your Grace, I really must have transportation to Gramarye.'

# Chapter Seven

They cut a particularly big blaze on a huge old willow overhanging the shore, then set off to the left, along the lakeside, heading north. After a half-hour's walk, they came out of the silver wood into an emerald-green meadow.

'Oh, *look*!' Cordelia gasped, pointing. 'The prettiest cow in the world!'

Rod looked, and swallowed, hard. The 'cow', even if it didn't have any horns, was definitely the biggest, toughest, meanest-looking old bull he'd ever seen. 'No, Cordelia, I don't think that's . . . '

'*Cordelia!*' Gwen gasped, and Rod whirled, just as a miniature witch on a branch of a broomstick shot past his nose.

'Too *late*!' Gwen clenched her fists in frustration. 'Oh, you dare not take your eyes from them for a second! *Milord, she is dangered!*'

'I know,' Rod ground out, keeping his voice low, 'but we don't dare charge out there, or we might spook it . . . No, put down that branch! I've got to stalk it . . . No you don't, young man!' He made a frantic grab for Magnus's collar, and yanked him back. 'I said *I'll* stalk it! One child in danger is enough, thank you! Gwen, hold on to 'em!' And he stepped out into the meadow, drawing his sword.

Geoffrey began to cry, but the sobs cut off quickly – Gwen's hand over his mouth, no doubt. She was right; they didn't dare make a sound. Rod moved very slowly, though every cell of his body screamed at him to hurry.

Especially since Cordelia was coming in for a landing! Not right under the bull's nose, thank Heaven – but only a few feet away! She plumped right down on the grass, though – at least she had the sense not to go running up to it.

'Here, Bossy!' He could hear her voice clearly, over a hundred feet of meadow grass – that might as well have been a thousand miles! 'Sweet moo-cow, come here!'

And the bull was turning its head towards her!

And now the rest of its body! It was moving! It was ambling towards her! Rod braced himself for a frantic mad dash . . .

And it nuzzled her outstretched hand.

Rod stood rigid, unable to believe it. But it was real – it liked her! It was gentle! It was nibbling grass from her hand! A father itself, no doubt – and sure enough of its own masculinity not to be insulted by her mistake as to its gender. Thank Heaven!

Not that he was about to stop trying to get to her – but carefully, now, very carefully; it was being gentle, let's not upset the cattle car! And move around to come at it from the side – if it charged him, Rod didn't want Cordelia in the way.

But there was no need to worry about that – she was going to be on top of the situation. Because the bull was folding its legs, and lying down beside her, in pure invitation! And she was climbing on! He choked back her name, and the impulse to shout it; don't spook the bull!

But it was climbing to its feet, and trotting away across the meadow – with his little girl on its back! 'Cor-deeel-iaaaa!'

She heard him; she waved – and turned the bull somehow, set it trotting back towards him! Rod breathed a sigh of relief, then stiffened again. This was only an improvement, not a solution – she was still on its back!

He pulled away, backing up toward his family, until his left hand brushed Gwen's arm. The boys could teleport out, if they had to, and there was a nice-sized boulder right next to Gwen – small enough for her to 'throw' by telekinesis, but large enough to knock the bull cold. He saw her glance flick over to it, and knew she was thinking along the same line.

But about twenty feet away, the bull started getting skittish. It slowed, and slewed around sideways, prancing to a stop, then pawing the turf.

'Oh, come, sweet cow, come!' Cordelia pleaded. 'Thou'rt so lovely, I wish to show thee to my family! *Please* do come!'

'No, now, dear don't push him – er, it. *We* can come over – can't we, dear?' And Rod stepped forward.

The bull stepped back.

Rod halted. 'I . . . don't think he likes me . . . '

'Mayhap he is wise enough not to trust males,' Gwen suggested. '*I* shall try.' And she took a step forward.

The bull stepped back again.

'Try it without the boys.' Rod caught Geoff's and Magnus's hands, and Gwen stepped forward again.

The bull held its place – warily, but holding.

Gwen took another step, then another, and another.

Great. Just great. Now Rod had *both* his womenfolk at peril!

Then the boys shouted with delight, and both little hands

wrenched out of his. '*Hey!*' Rod made a frantic grab – but he landed on his face, as two small *booms* told him they'd teleported. He scrambled back to his feet, just in time to see them reappear at the far end of the meadow, way over against the trees on the other side, along with . . .

*That* was the attraction – another little boy!

But what a boy – or at least, what an outfit! His doublet was dark green, with a golden surcoat; its sleeves belled out to brush the ground. His hose was buff, and fitted like second skins – and was that the glimmer of gold in his hair? Not a coronet, surely!

Whatever he was, he was moving very slowly toward a shaggy-looking horse that seemed to be waiting for him, head up and turned toward him, ears pricked forward. But it was bare-backed. Wild?

Magnus whooped a greeting, and the boy looked up. The horse tossed its head angrily, and sidled closer. Magnus ran toward the new boy, with Geoff hurrying after.

Rod squeezed his eyes shut, gave his head a quick shake in disbelief, and looked again. It *was*! The horse's body had grown longer – say, long enough for a couple of more riders!

Rod decided he didn't like its looks. He lit out running, sword in hand.

The boys had got past the opening wariness, and were shaking hands. Now the new boy was pointing to the horse – and Magnus was nodding eagerly – and the horse was kneeling down!

Then Gwen cried out in fright, and Rod whirled. She was running after him, waving frantically at the boys. Behind her, Cordelia was shrieking and kicking her heels against the bull's sides. It rumbled, and lumbered into motion.

The boys screamed behind him – high, hoarse, with raw, absolute terror! Rod spun about again, running. The horse was running flat-out toward the lake, and the boys were yanking and tugging, trying to pull themselves loose from its back.

Rod swerved, and fear shot a last ounce of adrenalin into his veins. He tore through the grass, shouting.

The horse hit the water with a huge splash; fountains of foam shot high. When they cleared, its back was bare; it reared up, wheeling about and plunging down at three small heads in the water, mouth gaping wide – and Rod saw carnivore's teeth!

He bellowed rage, and leaped.

Spray gushed about him as he hit, directly under the horse. It surged down, jaws gaping wide; he leaned to the side and slashed, back-handed, straight into its jaws. It screamed, rearing back, and lashed out at him with razor-edged hooves. Fire raked his side; then a thundering bellow shook the earth, and a juggernaut knocked him back, floundering. Water closed over his face; daylight glimmered through water. He fought his way back, broke surface, and stood – to see the horse twenty feet farther from shore, scrambling back upright, wheeling about in time to catch the bull's second charge.

The great dun beast slammed into the chestnut stallion. It folded over the bull, gleaming hooves slashing, needle-teeth ripping. The bull bellowed in anger and pain, and dived down. Blood sheened the water as both animals went under.

Rod didn't stay to wait for the curtain call. He floundered over to his boys, shot a hand down under water to grapple Geoff's collar and yanked him back above the surface, spluttering and wailing.

'Papa!' Magnus yelled. 'Elidor! He can't swim!'

Rod wallowed over to the sinking princeling, bellowing, 'Get to shore!' Water whooshed in as Magnus disappeared, shooting Elidor briefly to the surface. Rod caught him under the arms in a cross-body carry and backed toward shore, towing both boys. He stumbled and fell as he hit shallow water, scrambled back up, and hauled the two boys out onto the grass. And he kept hauling, yanking them up, one under each arm, and ran. He stopped when he fell, but Gwen was there by that time, with Magnus beside her, to catch Geoff in her arms. 'Oh, my boy, my foolish lad! We near to lost thee!'

Rod followed suit, yanking Magnus to him, hugging him tight to reassure himself the boy was still there. 'Oh, thank Heaven, thank Heaven! Oh, you fool, you little fool, to go near a strange animal like that! Thank the Lord you're alive!'

A high, piercing scream shattered the air.

They whirled, staring.

For a moment, the horse and bull shot out of the water, the horse leaping high to slash down at the bull with its teeth, catching it where neck joined shoulders. But the bull twisted, catching the horse's hind leg in its own jaws. Even a hundred feet away, they could hear the crunch. The horse screamed, and the bull bellowed, rearing up to drive down with its forelegs, slamming its opponent back under the water with the full force of its weight. It sank, too, but the water churned like a maelstrom, and the blood kept spreading.

Gwen shuddered and turned the children's heads away. ''Tis a horrid sight, and one that only thy father need watch, and he may warn us to flee if need be.' Then she noticed the blood dripping from Rod's doublet. 'Milord! Thou'rt wounded!'

'Huh?' Rod looked down. 'Oh, yeah! Now I remember. Unnnngh! Say, that's beginning to hurt!'

'Indeed it should,' Gwen said grimly, unlacing his doublet. 'Cordelia, seek out St John's Wort and red verbena! Boys, seek four-leafed clovers! Quickly, now!'

The children scampered to search. Elidor stood, blinking in confusion.

'Four-leafed clovers, lad,' Gwen urged. 'Surely thou mayst seek them, no matter how little herb-lore thou knowest! Quickly, now!'

Elidor stared at her indignantly; then fright came into his eyes, and he ran to join Magnus and Geoff.

'Strange one, that,' Rod said, frowning. 'Ow! Yes, dear, the skin's broken.'

''Tis not pretty,' Gwen said, tight-lipped. She tore a strip from the hem of her skirt.

'Here, Mummy!' Cordelia was back, leaves in hand.

'Good child,' Gwen approved. A flat rock lifted itself, a few feet away, and sailed over to land at her feet. She plucked Rod's dagger and dropped to her knees, pounding the herbs with the hilt.

'Here, Mama!' Magnus ran up, two four-leafed clovers in hand, with the other boys right behind him.

'Any will aid. I thank thee, lads.' Gwen added them to the porridge, then gave Rod's ribs a wipe with his doublet and plastered the herbs on the wound.

'St John's Wort, red verbena, and four-leafed clovers,' Rod winced. 'Not exactly the usual poultice, is it?'

'Nay, nor wast thou ripped by a usual beast.' Gwen wound the improvised bandage around his torso.

Rod tried to ignore the prickling in his scalp. 'As I remember, every one of those herbs is supposed to be a sovereign against fairies.'

'Indeed,' Gwen said, carefully neutral. 'Well, I have never seen such as these two beasts afore – yet I mind me of certain tales from my childhood. There, now!' She fastened the bandage and handed him his doublet. 'Walk carefully a week or so, mine husband, I pray thee.'

A long, piercing shriek echoed over the meadow. Before it died, a rumbling, agonized bellow answered it.

They spun about to face the lake. The maelstrom subsided; the waters grew calm. Finally, they could make out the body of the bull drifting toward shore.

'Children, be ready!' Gwen warned.

'No, I don't think so.' Rod frowned, and stepped carefully toward the lake. About twenty feet away, he could see a thick stew of blood and chunks of flesh drifting away toward the east. A passing crow noticed, too, circled back, and flew down for a sample. Rod shuddered and turned away. 'I don't think we'll have to worry about the horse, either.'

''Tis a courtesy of thy good rescue,' Elidor said solemnly. 'An thou hadst not come to our aid, this land had lacked a sovereign. A King's thanks go with thee!'

Rod looked down, startled. Then he darted a questioning glance at Gwen. She looked as startled as he felt, but she was nodding in confirmation.

Well, maybe she could read the kid's mind, but he couldn't. 'Are you the King of this land, then?'

'I am.' Elidor was wet to the skin; his fine clothes were torn and bedraggled, and he'd lost his coronet somewhere along the fray – but he straightened his shoulders, and bore himself regally. 'By courtesy of my mother the Queen, though I never knew her, and of Eachan, my father the King, dead these three years, I am King of Tir Chlis.'

Rod's face composed itself, hiding a stewpot of emotions – incredulity, sorrow for the boy, a yearning to take him in his arms . . . and the realization that this could be a huge stroke of good fortune for a family of wanderers, marooned in a strange world. 'It is my honour to greet Your Majesty. Yet I cannot help but notice your age, may I enquire who cares for you now?'

'A thousand thanks for kind rescue, brave knight and fair lady!' gasped an anxious voice.

Rod looked up, startled.

A gross fat man, a little shorter than Rod, with a gleaming bald pate surrounded by a fringe of hair around the back of his head, and a ruddy complexion, waddled toward them, swatched in an acre of white ankle-length robe topped with a brocade surcoat, and belted by a four-inch-wide strap. Behind him trooped thirty courtiers in bell-sleeved skirted coats and hose, and two peasants with a brace of belling hounds.

The courtiers all had swords, and the fat man had a lot of sweat and a look just short of panic. 'Gramercy, gramercy! If aught had happened to mine nephew through my lack of vigilance, I had never come out of sackcloth and ashes! Yet how didst thou know to set a bull of the Crodh Mara 'gainst the Each Uisge?'

'Ag whisky?' Rod was watching Elidor; the boy had drawn in on himself, staring at the fat man with a look that held wariness, but a certain longing, too . . . 'Er, well . . . to tell you the truth . . . '

'We but knew the old grannies' tales,' Gwen cut in hurriedly. 'The water-bull and the water-horse – all else followed from reason.' Her elbow tapped Rod lightly in the short ribs.

They were the wounded ones; the stab of pain cut through the murk of sentiment. 'Er, yes, of course! Opposite forces cancel out.'

'Indeed, an thou sayst it.' The fat man's brows were knit. 'Though I do not claim to understand. Thou must be a warlock most accomplished.'

Typed again! Rod winced. There must be something about him . . . 'A great part of wizardry is luck. By good fortune, we were here when we were needed.' He took a chance. 'Your Lordship.'

Fatso nodded, but his gaze strayed to Elidor, as though to assure himself the boy was all right. 'Fortunate indeed, else I had lacked a nephew – and this land, a King.' There was something of longing in his eyes, too.

He tore his gaze away from Elidor and turned back to Rod, forcing a little smile. 'Forgive me; I forget the courtesies. I am Duke Foidin, Regent to His Majesty, King Elidor.' He extended a beringed hand, palm down.

Gwen beamed, but there was uncertainty in her eyes. Rod tried to convert his puzzled frown to a polite smile, but he kept his hands on his hips, and inclined his head. 'Rodney d'Armand, Lord Gallowglass.' Some prick of caution kept him from using his real title. 'And my Lady Gwendylon – and our children.'

'I rejoice at thine acquaintance, Lord and Lady . . . Gallowglass?' The Duke seemed a little puzzled. ' 'Tis a title unfamiliar. Thou art, then, travellers from another land, far from thine own estates?'

'Very far,' Rod agreed. 'A foul sorcerer's curse has sped us here, far from our homeland; but we shall return with all due expedition.'

'Nay, not so quickly!' the Duke cried. 'Thou must needs let us honour thee – for thou hast saved a King!'

Somehow, Rod didn't want to spend a night under the man's roof. ''Tis courteously said – but time does press upon us . . . '

'Certes, not so much as that!' Wet and bedraggled, Elidor stepped up to his uncle's side – but still with that look of wariness about him. 'Surely thou'lt not deny the hospitality of a King!'

He was trying so very hard to be regal! Rod was about to cave in – but Gwen did, first. 'Well, a night's rest, then – we are sore wearied.'

But Rod was watching the Duke. The man's face lit up at Elidor's approach, and his hand hovered over the boy's shoulder, but didn't quite touch; Rod saw the longing in his face again, quickly masked, then a hint of a darker emotion that flashed upon his features, and was gone – but left Rod chilled. Somehow, he didn't think he'd want to be around if the Duke lost his temper.

Then Elidor smiled bravely up at his uncle, and the man's face softened. Troubled, he nodded reassuringly at the boy, forcing a smile; the hand hovered again, then fell to his side. He turned the smile up to Rod. 'Thou art in accord with thy Lady, then? Thou'lt guest within our castle this night, that we may honour thee?'

Gwen's elbow brushed his side again, and Rod winced again, too. She hadn't had to do that! The Duke seemed nice enough, or seemed to be honestly trying to be – but somehow, Rod didn't want to leave Elidor alone with him just yet. 'Indeed we shall. We are honoured to accept your invitation.'

'Most excellent!' The Duke's face split into a huge, delighted smile. 'Then come, in joy! To Castle Drolm!'

He whirled away, the hovering hand finally descending to clap Elidor's shoulder, and clasp the boy against his side. Elidor seemed to resist a little, and the Duke's hand immediately sprang free. *Insecure*, thought Rod, as he and his family were borne forward by the tide of the entourage that followed the Duke, roaring a victorious war-song.

'Papa,' Cordelia piped up through the din. 'I don't like going to that man's house.'

'Don't worry, dear,' Rod reassured her. 'We can always get out again – fast.'

# Chapter Eight

'The excitement, the glory of it!' Brother Chard burbled. 'Just think, Father, we may be the first clergy to contact these poor, benighted people in centuries!'

'Quite so, Brother.' Father Al couldn't help smiling at the young pilot's enthusiasm. 'On the other hand, we may arrive to find them quite well-equipped with their own clergy; one never knows.' He gazed at the viewscreen, letting his subconscious read ecclesiastical symbols into the random swirls of colour that hyperspace induced in the cameras.

'Roman Catholic clergy, in a society devoted to magic? Scarcely, Father! Just think, a whole new world of lost souls to save! We must try to get some estimate of the population, so that I can come back to His Grace with some idea as to how many missionaries we'll be requiring! How long before we get there?'

'Why ask me?' Father Al hid a smile. 'You're the pilot.'

'Oh! Yes, of course!' Brother Chard peered at his instrument panel. 'Let's see, ten light years . . . It should be about six more days.' He turned back to Father Al. 'Sorry the quarters are so cramped, Father.'

'It's easy to tell you've never spent much time inside a confessional. Don't worry, Brother, the quarters are positively luxurious. Why, we even have a separate cabin for sleeping! . . . Ungh!'

His body slammed into his shock webbing, as though the ship had suddenly rammed a wall. Then it took off like a bear with a fire on its tail, slapping Father Al back into his couch. His vision darkened, and he fought for breath, waiting for the bright little stars to stop drifting across his field of view. They didn't, but they did dim and fade, and the velvet blackness with them. Through its last tatters, he saw Brother Chard leaning forward groggily, groping toward his control console.

'Wha . . . what happened?'

'See for yourself!' The monk pointed at the viewscreen. Father Al looked, and saw the velvet darkness and bright little stars again;

but this time, they stayed still. 'We're back in normal space?'

Brother Chard nodded. 'And travelling at sub-light-speed. Very high, but still below C. We're lucky the difference in velocity didn't smear us against the forward bulkhead.'

'It would have, without the webbing. What went wrong?'

Brother Chard peered at a readout screen, punching keys. 'No significant damage; everything's padded as well as we were . . . There! The isomorpher quit!'

'Quit? Just . . . quit? Why?'

'That is a good question, isn't it?' Brother Chard loosed his webbing, smiling grimly. 'Shall we go have a look, Father?'

They climbed into pressure suits, cycled through the tiny airlock one at a time, clipped their safety lines to rings on the ship's skin, and clambered aft to the drive unit. Brother Chard slipped out a wrench and loosened the access hatch. He slid through headfirst; Father Al followed, groping for the rungs set into the hull, gaze riveted to the mirror-surfaced unit before him. 'Doesn't appear to be a break in the shielding.'

'No,' Brother Chard agreed. 'At least we can rule out any effects from stray radiation. Though you never know; if we can't find anything else, we'll have to go over it with a microscope.' He turned a knob, and the silver egg split open, the top half lifting up like a clamshell. A steady background of white noise faded in on Father Al's helmet speaker. He frowned. 'It *is* sick, isn't it?'

'Yes; we should be hearing a 1650 Hz tone.' Brother Chard looked up. 'I didn't know you knew electronics, Father.'

Father Al shrugged. 'Cathodeans pick up a lot from each other, especially during the seminary bull-sessions. I wouldn't claim to be an FTL mechanic, but I know basically how the isomorpher works.'

'Or how it doesn't. Well, let's see where the circuit broke.' Brother Chard pulled out a set of probes and started poking at the isomorpher's insides. Father Al crouched beside him in the crawl space, silent and intent, watching the meter on the forearm of Brother Chard's suit, atop the pocket that held the probes.

Finally, the monk looked up. 'No break, Father. Current's flowing through the whole beast.'

'Then you've got a grain that's passing current, but not doing anything with it. May I try?'

Brother Chard stared at him; then, reluctantly, he moved back. 'Certain you know what you're doing, Father?'

'Enough to know how to find out which grain is gone.' Father Al slipped the probes out of his sleeve pocket. 'We just test each pair of terminals, and when the needle goes into the red, we've found the trouble-spot, haven't we?'

'Yes, that's all,' Brother Chard said drily. 'Check your chronometer, Father, I think we'll have to go back for a recharged air cycler in about an hour.'

'Oh, I don't think it'll take us that long.' Father Al started probing.

Brother Chard was silent; when his voice came over the headphones, it was strained. 'I hope you're right, of course, Father – but it could take a week. If only we had a diagnostic computer aboard!'

'Well, a pinnace can't carry everything,' Father Al said philosophically. 'Besides, Brother Chard, I have a certain faith in the perversity of electronic circuitry.'

'You mean a faith in perversity, period, don't you, Father? I've heard some of the stories you Cathodeans tell about Finagle; sometimes I think you've fallen into heresy, and made a god of him!'

'Scarcely a god – but we might promote him to the status of demon, if he were real – which, fortunately, he's not. But the perversity he personifies is real enough, Brother.'

'True,' Brother Chard admitted. 'But the perversity's in us, Father, not in the universe.'

'But so much of our universe is man-made, Brother, so many of the things around us, the things that keep us alive! And it's so easy for us to build our own perversity into them – especially really complicated pieces of electronics!'

'Such as an isomorpher?'

'Well, yes. But computers, too, and 3DT cameras, and any number of other gadgets. Have you ever noticed, Brother, how they'll sometimes stop working for no apparent reason, then suddenly start again?'

'Now and then. But when you dig into them, Father, you can always find a reason.'

'When *you* dig into them, perhaps. Not when I do. But then, I seem to have an anti-mechanical personality; any chronometer I carry starts gaining about five minutes a day as soon as I touch it. On the other hand, there're people machines seem to like; let one of them walk in and lay his hand on the widget, and it works perfectly.'

'A little far-fetched, isn't that, Father?'

'Perhaps. But I'm fetching as far as I can, right now.' *Fetching aid from my patron, I hope. St Vidicon, no matter how far away you may be, please come to my aid now! Intercede with the Almighty for me, that this isomorpher may begin working again, long enough to get us to Gramarye and to get Brother Chard safely home again!* 'That might do it.' Father Al withdrew his probes. 'By the way, Brother Chard, you did disengage the isomorpher before we came out here, didn't you?'

'Of course, Father. There's just a trickle of current flowing through it now.'

'Good. Can you fire it up fully from in here?'

'I could.' The ghost of a smile tugged at Brother Chard's lips. 'But I wouldn't recommend it. The ship might not go into H-space, but we might.'

'Hm.' Father Al turned away toward the access hatch. 'Then let's go back to the bridge, shall we? We'll try it from there.'

'But you can't think it'll work again, Father! We haven't even found the trouble yet.'

'Perhaps not.' Father Al turned back with a smile. 'But I think we may have fixed it.'

'That's impossible!'

'Brother Chard, you should be ashamed of yourself! *All* things are possible – with God.'

'And St Vidicon of Cathode,' Brother Chard muttered; but he closed the isomorpher's shell, anyway, and followed Father Al.

On the way back to the airlock, Father Al finally let himself feel the dread at what might happen if the isomorpher *couldn't* be fixed. They'd be stranded light years away from any inhabitable planet, with only a month's supply of food and water. The air cycler would keep working for several years and, with strict rationing, the food might last an extra month; but no matter how you looked at it, even if they accelerated the ship to nearly the speed of light, by the time it came near enough to civilization for its beacon to summon aid, it would be carrying only two mummies.

Dread clutched at Father Al's belly; fear soured his throat. He took a deep breath, closed his eyes. *Thy will, Father, not mine. If it suits Thy purpose that I die in this place, then let it be as Thou wilt have it.*

Serenity filled him; the fear ebbed away. Smiling, he ducked into the airlock.

They loosened their helmets and webbed themselves into their couches. Brother Chard fed power into the engines, then engaged the isomorpher and fired it up.

The stars disappeared in a swirl of colours.

Father Al heaved out a huge sigh. 'Praise Heaven!' *And I thank you, St Vidicon, for interceding with Him for me.*

Brother Chard just sat staring at the viewscreen. 'I don't believe it. I see it, but I don't believe it.'

'Faith, good Brother,' Father Al chided gently. 'With faith, all things are possible.' He took out his breviary and began reading his Office.

# Chapter Nine

The Duke's Hall was huge, panelled in a greyish wood with silver highlights, and adorned with old weapons, bent and battered shields in a variety of coats-of-arms, and the skins of animals with the heads still on – not the most appetizing decoration in the world, Rod reflected, as he looked up into the eyes of a twelve-point stag while he chewed a mouthful of venison.

He noticed that Magnus was chewing his food very carefully, and wondered why. *Have to ask him about that, later.* Still, it seemed like a good idea. Seemed like a good idea to be careful about everything, with Duke Foidin for a host. In accordance with which thought, he made sure that he served himself only from platters that at least two other courtiers were eating from. He noticed Gwen was doing the same, and pointedly hadn't sipped her wine.

The Duke noticed, too. 'Do you not find my vintage sweet, Lord Gallowglass?'

Rod swallowed and smiled. 'Religious rule, Duke. We never touch intoxicating spirits.' *We have too many for friends.*

That drew startled looks from the whole table. A low mutter of gossip started up.

'Be ye paynim, then?' the Duke enquired, a little too carelessly.

'"Paynim"? . . . Oh, Moslems! No, not at all. Are you?'

'Sir!' The Duke drew himself up, affronted, and all the courtiers stared, aghast. 'What mockery is this? Are we not in Christendom?'

OK, so they were. At least Rod knew what the local religion was. 'No offence, Milord. But as you know, we're far-travellers; I honestly did not know that you're of the same religion as ourselves.'

Foidin relaxed. 'Ah, then, ye do be Christian folk. Yet how's this? I've never heard of a Christian would refuse wine.'

Rod smiled. '"Other lands, other rules", Milord. At least, in our land, the Church allows wine at Mass. I've heard of some Christians who won't even go *that* far.'

'Strange, most truly strange,' Foidin murmured. 'Are many of your folk warlocks, like yourself?'

*Careful, boy.* 'Not too many. It requires the Gift, the talent, and a great deal of study and training.'

'Ah.' The Duke nodded. 'Even as it doth here. I' truth, there be not four warlocks of any power in this land – and one of them's a vile recreant, who seeks to steal the person of the King, and usurp my regency!'

'No!' Now was the time to keep him talking – but Foidin wasn't the type to give any information away. What was he trying to pull?

Elidor nerved himself up. 'Nay, Uncle! Lord Kern . . . '

'Hush; be still, Majesty.' Foidin patted Elidor's hand with a paternal touch and gave him a steely glance. 'Thou'st had time a-plenty to speak with these good folk; do now allow your old uncle a modicum of conversation.'

Elidor met that steely gaze, and subsided.

'Well, I can't say I'm terribly surprised.' Rod turned back to his food. 'Wherever there's wizardry, there'll always be warlocks who misuse their power.'

'Aye, and so he doth!' Foidin fairly jumped on it. 'Indeed, his villainy surpasseth all imagining; he would seek to lay the whole of the land under the rule of magic!'

The table was noticeably silent. Elidor was reddening like a volcano, about to erupt.

Gwen caught his eyes and moved her hand, just a little, in a calming gesture. He stared at her, surprised; then he glanced up at his uncle, and back to his food.

'Indeed,' Gwen cooed, 'Tir Chlis is fortunate to have so godly a man as thyself, to defend it from such a knave.'

Nice try, Rod thought, but he was sure the Duke knew about flattery.

He did; he battened on it. He fairly expanded. 'Why, gently said, sweet lady – and true, quite true! Aye, the greater part of this land now dwells in peace and prosperity, under m— . . . His Majesty's beneficent rule.'

'Mmf!' A courtier across the table suddenly pressed a napkin to his mouth; bit his tongue, probably.

The Duke noticed, and frowned.

'Then thou must presently free the unhappy remainder,' Gwen said quickly.

'Ah, but 'tis not easily done, fair lady.' The Duke waved a forefinger sadly. 'Knowest thou that vasty range of mountains, in the north-east?'

'Nay; we came by magic.' Gwen smiled sweetly. 'We know only the meadow where thou didst find us, and the stretch of riverbank that curls on northward to the spot where we appeared.'

Northward? Rod could've sworn they'd *hiked* northward – which meant their entry-point lay southward!

'So newly-come as that!' The Duke was too surprised. Who was pumping whom, here? 'Yet let me assure thee, the mountains lie there, in the north-east, blocking off a poor eighth-part of this land; and 'tis there Lord Kern hath fled, to try to build a robber-force to steal the King away. I cannot go against him through those mountains, for he's blocked the only pass that's large enough for armies, with foul sorcery.'

'Yet he is thereby blocked himself!' Gwen crowed, delighted.

The Duke looked surprised, but he hid it quickly. 'Ye-e-e-s, there is that, sweet lady – for if he lifts his sorcery, my armies would be upon him in a moment!'

The courtier across the table was having trouble swallowing again.

'Yet there is coastline near him,' the Duke went on, 'and he hath attempted to land a force within our safe domain.'

'Thou hast repulsed him, then?'

'I have.' The Duke preened a little. 'My ships are of the best, most especially when I command 'em.'

The courtier grabbed for his wine cup.

'Thus have matters stood for three long years.' The Duke spread his hands. 'He cannot come out, nor can I go in, to free those miserable wretches who live beneath his yoke. Yet time will ripen my good designs, and rot his fell ones; my armies daily increase, as do my ships; and, when the time hath come, I'll strike at him by sea and grind him to the dust! Then will this land be whole again, to deliver up to Elidor when he doth come of age.'

The boy-King looked frightened at that last remark. Gwen caught his eyes briefly, then looked back at the Duke. 'Simply planned, but nobly, Milord. And thou art wise to bide thy time; disaster visits he who strikes before the iron's hot!'

'Well said, well said.' The Duke sat back, nodding, pleased. 'Thou art most rare of ladies. I am not accustomed to such intelligence in one so beautiful.'

Rod felt his hackles rising; but Gwen's foot touched his under the table, and he forced a smile. 'And we are fortunate to have so wise and prudent a host – and one who sets so goodly a table, as well!'

The Duke waved carelessly. 'My table's yours, whenever thou dost wish it. Yet dost thou wish to dine at my most noble banquet?'

Rod stared, caught short.

'Come, sir.' Gwen smiled roguishly. 'Wouldst thou have us think thou hast not laid forth thy finest for the rescuers of thy King?'

'Assuredly, I have,' the Duke said heartily. 'Yet I spoke not of game and pasties, but of battle.'

'Oh.' Rod nodded slowly. 'You speak of this gallant expedition to free the north-east corner of Tir Chlis.'

'Aye, indeed.' The Duke's eyelids drooped, and tension seemed to emanate from him, as from a lion who sees the antelope step near. 'As I have told thee, in that broil I'll face magics as well as spears. 'Twould soothe me, then, to have stout warlocks by my side. How say you, Lord Gallowglass? Wilt thou dine at my table, and aid King Elidor?'

'That's . . . a most attractive offer.' Rod found Gwen's eyes. 'To tell you the truth, nothing of the sort had occurred to me. We *had* been planning to get back home as fast as we could.'

''Tis a long and weary journey, I doubt not,' Gwen pointed out. 'And, to tell the truth, we know not even where our homeland lies, nor how far it is.'

'We *could* use a rest,' Rod agreed, 'and some time to find out where we are.' He glanced back at the Duke, and saw Elidor staring at him, suddenly tense.

But Magnus was sitting next to Rod, looking absolutely chirpy. Elidor noticed him, and relaxed a little.

'It *is* a very attractive offer,' Rod said to the Duke. 'But you'll understand, Milord, that w — *I* must consider it fully. I'll give you my answer over breakfast.'

'I shall await it eagerly,' the Duke said, smiling. 'Yet we have lingered long at table, and the hour doth grow late. No doubt thou'rt wearied.'

'Kind of,' Rod admitted. 'A soft bed would feel good.'

'Then let us have no more of talk.' The Duke clapped his hands, and a functionary in a glittering tunic stepped forward. 'Show these good people to their chambers!' The Duke stood. 'Myself am minded also of my rest; the day has been demanding. Elidor – Majesty! Wilt thou come with me?'

Elidor rose slowly, still wary – and almost, Rod would have said, hopefully.

His uncle seized his shoulder; Elidor winced, and bit back a cry. 'To bed, to bed!' the Duke sang jovially. 'Good night to all!'

# Chapter Ten

'*Amphibians?*' Father Al stared at the screen of the electron-telescope, unbelieving.

'I've noticed a couple of true lizards, but they're small.' Brother Chard shook his head. 'I'm sorry, Father. We've been around this planet four times in four separate orbits, and that's the highest form of life on any of the continents.'

'So there's only that one large island with humans; the rest of the planet is carboniferous.' Father Al shook his head. 'Well, if we needed anything to assure us that we're dealing with a colony instead of native sentients, we've found it. Could you call up the recordings of that island, Brother Chard?'

The monk pushed buttons, and a large island appeared in the main viewscreen, a huge, uncut emerald floating in a blue sea. 'Close in on that one large town, if you please,' Father Al murmured. A tiny hole in the greenery, a little north and west of the centre of the island, began to grow; the shorelines disappeared beyond the edges of the screen. The dot swelled into an irregular, circular clearing, and other dots began to appear around it.

'Really the only settlement large enough to be called a town,' Father Al mused.

The roofs filled the screen now, with the spire of a church and the turrets of a castle reaching up toward them, from the crest of a hill off to the eastern edge of the town.

'It's medieval architecture, Father – early Tudor, I'd guess.'

'Yes, but the castle's got to be thirteenth century; I'd swear it was almost a reproduction of Chateau Gaillard. And the church is late Gothic; fourteenth century at the earliest.'

'Church! It's a cathedral! Why does it look so familiar?'

'Possibly because you've seen pictures of the cathedral of Chartres. The original colonists don't seem to have been terribly original, do they?'

Brother Chard frowned. 'But if they were going to copy famous buildings from Terra, why didn't they make them all from the same period?'

Father Al shrugged. 'Why should they? Each century had its own beauties. No doubt some liked the fifteenth century, some the fourteenth, some the thirteenth . . . if we kept looking, Brother, I'm sure we'd find something Romanesque.'

Brother Chard peered at the screen as the camera zoomed in to fill it with an overhead view of a single street. 'Apparently they applied the same principle to their clothing; there's a bell-sleeved tunic next to a doublet!'

'And there's a doublet *with* bell-sleeves.' Father Al shook his head. 'I can almost hear their ancestors saying, "It's my world, and I'll do what I want with it!" '

Brother Chard turned to him with a sympathetic smile. 'You're going to have a bit of a problem with transportation, aren't you?'

'I never did learn to ride a horse.' Father Al felt his stomach sink. 'Appalling great brutes, aren't they?'

Brother Chard turned back to the viewscreen. 'Are you searching for just one man down there, Father? Or a community?'

'One lone individual,' Father Al said grimly. 'I can't just punch up a directory and scan for his name, can I?' He thought of Yorick and had to fight down a slow swell of anger; the grinning jester could've prepared him for this!

'Under the circumstances,' Brother Chard said slowly, 'I don't really suppose there's much point in following the usual protocol about landing.'

'Better try it, anyway, Brother,' Father Al sighed. 'You wouldn't want to be imprisoned on a technicality, now would you?'

'Especially not by all the King's horses and all the King's men.' Brother Chard shrugged. 'Wel, it can't do any harm. Who could hear our transmission down there, anyway?' He set the communicator to 'broadband' and keyed the microphone. 'This is Spacecraft H394P02173 Beta Cass 19, the Diocese of Beta Cassiopeia's *St Iago*, calling Gramarye Control. Come in, Gramarye Control.'

'We hear you, *St Iago*,' a resonant voice answered. 'What is your destination?'

Father Al almost fell through his webbing.

'Did I hear that correctly?' Brother Chard stared at the communicator, goggle-eyed. He noted the frequency readout and reached forward to adjust the video to match it. An intent face replaced the overhead view of the town street, a thin face with troubled eyes and a dark fringe of hair cut straight across the forehead. But Father Al scarcely noticed the face; he was staring at the little yellow screwdriver handle in the breast pocket of the monk's robe.

'What is your destination, *St Ia*— Ah!' The face lit up, and the man's gaze turned directly toward them as they came into sight on his screen. Then he stared, '*St Iago*, you are men of the cloth!'

'And your own cloth, too.' Father Al straightened up in his couch. 'Father Aloysius Uwell, of the order of St Vidicon of Cathode, at your service. My companion is Brother Chard, of the Order of St Francis Assisi.'

'Father Cotterson, Order of St Vidicon,' the monk returned, reluctantly. 'What is your destination, Father?'

'Gramarye, Father Cotterson. I've been dispatched to find a man named Rod Gallowglass.'

'The High Warlock!' Father Cotterson's voice turned sombre.

'You'll pardon my surprise, Father, but how is it you've retained knowledge of technology?' asked Father Al. 'I was told your ancestors had fled here to escape it.'

'How would you have known that?'

'Through a prophet, of a sort,' Father Al said slowly. 'He left a message to be opened a thousand years after he wrote it, and we've just read it.'

'A prophecy?' Father Cotterson murmured, his eyed glazing. 'About *Gramarye*?'

He was in shock; one of his prime myths had just focused on himself. The pause was fortunate; Father Al needed a little time to reflect, too.

High Warlock? Rod Gallowglass?

Already?

As to the rest of it, it was perfectly logical – there had been a Cathodean priest among the original colonists; and where there was one Cathodean, science and technology would be kept alive, somehow.

How? Well, that was nit-picking; it had any number of answers. The question could wait. Father Al cleared his throat. 'I think we have a great deal to discuss, Father Cotterson – but could it wait till we're face-to-face? I'd like to make planetfall first.'

Father Cotterson came back to life. He hesitated, clearly poised on the horns of a dilemma. Father Al could almost hear the monk's thoughts – which was the worst danger? To allow Father Al to land? Or to send him away, and risk his return with reinforcements? Father Al sympathized; myths can be far more terrifying than the people underlying them.

Father Cotterson came to a decision. 'Very well, Father, you may bring down your ship. But please land after nightfall; you could create something of a panic. After all, no one's seen a ship land here in all our history.'

Father Al was still puzzling that one over, three hours later, when the land below them was dark and rising up to meet them. If no spaceship had landed for centuries, how had Rod Gallowglass come to be there? Yorick had said he was an off-worlder.

Well, no use theorizing when he didn't have all the facts. He gazed up into the viewscreen. 'About two hundred metres away from the monastery, please, Brother Chard. That should give you time to lift off again, before they can reach us. Not that I think they *would* prevent you from leaving – but it never hurts to be certain.'

'Whatever you say, Father,' Brother Chard said wearily.

Father Al looked up. 'You're not still saddened at discovering they don't need missionaries, are you?'

'Well . . .'

'Come, come, Brother, buck up.' Father Al patted the younger man on the shoulder. 'These good monks have been out of contact with the rest of the Church for centuries; no doubt they'll need several emissaries, to update them on advances in theology and Church history.'

Brother Chard did perk up a bit at that. Father Al was glad the young monk hadn't realized the corollary – that those 'emissaries' might find themselves having to combat heresy. Colonial theologians could come up with some very strange ideas, given five hundred years' isolation from Rome.

And Rod Gallowglass could spark the grandaddy of them all, if he weren't properly guided.

The pinnace landed, barely touching the grass, and Father Al clambered out of the miniature airlock. He hauled his travelling case down behind him, watched the airlock close, then went around to the nose, moving back fifty feet or so, and waved at the nose camera. Lights blinked in answering farewell, and the St Iago lifted off again. It was only a speck against dark clouds by the time the local monks came puffing up.

'Why . . . did you let him . . . take off again?' Father Cotterson panted.

'Why, because this is my mission, not his,' Father Al answered in feigned surprise. 'Brother Chard was only assigned to bring me here, Father, not to aid me in my mission.'

Father Cotterson glared upward at the receding dot, like a spider trying to glare down a fly that gained wisdom at the last second. The monk didn't look quite so imposing in the flesh; he was scarcely taller than Father Al, and lean to the point of skinniness. Father Al's respect for him rose a notch; no doubt Father Cotterson fasted frequently.

Either that, or he had a tapeworm.

Father Cotterson turned back to Father Al, glaring. 'Have you considered, Father, how you are to leave Gramarye once your mission is completed?'

'Why . . . ' said Father Al slowly, 'I'm not certain that I will, Father Cotterson.' As he said it, the fact sank in upon him – this might indeed be his final mission, though it might last decades. If it didn't, and if the Lord had uses for him elsewhere, no doubt he would contrive the transportation.

Father Cotterson didn't look too happy about the idea of Father Al's becoming a resident. 'I can see we'll have to discuss this at some length. Shall we return to the monastery, Father?'

'Yes, by all means,' Father Al murmured, and fell into step beside the lean monk as he turned back towards the walled enclosure in the distance. A dozen other brown-robes fell in behind them.

'A word as to local ways,' Father Cotterson said. 'We speak modern English within our own walls; but without, we speak the vernacular. There are quite a few archaic words and phrases, but the greatest difference is the use of the second person singular, in place of the second person plural. You might wish to begin practise with us, Father.'

'And call thee "thee" and "thou"? Well, that should be easy enough.' After all, Father Al had read the King James Version.

'A beginning, at least. Now tell me, Father – why dost thou seek Rod Gallowglass?'

Father Al hesitated. 'Is not that a matter I should discuss with the head of thine Order, Father Cotterson?'

'The Abbot is absent at this time; he is in Runnymede, in conference with Their Majesties. I am his Chancellor, Father, and the monastery is in my care while he is gone. Anything that thou wouldst say to him, thou mayst discuss with me.'

A not entirely pleasant development, Father Al decided. He didn't quite trust Father Cotterson; the man had the look of the fanatic about him, and Father Al wasn't quite certain which Cause he served.

On the other hand, maybe it was just the tapeworm.

'The prophecy I told thee of,' Father Al began – and paused. Decidedly, he didn't trust Father Cotterson. If the man was the religious fanatic he appeared to be, how would he react to the idea that the High Warlock would become even more powerful?

So he changed the emphasis a little. 'Our prophecy told us that Rod Gallowglass would be the most powerful wizard ever known. Thou dost see the theological implications of this, of course.'

'Aye, certes.' Father Cotterson smiled without mirth – and also without batting an eye. 'Wrongly guided, such an one could inspire a Devil's Cult.'

'Aye, so it is.' Father Al fell into the monk's speech style, and frowned up at him. 'How is it this doth not disconcert thee, Father?'

'We know it of old,' the monk replied wearily. 'We have striven to hold our witchfolk from Satan for years. Rest assured,

Father – if no Devil's Cult hath yet arisen on Gramarye, 'tis not like to rise up now.'

'"Witchfolk"?' Suddenly, Father Al fairly quivered with attention to the monk's words. 'What witchfolk are these, Father?'

'Why, the warlocks and witches in the mountains and fens, and in the King's Castle,' Father Cotterson answered. 'Did not thy prophecy speak of them, Father?'

'Not in any detail. And thou dost not see thy High Warlock as any greater threat to thy flock?'

'Nay; he ha' been known nigh onto ten years, Father, and, if aught, hath brought the witchfolk closer to God.' Father Cotterson smiled with a certain smugness, relaxing a little. 'Thy prophet seems to have spake somewhat tardily.'

'Indeed he doth.' But Father Al wondered; the lean monk didn't seem to have noticed anything unusual about Rod Gallowglass. Perhaps there was a big change due in the High Warlock's life-style.

'At all odds, if thou hast come to guide our High Warlock, I fear thou hast wasted time and effort,' Father Cotterson said firmly. 'I assure thee, Father, we are equal to that task.' They came to a halt at the monastery gates. Father Cotterson pounded on them with a fist, shouting, 'Ho, porter!'

'I am sure that thou art,' Father Al murmured as the huge leaves swung open. 'Yet the prime task given me, Father, is to seek out the truth regarding our prophecy. If nought else, my mission is well-spent simply in the learning so much of a flock we had thought lost – and better spent in finding that they are not lost at all, but exceedingly well cared for.'

Father Cotterson fairly beamed at the compliment. 'We do what we can, Father – though we are sorely tried by too little gold, and too few vocations.'

'I assure thee, Father, 'tis the case on every world where humanity doth bide.' Father Al looked about him as they came into a wide, walled yard. 'A fair House you hold, Father, and exceedingly well-kept.'

'Why, I thank thee, Father Uwell. Wilt thou taste our wines?'

'Aye, with a right good will. I would fain see summat of this goodly land of thine, Father, and thy folk. Canst thou provide me with means of transport, and one to guide me?'

The thaw reversed itself, and Father Cotterson frosted up again. 'Why . . . aye, certes, Father. Thou shalt have thy pick of the mules, and a Brother for guide. But I must needs enjoin thee not to leave this our House, till the Lord Abbot hath returned, and held thee in converse.'

'Indeed, 'tis only courtesy, Father,' Father Al said easily.

'Yet most needful,' Father Cotterson said, in a tone of apology that had iron beneath it. 'Our good Lord Abbot must impress upon thee, Father, how strictly thou must guard thy tongue outside these walls. For these people have lived for centuries in a changeless Middle Ages, look you, and any hint of modern ways will seem to them to be sorcery, and might shake their faith. And, too, 'twould cause avalanches of change in this land, and bring ruin and misery to many.'

'I assure thee, Father, I come to verify what is here, not to change it,' Father Al said softly.

But something in the way Father Cotterson had said it assured Father Al that, if he waited for the Abbot, he might spend the rest of his life waiting. After all, he had taken an oath of obedience, and the Abbot might see himself as Father Al's lawful superior, entitled to give binding orders – and might resent it if Father Al chose to honour the Pope's orders over those of an Abbot. His resentment might be rather forcibly expressed – and, though Father Al valued times of quiet contemplation in his cell, he preferred that the cell be above ground, and that the door not be locked from the outside.

' . . . *per omnia saecula saeculorum*,' Father Cotterson intoned.

'Amen,' responded fifty monks, finishing the grace.

Father Cotterson sat, in his place at the centre of the head table, and the other monks followed suit. Father Al was seated at Father Cotterson's right hand, in the guest's place of honour.

'Who are servitors tonight?' Father Cotterson asked.

'Father Alphonse in the kitchen, Father.' One of the monks rose and stripped off his robe, revealing a monk's cloth coverall beneath. 'And myself, at the table.'

'I thank thee, Brother Bertram,' Father Cotterson answered, as the monk floated up over the refectory table and hung there, hovering face-down above the board. Father Alphonse bustled out of the kitchen with a loaded tray and passed it to Brother Bertram, who drifted down to the monk farthest from the head table and held the platter down for the monk to serve himself.

Father Cotterson turned to Father Al. 'Is this custom still

maintained in all chapters of the Order, Father – that each monk becomes servitor in his turn, even the Abbot?'

'Well . . . yes.' Father Al stared at Brother Bertram, his eyes fairly bulging. 'But, ah – not quite in this manner.'

'How so?' Father Cotterson frowned up at Brother Bertram. 'Oh – thou dost speak of his levitation. Well, many of our brethren do not have the trick of it; they, of necessity, walk the length of the tables. Still, 'tis more efficient in this fashion, for those that can do it.'

'I doubt it not.' Father Al felt a thrill course through him; his heart began to sing. 'Are there those amongst thee who can move the dishes whilst they remain seated?'

'Telekinesis?' Father Cotterson frowned. 'Nay; the gene for it is sex-linked, and only females have the ability. Though Brother Mordecai hath pursued some researches into the matter. How doth thy experiments progress, Brother?'

A lean monk swallowed and shook his head. 'Not overly well, Father.' The salt-cellar at the centre of the table trembled, rose a few inches, then fell with a clatter. Brother Mordecai shrugged. 'I can do no better; yet I hope for improvement, with practice.'

Father Al stared at the salt-cellar. 'But – thou didst just say the trait was sex-linked!'

'Aye; yet my sister is telekinetic, and we are both telepaths; so I have begun to attempt to draw on her powers, with the results thou dost see.' Brother Mordecai speared a slab of meat as Brother Bertram drifted past him. 'She, too, doth make the attempt, and doth draw on mine ability. To date, she hath managed to levitate three centimetres, when she doth lie supine.'

Father Cotterson nodded, with pursed lips. 'I had not known she had made so much progress.'

'But . . . but . . . ' Father Al managed to get his tongue working again. 'Is there no danger that she will learn of the technology thou dost so which to keep hidden?'

'Nay.' Brother Mordecai smiled. 'She is of our sister Order.'

'The Anodeans?'

Father Cotterson nodded, smiling. 'It doth warm my heart, Father, to learn that our Orders are maintained still, on other worlds.'

'Yet 'tis indeed a problem of security,' another monk volunteered. 'Our old disciplines seem to wear thin, Father Cotterson, in the closing of our minds to the espers without our Order.'

Father Cotterson stiffened. 'Hath one of the King's "witch-folk" learned of technology from our minds, Father Ignatius?'

'I think not,' the monk answered. 'Yet, the whiles I did meditate on mine electrolyte vies an hour agone, I did sense an echo, an harmonic to my thoughts. I did, of course, listen, and sensed the mind of a babe in resonance with mine. So 'tis not an immediate threat; yet the child will, assuredly, grow.'

'Might not his parents have been listening to his thoughts!'

'Nay; I sensed no further resonance. And yet I think it matters little; the babe's mind held an image of his mother, and 'twas the High Warlock's wife.'

Father Cotterson relaxed. 'Aye, 'tis small danger there; Lady Gallowglass cannot have escaped learning something of technology, and must assuredly comprehend the need of silence on the issue.'

'I take it, then, thou hast found ways of shielding thy minds from other telepaths?' Father Al burst in.

'Indeed.' Father Cotterson nodded. ''Tis linked with the meditation of prayer, Father, in which the mind is closed to the outside world, but opened toward God. Yet it doth seem we'll have to seek new ways to strengthen such closure. Brother Milaine, thou'lt attend to it?'

A portly monk nodded. 'Assuredly, Father.'

'Research is, of course, common amongst we who are cloistered within this monastery,' Father Cotterson explained.

Father Al nodded. ''Twould not be a House of St Vidicon, otherwise. Yet I assume such activity is forbidden to thy parish priests.'

'Nay; 'tis more simply done.' Father Cotterson started cutting his ounce of meat. 'Monks trained for the parishes are taught only their letters and numbers, and theology; only those who take monastic vows are trained in science and technology.'

'A practical system,' Father Al admitted, 'though I mislike secrecy of knowledge.'

'So do we, Father.' Father Cotterson's eyes burned into his. 'Knowledge ought to be free, that all might learn it. Yet 'twas only through subterfuge that Father Ricci, the founder of our Chapter, did manage to retain knowledge of science when he did come to Gramarye; and assuredly, he'd have been burned for a witch had he attempted to teach what he knew. Those who originally did colonize this planet were intent on forgetting all knowledge of science. We'd likely suffer burning ourselves, if we did attempt to disclose what we know – and 'twould throw the land into chaos. The beginnings of science did batten the turmoil of Europe's Renaissance, on Terra; what would knowledge of modern technology and science do to this medieval culture? Nay, we must keep our knowledge secret yet awhile.'

'Still, the High Warlock may ope us a path for the beginnings of teaching it,' Father Ignatius offered.

'Indeed he may.' Father Cotterson's eyes gleamed with missionary zeal.

'Saint Vidicon,' Father Al murmured, 'was a teacher.'

'As are we all – are we not?' Father Cotterson fairly beamed at him. 'Are we not? For how can we gain new knowledge, and not wish immediately to share it with others?'

This, Father Al decided, was the kind of fanaticism he could agree with.

Father Cotterson turned back to his monks. 'Apropos of which, Brother Feldspar, how doth *thy* researches?'

Brother Feldspar chewed his meat thoughtfully. 'Dost thou not wish more salt on this fowl, Father?'

'Indeed I do, but . . . '

The salt cellar appeared in front of Father Cotterson with a whoosh of displaced air.

He sat back sharply, eyes wide, startled.

The company burst into laughter.

After a second, Father Cotterson relaxed and guffawed with them. 'A most excellent jest, Brother Feldspar! Yet I must caution thee against thy proclivity for practical jokes.'

'Yet without it, Father, how would I ever have begun to seek methods of teleporting objects other than myself?'

'Truth,' Father Cotterson admitted. 'Yet I think thou didst make intermediate bits of progress in thine experiments that thou didst not inform us of. Beware, Brother; we might credit someone else with thy results! For a moment, I thought Brother Chronopolis had made progress.'

'Sadly, no, Father,' Brother Chronopolis smiled. 'The theory is sound, and I do think we *could* manufacture a quantum black hole – but we fear to do it on a planet's surface.'

Father Al tried not to stare.

'Indeed,' Father Cotterson commiserated. 'I shudder to think of the effects of so steep a gravity-gradient, Brother; and I've no wish to find myself atop a sudden new volcano! Nay, I fear the experiment will have to wait till we've access to space flight.'

Brother Chronopolis turned to Father Al. 'Father, when thou dost depart Gramarye . . . '

'Well, I could not perform the experiment myself.' Father Al smiled. 'I do be an anthropologist, not a physicist. Yet where I can provide aid, I will rejoice to do so.'

'The rest is for the Abbot to consider,' Father Cotterson said firmly.

*Manufacture* quantum black holes? The DDT's best scientists still thought they couldn't exist! Either the Gramarye monks were very mistaken – or very advanced. There was a way to find out . . . Father Al said casually, 'Hast thou made progress in molecular circuitry?'

The whole room was silent in an instant; every eye was fastened to him. 'Nay,' breathed Brother Chronopolis, 'canst thou make a circuit of a molecule?'

Well. They were very far behind, in *some* things. 'Not I, myself. Yet I do know that 'tis done; they do fashion single crystalline molecules that can perform all the functions of . . . ' What was that ancient term? Oh, yes . . . 'whole integrated-circuit chip.'

'But thou knowest not the fashion of it?'

'I fear I do not.'

' 'Tis enough, 'tis enough.' Brother Feldspar held up a quieting palm. 'We know it can be done, now; 'twill not be long ere we do it.'

Somehow, Father Al didn't doubt that for a minute.

'A most excellent evening, indeed,' Father Cotterson sighed as he opened the oaken door and ushered Father Al in. 'Thy presence did stimulate discussion wonderfully, Father.'

' 'Twas fascinating, Father – especially that account of the nun who doth surgery without opening the body.'

'Well, 'tis only the mending of burst blood vessels, and the massaging of hearts thus far,' Father Cotterson reminded him. 'Yet it doth hold great promise. I trust this cell will be to thy satisfaction, Father.'

'Luxurious,' Father Al breathed, looking around at the nine-by-twelve room with bare plaster walls, a straw mattress on an oaken cot-frame, a wash-stand and a writing-desk with a three-legged stool. 'True wood is luxury indeed, Father!'

'To us, 'tis the least expensive material,' Father Cotterson said with a smile. 'I'll leave thee to thy devotions, then, Father.'

'God be with thee this night, Father,' Father Al returned, with a warm smile, as Father Cotterson closed the door.

Then Father Al darted over to it, carefully pressing his ear against the wood. Faintly, he heard a key turn in a lock – and all his earlier forebodings came flooding back. Disappointment stabbed him; he'd found himself liking the monks' company so well that he'd hoped his suspicions were unfounded, then had become almost certain it was only his own paranoia.

Not that locking him in his cell proved they intended to imprison him, and not let him see the rest of Gramarye. In fact, the Abbot might be delighted to have him visit Rod Gallowglass.

But he also might not.

So Father Al charitably decided to avoid putting him to the test. Accordingly, he waited two hours, after which all the Brothers must certainly have been snoring on their cots. Then he took out his vest-pocket tool-kit, picked the huge old lock, and slipped down darkened hallways, as silently as a prayer. He drifted through the colonnade like a wraith of incense, found a ladder and a rope, and slipped silently over the wall.

They were such wonderful monks. It was so much better to remove temptation from their path.

# Chapter Eleven

'All sleep, except Elidor,' Magnus said, glowering.

He sat on the edge of a massive four-poster bed opposite a fireplace as tall as Rod. Tapestries covered cold stone walls; Rod paced on a thick carpet.

'He was . . . ' Cordelia burst out; but Gwen clapped a hand over her mouth, and stared at Magnus. He looked up at her, surprised, then nodded quickly, and closed his eyes, sitting very straight. He held it for a few minutes, then relaxed. 'I'm sorry, Mama; I was carried away.'

'No great harm is done,' Gwen assured him. 'They heard only that one sentence, and they cannot do so much with that.'

'Spies?' Rod frowned. 'How many of them *were* there?'

'Only the two,' Gwen assured him. 'One there, behind the knight on the tapestry o'er the hearth – thou seest that his eye is truly a hole? And one behind the panel next the door, where there's a knot dropped out.'

Rod nodded. 'Milford Foidin likes back-up systems – no doubt so he can check them against each other, and make sure no one's lying. Well, it kinda goes along with the rest of his devious personality; I think he's in the process of inventing the police state.' He turned to Magnus. 'How long are they out for?'

'Till dawn,' Magnus assured him, 'or after.'

Rod shook his head in amazement. 'How does he do it so *fast*?'

Gwen shook her head, too. 'I know not how he doth it at all.'

'Oh, that's easy! It's just projective telepathy. You just think "sleep" at 'em, right, son?'

'Not really, Papa.' Magnus frowned. 'I just *want* them to sleep.'

Rod shook his head again. 'You must "want" awfully loudly . . . Well! Can you tell what Duke Foidin's thinking?'

'I shall!' Cordelia said promptly.

'No, thou shalt not!' Gwen pressed her hands over her daughter's ears. 'Thou shalt not soil so young a mind as thine; that man hath filth and muck beneath the surface of his thinking that he doth attempt to hold back, but ever fails!'

'Oh.' Rod raised his eyebrows. 'You've had a sample already?'

'Aye, of the things he doth yearn to do to the folk in his part of Tir Chlis, but doth never, out of cowardice, and, be it said to his slight credit, some lingering trace of scruple. This I read in him, whilst he did speak of Lord Kern's "foul rule"!'

Rod nodded. 'If you could get him talking about one thing, all the related thoughts came to his mind, just below the surface.'

'Thou hast learned the fashion of it well, mine husband. Almost could I believe thou hast practised it thyself!'

'No, worse luck – but I've learned a lot about the human mind, from books.' He surveyed his children. 'I hope none of you were peeking into the Duke's mind.'

All three shook their heads. 'Mama forbade us,' Magnus explained.

'One of those little telepathic commands that I couldn't hear.' Rod sighed philosophically. 'Speaking of things I can't hear, what's the Duke doing right now?'

Gwen's eyes lost focus. 'Speaking to Elidor . . . ' Her voice suddenly dropped in pitch, in a parody of the Duke's. 'I was so *very* glad to find thee well, unharmed – believe, 'tis true!' Her voice rose, imitating Elidor's. 'I do believe it, Uncle.'

'Then believe it, also, when I tell thee that thou must not wander off again, alone! 'Tis too dangerous for an unfledged lad! There be a thousand perils in this world, awaiting thee! I own I have been harsh with thee, from time to time – yet only when thou hast tried mine patience overly, and ever have I repented of mine anger after! Stay, good lad, and I'll promise thee, I'll try to be more moderate.'

Very low: 'I'll bide, good Uncle.'

'Wilt thou! There's a good lad! Be sure, 'tis chiefly my concern for thee that moves me to this protest! Oh, I will not hide from thee my hatred for Lord Kern, nor have I ever sought to hide it – or my abiding fear that he may somehow seize thee from me, and use thee to gain power over me! For thou dost like him more than me, now dost thou not? . . . Dost thou not! . . . Answer!'

'He and his wife were kindly,' Elidor muttered.

'And was I not? Have I never treated thee with kindness? Nay, answer not – I see it in thine eyes. Thou dost remember only cuffs and blows, and never all the sweetmeats I did bring thee, nor the games that we did play! Nay, thou didst not wander off for mere adventure this day, didst thou? Thou didst seek to join Lord Kern! Didst thou not? Now answer to me! . . . What, wilt thou not?' Gwen's whole body shook; she shuddered, and her eyes focused on Rod again. Trembling, she said, 'He doth beat the lad. Most shrewdly.'

Rod's face darkened. 'The animal! . . . No, son!' He clamped a hand on Magnus's shoulder; the boy's body jolted, his eyes focusing again. 'You can't just teleport him away from the Duke; you'd raise a hue and cry that'd keep us penned in this castle for days. Poor Elidor'll have to last it out until we can find a way to free him.'

'He did not seem so bad a man, when first we met him,' Cordelia said, troubled.

'He probably wouldn't be, if he weren't a Duke, and a regent.' Rod ran his fingers through his hair. 'A burgher, say, where he could split the responsibility with a committee – or a clerk in an office. Without the pressure, his kind side'd be able to come through. But in the top position, he knows down deep that he can't really handle the job, and it scares him.'

'And when he's fearful, he will do anything to safeguard himself,' Magnus said sombrely.

Rod nodded. 'Good insight, son. Anyway, that's how I read him. Unfortunately, he *is* the regent, and he's out of control – even his own control.'

'Thus his power doth corrupt him,' Gwen agreed, 'and all his hidden evils do come out.'

'Evil he is,' Magnus said with a shudder. 'Papa, we must wrest Elidor from out his power!'

'I agree,' Rod said grimly. 'No kid ought to have a man like that in charge of him. But we can't just bull in there and yank him loose.'

'Wherefore not?' Cordelia's chin thrust out stubbornly.

'Because, sweetling, a thousand guardsmen would fall on us ere we'd gone fifty paces,' Gwen explained.

'Papa can answer for ten of them – and thou and Magnus can answer for the rest!'

'Nay, I fear not.' Gwen smiled sadly. 'There are some things that surpass even witches' power.'

'I *could* defeat a thousand!' Magnus protested.

Rod shook his head. 'Not yet, son – though I'm not sure you won't be able to, when you're grown. A thousand men, though, you see, they come at you from all sides, and by the time you've knocked out the ones in front, the ones behind have stabbed you through.'

'But if I took them all at one blow?'

Rod smiled. '*Can* you?'

Magnus frowned, looking away. 'There must be a way. How doth one do it, Papa? Without magic, I mean.'

'Only with a bomb, son.'

Magnus looked up. 'What is a "bomb"?'

'A thing that makes a huge explosion, like a lightning-blast.'

Magnus's face cleared. 'Why, *that* I can do!'

Rod stared at him, feeling his hair trying to stand on end. He might be able to do it – he just might. No one knew for sure, yet, just what the limits were to Magnus's powers – if there were any. 'Maybe you could,' he said softly. 'And how many would die in the doing of it?'

Magnus stared at him; then he turned away, crestfallen. 'Most, I think. Aye, thou hast the right of it, Papa. We cannot withstand an army – not with any conscience.'

'Stout lad,' Rod said softly, and felt a gush of pride and love for his eldest. If only the kid could pick it up, straight from his mind!

Instead, he had to content himself with clasping Magnus's shoulder. 'Well, then! How *will* we do it? First, we need some information. What did you get from him while you had him talking, dear?'

'She had a bonfire of craving,' Cordelia said. 'That, we could not shut out!'

Rod went so still that Magnus looked up at him, startled.

'Nought but what one would expect from so foul a man,' Gwen said quickly. 'Indeed, I doubt a lass doth cross his threshold that he doth not so desire!'

'But what doth he want them for, Mama?' Cordelia piped.

'That's one of the things we don't want you hearing from his mind, darling,' Rod said grimly.

'Papa, cool thy spirit,' Gwen cautioned.

'I will, for the time being. But when I can get him alone, I think Duke Foidin and I will have a very interesting exchange.'

'Of thoughts?' Magnus frowned.

'Interpret it as you will, son. But, speaking of thoughts, dear . . . ?'

'Well!' Gwen sat down on the bed, clasping her hands in her lap. 'To begin with, Lord Kern was the old King's Lord High Warlock.'

Rod stared.

Gwen nodded. 'And I do not ken the meaning of it, for none at that table could hear thoughts – of this, I'm certain. Still, the Duke is sure Lord Kern wields magic, and knows of several others – but none so strong as Kern.'

'No wonder he wants us! But what kind of magic do they do here, if they aren't espers?'

Gwen shook her head. 'I cannot tell; there were no clear events. Beneath the surface of his mind, there was but a feel of many mighty deeds unrolling.'

'There was making many men at once to disappear,' Magnus chipped in, 'and summoning of dragons, and of spirits.'

'And calling up the fairies! Oh! 'Twas pretty!' Cordelia clapped her hands.

'An' swords, Papa!' Geoff crowed in excitement. 'Swords that cut through all, and could fight by th'selves!'

Rod stared.

Then his gaze darkened, and he turned slowly, glowering down at each child in turn.

They realized their mistake, and shrank back into themselves.

'Mama only said not to listen to the Duke's mind,' Magnus explained. 'She said nothing of the other folk.'

Rod stilled.

Then he looked up at Gwen, fighting a grin.

''Tis true,' she said, through a small, tight smile. 'In truth, it may have been a good idea.'

'There *were* some with nasty, twisted thoughts,' Magnus said eagerly, 'But I knew that was why Mama did not wish us to "listen" to the Duke, so I shunned those minds, and bade Cordelia and Geoffrey to do the same.'

'Thou'rt not to command,' Cordelia retorted, 'Papa hath said so! . . . Yet in this case, I thought thou hadst the right of it.'

Rod and Gwen stared at each other for a moment; then they both burst out laughing.

'What, what?' Magnus stared from one to the other; then he picked it up from his mother's mind. 'Oh! Thou art *that* pleased with us!'

'Aye, my jo, and amazed at how well thou dost, without fully understanding what or why I bade thee,' Gwen hugged Geoff and Cordelia to her, and Rod caught Magnus against his hip. 'So! Magic works here, eh?' It raised a nasty, prickling thought; but Rod kept it to himself.

'It seems it doth, or there is something that doth pass for it. The old King sent Lord Kern away, to fight some bandits in the north-east country; then the King died. But Duke Foidin's estate's near by, and the Duke was the King's first cousin – so, even though he was out of favour with the King, he and his army were able to seize young Elidor and, with him, the strings of government. His army was the largest, three-quarters of the royal force being with Lord Kern; so when he named himself as regent, none cared to challenge him.' Her voice sank. 'It was not clear, but I think he had a hand in the old King's death.'

The children sat silent, huge-eyed.

'It fits his style,' Rod said grimly. 'What's this nonsense about a spirit having closed the pass?'

'No nonsense, that – or, at least, the Duke doth in truth believe it. Yet the spirit was not summoned by Lord Kern; it's been there many years. The High Warlock's force went to the north-west by sea.'

'Hm.' Thoughts of Scylla and Charybdis flitted through Rod's mind. 'Be interesting to find out what this "spirit" really is. But what keeps Lord Kern from filtering his troops through smaller passes?'

'The Duke's own army, or a part of it. Once he'd seized Elidor, he fortified the mountains; so, when Lord Kern turned his army southward, he was already penned in. Moreover, the ships that landed him, the Duke burned in their harbour. He has at most ten ships in his full-vaunted "Navy" – but they suffice; Lord Kern has none.'

'Well, he's probably built a few, by this time – but not enough. So he's really penned in, huh?'

'He is; yet Duke Foidin lives in fear of him; it seems he is *most* powerful in magic.'

'But not powerful enough to take the spirit at the pass?'

Gwen shook her head. 'And is too wise to try. Repute names that spirit *most* powerful.'

'*Must* be a natural hazard.' Rod had a fleeting vision of a high pass with tall, sheer cliffs on either side, heaped high with permanent snow. An army doesn't move without a *lot* of noise; an avalanche . . . 'Still, Duke Foidin no doubt lives in dread of Lord Kern's finding a way to fly his whole army in. Does he really think we'd work for him?'

'He doubts it; though what had he to lose in trying? Yet he's not overly assured by "our" victory o'er the *Each Uisge*; he doth not trust good folk.'

'Wise, in view of his character.'

'Yet even if we'll not labour for him, he doth want us.' Gwen's face clouded. 'For what purpose, I cannot say; 'twas too deeply buried, and too dark.'

'Mm.' Rod frowned. 'That's strange; I was expecting something straightforward, like a bit of sadism. Still, with that man, I suppose *nothing*'d be straightforward. I'd almost think that's true of this whole land.'

'What land is that, Rod?' Gwen's voice was small.

Rod shrugged irritably. 'Who knows? We don't exactly have enough data to go on, yet. It *looks* like Gramarye – but if it is, we've got to be *way* far in the future – at least a thousand years, at a guess.'

'There would be more witches,' Gwen said softly.

Rod nodded. 'Yes, there would. And where'd the *Each Uisge* come from, and the *Crodh Mara*? Same place as the Gramarye elves, werewolves, and ghosts, I suppose – but that would mean they'd have risen from latent telepaths thinking about them. And there weren't any legends about them in Gramarye – were there?'

'I had never heard of them.'

'None had ever told us of them,' Magnus agreed.

'And the elves have told you darn near every folk-tale Gramarye holds. But a thousand years is time for a lot of new tales to crop up . . . Oh, come on! There's no point in talking about it; we're just guessing. Let's wait until we have some hard information.'

'Such as, mine husband?'

'The year, for openers – but I don't feel like asking anyone here; there's no point letting them know just how much we don't know, other than to excuse our lack of local knowledge. We don't even know enough to know whose side we're on.'

'Elidor's,' Magnus said promptly.

'He is the rightful sovereign,' Gwen agreed.

'Fine – but who's on his side? Lord Kern?'

Magnus nodded. 'He slipped away from the Duke's men and was fleeing in hopes of reaching Lord Kern, for protection. This was in his mind whilst the Duke did whip him.'

Rod nodded. 'If only he hadn't stopped to play with the pretty horsey, hm?'

'He did not play, Papa! He knew he stood no chance without a mount!'

'Really?' Rod looked up. 'Then he's got more sense than I pegged him as having.'

Magnus nodded. 'Thou hast told me I have "roots of wisdom", Papa; so hath he.'

'We must defend him,' Gwen said quietly.

'We cannot leave him to that Duke!' Cordelia said stoutly.

Rod sighed and capitulated. 'All right, all right! We'll take him with us!'

They cheered.

# Chapter Twelve

'Ow! Cur— I mean, confound it!' Father Al fell back onto a grassy hummock, catching his poor bruised foot in both hands. It was the third time he'd stubbed it; Gramarye had uncommonly sharp rocks. They couldn't poke holes through his boots, but they could, and did, mash the toes inside.

He sighed, and rested his ankle over the opposite thigh, massaging it. He'd been hiking for six hours, he guessed – the sky to the east was beginning to lighten with dawn. And all that time, he'd been wandering around, trying to navigate by the occasional glimpse of a star between the bushy trees, hoping he was heading away from the monastery, and not around in a circle back toward it. He had no idea where he was going, really – all that mattered right now was putting as much distance as possible between himself and his too-willing hosts before daybreak. They'd given him one of their brown, hooded robes, but it was torn by thorns in a dozen places; his face and hands were similarly scratched, and he could've sworn he'd heard snickering laughter following him through the underbrush from time to time. All in all, he'd had better nights.

He sighed, and pushed himself to his feet, wincing as the bruised left one hit the ground. Enough hiking; time to try to find a place to hole up for the day . . .

There was a flutter of cloth, and a thump. He whirled toward it, sudden fear clutching his throat.

She was a teenager, with fair skin and huge, luminous eyes, and lustrous brown hair that fell down to her waist from a mob-cap. A tightly-laced bodice joined a loose blouse to a full, brightly-coloured skirt . . .

. . . And she sat astride a broomstick that hovered three feet off the ground.

Father Al gawked. Then he remembered his manners and regathered his composure. 'Ah . . . good morning.'

'Good . . . good morning, good friar.' She seemed shy, almost fearful, but resolved. 'May . . . may I be of aid to thee?'

'Why . . . I do stand in need of direction,' Father Al answered. 'But . . . forgive me, maiden, for I have been apart from this world almost since birth, and never before have I seen a maid ride a broomstick. I have heard of it, certes, but never have seen it.'

The girl gave a sudden, delighted peal of laughter, and relaxed visibly. 'Why, 'tis nothing, good friar, a mere nothing! Eh, they do keep ye close in cloisters, do they not?'

'Close indeed. Tell me, maiden – how did you learn the trick of that?'

'Learn?' The girl's smile stretched into a delighted grin. 'Why, 'twas little enough to learn, good friar – I but stare at a thing, and wish it to move, and it doth!'

*Telekinesis*, Father Al thought giddily, and *she treats it as a commonplace*. 'Hast thou always had this . . . talent?'

'Aye, as long as I can remember.' A shadow darkened her face. 'And before, too, I think; for the good folk who reared me told me that they found me cast away in a field, at a year's age. I cannot but think that the mother who bore me was afrighted by seeing childish playthings move about her babe, seemingly of their own accord, and therefore cast me out naked into the fields, to live or die as I saw fit.'

*Inborn*, Father Al noted, even as his heart was saddened by her history. Prejudice and persecution – was this the lot of these poor, Talented people? And if it was, what had it done to their souls? 'Ill done, Ill done!' He shook his head, scowling. 'What Christian woman could do such a thing?'

'Why, any,' the girl said, with a sad smile. 'Indeed, I cannot blame her, belike she thought I was possessed by a demon.'

Father Al shook his head in exasperation. 'So little do these poor country people know of their Faith!'

'Oh, there have been dark tales,' the girl said sombrely, 'and some truth to them, I know. There do be those harsh souls possessed of witch-power who have taken to worshipping Satan, Father – I have met one myself, and was fortunate to escape with mine life! Yet they are few, and seldom band together.'

'Pray Heaven 'twill never be otherwise!' And Father Al noted that most of these 'witches' were *not* Satanists, which pretty well assured that their Talent was psionic. 'Thine own charity shows the goodness of thine own sort, maiden – thy charity in seeking to aid a poor, benighted traveller; for I'd wager thou knew I had lost mine way.'

'Why, indeed,' the girl said, 'for I heard it in thy thoughts.'

'Indeed, indeed.' Father Al nodded. 'I had heard of it, yet 'tis hard to credit when one doth first encounter it.' In fact, his brain whirled; a born telepath, able to read thoughts clearly, not just to receive fuzzy impressions! And that without training! 'Are there many like thee, maiden?'

'Nay, not so many – scarce a thousand.'

'Ah.' Father Al smiled sadly. 'Yet I doubt me not that Holy Matrimony and God shall swell thy numbers.' And up till now, there had only been two real telepaths in the whole Terran Sphere!

'May I aid thee in thy journey, Father? Whither art thou bound?'

'To find the High Warlock, maiden.'

The girl giggled. 'Why, his home is half the way across the kingdom, good friar! 'Twill take thee a week or more of journeying!'

Father Al sagged. 'Oh, no . . . er, nay! 'Tis a matter of some import, and I mind me there is need for haste!'

The girl hesitated, then said shyly, 'If 'tis truly so, good friar, I could carry thee thither upon my broom . . . '

'Couldst thou indeed! Now bless thee, maiden, for a true, good Christian!'

She fairly seemed to glow. 'Oh, 'tis naught; I could carry two of thee with little effort. Yet I must needs caution thee, good friar, 'tis like to disconcert thee summat . . . '

'I care not!' Father Al ran around behind her and leaped astride the stick. 'What matter comfort, when a soul's welfare is at stake? Nay, then, let's be gone!'

In fact, he scarcely noticed when the broomstick left the ground.


# Chapter Thirteen

Opening a lock was women's work; it took telekinesis. The boys could make the lock disappear, but they couldn't open it.

'Let Cordelia attempt it. She must be trained, must she not?' Gwen ushered her daughter over to the door and set her in front of the lock. 'Remember, sweeting, to ease the bolt gently; assuredly the Duke hath posted guards on us, and they must not hear the turn.'

'Er, just a sec.' Rod held up a hand. 'We don't *know* they've locked us in.'

Gwen sighed, reached out, and tugged at the handle. The door didn't budge. She nodded. 'Gently, now, my daughter.'

Rod took up a position just behind the door. Cordelia frowned at the lock, concentrating. Rod could just barely hear a minuscule grating as the lock turned, and the bolt slid back. Then Gwen stared, and the door shot open silently.

Rod leaped out, caught the left-hand guard from behind with a forearm across the throat, and whacked his dagger-hilt on the man's skull. He released his hold and whirled, wondering why the other guard wasn't already over him . . .

And saw the man down and out, with Geoff crawling out from between the guard's ankles; Magnus standing over the man's head, sheathing his dagger; and Gwen beaming fondly as she watched.

Rod gawked.

Then he shook his head, coming out of it. 'How'd you keep him quiet?'

'By holding the breath in his lungs,' Magnus explained. 'Can I fetch Elidor now, Papa?'

Rod rubbed his chin. 'Well, I don't know. You could teleport him away from whatever room he's in – but are you sure you could make him appear right here?'

Magnus frowned. '*Fairly* certain . . . '

'"Fairly" isn't good enough, son. You might materialize him inside a wall, or in between universes, for that matter.' Why did that thought hollow his stomach? 'No, I think we'd better do this the old-fashioned way. Which way is he?'

'Thither!' Magnus pointed toward the left, and upward.

'Well, I think we'll try the stairs. Let's go.'

'Ah, by your leave, my lord.' Gwen caught his sleeve. 'If thou shouldst meet some guardsman, or even one lone courtier, 'tis bound to cause some noise.'

Rod turned back. 'You have a better idea?'

'Haply, I have.' Gwen turned to Cordelia. 'Do thou lead us, child, skipping and singing. Be mindful, thou'rt seeking the garderobe, and have lost thy way.'

Cordelia nodded eagerly, and set off.

'Thus,' Gwen explained, 'he who doth encounter her will make no outcry; 'twill be a quiet chat.'

'Even quieter, after we catch up with him.' Rod gazed after his daughter, fidgeting. 'Can't we get moving, dear? I don't like letting her go out alone.'

'Hold, till she hath turned the corner.' Gwen kept her hand on his forearm, watching Cordelia. The little girl reached the end of the hall and turned right, skipping and warbling. 'Now! The hall is clear before her; let us go.'

They went quickly, trying to match unseen Cordelia's speed, wading through the darkness between torches. Near the end of the hall, Gwen stopped, with a gentle tug at Rod's arm. The boys stopped, too, at a thought-cue from their mother. 'She hath encountered a guardsman,' Gwen breathed. 'Softly, now!'

Rod strained his ears, and caught the conversation:

'Whither goest, child?'

'To the garderobe, sir! Canst tell me where it is?'

'A ways, sweet lass, a ways! There was one near thy chambers.'

Oh. So *all* the guards knew where they were quartered. Very interesting.

'Was there, sir? None told us!'

'He curses in his mind, and she has turned him!' Gwen hissed. 'Go!'

Rod padded around the corner on soft leather soles. Three torchlight-pools away, Cordelia stood facing him, hopping from foot to foot with her hands clasped behind her back. The guardsman stood, a hulking shadow, between the child and Rod, his back to Papa. Rod slipped his dagger out of its sheath and leaped forward.

'Did not others, clad as I am, stand beside thy door to tell thee the way?'

'Why, no, good sir!' Cordelia's eyes were wide with innocence. 'Should there have been?'

'There should, indeed!' The guardsman began to turn. 'Nay, let me lead thee b— *Ungh!*'

He slumped to the floor. Rod sheathed his dagger.

Cordelia stared down at the guardsman. 'Papa! Is he . . . ' Then her face cleared with a smile. 'Nay, I see; he but sleeps.'

'Oh, he'll have a headache in the morning, honey – but nothing worse.' Rod glanced back over his shoulder as Gwen and the boys came running up. 'Well played, sweeting!' Gwen clasped Cordelia's shoulders. 'I could not ha' done it better. On with thee, now!'

Cordelia grinned, and skipped away, lilting the top part of a madrigal.

'If this's what she's doing when she's five,' Rod muttered to Gwen, 'I'm not sure I want to see fifteen.'

'If thou dost not, there are many lads who will,' Gwen reminded him uncharitably. 'Come, my lord, let us go.'

Five guardsmen, three courtiers, four varlets and a lady-in-waiting later, Gwen stopped them all at a corner. 'There lie Elidor's chambers,' she breathed in Rod's ear. 'Two guard the door, three keep watch in the antechamber, and a nursemaid sleeps on a pallet beside his bed.'

Rod nodded; Foidin definitely wasn't the sort to take chances.

'This is why I took care of the ones we met en route – so Magnus'd be well-rested. How many can you handle, son?'

'Four, at the least.' The boy frowned. 'Beyond that, their sleep might be light.'

Rod nodded. 'That'll do. Now, here's a routine your mother and I used to run . . . '

A few minutes later, Magnus frowned, concentrating; a minute later, there was a clatter and a pair of thumps, followed by a sigh in chorus, as the two door-guards sank into slumber. Rod peeked around the corner, saw them both sitting slouched against the wall, and nodded. 'OK, Geoff. Go to it!'

The three-year-old trotted eagerly around the corner and knocked on the door. He waited, then knocked again. Finally a bolt shot back, and the door swung open, revealing a scowling guardsman. He saw Geoff, and stared.

'Elidor come out 'n' play?' the little boy piped.

The guardsman scowled. 'Here, now! Where'd thou come from?' He grabbed, but Geoff jumped back. The guardsman jumped after him, and Geoff turned and scooted.

He sailed around the corner under full steam, with the guardsman a foot behind him, bent double, hand reaching, and another guard right behind him. Rod and Gwen kicked their feet out from under them, and they belly-flopped on cold stone with a shout. Magnus and Cordelia yanked their helmets off, and Rod and Gwen struck down with reversed daggers. A grace note of nasty double *chunks!* sounded, and the guardsmen twitched and lay still, goose eggs swelling on the backs of their heads.

'They'll sleep for an hour or two, at the least.' Gwen handed Magnus's dagger back to him.

'Hoarstane? Ambrine?' A hoarse voice called from around the corner.

Everyone froze. Rod's pulse beat high, with the hope that the third guard might follow the first two.

Unfortunately, he was a little too wary. 'Hoarstane!' he snapped again. There was silence; then the guardsman snarled again. Metal jangled as he turned away, and the door boomed shut; then a bolt snicked tight.

'Back in, and the door locked.' Rod shook his head. 'Well, we hadn't expected any more. You said you could handle four, son?'

Magnus nodded. 'Without doubt.' His eyes lost focus; he became very still.

Rod waited. And waited. Four he reminded himself, were bound to take a little time.

Finally Magnus relaxed and nodded. 'All sleep, Papa.'

'OK. You go get Elidor ready, while we get the door open.'

Magnus nodded, and disappeared.

He'd started doing it when he was a baby, but Rod still found it unnerving. With people who were only friends, such as Toby, OK – but his own son was another matter. 'Well, teamwork starts at home,' he sighed. 'After you, ladies.'

They tiptoed up to the door. Rod kept a firm hold on little Geoff's hand, to make sure he didn't try to teleport away to join Magnus. Gwen watched with fond pride as Cordelia stared at the lock, and they heard the sound of the bolt sliding back. The door swung open.

They stepped into a scene out of 'Sleeping Beauty'. The third guardsman sat slumped in a chair, chin on chest, snoring. Beyond him, a half-open door showed a nanny in a rocker, dozing over her needlework. Rod stepped forward and pushed the door the rest of the way open. Elidor looked up from belting on his sword. His hair was tousled, and his eyes bleary from slumber, red and puffy; Rod had a notion he'd cried himself to sleep.

'Almost ready, Papa.' Magnus picked up a cloak and held it out. Elidor stepped over; Magnus dropped it over his shoulders.

'God save Your Majesty.' Rod bowed. 'I take it Magnus has informed you of our invitation?'

'Aye, and with right good heart do I accept! But why art thou willing to take me from mine uncle's halls?'

'Because my sons have taken a liking to you.' You couldn't exactly tell a King that he triggered every paternal response you had. 'If you're ready, we shouldn't linger.'

'Ready I am!' The King clapped a hat on and headed for the door. Rod bowed him through, and waited as Magnus stepped through behind him.

He found Elidor staring at the snoring guard. 'Magnus had told me of it,' the boy whispered, 'but I scarce could credit it.'

'You're moving in magic circles.' Rod gave him a firm nudge on the shoulder. 'And if you don't keep moving, we'll wind up back where we started.'

Elidor paced on forward, pausing for a bow to answer Gwen and Cordelia's curtsies. Rod took the opportunity to dodge on ahead.

Magnus stepped up beside him, as pilot, and they padded silently through dim, torch-lit halls. Whenever Magnus stopped and nodded to Cordelia, she skipped on ahead, singing, to engage whatever unsuspecting person happened to be walking the halls at this late hour, in conversation, until Magnus could knock them out. After the fifth guardsman, Rod noticed the man was twitching in his sleep. 'Getting tired, son?'

Magnus nodded.

So did Rod. 'I'll take over for a while.'

Fortunately, there weren't too many more; the old-fashioned method is a little risky.

Elidor just followed along, his eyes getting wider and wider till they seemed to take up half his face.

Finally they crossed the outer bailey – it was really the only one; the castle had grown till it absorbed the inner. Rod's commando tactics couldn't do much about the sentries on the wall, so Magnus padded along, alert and ready; but the sentries were watching the outside, so they came to the main gatehouse without incident.

There they stopped, and Gwen gathered them into a huddle. 'Here's a pretty problem,' she whispered. 'A sentry stands on each tower, a porter by the winch, and six guardsmen in the wardroom – and thou art wearied, my son.'

Magnus *was* looking a little frayed around the edges. 'I can still answer for two, Mama, mayhap three.'

'That leaves six.' Rod frowned. 'What're they armed with, Gwen?'

Gwen gazed off into space for a moment. 'All bear pikes, save the Captain; he wears a sword.'

'Could you and Cordelia bop them with their own pike butts?'

'Aye, but they wear their helmets.'

'So.' Rod rubbed his chin. 'The problem is, getting them to take off their helmets.'

'Why, that can *I* do!' Elidor declared, and marched off towards the guardroom before anyone could stop him.

Rod looked up after him, startled, glanced back at Gwen, then turned and sprinted after Elidor. What was the kid trying to do, blow the whole escape?

But the boy moved fast, and he was hammering on the door before Rod could catch him. It swung open, and Rod ducked into the nearest shadow and froze. He could see through the open door, though, as Elidor marched in.

The guardsmen scrambled to their feet. 'Majesty!' The Captain inclined his head. 'What dost thou abroad so late o' night?'

Elidor frowned. 'I am thy King! Art thou so ill-bred as not to know the proper form of greeting? Uncover, knaves, and bow!'

Rod held his breath.

The soldiers glanced at the Captain, whose eyes were locked with Elidor's. But the boy-King held his chin high, glance not wavering an inch. Finally, the Captain nodded.

The guardsmen slowly removed their helmets and bowed.

Their pikes leaped to life, slamming down on the backs of their heads with the flats of their blades. They slumped to the floor with a clatter.

All except the Captain; he didn't have a pike near. He snapped upright, terror filling his face as he stared at his men. Then the terror turned to rage.

Rod leaped forward.

'Why, what sorcery is this?' the Captain snarled, coming for Elidor and drawing his sword.

The boy stepped back, paling – and Rod shot through the door and slammed into the Captain. He went down with a clatter and a *'whuf!'*, the wind knocked out of him; but his sword writhed around, the point dancing in Rod's face. Rod yanked the sword to one side, rolling the man half-over, and dived in behind him, arm snaking around the Captain's throat. He caught the larynx in his elbow, and squeezed. The Captain kicked and struggled, but Rod had a knee in his back, so all he could do was thrash about.

But Elidor was loose. He darted over to pluck the Captain's helmet, yanked his dagger out, and clubbed down with all his strength, just the way he'd seen Rod do. The Captain heaved, and relaxed with a sigh.

Rod let go and scrambled out. 'Well done, Your Majesty! You've got the makings of a King, all right.'

'There's more to that than battle,' the boy said, frowning.

'Yes, such as wisdom, and knowledge. But a lot of it's the ability to think fast, and the willingness to act, and you've got those. And style and courage – and you've just demonstrated those, too.' Rod clapped him on the shoulder, and the boy seemed to visibly expand. 'Come on, Your Majesty. I wouldn't say the rest of our party is dying to find out what happened, but they'll be vastly reassured to actually *see* us intact.' He ushered the boy out the door.

'Six down and three to go,' he whispered as they came up to Gwen and the children in the alcove.

Gwen nodded. ''Twas well thou followed Elidor. Well, if thou wilt hide thee near the porter, I think I can distract him for thee.'

Rod set his palms against his buttocks and leaned back, stretching. 'OK, but give me a minute. I'm beginning to feel it, too.'

A few minutes later, he waited just outside the doorway leading to the giant windlass that controlled the drawbridge. The porter paced the floor inside, humming to himself – trying to stay awake, probably.

Suddenly the rope that held the windlass slipped loose, and the ratchet chattered as the great drum began to turn.

The porter shouted and leaped for the crank-handle.

Rod leaped for the porter, plucked off his helmet, and clubbed him.

A few minutes later, he rejoined Gwen. 'All secure. I take it I should run back there and drop the bridge.'

'Aye, and raise the portcullis. Yet attend a moment.' She turned to Magnus. 'Son?'

Magnus was gazing off into space. A few seconds later, he relaxed and turned to her. 'The sentries on the towers are asleep.'

Gwen nodded at Rod.

He sighed, and trudged back to the windlass. Being a telepath must certainly save a lot of hiking.

The portcullis rose, the drawbridge fell, and Rod almost did, too. He straightened up, aching in every joint; it was getting to be a long day.

'My lord?' Gwen's head poked around the doorway. 'Wilt thou join us?'

'Coming,' he grumbled, and shuffled toward the doorway. How could she still look so fresh and cheery?

They went across the drawbridge, as fast as Geoffrey and Rod could manage. Fifty feet from the castle, Gwen stopped the party, and shooed them into the shadow of a big rock. She ducked her head around it, staring back at the castle. Curious, Rod peeked around the other side.

He saw the drawbridge slowly rise.

Startled, he darted a glance at Gwen. A wrinkle showed between her eyebrows; her lower lip was caught between her teeth. She was showing the strain – and so she should! That slab of wood had to weigh half a ton!

Cordelia was watching alertly, glancing from Gwen to the drawbridge and back. Finally, Gwen nodded, and Cordelia's face screwed up tight for a second. Then Gwen relaxed with a sigh. 'Well done; thou hast indeed secured the winch. Now slip the ratchet on the portcullis, sweeting – yet not altogether; thou dost not wish it to come a-crashing down.'

Cordelia frowned darkly for a few minutes, staring at the castle; then Rod heard a muted, deep-toned clang. Cordelia looked up at her mother, and nodded. ' 'Tis down.'

'Well done.' Gwen patted Cordelia's shoulder, and the little girl beamed. Mama turned to Magnus. 'Now wake the sentries, that they may think they've only dozed, and that nothing is amiss.'

Magnus gazed off into space a moment – it was a long moment, for he *was* tiring – then looked up at Gwen and nodded.

'Well enough.' Gwen nodded, satisfied. ' 'Twill be at least an hour ere the others awake, and we'll be long gone; let them search.' She turned to Rod. 'Yet we had best lose no time.'

'Agreed,' Rod affirmed. 'Make sure the sentries are looking the other way for a few minutes, will you? Otherwise, they can't help seeing us on this slope.'

'Hmf.' Gwen frowned. 'I *had* forgot that. Well . . . ' she held the frown for a few minutes, then nodded. 'They think they hear voices calling, towards the north. Lose no time.'

Rod nodded, and darted out across the slope, swinging Geoffrey up to his shoulders. The family followed. A hundred yards farther on and fifty feet lower, they stopped, panting, in the shade of a huge oak tree, sentinel for a crop of woodland.

'Whither away?' Gwen demanded.

Rod caught his breath and pointed southwest. 'That way, toward the grove where we came in. After all that talk about the High Warlock's holdout in the north-east, they'll expect us to head for him. They won't think we've got any reason for going back.'

'Have we?'

Rod shrugged. 'Not that I know of – except that I don't like travelling in totally unfamiliar territory at night, especially when I'm on the run.'

Gwen nodded. ' 'Tis as wise a course as aught else. Follow Father, children.'

# Chapter Fourteen

Father Al clung to the broomstick for dear life, knuckles white and forearms aching with the strain. At first, flight on so slender a craft had been a heady, delightful thing, almost like flying under his own power; but the sun had risen, and he'd happened to glance down. The world whizzed by below, treetops reaching up to snag at his robe. His stomach had turned over, then done its best to shinny up his backbone to safety. Since then, the ride had been a qualified nightmare. He just hoped the tears in his eyes were due only to the wind.

'Yon,' the girl called back to him, 'ahead, and below!'

He craned his neck to see over her shoulder. About a hundred metres ahead, a large cottage nestled within a grove, a half-timbered house with a thatched roof, and two outbuildings behind it. Then the ground was rushing up at them, and Father Al clung to the broomstick as he clung to his hope of Heaven, commanding his body to relax. His body didn't listen. The world rolled upward past them, then suddenly rolled back down. He clamped his jaw and swallowed, hard, just barely managing to keep his stomach from using his tongue as a springboard.

Then, incredibly, they had stopped, and solid earth jarred upward against his soles.

'We are come.' The witch-girl smiled back at him over her shoulder. Then her brows knit in concern. 'Art thou well?'

'Oh, most excellent! Or I will be, soon.' Father Al swung his leg over the broomstick and tottered up to her. 'A singular experience, maiden, and one I'll value till the end of my days! I thank thee greatly!' He turned, looking about him for a change of subject. 'Now. Where shall I find the High Warlock?'

'Oh, within.' The girl pointed at the cottage. 'Or if he is not, surely his wife will know when he may return. Shall I make thee acquainted with them?'

'Dost thou know them, then?' Father Al asked in surprise.

'Indeed; most all the witchfolk do.' She dismounted, picked up her broomstick, and led him toward the house. 'They are gentle souls, and most modest; one would scarcely think that they were numbered 'mongst the Powers of the land.' They were almost to the door, which was flanked by two flowering bushes. 'Their bairns, though, are somewhat mischiev— '

'Hold!' one of the bushes barked. 'Who seeks to pass?'

Father Al swung round to the bush in astonishment. Then, remembering what the girl had been saying, he realized one of the children was probably hiding inside the leaves, playing a prank. 'Good morn,' he said, bowing. 'I am Father Aloysius Uwell, come hither to call upon the High Warlock and his family.'

'Come hither, then, that I may best examine thee,' the voice demanded. Rather a deep voice, for a child; but the witch-girl was giggling behind him, so Father Al abided by his earlier guess – one of the children. And important to play along with the prank, therefore – nothing endears one to a parent like being cordial to the child. He sighed, and stepped closer to the bush.

'Why dost thou linger?' the voice barked. 'Come hither to me now, I say!'

It was coming from behind him.

Father Al turned about, reassessing the situation – there were at least two children involved. 'Why, so I do – if thou wilt hold thy place.'

The girl giggled again.

'Am I to blame if thine eyes art so beclouded that thou mistakest quite my place of biding?' The voice was coming out of a bush a little to Father Al's left, farther from the house. 'Come now, I say!'

Father Al sighed, and stepped toward the bush.

'Nay, here!' the voice cried from another bush, farther off to his left. 'Besotted shave-pate, canst thou not tell my bearing?'

'I would, if I could see thee,' Father Al muttered, and ambled patiently toward the new bush. Giggling, the girl moved with him.

'Nay, hither!' the voice commanded again, from yet another bush, off to his right and farther from the house. '*Wilt* thou come, I say!'

About then, Father Al began to get suspicious. The voice was plainly leading them away from the house, and he began to think this was no childish prank, but the work of some guardian who didn't trust strangers. 'Nay, I'll go no farther! I've come where thou hast said, not once, but several times! If thou dost wish that I should move another step, now show thyself, that I may *see* which way to step!'

'As thou wilt have it,' the voice grumbled; and, suddenly, the form of a broad and portly man rose up and came around the bush. Its head was shaven in the tonsure, and it wore a brown monk's robe with a small yellow-handled screwdriver in the breast pocket.

Father Al stared.

The girl burst into a peal of laughter.

'Dost thou not know me, fellow?' the monk demanded. 'Wilt thou not kneel to the Abbot of thine own Order?'

'Nay, that will I not,' Father Al muttered. Father Cotterson had said the Abbot was on his way back to the monastery, half a kingdom away – what would he be doing here, near a High Warlock's house, at that? Father Al's suspicions deepened, especially since he recognized an element out of folklore. So he began to whistle loudly, untied his rope belt, and took off his cassock. The witch-girl gasped and averted her eyes; then she looked back at him, staring.

'Friar!' the Abbot cried, scandalized. 'Dost thou disrobe before a woman? . . . And what manner of garb is it thou wearest beneath?'

'Why, this?' Father Al sang, improvising a Gregorian chant. ''Tis naught but the coverall all Cathodeans wear, which warms me in winter, and never doth tear.' He went back to whistling, turning his cassock inside-out.

The Abbot's voice took on a definite tone of menace. 'What dost thou mean by this turning of thy coat? Dost thou seek to signify that thou'lt side with the King against me?'

Interesting; Father Al hadn't known the old Church-State conflict was cropping up here. 'Why, nay. It means only,' he put the monk's robe on again, wrong side out, and wrapped it about him, 'that I wish to see things as they truly are.'

And before his eyes, the form of the Abbot wavered, thinned, and faded, leaving only a stocky, two-foot-high man with a pug-nosed, berry-brown face, large eyes, brown jerkin, green hose, green cap with a red feather, and a smouldering expression. 'Who ha' told thee, priest?' he growled. His gaze shifted to the witch-girl. 'Not thou, surely! The witch-folk ever were my friends!'

The girl shook her head, opening her lips to answer, but Father Al forestalled her. 'Nay, hobgoblin. 'Tis books have taught me, that to dispel glamour, one hath but to whistle or sing, and turn thy coat.'

'Thou'rt remarkably schooled in elfin ways, for one who follows the Crucified one,' the elf said, with grudging respect. 'Indeed, I thought that thee and thy fellows scarce did acknowledge our existence!'

'Nor did I.' In fact, Father Al felt rather dizzy – in spite of what Yorick had told him; he was frantically trying to re-evaluate all his fundamental assumptions. 'Yet did tales of thee and thy kind all fascinate me, so that I strove to learn all that I could of worlds other than the one I knew.'

'"Worlds?"' The elf's pointed ears pricked up. 'Strange turn of phrase; what priest would think that any world existed, but this one about us?'

Somehow, Father Al was sure he'd made a slip. 'In Philosphie's far realms . . . '

'There is not one word said of things like me, that do defy all reason,' the elf snapped. 'Tell me, priest – what is a star?'

'Why, a great, hot ball of gas, that doth . . . ' Father Al caught himself. 'Er, dost thou see, there is writing of seven spheres of crystal that surround the Earth . . . '

'"Earth?" Strange term, when thou most assuredly dost mean "world". Nay, thou didst speak thy true thought at the first, surprised to hear such a question from one like me – that do swing about the stars, and heavenly cars that sail between them. Is it not so? I charge thee, priest, to answer truly, by thy cloth – dost thou not believe a lie to be a sin?'

'Why, so I do,' Father Al admitted, 'and therefore must I needs acknowledge the truth whereof thou speakest; I could indeed tell thee of such wonders. But . . . '

'And didst thou not ride hither in just such a car, from such another world?' The elf watched him keenly.

Father Al stared at him.

The elf waited.

'Indeed I did.' Father Al's brows pulled down. 'How would an elf know of such matters? Hast thy High Warlock told thee of them?'

It was the elf's turn to be taken aback. 'Nay, what knowest thou of Rod Gallowglass?'

'That he is, to thee, indeed a puissant warlock – though he would deny it, had he any honesty within him – and doth come, as I do, from a world beyond the sky. Indeed, he doth serve the same Government of Many Stars that govern me, and came, as I did, in a ship that sails the void between the stars.'

''Tis even as thou sayest, including his denial of his powers.' The elf regarded him narrowly. 'Dost thou know him, then?'

'We never have met,' Father Al evaded. 'Now, since that I have told thee what thou didst wish to know, wilt thou not oblige me in return, and say to me how it can be that elves exist?'

'Why,' the elf said craftily, 'why not the way that witches do? Thou hast no difficulty understanding why *she* lives.' He nodded toward the witch-girl.

'That is known to me; she is like to any other lass, excepting that God gave to her at birth some gifts of powers in her mind; and I can see that, when first her ancestors did come to this world, those who chose to come had each within him some little germ of such-like powers. Thus, as generations passed, and married one another again and yet again, that germ of power grew, until some few were born who had it in good measure.'

''Tis even as Rod Gallowglass did guess,' the elf mused. 'Nay, thou art certainly from the realm that birthed him. But tell me, then, if such a marrying within a nation might produce a witch, why might it not produce an elf?'

'It might; it might indeed.' Father Al nodded thoughtfully. 'Yet were it so, my whistling, and the turning of my coat, would not dispel thy glamour as was told in Terran legend. Nay, there is something more than mortal's magic in thee. How didst thou come to be?'

'Thou dost see too well for easy liking,' the elf sighed, 'and I do owe thee truth for truth. I do know that elves are born of forest and of earth, of Oak, and Ash, and Thorn; for we have been here as long as they. And well ought I to know it, for I am myself the oldest of all Old Things!'

The phrase triggered memories, and *Puck of Pook's Hill* came flooding back to Father Al's mind from his childhood. 'Why thou'rt Robin Goodfellow!'

'Thou speakest aright; I am that merry wanderer of the night.' The elf grinned, swelling a little with pride. 'Nay, am I so famous, then, that all beyond the stars do know of me?'

'Well, all worth knowing.' Father Al silently admitted to a bit of bias within himself. 'For surely, all who know the Puck must be good fellows.'

'Dost thou mean that I should trust thee, then?' Puck grinned mischievously. 'Nay, not so – for some have known me to their own misfortune. Yet I will own thou dost not have the semblance of a villain. Nay, turn thy coat aright, and tell me wherefore thou dost seek Rod Gallowglass.'

'Why . . . 'tis thus . . . ' Father Al took off his robe, and turned it right side out again, getting his thoughts in order. He pulled it on, and began, 'A wizard of a bygone age foresaw that, in our present time, a change would come to thy High Warlock, a transformation that could make him a mighty force, for ill or good – a force so mighty as to cast his shadow over all the worlds that mortal folk inhabit. This ancient wizard wrote this vision down, and sealed it in a letter, so that in our present time, it might be opened and read, and we could learn, in time to aid Rod Gallowglass.'

'And bend him toward the good, if thou canst?' Puck demanded. 'Which means, certes, *thy* notion of the "good".'

'And canst thou fault it?' Father Al stuck out his chin and locked gazes with Puck, hoping against hope as he remembered the long hostility between Christian clergy and faery-folk, and the diminishing of the faeries' influence as that of the Christ had grown. And Puck glared back at him, no doubt remembering all that, too, but also reassessing the values the clergy preached.

'Nay, in truth, I cannot,' the elf sighed finally, 'when thou dost live by what thou preachest. Nor do I doubt thy good intention; and elves have something of an instinct, in the knowing of the goodness of a mortal.'

Father Al let out a long-held breath. 'Then wilt thou lead me to thy Warlock?'

'I would I could,' the elf said grimly, 'but he hath quite disappeared, and none know where.'

Father Al just stared at him, while panic surged up within him. He stood stock-still against it, fighting for calm, silently reeling off a prayer from rote; and eventually the panic faded, leaving him charged for otherworldly battle. 'Admit me to his wife and bairns, then; mayhap they hold a clue they know not of.'

But Puck shook his head. 'They have vanished with him, friar – all but one, and he's so young he cannot speak, nor even think in words.'

'Let me gaze upon him, then.' Father Al fixed Puck with a hard stare. 'I have some knowledge gleaned, sweet Puck; I may see things that thou dost not.'

'I doubt that shrewdly,' Puck said sourly, 'yet on the chance of it, I'll bring thee to him. But step warily, thou friar – one sign of menace to the child, and thou'lt croak, and hop away to find a lily pad to sit on, and wilt pass the rest of thy days fly-catching with a sticky tongue of wondrous length!'

He turned away toward the cottage. Father Al followed, with the witch-girl.

'Dost thou think that he could truly change me into a frog?' Father Al asked softly.

'I do not doubt it,' the girl answered, with a tremulous smile. 'The wisest heads may turn to asses', when the Puck besets them!'

They passed through the door, and Father Al paused, amazed at the brightness and cosyness of the house, the sense of comfort and security that seemed to emanate from its beams and rough-cast walls, its sturdy, homely table, benches, chests, two great chairs by the fire, and polished floor. If he looked at it without emotion, he was sure it would seem Spartan – there were so few furnishings. But it was totally clean, and somehow wrapped him in such a feeling of love and caring that he was instantly loath to leave. Somehow, he knew he would like the High Warlock's wife, if he should be lucky enough to meet her.

Then his gaze lit on the cradle by the fire, with the two diminutive, wizened old peasant-ladies by it – elf-wives! They stared up at him fearfully, but Puck stepped up with a mutter and a gesture, and they drew back, reassured. Puck turned, and beckoned to the priest.

Father Al stepped up to the cradle, and gazed down at a miniature philosopher.

There was no other way to describe him. He still had that very serious look that the newborn have – but this child was nearly a year old! His face was thinner than a baby's ought to be; the little mouth turned down at the corners. His hair was black, and sparse. He slept, but Father Al somehow had the impression that the child was troubled.

So did the witch-girl. She was weeping silently, tears streaming down her cheeks. 'Poor mite!' she whispered. 'His mind doth roam, searching for his mother!'

'Even in his *sleep*?'

She nodded. 'And I cannot say where he doth seek; his thoughts veer off beyond my ken.'

Father Al frowned. 'How can that be?' Then he remembered that the child was too young to have gained the mental framework that gives the human mind stability, but also limits. He found himself wondering where that little mind could reach to – and if, in a grown man, such searching would produce insanity.

He looked back at the child, and found its eyes open. They

seemed huge in the tiny face, and luminous, and stared up at him with the intensity of a fanatic. Father Al felt an eldritch prickling creep over his scalp and down his back, and knew to the depths of his soul that this was an extremely unusual baby. 'Child,' he breathed, 'would that I could stay and watch thine every movement!'

'Thou mayest not,' Puck said crisply.

Father Al turned to the elf. 'Nay, more's the pity; for my business is with the father, not the child. Tell me the manner of his disappearance.'

Puck frowned, like a general debating whether or not to release classified information; then he shrugged. ''Tis little enough to tell. Geoffrey – the third bairn – disappeared whilst at play. They called the High Warlock back from council with the King and Abbot, and he drew from his eldest son the place exact where the child had vanished, then stepped there himself – and promptly ceased to be. His wife and other bairns ran after him, dismayed, and, like him, disappeared.'

Father Al stared at the elf, while his mind raced through a dozen possible explanations. It could've been enchantment, of course, but Father Al wasn't quite willing to surrender rationality that completely just yet. A space warp or time warp? Unlikely, on a planet's surface – but who could say it was impossible?

Then he remembered Yorick, and his claim to be a time traveller. It could be, it could be . . .

He cleared his throat. 'I think that I must see this place.'

'And follow them?' Puck shook his head with a sour smile. 'I think that five lost are enough, good friar.'

Father Al hadn't really thought that far ahead, but now that Puck mentioned it, he felt a creeping certainty. 'Nay, I think that thou has said it,' he said slowly, 'for where'er thy High Warlock has gone, it could be just such a journey that could wake in him the Power that he knows not of. And I must be there, to guide him in its use!'

'Art thou so schooled in witchcraft, priest?' Puck fairly oozed sarcasm.

'Not in witchcraft, but in the ways of various magics.' Father Al frowned. 'For, look you, elf, 'tis been my life's study, to learn to know when a mortal is possessed of a demon and when he's not; and to prove how things that seem to be the work of witchcraft, are done by other means. Yet in this study, I've of necessity learned much of every form of magic known to mortals. Never have I ever thought *real* magic could exist; yet that letter that I told thee of warned us that Rod Gallowglass would gain real magic power. Still do I think his strength will prove to be of origins natural, but rare; yet even so, he'll need one to show him its true nature, and to lead him past the temptations toward evil that great power always brings.'

'I scarcely think Rod Gallowglass needs one to teach him goodness – an should he, I doubt me not his wife is equal to the task.' But doubt shadowed Puck's eyes. 'Yet I'll bring thee to the place. Thence, 'tis thy concern.'

The witch-girl stayed behind, to help with the baby if she could. Puck led Father Al down a woodland path – and the priest kept an eye on the direction of the sun, whenever it poked through the leaves, to make sure he was being led in a definite direction. Finally, they came out into a meadow. A hundred metres away, a pond riffled under a light breeze, bordered by a few trees. A huge black horse lifted its head, staring at them; then it came trotting from the pool.

''Tis the High Warlock's charger, Fess,' Puck explained. 'An thou dost wish to follow after his master, thou first must deal with him.' And, as the horse came up to them: 'Hail, good Fess! I present to thee a goodly monk, whose interest in thy master doth to me seem honest. Tell him who thou art, good friar.'

Well! Father Al had heard that elves had an affinity for dumb animals – but this was going a bit far! None the less, Puck seemed sincere, and Father Al hated to hurt his feelings . . . 'I am Father Aloysius Uwell, of the Order of St Vidicon of Cathode . . . ' Was it his imagination, or did the horse prick up its ears at the mention of the good Saint's name? Well, St Vidicon had influence in a lot of odd places. 'I am hither come to aid thy master, for I've been vouchsafed word that he might find himself in peril, whether he did know of it or not.'

The horse had a very intent look about him. Father Al must've been imagining it. He turned to Puck. 'Canst thou show me where the High Warlock did vanish?'

'Yon,' Puck said, pointing and stepping around Fess toward the pond. 'Indeed, we've marked the place.'

Father Al followed him.

The great black horse sidestepped, blocking their path.

' 'Tis as I feared,' Puck sighed. 'He'll let no one near the spot.'

Suddenly, Father Al was absolutely certain that he *had* to follow Rod Gallowglass. 'Come now! Certes no horse, no matter how worthy, can prevent . . . ' He dodged to the side, breaking into a run.

The horse reared up, pivoted about, and came down, its forefeet thudding to earth just in front of the priest.

Puck chuckled.

Father Al frowned. 'Nay, good beast. Dost not know what's in thy master's interest?' He backed up, remembering his college gymnastics.

Fess watched him warily.

Father Al leaped into a run, straight at the great black horse. He leaped high, grasping the front and back of the saddle, and swung his legs up in a side vault.

Fess danced around in a half-circle.

Father Al hit the ground running – and found himself heading straight for Puck. The elf burst into a guffaw.

Father Al halted and turned around, glowering at Fess. 'A most unusual horse, good Puck.'

'What wouldst thou expect, of the High Warlock's mount?'

'Apparently somewhat less than he doth expect of me.' Father Al hitched up his rope belt. 'But I know better now.' He set himself, watching Fess with narrowed eyes; then he raced straight at the horse, and veered to the left at the last second. Fess danced to the left, too, but Father Al was already zagging to the right. Fess reversed engines with amazing speed, getting his midsection solidly in front of the priest – and Father Al ducked under his belly.

Fess sat down.

Puck roared with laughter.

Father Al came reeling out of the fray, staggering like a drunk. 'I think . . . a change of tactics . . . might be in order.'

'So I think, too.' Puck grinned, arms akimbo. 'Therefore, try sweet reason, priest.'

Father Al frowned down at him, remembering Puck's legendary fondness for helping mortals make fools of themselves. Then he shrugged and turned back to Fess. 'Why not? The situation's so ridiculous, why should a little more matter?' He stepped up to the beast. 'Now, look thou, Fess – thy master's sore endangered. It may be that I may aid him.'

Fess shook his head.

Father Al stared. If he didn't know better, he would've thought the horse had understood him.

Then he frowned – just a coincidence, no doubt. 'We had a letter. It was writ a thousand years agone, by a man long dead, who foretold us that, in this time and place, one Rod Gallowglass would wake to greater power of magic than mortals ever knew.'

The horse moved to the side, tossing its head as though it was beckoning.

Father Al stared. Then he squeezed his eyes shut, gave his head a quick shake; but when he looked again, the horse was still beckoning. He shrugged, and followed, ignoring Puck's chortle.

Fess was standing by a patch of bare dirt, scratching at it with a hoof. Father Al watched the hoof, then felt a shiver run through him as he saw what the horse had drawn. There in the dirt, in neat block letters, lay the word 'WHO?'

Father Al looked up at the horse, facts adding themselves up in his head. 'The High Warlock's horse – and you came with him, from off-planet, didn't you?'

The horse stared at him. Why? Oh. He'd said, 'off-planet'. Which marked him. 'Yes, I'm from off-planet, too – from the Vatican, on Terra. And you . . . ' Suddenly, the priest shot a punch at the horse's chest.

It went *bongggggg*.

Father Al went, 'Yowtch!' and nursed bruised knuckles.

Puck went into hysterics, rolling on the ground.

Father Al nodded. 'Very convincing artificial horsehide, over a metal body. And you've a computer for a brain, haven't you?' He stared at the horse.

Slowly, Fess nodded.

'Well.' Father Al stood straight, fists on his hips. 'Nice to know the background, isn't it? Now let me give you the full story.'

He did, in modern English. Fess's head snapped up at the name of Angus McAran; apparently he'd had some contact with the head time-spider before. Encouraged, Father Al kept the synopsis going through his meeting with Yorick, at the mention of whose name, Fess gave a loud snort. Well, that had sort of been Father Al's reaction, too.

'So, if McAran's right,' Father Al wound up, 'something's going to happen to Rod Gallowglass, wherever he's gone, that's going to waken some great Power that's been lying dormant in him all along. Whatever the nature of that power, it might tempt him toward evil – without his even realizing it. After all, some things that seem right at the moment – such as revenge – can really lead one, bit by bit, into spiritual corruption, and great evil.'

The horse tossed its head, and began to scratch with its hoof. Father Al watched, holding his breath, and saw the words appear: POWER CORRUPTS. He felt relief tremble through him; he was getting through! 'Yes, exactly. So you see, it might be to his advantage to have a clergyman handy. But more than a clergyman – I'm also an anthropologist, and my life's study has been magic.'

Fess's head came up sharply.

Father Al nodded. 'Yes. I suppose you might call me a theoretical magician; I can't work a single spell myself, but I know quite a bit about how a man with magical Power might do so. There's a good chance I might be able to help him figure out how to use his new Power to bring himself and his family back here!'

But Fess lowered his head and scratched in the dirt again: AND A GREATER CHANCE THAT YOU, TOO, WOULD BE LOST.

Father Al thrust out his chin. 'That is my concern. I know the risk, and I take it willingly. It's worth it, if I can help this poor fellow and his family – and possibly avert a spiritual catastrophe. Have you considered the possible heresies that might arise, if a man should suddenly seem to have *real* magical powers?'

The horse's eyes seemed to lose focus for a few seconds, and Father Al was impressed; not many computers would have any theology on storage in their memory banks. Then Fess's eyes came back into focus again, and Father Al said quickly, 'So I have some vested interest in trying to help your master, you see. Properly instructed, he *could* be a mighty asset to the Church on this planet. But left to himself, he might fall into the temptations that power brings, find a way to return here from wherever he's gone, and become the leader of a heresy that could rock the Terran Sphere. We dare not leave him there.'

The horse lowered his head again, scratching with his hoof: HIS SAFE RETURN IS ALL.

Father Al frowned, puzzling it out, wishing the robot had been equipped with speech. Then he nodded, understanding. 'I see. It makes no difference to you if he comes back a heretic or a saint, as long as he comes back. But don't you see, with my knowledge of the workings of magic to aid him, his chances of returning are increased? *Much* increased, if you'll pardon my boasting.'

The synthetic eyes stared intently into Father Al's, for a few minutes that seemed to stretch out into aeons. Then, finally, the great horse nodded, and turned away, beckoning.

'I scarce can credit it!' Puck cried. 'Thou hast persuaded him!'

Father Al breathed a huge sigh of relief. 'I scarcely can believe it, either. It's the first time in my life I've ever made any headway with a computer.' He sent up a quick, silent prayer of thanks to St Vidicon, and followed Fess.

The black horse stopped, and looked back expectantly. Father Al trotted to catch up, and came to a halt to see a line of stones laid in the grass – the threshold of a Gate to where?

The great black horse stood to the side, waiting.

Father Al looked up at him, took a deep breath, and squared his shoulders. 'Wish me luck, then. You may be the last rational being I see for a long, long time.' And, without giving himself a chance to think about it, he stepped forward. Nothing happened, so he took another step – and another, and another . . .

. . . and suddenly realized that the trees had silver trunks.

# Chapter Fifteen

Gwen stopped suddenly. 'Hist!'

'Sure,' Rod said agreeably. 'Why not?'

'Oh, be still! I catch a trace of something I like not!'

'Pursuit?' Rod turned serious.

Gwen shook her head, frowning. ''Tis Duke Foidin, and in converse; yet I have only a sense of that which he doth speak with, and it's somewhat threatening.' She looked down at her children. 'Dost thou sense aught more?'

Silently, they shook their heads. ''Tis not altogether human, Mama,' Magnus contributed.

Out of the corner of his eye, Rod noticed Elidor trembling. He caught the boy's shoulder. 'Steady, there, lad. You're with us, now.' He turned back to Gwen. 'Of course, the wise thing to do would be to sneak on by.'

Gwen nodded.

Rod turned away. Silently, they picked their way between

white trunks in a dazzle of moonlight reflected off silver leaves. After about ten minutes, Gwen hissed, 'It doth grow stronger.'

Rod didn't falter. 'So they're on our line of march. We'll worry about avoiding them when we know where they are.'

Then, suddenly, they were out of the trees, at the top of a rise. Below them, in a natural bowl, rose a small hill. Light glowed around it, from glittering, moving figures.

'The faery knowe!' Elidor gasped.

'Hit the dirt!' Rod hissed. The whole family belly-flopped down in the grass. Rod reached up, and yanked Elidor down. 'No insult intended, Majesty,' he whispered. 'It's simply a matter of safety.' He turned to Magnus. 'You said the thought-pattern wasn't quite human?'

Magnus nodded. 'And therefore could I not comprehend it, Papa.'

'Well, you hit it right on the nose.' Rod frowned, straining his ears. 'Hold it; I think we can *just* make out what they're saying.'

Duke Foidin and his knights were easy to pick out by their dimness. They stood almost at the bottom of the bowl, off to Rod's left. The being facing him was taller by a head, and fairly seemed to glow. It had to be the most handsome male that Rod had ever seen, the fluidity of its movement, as it shifted from foot to foot continually, indicating musculature and co-ordination beyond the human. And he was brilliant; he fairly seemed to glow. His extravagant costume had no colour; it had only varying degrees of light. A silver coronet encircled his brow, tucking down behind pointed ears.

'The King of Faery?' Rod hissed to Elidor.

The boy shook his head. ''Tis a coronet, not a crown. A duke, mayhap, an they have such.'

The faery duke's arms chopped against each other. 'Be done! All this we've hearkened to aforetime, and found small reason in. This is no cause for we of Faery to embroil ourselves in mortal war.'

'Yet think!' Duke Foidin protested, 'the High Warlock doth champion the White Christ!'

'As have kings done these last two thousand years,' the faery replied.

*Two* thousand? It should've been more like eight hundred, from the medieval look of this land.

'The priests were threat to us at first,' the faery conceded, 'yet so was Cold Iron, which came not overlong before them – and we endure. The priests have learned they cannot expunge us, nor we rid ourselves of them.'

Duke Foidin took a deep breath. 'Then I offer price!'

The faery sneered. 'What could a mortal offer that a faery would desire?'

'Mortal wizards,' Foidin said promptly, 'two – a male and female?'

'Should we seek to breed them, then? Nay; we have some use for human captives, but wizards would be greater trouble than use, for they'd ever seek to learn our secrets.'

'Children.'

The faery stilled.

A stream of pure rage shot through Rod, almost seeming to come from somewhere, someone, else, scaring him by its intensity. He'd heard the fairy tales about changelings, aged elves left in mortal cradles for the pretty babes the fairies had carried off. The tradition had it that fairies liked mortal slaves, and definitely preferred to raise them themselves.

And, somehow, Rod thought he knew which children Foidin had in mind.

Foidin saw the faery duke was interested. 'And an infant, not yet a year of age; I'll have it soon.'

Rod almost went for him, right then and there. The snake was talking about Gregory!

But Gwen's hand was on his arm, and he forced himself to relax. No, of course not; Foidin didn't know Gregory existed. He wasn't even in this world.

' 'Tis the only mortal thing we value,' the faery said slowly, 'yet scarcely worth the fighting for. We've ways of gaining mortal children, at far less cost than war.'

And he turned on his heel, and strode away.

Duke Foidin stared after him, unbelieving, rage rising. 'Thou knavish wraith!' he fairly screamed. 'Will nothing move thee?'

The faery duke stopped, then slowly turned, and the air seemed to thicken and grow brittle, charged to breaking. 'Why should we of Faery care what mortals do?' His voice grew heavy with menace. 'Save to avenge an insult. 'Ware, mortal duke! Thou mayest gain the war which thou dost seek, but with the folk of Faery seeking *thy* heart's blood! Now get thee hence!'

Duke Foidin stood, white-lipped and trembling, aching to lash out, but too afraid.

'Mayhap thou dost doubt our power.' The faery duke's voice suddenly dripped with honey. 'Then let us show thee how easily we gain all that thou didst offer.' And his left hand shot up with a quick circling motion.

Suddenly, unseen cords snapped tight around Rod's body, rolling him over and pinning his arms to his sides and his legs to one another. He let out one terror-stricken, rage-filled bellow; then something sticky plastered itself over his mouth. He could still see, though – see Gwen and the children, even Elidor, bound hand and foot, and gagged, as he was, fairly cocooned in shining cords. Grotesquely ugly sprites leaped out of the grass all about them, stamping in a dance and squealing with delight. Their shaggy clothes looked to be made of bark; they had huge jughead ears, great loose-lipped mouths, and bulbous, warty noses dividing platter-eyes. The biggest of them was scarcely three feet high.

'They ever come, the prying big 'uns!' they cried.

'They never spy the sentry-spriggans!'

'Well caught, spriggans!' the faery duke called. 'Now bring them here!'

The spriggans howled delight, and kicked Rod up to the top of the rise, then shoved him over. Sky and grass whirled about him and about as he rolled down the hill, with spriggans running along, whooping, rhythmically pushing him, as a child rolls a hoop. Panic hit, fear for Gwen and the kids – and behind it, a feeling of some sympathetic Presence, its anger beginning to build with Rod's.

He brought up with a thump against the Duke's feet. Gwen slammed into his back, softening the bumps as the children knocked into her.

Foidin stared down at them, horrified. 'Elidor!'

'The King?' The faery duke looked up, interested. 'Of great account! We've never had a mortal king to rear!'

Foidin's gaze shot up at him, shocked. Then he glared down at Rod, pale and trembling. 'This is thy doing! Thou hast brought the King to this! But . . . how? What? How hast thou brought this thing to pass? I left thee safe, behind stout locks and guards!'

Rod mumbled through his gag.

The faery duke nodded contemptuously. 'Allow him speech.' A spriggan hopped to pull Rod's gag.

'Yeeeowtch!' The sticky plaster hurt, coming off. He worked his mouth, glaring up at the Duke. 'You should know, Milord Duke, that locks and guards cannot hold a warlock, if he does not wish it. Your lock did open without a human hand to touch it; your guards all sleep.'

'It cannot be!' the Duke fairly screeched, white showing round the borders of his eyes. 'Only magics most powerful can bring such things to pass!'

Rod smiled sourly. 'Be more careful of your guests – and hope this faery duke doth hold me fast. For now we have a score to settle, you and I.' He felt the touch of the helping spirit again, but its rage was growing – and so was his. 'You would have sold all my family, to gain this faery's aid! Be sure that never do I have a chance to come at thee alone – for I'll not trouble to use my magic! And this child' – it seemed, now, as though it weren't himself talking, suddenly, but the Presence – 'who was this babe you would have sold? How shall you gain possession of it?'

The Duke turned away to hide a sudden look of fear, trembling.

'Turn not away!' Rod barked. 'Face me, coward, and give answer – what child was this?'

'Indeed, do stay,' the faery duke murmured. 'Or wilt thou so straightaway abandon this thy King?'

'The King!' Foidin gasped, whirling back. 'Nay, assuredly, thou shalt not keep him – for if thou dost, my power fails!' He stared at the faery duke, drawn and palsied, nerving himself up to it – then his hand flashed to his sword.

The faery duke snapped his fingers contemptuously, and Foidin doubled over a sudden stabbing pain. 'Aieeengggh!'

Gwen seized the moment; Rod's sword shot out of its scabbard to slash his bonds, then whirled to cut Gwen's. Out of the corner of his eye, he saw Magnus's little blade shearing his ropes; then he sailed into the faery duke, knocking him back by sheer surprise, over Rod's knee, Rod's dagger at his throat. 'Release my family, milord – or feel cold iron in your veins.'

But Magnus had slashed his siblings' bonds, and he and Geoff were holding off a band of spriggans, who were throwing stones but retreating steadily before the boys' swords. Gwen and Cordelia crouched, waiting, as the faery band ran forward with a shout, glowing blades whipping through the air. 'Now!' Gwen cried, and a hail of stones shot toward the faeries, bruising and breaking. Some screamed, but most pressed on – and the thrown stones whirled back to strike at them again.

Duke Foidin saw his chance to curry favour, and whipped out his blade. 'Nay, Theofrin,' he grunted around his pain, 'I will aid thee!' And he leaped forward, blade slashing down at Rod.

Rod had no choice; his sword snapped up to guard, and Theofrin whiplashed out of his arms as though they were rubber. The Duke's blade slid aside on Rod's, but the faery duke Theofrin seized Rod's sword arm, snatched him high, whirled him through the air, and tossed him to the ground as though he'd been a bag of kindling. Rod shouted, and the shout turned into a shriek as he hit and felt something move where it shouldn't. His shoulder screamed raw pain. Through its haze, he struggled to his knees, right arm hanging limp – and saw Theofrin stalking towards him, elf-sword flickering about like a snake's tongue.

Beyond him, Duke Foidin and his men frantically parried faery blades; his try for favour hadn't worked. One courtier howled as a faery blade stabbed through him, and whipped back out; blood spurted from his chest, and he collapsed.

And Theofrin's blade danced closer. Rod whipped out his dagger – what else did he have left? Theofrin sneered, and lunged; Rod parried, but the faery duke had over-reached, and Rod flicked his dagger-blade out to nick the faery's hand. The faery shrieked at the touch of cold iron, and clasped his wounded hand, the elfin sword dropping to the ground. Rod staggered to his feet, and waded forward. Theofrin's face contorted with a snarl; his own dagger whisked out, left-handed.

'Papa!' Magnus's scream cut through the battle. Rod's head snapped up; he saw his eldest on the ground, spreadeagled, struggling against invisible bonds. A tall, thin faery stood above him, face lit with glee, as he chopped downward with his sword.

Adrenalin shocked through him, and Rod charged. Theofrin stepped to block his path. Rod barrelled into him, dagger-first, and the faery duke skipped aside with a howl of rage, the cold-iron dagger barely missing his ribs. Then Rod's shoulder caught his son's adversary in the midriff, and the sword-cut went wide, slicing his dangling right hand. Rod bellowed with the pain, but caught the hilt and wrenched the sword free. He howled again; it was cold, burning his flesh like dry ice; but he clung to it, lunging after the faery, stabbing. The sword cut into the faery's belly, and it folded with a scream, sprawling on the ground. Rod didn't stay to see if it were dead; he whirled back to his son, and saw the blood flowing from Magnus's shoulder as he struggled up on one elbow, the invisible bonds gone with the faery whose spell had forged them. 'Magnus!' Rod clasped the boy to him. 'What've they done to you!'

'Just . . . a cut . . . ' the boy choked out. His eyes had lost focus. 'Couldn't break his spell, Papa . . . Strange . . . too strong . . . ' Then he collapsed across Rod's arm.

Panic shot through Rod as he stared at his eldest son, dread clawing up into his throat. It couldn't be – so full of life! He couldn't be. . . .

'Dead?'

A metal point pricked his throat. Rod looked up, and saw Theofrin grinning down, with glowing, gloating eyes. 'Dead, as thou shalt be! Yet not too quickly. I'll have thine entrails forth for this fell insult, mortal, and pack hot coals in their place, whilst yet thou livest! Thy wife shall be our drudge and whore, thy children slaves, with torques about their necks!' His mouth twisted in contempt. 'Warlock, dost thou name thyself? An thou hadst been such, there'd have truly been a battle royal! Hadst thou been Lord Kern, now, our faery ropes would have crumbled ere they touched thee; our spriggans would have turned to stone! Cold iron in a thousand guises would have filled the air about thee, and thine every step would have waked the sound of church bells!'

Then Rod heard Gwen scream in rage. He darted a glance toward her, saw her kneeling with Cordelia and Geoffrey clasped against her. She had caught three fallen swords with her mind, and they wove a deadly dance about her, warding off a dozen faery courtiers; but the faeries' blades all flickered closer, closer . . .

'They are not done with her, quite yet,' Theofrin said. 'They'll play with her a while longer, then beat down her witch-swords. Then will they play with her again, and her witchling with her. When that is done, if they feel merciful, they may then slay them.' His eyes gleamed with a chill, self-satisfied light.

Rod glared up at him, terror for his family boiling into anger. He shot that energy into a craving wish for steel to fill the air, for church bells to ring – anything, to banish this fell faery!

And up beneath his rage it mounted, that sense of a kindly, outraged presence, a spirit other than his, reassuring him, but smashing out with all Rod's rage in one huge hammer blow.

Distantly, a bell began to toll.

Closer at hand, another bell began to peal.

Then another joined it, and another, north, east, south, and west – and more, and more, till the bells in every village church for miles around must have been clamouring.

He'd done it! He'd broken through his barrier, through to Gwen – and she'd set the bells to ringing!

The faery duke looked up, horrified; his glow seemed to dim. Then he threw back his head and let out a howl of rage. It echoed from every side as his court picked it up, till the whole of the glen was one huge scream.

Then, still screaming, they flew. A door swung open in the mound, and the faery folk lifted off the ground and whisked away toward it, like dry leaves borne on a whirlwind.

The duke tarried a moment, glaring down at Rod. 'I know not by what magics thou hast wrought this, wizard – yet be assured, I shall avenge it!' Then he shot up off the ground and towards the mound, with a long, drawn-out scream of wrath, that dwindled and cut off as the mound's door shut. For minutes more, there was screaming still, muted and distant, inside the knowe; then all was quiet. Moonlight showed a peaceful glen, silver leaves tinkling in the breeze; only a circle of flattened grass remained, to show where the fairies had danced.

And the Duke Foidin, and his henchmen. The Duke stood staring at the fairy mound; then, slowly, his eyes moved over the glen, till they fastened on Rod. He stared; then a leering grin broke his face, and he moved forward.

Slowly, Rod laid Magnus's body down and rose to his feet, albeit shakily, dagger at the ready.

Gwen turned and saw. Then she shifted her gaze, seeking and finding Rod's fallen sword. It lifted itself from the ground and shot to his side, point toward Duke Foidin, circling in the air. Through the numbed sorrow that filled him, Rod felt the comfort of her support. 'Whoever dies, milord, thou shalt be first.'

The Duke and his train stopped, grins vanishing. Foidin's eyes flicked from the floating sword to Rod's dagger, then to Rod's dangling arm, but back to the sword. He licked his lips, and swallowed. 'Deliver up mine ward and nephew.'

'He comes with me,' Rod grated.

The Duke's face darkened; he glanced back at his men, who

glanced at one another. Hands felt for sword hilts, but they darted uneasy glances at Rod.

Gwen whispered to Cordelia, and the little girl stared at the sword. Gwen transferred her gaze to a three-foot-high boulder fifty feet from the Duke. It shuddered, then rocked, then began to topple, to roll – over and over, faster and faster, right at the Duke and his men.

The courtiers broke, and fled. The Duke stayed an instant longer, to cast a venomous glance at Rod; then he ran, too.

Rod glared after them.

Little Elidor breathed out a shaky sigh.

The little sound broke Rod's trance; he dropped to the ground beside Magnus's still form. 'Gwen! Quickly!'

And she was there. She stared at her son, horrified.

Rod's thumb was on the inside of Magnus's wrist. 'There's still a pulse . . . '

'Quickly, children!' Gwen snapped. 'Four-leafed clovers, red verbena, and St John's Wort!' Leaning forward, she ripped open Rod's doublet and stripped the bandage from his wound. ' 'Twill do, until they find afresh! He needs it now!' She tore the poultice free; Rod winced, and watched as she flipped the fresh side down with one hand as she yanked Magnus's doublet loose with the other. She pressed the poultice down. 'Ah, if only chanting spells could work!'

It seemed reasonable – or at least, in harmony with everything else that'd been happening here. A strange sort of dizziness took hold of Rod, and with it came again that sense of a stern but kindly presence. His lips opened, and he found himself chanting:

'Red blood rise, to fill Life's way;
Close the wounds of weapons fey!
The elfin power hath lost its sway;
Warrior, rise, to greet the day.'

Gwen shot him a startled glance.

His right arm gave a terrific wrench, and something popped. Rod clasped his shoulder with a gasp of pain. 'Hahhhh . . . aieeee!' He gulped air, and swallowed hard. The glen swam before his eyes, then steadied, and the pain ebbed to a dull ache.

'My lord! What tortures thee?'

'Nothing – now.' Rod massaged his shoulder, marvelling. He

moved his arm; it was stiff, and ached, but it worked. 'Never mind me! How's Magnus?' He looked down, and saw the colour returning to the boy's face. Gwen stared, then slowly peeled back the poultice. Beneath it, only a faint red line marked the sword-cut. Rod could scarcely hear her whisper: 'He is healed!' Her head snapped up; she stared into Rod's eyes. 'Where didst thou learn that charm?'

Rod shook his head slowly. 'Just came to mind . . . Er – it *was* you who rang the church bells, wasn't it?'

Her gaze held his; she slowly turned her head from side to side. They knelt in silence, gazes locked.

Then Rod looked away. 'There *was* a feeling – a sense of some . . . something . . . helping . . . '

'A spirit?' Gwen demanded softly.

Rod shrugged. 'Good a name for it as any . . . '

Magnus groaned.

They both bent over him, holding their breath.

He levered himself up on his elbows, frowning and blinking. 'Papa . . . sorry . . . '

'*Sorry?* For *what?*'

'For that . . . I had to cry for aid. 'Twas . . . full puissant magic, do you see. The strength alone, I might have met, but . . . 'twas strange, unlike to any I had dealt with aforetime.'

Rod met Gwen's gaze. 'That makes sense; whatever kind of magic these elves use, it's probably not psionic. What kind of place *is* this, anyway?'

'One, I think, where magic truly reigns. Thou didst heal thy son with a spoken chant, didst thou not?'

'Well, yes – but the words just focused the power that did the healing.'

Gwen's eyes widened. 'Hast *thou* such power?'

'Well, it was in me at the time.' Rod frowned. 'That "spirit" that I told you of. Or maybe it *was* me . . . Well, it doesn't matter.' He looked back down at Magnus. 'Just how well *are* you, son?'

'I do feel stiff – but strong as ever.' Before they could stop him, Magnus rolled to his knees and stood. He took a few tentative steps, then nodded. 'I do feel wearied, Papa – but I am well.'

Rod let out a huge, shaky sigh of relief. 'Well, whatever magic it was that did it, I'm all in favour of it!'

'Yet what was it, indeed?' Gwen wondered. 'Or . . . whose?'

'I'm not so sure I want to know the answer to that,' Rod said slowly. 'Come on, let's get moving. As soon as Duke Foidin gets back to his castle, we're going to have an army on our heels.'

# Chapter Sixteen

Not only had the trees changed – so had the time of day. It had been morning when Father Al stepped past Fess, over the line of stones; now it was night, with rays of moonlight sifting down through the tinsel leaves. He caught his breath at the beauty of the woodland glade. *Yes. There could be magic here.*

Then he remembered his mission, and looked about him to see if he could find evidence of the Gallowglasses. The mould of the forest floor was thoroughly churned up; a number of people had been walking about, surely. Bending closer, he was able to distinguish the prints of small feet and large ones; the Gallowglasses and their children, surely. He straightened up and looked about him; immediately he saw two tracks going away from him: a small one and a broad one. He weighed the evidence and decided the small track was a preliminary foray, while the broad one would be the whole family moving together. It was an easy enough trail to follow – last year's fallen, mouldering leaves were scuffed up; twigs were broken; and small plants had been trodden down. He wasn't too far behind them, then – certainly no more than twenty-four hours. And if he hurried . . . He set off, following the moonlit trail.

He'd gone about twenty paces before he happened to glance up and see a blaze on a tree trunk.

He halted, grinning with delight. How considerate of them, to leave him so clear a way to follow! Not that they'd meant it for that purpose, of course – how could they have known someone would come after them? No doubt they'd wanted to make sure they could find their way back to the point they'd come from; presumably, it was the only place where this world was linked to their own.

World?

He looked about him, and silently revised that opinion. Silver trees had never grown on Terra, nor on any planet he'd ever heard of. Scarcely conclusive proof, that, but still . . . The chilling thought crept in that he might not even be in his own universe and, for the first time, it occurred to him that he should perhaps be concerned about getting back home.

Curiously, he wasn't. If God wanted him to return to Gramarye, or Terra, no doubt He would make the means available. And if He didn't, well, Father Al had long ago decided to do whatever work God sent him, wherever it should be. Dying on the planet of his birth mattered little, compared with doing God's will.

So he turned ahead and sauntered away between the forest trees, following the trail of blazes, and whistling – and not just out of good spirits.

He came out onto the bank of a stream, and looked to either side, to see which had trees with – What the blazes! Nothing! Not a single trunk was marked!

Of course – they would be returning back along the river bank; *they*'d know which direction they'd gone in. The stream itself was enough of a trail. They only needed to know at which tree to turn back into the wood.

Here was a knotty problem. Which way had they gone? Left, or right? Upstream, or down?

'Well met by moonlight, handsome stranger.'

She rose up out of the water, dark hair shimmering over her shoulders to cloak her breasts – and that was all that did. Her eyes were large, and slanted; her nose was small, but her mouth was wide, with full, red lips, and her skin was very pale. 'How fortunate am I,' she purred, 'that hath found a gentleman to company me.' She waded toward him, up out of the water. As she rose, watercress draped itself about her hips in a token tribute of modesty. Father Al managed to wrench his gaze back to her face, feeling the responses in his body that reminded him that priests are human, too. He swallowed thickly, turned his lips inward to wet them, and muttered. 'Greetings, Lady of the Waters.'

'No lady I,' she murmured, 'but a wanton, eager to do the bidding of a mortal man.' She twined her arms about his neck and pressed up against him.

It ran counter to every demand his body screamed, but Father Al pulled her arms loose, gently but firmly, and pressed her hands together in front of his chest, forcing her body away from his. She stared at him in surprise. 'How now! Do not deny that thou dost want me!'

'I do,' Father Al admitted, 'but 'twould be wrongful.' He

glanced down at her fingers, and noticed the tiny, vestigial webs between them.

'Wrongful, because thou art a mortal, and I a nymph?' She laughed, revealing small, perfect, white teeth. 'Come, now! It hath been often done, and always to the man's delight!'

Delight, yes – but Father Al remembered some old tales, of how a water-maid's seduction had led to death – or, failing that, to a steadily-worsening despair that had surely torn apart the mortal lover's soul. He clung to the memory to give him strength, and explained, 'It must not be – and the fact that I am human and you are not has little enough to do with it; for see you, lass, if thou dost give out favours of thy body where thou art lusted for, but are not loved, thou dost break thine own integrity.'

'Integrity?' She smiled, amused. ''Tis a word for mortals, not for faery folk.'

'Not so,' Father Al said sternly, 'for the word means "wholeness", the wholeness of thy soul.'

She laughed, a dazzling cascade of sound. 'Surely thou dost jest! The faery folk have no immortal souls!'

'Personalities, then.' Father Al was miffed at himself for having forgotten. 'Identity. The sum and total of thyself, that which makes thee different, unique, special – not quite like any other water-nymph that ever was.'

She lost her smile. 'I think thou dost not jest.'

'Indeed, I do not. Thy identity, lass, thy true self, hidden away and known only to thyself, is what thou really art. 'Tis founded on those few principles that thou dost truly and most deeply believe in – those beliefs which, when manners and graces and fashions of behaving are all stripped away, do still remain, at the bottom and foundation of thy self.'

'Why, then,' she smiled, 'I am a wanton; for in my deepest self, my chiefest principle is pleasure sexual.' And she tried to twine her arms about his neck again.

Well, Father Al had heard *that* one before, and not just from aquatic women, either. He held her hands firmly, and held her gaze, looking deeply into her eyes. ''Tis an excuse, I trow, and will not serve. Some male hath wronged thee deeply, when thou wast young and tender. Thou didst open thy heart to him, letting him taste thy secret self, and didst therefore open, too, thy body, for it seemed fully natural that the one should follow the other.'

She stared at him, shocked, then suddenly twisted, trying to yank herself free. 'I'll not hear thee more!'

'Assuredly, thou wilt,' he said sternly, holding her wrists fast, 'for this young swain, when he had had his fill of thee, tore himself away, and tore a part of thy secret self with him. Then went he on his merry way, whistling, and sneering at thee – and thou wast lost in sorrow and in pain, for he had ripped away a part of thine inner self that never could be brought and mended back.'

'Mortal,' she fairly shrieked, 'art thou crazed? I am a *nymph!*'

Father Al had heard that one before, too. 'It matters not. There was never a thinking creature made to tear her secret self to bits, and toss the pieces out to passers-by; thus thou wouldst slowly shred thy secret self away, till naught was left, and thou didst not truly exist – only a walking shell would then be left. And this doth happen whenever thou dost open thy body to one who loves thee not, and whom thou dost not love. That breaks the wholeness of thy secret self, for we are made in such a wise that our inner selves and bodies are joined as one, and when the one doth open, the other should. So if thou dost open thy body while keeping thy secret self enclosed, thou dost break the wholeness of thy self.'

'A thousand times have I so done,' she sneered, 'yet I am whole within!'

'Nay, thou'rt not. Each time, a tiny piece of thee hast gone, though thou didst strive to know it not.'

'Nay, not so – for 'tis my nature to give my body and retain my self untouched! I am a *nymph!*'

'This is a thin excuse that thou didst first concoct, when first thy secret self was torn. Thou then didst say, "It matters not; I am untouched. This is my nature, to give of my body and not of my soul; mine only true desire is pleasure." And to prove it to thyself, thou didst seek to couple with every male that happened by – yet each time, thou wast more torn, and didst need to prove it more – so thou didst seek out more to pleasure thee, quite frantically – though in thy depths, thou knew it pleasured thee not at all. For in truth, 'twas only an excuse.'

'And what of thee?' she demanded angrily. 'Why dost thou rant thus at me? Why dost thou make me stay to listen, when I would turn away? Is not this thine own excuse, for the hot lust that doth throb within thee at the sight of me?'

*Touché*, Father Al thought. 'It is indeed. Yet hath mine excuse done harm to thee? Or me?'

She frowned prettily, searching his eyes. 'Nay . . . none to me. Yet I think that it doth harm to thee – for what is natural to thyself would be to grapple me, and couple here in wildness and in frenzy.'

'Thou dost read me shrewdly,' Father Al admitted. 'Yet though 'tis "natural", lass, it is not right – for thereby would a part of me be ripped away, even as a part of thee would.' He sighed. 'It is a male conceit that a woman's self may be rended by a one-night's coupling, while the man's is not – but 'tis only a conceit. We, too, are made all of one piece, body and soul so shrewdly welded together that we cannot give of the one without giving of the other. And we, too, can be rended by a first coupling with a one who loves us not, and may we seek to deny that hurt by seeking to lie with every maid we may. Thus is the legend born of prowess male, and many a young man's soul is rended by the promiscuity that comes of thus attempting to prove himself a legend – which is to say, a ghost. But if young men would speak the truth, they would own that there is little enough pleasure in it – for loveless coupling, at the moment when pleasure should transform itself to ecstasy, truly turns itself to ashes, and the taste of gall.'

'I think,' she said slowly, 'that thou dost speak from hurt that thou hast known.'

He smiled ruefully. 'All young men commit the same mistakes; all step upon the brush that covers o'er the pitfall, no matter how loudly their seniors blare the warnings in their ears. I was once young; and I was not always of the Cloth.'

Her eyes widened in horror. She leaped back, looking him up and down in one quick glance, and pressed her hands to her mouth. 'Thou art a monk!'

He smiled. 'Hadst thou only seen that I was male?'

She nodded, eyes huge.

'If thou hadst looked, thou wouldst have known that I did not walk the stream-banks in search of pleasure.'

'Nay, that follows not,' she said with a frown, 'for I have known – nay, never mind. Yet if thou didst not hither come for sport, why *hast* thou come?'

'Why, I do seek an husband, wife, and children three,' Father Al said slowly. 'They would have come out from this wood some time ago, mayhap whilst sunlight shone. Wouldst thou have seen them?'

'Indeed I did,' the nymph said slowly, 'they woke me from my daytime sleep – the wee ones made some noise, thou knowest.'

'I do indeed.' Father Al had delivered sermons at family churches. 'Canst thou say which way they went?'

She shook her head. 'I did not look so long. One quick glance sufficed to show a woman with them – and she was quite beautiful.' The nymph seemed irritated by the memory. 'I saw no prospect of a satisfaction there, though the man and boys were comely – so I sought my watery bed again.'

'Out upon it!' Father Al glared up at the leaves, clenching a fist. 'How can I tell which way to go?'

'If 'tis a matter of so great an import to thee,' the nymph said slowly, 'mayhap that I can aid. Do thou sit here, and wait, and I will quickly course the stream, and seek for sign of them.'

'Wouldst thou, then!' Father Al cried. 'Now, there's a wench for thee! Why, thank thee, lass! The blessings of . . . '

'I prithee, hold!' The nymph held up a hand. 'Name not thy Deity, I beg thee! Do thou abide; I'll search.' She ducked under the water, and was gone.

Father Al stared after her a moment; then he sighed, and lowered himself carefully to the river bank. Not so young as he had been – but still too young for comfort in some ways, eh? He wondered if his hectoring had done any good, if the nymph would even remember it. Probably not; the young never seemed to learn where sex was concerned, and she was eternally young. Nice of her to offer to help, though – or had it just been a convenient excuse for getting away from a garrulous old man?

With that thought in his head, he sat there on tenterhooks, tense in waiting, wondering if the nymph would even return.

Then, suddenly, the water clashed in front of him, and the nymph rose up, pushing her hair back from her face. 'They come, good monk. Back up the stream-bank they do wander.' She pointed downstream. 'Though why, I cannot say.'

'A thousand blessings on thee!' Father Al cried, surging to his feet. The nymph gasped in horror, and disappeared in a splash.

Father Al stared at the widening ripple-rings, biting his tongue in consternation at his *faux pas*. Well, no doubt she'd realize he'd just been carried away, and would credit him with good intentions.

Then he turned away, the nymph receding to the back of his mind, and plunged into the underbrush that lined the bank, heading back into the trees and downstream, excitement rising high within him at the thought of finally meeting the Gallowglasses.

# Chapter Seventeen

They dodged through the silver woods, trusting to Gwen's sense of direction, until they came out on the lake shore. Rod sighed with relief. 'OK, into the water. If they're tracking us with hounds, we want to break the trail.' He was about to jump in when he noticed his family all hanging back. 'Hey, what's the matter? Jump in!'

'My lord,' Gwen said delicately, 'it doth occur to us to remember the *Each Uisge* . . . '

'What of it? It's dead!'

'Aye; but it may not have been alone. We know so little of this land . . . '

Rod felt a sudden dislike of water, himself. 'Er . . . how about it, Elid— er, Your Majesty? Are there other unfriendly beasties in the water?'

'Oh, aye!' Elidor said promptly. 'There do be Fuathan of all sorts and shapes! Shellycoats, peallaidhs, fideal, urisks, melusines . . . '

'Er, I think that's enough,' Rod interrupted. 'We'll take our chances with the hounds.'

They moved along the lake shore. It was quicker going; the trees didn't come down right to the water's edge; they generally had a path at least two feet wide.

'We do seem to have come into a country with a rather strange population,' Rod admitted to Gwen.

'We do indeed,' she agreed. 'The Faery, and some of the spirits Elidor doth mention, I have heard of – yet some are total strangers. Can we be in Gramarye, Rod?'

Rod shrugged. 'Sure. Given a population of latent telepaths, who can persuade witch-moss to adopt any shape they're collectively thinking of, and a thousand years to work in, who can say *what* would show up?'

'Yet I cannot think the elves would disappear,' Gwen pointed out, 'and some magics that the faery duke did speak of, no witch or warlock in all Gramarye possesseth.'

'True,' Rod admitted, 'both points. The spriggans' ropes *are* something new – and so is making them crumble to dust *before* they touched Lord Kern – if the faery duke wasn't just making that up. Still, I could see a way telekinesis might do that. But, turning faeries to stone? No. That's *really* new – if he meant it literally.'

'Yet if we be on Gramarye,' Gwen said softly, 'where do we be?'

'Nice question.' Rod looked up at the starry sky above the lake. 'Could be anywhere, dear. McAran's time machine was a matter transmitter as well as a time shifter. I suppose we could be on any world, around any star in the universe.' He frowned, squinting up at the sky. 'Though, come to think of it, there's something familiar about those constellations . . . ' He shook his head. 'Can't place it. But I *know* I've seen that stellar layout before!'

'Yet 'tis not the sky of Gramarye,' Gwen said softly.

Rod was silent for a moment. Then, slowly, he shook his head. 'No, dear. It's not.'

They walked silently for a few minutes, looking away from the sky and down toward the ground, hand in hand. The children picked up Gwen's thoughts, and crowded close for comfort. Elidor watched, not understanding, alone and to the side.

Gwen reached out and gathered him in. 'Well, 'tis not so great a blow as all that; I've had suspicions. There're far too few folk here with any Power, for it to ha' been our Isle of Gramarye.'

'Yes,' Rod said sombrely. 'We haven't run into so much as a telepath. Not that I'm used to having people read *my* thoughts . . . ' He looked up at Gwen, frowning. 'Strange, isn't it? When I first came to Gramarye, the Queen's witches could read my mind – but by the time I met you, no one could.'

'Oh, really?' said a mellow baritone behind him. 'That's interesting!'

Rod whirled about.

A friar in a brown robe with a black rope belt picked his way through the trees toward them. Moonlight gleamed off his tonsure. 'Can you think of anything that could cause that effect?'

'Not offhand,' Rod said slowly. 'And you'll pardon my noticing that you don't quite speak like the rest of the local population.'

'Not surprising; I'm from out of this world.' The friar thrust out a hand. 'Father Aloysius Uwell, at your service.'

'I hope so.' Rod searched the man's face. He was definitely on the fat side, with brown hair and a library pallor, wide, frank eyes, and a firm mouth; and something immensely likeable about him. Rod warmed to him, albeit reluctantly. He took Father Uwell's hand. 'Good to met you.' Then he noticed the tiny yellow screwdriver in the priest's breast pocket. 'You're a Cathodean!'

'Is that so surprising?' Father Uwell smiled. 'I told you I wasn't of this world.'

'Or the next?' But Rod couldn't help smiling. 'What world *are* you from?'

'McCorley, originally – but I've been on Terra, at the Vatican, for the last twenty years. Except for jaunts to trouble-spots, of course – such as Gramarye.'

'Gramarye?' Rod's eyebrows shot up. 'So you came in the same way we did?'

'Yes, and it wasn't very easy, I don't mind telling you! Here I've been outbound from Terra for most of a month, just to meet you – and when I get to Gramarye, I find you've just left! Not very hospitable of you, sir.'

'Er, yeah, well, I'm sorry, but your reservation got mislaid. Pardon my curiosity, but I wouldn't think the Vatican would even have *heard* about me, let alone have been interested in me!'

'We hadn't, until the Pope opened a letter that's been waiting in the vaults for a thousand years or so.'

'A thousand *years?*' Rod did some quick subtraction. 'Who knew about me in 2000 AD?' Then it hit him. 'Oh. No. Not McAran.'

'Ah, I see you've met! Yes, it was from a Dr Angus McAran. He informed the Pope that Rod Gallowglass, of Gramarye – and he gave the co-ordinates – was potentially the most powerful wizard ever born.'

Gwen gasped.

The kids stared.

Rod squeezed his eyes shut and gave his head a quick shake. 'Oh, no, not again! That skinny old b— .' He remembered the children and took a deep breath. ''Fraid it's a wild goose chase, Father. I've never shown the faintest trace of any magical ability.'

'He did say "potential",' Father Uwell reminded him, 'and I find this sudden telepathic blockage of yours quite interesting – oh, yes, I do believe telepathy works, especially since I've visited Gramarye.'

Rod smiled. 'Met some of our witches, huh?'

Father Al winced. 'Just one – and an elf. I'd really rather call your "witches" espers, if you don't mind. "Witch" is a supernatural term, and there's nothing metaphysical about psionic powers. Oh, and by the way, I saw your youngest.'

'Gregory!' Gwen's gaze riveted on the priest. 'How doth he, good Father?'

'Quite well, I assure you, madame,' Father Al said kindly. 'Two old elf-wives are watching over him, and the witch-girl who brought me to your house is helping them now. And Puck himself is guarding the door.'

Rod smiled, feeling a weight lift off his shoulders. 'Well, with him there, no enemy could even get close to the door.'

'Doth he fret?' Gwen said anxiously.

'Not visibly.' Father Al frowned. 'In fact, he's very quiet. But the witch-girl read his thoughts, and told me that his mind searches for you ceaselessly – even when he's asleep. Well did you name him "Gregory", the watcher, the sentinel.'

But Gwen wasn't listening any more; her eyes had lost focus as her mind probed. Suddenly she gasped. 'I do feel his touch!'

'Across *time*?' Rod cried. Then he frowned. 'Wait a minute – McAran had a technique like that, where the mind travelled through time to a host-body. But how could a baby learn it?'

'He's too young to know about time,' Father Al suggested. 'Perhaps, to him, all moments are the same.'

'There are words!' Gwen cried, eyes huge.

'Words? But the kid doesn't know how to talk!'

'Nay . . . 'tis Fess.' Gwen's brows knit. 'Do not ask me the manner of it.'

Rod slammed a fist into his palm. 'Transmitting on my thought-frequency – and Gregory's my baby, so his frequency resonates with mine! He's picking up Fess's thoughts, and Gregory's tele-pathic waves are acting as a carrier wave for Fess! What's he saying, Gwen?'

She frowned. ''Tis too faint to make much of . . . There is something said of a machine, and of Brom O'Berin and Dr McAran . . . And something of the Abbot and the King, also. I think . . . 'tis that the Abbot unaccountably turned back, return-ing to Their Majesties full wroth. He thought he had been duped . . . their bargain was broken . . . the Abbot doth storm away, back to his monastery . . . Tuan hath sent out the summons to his barons, to send him levies of knights and men, and doth gird himself for war . . . ' Her voice broke. 'Husband – they may come to battle, and our babe lies there defenceless!'

'Not defenceless, not with Puck guarding his door,' Rod re-assured her quickly. 'And you can be sure, if Puck's there, Brom

O'Berin's getting hourly reports. If there's any threat to the kid, he'll whisk him away to Elfland so quickly that Gregory won't even know he's been moved!'

'Dost thou truly think he will?' Tears filled Gwen's eyes.

'Of course! After all, he's the kid's gr— *god*father! Believe me, you can trust him. But cut the talking, dear – reassure the poor baby, while the contact lasts.'

'Aye . . . ' Gwen's gaze seemed to turn inward; she sat alone, hands in her lap, mind reaching out to enfold her baby's.

Father Al coughed politely. 'Ah, may I enquire – who is "Brom O'Berin"?'

'The King of the Elves,' Rod said absently, then quickly, 'Er, that's semi-classified information! Do you still honour the Seal of the Confessional, Father?'

'We do, though we don't use that term any more.' Father Al smiled, amused. 'And what you've just let slip is protected by it. Would it reassure you if I called you, "my son"?'

'No, that's not necessary.' Rod smiled, warming even more to the priest. 'Brom's also the Royal Privy Counsellor, you see – so there is a need for secrecy.'

'Hm.' Father Al frowned. 'Then should your children hear it?'

'The kids?' Rod glanced at the grassy bank; the children lay tumbled on it, asleep. 'It *has* been a long day, hasn't it? No, I don't think they heard, Father.'

'So I see.' Father Al smiled fondly.

Rod cocked his head to one side, watching him. 'Little sentimental, aren't you? I mean, considering they're supposed to be little warlocks and a little witch.'

Father Al stared at him, startled. 'Come now, sir! These children's souls are perfectly normal, from all that I can see! There's nothing supernatural about psionic powers!'

'Sure about that?' Rod eyed him sideways. 'Well, it's your field, not mine. Er – you *are* a specialist, aren't you?'

Father Al nodded. 'A cultural anthropologist, really, but I specialize in the study of magic.'

'Why?'

Father Al blinked. 'How's that again?'

'Why would the Church of Rome be interested in magic?'

The priest grinned broadly. 'Why, to prove it doesn't exist, for one thing – and that takes some meticulous work on occasion, believe me; there've been some extremely clever hoaxes. And, of course, the rare actual esper can very easily be mistaken for a sorcerer. Beyond that – well, the whole concept of magic has a strange domination over men's souls, in many cultures; and the soul is our concern.'

'Meaning that if any real magic ever does show up, you want to know how to fight it.'

'If it's demonic, yes. For example, exorcism has a long history. But the Church didn't really begin to become interested in magic until the twenty-fifth century, when provable espers began to become visible. They weren't Satanists, nor possessed by evil spirits; that didn't take long to establish. On the other hand, they weren't saints either – that was even more obvious. Good people, most of them, but no better than the average, such as myself.'

'So,' Rod said, 'you had to decide there was a "magic" force that had nothing to do with the supernatural.'

Father Uwell nodded. 'Then we were off the hook, for the time being. But some of the Cathodeans began to wonder how the Church should react if it ever ran into some sort of *real* magic that was neither witchcraft nor miracle.'

Rod frowned. 'Just what'd you have in mind? I mean, if esper powers don't fit that description, what does?'

'Oh, you know – fairy-tale magic. Waving your hands in the air, and chanting an incantation, and making something happen by a ritual process, *not* by the power of your mind.'

'Saying "Abracadabra" and waving a magic wand, huh? All right, I'll bite – how *should* the Church react?'

Father Uwell shrugged. 'How should I know? We've only been discussing it for five hundred years.'

Rod eyed him sideways. 'I should think that'd be time enough to arrive at a few tentative conclusions.'

'Oh yes, hundreds of them! That's the problem, you see – we have a notion about how we should respond if we ever do encounter a case of real magic – but so far, we haven't.'

'O-o-oh.' Rod nodded. 'No one to test your theories on, huh?'

'Exactly so. Of course, we've looked for a real magician; we've investigated hundreds of cases. But most of them proved to be espers who didn't know what they were; and there were a few cases of demonic possession, of course. The rest were hoaxes. So if we ever do find a real "wizard", we *think* we'll know how to react, but . . .'

'How?'

Father Uwell shrugged. 'The way we should've reacted to the introduction of science, and eventually did – that it's something neither good nor evil, but does raise a deal of questions we have to try to answer.'

Rod tilted his head back, lips forming the syllable quite a while before he said it. 'Oh. So if a real wizard should happen to come waltzing along, you want to be there from the very beginning, so you can figure out what questions he's raising.'

'And bat them to the theologians, to find answers for.' Father Uwell nodded. 'And there is the danger that a neophyte wizard might start meddling with the supernatural, without realizing what he's doing. If that did happen, someone should be there to steer him back into safe territory.'

'And if he doesn't steer?'

'Persuade him, of course.'

'And if he doesn't stop?'

Father Uwell shrugged. 'Batten down the hatches and get braced for the worst – and try to figure out how he does what he does, so that if he lets loose some really evil power, we can counter it.'

Rod stood very still.

Then he nodded, slowly. 'So. It does behove the Church to study magic.'

'And we have. We've worked out a great deal, theoretically – but who's to say if any of it's really valid?'

Rod shook his head. 'Not me, Father. Sorry, but if you're looking for a wizard, you haven't found him. I've never worked a trick in my life that didn't have a gadget behind it. I did bump into McAran once, coming through a time machine – but I wasn't a wizard then, either. And he knew it!'

The priest thrust his head forward. 'A time machine. He could've used it to take a look at your personal future.'

Rod stood stock-still for a moment.

Then he shook his head vigorously. 'No. Oh, no. No. There's no way I *could* turn into a wizard – is there?'

'Well, there is the question of your suddenly becoming telepathically invisible – but that's more a matter of psi phenomena than of magic. Still, it indicates you may have some powers you don't know about. Has something improbable ever happened, when you wanted it to happen, for no visible reason?'

Rod frowned, shaking his head. 'Never, Father. Can't think of a single.'

'Mine husband,' Gwen reminded, 'the bells . . . '

Rod looked up, startled. Then he turned back to the priest, slowly. 'That's right. Just a little while ago, I wanted church bells to ring, very badly – wished it with all my might, actually – I was trying to break through to Gwen, hoping she'd read my mind and start ringing them telekinetically.'

'And they rang,' Gwen said softly, eyes wide, 'though I did not do it.'

'Nor the kids either,' Rod said grimly. 'You don't suppose . . . ?'

'Oh, I do – but it's only a supposition. One incident isn't quite enough to construct a theory. Excuse me – you did say your wife is telekinetic?'

'Among other things.' Rod nodded. 'And our little girl too. The boys teleport. That's the usual sex-linked breakdown on Gramarye, for espers. But Magnus is telekinetic, too, which breaks the rules – and he's got some powers we're not sure about at all.'

'It runs in the family, then.'

'Runs? It never even slows down to a trot!'

'Yes, I see.' Father Uwell frowned. 'I'd heard about this all, of course, but . . . doesn't it strike you as strange that your children should breed true, in esper powers, when only one of their parents is an esper?'

Rod stared. Gwen's eyes lit.

'I'd assumed it was a dominant trait,' Rod said slowly.

'Which it well might be, of course. But how do you explain your son's additional powers?'

'I don't.' Rod threw up his hands. 'I've been trying for eight years and I still can't. How's "mutation" sound to you?'

'About the same way "coincidence" does – possible, but also improbable, and therefore suspect.'

'So.' Rod steadied his gaze on the chubby, gently-smiling face. 'You think he might've inherited it from both sides.'

Father Uwell spread his hands. 'What can I say? It's possible – but three bytes of data are scarcely a full meal.'

'About what I expected.' Rod nodded. 'So. Keep on observing, and hope for the best, eh?

'If you don't mind.'

'Oh, not at all! Me, mind? Just because we're hiking through unknown territory, where there might be an enemy on every side? Just because we've got supernatural beasties with long, sharp teeth coming out of roadside pools? No, I don't mind at all, Father – but you should, I mean, it's not exactly going to be a church picnic, if you'll pardon the phrase.'

'Certainly,' the priest said, smiling. 'And as to the danger – well, we'll have to take it as it comes, eh?'

'Sure will.' Rod couldn't help smiling; there was something *very* likeable about this brown-robe. Not to mention reassuring; it never hurt to have another adult male in the party, even if he wasn't exactly a warrior. 'But there might be a way to limit that. You just came in from Gramarye, you say.'

Father Uwell nodded.

'Is the door still open?'

The priest blinked. 'Why, as far as I know, it was never shut.'

'*What!*'

Father Uwell nodded. 'I understand there's been quite a loss of game in the area, and several peasants are complaining about missing livestock. No other people have "fallen in", though. There's a great black horse on patrol there, and he won't let anyone near.'

'Fess!' Rod slapped his thigh. 'He's still standing there, waiting for us to come out!'

'Trying to figure out how to *get* you out, I think. At least, that's the only reason he let me past.'

Rod frowned. 'You don't mean he talked to you.'

'No, but I wouldn't have been surprised if he had. I came to your house, and, not finding you home, I set out to the woods near by, with Puck for a guide. As I went toward the pond, your horse galloped up to block me. I dodged to the side, but he dodged with me. I ducked under his belly, but he sat on me. I tried to vault over him, and he swivelled around so that I jumped off exactly where I'd jumped on. I finally decided I was dealing with an unusual specimen.'

Rod nodded. 'You should only know *how* unusual.'

'I have some idea; when I struck him, he clanged. So I tried to reason with him.

'He eventually escorted me to the point at which you'd disappeared. I walked ahead – and found myself surrounded by silver leaves! I whirled about, and found myself facing a great white-trunked tree with a big "X" carved on it. I tried to step back into it, but I thumped roundly against the bark and sat back on my cassock. I fancy I must have looked rather ridiculous.'

'So did I,' Rod said grimly. 'Don't worry about it, Father.

So. The gate's still open, but it only works one-way, eh?'

The priest nodded. 'It would require a transmitter on this end, I fancy.'

Rod's head snapped up, staring.

Then he hit his forehead with the heel of his hand. 'Of course! What's the matter with me? They just set up a transmitter, and didn't worry about who was going to stumble in here, as long as all of *us* did!' He shook his head, feeling the anger boil. 'Can you believe how callous those futurians are? What do they care if a hundred peasants get torn away from their families, just so long as they get the ones they're after!'

'I take it you have enemies,' Father Uwell said carefully.

'You might say that, yes.' Rod smiled sardonically. 'Enemies with time machines – so I was thinking of Doc Angus's time machine, which *can* pass any amount of material, and which *can* pull you back out of whenever it lands you. I forgot that the man at the controls has to *want* to pull you back.'

'Which your enemies obviously don't,' Father Uwell agreed. 'So they gave you a one-way ticket here, you might say.'

'You might, yes. So getting home will be something of a problem, won't it? Well, you're welcome to poke around in my subconscious all you want, Father, if that'll help get us out of here – but frankly, I can't offer much hope.'

'We'll worry about that when the time comes,' the priest said, with a faint smile. 'But how *were* you planning to get home?'

Rod looked at Gwen. 'Well, at the moment, our best bet looks to be one Lord Kern, whose got the title of High Warlock.'

'*Your* title.' Father Uwell frowned. 'Interesting.'

'Is it? But it seems that magic works, here; I'm sure you'll find Lord Kern oodles of fun, if we ever get to him. There are definitely faery folk here, I'll tell you that – we just escaped from a bunch of them. *They* had some interesting tricks, too.'

'Really?' Father Uwell's eyes fairly glowed. 'You must tell me about them – when you have time. But as to Lord Kern – how do you plan to persuade him to help you?'

Rod shrugged. 'I expect Gwen and I'll have to fight on his side in a little war, first, to earn it – unless he's grateful enough just for our helping his child-King ward escape to him. Father Uwell, meet His Majesty, King Elidor . . . ' He turned toward the boy – and frowned. 'Elidor? Gwen, where did he go?'

'Elidor . . . ?' Gwen's eyes slowly came back into focus.

'Oh! I'm sorry, dear!' Rod's mouth tightened in self-anger. 'I didn't mean to break you off from Gregory. I didn't know you were still in contact.'

'I was not.' Gwen bowed her head, forlorn. 'I but sat in reverie, some while after the touch of him faded . . . ' She straightened up, forcing a smile. 'I must bear it; surely his touch will come again. What didst thou wish, mine husband?'

'Elidor? Where'd he go?'

'Elidor?' Gwen glanced about quickly. 'My heaven, I had forgot! Elidor! Where . . . '

'Mama!'

It was small, bald, and wizened, with great luminous eyes and pointed ears. Its mouth was wide, with loose, rubbery lips, and its nose was long and pointed. It wore a rusty-brown tunic and bias-hosen, with cross-gartered sandals.

Gwen screamed, clasping her hand over her mouth.

Rod's eyes bulged; all he could manage was a hoarse, strangled caw.

The noise woke the children. They sat bolt-upright, eyes wide and staring, darting glances about for the danger.

Then they saw the kobold.

Cordelia screamed, and flew into her mother's arms, burying her head in Gwen's breast and sobbing. Geoffrey darted to her, too, bawling his head off.

But Big Brother Magnus clamped his jaws shut around a neigh of terror, plastered his back against a tree, then drew his sword and advanced slowly, pale and trembling.

Rod snapped out of his horrified daze and leaped to Magnus's side, catching his sword-hand. 'No, son! Touch him with cold iron, and we'll never see him again!'

'Good,' Magnus grated. 'I have small liking, to gaze upon such an horror. I beg thee, free my hand, Papa.'

'I said *no!*' Rod barked. 'That's not just an average haunt who happened by, son – it's a changeling!'

Magnus's gaze shot up to Rod's, appalled. 'A *what?*'

'A changeling. Theofrin's faeries must've been following us, waiting for their chance – and while you three were asleep, and Gwen was preoccupied with Gregory's thoughts, and I was talking with Father Al,' his lips tightened, again in self-anger, 'no one was watching Elidor, so they kidnapped him, and left this thing in its place.' He took a quick glance at his own three, to reassure himself they were all there. They were, thank Heaven.

'We must not afright it,' Gwen said grimly.

'Your wife is right,' Father Al murmured, stepping behind a tree. 'We must not scare it away, and the sight of me might do just that. I see you know what a changeling is. Do you know that it holds a correspondence to the child who was kidnapped?'

Rod scowled. 'You mean you can use it to work a spell that'll recover Elidor?'

Father Uwell nodded. 'And it's our only link to him. If it leaves, we'll have no way of regaining him.'

'All right.' Rod nodded. 'I'll bite. How do we use the changeling to get Elidor back?'

'Well, first you take an egg . . . ' He broke off, frowning. 'What's that chiming?'

'Just the breeze in the trees; the leaves rustle strangely here.'

The priest shook his head. 'No, beyond that – the tinkling. Do you hear it?'

Rod frowned, turning his head. Now that the priest mentioned it, there *was* a sound of chiming bells. 'Yeah, come to think of it. Strange. What do you suppose it is?'

'Given the terrain and what you've told me about the inhabitants, it could be any of several things, none of which would exactly welcome the sight of a priest. I'd recommend you trace the sound to its source. I'll follow, but I'll stay back out of sight.'

'Well, it's your field, not mine,' Rod said dubiously. 'Come on, kids! And stay close to your mother and me.' He glanced back at Magnus. 'Er, bring . . . Elidor?'

'Aye, Papa.'

Gwen caught Geoff's and Cordelia's hands, and looked back at the changeling. 'Come, then!' She shuddered as she turned away from it. Cordelia clung to her, trembling.

They wound through the silver forest, hands clasped, following the tinkling sound. It began to fall into a tune; and, as it became louder, Rod began to hear a thin piping of reeds, like very high-pitched oboes; underneath it, and, lower in pitch, a flute. Then the trees opened out into a little clearing, and Gwen gasped.

Faery lights wavered over the grove, mostly gold, but with occasional flickers of blue and red. Looking more closely, Rod saw that the air was filled with fireflies, so many that their winking lights lent a constant, flickering glow that supplemented the moonlight, showing a ring of delicate, dark-haired women, supple and sinuous, in diaphanous shifts, dancing to the tune played by a three-foot-tall elf with a bagpipe, and another who sat atop a giant mushroom with a set of pan-pipes. The ladies, too, couldn't have been more than three feet high – but behind them, beaming down fondly, sat a woman of normal size.

Of more than normal size – in fact, of epic proportions. She would've tipped the scales at three hundred pounds, and kept on tipping them. She wore a mile or so of rose-coloured gown, the skirts spread out in a great fan in front of her. A high, square-topped head-dress of the same cloth exaggerated her height, with folds of veil framing her face. It was a quiet face, and calm, layered in fat but surprisingly little, compared to her body. Her eyes were large and kind, her nose straight, and her mouth a tuck of kindness.

Rod glanced out of the corner of his eye; the changeling was hanging back in the shadows. Then he turned back to the ample beldame, and bowed. 'Good evening, Milady. I am Rod Gallowglass; whom have I the pleasure of addressing?'

'I am called the Lady Milethra, Grand Duchess of Faery,' the dame answered with a smile. 'Thou art well come among us, Lord Gallowglass.'

Rod hiked his eyebrows; she knew his title. He decided not to remark on the subject. 'Er, in my company are my wife, the Lady Gwendylon, and our children – Magnus, Cordelia, and Geoffrey.'

Gwen dropped a curtsy, and Cordelia mimicked her. Magnus bowed, and Geoff needed prompting.

The Grand Duchess nodded graciously. 'Well come, all. A fine crop of young witch-folk, Lord Gallowglass – and please inform your clerical acquaintance that his tact in remaining unseen is appreciated.'

'"Clerical acquaintance"? Oh, Father Uwell. I will, Your Grace. If you'll pardon my saying so, you're remarkably well-informed.'

'Prettily said,' she answered, with a pleased smile. 'Yet 'tis not so remarkable as all that; little escapes mine elves' notice.'

The piper grinned up mischievously at Rod, then went on with his piping.

'Ah – do I take it Your Grace, then, knows of our recent loss?'

'Thou speakest of my godson, Elidor.' The Lady folded her hands, nodding. 'Indeed, I do know of it.'

A fairy godmother, yet! And was Rod in for a roasting, or a basting? 'Your pardon for our lapse of vigilance, Your Grace.'

She waved away the apology with a lacy handkerchief. 'There is naught to pardon; with Eorl Theofrin's spriggans out to seize the lad, there was little thou couldst do to protect him. Indeed, I am grateful to thee for saving him from the *Each Uisge*; mine elves would have been sore tried to vanquish that monster.'

Which meant they might've had to sweat. 'Er – I take it Eorl Theofrin is the faery lord who had us in his power not too long ago?'

'The same. Now, as bad fortune hath it, Elidor is within his power again, where I may not run to save him. Since thou hast aided him in this wise once already, may I ask thee to aid him so again?'

'With all heart!' Gwen said quickly.

'Well, yeah, sure,' Rod said, more slowly. 'But I confess to some puzzlement as to why you should wish to employ us in this, Your Grace. Doesn't a Grand Duchess kind of outrank an Eorl?'

'I do, indeed – yet there is the practical matter of force. Eorl Theofrin's forces far outweigh mine – and my rank, of itself, suffices only if there is one of paramount rank to whom to appeal.'

'And Oberon's out of the country, at the moment?'

The Grand Duchess's eyebrows rose. 'Thou dost know the name of the Faery King? Good, good! Aye, he is afield, in the land of the English, for some time. Some trifling quarrel with Titania, it is, over some tedious Hindu lad . . . Ever did I mistrust that shrewish and haughty demoiselle . . . Enough!' She turned back to Rod with determination. 'There is some hope of welding an alliance 'twixt some other of the Faery Lords; yet few would wish to move against Theofrin, and all dread the illnesses that a war 'twixt the Faery demesnes would work upon the land, ourselves, and the mortals.'

'And it would take a while to get them all working together.'

'Even so; and the longer Elidor remains under Theofrin's hand, the harder 'twill be to pry him loose. Yet mortals stand removed from our quarrel.'

Rod nodded. 'We're a third force that can upset the balance, right?'

'Even so. Most mortals' power would be too little to counter a faery's; yet there are some spells which, if wielded by a warlock or witch, can own to far more power than any slung by one faery 'gainst another.'

Rod frowned. 'I don't quite understand that. If mortals are magically so much weaker, how could our spells be so strong?'

'Why,' said the Grand Duchess, with a disarming smile, ''tis because ye have souls, which we lack.'

'Oh.' Now that Rod thought of it, there *was* that old tradition about fairies having no souls. He swallowed hard, wondering what shape his own was in.

'Not so bad as all that,' the Grand Duchess assured him.

'Well, that's a relief to hear . . . *Hey!* I didn't say that aloud! How'd you know what I was thinking?'

'How not?' The Grand Duchess frowned. 'Ah, I see – no other mortals can hear thy thoughts! Rest assured, 'tis nothing inborn; 'tis only that, deep within thee, thou dost not *wish* them to.'

Gwen was staring at him with joy that was rapidly giving place to suspicion.

Rod swallowed. 'But why wouldn't I? Never mind, let's not go into that just now! Er – I take it the Faery folk have more thought-reading power?'

'Nay; but we have spells we may use, when we wish it – quite powerful ones. Since that thou art somewhat new to this world, I did wish it.'

'Oh.' Rod felt as though he ought to feel outraged that she hadn't given him official notice at the beginning of the interview; but he was scarcely in a position to bargain. He wanted Elidor *back!*

'As do I,' the Grand Duchess agreed. 'Yet I confess I am mystified as to why it should matter to thee; he is no kin of thine.'

Good question. Rod spoke the first answer that came to mind. 'I seek to return to my own place and time, Your Grace. I think I'm going to need magical help to do it; and getting Elidor to Lord Kern ought to win me a return favour. From you, too, come to that.'

The Grand Duchess leaned forward, peering closely at him. Gwen was staring at him, thinking about getting angry.

'Aye, there is some of that in thy mind,' the Grand Duchess said slowly, 'yet there is more of a . . . guilt.'

Rod winced.

The Grand Duchess nodded. 'Aye, 'tis that – that thou didst

take him under thy protection, then failed him. Yet beneath that lies sympathy, sorrow for a poor orphaned child among folk who love him not – and under that lies fear for thine own bairns.' She sat back, satisfied.

Gwen, however, was another matter. She was watching Rod narrowly. Then, slowly, she nodded, too.

Rod felt something snap around his knee. He looked down, and saw it was Geoffrey, hugging his daddy's leg and peering out wide-eyed at the great big lady.

Rod turned back to the Grand Duchess. 'OK – so I'm trustworthy.' He reached down and patted Geoff's head. 'What do we do?'

'Eorl Theofrin and all his court do ride nightly from Dun Chlavish to Dun Lofmir,' she answered. 'If the child's mother were alive, it would be she, closest to him, who would have to do the worst of it; in her absence, 'tis thy wife's place.'

Gwen nodded. 'I am ready.'

Suddenly, Rod wasn't so sure *he* was; but the Grand Duchess was ploughing on. 'Do thou hide in the furze by the side of the track, where it tops a rise, for there will they be going slowest. When Elidor's horse comes nigh, thou must seize him, drag him down, take off his cloak and doublet, turn them inside out, and set them on him again. Then mayest thou lead him hence, with none to hinder thee.'

Gwen frowned. 'This will take some time, Your Grace; I have dressed little ones aforetime.'

'I know thou hast; and buying thee the time must be thy husband's place.'

'Oh?' Rod raised an eyebrow. 'And how am I to do *that*, Your Grace?'

'Why, that is thy concern; thou art the man of war, not I.' The Grand Duchess sat back placidly, hands folded in her lap. 'Yet what e'er thou dost, be minded – bear wood of ash, and rowan berries in thy cap, and keep cold steel about thee.'

Rod started to ask why, then decided against it. 'Well enough – if I can't think up a diversion by now, I should be drummed out of the Heroes' Union. But tell me, Your Grace – do you have any idea *why* Eorl Theofrin stole Elidor back?'

'Why, 'twould be a triumph for him, to number a king amongst his mortal captives,' the Grand Duchess answered, 'and besides – he hath a score to settle with thee, hath he not?'

Rod remembered the Faery Lord's last threat. Slowly, he nodded.

So did the Grand Duchess. 'Belike he guessed thou wouldst seek to rescue Elidor, and thereby put thyself again within his grasp.'

# Chapter Eighteen

'Worked, too, didn't it?' Rod said, with a sardonic smile.

'That *is* a problem with goodness,' Father Uwell sighed. 'It can be used against you. Not that the evil ones don't overbalance themselves occasionally, too . . . Here she comes!'

Cordelia swooped down over the treetops, skimmed low over the meadow grass, and brought her broomstick in for a two-point landing. She hopped off, and reported to Gwen, 'There is the mound we saw last night, Mama, and another like it perhaps a mile away. And a track connects them.'

Gwen nodded. 'The one we saw last night would be Lofmir, then; they would dance at the end of the ride.' She turned to Rod. 'What land dost thou seek, husband?'

Rod shrugged. 'Well, a rise, with a good thicket just beside the trail, as the Grand Duchess said – preferably with a nice high cliff-top right behind it. And plenty of room across from the cliff.'

Cordelia nodded. 'There is a rise beneath a hill's brow, and the ground falls away on the other side in a long, long slope.'

Rod grinned. 'Perfect! OK, scout – lead us to it.'

Cordelia hopped back on her broom.

'Er, hold it, there.' Rod caught the straw. 'We've got to keep our heads down.'

'But, Papa,' Magnus protested, ''twould be so easy just to fly there!'

'Yeah, and easy for Duke Foidin's sentries to spot us, too – or are you forgetting it's daylight now? It was taking enough of a chance, having Cordelia fly reconaissance – and you'll notice I chose the smaller body for the purpose.'

''Tis as when we came,' Magnus grumbled. 'We had to walk because Papa could not fly.'

'Hey, now!' Rod frowned. 'No looking down on your old man, mind! Or do I have to prove I can still get in one good spank before you can teleport?'

Magnus glowered truculently up at him, but Rod just held a steady glare, and the kid finally began to wilt.

'It *was* unkind,' Gwen said softly.

Magnus let go, and looked down at the grass. 'I'm sorry, Papa,' he mumbled.

'S'okay.' Rod clapped him on the shoulder. 'We didn't fly then for the same reason, son – don't attract attention until you know whether or not the territory's friendly – and always keep a few surprises handy. Let's go, folks.'

They set out across the meadow, Cordelia skimming the top of the grass with Geoff hitch-hiking behind her, Magnus floating along in their wake to keep pace with the grownups. Father Uwell looked startled at first, but he adapted quickly. 'I admire your discipline,' he murmured to Rod.

Rod watched the kids warily, then dropped back a few paces. 'Just a matter of getting through to them while they're young enough to hang onto, Father.'

'Yes, surely,' the priest agreed. 'Tell me – *could* you punish him now, if you wanted to?'

Magnus perked his ears up.

'I'd rather not say,' Rod muttered.

Father Uwell followed the direction of his gaze, and nodded. 'I see. Sometimes it helps, being telepathically invisible, eh?'

Rod gave him a very dirty look.

The priest rolled his eyes up, studying the sky.

'What're you looking for,' Rod demanded, 'constellations?'

'Oh, no. I noticed those last night, as soon as I came to a clearing.'

'Really?' Rod perked up. 'Recognize any?'

'Oh, all of them, of course.'

'Of *course*?' Rod frowned. 'What is this – your home world?'

'No, but I've spent half my life here.' The priest cocked his head to the side. 'You've never been to Terra?'

Rod stared.

'I take it you haven't.'

Rod gave his head a quick shake. 'Well, yes, once or twice – but I didn't exactly have time to study the stars. Er – isn't the scene here a little rural for Terra?'

'The whole planet *is* rather overgrown with cities,' Father Uwell agreed, 'so, obviously, it's not the same Terra.'

Rod stopped.

So did the priest. 'You hadn't guessed?'

'Well, yes and no.' Rod gestured vaguely. 'I mean, I knew we were several thousand years in the future . . . '

Father Uwell shook his head.

Rod just watched him for a minute.

Then he said, 'What do you mean, "no?"'

'The stars are the same as they were when I left,' the priest answered. 'The whole sphere's rotated a little – I'd guess we're somewhere on the North American continent, whereas I'm used to the Italian sky – but there's no star-drift, no distortion of the constellations. We're just about 3059 AD.'

'I can't accept that,' Rod snapped.

'I think the Pope said that to Galileo, once,' Father Uwell sighed. 'But I see a peasant, over there; why don't you ask him?'

Rod looked up. A labourer was out early with his sickle, mowing hay. Rod glanced at his family, decided he could catch up quickly enough, and trotted over to the peasant. He stopped suddenly, remembering where they were. He turned back toward Gwen, and whistled. She looked up, saw the peasant – and all three children dropped to the ground and started walking.

Unfortunately, the peasant had noticed. When Rod got to him, he was still rubbing his eyes. 'Good morrow,' Rod called. 'Eyes troubling you?'

The peasant looked up, blinking. 'I have not waked quite, I think. Were yon children *flying?*'

Rod glanced over at the kids, then back. 'No, you're still dreaming.'

'Art thou certain?'

'Of course I'm sure! I'm their father. Say, would you happen to know the date?'

The man blinked again. 'Date?'

'Er, the year will do.' Rod took a deep breath. 'See, we're from out of town, and we want to make sure we count the years the same way you do.'

'I see.' He didn't. 'Well . . . 'tis the Year of Our Lord 3059 . . . Art thou well?'

Rod realized he was staring. 'Er, just asleep on my feet. I hate it when the day starts so early.'

'Assuredly,' the man said, wondering, 'how *can* it begin, but with sunrise?'

'A good point,' Rod admitted. 'Well, thanks for the information. Have a good day!' He turned, and trotted back to Gwen and the kids. As he came up to them, he glanced back; the labourer was still staring at them. Rod grabbed Magnus's shoulder. 'Son, give that guy a quick cat-nap, will you? I want him to think he dreamed us.'

Rod surveyed the site from the hill-top, and nodded. 'Good. Very good. Gwen, there's your thicket . . . ' he pointed to a stand of furze on the near side of the trail, ' . . . and here's my station on the slope.'

'Where shall we be, Papa?' Magnus asked eagerly.

'Up here, with Father Uwell, for protection.'

'*Their* protection?' The priest smiled, amused. 'Or mine?'

'Ours,' Rod answered, 'Gwen's and mine. And Elidor's.'

'Mama,' Geoffrey piped up, 'hungry.'

'Me too, come to think of it.' Rod's stomach growled. He shrugged. 'OK, kids – go find breakfast.'

The children whooped and ran, tumbling down the hillside.

'What will they find?' Father Uwell asked.

Gwen shook her head, smiling. 'Only Heaven may know, Father.'

'Care to ask?' Rod prompted.

Father Uwell shook his head, smiling. 'I'm afraid my pipeline doesn't go beyond the Vatican.'

'Yes – the place with the constellations.' Rod frowned.

'Have you absorbed it?' the priest said gently.

'Pretty much. You updated, Gwen?'

She nodded. 'I was aware of Father Uwell's thoughts.'

It didn't faze him. Rod gave him points. 'So, Father . . . '

'Please.' The priest held up a hand. 'We're apt to be together awhile. My friends call me "Al".'

'Right. Well, Father Al, what do you make of it?'

The priest frowned for a second; then he shrugged and smiled. 'We're on Terra, but it's not the Terra we know – and, by the constellations, it can't be any other planet.'

'Alpha Centauri A?' Rod said, trying feebly.

The priest shook his head. 'No, my friend. Four point three seven light years makes a noticeable difference in the constellations.

Besides, I've been on its habitable planet, and it looks nothing like this – you might say the terraforming still hasn't quite taken hold.'

'No, it hasn't.' Rod had been there, too; it was nice, if you liked wide, empty spaces. 'So it's Terra, and there's no way out of it.' He swallowed as he realized the double meaning.

Father Al caught it, too. 'If humankind can make a way in, they can make a way out,' he said firmly, 'but we'll have to learn a new set of ground rules.'

'Yes,' Rod said grimly. 'Let's stop skirting around it and say it, Father – we're in another universe.'

'Of course.' Father Al seemed mildly surprised. 'You've adapted to the concept very well.'

Rod shrugged. 'I'm getting used to the place.' He turned to Gwen. 'How you feel about it, dear?'

She shrugged. 'Is it harder to get home over the void between universes, than over a thousand years?'

'I dunno,' Rod said, 'but I bet we'll find out. Here comes brunch, Father.'

The children came toiling back uphill. Magnus held a few partridge, Geoff proudly bore a rabbit skewered on his sword, and Cordelia had her apron full.

'Rowan, Papa.' She held up some red berries as she came to Rod. 'You forgot.'

'You're right, dear – I did.' Rod accepted the berries ruefully and turned to the priest. 'Know what an ash tree looks like, Father?'

They woke about sunset. The children scouted up dinner, and rolled the leftovers in a fresh rabbit-skin for Elidor. 'For,' said Gwen, 'he'll surely have had the sense to eat no fairy food.'

'We hope,' Rod said grimly. 'If he has, it'll take more magic than ours to pry him loose from Theofrin.'

'Have no fear,' Magnus assured him, 'he hath neither eaten nor drunk. His godmother hath told him tales.'

Rod looked down, startled. 'You're still tuned in on him?'

Magnus nodded.

'Hmm.' Rod rubbed his chin, gazing southward along the track. 'OK, son – when you "hear" him getting close, give an owl-hoot. Any questions?'

Everyone shook their heads.

Except Father Al. 'I have several – but I think I'll have to observe, and work out the answers for myself.'

Rod gave him a withering glance. 'I wasn't talking about theology.'

'Neither was I.'

'That does it.' Rod clapped his hands. 'Battle stations, everyone – and keep an eye peeled for spriggans.'

They took their assigned positions, and waited. And waited.

Rod took a stout hold on his ash staff and reminded himself that midnight was the witching hour. Probably a long wait yet . . .

An owl hooted.

Rod looked up, startled. The real thing, or Magnus? But it hooted again, and it was coming from across the track, high up. He glanced up at the sky, saw only stars, moon, and the light grey of clouds.

Magnus.

Then be began to hear it – tinkling, like tiny cymbals, and a weird skirling of pipes. Over it all ran a wavering drone, like an army of bees, but soaring from one end of the scale to the other.

Then came the clatter of harness.

Rod glanced up at the thicket above him, but there was no movement. Of course not – Gwen was an old campaigner in her own right.

Then the vanguard appeared.

They wound around a hill at the southern end of the track, a host of small, bright, dancing figures, followed by tall, impossibly slender, elongated horses, coats sheening golden by moonlight. And the riders! They caught Rod's breath. Extravagantly dressed, in a rainbow of colours – tall, slender, and beautiful. And glowing. Each of them.

And one tiny rider, in the centre of the company, slouched over, head low – Elidor!

Rod rolled to his feet. Time to get moving.

He set off across the hillside, angling downward, then hiking back upward, as though he were trying to keep a straight line and failing. He let his gait wobble and started singing, slurring his voice as much as he could.

He heard a multiple whoop of glee behind him and choked down the surge of panic, forcing himself to keep his feet steady.

He heard hisses behind him. ' 'Tis a toss-pot!' 'Nay, 'tis a long road home he'll have tonight!' 'Do thou afright him from the front!'

Suddenly a huge dun-coloured dog rose up before him, growling, mischief dancing in its eyes.

Rod jerked to a stop, trying to stay in character. ''Ere, now! 'Owzh it wizh 'ee, Bowzher?'

'Nay, look behind thee!' a voice giggled, and he whirled about, stumbled, caught himself on his staff, and found himself staring straight into the dancing eyes of a snake, reared to strike. He let out a shriek and stumbled back, into the multiple arms of a giggling thing with a mouth like a slice of melon. He screamed and thrashed about, but its hold tightened – and touched his staff.

It shrieked, yanking an arm back, and fell over around the wound, screaming like a burn victim. 'His staff! 'Tis ash, 'tis ash! Oh, mine arm, mine arm!'

'*Ash! Ash! Ash!*' whispered through the crowd of faeries; and they drew back, leaving a wide space around Rod. Many more came flitting over from the caravan, leaving only the lordly faery folk on their horses; and they were watching closely.

So far, so good. Rod stumbled to his feet, doing his best to tremble. 'Nay, good shtaff, pertect me! Ay, poor old Josh! The fairy-folk've come to claim thee!'

A dancing light appeared in front of him, coalescing into the form of a beautiful woman. She smiled, as though amused at a hidden joke, and beckoned.

Staring, he took a few stumbling steps toward her.

She drifted away from him, beckoning again. Exactly what it was, he didn't know; some kind of will-o'the-wisp, no doubt. But why were they springing her on him? He played along, though, stumbling after her, faster and faster. 'Nay, pretty shing! Tarry now; let me shee thee!'

The surrounding watchers giggled, and it wasn't a pleasant laugh. Out of the corner of his eye, Rod noticed the faery gentry staring, fairly glued to the scene. Then he saw the reason why; the phantom was floating out over a sudden drop-off. They couldn't touch him, because of the ashen staff; but they could lure him to his death. Then he noticed Elidor suddenly disappear from his saddle, and knew it was time to escalate. He tripped and fell sprawling. An angry moan of disappointment went up all about him; he was a few inches short of the drop-off; but he opened his hand and let the staff roll away, and the moan slid up to a shriek of delight. Then they were on him, pinching and tickling; his skin itched in a thousand places, and his ears were filled with gibbering giggles.

But he had to hold attention, and hold it completely, to buy Gwen time. It was the moment for taking off the mask. He set his hands against the earth and shoved with all his might, surging to his feet and scattering elves left and right. The spriggans howled with glee and lurched in.

Rod whipped out his sword.

A moan of terror swept through the mob. They scuttered back away, wailing, 'Cold iron! Cold iron!'

'He is no drunkard!' screamed a spriggan.

'Nay, but a sober warrior in his prime!' Rod called back. 'Take me now if you can!' And he wrenched his doublet open, showing a necklace of rowan berries.

The host moaned in fear, and pressed backward – but Rod saw, beyond them, the faery horsemen galloping toward him, with Eorl Theofrin at their head.

The Eorl drew up thirty feet away, calling, 'Whoever hath advised thee, mortal, hath ill-advised thee! Thou art marked for faery vengeance now!'

'I was already,' Rod jeered, 'last night. Recognize me?'

Theofrin stared. 'Cold bones! It is the wizard!'

He whipped about in his saddle, staring back at the trail. 'The mortal king! The boy is gone!'

Five riders wheeled their horses about and went plunging toward the track.

Gwen stepped up on the trail, holding Elidor's hand. His doublet and cloak showed seams and lining.

The elf-horse beside him reared, screaming and pawing the air. Then it leapt up and whipped away, blown on a sudden gust of northern wind.

The five riders shrieked in frustration, jumping their mounts high to meet the gust. So did all the faery host, leaping into the air with a scream, and the breeze swept them away round the hill to the south, like autumn leaves.

Only Eorl Theofrin remained, his horse neighing and dancing as though it stood on hot coals. He himself winced and hunched his shoulders against pain, but managed to pull a crossbow from its place on his saddle, cranking the string back. 'Thou hast cheated me full, wizard! Yet ere I succumb to pain and fly, I'll break thee for thy life!'

There wasn't a rock big enough to hide behind for a thousand paces. Rod stood his place, sword lifted, fighting a surge of panic.

What that bolt could do, he didn't know – but he knew it was deadly. His one chance was to try to block it with his sword – but crossbow bolts moved *very* fast.

Theofrin levelled the bow.

Dimly, Rod was aware of that kindly, stern Presence with him again, reassuring, urging.

Fervently and with his whole being, he wished the faery lord would go follow one of his own phantoms off a cliff – and wherever else it led him, all night long.

Theofrin suddenly dropped his bow, staring off to his left.

Rod stared, too. He glanced over toward where the Eorl was looking, then quickly back to Theofrin. He'd seen nothing.

'Nay, pretty maiden,' Theofrin crooned, 'come nigh to me!' And his horse began to move forward. 'Nay, dost thou flee?' Theofrin grinned. 'I'll follow!' And his horse leaped into a gallop.

Straight over the cliff.

And on up into the sky – it was a faery steed, after all – with Theofrin carolling, 'Nay, come nigh! Nay, do not flee! I'll do thee no harm, but show thee great delights! Ah, dost thou fly still? Then I'll follow thee, while breath doth last!'

Rod stared after him, stupefied, until Theofrin was only a lighted speck off to the east, that sank below a horizon-line of trees, and was gone.

'My lord!'

He turned. Gwen came running up, clasping Elidor's hand firmly. 'My lord, I saw it all! Thou art untouched?'

'Er . . . ' Suddenly, Rod became aware of aches all over. 'I wouldn't say that. Those pinches *hurt*! But nothing lasting – I hope.'

'There shouldn't be, if Terran folk-tales hold true here.' Father Al came puffing up. 'But if he'd hit you with that crossbow bolt, it might've been another matter.'

'Oh?' Rod looked up, dreading the answer. 'What kind of effects do those things produce, Father?'

The priest shrugged. 'Oh, epilepsy, rheumatism, a slipped disc, partial or full paralysis – it would be the same as any elf-shot, I assume.'

'Oh, really.' Rod felt his knees turn to water. 'Gee, isn't it too bad he had to leave so suddenly.'

'Yes, I was wondering about that.' The priest frowned. 'What was he chasing?'

Rod shook his head. 'Hanged if I know, Father. All I know is, I was wishing with all my might that he'd go follow one of his own will-o'the-wisps over a cliff – and he did.'

'Hm.' Father Al's face instantly went neutral. 'Well. Another datum.'

Rod frowned; then he levelled a forefinger at the priest. 'You're suspecting something.'

'Well, yes,' the priest sighed, 'but you know how foolish it is to state a thesis prematurely.'

'Yeah.' Rod *should* know – Fess'd told him often enough. He sighed and straightened up. 'OK, Father – play 'em close to your chest. I'll just be real careful what I wish, from now on.'

'Yes.' The priest nodded grimly. 'I'd do that, if I were you.'

# Chapter Nineteen

A soft tinkling sounded.

The whole company stilled.

Reed pipes overlaid the tinkling; a flute underscored them.

Rod turned to Gwen. 'I think we've got company.'

'Godmother!' Elidor cried.

They turned to watch as he scooted over the grass to the wealth of woman beneath the firefly canopy. He leaped into her lap, arms outflung, and she gathered him in, pressing him against her more-than-ample bosom, resting her cheek on his head and crooning softly to him.

'Ever feel superfluous?' Rod asked.

'And never was so glad to feel so,' Gwen affirmed. 'Yet I think there is some business for us here. Come, my lord.' She gathered her children's hands, and marched forward.

Rod sighed, caught Magnus's shoulder, and limped after her, while Father Al did a fast fade.

Gwen dropped a curtsy, and Cordelia imitated her. The boys bowed, and Rod bent forward as much as he could.

The Grand Duchess noticed. 'Does it pain thee so greatly, High Warlock?'

Elidor looked up, startled.

'Not *that* High Warlock,' Rod assured him. 'And, well, I've

felt this way before, Your Grace – say, the day after the first
time I went horse-back riding. It won't last, will it?'

'Nay; 'tis only soreness,' she assured him. 'Yet trust me, 'tis
suffering well-endured; though hast given him good rescue, as I
knew thou wouldst.'

'I'm glad somebody did. Well, you've got him safe, now
– so, if you'll forgive us, we'll be on our way. Come on, kids.'

The Grand Duchess looked up, startled. 'Thou wilt not take
him to Lord Kern?'

Gwen caught Rod's sleeve. 'Assuredly, an thou wishest it . . . '

'Er, Gwen . . . '

' . . . yet will the royal lad not be safer with his godmother?'
Gwen finished.

The Grand Duchess smiled sadly. 'Safer, aye; but he'll not
die 'mongst mortal men – both sides need him. And duty doth
summon him.'

Elidor clung to her, and buried his face in her bosom.

'Nay, sweet chick,' she crooned softly, 'thou dost know that I
speak aright. Nay, nay, I would liefer keep thee all thy life beside
me – but therein would I wrong mine old friends, the King and
Queen thy parents, who bade me see that thou wouldst grow into
a King; and the folk of thy land, who need thee grown. And lastly
would I wrong thee, for I'd abort thy destiny. Come now, sweet
chuck, bear up; sit tall, and give thyself a kingly bearing.'

Slowly, the little boy sat up, sniffling. He looked at her
forlornly, but she pinched his cheek gently, smiling sadly, and he
smiled in spite of himself, sitting up more firmly. Then he turned
to face the Gallowglasses, straightening and lifting his chin, once
again a Prince.

'See thou, he is to be a King of men,' the Grand Duchess said,
low, 'and therefore must he learn what men are, and not from
written words alone. He must live and grow among them, good
and bad alike, that when he comes to be a king, he'll recognize
them both, and know their governance.'

Gwen nodded sadly. 'And therefore canst thou not keep him
here, to hide him from the troubles of these times. But might
thee not, at least, conduct him to Lord Kern?'

The Grand Duchess sighed. 'I would I could; but know this
of us faery folk: we are bound to our earthly haunts. Some among
us, like myself, can claim demesnes of miles' width, and freely
move within them; but few indeed are they who move wherever

they please, and to none of those would I entrust this lad – or any folk, of whom I cared.'

'But you would trust us.' Rod could feel it coming.

The Grand Duchess nodded.

Gwen looked up at him, pleading.

'Oh, all right!' Rod clapped his hands. 'Keeping track of children is mostly your job, anyway. Sure, Your Grace, we'll take him along.'

The children cheered.

Elidor looked surprised; then he smiled, a slow, shy smile.

Magnus ran forward, caught Elidor's arm, and yanked him off the Grand Duchess's lap. 'We'll keep thee close, coz! Yet mark thou, stay within mine eye this time!'

'I will stay near,' Elidor promised.

'As near as one of mine own.' Gwen gathered him in.

'Of course,' Rod said, 'it would help if we had someone to point us on our way.'

'Elidor will show you.' The Grand Duchess was clasping her hands tightly, and her smile seemed a little strained. 'He hath conned his charts, and doth know the shape of every track and pathway in his land.'

'Well, that'll help,' Rod said dubiously, 'but real hills and lakes don't match a map all *that* well. It'd be better to have someone who's been there, too.'

The Grand Duchess shook her head firmly. 'The sprites cannot leave their lands or waters, as I've told thee.'

'Tell us, then,' Gwen asked, 'what we must do to see him safely to Lord Kern.'

The Grand Duchess nodded, her eyes lighting. 'Thou must first rid the rower of Gonkroma of its Redcap.'


# Chapter Twenty

'I don't really see what chasing some sort of elf has to do with getting safely to Lord Kern,' Rod called.

Gwen said something back, but the roaring wind drowned out her answer.

'Come again, dear?' Rod called. 'Louder, please; it's hard

to hear, when I'm behind you, and the wind's whistling in my ears.'

He was riding pillion on a makeshift broomstick.

'I said,' Gwen called, 'that I know no reason, but do trust her judgement.'

'That's what it seems to come down to, here,' Rod sighed, 'faith. Wasn't that the medieval ethic, Father?' He looked back over his shoulder. Father Al was clinging to the broomstick for dear life, and was definitely looking a little green around the gills; but he swallowed, and nodded manfully. 'Something like that, yes. It's a little more complicated, though.'

'Well, I like to deal in over-simplifications. You sure you're OK, now?'

'Oh, fine, just fine! But are you sure your wife can carry all three of us for so long?'

'If I can bear four children,' Gwen called back, 'I can bear two men.'

'There's some truth in that,' Rod acknowledged. 'After all, she's managed to bear with me for almost ten years now.' He turned to the children, floating beside him. 'Geoff, you be sure and tell us if you start feeling sleepy, now!'

'Fear not,' Gwen called. 'They napped well ere we left the Grand Duchess.'

'Yes, thanks to Magnus. But Geoff, make sure you tell me if you start feeling tired – after all, Cordelia can give you a lift for a few minutes.'

'For an *hour*,' Cordelia carolled, swooping her broomstick in a figure-eight, 'and not even feel it!'

'Hey, now! Straighten out and fly right! We've got a long way to go; no time or energy for fancy stuff!'

'Killjoy!' Magnus snorted. 'Night flying's *fun!*'

'This, from the expert who thought I was wrong wanting to fly this time,' Rod snorted.

'Well, Papa, you said yourself it'd attract too much attention.'

'Yeah, but we've got a hundred miles to go before dawn; we don't have much choice this time. Besides, we're not too apt to be noticed at night; and if we are, by the time Duke Foidin can get troops after us, we'll be out of reach. And we're certainly going faster than any courier he can send!' He peered over Gwen's shoulder. 'How's Elidor holding out, dear?'

Gwen glanced down at the small shape huddled against her,

between her arms. 'Almost beginning to enjoy it, I think.'

'He *is* the stuff of which kings are made,' Father Al gulped.

Rod decided the priest could use a distraction. 'Figured out how magic works here, Father?'

'Oh, it seems to be fairly straightforward. I postulate three forces: Satanic, Divine, and impersonal. Most of what I've seen today, and tonight, falls in the "impersonal" category.'

Rod frowned. 'What's "impersonal"?'

'Essentially, it's the same force espers use. Everyone has it, to some degree. An esper has so much of it that he can work "magic" by his own power; but everyone "leaks" their little bit, and it goes into the rocks, the earth, the water, the air, absorbed into molecules. So it's there, ready to draw on; and, in a universe such as this, a few gifted individuals have the ability to tap that huge reservoir, and channel its force to do whatever they want.'

Rod nodded. 'Sounds right. Seen anything here that would disprove that?'

'No, but I think I'm going to have to come up with a corollary theory for the faery folk.'

'You do that. Any idea why the whole world is still medieval, even though it's 3059 AD?'

'Well, at a guess, I'd say it's because technology never advanced much.'

'Fine.' Rod smiled. 'So how come technology didn't advance?'

Father Al shrugged. 'Why bother inventing gadgets, when you can do it by magic?'

That gave Rod pause. He was quiet for the rest of the flight.

Well, most of the time, anyway. 'No, Cordelia – you may *not* race that owl!'

'You *sure* you're not getting tired, Geoff?'

'Magnus, leave that bat alone!'

The land rose beneath them, rippling into ridges and hills, then buckling into mountains. Finally, as dawn tinged the sky ahead and to the right, Elidor's finger stabbed down. 'Yonder it lies!'

Rod peered ahead around Gwen and saw the ruins of a great, round tower, perched high on a crag. 'Be fun getting up to that.'

Magnus veered close and pointed downward. 'I see a ledge of rock beside it, that trails away behind for a good hundred yards.'

'Yeah, but then it blends back into the side of the mountain. How do I get to it in the first place?'

'Why, I will land thee on it, when thou dost wish,' Gwen called back. 'But, husband, we have flown half the night, and even I begin to weary. Would we not do well to rest ere we advance?'

'Yes, definitely.' Rod looked around. 'Where's a good place to rest?'

'There, and a safe one.' Father Al nodded down toward a valley, but did *not* point. 'That little village, with the small steeple. There's a patch of woods near it, to hide our descent.'

Rod looked down. 'Well, it looks snug enough. But will we be welcome? As I recollect, mountaineers aren't generally too hospitable to outsiders.'

'Oh, the parish priest will let us in,' Father Al assured him. 'I have connections.'

Rod shrugged. 'Good enough for me. Wanna let me off this thing, dear?'

'Aye, if thou wilt wait till I do land.' Gwen tilted the broomstick down. Father Al gulped, and held on tight.

They found a clearing just big enough, and brought everyone in, in orderly fashion. Little Geoff fell the last two feet and pushed himself up out of the meadow grass, looking groggy. Rod ran over to him. 'I *told* you to tell me when you were getting tired! Here, son, why don't you ride a little, now?' He hoisted the boy up onto his shoulders, and turned to Gwen. 'Now – which way's the village?'

They found it, webbed in the birdsong of early morning. The parish priest was just closing the back door as they came up.

'Good morning, Father!' Father Al called cheerily, in spite of his rubber legs.

The old priest looked up, blinking. He was bald, and his long beard was grey. He was slim with a lifetime of fasting, and rock-hard as his mountains. 'Why . . . good morrow, Father,' he returned. ''Tis early, for travellers to come walking.'

'We've been on the road all the night; 'tis a matter of some urgency,' Father Al replied. 'I am these goodfolks' protection from the powers that walk at night; yet even I must sleep sometime. Canst thou spare us hospitality for a few hours?'

'Why . . . assuredly, for the Cloth,' the old priest said, bemused. 'Yet there is only my poor small room, behind the chapel . . . '

'No matter; we'll sleep in the nave, if thou dost not object, under the Lord's protection. We'll need every ounce we can get.'

'Father,' the old priest said severely, 'one ought not to sleep in church.'

'Tell that to the goodfolk who must listen to my sermons.'

The old priest stared for a moment; then he smiled. 'Well said, well said! Avail thyself of what little thou canst find, then – and pardon my poor hosting. I must bless three fields and see to a woman whose hands pain her.'

'Arthritis?' Rod asked, coming up behind Father Al.

'Nay, only a swelling of the joints, and pain when she moves her fingers. Elf-shot, belike. A drop of holy water, a touch of the crucifix, and a short prayer will set her to rights.'

Rod stared.

Father Al got the thoughtful look again. 'Hast thou ever known the treatment to fail, Father?'

'Aye; there do be stronger spells. Then must I ask the Bishop to come – or take my poor souls to him, if they can walk.'

'And the blessing of the fields – are the crops in danger?'

'Oh, nay!' the old priest laughed. 'I can see thy mind; but do not trouble thyself, Father; thou hast journeyed long, and hast need of thy rest. Nay, 'tis only the usual blessing, without which the fields will yield scarcely half their corn.'

'Of course.' Father Al smiled. 'Well, it doth no harm to be certain. Thou wilt send for me if thou dost need me, though?'

'Be assured that I will – but be also assured that I'll have no need. Be welcome in my home, and make thyselves free of what little thou'lt find in the larder. Have no fear for me – the Lord will provide.'

'And He probably will,' Father Al noted as they watched the old man leave, with an almost-youthful stride. 'After all, magic works, here.'

'Small magics,' Rod agreed, 'daily ones. It seems the village priest is the mundane magician, here. How does *that* fit into your theories, Father?'

'Perfectly. As I mentioned, I posit three sources of Power, and one of them is Divine – though I have a notion that some of his spells work more by "secular", impersonal magic than by God's Power. Some trace of magical ability could well be a requirement for admission to the seminary.'

'Probably,' Rod agreed. 'But the old man's abilities notwithstanding, I think it might be in order to keep our hands off his

food, if we can.' He turned to his son. 'Magnus, Geoff's about
tuckered. How much grub do you think you could scare up by
yourself?'

Magnus pulled a hare out from behind his back. 'I was hungry,
Papa.'

'So was I.' Cordelia held out an apronful of birds' eggs and
berries.

'Nice thing about kids – they never lose track of the important
things,' Rod noted to Father Al. 'What do you say I take the
skillet, Gwen? You're looking pretty tired yourself.'

'Aye, but I wish to eat before noon.' Gwen caught up the
hare and brushed past him into the 'rectory'. 'Come, Cordelia.'

'Well, I guess we get to decide the fate of the world.' Rod
sat down on the step as the door closed behind the ladies.
'Magnus, keep your brother busy until breakfast, so he doesn't
fall asleep.'

'Doing what, Papa?'

'Oh, I dunno . . . go play tag with a wolf, or something.
Er, cancel that,' he added quickly, as he saw Magnus's eyes
light up. 'No sense in cruelty to animals. Go cut a couple of
willow wands and drill him on fencing – he's a little slow on the
riposte.'

'As thou dost wish, Papa.' Magnus turned away, crestfallen.
'Come, Geoffrey.'

'And stay where I can see you!'

Magnus gave a martyr's sigh. 'We will.'

'Would you really have worried more about the wolf than
about them?' Father Al asked, sitting beside Rod.

'Not completely,' Rod admitted, 'but I've seen Magnus drive
a wolf to distraction. He disappears just before the wolf gets him,
and reappears behind it. Then the wolf turns around to charge him
again, and he disappears in the nick of time, bobbing up behind
it again. When I caught him, he had it chasing its own tail.'

Father Al shook his head in wonder. 'I think I begin to
understand why you adjusted to a world of magic so easily.'

'Kids do keep your mind limber,' Rod admitted.

'Limber enough to understand why technology never went
beyond the hammer and anvil here?'

'Oh, there's not much question there. Why do you need to
develop fertilizers when the average parish priest can do the same
thing with a blessing?'

Father Al nodded. 'I'll have to worm the wording of the prayers out of him, to see whether it's the prayer that does it, or the charm.'

'So you can know which Power is working?'

Father Al nodded. 'Increasing crop yields isn't exactly what we mean by "small miracles happening everywhere".'

'Like medical technology? It sounds as though he can cure arthritis, though he doesn't know it by that name. Our own doctors can't do much better. I'd imagine the same kind of thing's happening in all areas of technology.'

Father Al nodded again. 'Smiths producing case-hardened alloys by singing to the metal as they pound it; carriages riding smoothly, cushioned by spells instead of steel leaves, perhaps even spell-propelled; ships communicating with shore by crystal balls . . . Yes, why bother inventing anything?'

'But,' said Rod, 'magicians being rare, the average man couldn't afford battle-spells; so martial power remained an aristocratic monopoly. Which meant . . . '

'That the political system remained essentially feudal.' Father Al's smile grew hard. 'Though, with wizards providing kings with efficient communications, and even intelligence abilities, there's a chance centralized governments may have evolved.'

'But never terribly absolute,' Rod noted. 'The barons could get wizards, too. So they'd think of themselves as "Christendom" as much as separate countries.'

'Not much nationalism,' Father Al agreed. 'But how would the New World have been colonized?'

Rod shrugged. 'No problem; Columbus came over shortly after the Wars of the Roses, and the Vikings set up a colony before him. With wizardry to help them, they shouldn't've had as much trouble with the "skralings".'

'The Amerinds, yes. I notice that most of these people are nowhere nearly as pale as Northern Europeans of the period.'

'Probably hybrids. And with their shamans' magic added in, you'd have quite an assemblage of magic. But that indicates a big emphasis on trade, which means mercantilism. How come there's no rise of the middle class?'

'There probably was, to a point. But the kings and barons would've entrusted fund-raising to their wizard-advisers, who, being probably of common birth, could participate in trade for them. No, I'd guess the "merchant princes" *were* princes. And trade not being their means to rise, they wouldn't push its development as hard.'

Rod spread his hands. 'But – fifteen hundred years! Could a society really last that long, without changing?'

'Well, there was ancient Egypt – and the Chinese Empire. Dynasties changed, and styles; technology even improved a little, from time to time – but the society remained the same. And, come to think of it, India, before the Mongols . . . You know, Europe may have been the exception, not the rule, with its changing society.'

Rod shook his head in wonder. 'All because they started being able to make magic work! What do you think was the dividing point – the alchemists?'

' "Dividing point"? Oh, you mean when this universe split off from ours. It didn't have to, you know – both universes *could* have started at the same time, and evolved independently.'

'Could have,' Rod admitted, 'but there're just too many resemblances between this universe and ours. The language is even close enough to Gramarye's so that I didn't have any problem understanding.'

'Hmf. A good point.' Father Al frowned. 'Who knows? Perhaps both theories are true. It may be that the model for multiple universes isn't just one branching tree, with universes splitting off from one another at major historical events, but a forest – several root universes, each one branching at decision-points.'

'Maybe – but this one looks to have branched off from ours.'

'Or ours from it – we're not necessarily the centre of Creation, you know.' Father Al grinned wickedly.

'A point,' Rod admitted. 'So what was it – the alchemists?'

'Perhaps. There was much talk of wizardry before that, of course – but the alchemists *were* the first ones to approach the topic rationally. And the astrologers, of course.'

Rod nodded. 'So some alchemist-astrologer, probably totally forgotten in our own universe, happened to have the Power, and figured out some rules for its use. He probably wouldn't have let anyone else in on the secret – but once he proved it could be done, others would figure out how. When would this have happened – fourteenth century?'

Father Al nodded. 'Sounds about right – I haven't seen any gunpowder here. That would be the latest point it *could've* happened, at least.'

'And styles have continued to change, and they've kept pieces of all of them – but the social set-up hasn't.' Rod nodded. 'Makes sense. A little on the sick side, but sense. Where did the elves come from?'

Father Al shrugged. '"Summoned" from another universe, or extremely thorough illusions made by a wizard, and kept "alive" by the popular imagination. But they may have been there all along, and were only chased out of our universe by the combination of cold-iron and Christianity, which gradually eroded the people's belief in them. There's some evidence for that last one – the Grand Duchess told us that the faery folk are tied to their own particular piece of countryside. that would seem to indicate that they grew out of the land itself, or rather, out of its life-forms. We aren't the only beings that set up minute electromagnetic fields around themselves.'

Rod nodded slowly. 'Ye-e-e-s. And in our universe, it would have been the nineteenth century that finally undid that completely, as it laid Europe under a grid of railway tracks, and sent telegraph wires all over the countryside, disrupting local field-forces.'

'Well, there were still tales told in the twentieth century – its early years, at least. But radio and television would have finished the job – those, and concrete. They *are* basically nature sprites, after all.'

The door swung open behind them. 'We dine, gentlemen.'

'Well, enough of the fate of this world.' Rod slapped his knees and stood up. 'Let's get to the important stuff, Father.'

The boys cheered and beat them to the door.

They waked to the ringing of the noon bell. The old priest had returned, and the boys scampered out to find lunch. The old man was amazed at the table they set for him. 'Cold hare, wild strawberries, grouse eggs, and trout simmering – thy children are most excellent hunters, Milord!'

'Why?' Rod asked around a mouthful. 'Game getting scarce?'

'Aye, for some years. There were folk here who lived by trade through the mountains; and, when it ceased, they had need to scour the countryside for victuals. Many have wandered away, but there are still so many that our few farms can scarce feed them all.'

'Well, if it moves and is edible, my boys'll find it. What stopped the trade, Father – Duke Foidin's garrisons?'

'That, and the Redcap who lives in the Tower. Not even a pedlar can make his way past it, now.'

'Oh.' Rod glanced at Father Al. 'What does he do to them?'

'And what manner of sprite is he?' Father Al chipped in.

The old priest shuddered. 'He doth take the form of an aged man, squat and powerful, with long snaggled teeth, fiery eyes, long grizzled hair, and talons for nails. He doth wear iron boots and beareth a pikestaff. As to what he doth to travellers, he hath no joy so great as the redying of his cap in human blood.'

'Oh.' Suddenly, cold roast hare didn't taste quite so good. 'Can't anyone do anything to stop him?'

The old priest gave a short laugh. 'What wouldst thou have? Armies cannot stand against him! 'Tis said that reading him Scripture, or making him look upon a cross, will rout him – but how canst thou force him to listen or look?'

'Good question.' Rod turned to Father Al. 'Any ideas?'

'One.' The priest nodded. 'If religious symbols will repel him when he perceives them, a stronger symbol should banish him by its touch.'

The old priest chuckled. 'Certes, Father – but where wilt thou find the man to chance the doing of it?'

'Papa will,' Geoff piped.

The old priest chuckled again, till his eyes met Rod's, and the chuckle died. Then he paled. 'Nay, thou wilt not attempt it!' He looked from Rod to Father Al, then to Gwen, and sat very still. Then he scrambled up, turning toward the door.

'Father,' Father Al said quietly, 'I shall require thine altar stone.'

The old priest stopped.

Then he turned about, trembling. 'Thou mayest not! The Mass must be said on the bones of the saints, embedded within the altar stone! How shall I say Mass without it?'

'We shall return it this evening.'

'Wilt thou?' The old man strode back, pointing to Father Al with a trembling forefinger. 'Wilt thou come back at all? Redcap can stand against armies; how wilt two of thee beat him?'

'Three,' Gwen said quietly. 'I have some powers of mine own, Father.'

'In fact, it's a family affair,' Rod corroborated. 'You'd be surprised at what my kids can do, without getting in range.'

The old priest darted glances from one to another, as though

they were mad. 'Give over, I beg thee! And these poor wee bairns
– do not subject them to such hazard!'

'We couldn't leave them behind if we wanted to,' Rod said
grimly.

'We will triumph, Father,' Gwen said gently. 'We have but
lately set the *Crodh Mara* to defeat the *Each Uisge*, and have,
together, put a faery lord's court to flight.'

'Yet the faery lords are not Redcap! They do not *delight* in
murder and bloodshed! No! Do not go! But if thou must, thou
shalt go without mine altar stone!'

Father Al sighed and pulled a rolled parchment out of his robe.
Rod saw fold lines in it, and guessed it had been in an envelope
before Father Al got to Gramarye. The Terran monk said, 'I had
hoped to avoid this, but . . . look upon this writ, Father.'

The old man stared at him, frightened. Then, reluctantly,
he took the parchment and unrolled it. He read it, gasped,
and grew paler the more he read. At last he rolled it back up
with trembling hands and lifted his head, eyes glazed. 'It . . . it
cannot be! He . . . he is in Rome, half-way 'cross the world! Rarely
doth he speak to those of us in this far land, and then only to
Archbishops! How doth it chance . . . Aiiieee!' He dropped the
parchment, clasping his head in his hands. 'What have I done?
What sin lies on my soul, that *he* should write to *me*?'

'No sin, Father, surely!' Father Al cried in distress, clasping
the old man's arm. 'In truth, I doubt he doth know that thou
dost live! He doth address this Writ to any who should read it,
should I choose to show it them, having need of their aid!'

'Aye, oh! Aye.' The old man lifted a haggard face. 'Yet what
mischance doth befall, that *I* should be the one from whom thou
dost require aid? Why doth this chance befall to *me*? Nay, surely
have I failed in my duty to my God and to my flock!'

'Thy humility doth thee credit,' Father Al said gently, but
with the firmness of iron underlying it. 'But thy common sense
doth not. This lot doth fall to thee only because thy flock doth
live near the Tower of Gonkroma, whither I and my friends must
go to challenge Redcap.'

Slowly, the old man's eyes focused on Father Al. He nodded,
and his face began to firm up. 'Aye. 'Tis even as thou dost say.'
He straightened his shoulders and rose. 'Well, then, if it must be
so, it must – and I do not doubt it; I cannot ready his hand, yet
I've seen the picture of his Seal in books.'

'And now thou dost see the impression of the Seal itself. Wilt thou render up thine altar stone, good Father?'

'Aye, that will I. If His Holiness would wish it, then thou shalt have it. Come; I will lift it for thee.'

They came out of the chapel a few minutes later, Father Al holding the stone wrapped securely under his arm.

'That wasn't quite honest, was it?' Rod asked.

Father Al looked up, startled. 'Why not? The letter's genuine, I assure you! That *is* the impression of the real Papal Seal, and the signature of the real Pope!'

'Yes, but not *his* pope.'

Father Al frowned. 'What do you mean? John XXIV *is* Pope . . . Oh.'

'Yes.' Rod nodded. 'In *our* universe.'

'But he is not, in this universe?'

'How could he be?'

'Why not?' Father Al turned a beaming smile on him. 'This Earth is very much like the Terra of our universe; the constellations are the same; the language is the same as that of Renaissance England. Why might there not be people who are the same in both universes, too?'

'You don't seriously believe that, do you?'

Father Al shrugged. 'I'm willing to consider it. But it doesn't really matter greatly. We Catholics believe that the Pope speaks for God, when he speaks *as* Pope, not just as himself – *ex cathedra*, we call it.'

Rod stopped dead still, ramrod-straight, eyes closed. He counted to ten, then said carefully, 'Father – doesn't that strike you as a little medieval?'

'Have you looked around you lately?'

'Cheap rejoinder, Father.' Rod fixed him with a gimlet eye. '*Our* universe isn't medieval – but your belief is.'

'Not really,' Father Al said earnestly. 'Spiritual beliefs really can't be proven or disproven by physics or chemistry, any more than theology can deduce the formula for a polymer. It comes down to faith, after all – and we believe that Christ gave Peter the power to speak for Him, when He told that first Bishop of Rome, "I give to you the keys to the Kingdom of Heaven. What you bind on Earth, it shall be bound in Heaven; what you loose on Earth, it shall be loosed in Heaven." We also believe that Peter's "keys" descended to his successors, down to the present Pope.'

'Very interesting, but I don't see . . . ' Rod broke off, staring. 'Oh, no! You don't mean . . . '

'Why not?' Father Al smiled. 'Did you think there would be a different God for each universe? I can't prove it with physical evidence, but I believe in a God who existed before anything else did, and who created everything – one God who began *all* the universes. I've noticed that the people here are Christians – Roman Catholics, in fact. So, if it's the same God for both universes, and the Pope speaks for Him, says what God wants said, surely the Pope in this universe will give the same answer to any given question as the Pope in our universe would.'

'So your Writ from your Pope says what the Pope in *this* universe wants that old priest in there to do.' Rod gave Father Al a sidelong look. 'Doesn't that sound just a teeny bit lame to you, Father?'

'Of course,' said Father Al, with a disarming smile. 'Because, when my Pope wrote this letter, he wasn't speaking *ex cathedra*; so he was speaking as John XXIV, not as Pope. None the less, I've no doubt the Christians here hold basically the same beliefs as Christians in our home universe; so I don't doubt the Pope here would want me to have this altar stone.' He frowned, gazing at the sky.

'Pretty problem, though, isn't it?' Then his face cleared. 'Well, I'll tell the Jesuits about it, when we get back. Shall we get down to business?'


# Chapter Twenty-one

Gwen brought her broomstick hovering over the ledge, a hundred yards from the Tower, and brought it slowly to ground. Rod and Father Al dismounted, just as Magnus and Geoff popped into sight beside them.

'What're *you* two doing here?' Rod demanded. 'I want you up on top of that crag!'

'Aw, Papa! Do we *have* to?'

'Yes, you do! I want you watching from a safe distance, ready to teleport me out of there if it looks like he's really apt to kill me! And where's Elidor?'

Magnus's eyes widened; then guilt rose in them. 'Er – we left him atop the crag.'

'Er-huh!' Rod nodded grimly. 'So what's to stop a spriggan from hopping in and snatching him again, huh? Now, you two get back there – fast!'

'Yes, Pap— ' They disappeared before they finished the syllable.

'And that goes for you, too.' Rod glowered at the witchling who hovered before him on a makeshift hearth-broom. 'Stay out of the fight, Cordelia! But help your Mama, and be ready to drop a few rocks on the meany!'

'Oh, all *right*, Papa!' Cordelia huffed, and wheeled her broomstick up and away toward the top of the mountain.

'You, too, dear.' Rod caught Gwen's hand. 'Out.'

'I will.' Tears stood in her eyes. 'Take care of thysel'.'

'I will,' Rod promised. 'You take care of me, too, huh?' And he gathered her in.

Father Al turned away to study the local geology for a few minutes.

Rod turned back to him with a happy sigh. Air whooshed behind him as Gwen swooped back up to the top of the mountain.

'Some very interesting stratification, here.' Father Al pointed to the rockface. 'At a guess, I'd say this was a seabed a few million years ago.'

'I'm sure it was – and thank you for your delicacy, Father. Come on, let's go meet the monster.'

They strode down the rock ledge, Rod saying, 'Now, I want this clear. I go in first, to draw his attention; then, while I've got him occupied, you sneak up behind and brain him with the stone.'

'I think a touch will suffice,' Father Al murmured. 'What happens if he knocks you over the ledge, and still turns around in time to brain me?'

'Wear a crucifix, don't you?'

'Not ordinarily; but it's a good thought.' Father Al pulled out a rosary and slipped it over his head. 'Now! The crucifix will protect me – because he'll have to look away from me to avoid seeing it.'

Rod nodded. 'Right.'

'And since I'm protected, *I* should go in first.'

Rod stopped dead.

'You must admit, it's more logical.'

Rod sighed. 'Well, I never did have too much luck against logic. All right, Father, you win. You first, into the lion's den – but I'll be right behind you.'

'Your reference was to Daniel,' Father Al mused as they started up again. 'I wonder – is your soul in as good a shape as his was?'

Rod was quiet for a few paces. Then he admitted, 'I *was* raised Roman Catholic . . . '

'And how long has it been since you took the Sacraments?'

Rod sighed. 'My wedding, Father – nine years ago. And you've got a point – if a lion's in there, I'd better be in top shape. Give me a few minutes to examine my conscience.'

And they moved slowly toward Redcap, murmuring softly together.

'*Ego te absolvo*,' Father Al said finally, making the sign of the Cross. 'And I think you're about to meet your penance.'

They rounded a curve, and the Tower loomed over them.

The ledge around the tower was strewn with human bones and a few skulls. That almost did Rod in, right there. The fear hit, suddenly and totally. He paused, letting it wash over and through him. the tidal wave passed, leaving that old, familiar, clutch-bellied, knee-jellied feeling; but he could cope with that. He glanced at Father Al; the priest looked to be feeling it, too. His face was drawn and pale, but his lips firmed with resolve. He unwrapped the altar stone and held it out with both hands. 'Are we ready, then? . . . Good. "Then into the Valley of Death." '

And he strode forward before Rod could say anything, chanting:

"He who digs a pit may fall into it
And he who breaks through a wall
May be bitten by a serpent!
He who moves stones may be hurt by them,
And he who chops wood is in danger from it!
If the iron becomes dull,
Though at first he made easy progress,
He must increase his efforts;
But the craftsman
Has the advantage of his skill!"

With a roar, the Redcap was on him.

It bolted out of the tower, crusted with filth and crazed with hatred and loneliness – about five feet high; shoulders as wide as a barrel; greasy, grizzelled hair flying about its shoulders, huge eyes afire with bloodlust. Its tunic and leggings were stiff with grease and covered with dirt; its iron boots rang on the stone and crunched through bone. It whirled a pikestaff high with one hand, like a hatchet; then its rusty edge sliced down at the priest.

Then Redcap saw the altar stone, and clanked to a halt.

They stood frozen for a moment, the priest holding out the stone like a shield, the monster glaring at it balefully.

Rod drew his sword and came running.

Father Al began to chant again:

" . . . a live dog is better
Than a dead lion. For the . . . "

Redcap roared and slashed out with his pikestaff.

The flat of the blade slammed into Father Al's side; he went flying, landed ten feet away, the altar stone jarring out of his hand. Redcap grabbed a small boulder, still roaring, and heaved it at the stone. It swerved aside at the last second, narrowly missing Father Al's head.

Then Rod leaped in, shouting, '"O ye dry bones, now hear the word of the Lord! . . . I heard a noise; it was a rattling as the bones came together . . . "' and lunged full-out for Redcap's belly. The sword shot into the monster's smock with a CLANK! that shocked through Rod's arm and into his body. The blasted critter was made of rock!

Redcap brayed laughter and swatted out at Rod back-handed. Pain flared through Rod's side, and the cliff and tower tumbled past him. Then, with a crack that exploded through him, he stopped, and got a close-up view of a rock wall sliding upward past him. He realized he was sliding down the cliff face and turned, frantically, as he jolted to a stop on the ledge. He was just in time to see two small figures appear right next to Redcap, inside his guard, and start chopping at his legs with small swords. 'Boys, no!' he tried to yell, 'Get back to your mother!' but it came out more like a chorus from a frog-pond. He could scarcely hear it himself, anyway; Redcap was roaring loudly as he reached down toward the mites . . .

A boulder slammed into the back of his head.

Redcap jolted forward, tripped over Magnus, and went sprawling. Small rocks bombarded him; then a boulder crashed down, just as he was getting up to his hands and knees. It crashed into his back, flattening him again.

Magnus and Geoffrey ran to finish him off.

Panic surged as Rod scrambled to his feet, lashing over him like a coating of fire. He had to get his boys out of there! He stumbled forward as Redcap heaved mightily, shaking the rock off his back, and rolled to his feet just in time for the boys to carom off his legs. He laughed wickedly, and bent toward them, then straightened suddenly and reached up to catch a boulder. He swung around following its inertia, and hurled it back up toward the mountaintop.

The bastard! If he'd hit Gwen or Cordelia . . . Boiling rage surged up in Rod, seeming almost to come from somewhere outside himself, flaming hatred at a monster who dared injure *his* child! He slammed into the back of Redcap's knees, and pain howled through his shoulder; then a small mountain crashed down on his back. Dimly, he heard Magnus howl, and fought his head up just in time to see Father Al, on hands and knees, reach out toward Redcap, who lay fallen backward across Rod. The stone was in the priest's hand; it touched the monster's forehead. Redcap howled, his body bucking in agony—

And disappeared.

Rod stared, not believing.

Then the whole scene turned dim; stars shot through it, a cascade of stars, leaving darkness in their wake . . .

' . . . three broken ribs. That nosebleed is stopped? Then the flow's from his mouth.'

'Oh, Father! His lung . . . ?'

'Pierced? Could . . . '

The sound faded out, then faded in again. ' . . . shoulder's broken, and the collarbone. How . . . ' Roaring came up like the surf, then faded. ' . . . on his feet again?'

'His back is broken?'

'No, but I think there're cracked vertebrae.'

Rod felt awfully sorry for the poor slob they were talking about. Who, he wondered?

Then an inspiration hit; look. Just open the eyes, take a look. Who was that, crying in the background?

Trouble was, there was this sandbag on each eyelid. And pain, that blasted pain, all through him! But he could do it; he'd done tougher things. He just fought a giant, hadn't he? A five-foot giant . . .

'Please, Magnus, staunch thy tears, and comfort thy sister and brother! Elidor, canst not help with Geoffrey? I must work!'

Agony seared through his shoulder. His eyes snapped open, and he bawled like a dogie who'd bumped a branding iron.

A lovely face hovered over him, framed with flaming hair. 'He wakes! Husband! Dost hear me?'

Reason turned for an afterthought: Gwen was trying to mend his shoulder telekinetically. 'Stop . . . please . . . Pain . . . '

'It will take time.' She nodded, tense-lipped. 'But it must be done. Oh, Rod! So many wounds . . . '

'It won't work; there's too many, and it'll take too long.' Father Al's face slid into view as Gwen's slid out. 'High Warlock! Hear me! Wish, as you've never wished before! Wish, with all your might, all your being, for your body to be whole again, completely mended, as it was before you ever were wounded!'

'I do,' Rod croaked. Now that the priest mentioned it, he did! Oh, how he wished! If anything could stop this agony, let it happen! He wished, fervently, for total health, for an unmarked body, for the wounds to go away, and never come back . . . !

And the helping spirit was there again, sliding inside, up, and all through him, kindly, reassuring, healing, absorbing the hurt . . .

Then it was gone – and so was the pain.

Rod stared, unbelieving.

Then he lifted his head, slowly, and looked down at his body. He was covered with blood, and his clothing was torn to rags – but the blood was still, there was nothing new running. And he felt well. In fact, he felt wonderful.

'Er . . . Gwen . . . '

'Aye, husband.' She was there, her hand cradling his head.

'Just to be on the safe side, I'd better not move. Check the shoulder, will you?'

He felt her fingers probing – rather pleasant sensation, really. In fact, more than pleasant . . .

' 'Tis whole, Rod.' There was wonder in her voice.

He relaxed with a sigh, letting his head fall back. 'Thank Heaven for that! Was there anything else wrong?'

'Quite a bit,' Father Al admitted.

The children had hushed.

'Check it out, would you? I'd hate to move if I'm going to start hurting again.'

'I will, husband.' He felt her fingers probing his side, his collarbone, his nose, rolling him a little to test his back.

'Thou'rt whole, husband.' The wonder gave way to rejoicing. 'Oh, thou'rt healed!'

'Well, then, let's get back into action.' He sat up and gathered her in. She clung to him as though he were a rock in the rapids, sobbing. 'There, now – there, love,' he murmured. 'I'm OK now. There, be a good girl, don't cry, we'll go find a haystack as soon as the kids're asleep, and I'll prove it.'

She smiled up at him, blinking through her tears. 'Well, if I'd any doubts, they're resolved. Thou *art* healed.'

'Papa!' shrieked three jubilant voices, and the kids piled onto him.

He just barely managed to remain upright, patting and hugging. 'There, now, children, don't worry. Papa had a bad time, but he's clear now . . . Gwen, watch Elidor, would you? We don't want to lose him again . . . No, now, there, I'm all right!'

'Aye,' Gwen breathed, eyes glowing. 'Father Al hath cured him.'

'No – *he* did,' the priest insisted. 'I just told him what to do.'

Rod stilled.

Then he cleared the children gently out of his line of sight. 'You mean *I* wrought that miracle cure?'

'Well . . . ' Father Al spread his hands. 'We'd already established that what you wished, happened . . . '

'Yes, we had,' Rod agreed. 'Ready to try a hypothesis yet, Father?'

'No-o-o-o,' the priest pursed his lips. 'But I *am* getting closer . . . '

'You and my robot,' Rod sighed, getting to his feet. 'He never would state a hypothesis until it was established fact. Hey, I don't even feel any of the aches from those faery pinches last night!'

'Interesting,' Father Al breathed. 'Have any old scars?'

'Hm – that's a thought.' Rod glanced at Gwen. 'We'll have to check that tonight, dear.'

She blushed, and explained to the priest, 'Some of them are where he cannot see them.'

'I always did like a good Christian marriage,' Father Al agreed.

'Well! If we've picked up all the pieces, can we get back to the chapel? I have an altar stone to return.'

'Yeah, I don't see any reason for hanging around here.' Rod surveyed the scene, turning grim. 'Hey! What're you doing, Magnus?'

'Picking up the pieces.' The boy straightened, holding up a long, sharp tooth. 'Can I keep this for a trophy, Papa?'

'What – the monster left a tooth behind?' Rod shuddered. 'Why would you want to remember *him*, son?'

'I do not know, Papa.' Magnus's chin thrust out a little. 'I only know that I think 'twould be wise.'

Rod frowned down at him. Then he said, 'Well, I've learned that your hunches generally turn out to be worth having. OK, take it along – but wrap it up tight, and swab it down with alcohol first chance you get.'

'I will, Papa.' Magnus blossomed into a smile and pulled a rag from his wallet.

It *had* been a handkerchief, once. Rod turned to Gwen. 'Ready to go, dear?'

'Aye.' She picked up her broomstick.

'And I.' Father Al came up, tucking the wrapped altar stone under his arm. He looked up at the tower. 'Whose army will garrison this place now, do you think – Duke Foidin's, or Lord Kern's?'

'Whichever gets here fastest.' Rod turned away. 'Frankly, Father, right now, I'd love to see the blasted thing fall apart.' He looked up sharply at the gleam in Magnus's eye. 'Don't you dare!'

They came out of the copse toward the back door of the church as the sun was setting. Rod looked around the town, frowning. 'Little quiet, isn't it?'

'It *is* the hour for supper,' Gwen mused.

'Well, it's been a strange day all around.' Father Al knocked on the 'rectory' door. 'No doubt the good Father will explain.'

The door opened a crack, showing an eye and a slice of beard. The eye widened, then so did the door. 'Thou livest!'

'Was there any doubt of it?' Father Al smiled and held out the altar stone. 'We had a saint on our side!'

The old priest took it gingerly, as though not quite believing it was real. 'And the Redcap? Is he dead?'

'Well, vanished, anyway.' Rod smiled. 'I don't think he'll come back.'

'Nay, they never return, once they've been routed; none of the faery folk do!' The old priest breathed a long, shaky sigh. 'We heard thunder in the mountains, and hid our heads. I and half the parish are here, besieging Heaven with prayers for your safety.'

'Well, that explains my quick recovery.' Rod locked gazes with Father Al. 'I had reinforcements.'

'A very intense field to draw from, near by?' The priest pursed his lips. 'Perhaps . . . '

'Dost thou know what thou hast done?' the old priest burst out. 'Caravans once did move through that pass above us – whole armies! None ha' dared venture there for ten years, since the King's army attempted, and lost!'

Rod stared, his eyes growing huge. Then he stabbed his finger toward the mountain pass a few times, making noises in his throat.

'Milord?' the old priest said humbly.

'You mean . . . ' Rod finally got his voice in gear. 'You mean *that* was the monster that's been blocking Lord Kern from coming out of the north-west?'

'Aye,' the old priest said, ''twas, indeed.'

Rod clasped his hands tight to stop the trembling, then had to clench his teeth to stop the chattering.

The old priest blinked, bemused, then turned to Father Al. 'Should I not ha' told him?'

'Oh, no, it's all right, it's all right!' Rod protested. 'I'm just glad you didn't tell me *before* we went up there . . . '

# Chapter Twenty-two

They camped that night by a mountain stream. When the trout had been eaten and the bones buried, and the children and Father Al lay bundled up in blankets the villagers had been only too glad to contribute, Gwen cosied up to Rod with her eyes on the campfire. 'Thou dost lead us north-west now, husband.'

Rod shrugged. 'Why not? Somehow, I think we'd better keep moving – and we *are* trying to get to Lord Kern. Though why, I don't know,' he added as an afterthought. 'We could just sit back now, and wait for him to come to us.'

'Indeed. He will likely march down through the pass with all his army, to rend Duke Foidin from the seat of power.' Her eyes strayed to the sleeping children. 'There should be one more amongst them, husband.'

'There should.' Rod felt the aching longing for his baby. 'But remember, dear – he's safer where he is . . . '

'Would I could be sure of it, with King and Abbot like to rend the land with civil war.' Her eyes lost focus; suddenly, she stiffened. 'I do hear his thoughts again!'

'Whose! Gregory's?'

'Aye.' She clutched Rod's forearm, gazing off into space. 'Aye, 'tis the touch of his mind. Oh, my bairn! . . . He seems alive and well. Be comforted, sweeting; thy mother and thy father strive to rejoin thee, as certainly as thou seekest us! . . . His touch is stronger now, mine husband.'

Sronger? Rod frowned. Why should that be? The two universes couldn't have come closer together!

'And Fess – his words begin!' Gwen frowned, concentrating. 'Still, I cannot quite discern the words. Summat there is, about Dr McAran, and the crafting of the weird engine . . . and the Crown and Church; the southern barons do declare they cannot, in all good conscience, fight against their Holy Mother Church . . . The northern barons have sent men and knights to Tuan . . . And the Abbot hath sent out a call to all nobles, summoning them with men and arms, to fight against the tyranny he doth say doth threaten Holy Mother Church!'

Rod groaned. 'They're shaping up to start a civil war for sure! Of course, the southern lords see this as their big chance to break their oaths of fealty to Tuan with some moral justification, and without losing the support of their people!'

'Yet they have not declared allegiance to the Abbot, nor defiance to the Crown,' Gwen said hopefully.

'Only because the Abbot just got around to issuing the call to arms! Mark my words, Gwen, there're futurian agents showing their hands in this. Someone's got to the Abbot – why else would he turn around to nullify his agreement with Tuan, before he'd even arrived home at his monastery? One of his entourage is a totalitarian agent, and talked him into it on the road! The totalitarians would love to have the Church take over the government;

a medieval theocracy could turn into a very tight police state, if
it were given a few modern techniques! And the anarchists are
probably advising the lords again – they'd love to see the barons
band together under the Church's banner, just long enough to
topple the monarchy, then fall to bickering between themselves
until the whole country fell into warlordism!' He slammed a
fist into his palm. 'Damn! And I'm stuck here, where I can't
fight 'em!'

'I believe 'tis as they planned,' Gwen murmured.

'You bet it is! And in the middle of all of that is my *baby*!'

'Peace, mine husband,' Gwen soothed. 'We do come nigh
Lord Kern; quite soon enough, we shall return to our own time
and place; sweet chuck, doubt it not! Then shalt thou make all
things well.'

'You've got more faith in me than I do,' Rod grated – but he
was calming down a bit. 'But maybe you're right. OK, darling –
you go "talk" to baby; reassure him, tell him we're still with him,
at least in spirit – and our bodies will be joining him, as soon as
they can.'

'I will,' she murmured, and leaned against his shoulder, eyes
glazed. He sat as still as he could, gazing out at the stream, his
thoughts in turmoil, worry about his baby son alternating with
stewing about the war, and ways to avert it. He sorted through
a dozen different plans or information he could send back to Fess
through Gwen's telepathy, that might brake the conflict – but none
of them could work. If he were there in person, his stature as High
Warlock, and as the architect of the Crown's previous victories over
the lords and the mob, would turn the balance; both sides would
listen to what he said and, to some extent, would back off due to
sheer intimidation. But that required his personal presence; there
wasn't much string-pulling he could do, without at least being on
the puppet stage.

But the scheming did dissipate the adrenalin; that, and maybe
some spillover from Gwen's comforting of Gregory. He began to
feel more relaxed. Then he glanced at his sleeping children, and
let the warmth and security of the family seep in to calm him. He
put his arm around Gwen, resting his cheek on her head.

' 'Tis faded,' she murmured. 'Yet I think I left him comforted.'

'Me, too. You seem to have a wonderful effect on males.'

Gwen smiled. 'I would thou hadst thought of that ere we
left the village.'

Rod frowned. 'Why?'

'For that we could ha' stayed the night there – and mayhap found a chamber to ourselves.' She looked up at him, eyes wide; and he felt himself being drawn down into them, down, down . . . He let himself go, but only as far as her lips. Still, it was a very long, and very satisfying, kiss.

Unfortunately, it was also very stimulating.

He pulled himself out of the kiss with a sigh. 'Well, when we find Lord Kern, maybe he'll spare us a room for the night – alone.'

'Aye.' She smiled sadly. 'Till then, we must needs bide in patience.' She let go, and lay back, rolling her blanket around her. 'Good night, husband – and wake me if thine eyelids droop.'

He'd rather have waked for other reasons, but he only said, 'I will. 'Night, love,' and caressed her hair.

She smiled contentedly, and wriggled under his touch, then lay still.

The whole night was still. He sat beside the dwindling fire, watching the woods and thinking long thoughts. When the moon had set, he woke Father Al, and rolled up in his own blanket.

Then a small earthquake rocked him. He looked up blearily, frowning; he'd *just* managed to doze off . . .

'Lord Gallowglass, we've got company,' Father Al informed him, 'and it wishes to speak to you.'

'"It"!' Rod scrambled out of his blanket.

'Yes. In fact, it ducked back down under the water at sight of me; it just barely had time to call for "the wizard".'

'I thought there were supposed to be *fewer* interruptions, at night.' Rod glanced toward the east. 'Mm. Not all that much "night" any more, is it? Well, I'll take the call.' He went over to the stream, and called out, 'This is the wizard speaking.'

A splash, and a gush of water, and a great, green, round head on a huge pair of shoulders, with a red cocked hat on its head (a feather in it, yet!) popped out of the stream. It was covered with scales; its nose was long, sharp, and red at the tip; it had little pig's eyes, and was covered with green scales. It held up a webbed hand, and grinned. 'Good morn to thee, wizard!'

Rod squeezed his eyes shut and gave his head a shake, then looked up again. 'Er – good morning.'

'Aye, I'm real.' The water-man grinned. 'Thou'st never seen a Merrow afore?'

''Fraid not, I wasn't quite ready for it. Er – don't you find that stream a little confining?'

'Aye, but we go where we must. I am sent with word for thee.'

'What word?'

'Word of the Redcap thou'st routed from the Tower of Gonkroma.'

Rod shuddered. 'I'm not really interested in where that critter is, thank you.'

'Then thou'lt wish to know where it ha' been – or so says the Grand Duchess.' The Merrow rolled an eye at him. 'The fellow appeared out of nowhere, struck away guards, and stole a yearling child away.'

Rod stared, electrified.

Gwen rolled over and sat up sleepily. 'What moves, husband?' Then she caught sight of the Merrow; her eyes widened.

So did his, and his grin turned toward a leer.

'Good morrow,' Gwen said graciously.

'No, good Merrow,' Rod corrected. 'At least, he'd better be.' He let his hand rest on his dagger-hilt.

The Merrow held up both webbed hands and bowed its head. 'Ha' no fear o' me. I am nothing if not willing, and seek naught else in return. I only seek to discharge my message, naught more.'

'What message?' Gwen frowned up at Rod.

'It seems Redcap wanted revenge,' Rod said slowly. 'He's stolen an infant, and disappeared.'

Gwen gasped.

'I know,' Rod said grimly, 'but we've got to get home; we've lost enough time playing Good Samaritans. I mean, I feel sorry for the kid and its parents, but . . . ' He ran down under Gwen's glare.

'Be shamed,' she said severely. 'The child would rest securely, had we not routed Redcap.' She turned to the Merrow. 'Who sent thee?'

'The Grand Duchess.'

'Then tell her we will seek out Redcap, and have the child back.'

The Merrow looked questioningly at Rod.

'All right, all right!' Rod threw up his hands. 'I know when I'm beaten, between you and my conscience! Might be the same thing, come to think of it . . . All right, Monsieur. We'll do it. And if I know the Grand Duchess, she's got thorough information about the specifics. Who's the child?'

'Whose? Why, Lord Kern's, of course.'

Rod and Gwen both stared.

Then Rod said slowly, 'Does Duke Foidin know about this?'

'Aye. A troop of his men doth race hotfoot to seize the child –
though, knowing Redcap's repute, I misdoubt me that they make
quite so much speed as they might.'

'I don't blame 'em,' Rod said grimly. 'But *if* they succeed,
Foidin will have the best hostage he could hope for. He might
even be able to make Kern surrender. Who told Foidin about the
kidnapping?'

'Eorl Theofrin, who knew from a gazing-crystal, belike.'

'Theofrin?' Rod frowned. 'Why would he suddenly be helping
the Duke?'

'For the enmity he bears thee.' The Merrow grinned.

Rod just watched him for a minute, trying to figure it out.
Then he gave up. 'All right, I'll ask the obvious question:
how does telling Foidin about the kidnapping help Theofrin
hurt *me*?'

The Merrow spread his hands. 'I know not, milord.'

'' 'Tis a trap, mine husband,' Gwen said softly.

Rod nodded. 'They must be figuring we'll run to the kid's
rescue – and they're right. Then the troops come in, and capture
the kid *with* us. Well, I think we can have a little surprise waiting
for them.'

'But do we guess aright?'

'We'll know when we get there.' Rod slapped his scabbard.
'If we see a battle in progress when we get there, we've guessed
wrong – in which case, we'll puzzle it out later. Did the Grand
Duchess say where Redcap's hiding?'

'Aye.' The Merrow nodded. 'He ha' found an auld tower,
at Dun Kap Weir.'

'Yonder.' Elidor pointed down at a ruined tower atop a mound
in the middle of a plain. ''Tis Dun Kap Weir. Foul deeds were
done there, long years ago.'

'Of course.' Rod smiled sardonically. 'What other kind of lair
would Redcap choose? I don't like this coming east again, back
into the Duke's country.'

'We are warned against his troops,' Gwen reminded him.
'Hai! They are there!'

Rod peered down over her shoulder, at a battle raging in front
of the tower. A dozen foot soldiers fought frantically, shouting,

pikes flashing in the early sunlight. Underneath their clamour was roaring.

'I guess they weren't planning to ambush us,' Rod mused.

Suddenly, two men went flying. They hit twenty feet downslope and lay still, among a score of their fellows.

'What a fighter!' Rod shook his head in admiration. 'Redcap against thirty soldiers, alone! Too bad he's on the wrong side . . . '

'Do not think of converting him,' Gwen said grimly.

Five more soldiers went flying. The rest drew back, leaving an open half-circle; for a moment, the stunted ogre stood at bay, facing his enemies.

Then he whirled up his pike and charged them, bellowing. They howled in fear and ran. Redcap followed them to the brow of the hill and stood, glowering down, breathing heavily, watching as they tripped over their fallen comrades and went rolling, scrambling back to their feet, then running on down the hill and over the meadow to the shelter of nearby trees.

Redcap tossed his head and turned back to his tower.

'What do we do now?' Father Al asked.

'Let me.' Magnus suddenly disappeared.

'Magnus – NO!' Rod and Gwen shouted together, and the broomstick went into a power dive.

Redcap whirled, looking up at the shout – so they had a great view as Magnus appeared in front of the monster, holding up its missing tooth. Redcap just stared at it, frozen, wide-eyed. Then he began to tremble.

'My father comes, with the priest,' Magnus warned. 'Begone, foul monster, and never come near human places again!'

Redcap threw back his head with a shriek of dismay, and disappeared.

Cordelia shot past Gwen on her broomstick, and darted through the tower doorway.

'Cordelia! Thou knowest not what may dwell there!' Gwen cried, and shot after her.

Rod leaped off five feet above ground and landed running. He jumped up against the side of the tower to brake his momentum, and rebounded to face his son.

Magnus was calmly picking up something from the spot where Redcap had been standing. He held it up for his father to see – another long, nicked tooth.

'Well – it worked out OK.' Rod stepped up to his boy and caught him against his hip in a bruising hug. 'But don't do something like that again, son – please! I could swear you took five years off my life, and your mother's! What would've happened if you'd been wrong? If the sight of his own tooth *hadn't* banished him?'

'But it did,' Magnus's voice said, muffled.

Rod sighed. 'And I'll admit, I'll never question your hunches – but couldn't *you* learn to?'

Cordelia appeared in the tower doorway. 'Papa! Come quickly!'

Rod ran.

He braked to a halt beside Gwen, saw an infant wrapped in her arms. He sighed and relaxed, the ebb of adrenalin leaving him weak. '*This* is an emergency?'

She turned an unfocused, faraway gaze up to him. ''Tis Gregory.'

Rod stared down at the baby. Dark hair, big grey eyes – and that look. That solemn, solemn look. 'But – it can't be! Not here!'

But it made sense – almost. If someone had thrown Gregory through the Gate, Redcap would have sensed he was Rod and Gwen's baby, and have gone after him in revenge!

'The *child* is not.' Gwen's voice was remote. ''Tis almost more like him than himself – yet 'tis not him; I would know.'

'Then what . . . ?'

'His thoughts.' Her eyes searched for his face, but stayed far away. 'This child carries Gregory's thoughts.'

Of course! That was why they'd been able to hear Gregory's thoughts twice before – and why the second contact was clearer; they had been further north-west, closer to this child!

'It could happen,' Father Al said quietly. 'In another universe, there *could* be a child that exactly corresponds to your own. And your Gregory has been searching, yearning outward, achingly, with every iota of his tiny strength – enough for his thoughts to resonate through another mind, exactly like his own. Then, once *this* child was stolen from *his* parents, his mind would do the same – and their thoughts would meld, so that Gregory's would become much more clear.'

'So their minds form a link between universes?'

Father Al nodded. 'If the two individuals are analogues of one another.'

'Words come,' Gwen said suddenly. ''Tis Fess . . . "—attempted to turn off the transmitter and close the Gate, but I prevented them, and remanded them to King Tuan; they are in his prison. They admit to being futurian anarchists, but nothing more; and King Tuan, in accordance with your joint policies, continues to resist Queen Catharine's insistence on using torture. Brom O'Berin summoned Yorick—''

Father Al started.

Rod cocked an eyebrow at him.

'"—Yorick, who identified the device as *not* being a time machine, and brought Dr McAran, who tentatively identifies it as a mechanism allowing travel between alternate universes. He is currently working at fever-pitch, attempting to construct such a device of his own. He attempted to dismantle this one, but I would not permit him to turn it off. So, if you can endure, help should be forthcoming – eventually. Meanwhile, in your absence, the Church and Crown have moved toward war. The Abbot has issued a formal declaration that the Crown encroaches so far upon the authority of the Church that all folk of good conscience should resist their King and Queen as tyrants. He has absolved the barons from their oaths of fealty, and summoned them to attack Their Majesties in force. Four southern barons have answered his call, with all their knights and men. Three northern lords have brought their armies to Tuan. The other five lords claim the conflict is no concern of theirs, but is only between the Church and Crown; they therefore stand neutral.''

'Ready to jump in and take over when the other barons have torn each other, and the Crown, apart,' Rod growled.

There was time for it; Gwen had paused, eyes glazed, lips parted, waiting. Now she spoke again. '"FCC robot number 651919, transmitting on human-thought frequency, near the Gate through which the Gallowglass family disappeared, in an attempt to contact them. Though I think it extremely unlikely that the Gate will re-transmit my signal into another universe, I must attempt it. Situation report: The agents responsible for your exile attempted to turn off the transmitter and close the Gate . . . "' She blinked, eyes focusing again. 'He repeats himself.'

Rod nodded. 'Faithful old Fess, standing twenty-four-hour watch at the Gate, trying somehow to reach us. He probably doesn't even realize Gregory's his transmission link. Just keeps repeating the message over and over, hoping against hope – and updating the situation report, of course.'

Father Al nodded. 'I was wondering when you'd get around to confirming that your horse was a robot.'

Rod jerked his head impatiently. 'No point in giving away information, is there? Though I might as well have; you do a very nice job of putting together comments I've dropped here and there.' He turned to Gwen. 'Did you reassure him?'

She nodded. 'As well as I could – that we still do live, and *will* come home.'

'But not when.' Rod's mouth tightened. 'Well, you do have to at least *try* to be honest with a child.' He looked up. 'And with ourselves. The situation at home just keeps getting worse, and here we stick!'

'Thou didst say, husband, that even should it come to open war, our babe will not be endangered.'

'Yeah, *probably* not but even two per cent sounds like too high a probability, when we're talking about our own baby! Come on, Gwen, let's get out of here and return this infant to his rightful parents, so we can get busy collecting the favour his father owes us – a quick burst of magic that'll send us back to Gramarye. If he can do it. Let's go.' He turned away to the doorway, looking about him, frowning. 'Magnus and Geoff and Elidor stayed outside, eh?'

He stepped through the doorway, and saw his sons lying unconscious at the feet of soldiers dressed in the Duke's livery.

Then something exploded on the back of his head, and he just had time for one quick thought, before the stars wiped out the scene:

*Of course. The Duke kept some forces in reserve for an ambush, just in case we did show up . . .*

# Chapter Twenty-three

When he saw the light of day again, it was golden-orange, and dim. Turning a head that seemed as large as an asteroid and rang at the slightest touch, he saw the reason for the dimness – a tiny window, barred, and up near the low ceiling. Turning his head again in spite of the pain, he saw walls of rough-hewn rock, damp and splotched with fungus.

He levered himself up on his elbows. Consciousness tried to slide away again, but he hauled it back. Little Geoff huddled next to him, curled into a ball. Beyond him, Father Al sat gravely watching.

They were both shackled to the wall by four-foot lengths of heavy chain.

'Good afternoon, my friend,' the priest said softly.

Geoff's head snapped up. He saw Rod's eyes open, and threw his arms around his neck. 'Papa!' He began to cry.

'There, there, now, son,' Rod soothed. Chains clanked as he wrapped his arms around Geoff. 'Papa's all right. It'll be OK.' He looked up at Father Al. 'Where're Gwen and Cordelia and Magnus?'

'In a room like this one, I'd guess. The soldiers carrying them split off one floor up; I gather they've two layers of dungeons here.'

'You were conscious.'

'By then I was, yes.' Father Al fingered a bruise in the middle of his tonsure. He had several more on his forehead and cheeks, and there was clotted blood around his nostrils. 'It wasn't much of a fight. Your wife stepped out just as you started to crumble, and they caught her on the back of the head with a cudgel; she was out before she could do anything. Your little daughter and I made something of a try – the air was quite thick with flying stones for a few minutes there, till a soldier caught her from behind with a pike-butt. For myself, I found a reasonably solid stick, and actually managed to lay out a couple of them, myself.' He sounded surprised.

'Which lost you your clergy's right to not get hit.' Rod found his respect for Father Al going up still more, while dull anger grew at the bastards who'd struck his wife and daughter – and clouted a priest, besides!

He took Geoff by the shoulders and held him back a little. 'Try to stop crying, son. I've got to check you over. Where does it hurt?'

Geoff pointed to his head, and Rod fingered the spot gently – there was a large goose-egg. Geoff winced as he probed, but didn't cry out; and the bone didn't give when he pressed it. Good. 'Look at me, son.' He stared into Geoff's eyes – the pupils were the same size. 'No, I think you're OK.' *Thank Heavens!* 'You'll have a headache for a while, though. Now, close your eyes, and see if you can hear Mama's thoughts.'

Obediently, Geoff sat back against the wall and squeezed his eyes shut. After a few minutes, he said, 'She there, Papa – 'n' Mag'us 'n' 'Elia near. But everyone aseep!'

'Haven't come to, then.'

'*Big* sleep, Papa – bigger 'n' you just had!'

'Bigger?' Rod didn't like the sound of that – it smacked of drugs.

A key clanked in the lock, and the door groaned open. Duke Foidin stepped in, grinning, flanked by guards. 'Well, well! The gentlemen wake!'

'Yes, we do.' Rod glowered up at him. 'Gonna slip us a sleeping potion now, like you did to my wife and other children?'

The Duke couldn't quite mask the surprise. 'Well, well! Thou dost have some power! And to think Eorl Theofrin assured me 'twas the other three who were dangerous.'

'We operate as a unit,' Rod snapped. 'What're you planning to do with us?'

'Why, turn thee over to the Eorl, naturally – his help thus far has been rather half-hearted, being solely concerned with capturing thyself. Thou must have offended him deeply.'

'I didn't exactly find him complimentary, myself.'

'Delightful, delightful!' The Duke rubbed his hands. 'He should be quite eager to seize thee and thine – eager enough to pledge full support. To assure it, I believe I'll give him thy family, but save thee till Lord Kern's defeated.'

Rod studied the Duke's face, deciding that his usual squeamishness about murder could be waived in this case.

'Oh, and thy wife! I had forgot!' The Duke raised a finger. 'I ha' not had time to attend to her properly – but I shall.' A leering grin spread over his face. 'Be assured that I shall.'

Rod held himself wooden-faced, but the anger and loathing condensed and hardened into iron resolve.

Footsteps clattered in the hall, and a soldier burst in, covered with dust and caked blood. He dropped to one knee. 'Milord Duke! Foul sorcery! Lord Kern's troops filled the pass ere ours could come there! We battled to hold them within, but a horde of monsters turned our flank, and . . . '

'Be still, fool!' The Duke snapped, with a furious glance at Rod. 'Well, I must attend to this matter, wizard – but I'll see thee again, at my leisure! Come!' he snapped to his guards, and whirled out the door. The messenger scrambled to his feet and stumbled after him. The guards clanked out and slammed the door; the key grated in the lock.

'I don't think he'll have much leisure for anything, now,' Rod said, with vindictive pleasure. 'Lord Kern'll come down like a whirlwind, and mop him up. Unless . . . ' his face darkened.

'Unless Eorl Theofrin joins him whole-heartedly?' Father Al nodded. 'But he has to buy Theofrin's support. I suggest we do what we can to eliminate his buying power.'

'Yes – and now, while he's busy!' Rod turned to Geoff. 'Try to wake Mama, son! She can get us out of these shackles. Try really hard.'

'I . . . will, Papa,' the little boy said hesitantly. 'But sleeps *real* hard.' None the less, he screwed his eyes shut, concentrating. His whole little face knotted up with trying.

Then he yawned.

'Son? . . . Geoff. Geoff!' Rod reached out and shook him. Geoff's head lolled over against him, with a little smile, and the boy breathed deeply and evenly.

'Damn! Whatever they put into her must've been *really* strong – it put him to sleep, too! What do we do now, Father?'

'A good point.' The priest frowned down at his hands. 'We are, as they say, thrown back on our own resources.'

'Which means me,' Rod said slowly. 'Ready to try a theory now, Father?'

The priest sighed and straightened up. 'I don't have much choice now, do I?'

'We *have* come to the crunch,' Rod agreed.

'All right.' Father Al slapped his hands on his thighs. 'Try to follow me through this. First, the Gramarye espers could read your mind – until you fell in love with one of them.'

'Hey, now, wait a minute . . . '

Father Al held up a hand. 'It was your falling in love that did it. You can't remember the precise moment you became psionically "invisible", of course; but you weren't before you met her, and you were afterwards. What other event could have triggered it?'

'Mmf. Well, maybe,' Rod grumbled. 'But why? I want her to be able to read my mind, more than anyone!'

'No, you don't.' Father Al waved a forefinger. 'Not subconsciously, at least. She may be your greatest blessing, but she's also your greatest threat. A man's vulnerable to his beloved when he's vulnerable to no one else; because you've "let her into your heart", she can hurt you most deeply. You needed some defence, some way of keeping the core of yourself inviolate – which you couldn't do, if she could read your mind.'

'It *sounds* sensible. But Lord, man, it's been nine years and four children! Wouldn't I have outgrown that by now? I mean, shouldn't my subconscious be convinced it can trust her?'

'Should,' the priest agreed.

Rod was silent, letting the implications sink in.

Father Al gave him a few minutes, then said, 'But that's beside the point. What matters here is that the ability to shield your mind from a telepath indicates some power in you, some sort of esper ability that you've never been aware of. Not the ones we ordinarily think of – I'd imagine there've been some rather desperate moments in your life, when you could've used such powers badly.'

'Quite a few,' Rod said sourly. 'In fact, my subconscious should've dredged them up out of sheer instinct for survival.'

'But it didn't; therefore, you don't have them. What I think you *do* have is the ability to use the psionic force that espers, and latent espers, leak into the general environment.'

Rod frowned. 'But there must've been plenty of that power leaking into the rocks and trees of Gramarye; in fact, the place must've been permeated with it. Why couldn't I use that?'

'Because you didn't know how. You didn't even know you could. You needed something to trigger it in you, to release it, and to teach you how to use it.'

'So what did it? Just being in a universe where magic works?'

'Not quite.' Father Al held up a forefinger. 'When Redcap finished with you, you were so thoroughly chewed up that I doubt the most advanced hospital could've put your insides back together – but you wished for it, didn't you?'

Rod nodded slowly.

'And it worked.' Father Al smiled. 'That wasn't the doing of a neophyte wizard – it was the work of a master. And I suspect it took a bit more power than your own.'

Rod frowned. 'So where did it come from?'

'Lord Kern.'

Rod looped his head down and around, and came up blinking. 'How did you figure *that* one?'

'The child, the one we saved from Redcap. He's an exact double for your own infant son – and his analogue.' He stopped, watching Rod closely.

Rod watched back – and, slowly, his eyes widened. 'Holy Hamburg! If the kid's Gregory's analogue – then his parents have to be analogues of Gwen and me!'

Father Al nodded again.

'And if Lord Kern's his father – then Kern's my analogue.'

'But of course,' Father Al murmured. 'After all, he, too, is High Warlock.'

'And if he's my analogue – then he and I can blend minds, just as his baby and Gregory did!'

'If you could learn to drop your psionic shield, yes – which, in a moment of great emotional stress, you did.'

'At least for the moment.' Rod frowned. 'I never told you, Father – but each of those times I worked a "spell", I felt some . . . presence, some spirit, inside me, helping me.'

'Lord Kern, without a doubt!' Father Al's eyebrows lifted. 'Then perhaps there is something of the telepath about you – or about Lord Kern. For, do you see, whether or not you can hear his thoughts, you can apparently draw on his powers.'

Rod shivered. 'That's a little intimidating, Father. Well, at least he's a nice guy.'

'Is he?' Father Al leaned forward, suddenly very intent. 'What is he like?'

Rod frowned. 'Well – from what I've felt when I was wanting some magic to happen – he seems kind, very kind, always willing to help anybody who needs it, even an interloper like me. But he's stern; he knows what he wants and what he believes is right, and he's not going to put up with anyone going against it.'

'Hm.' Father Al frowned. 'That last sounds troubling.'

'Oh, no, he's not a fanatic or anything! He's just not willing to watch someone hurt somebody else! Especially children . . . '

'Yes?' Father Al prompted. 'What about children?'

Rod shuddered. 'Threaten a child, and he goes into a rage. And if it's *his* child . . . '

'He loses control?'

'Well, not quite berserk . . . '

'It sounds somewhat like yourself,' the priest said gently.

Rod sat still a moment; then he looked up. 'Well, shouldn't it?'

'Of course.' Father Al nodded. 'He's your analogue.'

Rod nodded. 'But where's *your* analogue, Father?'

'Either we haven't met him or he doesn't exist.' The priest

smiled. 'Probably the latter – and that's why *I* can't work magic here.'

Rod frowned. 'But how come I'd have an analogue, and you wouldn't?'

Father Al held out his hand with the fingers spread. 'Remember our theory of parallel universes – that there's a set of "root" universes, but any one "root" will branch? Every major historical event really ends both ways – and each way is a separate universe, branching off from the "root". For example, in our set of universes, the dinosaurs died, and the mammals thrived – but, presumably, there was another "main branch" in which the *mammals* died, and the dinosaurs survived, and continued to evolve.'

'So there might be a universe in which Terra has cities full of intelligent lizards.' Rod gave his head a shake. 'Sheesh! And the further back in time the universes branched off from one another, the further apart they are – the more unlike each other they are.'

Father Al nodded slowly, gazing steadily at him.

Rod frowned. 'I don't like being led. If you've got the next step in mind, *say* it.'

Father Al looked surprised, then abashed. 'Pardon me; an old teacher's reflexes. You see, this can't be the universe next to ours – we've skipped a whole set in which science rules, and magic's just fantasy. There should be a universe in which the DDT revolution failed, for example, and PEST still rules – and one in which the IDE never collapsed, the old Galactic Union. And on, and on – one in which humankind never got off of Terra, one where they made it to the Moon but no farther, one in which the Germans won World War II, one in which they won World War I and World War II never occurred . . . millions of them. We skipped past all of them, into a universe far, far away, in which magic works, and science never had a chance to grow.'

Rod stared, spellbound.

'Now, logically,' Father Al went on, 'since the farther you get from your "home universe", the more it changes – the number of people who have analogues grow fewer. For example, think of all the soldiers who came back from World War II with foreign brides. In the universe in which World War II never happened, those couples never met – so their descendants have no analogues in that universe, nor in any of the universes that branched off from it.'

Rod scowled. 'Let me head you off – you're working around to saying that, by the time we get this far away, there're damn few analogues left.'

'Exactly.' Father Al nodded. 'Very few, my friend. You seem to be a very rare case.'

Suddenly, the stone floor felt very uncomfortable. 'What makes me so special?'

'Oh, no!' Father Al grinned, holding up a palm. 'You're not going to get me to make *any* guesses about that – not without a great deal more research! After all, it could just be a genetic accident – Lord Kern and yourself might not even have analogous grandfathers!'

'I doubt it,' Rod said sourly.

'Frankly, so do I – but who's to tell? I don't quite have time to work out a comparative genealogy between yourself and Lord Kern.'

'But how many universes *do* I have analogues in?'

'Again – who knows? I'd guess you don't have any in universes that never developed *Homo sapiens* – but I wouldn't want to guarantee it.'

Rod chewed at the inside of his lower lip. 'So I might be able to draw on the powers of wizards in still other, more magical, universes?'

'It's conceivable. Certainly you've got to have a great many analogues, to have come even this far.'

'That makes two "I don't knows" – or is it three?' Rod folded his legs. 'Time to quit speculating and get down to practicalities, Father. How do I control this gift? How do I go about drawing on Lord Kern's powers? I can't just wish – it's a little too chancy.'

'It surely is. But when you're wishing with great emotional intensity, all you're doing is opening yourself up – and there are techniques for doing that deliberately.' Father Al leaned forward. 'Are you ready?'

Rod settled himself a little more comfortably, swallowed against the lurking dread that was trying to form in his belly, and nodded. 'What do I do?'

'Concentrate.' Father Al held out his rosary, swinging the crucifix back and forth like a pendulum. It caught the remaining ray of golden sunlight and glittered. 'Try to let your mind go empty. Let your thoughts roam where they will; they'll settle down and empty out. Let the dancing light fill your eyes.'

'Hypnotism?'

'Yes, but you'll have to do it yourself – all I can do is give directions. Let me know when I seem a little unreal.'

'As of three days ago, the first time I met you.'

The priest shook his head. 'That kind of joke's a defence, my friend – and you're out to let the walls fade away, not make them thicker. Let your mind empty.'

Rod tried. After a little while, he realized that's what he was doing wrong. He relaxed, letting his thoughts go wherever they wished, keeping his eyes on the glittering cross. Words whirled through his mind like dry leaves; then they began to settle. Fewer and fewer remained – and he felt as though his face were larger, warmer, and his body diminished. The cross filled his eyes, but he was aware of Father Al's face behind it, and the stone room behind that – and he was aware of the ceiling and floor lines slanting together toward an unseen vanishing point, as though the whole thing was painted on a flat canvas. There seemed to be a sort of shield around him, unseen, a force-field, four feet thick . . . 'I'm there.'

'Now – reach out.' The droning voice seemed both distant and inside his head. 'Where's your mind?'

It was an interesting question. Rod's head was empty, so it couldn't be there. 'Far away.'

'Let your consciousness roam – find your mind.'

It was an interesting experience – as though he were groping with some unseen extension through a formless void; but all the while, he still saw only the dungeon, and the priest.

Then the extension found something, and locked into place. 'I've got it.'

And power flowed to him – blind, outraged anger, a storm of wrath, that filled him, he could feel his skin bulging, feel it trying to get out of him and blast everything to char.

The crucifix filled his eyes again, and the priest was barking something, in Latin, Rod couldn't follow it, but it was a thundering command, with the power of Doom behind it.

Then the crucifix lowered, and the priest's voice was muffled, distant. 'Whatever it is, it's not supernatural.'

Rod shook his head, carefully. 'It's human.' His voice seemed to echo up through a long channel, and also be right there at his eardrums. It occurred to him that he should be scared, but he was too angry. Slowly, he rose to his knees, keeping himself carefully upright. 'What do I do now?'

'Use it. First . . . '

A sudden shock shook Rod. 'Hold it. It's using me.'

'For what!'

'I don't know . . . No, I do. It's Lord Kern, and he's not a telepath, but I'm getting the bottom level of what he's going through. He just used me for a beacon, and he's drawing on me in some way, to teleport a chunk of his army in . . . ' He convulsed again. 'Another chunk of infantry . . . Cavalry . . . archers . . . they're all here now, very close by . . . Now he's done with me.'

'Do you still have his power?'

Rod nodded.

'Wake your family.'

Rod didn't try to slide into Geoff's mind; he just willed him awake, pushing a bit of power into him to throw off the effects of the drug. The little boy yawned and stretched, and looked up at his father with a sleepy smile. Then his eyes shot wide open, and he scrambled to his feet.

Rod reached over to grasp his shoulder. 'It's OK, son. I'm still me. Now I've got to wake your brother and sister. Find them for me.'

Geoff gulped, paling, and squeezed his eyes shut. It was almost as though Rod could see the line of his thought, arrowing off through the stone wall. He turned his eyes that way, glaring up at the ceiling, pushing power out to his family and willing them awake.

'They awake.' Geoff's voice was hushed and subdued. Father Al gathered him in.

'Are they chained?'

'No, Papa. They were asleep.'

'Then tell them to meet us at the stairwell. We're going to find Elidor.'

'How, Papa?' Geoff held up his manacle.

Rod glared at the iron cuff, and it shattered. Geoff screamed and cowered back against Father Al. Rod glared at his other wrist, and the iron shattered again.

Slowly, Father Al held up his own wrists, side by side. The manacles shattered. Then Rod pushed his arms straight forward, and his manacles crumbled. He stood up, very slowly, keeping his body very straight; he felt as though his head were swollen, his face two feet in front of itself. 'Guide me, Father. I can't feel the floor.'

And he couldn't – he could feel nothing but the tremendous, vibrating power that filled him, the towering rage that he fought to contain. He reached out to grasp the priest's arm, and Father Al gasped. Rod lightened his hold, and the priest guided him slowly toward the door. Geoffrey followed, eyes huge.

They paused at the huge oaken panel. The lock erupted in a cloud of wood-dust; when it settled, they saw the lock twisted half-out of the door. Rod kicked it open and staggered out into the hall. Father Al scurried along, holding him up, bracing him. Rod's head was beginning to ache now, with a savage throbbing. They moved toward the stairway.

There were a handful of guards at the iron gate. They looked up, saw Rod coming, stared, then caught up their pikes.

The iron gate suddenly wrenched itself out of shape, and the pikestaves exploded into flame. The soldiers shrieked and dropped their weapons, and spun toward the oaken door behind the gate – as it exploded into flame, too. They fell back, howling, as the centre of the door blew out, scattering burning wood through the passage.

'I didn't do that,' Rod croaked, 'any of it.'

And Gwen stalked through the door, surrounded by flame, eyes burning in wrath, coming to claim her man. Magnus and Cordelia leaped up one each side of her, faces flint, hounds of war.

She saw him coming, and the anger hooded itself. She came to him, caught his arm. 'Husband – what hath thee?'

'Power,' he croaked. 'Lead me.'

Up the stairwell, then, and through the halls. Soldiers came running, shouting, pikes at the ready. A huge invisible fist slammed them back against the walls. Courtiers leaped out with swords arcing down; something spun them aside and threw them down. The family stepped over their bodies, advancing.

They climbed the Keep. On the last step, Magnus suddenly screamed in rage and disappeared. Geoff yelled and disappeared after him.

'Where've they gone?' Rod grated.

'To the King's chamber!' Gwen's fingers tightened on his arm. 'Hurry! Duke Foidin seeks to slay Elidor!'

Rod grabbed Cordelia's arm and closed his eyes, swaying, concentrating. The ache pounded in his temples; blood roared in his ears and, behind it, a singing . . .

He felt a jolt, and opened his eyes.

He stood in a richly-furnished room, with an oriental carpet and tapestried hangings. A huge, canopied bed stood against the far wall, with Elidor huddled against the headboard. Near it, under a tall slit of a window, stood a cradle.

The Duke stood before the bed with his sword drawn. Between it and Elidor, Geoff and Magnus wove like cobras, fencing madly against the Duke. He roared, laying about him with huge sweeps of his sword, maddened at not being able to touch them.

Elidor uncurled and plunged a hand under the featherbed, snatching out a dagger.

A huge blue face appeared at the window, and a blue arm with iron nails poked through, groping toward the cradle.

Cordelia shrieked, and the hag's arm suddenly twisted. It bellowed, and Geoff looked up, startled, then whirled away to the cradle, to thrust up at the monster. With a howl of glee, it scooped him up. Geoff wailed, suddenly only a very frightened three-year-old, struggling madly.

'Aroint thee!' Gwen screamed, and the monster's arm snapped down against the window ledge with a crack like a gunshot. The hag shrieked, but her hold on Geoffrey tightened; his face was reddening too much. Then the blue face fell back, and the hand yanked Geoffrey out of the window.

Rod leaped to the window and bent out, looking down.

Below him, the hag scuttled down the wall of the keep, like a spider, waving Geoffrey in the air. Rod's eyes narrowed, and the cold rage that filled him left no room for pity. Suddenly, the hag's arm twisted, and twisted again, ripping free from her shoulder. Her screams drilled through Rod's head as she fell, turning over and over, to slam into the ground.

But her arm floated high in the air, with Geoffrey.

Then Gwen was beside Rod, staring at the huge blue hand. One by one, the fingers peeled back, opening, and Geoffrey floated up toward them, cradled by his mother's thoughts, sobbing.

Rod didn't stay to see the rest; his younger boy was safe, but his oldest wasn't. He turned, deliberately, cold glare transferring to the Duke.

Duke Foidin still fought; but he fenced with a gloating grin, for Magnus was tiring. His parries were slower, his ripostes later. The Duke slashed at his head, and Magnus ducked – and tripped on the carpet's edge, falling forward. The Duke roared with savage satisfaction and chopped down at Magnus.

His arm yanked back hard, slamming him against the wall; he

screamed. Then he looked up into Rod's eyes, and dread seeped into his face. Rod's eyes narrowed, and the Duke's body rocked with a sudden, muffled explosion. The colour drained out of his face as his head tilted back, eyes rolling up; then he crumpled to the floor.

'What hast thou done?' Gwen murmured into the sudden silence.

'Exploded his heart,' Rod muttered.

A scream erupted from the cradle.

Gwen ran over to it, scooped up the baby. 'There, there, now, love, shhh. 'Tis well, 'tis well; none here would hurt thee, and thy mother shall come presently to claim thee.' She looked up at Rod. 'Praise Heaven we came!'

Father Al nodded. 'The Duke's sentries must have told him, Lord Kern was virtually at his gate – so he tried to kill Elidor, in spite.'

'And would've gone on to kill the baby!' Suddenly, the anger soared up in Rod again, bulging him out, shaking him like a gale – and Father Al was there beside him, shaking his shoulders and crying, 'The deed is done, the Duke's dead! Elidor's safe, the baby is safe, *your* children are safe! *All* the children are safe – and you are Lord Gallowglass, not Lord Kern! You are Rod Gallowglass, Rodney d'Armand, transported here from Gramarye, in another universe – and by science, not magic. You are Rod *Gallowglass*!'

Slowly, Rod felt the anger beginning to ebb, the Power to fade. It slackened, and was gone – and he tottered, his brain suddenly clouded; stars shot through the room.

'My lord!' Gwen was beside him, baby cradled in one arm, the other around him.

'Yes, I know you are drained.' Father Al had a shoulder under his arm. 'That use of magic took every bit of reserve your body had. But pull yourself together – it's not over yet! Hear that?'

Hear? Rod frowned, shaking his head, trying to clear it. He strained, and dimly, through the ringing in his ears, he heard shouts, and the clash of steel. War!

'Lord Kern's troops are battling the Duke's,' Father Al snapped.

Adrenalin shot its last surge, and Rod straightened up. 'No . . . no, I can stand.' He brushed away their hands and stood by himself, reeling; then he steadied.

And a voice thundered through the castle, coming from the walls themselves: 'THY DUKE IS DEAD! THROW DOWN THINE ARMS!'

There was a moment's silence; then a low moan began, building to despair. As it died, Rod heard, dimly, the clatter and clank of swords, shields, and pikes rattling on cold stone.

'That voice,' Gwen murmured.

'What about it?' Rod frowned. 'Sounded ugly, to me.'

'It was thine.'

'I believe our counterpart has come,' Father Al murmured, 'to reclaim his own.'

'Good,' Rod muttered. 'He's welcome to it.'

Mailed footsteps rang on the stone of the hallway.

'Quickly!' Father Al snapped. 'Hold hands! Link your family together!'

Rod didn't understand but he reacted to the urgency in the priest's voice. 'Kids! Children-chain! Quick!'

They scurried into place, Magnus and Cordelia catching Geoff's hands, Cordelia holding Gwen's hand and Magnus holding Rod's.

Just to be sure, Rod grabbed Father Al's arm. 'What's this all about?'

'Just a precaution. Do you know what to do when you see your fetch?'

'No.'

Father Al nodded. 'Good.'

Then the doorway was filled, and Gwen's exact double stepped into the room.

Well, not exact – her hair was darker, and her lips not as full – but it was unmistakably her.

The 'real' Gwen held out the baby. 'Here is thy bairn.'

The woman gave a little cry, and leaped to scoop the child out of Gwen's arms. She cuddled it to her, crooning to it in the same tones Gwen used.

'My thanks.'

Rod looked up.

The hair swept the shoulders, and he wore a jawline beard and close-clipped moustache – but it was Rod's face behind all the hair. 'I give thee *greatest* thanks, for the lives of my babe, and my King.'

Then Lord Kern's face darkened, and he bellowed, 'What dost thou here, what dost thou here? Seekest thou mine end? Get thee hence! Get thee gone!'

And the scene exploded into a riot of colour.

Swarming colours, sliding into one another and back out, wavering and flowing all about him. Rod couldn't see anything else; he was floating in a polychrome void; but he could feel the pressure of Magnus's hand within his, and Father Al's arm. And he felt yearnings and longings in different directions, like unseen hands trying to pull him five ways at once; but one was stronger than the others, and pulled him harder. He moved toward it; it was the direction Magnus's hand was pulling in, anyway. Gregory, he realized – baby Gregory, calling Mama home. And Papa, too, of course – but who's really important to an infant, anyway?

Then the colours began to thicken, blending into one another, then separating out again – brown stripes, and multi-hued ones, that coalesced into wooden beams and draperies; white, that bristled into stucco . . .

There was a floor under him. He let go of Magnus and Father Al and shoved against it, levering himself up, feeling dizzy – and gazed around the big room in his own home.

Near the fireplace stood a cradle, with Brom O'Berin bulking over it, scarcely larger than it was, staring.

Gwen scrambled up with a glad cry, and ran to catch up the baby. Brom bellowed in joy and flung his arms around her.

'Uncle Brom!' the children shouted, and piled onto both of them.

'Fess?' Rod muttered, not quite believing it.

'Rod!' The voice crackled in his ear; he winced. 'Is it feedback in my circuits? Rod! Are you real?'

'I'll have to admit to it,' Rod muttered. 'Never knew I'd be so glad to hear your tinny voice. You can shut down the transmitter, now.'

'Oh, Papa!' Cordelia scampered up to him, disappointed. 'Just one more time?'

'No! Definitely not! . . . At least, not today.' He turned to see Father Al picking himself up off the floor. 'If you don't mind, Father, I definitely prefer technology.'


# Chapter Twenty-four

Not that they made a practice of it, you understand – but this was one occasion when the Gallowglass family just *had* to have a horse for dinner.

Not that Fess ate as he stood at the end of the table – though he did stick his nose in a feedbag, to keep up appearances. After the mad flurry of greetings and rejoicings, Gwen had quickly parcelled out victuals, and the whole family had sat down to their first meal in a day. Cordelia and Geoff had been packed off to bed (protesting), and the adults (and a bleary-eyed Magnus) sat down to tell Brom (and Fess) their adventures.

'The varlet!' Brom cried, when they were done. 'Thou hadst oped his road to victory, slain his chief enemy, and succoured his son – and what is his thanks? To bid thee get hence!'

'Oh, it's not as bad as all that,' Father Al explained. 'In fact, he probably *was* very grateful – but not so grateful as to be willing to die.'

'To die?' Brom scowled at him. 'What is thy meaning, shavepate?'

'He thought Rod was his fetch.'

Brom stared.

Then he slapped the table and threw back his head, roaring laughter. 'Nay, o' course, then, o' course! What recourse had he, save spells of banishment?'

Rod looked from him to Father Al, then to Gwen; but she shook her head, as lost as he was. 'Somebody wanna let us in on the joke?' Rod said mildly.

'A "fetch",' Father Al explained, 'is your exact double, and seeing it usually means you'll die in the near future. It's also called a co-walker, or in German, a *doppelgänger*.'

'Oh.' Slowly, Rod grinned. 'And in this case, the superstition would've proved true?'

'Well, we'll never know now. But it could be that, with both of you in the same place, that universe might've cancelled both of you.'

'Wasn't room enough in that universe for both of us, huh? Not the original *and* the analogue?'

'Perhaps. At any rate, Lord Kern took no chances. He pronounced the traditional phrases for banishing a fetch – and it worked.'

'Banished me right back to my own universe.' Rod lifted his wineglass. 'For which, I thank him.'

'Exactly,' Father Al agreed. 'No harm or ingratitude intended, I'm sure.'

'Yes, nothing personal. So he gets to keep his universe – but do I get to keep his powers?'

'An interesting point.' Father Al pursed his lips. 'I'm sure he retains them – but the experience of using his powers certainly should've eliminated any blocks you'd unconsciously set up, freeing you to use whatever powers you *do* have – and we'd already established that you had *something* of your own before you went to that universe.'

'Such as the power to manipulate the "magic field"?'

Father Al nodded. 'You may still have that. And from what you've told me of Gramarye, the population here should be providing a very powerful magic field.'

'Then he is a warlock?' Gwen demanded.

Rod shrugged. 'No way to say until I try, dear – and if you don't mind, I'd rather not, just now.'

'Of course,' Father Al reminded him, 'you *could* always draw on the power of one of your analogues . . . '

Rod shuddered. 'I'd *really* rather not. Besides, their powers couldn't work, in this universe.'

Father Al got a faraway look in his eyes. 'Well, in theory . . . '

'Er, some other time,' Rod said nervously. 'Wait till it scabs over, will you, Father? Somehow, I don't think any of us are going to be the same after this.'

He heard Gwen murmur, 'Aye. I fear 'twill mark Gregory for life.'

'Yes,' Rod agreed sombrely. 'Going through this at less than one year of age, the effect could be massive. I just wish we could know what that effect will be.' He turned to her, meeting her gaze with a smile that he hoped was reassuring.

But she was staring, shocked. 'My lord . . . '

Suddenly, it was very silent. Brom frowned, perplexed.

Father Al coughed delicately.

Rod scowled, looking from one to another. 'Would someone please tell me what this is all about!'

'Papa,' Magnus said, round-eyed, 'she did not speak.'

Now *Rod* stared.

Fess cleared his oscillator. 'Ah, Rod – I hate to trouble you at a time like this . . . '

'Oh, no problem!' Rod jumped at the shred of relative sanity. 'Trouble? Yes, yes! Tell me!'

'We do have the matter of the conflict between the Abbot and the Crown . . . '

'Oh, yes! Been meaning to get to that. Thanks for your bulletins, by the way – we *did* receive them. I'll tell you how sometime, when you'll have an hour or so to recover. Your last dispatch said four southern lords had answered the Abbot's call to arms, and three northern barons had risen to the King's banner . . . '

'Precisely. Tuan marched his armies toward the monastery of St Vidicon; the Abbot, hearing of his approach, rode out to meet him with four armies at his back. As of sunset, they were camped in sight of one another, and the King and the Abbot were exchanging dispatches.'

'I'm a little too cynical to think they'll have reached a compromise.' Rod glowered at the floor. 'In fact, I'd bet that the final words of defiance arrived by special messenger before they bedded down for the night.' He glanced out the window at the sun. 'Think we can still get there before the first charge, Fess?'

'We can but try, Rod.'

'Then let's get going.' Rod headed toward the door, calling back to Gwen, 'Sorry, dear – the boss just called.'

Gwen jolted out of her stupor. 'Oh, aye! I shall hold dinner for thee!'

'I *hope* we'll be done by then.' In fact, if they weren't, they'd probably be in the middle of a battle. He bolted out the door, not a moment too soon, with the great black horse on his heels. Clear of the doorway, he swung aboard, and kicked his heels into Fess's sides.

Something jolted behind him. He looked back to see Father Al riding Fess's rump. 'From what little I heard in that one-sided conversation, I thought I had better come along.'

Rod shrugged. 'Suit yourself, Father – but hold on tight; this ride's going to make a broomstick look cosy!'

Fess galloped over the meadow, extruding jet engines from his flanks, leaped into the air, and roared away.

# Chapter Twenty-five

'There they are.' Rod pointed downward.

Ahead and below, the trees gave way to a plain. In its centre two long lines of armoured knights faced each other, two hundred yards apart. As Rod watched, the two lines seemed to lean forward, then began to move. The horses broke into a trot, then a canter . . .

'Hold on! They can't start, now that we're almost there! Buzz 'em, Fess! And make all the noise you can!'

The great black horse stooped like a falcon, and the engines' roar suddenly increased by half. Father Al gasped and held on for dear life.

The black horse shot down the alley between the two lines of charging knights, five feet above the plain, jets racketing. Horses screamed, rearing back and throwing their riders. Other knights reined in their mounts with oaths of dread. Behind them, the soldiers roared with panic and turned about, trying to scramble over each other to get away from the roaring spirit.

Fess climbed up, circling. Rod looked back over his shoulder with a nod of satisfaction. 'That oughta do it. It'll take 'em a while to straighten out *that* mess.' He felt a certain smug pleasure at the thought that, near the Abbot and near each baron, there must be a futurian agent who was gnashing his teeth in frustrated rage at the appearance of the High Warlock.

'We can't do much good up here,' Father Al bellowed in his ear.

'Oh, I'd say we haven't done too badly so far,' Rod yelled back. 'But you're right; the rest of it's gotta be done on foot. Mechanization can only go just so far . . . Bring us in, Fess.'

The great black horse circled around, slowing, its engines lowering in pitch, then dived along the same path as its first run. Hooves jolted on the ground; shock absorbers built into his legs took up the impact. He landed at a full gallop, slowing to a canter, then a trot as he came up to the centre of the line, and King Tuan.

Tuan snapped up his visor, staring in disbelief. Then a huge smile spread over his face, and he spurred his mount forward to grasp Rod by the shoulders. 'Lord Gallowglass! Praise Heaven thou dost live! But how comes this? We had heard that thou wert witched away!'

Rod grinned and slapped him on the shoulder. Then he winced; armour is hard. Something jolted behind him, and he whirled around, to see Father Al running across the plain toward the opposing line – and the Abbot! For a moment, anger shot through Rod. What was this – treachery? Then his anger turned into chagrin. Of course, he couldn't blame the man for adhering to the side he was sworn to.

'Who was that monk?' Tuan demanded. 'And how wast thou ensnared in sorcery, with thy wife and bairns? Where hast thou been? How comest thou back? Nay, tell me who ensorcelled thee, who doth command those wretches in my dungeons, and I will turn these knights and men upon him!'

Rod grinned and held up a hand. 'One question at a time, Your Majesty, I beg you! But I'm very gratified by your welcome.'

'Thou dost not know how sorely we have needed thee. But what of the Lady Gwendylon and thy little ones?'

'Returned with me, and all well. As to the rest of it . . . Well, it's quite a story, and I think it'd be a little easier to understand if I told it to you straight through, from beginning to end. Let's let it wait a while, shall we?'

'It seems we must,' Tuan said reluctantly, 'for there is this boiling coil to consider. Thou hast stopped the beginning of this battle, High Warlock – but I think that thou canst not prevent its end.'

'It's worth a try, though, isn't it? Reconciliation is always possible.'

'An thou sayest it, I will try.' Tuan shook his head. 'But there have been harsh words spoke, Lord Warlock, and I fear it hath gone beyond all hope of healing.'

'You're probably right – but I'd like a chance to prove it to myself.' Rod turned about. 'Let's call for a parley.'

But they would have to wait. Across the field, Father Al stood beside the Abbot's horse, and the Abbot stared down at a parchment in his hand. Even across the distance, their voices carried.

'The *Pope*?' the Abbot cried, in shock and dismay. 'Nay, but surely he is legend!'

'Thou knowest he is not,' Father Al replied, politely but firmly. 'Thou dost know how long the line of Peter did persevere, and know within thee that some few centuries' time would not obliterate it.'

The Abbot lowered the parchment with a shaking hand. 'And yet I think it cannot be. What proof have I that this is real, or that the Seal is genuine?'

'Thou hast seen it in thy books, Lord Abbot. Dost thou truly doubt its authenticity?'

They locked gazes for a moment; then the Abbot's face clouded with doubt. 'Nay, not truly so. Yet for five long centuries, the

Vatican hath forgot our presence here. How is't that, now, only *now*, do they deign to notice us, and then only to command?'

'This was a grievous omission,' Father Al admitted. 'Yet, did the founder of this branch of our Order seek to notify the Vatican of his intentions, or his presence here? And canst thou truly say that thou, or any of thy predecessors, have attempted to renew the contact? And tell me not that thou couldst not have done so; I have met thy monks.'

The Abbot locked gazed with him, still trembling. Then, slowly, he nodded. 'Nay, I must own there is omission on both sides. Yet how doth it chance now, when — *interference* is calamitous, that it doth come?'

Now Father Al's face softened into rueful sympathy. 'Milord — thou art a Cathodean; thou dost know of Finagle.'

The Abbot folded. 'Aye, certes, certes! "When the results will be most frustrating . . . " Aye, aye.' He sighed, straightening in his saddle. 'Well, we must adapt to these vicissitudes, so that we can turn perversity back upon itself, must we not? Therefore, tell to me, Father, what His Holiness doth, through thee, command.'

'If we might have converse aside, Milord?'

'If we must, we must.' The Abbot climbed down from his mount, his breastplate and helm suddenly incongruous atop a monk's robe. They stepped out into the plain, between the two armies, muttering in low voices.

Tuan frowned. 'Who is this shave-pate thou hast brought to our midst, Lord Warlock?'

'An honest man, and a goodly,' Rod said promptly. 'If it weren't for him, I'd still be . . . where I was. Or dead.'

Tuan nodded. ''Tis warrant enough. Yet goodly or not, in this fell broil, thou canst not be assured that he will not now turn against thee.'

'No,' Rod said slowly, 'I can't.'

'As I thought.' Tuan squared his shoulders and sat straighter on his mount. 'Well, we'll learn it presently. They do come, to parley.' He touched his spurs to his horse's side, and rode out to meet the Lord Abbot, who was pacing toward him. Fess trotted after him. Tuan swung down to stand beside the Abbot — a good touch, Rod thought. There was no hope of reconciliation if you insisted on looking down at your opponent. Accordingly, he dismounted, too.

'Well, Milord Abbot,' Tuan said, 'Heaven hath interceded,

and aborted this battle when all mortals would have thought 'twas far too late. May we not now discover some fashion of preserving this gift of peace, thou and I?'

The Abbot was pale and drawn, but his lips were tight with resolution. 'An thou dost wish it, Majesty, I am not loath to attempt it. Yet we must consider deeply.'

'I will,' Tuan promised. 'Say on.'

The Abbot took a deep breath. 'We must consider that the Church and State must needs be separate in their powers and functions.'

Tuan blinked.

Then slowly, he inclined his head. 'Even as thou sayest, Milord. Reluctantly I do admit it; but we must agree to the principle. We cannot claim authority in matters spiritual.'

The *Abbot* blinked, this time; he hadn't been expecting quite so gracious a response to his about-face. 'Ah – I own to great joy to hear Your Majesty speak so. Accordingly, following from this principle, we must own that Holy Mother Church can claim no authority in the distribution of State funds.'

Tuan stood, expressionless, still.

Then he nodded slowly. 'Even as thou sayest, Milord; yet I would hope that we may rely on your good counsel in this matter, especially as regards those areas within our domain whose needs are not adequately met.'

'Why – certes, certes!' the Abbot cried, startled. 'My counsel is thine, whenever thou dost wish it! Yet . . . ' His face darkened. 'In like fashion, Majesty, we must insist on the authority of Holy Mother Church to appoint her priests to her own parishes!'

Tuan nodded. 'Of this, the Queen and I have spoken at some length, Lord Abbot; thou wilt comprehend that, to us, 'tis sore trial to give up such power.'

The Abbot's face hardened – reluctantly, Rod thought.

'Yet,' Tuan went on, 'when we consider our adherence to the principle of separation that thou hast enunciated – why, there can be no question. The appointments of clergy must rest within thy hands; henceforth, we wish naught to do with such.'

The Abbot stared, speechless.

'We would ask that thou be mindful of thy pledge,' Tuan said, somewhat severely, 'to inform us where and when aid to the poor is lacking, and to bring to our notice any devices for the better relief of the indigent that thou dost encompass!'

'With all my heart!' cried the Abbot. 'Be assured, I shall advise thee of all good knowledge we gain, and all ideas we may devise! Indeed, I shall set my brethren to meditating upon such means as soon as I am arrived again at mine abbey!'

'Oh, come, 'tis not needful!' Tuan protested. 'Still, an thou wouldst . . . '

There was more of it, in the same vein; in fact, they virtually swore to a mutual crusade against injustice and poverty right there.

And, after the Abbot had disappeared within his own ranks, wobbling with relief and fairly glowing with good intentions, Tuan rounded on Rod. 'Now, warlock! By what wizardry hast thou brought about *this* seachange?'

'Why, I had nothing to do with it,' Rod said virtuously, 'except to bring along Father Uwell – and you wouldn't expect *him* to tell, would you?'

'All right, Father, let's have it,' Rod shouted over the roar of Fess's jets.

'Oh, come now!' Father Al roared back. 'Can't I claim a professional privilege?'

'You showed him that writ from the Pope, didn't you? And he *did* recognize the signature!'

'No, but he knew the Seal. Beyond that, all I did was explain the Holy Father's policy on relations between Church and State.'

'Which he proceeded to quote, chapter and verse.' Rod nodded. 'Even so, I wouldn't've expected him to cave in *that* quickly. How'd you do it?'

Father Al shrugged. 'Probably shock, mostly. They haven't heard from Rome in more than five hundred years.'

# Chapter Twenty-six

Finally, he was able to close the bedroom door (an innovation, on Gramarye) and shuck off his doublet. 'What's the matter with the kids?'

'Why, naught, I should think,' Gwen answered from the pillow. 'They have been perfectly behaved, all afternoon!'

'That's what I mean. What's wrong with them?'

'Oh.' She rolled over on her side with a cat-smile. 'They do fear thou'lt hear their thoughts.'

'Oh.' Rod grinned. 'So they can't even think about being naughty, huh? Well, I do sort of hear them – but so far, it's only a mutter in the background. Of course, I haven't been trying.' He stripped off his hose and slipped into bed.

'Thou'st forgot thy nightshirt,' Gwen murmured.

'I haven't forgotten anything.' Rod reached out, caressing; she gasped. 'Hmmmm, yes, just as I remembered. Sure that's all that was bothering them?'

'That, and the memory of thine aspect as thou slew the Duke.' She shuddered. ''Twould shake a grown man, let alone a child.'

'Hmm, yes.' Rod frowned. 'I'd like to say I'd never even try to do that again, dear – but you know occasions are bound to arise.'

'They are indeed.' Her voice was hushed; she cuddled close. 'I doubt not thou'lt be enforced to draw on such powers again.'

'If I can,' he agreed. 'And if I do, dear – well, I hate to say it, but, as wife, you sort of have signed on for the job of keeping me sane while I do it, of being my link with who I really am.'

She only smiled, but her words murmured inside his mind: *Have I not always done so?*

He grinned, and agreed, his words wrapping themselves in her mind, while his arms wrapped her in a much closer, much warmer embrace than she'd ever known.

# The
# Warlock
# Enraged

# Chapter One

*For some time now, I've been getting worried about the steadily increasing number of hopeful historians on this Isle of Gramarye. There weren't any when I came here – none that I was aware of, anyway. Then Brother Chillde started keeping his chronicles, and, first thing I knew, there were five more just like him. Not that this is all bad, of course – Gramarye'll be much better off if it has an accurate record of its history. What bothers me is that each one of these young Thucydideses is conveniently forgetting all the events that make his own side look bad, and definitely overdoing it more than a bit, about the happenings that make his side look good. I'm mostly thinking of the Church here, of course, but not exclusively – for example, I know of one young warlock who's taken to keeping a diary, and a country lord's younger son who's piling up an impressive number of journals. So, in an effort to set the record straight, I'm going to set down my version of what happened. Not that it'll be any more objective, of course; it'll at least be biased in a diff—*

''Tis *my* place, 'Delia!'

'Nay, Geoffrey, thou knowest 'tis not! This end of the shelf is mine, for the keeping of my dolls!'

''Tis not! I've kept my castle there these several weeks!'

Rod threw down his quill in exasperation. After three weeks of trying, he'd finally managed to get started on his history of Gramarye – and the kids had to choose this moment to break into a quarrel! He glared down at the page . . .

And saw the huge blot the quill had made.

Exasperation boiled up into anger, and he surged out of his chair. 'Delia! Geoff! Of all the idiotic things to be arguing about! Gwen, can't you . . . '

'Nay, I cannot!' cried a harried voice from the kitchen. 'Else thou'll have naught but char for thy . . . Oh!' Something struck with a jangling clatter, and Rod's wife fairly shrieked in frustration. 'Magnus! How oft must I forbid thee the kitchen whiles I do cook!'

'Children!' Rod shouted, stamping into the playroom. 'Why'd I ever *have* 'em?'

'Di'n't, Papa.' Three-year-old Gregory peeked over the top of an armchair. 'Mama did.'

'Yeah, sure, and I was just an innocent bystander. Geoffrey! Cordelia! *Stop* it!'

He waded into a litter of half-formed clay sculptures, toys, and pieces of bark twisted together with twigs and bits of straw that served only to those below the age of thirteen. 'What a mess!' It was like that every day, of course. 'Do you realize this room was absolutely spotless when you woke up this morning?'

The children looked up, startled, and Cordelia objected, 'But that was four hours ago, Papa.'

'Yeah, and you must've really worked hard to make a mess like this in so short a time as that!' Rod stepped down hard – into a puddle of ochre paint. His foot skidded out from under him; he hung suspended for a split second, arms thrashing like the wings of a dodo trying to fly; then his back slammed down to the floor, paralysing his diaphragm. For an instant of panic, he fought for breath, while Cordelia and Geoffrey huddled back against the wall in fright.

Then Rod's breath hissed in and bounced back out in a howl of rage. 'You little *pigs*! Can't you even clean up after yourselves!'

The children shrank back, wide-eyed.

Rod struggled to his feet, red-faced. 'Throwing garbage on the floor, fighting over a stupid piece of shelf space – and to top it off, you had the gall to *talk back*!'

'We didn't . . . We . . . '

You just did it *again*!' Rod levelled an accusing forefinger. 'Whatever you do, don't contradict me! If I say you did it, you *did* it! And don't you *dare* to say you didn't!'

He towered over them, a mountain of wrath. 'Naughty, *stupid*, asinine brats!'

The children hugged each other, eyes huge and frightened.

Rod's hand swept up for a backhanded slap.

With a crack like a pistol shot, big brother Magnus appeared in front of Cordelia and Geoffrey, arms outspread to cover them. 'Papa! They didn't mean to! They . . . '

'Don't try to tell me what they were doing!' Rod shouted.

The eleven-year-old flinched, but stood up resolutely against his father's rage – and that made it worse.

'How *dare* you defy me! You insolent little— '

'Rod!' Gwen darted into the room, wiping her hands on her apron. 'What dost thou?'

Rod whirled, forefinger stabbing at her. 'Don't you even *try* to speak in their defence! If you'd just make your children toe the line, this wouldn't happen! But, oh no, you've got to let them do whatever they want, and just scold them, and that's only when their behaviour's *really* atrocious!'

Gwen's head snapped back, stung. 'Assuredly, thou'rt scarce mindful of what thou sayest! 'Tis ever *thou* who dost plead leniency, when I do wish to punish . . . '

'Sure, when!' Rod glared, striding towards her. 'But for the thousand and one things they do that deserve spanking, and you let them off with a scold? Use your head, woman – if you can!' His gaze swept her from head to toe, and his lip lifted in a sneer.

Gwen's eyes flared anger. ''Ware, husband! Even to thine anger, there doth be a boundary!'

'Boundaries! Limits! That's all you ever *talk* about!' Rod shouted. '"Do this! Do that! You *can't* to this! You *can't* do that!" Marriage is just one big set of limits! Will you ever— '

'Peace!' Magnus darted between them, holding out a palm towards each. 'I prithee!' His face was white; he was trembling. 'Mother! Father! I beg thee!'

Rod snarled, swinging his hand up again.

Magnus stiffened; his jaw set.

Rod swung, with his full weight behind it . . .

. . . And shot through the air, slamming back against the wall.

He rolled to his feet and stood up slowly, face drained of colour, rigid and trembling. 'I told you never to use your "witch powers" on me,' he grated, 'and I told you why!' He straightened to his full height, feeling the rage swell within him.

Geoffrey and Cordelia scurried to hide behind Gwen's skirts. She gathered Magnus to her, but he kept his face towards his father, terror in his eyes, trembling, but determined to protect.

Rod stared at them, all united against him, ready to pick him up with their magic and hurl him into his grave. His eyes narrowed, pinning them with his glare; then his eyes lost focus as he reached down inside himself – deep down, reaching across an abyss – to the psi powers that had lain so long dormant, but which had been awakened by the projective telepathy of Lord Kern, in another universe, one in which magic worked. His powers weren't as readily accessible as his family's; he couldn't work magic just by willing it, as easily as thinking, but once he'd drawn them up, his were at least as great as theirs. He called those powers up now, feeling their strength build within him.

'Mother,' came Magnus's voice, across a huge void, 'we must— '

'Nay!' Gwen said fiercely. 'He is thy father, whom thou dost love – when this fit's not on him.'

What did that mean! The powers paused in their building . . .

A smaller figure entered his blurred field of vision, to the side and a little in front of the family group, gazing up at him, head tilted to the side – three-year-old Gregory. 'Daddy is'n' there,' he stated.

That hit Rod like a bucketful of cold water; the complete, calm, sanity of the child's tone – so open, so reasonable – and the totally alien quality of the words. His eyes focused in a stare at his youngest son, and fear hollowed his vitals – fear, and a different anger under it; anger at the futurians who had kidnapped him and the rest of his family away from this child while Gregory was still a baby. The desertion, Rod feared, had totally warped the boy's personality, making him quiet, indrawn, brooding, and sometimes, even weird. His gaze welded to Gregory's face, his fear for Gregory burying his anger at the rest of the family; it ebbed, and was gone.

'Who's not there?' he whispered.

'Lord Kern,' Gregory answered, 'that Daddy like thee, in that Faerie Gramarye thou talk'st of.'

Rod stared at him.

Then he stepped closer to the boy. Magnus took a step towards Gregory, too, but Rod waved him away impatiently. He dropped to one knee, staring into the three-year-old's eyes. 'No . . . no, Lord Kern isn't anywhere – except, maybe, in his own universe, that Faerie Gramarye. But why should you think he was?'

Gregory cocked his head to the other side. 'But didst thou not, but now, reach out to touch his mind with thine own, to draw upon his powers?'

Rod just gazed at the boy, his face blank.

'Gregory!' Gwen cried in anguish, and she took a step towards him, then drew back for Rod still knelt staring at the child, his face blank.

Then he looked up at Gwen, with an irritated frown. 'What am I – a bear? Or a wolf?' He raked the children with his glare. 'Some kind of wild animal?'

They stared back at him, eyes huge, huddled together.

His face emptied again. 'You think I am. You really think I am, don't you?'

They stared back, wordlessly, eyes locked on him.

He held still, rigid.

Then he swung up to his feet, turning on his heel, and strode to the door.

Cordelia darted after him, but Gwen reached out and caught her arm.

Rod paced out into the bleakness of a day veiled by clouds. A chill wind struck at him, but he didn't notice.

Rod finally came to a halt at the top of a hill, a mile from home. He stood, staring down at the broad plain below, not really seeing it. Finally, he sank down to sit on the dry grass. His thoughts had slowed in their turmoil as he walked; now, gradually, they sank away, leaving a blank in his mind. Into that, a niggling doubt crept. Softly, he asked, 'What happened, Fess?'

The robot-horse answered, though he was a mile away in the stable. Rod heard him through the earphone embedded in his mastoid process, behind his ear. 'You lost your temper, Rod.'

Rod's mouth twitched with impatience. The robot's horse body might be a distance away in the stable, but the old family retainer could see into him as well as if they were only a foot apart. 'Yes, I do realize that much.' The microphone embedded in his maxillary, just above the teeth, picked up his words and transmitted them to Fess. 'But it was more than simple anger, wasn't it?'

'It was rage,' Fess agreed. 'Full, thorough, open wrath, without any restraints or inhibitions.'

After a moment, Rod asked, 'What would have happened if my family hadn't been able to defend themselves so well?'

Fess was silent. Then he said, slowly, 'I would hope that your inborn gentleness and sense of honour would have protected them adequately, Rod.'

'Yes,' Rod muttered. 'I would hope so, too.'

And he sat, alone in his guilt and self-contempt, in silence. Even the wind passed him by.

Quite some while later, cloth rustled beside him. He gave no sign of having heard, but his body tensed. He waited, but only silence filled the space of the minutes.

Finally, Rod spoke, 'I did it again.'

'Thou didst,' Gwen answered gently. Her voice didn't blame – but it didn't console, either.

Something stirred within Rod. It might have risen as anger, but that was burned out of him, now. 'Been doing that a lot lately, haven't I?'

Gwen was silent a moment. Then she said, 'A score of times, mayhap, in the last twelvemonth.'

Rod nodded, 'And a dozen times last year, and half-a-dozen the year before – and two of those were at the Abbot, when he tried his schism.'

'And a third with the monster which rose from the fens . . . '

Rod shrugged irritably. 'Don't make excuses for me. It still comes down to my losing my temper with you and the kids, more than with anyone else – and for the last three months, I've been blowing up about every two weeks, haven't I?'

Gwen hesitated. Then she answered, 'None so badly as this, my lord.'

'No, it never has been quite as bad as this, has it? But every time, it gets a little worse.'

Her answer was very low. 'Thou hast offered hurt to us aforetime . . . '

'Yes, but I've never actually tried it, have I?' Rod shuddered at the memory and buried his head in his hands. 'First, I just threw things. Then I started throwing them without using my hands. Today, I would've thrown Magnus – if Gregory hadn't interrupted in time.' He looked up at her, scowling. 'Where in Heaven's name did you get that boy, anyway?'

That brought a hint of smile. 'I did think we had, mayhap, borne him back from Tir Chlis, my lord.'

'Ah, yes!' Rod stared out over the plain again. 'Tir Chlis, that wonderful, magical land of faeries and sorcerers, and – Lord Kern.'

'Even so,' Gwen said softly.

'My other self,' Rod said bitterly, 'my analogue in an alternate universe – with magical powers unparalleled, and a temper to match.'

'Thou wert alike in many ways,' Gwen agreed, 'but temper was not among them.'

'No, and witch powers weren't either – but I learned how to "borrow" his wizardry, and it unlocked my own powers, powers that I'd been hiding from myself.'

'When thou didst let his rage fill thee,' Gwen reminded gently.

'Which seems to have also unlocked my own capacity for wrath; it wiped out the inhibitions I'd built up against it.'

'Still – there were other inhibitions that thou didst learn to lay aside, also.' Gwen touched his hand, hesitantly.

Rod didn't respond. 'Was it worth it? OK, so I had been psionically invisible; nobody could read my mind. Wasn't that better than this rage?'

'I could almost say the sharing of our minds was worth the price of thy bouts of fury,' Gwen said slowly, 'save that . . . '

Rod waited.

'Thy thoughts grow dim again, my lord.'

Rod only sat, head bowed.

Then he looked up. 'I'm beginning to hide myself away from you again?'

'Hast thou not felt it?'

He stared into her eyes; then he nodded. 'Is that any surprise? When I can't trust myself not to explode into wrath? When I'm beginning to feel as though I'm some sort of subhuman beast? Sheer shame, woman!'

'Thou art worthy of me, my lord.' Her voice was soft, but firm, and so was her hand. 'Thou art worthy of me, and of my children. I' truth, we are fortunate to have thee.' Her voice shook. 'Oh, we are blessed!'

'Thanks.' He gave her hand a pat. 'It's good to hear . . . Now convince me.'

'Nay,' she murmured, 'that I cannot do, and thou'lt not credit what I say.'

'Or even what you do.' Rod bowed his head, and his hand tightened on hers. 'Be patient, dear. Be patient.'

And they sat alone in the wind, not looking at each other, two people very much in love but very much separated, clinging to a thin strand that still held them joined, poised over the drop that fell away to fallow lands below.

Magnus turned away from the window with a huge sigh of relief. 'They come – and their hands are clasped.'

'Let me see, let me see!' The other three children shot to the window, heads jammed together, noses on the pane.

'They do not regard one another,' Cordelia said dubiously.

'Yet their hands are clasped,' Magnus reminded.

'And,' Cordelia added, troubled, 'their thoughts are dark.'

'Yet their hands are clasped. And if their thoughts are dark, they are also calm.'

'And not all apart,' Gregory added.

'Not *all* – not quite,' Cordelia agreed, but with the full, frank scepticism of an eight-year-old.

'Come away, children,' a deep voice bade them, 'and do not leap upon them when they enter, for I misdoubt me an they'd have much patience now with thy clasping and thy pulling.'

The children turned away from the window, to a foot and a half of elf, broad-shouldered, brown-skinned, and pug-nosed, in a forester's tunic and hose, wearing a pointed cap with a rolled brim and a feather. 'Geoffrey,' he warned.

The six-year-old pulled himself away from the window with a look of disgust. 'I did but gaze upon them, Robin.'

'Indeed – and I know that thou'rt anxious. Yet I bethink me that thy parents have need of some bit more of room than thou'rt wont to accord them.'

Cordelia flounced down onto a three-legged stool. 'But Papa was so angered, Puck!'

'As thou hast told me.' The elf's mouth tightened at the corners. 'Yet thou dost know withal, that he doth love thee.'

'I do not doubt it . . . ' But Cordelia frowned.

Puck sighed and dropped down cross-legged beside her. 'Thou couldst scarce do otherwise, if he did truly become as enraged as thou didst tell.' He turned his head, taking in all four children with one gaze. 'Gentles, do not reprehend; if you pardon, he will mend.'

They didn't look convinced.

'Else the Puck a liar call!' the elf cried stoutly.

The door opened, and the children leaped to their feet. They started to back away, but Puck murmured, 'Softly,' and they held their ground – warily.

But their father didn't look like an ogre as he came in the door – just a tall, dark, lean, saturnine man with a rough-hewn face, no longer young; and he seemed dim next to the red-haired beauty beside him, who fairly glowed, making the question of youth irrelevant. Still, if the children had ever stopped to think about it, they would have remarked how well their parents looked together.

They did not, of course; they saw only that their father's face had mellowed to its usual careworn warmth, and leaped to hug him in relief. 'Papa!' Magnus cried, and 'Daddy!' Geoffrey piped; Cordelia only clung to his arm and sobbed, while Gregory hugged the other arm, and looked up gravely. 'Daddy, thou hast come back again.'

Rod looked into the sober gaze of his youngest, and somehow suspected that the child wasn't just talking about his coming through the door.

'Oh, Papa,' Cordelia sniffled, 'I do like thee so much better when thou'rt Papa, than when you thou'rt Lord Kern!'

Rod felt a chill along his spine, but he clasped her shoulder and pressed her against his hip. 'I don't blame you, dear. I'm sure his children feel the same way.' He looked up over the children's heads, at Puck. 'Thanks, Robin.'

'Now, there's a fair word!' Puck grinned. 'Yet I misdoubt me an thou wilt have more such; for there's one who doth attend thee.' He jerked his head towards the kitchen.

'A messenger?' Rod looked up, frowning. 'Waiting inside the house? Toby!'

A dapper gentleman in his mid-twenties came into the room, running a finger over a neatly trimmed moustache. Hose clung to well-turned calves, and his doublet was resplendent with embroidery. 'Hail, Lord Warlock!'

Gwen's face blossomed with a smile, and even Rod had to fight a grin, faking a groan. 'Hail, harbinger! What's the disaster?'

'Nay, for once, the King doth summon thee whiles it's yet a minor matter.'

'Minor.' The single word was loaded with scepticism. Rod turned to Gwen. 'Why does that worry me more than his saying, "Emergency"?'

''Tis naught but experience,' Gwen assured him. 'Shall I company thee?'

'I'd appreciate it,' Rod sighed. 'If it's a "minor" matter, that means social amenities first – and you know how Catharine and I don't get along.'

'Indeed I do.' Gwen looked quite pleased with herself. Catharine the Queen may have spread her net for Rod, but it was Gwen who had caught him.

Not that Catharine had done badly, of course. King Tuan Loguire had spent his youth as Gramarye's most eligible bachelor, and it must be admitted that Rod had been a very unknown quantity.

Still was, in some ways. Why else would Gwendylon, most powerful witch in circulation, continue to be interested in him?

Rod looked up at Puck. 'Would you mind, Merry Wanderer?'

The elf sighed and spread his arms. 'What is time to an immortal? Nay, go about the King's business!'

'Thanks, sprite.' Rod turned back to Gwen. 'Your broom, or mine?'

Gwen bent over the hanging cradle swathed in yards of cloth-of-gold, and her face softened into a tender smile. 'Oh, he is dear!'

Queen Catharine beamed down at the baby. She was a slender blonde with large blue eyes and a very small chin. 'I thank thee for thy praise . . . I *am* proud.'

'As thou shouldst be.' Gwen straightened, looking up at her husband with a misty gaze.

Rod looked around, hoping she was gazing at someone else. On second thought, maybe not . . .

Catharine raised a finger to her lips and moved slightly towards the door. Rod and Gwen followed, leaving the child to its nanny, two chambermaids, and two guards.

Another two stood on either side of the outer doorway, under the eagle eye of the proud father. One reached out to close the door softly behind them. Rod looked up at King Tuan, and nodded. 'No worries about the succession now.'

'Aye.' Gwen beamed. 'Two princes are a great blessing.'

'Well, I can think of a few kings who would've argued with that.' Rod smiled, amused. 'Still, I must admit they're outnumbered by the kings who've been glad of the support of their younger brothers.'

'As I trust our Alain shall be.' Tuan turned away. 'Come, let us pass into the solar.' He paced down the hall and into another chamber with a wall of clerestory windows. Rod followed, with the two ladies chattering behind him. He reminded himself that he and Gwen were being signally honoured; none of the royal couple's other subjects had ever been invited into their majesties' private apartments.

On the other hand, if Gwen had been the kind to brag, *they* might not have been invited in, either.

And, of course, there was old Duke Loguire. But that was different; he came under the alias of 'Grandpa'. And Brom

O'Berin; but the Lord Privy Councillor would, of course, have access to the privy chambers.

On the other hand, Rod tried not to be too conscious of the honour. After all, he had known Tuan when the young King was an outlaw; exiled for courting Catharine; and hiding out in the worst part of town, as King of the Beggars – and unwitting party to the forming of a civil war. 'As long as they grow up friends,' he reminded Tuan, 'or as much as two brothers can.'

'Aye – and if their friendship doth endure.' A shadow crossed Tuan's face, and Rod guessed he was remembering his own elder brother, Anselm, who had rebelled against their father, and against Queen Catharine.

'Then must we take great care to ensure their friendship.' Catharine hooked her arm through Tuan's. 'Yet I misdoubt me, my lord, an our guests did come to speak of children only.'

'I'm sure it's a more pleasant subject than whatever he had in mind,' Rod said quickly.

'And 'twould have been cause enow, I do assure thee,' Gwen added.

Catharine answered with a silvery laugh. 'For thou and I, mayhap – but I misdoubt me an 'twould interest our husbands overlong.'

'Do not judge us so harshly,' Tuan protested. 'Yet I must own that there are matters of policy to be discussed.' He sighed, and turned away to a desk that stood beneath the broad windows, with a map beside it on a floor stand. 'Come, Lord Warlock – let us take up less pleasant matters.'

Rod came over, rather reassured; Tuan certainly didn't seem to feel any urgency.

The young King tapped the map, on the Duchy of Romanov. 'Here lies our mutual interest of the hour.'

'Well, as long as it's only an hour. What's our bear of a Duke up to?'

' 'Tis not His Grace,' Tuan said slowly.

Rod perked up; this was becoming more interesting. 'Something original would be welcome. Frankly, I've been getting a bit bored with the petty rebellions of your twelve great lords.'

'Art thou so? I assure thee,' Tuan said grimly, 'I have never found them tedious.'

'What is it, then? One of his petty barons gathering arms and men?'

'I would it were; of that, I've some experience. This, though, is a matter of another sort; for the rumours speak of foul magics.'

'Rumours?' Rod looked up from the map. 'Not reports from agents?'

'I have some spies in the north,' Tuan acknowledged, 'yet they only speak of these same rumours, not of events which they themselves have witnessed.'

Rod frowned. 'Haven't any of them tried to track the rumour to its source?'

Tuan shrugged. 'None of those who've sent word. Yet I've several who have sent me no reports, and mine emissaries cannot find them.'

'Not a good sign.' Rod's frown darkened. 'They might have ridden off to check, and been taken.'

'Or worse,' Tuan agreed, 'for the rumours speak of a malignant magus, a dark and brooding power, who doth send his minions everywhere throughout the north country.'

'Worrisome, but not a problem – as long as all they do is spy. I take it they don't.'

'Not if rumour speaks truly. These minions, look you, are sorcerers in their own right; and with the power they own, added to that which they gather from their sorcerer-lord, they defeat the local knights ere they can even come to battle. Then the sorcerers enthral the knights, with their wives and children, too, and take up lordship over all the serfs and peasants of that district.'

'Not too good a deal for the knights and their families,' Rod mused, 'but probably not much of a difference, to the serfs and peasants. After all, they're used to taking orders – what difference does it make who's giving them?'

'Great difference, if the first master was gentle, and the second was harsh,' Tuan retorted. His face was grim. 'And reports speak of actions more than harsh, from these new masters. These sorcerers are evil.'

'And, of course, the peasants can't do much, against magic.' Rod frowned. 'Not much chance of fighting back.'

Tuan shuddered. 'Perish the thought! For peasants must never resist orders, but only obey them, as is their divinely appointed role.'

What made Rod's blood run cold was that Tuan didn't say it grimly or primly, or pompously, or with the pious air of self-justification. No, he said it very matter-of-factly, as though it were as much a part of the world as rocks and trees and running water, and no one could even think of debating it. How could you argue about the existence of a rock? Especially if it had fallen on your toe . . .

That was where the real danger lay, of course – not in the opinions people held, but in the concepts they knew to be true – especially when they weren't.

Rod shook off the mood. 'So the chief sorcerer has been knocking off the local lordlings and taking over their holdings. How far has his power spread?'

'Rumour speaks of several baronets who have fallen 'neath his sway,' Tuan said, brooding, 'and even Duke Romanov, himself.'

'*Romanov?*' Rod stared, appalled. 'One of the twelve great lords? How could *he* fall, without word of it reaching us?'

'I could accomplish it – and I am no wizard.' Tuan shrugged. ''Tis simplicity – close a ring of iron around his castle under cover of night, then hurl an army 'gainst his barbican, and siege machines against his towers. Invest the castle, and trust to thy ring of knights and men-at-arms to see that not a soul wins free to bear off word.'

Rod shuddered at Tuan's sang-froid. 'But he had a couple of esp— er, witches, guesting in his tower!'

'More than "guesting", as I hear it,' Tuan answered, with a grim smile. 'They were thoroughly loyal to Milord Duke, for he had saved them from the stake and embers. They've been of great service tending to the ill and injured and, I doubt not, gathering information for him.'

Rod frowned. 'They must have been very discreet about it. We make it a practice, in the Royal Coven, not to pry into the minds of anyone except our enemies.'

'Or those who might become so,' Tuan amended. 'Who's to say his witches did more? Nay, once Catharine showed them the way of it, and thou and thy good wife did aid her in forming that band into a battle-weapon, all the lords did learn, and followed suit.'

'And Romanov's witches couldn't give him enough advance warning?' Rod pursed his lips. 'This sorcerer is effective. But speaking of mental eavesdropping, that's a way to check on the rumours. Did you ask any of the Royal Witchforce to try and read Romanov's mind?'

'I did. They could not find him.'

'So.' Rod pursed his lips. 'What minds did they hear, to the north?'

Tuan shrugged. 'Only what should be. The ploughman followed his oxen, the milkmaid coaxed her swain – naught was there to bring alarm, save that the warlock who listened could not find the minds of any knights or barons.'

'How about vile thoughts, from evil sorcerers?'

Tuan turned his head slowly from side to side.

'So.' Rod's gaze strayed back to the map. 'On the face of it, nothing's wrong; it's just that the Duke of Romanov seems to have taken a vacation to parts unknown, with all his aristocratic retainers.'

'Thou dost see why I do suspect.'

Rod nodded. 'Sounds fishy to me, too . . . not that I can't understand why the noble Duke would want to take off for a while, though. I've been feeling a bit too much stress lately, myself . . . Gwen?' He turned, to find Gwen standing near. 'Been listening?'

'I have.' She smiled. 'And I do think thou dost make a great coil of naught.'

'Well, I wouldn't exactly say we're making a lot of fuss.' Rod locked gazes with Tuan. 'Where's the weeping and wailing? The yelling and hair-tearing?'

''Tis even as thou sayest,' Tuan turned to Gwen. 'I do not see great danger here, Lady Gwendylon – only the abuse of witch-power, over those who have it not.'

'And witches ganging up on normals,' Rod added. 'But that can all be cured by even more witches – from the good guys. After all, we have a vested interest in the public's opinion of witches, dear.'

'In truth,' Gwen said firmly, 'and we cannot have the folk afeard that witches will seek to govern by force of magic.'

'Of course not,' Rod murmured, 'especially when every right-thinking individual knows it has to be done by force of arms.'

Tuan frowned. 'How didst thou speak?'

'Er, nothing.' Rod turned to Gwen. 'How about it, dear? A family vacation, wandering towards the north?' When Gwen hesitated, he added, 'I don't really think there's any danger – at least, none that you and I can't handle between us.'

'Nay, surely not,' Gwen agreed, but her brow was still furrowed.

'What, then? The kids? I really don't think they'll mind.'

'Oh, certes they will not! Yet hast thou considered the trials of shepherding our four upon the road?'

'Sure.' Rod frowned. 'We did it in Tir Chlis.'

'I know,' Gwen sighed. 'Well, an thou sayest 'tis for the best, my husband, we shall essay it.'


# Chapter Two

Rod turned the key in the lock, pulled it out, set it in Gwen's palm, and wrapped her hand around it. 'Your office, O Lady of the House.' He studied her face for a second and added gently, 'Don't worry, dear. It'll still be here when you get back.'

'I know,' she sighed, 'yet 'tis never easy to leave it.'

'I know.' Rod glanced back at the house. 'I'll get half-way down the road, and start wondering if I really *did* put out the fire on the hearth.'

'And thou dost, but call it out, and an elf shall bear word to me,' Brom O'Berin rumbled beside them. 'Mere minutes after thou hast uttered it, an elf shall spring out of the inglenook to douse thy hearth – if it doth need.'

'I thank thee, Brom,' Gwen said softly.

The dwarf scowled, becoming more gruff. 'Nay, have no fear for thine house. Elves shall guard it day and night. Ill shall fare the man who doth seek to enter.'

Rod shuddered. 'I pity the footpad Puck catches! So come on, dear – there's nothing to worry about. Here, anyway. Time for the road.' He grasped her waist, and helped her leap to Fess's saddle.

'May we not fly, Papa?' Cordelia pouted. Her hands were clasped behind her back, and a broomstick stuck out from behind her shoulder.

Rod smiled, and glanced at Gwen. She nodded, almost imperceptibly. He turned back to Cordelia. 'As long as you stay near your mother and me – yes.'

Cordelia gave a shout of joy and leaped onto her broom. Her brothers echoed her, drifting up into the air.

'Move out, Old Iron,' Rod murmured, and the great black

robot-horse ambled out towards the road. Rod fell into step beside him, and turned back to wave to Brom.

'A holiday!' Geoffrey cried, swooping in front of him. ''Tis ages since we had one!'

'Yeah – about a year.' But Rod grinned; he seemed to feel a weight lifting off his shoulders. He caught Gwen's hand and looked up at her. 'Confess it, dear – don't you feel a little more free?'

She smiled down at him, brightening. 'I do, my lord – though I've brought my lock and bars along.'

'And I, my ball and chain.' Rod grinned. 'Keep an eye on the links, will you? . . . Magnus! When I said, "Stay near", that meant altitude, too! Come down here right now!'

The tinkers strolled into the village, gay and carefree, smudged and dirty. Their clothes were patched, and the pots and pans hanging from their horse's pack made a horrible clattering.

'This is rather demeaning, Rod,' Fess murmured. 'Additionally, as I have noted, no *real* tinker family could afford a horse.'

'Especially not one fit for a knight. I know,' Rod answered. 'I'll just tell them the last stop was a castle, and the lord of the demesne paid us in kind.'

'Rod, I think you lack an accurate concept of the financial worth of a war-horse in medieval culture.'

'Hey – they had a *lot* of pots.' Rod grinned down at his own primitive publicity agents. 'OK, kids, that's enough. I think they know we're here.'

The four little Gallowglasses slowed their madcap dancing, and gave their pots and pans one last clanging whack with their wooden spoons. 'You spoil *all* the fun, Papa,' Cordelia pouted as she handed him the cookware.

'No, just most of it. Magnus? Geoff? Turn in your weapons, boys. Gregory, you too – ah, a customer!'

'Canst mend this firkin, fellow?' The housewife was plump, rosy-cheeked, and anxious.

Rod took the little pot and whistled at the sight of the long, jagged crack in the cast iron. 'How'd you manage *that* kind of break?'

'My youngest dropped it,' the goodwife said impatiently. 'Canst mend it?'

'Yeah,' Rod said slowly, 'but it'll cost you a ha'penny.'

The woman's face blossomed in a smile. 'I have one, and 'twill be well worth it. Bless thee, fellow!'

Which sounded a little odd, since 'fellow' was a term of semicontempt; but Rod blithely took out a hammer and some charcoal, laid a small fire, and got busy faking. Magnus and Gregory crouched on either side of him, ostensibly watching.

'This is the manner of the crafting of it, Gregory,' big brother Magnus said softly. 'Let thy mind bear watch on mine. The metal's made of grains so small thou canst not see them . . . '

'Molecules,' Rod supplied.

'Aye. And now I'll make these molecules move so fast they'll meld one to another. Yet I must spring them into motion so quickly that their heat will not have time to spread through the rest of the metal to Papa's hands, the whiles he doth press the broken edges together – for we'd not wish to burn him.'

'Definitely not,' Rod muttered.

Gregory watched intently.

So did Rod. He still couldn't quite believe it, as he saw the metal spring into cherry-redness all along the crack, brighten quickly through orange and yellow to near whiteness. Metal flowed.

'Now quickly, cool it!' Magnus hissed, drops of sweat standing out on his brow. 'Ere the heat can run to Papa's hands!'

The glow faded faster than it had come, for Gregory frowned at it, too; this part was simple enough for a three-year-old.

Simple! When only witches were supposed to be telekinetic, not warlocks – and even the best of them could only move objects, not molecules.

But there the pot stood, round and whole! Rod sighed, and started tapping it lightly with the hammer, far from where the crack had been – just for appearances. 'Thanks, Magnus. You're a great help.'

'Willingly, Papa.' The eldest wiped his brow.

'Papa,' Gregory piped up, 'thou dost know that elves do company us . . . '

'Yeah.' Rod grinned. 'Nice to know you're not alone.'

'Truth. Yet I've thought to have them ask for word from their fellows in the north . . . '

'Oh?' Rod tried not to show it, but he was impressed. Three years old, and he'd thought of something Tuan and Rod had both overlooked. 'What did they say?'

'The goodwives no longer call warnings to the Wee Folk ere they empty garbage out upon the ground.' Gregory's eyes were large in his little face. 'They no longer leave their bowls of milk for the elves, by their doors. Each house now hath cold iron nailed up over its door, whether it be a horseshoe or some other form, and hearths go unswept at eventide.'

Rod felt a chill and glanced at a nearby tree, but its leaves were still. 'Well, I guess no housewife there is going to find sixpence in her shoe. What are the elves doing about it?'

'Naught. There is some spell lies o'er the ploughed land there, that pushes against all elfin magic. They have turned away in anger, and flitted to the forests.'

Rod struck the pot a few more times, in silence.

'Is this coil in the north so light as thou hast told us, Papa?' Gregory finally asked.

Rod reflected that, for a three-year-old, the kid had one hell of a good vocabulary. He put down his hammer and faced the child squarely. 'There's no *real* evidence, yet, that it's anything major.'

'But the signs . . . ' Magnus murmured.

'Are not evidence,' Rod answered. 'Not firm evidence – but I'm braced. That's why we're travelling in disguise – so we can pick up any rumours, without letting people know we're the High Warlock and Company.'

'Thou does not wish our presence known, for fear the evil folk will hide till we've gone by?' Magnus asked.

'No, because I don't want to walk into an ambush. Not that I expect to, mind – I just don't want to take any chances.' He gave the pot a last tap and held it up to admire. 'You boys did a good job.'

'We shall ever do our best, for thee,' Magnus responded. 'Papa . . . if thou dost gain this firm evidence that thou speakest of . . . what then?'

Rod shrugged. 'Depends. If it's nothing major, we'll fix whatever's wrong, and go on to the northern coast for a couple of weeks of swimming and fishing. You've never tried swimming in the ocean, boys. Let me tell you, it's very different from the little lake near our house.'

'I shall hope to discover it,' Gregory piped. 'Papa . . . what if the evidence is of great wrongness?'

'Then you three boys will turn right around, and take your

mother and your sister right home,' Rod said promptly.

'And thou . . ?'

'I'm the High Warlock, aren't I?' Rod grinned at them. 'They gave me the title. I've got to live up to it.'

Gregory and Magnus looked at each other, and locked gazes.

'I prithee, my lord, calm your heart,' Gwen eyed him anxiously as she laid the campfire. ''Twas not the forester's fault that we may not hunt.'

'Yeah – but the way he dragged Magnus in, as though he were some kind of criminal!' Rod folded a hand around his trembling fist. 'He should only know how close he came to disaster! Good thing Magnus remembered his disguise.'

''Twas not the child's self-rule that troubled me.' Gwen shuddered. 'My lord, if thou couldst have but seen thine own face . . . '

'I know, I know,' Rod snapped, turning away. 'So it's not surprising he reached toward his knife. But so help me, if he had touched it . . . '

'He would have died,' Gwen said simply, 'and men-at-arms would have caught us on the morrow.'

'Oh, no, they wouldn't,' Rod said grimly. 'They wouldn't've dared touch the High Warlock!'

'Aye – and all the land would have known we ride north.' She sighed. 'I rejoice thou didst throttle thy temper.'

'No, I didn't, and you know it! If you hadn't butted in and taken over, raining thanks and praise on the forester, as though you were a waterfall . . . '

Gwen shrugged. ''Twas naught but his due. A less kind man would have beaten the child, and haled him off to his knight's gaol.'

Rod stared, appalled.

Gwen nodded. 'Oh, aye, my lord. And the law allows it. Nay, more; for this good warden who did find our son, might be censured if his lord did know of his forbearance.'

Rod shuddered. 'I'm glad I let him go, then. But, my lord! It's not as though the boy'd been trying to bring down a deer! All he was after was a rabbit!'

'Even so, the Forest Laws would say 'twas theft,' Gwen reminded him. 'Every hare and goose – nay, each mouse and sparrow – doth belong unto the manor's lord; and to hunt them is to steal!'

'But how do these people *live*?' Rod cupped an empty hand. 'We didn't do badly today, for tinkers – we made a penny and a half! But we had to spend the penny for a chicken, and the half for bread! What would we live on, if nobody broke a pot?'

'The law . . . ' Gwen sighed.

'Well, it won't, for long.' Rod curled the hand into a fist. 'I'm going to have a few words with Tuan, when we get back to Runnymede!'

'Do,' Gwen said softly, 'and thou'lt have proved the worth of this journey, even an we find naught wrong i' the north.'

'I'm afraid that's not very apt to happen.' Mollified, Rod watched her stare at the kindling. It burst into flame, and he sighed. 'I'd better see how the kids are coming along with their foraging.' He stiffened at a sudden thought, staring at her. 'We *are* allowed to gather berries, aren't we?'

Rod sat bolt upright with a hissing-in of breath, staring about him, wide-eyed.

The night breathed all around him, hushed. Far away, crickets and frogs wove counterpoint that darted harmony with the myriad of stars. The land lay deep in peace.

Rod sagged against the prop of his arm, relieved by reality. Adrenalin ebbed, and his hammering heart began to slow. He couldn't even remember the nightmare – only that, vaguely, the face was Lord Kern's.

This had to stop. Somehow, he had to break this spell. Somebody moaned; not surprising, the way he felt.

Then he stiffened, all his attention concentrated on his ears. Whoever had moaned, it hadn't been him.

Then, who . . ?

The sound came again, louder and closer. It wasn't a moan, really – more of a grinding sound. Not moving, Rod murmured, 'Fess?'

'Here, Rod.' Being a robot, Fess never slept. In fact, he scarcely ever powered down.

'Hear anything out of the ordinary?'

'Yes, Rod. The sound is that of rock moving against rock. When the frequency of its repetitions is accelerated, there is discernible Doppler shift . . . '

'Coming, or going?'

'Coming – and rather rapidly, I should— '

Trees at the edge of the meadow trembled, and a huge dark form came into sight. The silhouette was crudely human.

Rod was on his feet and darting over to Fess. He yanked a light out of the pack, aimed it at the dark form, and pressed the tab. 'Gwen!'

Gwen raised her head just as the beam struck the huge figure.

If it was female, it was a caricature. It it had breasts, it also had shoulders like a fullback's and arms like a gorilla's. It did have long fingernails, though – and they glinted dangerously in the actinic glare. Its face was blue. It flinched at the sudden stab of light, lips drawing back in a snarl – revealing fangs.

'Black Annis!' Gwen gasped in horror.

The monster froze for a moment, startled by the beam – and Rod snapped, 'Magnus! Cordelia! Wake the babies and get into the air!'

The elder children snapped out of sleep as though they'd been jabbed, galvanized by Gwen's mental alarm. Geoffrey rolled up, sitting, knuckling his eyes and muttering. '*Not* a baby! Six!' But Gregory just shot straight into the air.

Then the monster roared, charging, and caught up Geoffrey with one roundhouse swipe. He squalled, but in anger, not fright, and wrestled his dagger out of its sheath. But Rod thundered rage, and the monster rose into the air, then slammed down onto his back. Geoffrey jabbed the huge hand with his dagger, and Black Annis howled, dropping him. He shot into the air, while Rod stalked towards the horror. Red haze blurred his vision, obscuring all but Black Annis struggling to its feet in the centre of his field of view. The familiar roaring thundered in his ears, and power thrilled through every vein. One thought filled him, only one – to see the creature torn to bits.

Behind him, though, Gwen retreated, keeping her face towards the monster, pulling Magnus and Cordelia by their hands, along with her.

The monster floundered to its feet and turned towards Rod, its face contorted with hate, claws lifting to pounce; but Rod's arm was raising, forefinger stiffened to focus his powers.

Gwen's eyes narrowed, and her children squeezed their eyes shut.

Black Annis exploded into a hundred wriggling fragments.

Rod roared in rage, cheated of his revenge; but Gwen cried to her two youngest, 'Rise and follow!'

For the wriggling fragments kept writhing and, as they fell to earth, ran leaping away, long-eared and puff-tailed, fleeing back toward the wood.

Rod clamped his jaw and ran after them.

But Gwen was beside him, pacing him on her broomstick, gripping his arm and calling to him through the blood-haze. Distantly through the roaring, he heard her: 'My lord, it was not real! 'Twas a phantom, made of witch-moss!'

That stung through; for 'witch-moss' was a fungus peculiar to this planet, telepathically sensitive. If a projective esper thought hard at a lump of it, it would turn into whatever he or she was thinking about.

Which meant there had to be a projective esper around.

Gwen was tugging at his arm, falling behind. 'Softly, mine husband! Fall back, and wait! If this monster was made o' purpose, 'tis towards the purposer that these conies we've made from it do flee! Yet if that villain doth take sight of thee, he'll flee ere we can seize him!'

'I'll blast him into oxides,' Rod muttered, but sense began to poke through his battle-madness.

'A pile of dust cannot tell us what we wish to know!' Gwen cried, and, finally, Rod began to slow. The master who had made this monster, was nothing; what mattered was the one who'd pulled *his* strings. *That* was the ogre who'd threatened Rod's children. 'Black Annis eats babies,' he muttered, and the rage began to build again.

'Black Annis is an old wives' tale!' Gwen's voice whipped, and stung through to him. 'In Tir Chlis she did truly live, mayhap, but not in Gramarye! Here, she's only crafted out of witch-moss! Here, 'tis a sorcerer who doth scorn babes!'

Rod halted, trembling, and nodded. 'And it's the sorcerer we've got to catch – yes! But to find him, we have to question the minion that sent the monster against us!' His lips pulled back against his teeth. 'That questioning, I think I'll enjoy!'

Gwen shuddered, and implored, 'Hold thyself in check, I prithee! Knowledge is our goal, not joy in cruelty.'

'Just tell me where he is. Who's spotting? . . . Oh. The kids.' He stilled, listening mentally for his children's call – and muttering, 'Fess, to me. When we need to ride, we'll need full speed.'

The great black horse drummed up beside him, just as Cordelia's cry came, 'Here!'

Rod leaped astride Fess, and they tore off through the night. The robot's radar probed the darkened landscape, and Fess hurdled fallen trunks and streams as though he rode a close-clipped steeplechase course. Gwen swooped above the trees; but Fess broke from cover as she began her downward strike.

Her target was a high-walled wagon with a roof. A woman stood in its open door, silhouetted by candlelight. She darted a glance at Gwen, then whirled, to stare first toward the north, and Cordelia, then towards the east, and Gregory, then toward Geoffrey, then Magnus. She darted back inside, slamming the door; but she reappeared at the driver's seat, catching up the reins. Her horses lifted their heads and turned into the meadow, pulling the caravan about . . . And she stared, appalled, at the horde of rabbits who filled the meadow – and the great black horse who thundered up behind them.

Then both her arms snapped out straight, fingers pointing – the rabbits leaped together, melded, coalesced, metamorphosed – and lion, wolf, and bear whirled about, to turn on Rod.

He howled in rage and glee as the blood-haze enfolded him again, obscuring all but the monsters. They were release; they were justification for lashing out with his power. He would blast them; then his path would be clear, to smear the woman over the meadow grass.

The wolf was gaunt, with eyes of fire, impossibly huge. The bear, shambling upright, had a human face; and the lion's mane was flame, its teeth and claws were steel.

Rod hauled on the reins and Fess dug in his hooves, throwing his weight back, ploughing up the meadow in his halt, as Rod rose in the stirrups, stiffened arm spearing out.

The wolf exploded.

Rod's head pivoted deliberately.

The lion's mane expanded, flame sweeping out to envelop its body. But the beast didn't seem to notice; it bounded on towards Rod, roaring.

Rod's eyebrows drew down, his brow furrowing.

The lion's head whipped around in a full turn and whirled spinning away. Fess sidestepped, and the body hurtled on by, to collapse in a writhing heap.

Rod pivoted towards the bear, his sword hissing out of its sheath; then the beast was on him. A great paw slammed against the side of Rod's head. For a moment, he was loose in space, the blackness shot with tiny sparks; then the earth slammed into his back, and his insides knotted, driving the breath out of him. But the blood-haze still filled his sight; he saw Fess rearing up to slam forehooves into the bear's shoulder. It stumbled, but came on, manlike face contorted in a snarl.

Rod clenched his jaw, waiting for breath, and glared at his sword-blade. Flame shot down its tip, billowing outward as though it were a blowtorch with a three-foot blast.

The bear halted, and backed away, snarling.

Rod's diaphragm unkinked, and he drew a laboured breath, then thrust himself to his feet, staggering towards the bear.

It threw itself on him with a roar.

He swung aside, squinting against pain, glaring at it. It flared like magnesium; but it had barely begun its death-howl when its fires flickered, guttered, and went out. Where it had stood, only ashes sifted to the ground.

Rod stood alone in the darkness, swaying, as the haze that filled him darkened, faded, and retreated back within him. He began to realize that a breeze was blowing . . .

Fire.

He'd left a burning corpse. The breeze could spread that flame over all the meadow, and into the woods.

He swung toward the remains of the lion – and saw Gregory floating near it, ten feet away, staring at the charred hulk. Even as Rod watched, bits of it were breaking loose, and moving off through the meadow grass. He turned toward the bear, and saw Geoffrey turning it into a herd of toy horses, which galloped toward the wood.

'We cannot leave such large masses of witch-moss whole,' Gwen's voice said softly behind him, 'or the first old aunt, telling of a frightful tale, will bring it up unwittingly, in some horrible guise.'

'No.' The last of the anger ebbed, and remorse rushed in to fill its place. Rod spoke roughly to counter it. 'Of course you couldn't. What happened to the witch?'

'She fled,' Gwen said simply.

Rod nodded. 'You couldn't follow her.'

'We could not leave thee here, to fight unaided.' Cordelia clung to her mother, watching her father out of huge eyes.

'No.' Rod turned to watch his two youngest dismember the remains of what had been horrors. 'On the other hand, if I hadn't stayed to fight them, you could've just taken them apart, and still had time to follow her.'

Gwen didn't answer.

'Where's Magnus?' Rod sighed.

'He did follow the witch,' Cordelia answered.

Air blew outward with a bang, and Magnus stood beside them. Rod usually found his son's appearances and disappearances unnerving, but somehow, now, it seemed remote, inconsequential. 'She got away?'

Magnus bowed his head. 'She fled into the forest, and I could no longer see her from the air.'

Rod nodded. 'And it would've been foolish for you to try to follow low enough for her to get at you. Of course, if I'd been following on Fess, it would've been another matter.'

Nobody answered.

He sighed. 'How about her thoughts?'

'They ceased.'

Gwen stared down at Magnus. 'Ceased?' She looked up, eyes losing focus for a few seconds; then her gaze cleared, and she nodded affirmation. ''Tis even as he saith. But how . . . ?'

'Why not?' Rod shrugged. 'I was telepathically invisible for years, remember? Sooner or later, somebody was bound to learn how to do that whenever they wanted.'

'My lord,' Gwen said softly, 'I think there is more danger in these northern witches than we had thought.'

Rod nodded. 'And, at a guess, they're better mind readers than we gave them credit for – 'cause they certainly knew we were coming.'

Gwen was silent, digesting that.

Rod shrugged, irritably. 'Oh, sure, it's possible this one sorceress has a hatred for tinkers, especially when they come in families – but, somehow, I doubt that. Conjuring up a Black Annis for the average wanderer is a bit elaborate. No, they've spotted us.'

He straightened his shoulders and clapped his hands. 'All right, so much for our night's adventure! Everybody back to bed.'

The children looked up, appalled.

'Don't worry, Mummy'll give you a sleep spell.' Gwen's lullabies were effective projective telepathy; when she sang, 'Sleep, my child', they really did.

'My lord,' Gwen said softly, 'if they do know of our presence . . . '

'We'd better post sentries. Yes.' Rod sat down cross-legged. 'I'll take first watch. I haven't been sleeping well lately, anyway.'

When the night noises prevailed again, and the only child-sound was deep and even breathing, Rod said softly, 'They're being very good about it – but the fact is, I blew it.'

'But it is distinctly improbable that you could have caught the projective, in any event,' Fess's voice answered him. 'Banished her, certainly – possibly even destroyed her, though that certainly would have been quite dangerous. But attempting to immobilize an esper, without killing her, would be ten times more dangerous.'

Rod frowned. 'Come to think of it, why didn't she just hop the next broomstick?' He had a sudden, vivid vision of Gwen in an aerial dogfight, and shuddered.

'Why leave her caravan, if she did not have to?' Fess countered.

Rod winced. '*That* hurts – that my rage hamstringed things so much that she didn't even have to strain to get away!'

'Still, that is only a blow to your pride,' Fess reminded him. 'The object was accomplished; the danger was banished.'

'Only temporarily,' Rod growled, 'and the next time, it might banish *us*, if I let rage block off my brain again.'

'That is possible,' Fess admitted. 'And the danger must be considered greater, now that there is reason to believe the enemy knows your identities and direction.'

'And can guess our purpose,' Rod finished. 'Yes, we can be sure they'll attack again, and as soon as possible . . . Fess?'

'Yes, Rod?'

'Think it's time yet to send Gwen and the kids home?'

The robot was silent for a moment; then he answered, 'Analysis of available data does not indicate a degree of danger with which your family, as a unit, cannot cope.'

'Thank Heaven,' Rod sighed. 'I don't think they'd be very easy to send home, just now.'

'Your children *have* become intrigued.'

'Children, my eye! It's Gwen I'm worried about – her dander's up!'

Fess was silent.

Rod frowned at the lack of response; then his mouth tightened. 'All right, what am I missing?'

The robot hesitated, then answered, 'I don't think they trust you out alone, Rod.'

# Chapter Three

'We're getting pretty close to the Romanov border now, aren't we?'

'Aye, my lord. 'Tis mayhap a day's journey further.' Gwen was holding up bravely, but she did seem tired.

Rod frowned. 'Look – they know we're coming; there's no point in keeping our disguise. Why're we still walking?'

'To save fright, Papa.' Gregory looked down at his father, from his seat on Fess's pack. 'If the good peasant folk see us flying north, they would surely take alarm.'

Rod stared at his youngest for a moment, then turned to Gwen. 'How old did you say he was? Three, going on *what*?'

But Gwen frowned suddenly, and held up a hand. 'Hist!'

Rod frowned back. 'The same to you.'

'Nay, nay, my lord! 'Tis danger! Good folk come, but flee toward us in full terror!'

Rod's face went neutral. 'What's chasing them?'

Gwen shook her head. 'I cannot tell. 'Tis human, for I sense the presence – yet there's a blank where minds should be.'

Rod noted the plural. 'All right, let's prepare for the worst.' He put two fingers to his mouth, and blasted out a shrill whistle.

Like tandem firecrackers, Magnus and Geoffrey popped out of nowhere, and Cordelia swooped down to hover behind them. 'Why didst thou not but think for us, Papa?' Magnus enquired.

'Because we're up against an enemy that can hear thoughts farther than whistles. All right, kids, we've got to set up an ambush. I want each of you high up in a tree, doing your best imitation of a section of bark. Your mother and I'll take the ground. When the enemy shows up, hit 'em with everything you've got.'

'What enemy, Papa?'

'Listen for yourself. Mama says it's human, but nothing more.'

All four children went glassy-eyed for a moment, then came out of their trances with one simultaneous shudder. ''Tis horrible,' Cordelia whispered. ''Tis there, but – 'tis not!'

'You'll know it when you see it,' Rod said grimly, 'and just in case you don't, I'll think, Havoc! as loudly as I can. Now, scoot!'

They disappeared with three pops and a whoosh. Looking up, Rod spotted three treetops suddenly swaying against the wind, and saw Cordelia soar into a fourth. 'Which side of the road do you want, dear?'

Gwen shrugged. 'Both sides are alike to me, my lord.'

'What do you think you are, a candidate? OK, you disappear to the east, and I'll fade into the left. I keep trying, anyway.'

Gwen nodded, and squeezed his hand quickly before she sped off the road. Leaves closed behind her. Rod stayed a moment, staring north and wondering; then he turned to the underbrush, muttering, 'Head north about ten yards, Fess.'

The robot sprang into a gallop, and almost immediately turned off the road onto Rod's side.

The leaves closed behind him, and Rod turned to face the roadway, peering through the foliage. He knelt, and let his body settle, breathing in a careful rhythm, watching the dust settle.

Then, around the curve of the roadway, they came – a dozen dusty peasants with small backpacks and haunted faces. They kept glancing back over their shoulders. The tallest of them suddenly called out, jerked to a halt. The others hurried back to him, calling over their shoulders to their wives, 'Go! Flee!' But the women hesitated, glancing longingly at the road south, then back at their husbands. The men turned their backs and faced north, toward the enemy, each holding a quarterstaff at guard position, slant-wise across his body. The women stared at them, horrified.

Then, with a wail, one young wife turned, hugging her baby, and hurried away southward. The others stared after her; then, one by one, they began to shoo their children away down the road.

Then the men-at-arms strode into sight.

Rod tensed, thinking, Ready! with all his force.

They wore brown leggings with dark green coats down to midthigh, and steel helmets. Each carried a pike, and a saffron badge gleamed on every breast. It was definitely a uniform, and one Rod had never seen before.

The soldiers saw the peasants, gave a shout, and charged, pikes dropping down level.

Rod thought the word with all his might, as he muttered it to Fess: 'Havoc!'

He couldn't have timed it better. Fess leaped out of the underbrush and reared, with a whinnying scream, just as the last soldiers passed him. They whirled about, alarmed, as did most of their mates – and Rod leaped up on the roadway between peasants and soldiers, sword flickering out to stab through a shoulder, then leaping back out to dart at another footman even as the first screamed, staggering backward. Two soldiers in the middle of the band shot into the air with howls of terror, and slammed back down onto their mates, as a shower of rocks struck steel helmets hard enough to stagger soldiers, and send them reeling to the ground.

Rod threw himself into a full lunge, skewering a third soldier's thigh, as he shouted to the peasants, 'Now! Here's your chance! Fall on 'em, and beat the hell out of 'em!'

Then a pike-butt crashed into his chin and he spun backward, vision darkening and shot through with sparks; but a roar filled his ears and, as his sight cleared, he saw the peasant men slamming into the soldiers, staves rising and falling with a rhythm of mayhem.

Rod gasped, and staggered back toward them; there was no need for killing!

Then another thought nudged through: they needed prisoners, for information. He blundered in among the peasants, took one quick glance at the remains of the mêlée, and gasped, 'Stop! There's no need . . . They don't deserve . . . '

'Thou hast not seen what they've done,' the peasant next to him growled.

'No, but I intend to find out! Look! They're all down, and some of 'em may be dead already! Stand back, and leave them to me!'

A rough hand grasped his shoulder and spun him around. 'I' truth? And who art thou to command, thou who hast not lost blood to these wolves?'

Rod's eyes narrowed. He straightened slowly, and knocked the man's hand away with a sudden chop. It was ridiculous, and really shouldn't have made any difference to anybody – but it would work; it'd get their co-operation. 'I am the High Warlock, Rod Gallowglass, and it is due to my magic and my family's that you men stand here victorious, instead of sprawling as buzzard's meat!'

He didn't have to add the threat; the man's eyes widened, and he dropped to one knee. 'Your pardon, Lord! I . . . I had not meant . . . '

'No, of course you didn't. How could you tell, when I'm dressed as a tinker?' Rod looked around to find all the peasants kneeling. 'All right, that's enough! Are you men or pawns, that you must kneel? Rise, and bind these animals for me!'

'On the instant, milord!' The peasants leaped to their feet, and turned to begin lashing up the soldiers with their own belts and garters. Rod caught the belligerent one by the shoulder. 'How are you called?'

Apprehension washed his face, and he tugged at his forelock. 'Grathum, an it please thee, milord.'

Rod shrugged. 'Whether or not it pleases you, is a bit more important. Grathum, go after the women, and tell them the good news, will you?'

The man stared, realization sinking in. 'At once, your lordship!' And he sped away.

Rod surveyed the knot-tying party and, satisfied everything was well under way with the minimum of vengeful brutality, glanced up at the trees and thought, Wonderful, children! I'm a very proud daddy!

The branches waved slightly in answer. Rod could have bent his mind to it, and read their thoughts in return; but it still involved major effort for him, and he couldn't spare the concentration just now. But he turned toward the underbrush, and thought, Thanks, dear. It was nice to see you throwing somebody else's weight around for a change.

'As long as 'tis not thine, my lord? Thou art most surely welcome!'

Rod looked up, startled – that was her voice, not her mind. Gwen came marching up with the women and the children behind her. Grathum hurried on ahead, face one big apology. 'Ere I could come unto them, milord, thy wife had brought word, and begun their progress back.'

She had obviously run the message on her broomstick; the wives were herding their children silently, with covert glances at her, and the children were staring wide-eyed.

Rod turned back to Grathum. 'Any more of these apes likely to be following you?'

The peasant shook his head. 'Nay, milord – none that we know of. There were more bands – but they chased after others who fled. Only these followed the high road, when we who escaped to it so far as this, were so few.'

'Others who fled?' Rod frowned, setting his fists on his hips. 'Let's try it from the beginning. What happened, Grathum? Start back before you knew anything was wrong.'

'Before . . . ?' The peasant stared at him. ''Tis some months agone, milord!'

'We've got time.' Rod nodded towards the north. 'Just in case you're worried, I've got sentries out.'

Grathum darted quick looks about him, then back at Rod, fearfully. Rod found it unpleasant, but right now, it was useful. 'Several months back,' he prompted, 'before you knew anything was wrong.'

'Aye, milord,' Grathum said, with a grimace. He heaved a sigh, and began. 'Well, then! 'Twas April, and we were shackling our oxen to the ploughs for the planting, and a fellow hailed me from the roadway. I misliked his look — he was a scrawny wight, with a sly look about him — but I'd no reason to say him nay, so I pulled in my ox and strode up to the hedge, to have words with him.'

'"Whose land is this?" he did ask me; and I answered, "Why, o' course, 'tis the Duke of Romanov's; but my master, Sir Ewing, holds it enfeoffed from him."

'"Nay," quoth this wight, "'tis not his now, but the Lord Sorcerer Alfar's — and I hold it enfeoffed from him."

'Well! At this I became angered. "Nay, assuredly thou dost not," I cried. "An thou dost speak such treason, no man would blame me!" And I drew back my fist to smite him.'

Rod's mouth tightened. That sort of fitted in with his overall impression of Grathum's personality. 'And what'd he do about it?'

'Why! He was gone ere I could strike — disappeared! And appeared again ten feet away, on my side of the fence! Ah, I assure thee, then fear did seize my bowels - but I ran for him anyway, with a roar of anger. Yet up he drifted into the air, hauling a thick wand out from his cloak, and struck down at me with it. I made to catch it, but ever did he seem to know where I would grasp next, and ever was his stick elsewhere; and thus did he batter me about the head and shoulders, till I fell down in a swoon. When I came to my senses, he stood over me, crowing, "Rejoice that I spared thee, and used only a wooden rod — nor tossed a ball of fire at thee, nor conjured a hedgehog into thy belly!" Could he do such, milord?'

'I doubt it highly,' Rod said, with a dry smile. 'Go on with your story.'

Grathum shrugged. 'There's little more to tell of that broil. "Be mindful," quoth he, "that thou dost serve me now, not that sluggard Sir Ewing." The hot blood rushed to my face to hear my lord so addressed; but he saw it, and struck me with the wand again. I did ward the blow, but he was behind me on the instant, and struck me from the other side – and I could not ward myself, for that the arm that should have done it, was beneath me. "Be mindful," quoth he again, "and fear not Sir Ewing's retribution; ere the harvest comes, he'll not be by to trouble thee further." Then he grinned like a broad saw, and vanished in a crack of thunder.'

Rod noted that all his junior wizard seemed to have done was teleport and levitate – but he has used them to give him an advantage in a fight!

'This worm of a warlock was fully lacking in honour,' Gwen ground out, at his elbow.

'Totally unethical,' Rod agreed, 'and, therefore, totally self-defeating, in the end. If witches and warlocks went around behaving like *that*, the mobs would be out after them in an instant – and how long could they last then?'

'For ever,' Grathum said promptly, 'or so this Lord Sorcerer and his sorcery-knights do believe. They fear no force, milord, whether it come from peasants or knights.'

The fright in his tone caught at Rod. He frowned. 'You sound as though you're talking from experience. What happened?' Then he lifted his head as he realized what someone like Granthum might have done. 'You *did* report this little incident to Sir Ewing, didn't you?'

'I did.' Grathum bit his lip. 'And I wish that I had not – though it would have made little difference, for each and every ploughman on Sir Ewing's estates told him likewise.'

'The same warlock in each case?'

'Aye; his name, he said, was Melkanth. And there was no report of him, from any other manor; yet each had been so visited by a different warlock or witch. Naetheless, 'twas our Sir Ewing who did rise up in anger and, with his dozen men-at-arms, rode forth to seek out this Melkanth.'

Rod clamped his jaw. 'I take it Sir Ewing found him.'

Grathum spread his hands. 'We cannot think otherwise; for he did not come back. Yet his men-at-arms did; but they wore this livery thou seest on those who pursued us.' He jerked his thumb back over his shoulder at the heap of bound soldiers. 'Aye, they came back, these men that we'd known since childhood; they came back, and told us that Sir Ewing was no more, and that we served His Honour Warlock Melkanth now.'

Rod stared, and Gwen caught at his arm. That jarred Rod

back into contact with reality; he cleared his throat, and asked, 'Anything odd about 'em? The way they looked?'

'Aye.' Grathum tapped next to his eye. ''Twas here, milord – in their gazes. Though I could not say to thee what 'twas that was odd.'

'But it was wrong, whatever it was.' Rod nodded. 'What'd the soldiers do? Stay around to make sure you kept ploughing?'

'Nay; they but told us we laboured for Melkanth now, and bade us speak not of this that had happed, not to any knight nor lord; yet they did not say we could not speak to other peasant folk.'

'So the rumour ran?'

'Aye. It ran from peasant to peasant, till it had come closer by several manors to our lord, Count Novgor.'

Rod kept the frown. 'I take it he's vassal to Duke Romanov.'

'Aye, milord. The Count called up his levies – but scarce more than a dozen knights answered his call; for the others had all marched forth to battle the warlocks who challenged them.'

'Oh, really! I take it rumour hadn't run fast enough.'

Grathum shrugged. 'I think that it had, milord; but such news only angered our good knights, and each marched out to meet the warlock who claimed his land, thinking his force surely equal to the task.'

'But it wasn't.' Rod's lips were thin. 'Because they went out one knight at a time; but I'll bet each one of them ran into this Lord Sorcerer and all his minions, together.'

Grathum's face darkened. 'Could it be so?'

Rod tossed his head impatiently. 'Your peasants have got to stop believing everything you're told, Grathum, and start trying to find out a few facts on your own! . . . Oh, don't look at me like that, I'm as sane as you are! What happened to Count Novgor and his understrength army?'

Grathum shook his head. 'We know not, milord – for fear overtook us, and we saw that, if the sorcerer won, we would be enslaved to fell magic, and our wives and bairns with us. Nay, then we common folk packed what we could carry and sin' that we would not have the chance to fight, fled instead, through the pasture lanes to the roadway, and down the roadway to the High Road.'

'So you don't know who won?'

'Nay, but early the next morning, when we'd begun to march

again, word ran through our numbers – for it was hundreds of
people on the road by then, milord; we folk of Sir Ewing's were
not alone in seeing our only chance to stay free – and word ran
from the folk at the rear of the troupe, to us near the van, that
green-coated soldiers pursued. We quickened our pace, but word
came, anon, that a band of peasants had been caught up by
soldiers, and taken away in chains. At that word, many folk
split away, village by village, down side roads toward hiding. But
when we came to high ground, we looked back, and saw squadrons
of soldiers breaking off from the main host, to march down the side
roads; so we turned our faces to the south, and hurried with Death
speeding our heels – for word reached those of us in the van that the
soldiers had begun slaying those who fought their capture. Then did
we take to a byway ourselves; but we hid, with our hands o'er our
children's mouths, till the soldiers had trooped by, and were gone
from sight; then back we darted onto the High Road, and down
toward the south again. Through the night we came, bearing the
wee ones in litters, hoping that the soldiers would sleep the whiles
we marched; and thus we came into this morning, where thou hast
found us.'

Rod looked up at the sky. 'Let's see, today . . . yesterday . . .
This would be the third day since the battle.'

'Aye, milord.'

'And you, just this little band of you, are the only ones
who made it far enough south to cross the border?'

Grathum spread his hands. 'The only ones on the High Road,
milord. If there be others, we know not of them . . . and had it
not been for thee and thy family, we would not be here either.'
He shuddered. 'Our poor Count Nogvor! We can only pray that
he lives!'

Air cracked outward, and Gregory floated at Rod's eye level,
moored to his shoulder by a chubby hand.

The peasants stared, and shrank back, muttering in horror.

'Peace.' Rod held up a hand. 'This child helped save you from
the sorcerer's soldiers.' He turned to Gregory, nettled. 'What is
it, son? This wasn't exactly a good time.'

'Papa,' said the boy, eyes huge, 'I have listened, and . . . '

Rod shrugged. 'Wasn't exactly a private conversation. What
about it?'

'If this Count Nogvor had won, these soldiers in the sorcerer's
list would not have been marching after these peasant folk.'

The folk in question gasped, and one woman cried, 'But the bairn can scarcely be weaned!'

Rod turned to them, unable to resist a proud smirk. 'You should see him think up excuses not to eat his vegetables. I'm afraid he's got a point, though; I wouldn't have any great hopes for Count Nogvor's victory.'

The peasants sagged visibly.

'But it should be possible to get a definitive answer.' Rod strode forward.

The peasants leaped aside.

Rod stepped up to the bound soldiers. He noticed that one or two were struggling against their ties. 'They're beginning to come to. I think they might know who won.' He reached out to yank a soldier onto his feet, then turned to the peasants. 'Anybody recognize him?'

The peasants stared and, one after another, shook their heads. Then, suddenly, one woman's finger darted out, to point at the soldier on top of the third pile. 'But yonder is Gavin Arlinson, who followed Sir Ewing into battle! How comes he to fight in the service of his lord's foe?'

'Or any of them, for that matter? Still, he'll do nicely as a representative sample.' Rod gave the soldier he was holding a slight push; the man teetered, then fell back down onto his comrades. Rod caught him at the last second, of course, and lowered him the final inch; then he waded through the bound men, to pull Gavin Arlinson onto his feet. He slapped the man's face gently, until the eyelids fluttered; then he called, 'Magnus, the brandy – it's in Fess's pack.'

His eldest elbowed his way through to his father, holding up a flask. Rod took it, noting that nobody seemed to wonder where Magnus had come from. He pressed the flask to Arlinson's lips and tilted, then yanked it back out quickly. The soldier coughed, spraying the immediate area, choked, then swallowed. He squinted up at Rod, frowning.

Just the look of the eyes made Rod shiver. Admittedly, the glassiness of that stare could be due to the head knock he'd received, but the unwavering, unblinking coldness was another matter.

Rod pulled his nerve back up and demanded, 'What happened to Sir Ewing?'

'He died,' the soldier answered, his tone flat. 'He died, as must any who come up against the might of the Lord Sorcerer Alfar.'

Rod heard indignant gasps and muttering behind him, but he didn't turn to look. 'Tell us the manner of it.'

''Tis easily said,' the soldier answered, with full contempt. 'He and his men marched forth to seek the warlock Melkanth. They took the old track through the forest, and in a meadow, they met him. But not Melkanth alone – his brother warlocks and sister witches, all four together, with their venerable Lord, the Sorcerer Alfar. Then did the warlocks and witches cause divers monsters to spring out upon Sir Ewing and his men, while the witches cast fireballs. A warlock appeared hard by Sir Ewing, in midair, to stab through his visor and hale him off his mount. Then would his soldiers have fled, but the Lord Sorcerer cried out a summoning, and all eyes turned toward him. With one glance, he held them all. Then did he explain to them who he was, and why he had come.'

'I'll bite.' Rod gave him a sour smile. 'Who is he?'

'A man born with Talent, and therefore noble by birth,' the soldier answered tightly, 'who hath come to free us all from the chains in which the twelve Lords, and their lackeys, do hold us bound.'

'What chains are these?' Rod demanded. 'Why do you need freeing?'

The soldier's mouth twisted with contempt. 'The "why" of it matters not; only the fact of enslavement's of import.'

'That, I can agree with – but not quite the way you meant it.' Rod turned to his wife. 'I call it hypnosis – instant style. What's your diagnosis?'

'The same, my lord,' she said slowly. ''Tis like to the Evil Eye with which we dealt these ten years gone.'

Rod winced. 'Please! Don't remind me how long it's been.' He submitted to a brief but intense wave of nostalgia, suddenly feeling again the days when he and Gwen had only had to worry about one baby warlock. And, of course, a thousand or so marauding beastmen . . .

He shook off the mood. 'Can you do anything about it?'

'Why . . . assuredly, my lord.' Gwen stepped up to him, looking directly into his eyes. 'But dost thou not wish to attempt it thyself?'

Rod shook his head, jaw clamped tight. 'No, thanks. I managed to make it through this skirmish without rousing my temper – how, I'm not sure; but I'd just as soon not tempt fate. See what you can do with him, will you?'

'Gladly,' she answered, and turned to stare into the soldier's eyes.

After a minute, his lips writhed back from his teeth. Rod glanced quickly at the thongs that held his wrists, then down to his lashed ankles. His muscles strained against the leather, and it cut into his flesh, but there was no sign it might break. He looked back up at the soldier's face. It had paled, and beads of sweat stood out on his forehead.

Suddenly, he stiffened, his eyes bulging, and his whole body shuddered so violently that it seemed it would fall apart. Then he went limp, darting panicked glances about him, panting as though he'd run a mile. 'How . . . Who . . . '

Gwen pressed her hands over her eyes and turned away. Rod looked from her to the soldier and back. Then he grabbed Grathum and shoved the soldier into his arms. 'Here! Hold him up!' He leaped after his wife, and caught her in his arms. 'It's over, dear. It's not there anymore.'

'Nay . . . I am well, husband,' she muttered into his doublet. 'Yet that was . . . distasteful.'

'What? The feel of his mind?'

She nodded, mute.

'What was it?' Rod pressed. 'The sense of wrongness? The twisting of the mind that had hypnotized him?'

'Nay – 'twas the lack of it.'

'*Lack?*'

'Aye.' Gwen looked up into his eyes, a furrow between her eyebrows. 'There was no trace of any other mind within his, my lord. Even with the beastmen's Evil Eye, there was the sense of some other presence behind it – but here, there was naught.'

Rod frowned, puzzled. 'You mean he was hypnotized and brainwashed, but whoever did it was so skilful he didn't even leave a trace?'

Gwen was still; then she shrugged. 'What else could it be?'

'But why take the trouble?' Rod mused. 'I mean, any witch who knows more than the basics would recognize that spell in a moment.'

Gwen shook her head, and pushed away from him. ''Tis a mystery. Leave it for the nonce; there are others who must be wakened. Cordelia! Geoffrey, Magnus, Gregory! Hearken to my thoughts; learn what I do!' And she went to kneel by the bound soldier. Her children gathered about her.

Rod watched her for a moment, then turned back to Arlinson, shaking his head. He looked up into the man's eyes, and found them haunted.

The soldier looked away.

'Don't blame yourself,' Rod said softly. 'You were under a spell; your mind wasn't your own.'

The soldier looked up at him, hungrily.

'It's nothing but the truth.' Rod gazed deeply into the man's eyes, as though staring could convince him by itself. 'Tell me – how much do you remember?'

Arlinson shuddered. 'All of it, milord – Count Novgor's death, the first spell laid on us, the march to the castle, the deepening of the spell . . . '

Rod waited, but the soldier only hung his head, shuddering. 'Go on,' Rod pressed. 'What happened after the deepening of the spell?'

Arlinson's head snapped up, eyes wide. 'What more was there!'

Rod stared at him a moment, then said slowly, 'Nothing. Nothing that you could have done anything about, soldier. Nothing to trouble your heart.' He watched the fear begin to fade from the man's eyes, then said, 'Let's back it up a bit. They – the warlocks, I mean – marched you all to the castle, right?'

Arlinson nodded. 'Baron Strogol's castle had it been, milord.' He shuddered. 'Eh, but none would have known it once they'd passed the gate house. 'Twas grown dank and sour. The rushes in the hall had not been changed in a month at least, mayhap not since the fall, and each window and arrow slit was shuttered, barring the daylight.'

Rod stored it all away, and asked, 'What of the Count?'

Arlinson only shook his head slowly, eyes never leaving Rod's. Rod leaned back on one hip, fingering his dagger. 'How did they deepen the spell?'

Arlinson looked away, shivering.

'I know it's painful to remember,' Rod said softly, 'but we can't fight this sorcerer if we don't know anything about him. Try, won't you?'

Arlinson's gaze snapped back to Rod's. 'Dost thou think thou canst fight him, then?'

Rod shrugged impatiently. 'Of course we can – but I'd like

to have a chance of winning, too. Tell me how they deepened the spell.'

The soldier only stared at him for a time. Then, slowly, he nodded. ''Twas done in this manner: they housed us in the dungeon, seest thou, and took us out from our cage, one alone each time. When my turn came, they brought me into a room that was so dark I could not tell thee the size of it. A lighted candle stood on a table, next to the chair they sat me in, and they bade me stare at the flame.' His mouth twisted. 'What else was there?'

Rod nodded. 'So you sat and stared at the flame. Anything else?'

'Aye. Some unseen musicians played a sort of music I never heard aforetime. 'Twas a sort of a drone, seest thou, like unto that of a bagpipe – yet had more the sound of a viol. And another unseen beat on a tambour . . . '

'Tap it out,' Rod said softly.

The soldier stared, surprised. Then he began to slap his thigh, never taking his eyes from Rod's.

Rod recognized the rhythm; it was that of a heartbeat. 'What else?'

'Then one who sat across from me – but 'twas so dark, I could tell his presence only by the sound of his voice – one across from me began to speak of weariness, and sleep. Mine eyelids began to grow heavy; I remember that they drooped, and I fought against drowsiness, yet I gave into it, finally, and slept – until now.' He glanced down at his body, seeming to see his clothing for the first time. 'What is this livery?'

'We'll tell you after you've taken it off,' Rod said shortly. He slapped the man on the shoulder. 'Be brave, soldier. You'll need your greatest courage when you find out what's been happening while you were, er . . . while you "slept".' He turned to Grathum. 'Release him – he's on our side again.' And he turned back to Gwen, just in time to see the children, as a team, wake the last soldier, while Gwen supervised closely. 'Gently, Magnus, gently – his mind sleeps. And Geoffrey, move slowly – nay, pull back! Retreat! If thou dost wake him too quickly thou'lt risk driving him back into the depths of his own mind, in shock of his waking so far from his bed.'

The soldier in question blinked painfully, then levered himself up on one elbow. He looked down and stared at his bound wrists. Then he looked up, wildly – but even as he began to struggle up, his eyes lost their wildness. In a few seconds he sank back onto one elbow, breathing deeply.

'Well done, my daughter,' Gwen murmured approvingly. 'Thou dost soothe him most aptly.'

Rod watched the man growing calmer. Finally, he looked about him, wide-eyed. His gaze anchored on Gwen, then took in the children – then, slowly, tilted up towards Rod.

'All are awake now, husband, and ready.' Gwen's voice was low. 'Tell them thy condition, and thy name.'

'I am named Rod Gallowglass, and I am the High Warlock of this Isle of Gramarye.' Rod tried to match Gwen's pitch and tone. 'Beside me is my lady, Gwendylon, and my children. They have just broken an evil and vile spell that held you in thrall.' He waited, glancing from face to face, letting them take it in and adjust to it. When he thought they'd managed, he went on. 'You have been "asleep" for three days, and during that time you have fought as soldiers in the army of the Lord Sorcerer, Alfar.'

They stared at him, appalled. Then they all began to fire questions, one after another, barking demands, almost howling in disbelief.

They were building towards hysteria. It had to be stopped.

Rod held up his hands, and bellowed: *'Silence!'*

The soldiers fell silent, as military discipline dug its hooks into their synapses. But they were primed, and ready to explode, so Rod spoke quietly. 'What you did during those days was not truly your doing – it was the "Lord" Sorcerer's and his minions. They used your bodies – and parts of your minds.' He saw the look that washed over the soldiers' faces, and agreed, 'Yes. It was foul. But remember that what you did was *their* crime, not yours; there is no fault of yours in it, and you cannot rightly be blamed for it.' He saw their foreboding. Well, good – at least they'd be braced, when Grathum and his peasants told them what had been happening. He glanced from face to face again, holding each set of eyes for a moment, then breathed, 'But you can seek justice.'

Every eye locked onto him.

'You have pursued these goodfolk, here . . . ' Rod jerked his head towards the peasants ' . . . southward. You have passed the border of Romanov, and are come into Earl Tudor's land. Wend your way on to the south, now, with the folk you did chase – only now, be their protectors.'

He saw resolve firm the soldiers' faces.

Rod nodded with satisfaction. 'Southward you go, all in one body, to King Tuan at Runnymede. Kneel to him there, and say the High Warlock bade you come. Then tell him your tale, from beginning to end, even as Gavin Arlinson has told it to me. He will hear you, and shelter you – and, if you wish it, I doubt not he will take you into his army, so that, when he marches north against this tyrant sorcerer, you may help in tearing him down.'

Rod glanced from face to face again. He hadn't said anything about guilt or expiation, but he could see remorse turn into fanaticism in their expressions. He turned to Grathum. 'We can trust them. Strike off their bonds.'

Grathum eyed him uncertainly, but moved to obey.

Rod felt a tug at his belt, and looked down.

'Papa,' said Gregory, 'will the guards allow them to speak to the King?'

'I'll have to see if I can get you a job as my memory.' Rod turned away to fumble in Fess's pack, mumbling, 'We did bring a stylus and some paper, didn't we?'

'We did,' the robot's voice answered, 'but it is at the bottom, under the hardtack.'

'Well, of course! I wasn't expecting a booming correspondence on this jaunt.' Rod dug deep, came up with writing materials and wrote out a rather informal note, asking that the bearer be allowed to speak with Their Majesties. He folded it, tucked the stylus away, and turned to Cordelia. 'Seal, please.'

The witchlet stared at it, brow puckering in furious concentration. Then she beamed, and nodded.

'All done?' Rod tested it; the paper was sealed all around the edges; molecules from each half of the sheet had wandered in among the other half's. Rod grinned. 'Thanks, cabbage.' He turned to Grathum, handing him the letter. 'Present this to the sentry. Not being able to read, he'll call the captain of the guard, who'll call for Sir Maris, who'll probably allow only two of you to come before Their Majesties – and even then, only when you're surrounded by ten of the Queen's Own Bodyguard. Don't let them bother you – they'll just be decoration.' He pursed his lips. 'Though I wouldn't make any sudden moves, when you're in the throne room . . . '

Grathum bobbed his head, wide-eyed. 'E'en as thou dost say, milord.' Then he frowned. 'But . . . milord . . . '

'Go ahead.' Rod waved an expansive gesture.

Grathum still hesitated, then blurted, 'Why dost thou call thy lass a "cabbage"?'

''Cause she's got a head on her shoulders,' Rod explained. 'Off with you, now.'

# Chapter Four

The family watched the little company march southward. When they had disappeared into the woodland, Rod turned back to his family. 'Thank you, children. I was very proud of you.'

They blossomed under his praise. Cordelia caught his hand and returned, 'And *I* was proud of *thee*, Papa, that thou didst not lose thy temper!'

Rod fought to keep his smile and said only, 'Yes. Well, every little improvement counts, doesn't it?'

He turned to sit on a convenient rock. 'We could use a little rest, after all that excitement.'

'And food!' Geoffrey plopped himself down on the grass in front of Rod. 'May I hunt, Papa?'

'No,' Rod said slowly, 'there are those laws against poaching, and this tinker disguise still seems to be useful.'

'But it doth not deceive the sorcerer and his coven,' Magnus said, folding himself down beside Geoffrey.

'True, but it does seem to make the folk we encounter more willing to talk. Grathum said things to the tinker, that he was careful to hold back from the Lord High Warlock.'

'Indeed,' Gwen confirmed. 'He was so overawed that his true feelings did not even come into his mind, when he knew thou wert noble.'

'Which I still don't believe,' Rod noted, 'but he did. That's what's important. So we remain a tinker family, on the surface.'

'Then, no hunting?' Geoffrey pouted.

'Yes,' Rod nodded. 'No.'

'But we're *hungry*!' Cordelia complained.

'There is an answer to that.' Gwen opened a bundle and spread it out. 'Biscuits, cheese, apples – and good spring water, which Magnus may fetch.'

Magnus heaved a martyred sigh and went to fetch the bucket.

'I know,' Rod commiserated. 'It's not easy, being the eldest.'

Magnus set the bucket down in the centre of the family ring and scowled at it. With a sudden slosh, it filled with water.

Rod gazed at it, then lifted his eyes to his eldest. 'I take if you remembered the last brook we crossed?'

Magnus nodded, folding himself down cross-legged. 'Though milk would be better.'

'You may *not* teleport it out,' Rod said sternly. 'How do you think the poor cow would feel? Besides, it'd take too long to cool after Mama pasteurised it.'

'She could heat it in the cow,' Cordelia offered.

'Haven't we done that poor beast enough meanness already?'

'Rabbit would be better,' Geoffrey groused.

Gwen shook her head. 'There is no time to roast it. We must yet march northward a whiles this day, children.'

Geoffrey sighed, and laid a slice of cheese on a biscuit.

'Will we cross into Romanov this night, Papa?' Magnus asked.

'Not if I can help it. That's one border crossing I want to make in daylight.'

'There are surprises enough, under the sun,' Gwen agreed. 'We need not those of the moon, also.'

Cordelia shrugged. 'We know the range of witch-powers. What new thing could they smite us withal?'

'An we knew of it,' Gwen advised her, ''twould not be surprise.'

'Besides,' Rod said thoughtfully, 'I don't like what your Mama said about that depth-hypnosis not having any feel of the mind that did it.'

The children all stared up at him. Magnus voiced for them. 'What dost thou think it may be, Papa?'

But Rod shook his head. 'There are too many factors we don't know about.'

'We do know that the Tyrant Sorcerer is aged,' Gregory piped up.

The others stared at him. 'What makes thee say so?' Cordelia demanded.

'I heard the soldier speak thus, when he told Papa of the battle with Count Novgor.'

'Such as it was.' Rod searched his memory, and realized Gregory was right. But it was such a slight reference! And 'venerable' didn't necessarily mean 'old'. He glanced at Gwen, and found her eyes on him. He turned back to Gregory. 'Very good, son. What else do we know?'

'That he has gathered other witches and warlocks about him!' Cordelia said quickly.

'That they are younger than he,' Magnus added, 'for Grathum did not mention age when he spoke of the warlock Melkanth.'

'He did not say Melkanth was young, though,' Gregory objected, 'and neither he nor the soldier said aught of the other sorcery folk.'

Magnus clamped his jaw, and reddened. 'Other than that there were more than a few of them – and enough to defeat a dozen armed men!'

'Well, he did use the plural,' Rod temporized, 'and Grathum and Arlinson both probably would've mentioned it, if they'd been old.'

Magnus glanced up at his father gratefully.

'Still . . . ' Rod glanced at Gregory, whose face was darkening into obstinacy, ' . . . that *is* something we've guessed, not something we *know*. We've got to be ready to change that opinion in a hurry.'

Gregory's expression lightened.

'We know there is a crafter of witch-moss among them,' Gwen said slowly, 'and I would presume 'tis the one we met with two nights agone.'

'Probably,' Rod agreed, 'and at least one of their witches is good enough at telekinesis to come up with fireballs.'

'That doth take skill,' noted Gwen, who could light both a match and a barn a mile off.

'And a projective who can manage a quick hypnotic trance that's good enough to hold a dozen demoralized soldiers,' Rod mused. 'Presumably, that's the tyrant himself.'

'Thou dost guess, Papa,' Gregory reminded.

Rod grinned. 'Good boy! You caught it.'

'And one among them can plan the use of all these powers, in such wise as to easily defeat an armed force,' Geoffrey said suddenly.

Rod nodded. 'Good point – and easy to miss. What was their strategy?'

'To gobble up first the peasants, then the knights.' Geoffrey's eyes glowed. 'They began with the small and built them into strength, then used them to catch something larger. They should

therefore attack Duke Romanov and, after him, some others of the
Great Lords – Habsburg and Tudor, most likely, sin' that they are
nearest neighbours. Then they might chance attack on the King
and Queen, sin' that they'll have the Royal Lands encircled – or,
if they doubt their own strength, they might swallow up Bourbon,
De Medici, and Gloucester ere they do essay King Tuan.'

The family was silent, staring at the six-year-old. Rod reflected
that this was the child who hadn't wanted to learn how to read until
Rod told him the letters were marching. 'That's very good,' he said
softly, 'very good – especially since there wasn't much information
to go on. And I did say strategy, when I really meant tactics.'

'Oh! The winning of that one battle?' Geoffrey shrugged.
'They sent witch-moss monsters against the armed band, to busy
them and afright them. Then, the whiles the monsters held their
attention, the other warlocks and witches rained blows on them
from all sides. 'Twas simple – but 'twas enow; it did suffice.'

'Hm.' Rod looked directly into the boy's eyes. 'So you don't
think much of their tactician?'

'Eh, I did not say that, Papa! Indeed, he did just as he should
have – used only as much force as was needed, and when and where
it was needed. I doubt not, had Count Novgor proved stronger than
he'd guessed, he'd have had magical reserves to call upon.' Geoffrey
shook his head. 'Nay, I could not fault him. His battle plan in this
skirmish may have been, as thou hast said, simple – but he may
also be quite able to lay out excellent plans for elaborate battles.'
He shrugged. 'There is no telling, as yet.'

Rod nodded slowly. 'Sounds right. Any idea on the number
of subordinate warlocks and witches?'

'Four, at least – one to craft witch-moss, and direct her con-
structs; one to fly above, and drop rocks; two, at least, who did
appear and disappear, jumping from place to place within the
melee, wreaking havoc and confusion. There may be a fifth, who
threw fireballs; and also a sixth, who did cast the trance spell.'

'Hypnosis,' Rod corrected.

'Hip-no-siss.' Geoffrey nodded, with intense concentration. 'As
thou sayest. And, of course, there was the Tyrant-Sorcerer, this
Alfar; it may have been he who cast the trance spell, which would
make his lesser warlocks and witches only the five.'

Rod nodded. 'So. We can be sure there're Alfar, and four
subordinates – but there may be more.' He checked his memories
of Gavin Arlinson's account, but while he was checking, Gregory

confirmed, ''Tis even as Geoffrey doth say. Word for word, he hath counted them.'

Geoffrey cast him a look of annoyance. 'Who did ask thee, babe?'

Gregory's face darkened.

'Children!' Gwen chided. 'Canst thou not allow one another each his due share of notice?'

Cordelia sat up a little straighter, and looked virtuous.

Rod leaned back on his hands, staring up at the sky. 'Well! I didn't know we knew all that much! I expected you children to help out on the odd jobs – but I didn't expect *this*!' He looked down at his brood, gloating. 'But – if they've got all that going for them – why did they worry about some escaping peasants? Why did they send their brand-new army to chase them down?'

'Why, 'tis simply said!' Geoffrey looked up, startled. ''Twas done so that they might not bear word to Duke Habsburg, or Earl Tudor – or e'en Their Majesties!'

They were quiet again, all staring at him.

Geoffrey looked from face to face. 'But – 'tis plain! Is't not?'

'Yes, now that you've told us,' Rod answered. 'But what bothers me, is – *why* doesn't Alfar want anyone to know what he's doing?'

'Why, 'tis even plainer! He means to conquer the Duke, and doth not wish any other Lord to send him aid!'

His brothers and sister watched him, silent.

Rod nodded, slowly. 'Yes. That's what I was afraid you were going to say.'

Count Drulane and his lady rose, and all their folk rose with them. At the farthest end from their dais, the family of tinkers rose, too – though Gwen had to prod Geoffrey into putting down his trencher long enough to remember his manners.

'A good night to you all, then,' the Count intoned. 'May your dreams be pleasant – and may you wake in the morning.'

The habitual phrase fell rather sombrely on their ears, considering the tenor of the table conversation. The Count may have realized it; certainly, his departure through the door behind the dais, with his lady, was a bit brusque.

Gwen leaned over to Rod and murmured, 'Is such fear born only of silence?'

Rod shrugged. 'You heard what they said. The peasants are used to meeting Romanov peasants at the markets, and suddenly, they're not there. And the Count and Countess are used to the occasional social call – but there haven't been any for two weeks, and the last one before that brought rumours of the Romanov peasants being upset about evil witches.'

'*I* would fear,' said Magnus, 'if such visits stopped so suddenly.'

'Especially if you had relatives up there,' Rod agreed, 'which most of them seem to. I mean, who else are the knights' daughters going to meet and marry?' He clasped Magnus's shoulder. 'Come on, son. Let's help them clean up.'

Geoffrey, *now*!' Gwen said firmly and the six-year-old wolfed the last of his huge slice of bread as he stepped back from the table. Then he reached out and caught his wooden cup just as Rod and Magnus lifted the board off its trestles and turned it sideways, to dump the scraps onto the rushes.

' 'Tis not very cleanly, Papa,' Cordelia reminded.

'I know, dear – but when you're a guest, you do what your hosts do. And make no mistake – the Count and Countess are being very kind to let a family of poor tinkers spend the night in their castle.'

'Especially sin' that their own smith doth mend their pots,' Magnus added as he turned to carry the board over to the wall. Rod followed, and they waited their turn to drop their board onto the growing stack.

'It must be that the witches have done it,' the serf in front of them was saying to his mate. 'When last I saw Horth – mind thou, he that is among Sir Orlan's hostlers? – he did say an evil warlock had come among the peasants, demanding that they pay him each a penny ere Midsummer.'

'And Midsummer hath come, and gone.' The other peasant shook his head. 'What greater mischief ha' such warlocks brewed, ere now?'

As they dropped their board, Magnus looked up at Rod. 'Such words strike greater fear into my breast than doth the silence itself, Papa.'

'Yes,' Rod agreed, 'because it threatens us, personally. That's the real danger, son – and not just to us.' He clasped Magnus around the shoulder as they went back. 'The peasant reaction. Your mother and I, and Queen Catharine, with Tuan's help, were beginning to build up the idea that espers could be good guys – but one power-grabber can undo all that, and send the peasants out on witch-hunts again.' He broke off, grinning at the sight of Cordelia and Geoffrey, struggling towards him with one of the trestles between them. 'Hold it, you two! You're just not big enough to handle one of those things, yet – with just your hands, anyway!'

Cordelia dropped her end and glared up at him, fists on her hips. 'I'm a *big* lass, Papa!'

'Not yet, you're not – and you won't be for at least five more years.' Under his breath, Rod added, *God willing.* 'But you're a real sweetheart, to try and help. Mama needs you, though, to help clean a spot for our blankets.'

Cordelia shuddered, and Geoffrey pointed out, 'It'd be more pleasant outside, Papa.'

'We're after gossip, not comfort.' Rod turned him around and patted him on his way. 'Go help Mama; she needs someone to talk a cat into staying near us all night.'

Geoffrey balked.

'Cats *fight* rats,' Rod reminded.

Geoffrey's eyes gleamed, and he scurried back towards Gwen.

Rod picked up his end of the trestle. 'OK, up!'

Magnus hoisted his end, and turned towards the wall. 'E'en an witches could conquer all of Gramarye, Papa, they could not hold it – against such peasant fear and hate.' He shrugged. 'We number too few.'

'Watch the personal references.' Rod glanced quickly about, but none of the peasants were close enough to have heard. 'Good thing none of them wants to be seen near a tinker . . . No, son, an evil esper, such as this Alfar, *could* hold power – but only by a very harsh, cruel, obsolete rule.'

Magnus scowled. ''Tis as bad as witch-hunts.'

'Worse, for my purposes – because it'd stifle any chance of democracy on this planet. And I want Gramarye's telepaths to be the communications system for an interstellar democracy, some day.' Rod straightened, eyes widening. 'So *that's* it!'

Magnus looked up, startled. 'What, Papa?'

'Where the futurians come in – you know, the villains who kidnapped us all to Tir Chlis?'

Magnus's face darkened. 'I mind me of them – and of the peril they place us in. But what sign of them is there in this coil, Papa? I see naught but an aged wizard, who hath at long last struck out in bitterness and sense of being wronged.'

'That's what they want you to see. OK, son, up onto the stack

– heave!' They swung the saw-horse up onto the top of the stack, and turned away to get the other one. 'But if there's the likelihood of a repressive government showing up, there's a high probability of totalitarians from the future being behind it.'

Behind his ear, a methodical voice intoned, 'Generalizing from inadequate data . . . '

'But surely that is not enough sign of their presence,' Magnus protested, 'only the harshness of Alfar's rule!'

'You've been talking to Fess again,' Rod accused. 'But keep your eyes open, and you'll see more signs of their hand behind Alfar. Myself, I've been wondering about what your mother said – that there's no trace of a mind behind that "instant" hypnosis spell Alfar used on these soldiers.'

Magnus stared in consternation. 'But . . . Papa . . . how could that . . . '

'Up with the trestle,' Rod reminded, and they bent to pick it up, and started towards the wall again. 'Think, son – what doesn't? Think, that is. What can do things, but doesn't think?'

Magnus was silent as they hoisted the trestle to the top of the stack. As they turned away, he guessed, 'A machine?'

'You *have* been talking to Fess, haven't you?' There was a brief, nasty buzz behind his ear. 'I'd call that a good guess.'

'But only a guess,' Magnus reminded him.

'Of course.' They strolled up to Gwen where she knelt, just finishing spreading their blankets out over the rushes. 'Managed to banish the vermin, dear?'

'Indeed.' She glanced at him. 'Cordelia and I did think to gather fresh rushes the whiles we were on our way here, so we'll sleep sweetly enow.'

Something about the phrase caught Rod's attention. He stared down at the blanket, then lifted his gaze slowly to look deeply into Gwen's eyes.

She tilted her chin up and turned to her sons. 'And bear thy manners in mind, for we sleep in company, here.'

The children stared at her, then frowned at one another in puzzlement, then turned back to her. 'Why wouldst thou think we might not?' Magnus asked. Geoffrey piped in, 'We're *good* boys, Mama!'

'Aye,' Gwen answered, turning to Rod, 'and so must thou *all* be.'

\* \* \*

In the middle of the night a low groan began, swelling in volume and bouncing back and forth between the stone walls, until it filled the whole hall.

Rod shot bolt upright, panic clamouring up inside him jarring his brain. Rage answered, and struggled against it.

A bluish white light filled the hall, showing all the servants shocked upright, staring in fear and horror. Cordelia screamed, burying her face in Rod's midsection, and Gregory burrowed into Gwen's skirts.

Magnus and Geoffrey glared truculently upward, even as they backed away against the wall.

Above them all, the great hall was filled with a throng of pale, glowing spectres in antique gowns and ancient armour, all blue-white and translucent.

And facing the Gallowglass family.

The male closest to them lifted an arm with the weight of centuries, and his voice rolled out, thundering, 'Thou! 'Tis thou who dost disturb our rest, thou and thy get! Name thyself, and step forth from thy craven guise!'

Gwen laid a restraining hand on Rod's arm, but the rage was building, and he shrugged her off, incensed that she should dare to remonstrate with him. He glared up at the ghost, throwing his shoulders back and issuing his words one by one. 'I am Rodney Lord Gallowglass, High Warlock of Gramarye! And who are you, who dares so address me?'

'I am Arendel, first Count of Drulane!' the ghost bellowed. ''Tis in my hall thou dost stand! Wherefore hast thou come, and why hast thou disturbed my rest – mine, and all of my line's! Speak, sirrah! Now!'

The rage surged higher. 'Speak with respect to thy betters, feeble ghost! Or from this place I shall banish thee, to leave thy wraith wailing in the void between worlds!'

The ghost stared a moment, with the empty darkness of its eyes. Then its face creased, and broke open, and laughter spilled out – harsh, mocking laughter, that all the ghosts echoed, ringing from one to another, clamouring and sounding like brazen gongs, until all the Great Hall rang with it, while spectral fingers pointed at Rod.

And the rage built to fill him, striving to master him; but he held himself rigid against it and, in a last attempt to avoid it, cried, 'Fess! To me, now! In the great hall!'

'Why, then, mannikin, work thy will!' the ghost sneered. 'Hale me down, and grind me under! Work thy wonders! Show us this power thou canst employ, against ghosts!'

Steel hooves rang on stone, and the great black horse charged into the hall, rearing to a halt bare inches from a peasant couple, who scrambled away in panic.

Arendel turned his wrathful gaze on Fess, staring in outraged anger. 'What beast is this thou dost summon! Hast thou no shred of courtesy within thee, that thou wouldst bring thine horse into a lord's hall?'

'Fess,' Rod bellowed in agony. 'What are they?'

'Rr . . . Rrrodd . . . in-they awwrr . . .' Suddenly, Fess's whole body heaved in one great convulsion, neck whiplashing; then his head plummeted down to swing between his fetlocks. He stood spraddle-legged, each knee locked stiff.

'Seizure,' Rod snapped. 'They're real!'

Arendel stared in disbelief for a moment; then he threw back his head, and his laughter rocked the hall. 'Elf-shot! He summons his great aid, his model of all that is powerful and perfect – and 'tis elf-shot!' And his merriment rolled forth, to batter against Rod's ears.

Then Rod's own natural fury broke loose, his indignation that anyone should mock disability, make a joke of the truest companion he had known from earliest memory – and that fury poured into the building rage to boil it over the dam of Rod's willed control. The red haze enveloped him, and the icy, insane clarity stilled his thoughts, ringing one clear idea: *Ghosts could be exorcized.* Rod bent his brows, eyes narrowing, and a thunderclap exploded through the hall, crashing outward from a short, balding man wearing spectacles and a green chasuble over a white robe. He blinked about him, stupefied. 'I was . . . What . . . How . . . '

'Welcome, Father,' Rod breathed, in a voice of dry ice.

The priest blinked, seeking Rod out with watery eyes. 'But I was even now saying Matins, in the monastery chapel! How came I here?'

'Through my magic,' Rod grated, 'in response to the ill manners of this churlish dead lord! Exorcize him, Father – for his soul's barred from Heaven whiles he lingers here!'

The ghost roared with rage, and his fellows all echoed him, with screechings and roarings that made the priest wince and cry. ' 'Tis a foretaste of Hell!'

'Banish them,' Rod cried, 'ere they linger to damn themselves!'

The priest's face firmed with resolve. ''Tis even as thou sayest.' And he held up one palm toward the ghosts while he fumbled in a pocket with the other, beginning a sonorous Latin prayer.

Lord Arendel shrieked, and disappeared.

With a wave of wailing despair, the other ghosts faded.

In the sudden, soft darkness, Magnus cried, 'There! Against the eastern wall! Nay, stop her, seize her! Mother, a light, I prithee!'

Sudden light slashed the darkness – a warm, yellow glow from a great ball of fire that hung just below the ceiling, and Magnus and Geoffrey were diving toward a woman in a blue, hooded cloak, who hauled out a broomstick and leaped onto it, soaring up through the air to leave them in a wave of mocking laughter. Magnus shouted in anger, and banked to follow her, but she arrowed straight toward the window, which was opened wide to the summer's night. She trilled laughter, crying, 'Fools! Dost not know the witches are everywhere? Thou canst not escape Alfar's power, nor hope to end it! Hail the Lord Sorcerer as thy master, ere he doth conquer thee – for Alfar shall rule!'

With a firecracker-pop, Gregory appeared directly in front of her, thrusting a stick toward her face. It burst into flame at its tip. The witch shrieked and veered to the side, plummeting toward the open door, but Cordelia swirled in on her broomstick to cross the witch's path, hurling a bucketful of water. The fluid stretched out into a long, slender arrow, and splattered into the witch's face. She howled with rage and swirled up and around the great hall while she dashed the water from her eyes with one swipe of her hand. Magnus and Geoffrey shot after her, closing in from either side. At the last second, the witch clutched at a great whorl of an amulet that hung on her breast, cried, 'Hail, Alfar,' and disappeared in a clap of thunder.

The hall was silent and still.

Then a low moan began, and spread around the outside of the chamber. It rolled, building toward a wail.

Magnus hung in the centre of the hall, beneath the great fireball, his eyes like steel. Slowly, his mouth stretched wide.

Gwen's voice cut like a knife blade. 'Nay, Magnus! Such words are forbidden thee, for no gentleman may use them!'

For an instant, shocked stillness fell again. Then one woman began to giggle incredulously. Another gave a little laugh, but another laughed with her, then another, and another, and the horror in the hall turned into full-throated laughter – with an hysterical edge to it, perhaps, but laughter none the less.

Then the Count of Drulane stood on the dais with his quaking wife behind him, gazing about his hall silently. One by one, his servants and thralls saw him, and fell silent.

When the whole hall was quiet, the Count turned to a waiting servant. 'Light fires, that we may thank this lady for her good services, and be done with her flaming light.'

The servant turned to the task, and others leaped to join him.

The Count turned to the priest and said gravely, 'I must thank thee, reverend Father, for thy good offices.'

The priest bowed. 'My office it was, and there was small need to thank me.'

'Naetheless, I do. Still, Father, I own to some concern, for these were the spirits of mine ancestors. Are their souls destroyed, then?'

'Nay, milord.' The priest smiled. 'I' troth, I misdoubt me an a soul can be annihilated. Yet even an 'twere, 'twould not be now; for I saw no need for exorcism. Nay, I merely did bless this hall, and pray for the souls of all who have dwelt here, that they might find rest – which they did.'

'And I had feared thou wouldst attempt to blast them with power of thine own,' Gwen said softly to her husband. 'How is't thou didst think of the clergy?'

But the rage had ebbed, and Rod was filled with guilt and remorse. He shrugged impatiently. 'Just an odd fact.'

'It was, i' truth, for thou hast never been greatly pious. Where didst thou learn it?'

The question poked through Rod's miasma; he frowned. Where *had* he learned that ghosts could be banished by clergy? 'Common knowledge, isn't it?' He glowered at her. 'Just came to me, out of the blue.'

'Nay,' said little Gregory, reaching up to catch his hand. ''Tis not from the blue . . .'

'Who asked *you*?'

Gregory flinched away, and self-disgust drowned Rod's irritation. He reached out to catch the child around the shoulders and jam him against a hip. 'Oh, I'm sorry, son! You didn't deserve that!'

The priest was still reassuring the Count. 'They have fled back to their graves, milord – and, I hope, to their well-earned afterlives.'

'For some, that will be a blessing,' the Count said noncommittally.

Rod looked up from the shame-filled ashes of his wrath. 'Shall I send you home now, Father?'

The priest looked up, appalled, and the Count said quickly, 'Or, an thou dost wish it, Father, we can offer thee hospitality and, when thou art rested, guardsmen and a horse, to escort thee south, to thy monastery.'

'I thank thee, milord,' the priest said, not managing to hide his relief.

The Count inclined his head. Then, slowly, he turned to Rod; and he spoke softly, but his words cut like fire. ''Twas ungentlemanly of thee, Lord Warlock, to come, unannounced and disguised, into mine household.'

Rod met his gaze, despite the shame that permeated him. He'd lost his head in fear and panic, and aimed at the wrong enemy – and now, to top it off, the Count was right.

How dare he be!

It worked; he summoned up enough indignation to raise his chin. 'Deeply do I regret the need for such deception, milord Count – but need there was.'

'What?' The Count frowned. 'Need to wake mine ancestors from their sleep?'

Rod answered frown for frown. 'Be mindful, milord – that raising was no work of ours. 'Twas the doing of a vile wi — er, sorceress.'

'Aye.' The Count seemed embarrassed. ''Tis even so, milord; I had forgot.'

'But the witch would not ha' been here,' Geoffrey whispered, 'had we not been.'

'Shut up, kid,' Rod muttered.

'I prithee, judge not all us witches by her,' Gwen pleaded. 'There be only a few such wicked ones. And, as thou hast seen, ever will they flee the might of the Royal Coven.'

The peasants didn't seem all that much reassured.

'Make no mistake,' Rod advised. 'The Tyrant Sorcerer, Alfar, does send his agents out to prepare his conquests – and, as you've seen, he has come this far to the south already.' He turned back to

Count Drulane. 'That is why we have come in disguise – to learn all we can of Alfar's doings.'

The Count gazed at him for several seconds, then nodded slowly. 'Aye, I am captain enough to understand the need of that.'

'I thank you for understanding,' Rod gave him a slight bow. 'But we must not trouble your keep further this night. The witch has fled, and we have learned all that we can.' *Especially now that our cover's blown.* 'We will thank you for your hospitality, and take our leave.'

The Count returned the bow, not quite managing to hide his relief.

Rod smiled, turned, and marched toward the door.

Magnus blinked, then jumped to follow his father, shoulders squared and chin high.

The other children looked about them, startled, then hurried after Magnus, with Gwen shooing them along.

The peasants pressed back, making way for them.

Rod stopped by Fess and reached under the saddle for the reset switch. He thew it, and the robot's head came up slowly. Rod caught the reins and led the black horse away with them.

They came out into the open air, and Geoffrey heaved a sigh of relief.

'Clean!' Cordelia gasped.

Rod was silent for two paces; then he nodded. 'Yes. You did want to sleep outdoors, didn't you?'

'Crickets be more musical than snores,' Magnus assured him.

'And if I must needs sleep with animals, I had liefer they be large enough to see clearly.' Gwen brushed at her skirts. 'Faugh!'

'No argument there,' Rod assured her. 'Come on, we'll just go a quarter-mile or so past the gate, and bed down for the rest of the night.'

They passed through the gatehouse, across the drawbridge, and set out into the night.

After a few paces, Rod let a sigh explode out. 'Now! Next time you disagree with me, Gregory, *please* wait until we're alone! Because you never know, I might be right.'

'Yes, Papa,' the little boy said, in a little voice.

Rod frowned. 'I don't mean to be hard, son – but there's a very good chance that, if that witch hadn't been there to harry us, there might've been another one of Alfar's crew, to try to spy out the territory *and* spread rumours that'd worry the folk. I mean, all that worried dinner-table talk was *probably* genuine – but it is strangely convenient for Alfar, isn't it?'

Gregory was silent.

To cover his guilt feelings, Rod turned to Fess, muttering, 'Recovered, Circuit Rider?'

'Nearly,' answered the robot's voice. 'I had never encountered convincing evidence of the existence of a medium, before this night.'

'Well, maybe you still haven't,' Rod mused.

'Who hath not what?' Magnus looked up with a frown. 'Oh! Thou didst speak with Fess.' He nodded, satisfied; the children had long ago learned that they could not hear Fess's thoughts, unless he wanted them to.

'Mayhap he still hath not what?' Cordelia asked.

'Seen a medium,' Rod explained, 'a person who can talk to ghosts, or make them appear.'

'Oh.' Cordelia nodded. 'Thou speakest aright, Papa. He hath not.'

'Oh, really? Those ghosts looked genuine to me.'

'They were not,' Magnus assured him. 'They had no greater thought than a mirror.'

Rod frowned. 'Odd simile.'

'Yes 'tis apt,' Gwen affirmed. 'They had no true thoughts of their own; they mimicked what was there laid down for them.'

'Laid down?' Rod still frowned. 'By whom?'

'By the witch,' Magnus explained. 'She did call up the memories laid in the stones, and throw them out to us.'

Rod stared. After a few seconds, he said, 'What?'

'Some witches there be, milord,' Gwen explained, 'who can lay a hand on a ring, and gain the full sense of the person who wore it, even to the pattern of his or her thoughts.'

Rod gazed off into space. 'Yeah . . . I think I've heard of that. They call it "psychometry", don't they?'

Gwen shrugged. 'I know not, my lord; such are the words of thy folk, not ours.'

' 'Tis all one,' Cordelia added.

'Thanks for the lesson,' Rod said sourly. 'But how did you know about this, Magnus?'

The boy reddened. 'I did not wish to trouble thee, Papa . . . '

'Oh, really?' Rod looked the question at Gwen; she shook her head. 'Didn't want to worry Mama either, I gather. Which is fine, until we find out about it. From now on, we'll *always* be worried – that you've discovered a new way to use your power, and are trying dangerous experiments without letting us know.'

Magnus looked up, startled. 'I had not meant . . . '

'I know. So don't. Worry me, son – that's what I'm here for.' For a second, he wondered if that was truer than he knew.

Magnus sighed. 'Well enough, then. I have found thoughts in things people have used, Papa.'

Rod nodded. 'Let Mama be near next time you experiment with it, OK? So much for the "calling up" part. I take it the "throwing out" is talking about projective telepathy?'

'By that,' Gwen explained to the children, 'he doth mean a witch or warlock who can send their thoughts out to folk who have not witch power.'

'Oh!' Cordelia nodded. 'Such she was, Papa. What she saw in her mind, she could make others see, also.'

Rod nodded. 'So we weren't seeing real ghosts – just reflections of the memories "recorded" in the rocks of that hall . . . er, Gwen?'

'Aye, my lord.'

'Remember those ghosts we met, way back, when in Castle Loguire?'

'Aye, my lord. Mayhap they were, at first, raised in just such a manner.'

'Why the "at first"?'

'Why, for that they endured after the witch who raised them – long after, by accounts.'

'Oh, yeah.' Rod nodded. 'That's right – that castle was supposed to have been haunted for a century or two, wasn't it?' He glared at the sudden gleam in Magnus's eye. 'Don't go trying any surprise visits. Those ghosts weren't harmless.'

'Save for thy father.' Gwen couldn't resist it.

Rod gave her a glower. 'That was diplomacy, not necromancy. And, come to think of it, this witch of Alfar's wasn't too bad at persuasion herself.'

'Aye,' Gwen agreed. 'Her words, when we had unmasked her, were meant more for Count Drulane and his folk, than they were for us.'

'Trying to boil up all the old fears of witches, to boost their

Reign of Terror,' Rod growled. 'Never mind what the peasants might do to the witches in the rest of the kingdom.'

'Nay, *do* mind it!' Gregory cried. 'For if they take fright, and are hurted enough to become bitter and hateful, might they not flee to Alfar, and swell his strength?'

Rod thought about it, then slowly nodded. 'I hate to admit it, son, but you're right.' He turned a sombre gaze on Gwen, then dropped his gaze to look at his children, one at a time.

'What thoughts dost thou engender, husband?' Gwen asked softly.

Rod lifted his gaze to her again. 'This mission has definitely turned dangerous, darling. Time for you and the children to go home.'

The night was silent for a moment. Then: ' 'Tis not fair!' Cordelia cried.

'Only now doth it gain interest!' Gregory protested.

'None the less . . . ' Rod began.

' 'Tis the tactics of magic!' Geoffrey cried. 'Assuredly, Papa, thou'lt not deny me the chance to witness such!'

'You're apt to get hurt!' Rod snapped. 'And preventing that is my main job in life!'

'Then wither wouldst thou be, without us?' Magnus demanded, catching at his sleeve.

'Lonely,' Rod snapped, 'but effective. A lot *more* effective than if I'm worrying about you while I'm in the middle of a fight!'

'Yet thou hast no need to fear for us!' Cordelia cried.

'Send an *army* 'gainst us, ere thou dost fear!' Geoffrey howled.

'Yeah.' Rod's jaw tightened. 'You'd just love to have an army to box with, wouldn't you? Unfortunately, it just might have a stronger arm than you, and . . . '

'Husband.' Gwen's low voice bored through his building anger. 'Thou didst say, even now, that thou didst protect them.'

Rod's head snapped up, indignation flaring. 'Are you imply-ing— ?'

But Gwen was already talking to the children, rapidly. 'Thy father has said there is danger in this; and if thou dost believe thyselves strong, only think – how wouldst thou fare if thou didst confront a grown warlock, at the height of his powers, an thou wert alone? If thou hadst been split away from thy brothers and sister – how then?'

Geoffrey started to answer.

Gwen pressed a hand over his mouth. 'Nay, do think carefully ere thou dost speak! There is a thrill of pleasure in it, aye – but only till thou dost truly fear! Then all of thy joy in it doth die a-borning.' Her gaze came up to meet Rod's. ''Tis even as thy father doth know, for he hath been in peril. Nay, if he saith 'tis dangerous, then assuredly the danger could strike deepest fear in thee, could kill thee.'

The children stared up at her gravely, thinking they understood.

'Yet, husband, be mindful.' Gwen looked straight into Rod's eyes. 'The foes Alfar hath sent against us thus far have scarce begun to tax our powers. Were Alfar to send all his force against us, 'twould be great danger, aye; but I misdoubt me an he would risk more than a moiety of his force, when he knoweth not the true depth or breadth of our power. Were he to send an army, in truth, we ought then to flee; yet if he sends only witches, the High Warlock and his family have little fear.'

'Only enough to make it fun, eh?' Rod managed a harsh smile.

'I could not deny it,' Gwen admitted. ''Tis but exercise, for a brood such as ours.'

'Yes . . . ' Rod frowned. 'He's testing us, isn't he?'

Geoffrey spun around, wide-eyed. 'Papa! Wherefore did I not see that?'

'Experience,' Rod assured him. 'But that means the attacks will become stronger, until he thinks he knows our limits. *Then* he'll hit us with twice the force he thinks he needs, just to make sure.'

Geoffrey had a faraway look in his eyes. 'Therefore . . . it doth behove us to use as little power as we must, to defeat them.'

Rod nodded. 'Which we haven't exactly been doing, so far.'

'We may stay then?' Cordelia cried, jumping up and down.

Rod fixed them all with a glare.

They pulled themselves into line, hands clasped in front of them, heads bowed a little – but looking up at him.

'Do I have your *absolute* promise that you'll all go right home, without any argument, the next time I say so?'

'Oh, yes, Papa, yes!' they cried. 'We will flee, we will fly!' Cordelia avowed.

'We wouldn't *want* to stay, if this sorcerer really were dangerous, Papa,' Magnus assured him.

'But you don't believe he could be, eh?' Rod fixed his eldest with a glare.

'Well . . . '

'That's all right.' Rod held up a palm. 'I've got your promise. It's OK – you're still on board, at least until the next attack. And if it's too close to being dangerous, home you go!'

'Home,' they averred.

'Still don't believe me, eh?' Rod looked up at Gwen. 'How about you? Promise?'

'I shall heed thee as strongly as ever I have done, my lord,' she said firmly.

'That's what I was afraid of,' Rod sighed. 'Well, I suppose I'll have to be content with that. C'mon kids, let's set up camp.'

Gwen threw her head back with a happy sigh. 'Ah, 'tis good to be aloft again.'

'I'm glad for you.' Rod gripped the broomstick tighter and swallowed heavily. His idea of flying was inside a nice, warm spaceship, with a lounge chair and an autobar. 'This shooting around on a broomstick is strictly for the birds. On second thoughts, strike that – even the birds wouldn't touch it.'

'Oh, certes, they would, Papa.' Cordelia shot up alongside, matching velocities. A robin sat on the tip of her broomstick, chirping cheerily.

Rod gave the bird a jaundiced glance. 'Odd friends you're making up here.'

Gregory shot past them, flipping over onto his back to look back and wave bye-bye.

'Show-off,' Rod growled, but his heart sang at the sight of a smile on the face of his sober little son. It was good to see him be child again.

'Regard thy way,' Gwen called after him. Gregory nodded cheerfully and flipped over onto his tummy again.

Magnus swung up alongside. 'I thank thee, Papa! We are free again!'

'Delighted.' Rod tried to mean it. 'Might as well, since Alfar knows who we really are, anyway.'

'Yonder.' Magnus pointed ahead. Rod looked up, and saw a line of hills, blued by distance. Magnus informed him, ''Tis the Titans' Rampart.'

'The Romanov boundary.' Rod felt his stomach suddenly grow

hollow. 'Somehow, I find myself less than eager to cross it.'

'But 'twill be exciting, Papa!' Geoffrey cried, flying up on his port side.

'That's a kind of excitement I think I can live without. Besides, I'm hungry. Darling, what do you say we find a town large enough to have an inn, this side of the boundary?'

'I misdoubt me an they'd welcome folk so poorly dressed, my lord.'

'Yeah, but they'd let us sit in the innyard, if we buy our food with real silver.'

'Hot sausage!' Geoffrey cried.

'Stew!' Magnus carolled.

'Toasted cheese!' Cordelia exulted.

'Hungry children,' Gwen sighed. 'Well, husband, an thou dost wish it.'

'Great. Land us in a nice little copse, about half a mile out, will you? Tinkers they might accept in the innyard, but not if they use it for a landing strip.' He stared ahead hungrily. 'Terra firma!'

# Chapter Five

As they came into the town, Cordelia gave a happy little sigh. ''Tis *so* nice that the nasty old sorcerer knows we come toward him!'

'Oh, indeed yes,' Rod muttered. 'This way he can have a wonderful reception all ready for us! Why do *you* like it, dear? Because you can fly?'

'Oh, aye!'

'I dislike disguise, Papa,' Geoffrey explained.

Rod gave his son a measuring stare. 'Yes, I suppose you would – even when you see it's necessary.'

'As 'tis, I know,' the little boy sighed. 'Yet doth it trouble me, Papa.'

'I understand.' Rod frowned. 'What bothers *me*, is trying to figure out how Alfar saw through our disguises.'

The family walked on in brooding silence – for a few seconds. Then Gwen said, ''Tis widely known that the High Warlock doth have a wife, and four bairns – and that one is a lass, and the other three lads.'

Rod scowled. 'What are you suggesting – that they had their illusionist attack on every family who came north?' His gaze wandered. 'Of course, I suppose there aren't that many families *coming* north . . . and the kids' ages are pretty much a matter of public record . . . '

'It doth seem unlikely,' Gwen admitted.

'And therefore must be seriously considered. But we would have heard about it, wouldn't we? Monsters, attacking families?'

'Not if the witch and her monsters won out,' Geoffrey pointed out.

'But no sooner would they have attacked, than the witch would have seen the families had no magical powers!' Cordelia protested. 'Surely she would then have called off her monsters.'

Geoffrey's eyes turned to steel. 'She would not – if she wished to be certain no word reached the King.'

'That does seem to be their strategy,' Rod agreed.

'But – to kill *bairns*?' Cordelia gasped.

'They are not nice people,' Rod grated.

The children were silent for a few minutes, digesting an unpleasant realization. Finally, Gregory pointed out, 'We do not *know* that, Papa.'

'No, but I wouldn't put it past them. Still, it does seem a little extravagant.'

'Mayhap they did post sentries,' Geoffrey suggested.

Rod nodded. 'Yes, well, that's the most likely way – but what kind of sentries? I mean, we haven't seen any soldiers standing around in Alfar's livery. So his sentries must be disguised, if he has them. And I suppose they'd have to know what we looked like . . . '

'Eh, no!' Magnus cried, grabbing Rod's wrist. 'They need only be— '

'Telepaths!' Rod knocked his forehead with the heel of his hand. 'Of course! Just station mind readers on each of the main roads – and maybe even out in the pastures, if you're the suspicious type – and they'd be almost impossible to spot! They could be anybody – the farmer who passes in his cart, the varlet in the kitchens, the merchant and his draymen . . . '

The children looked around them, suddenly alert.

' . . . and they'd be almost impossible to spot,' Rod finished, 'since all they have to do is sit there, with their minds wide open for every stray thought!'

'We *could* have masked our minds,' Geoffrey mused.

'Yes, but we didn't.' Rod shook his head. 'Besides, it's not as easy as it sounds. You're all beginning to get pretty good at it – ' he caught Gwen's glance – 'every time you're doing something you don't want Mama and me to know about.'

The children exchanged quick, guilty glances.

'Of course, Mama and I are getting even better at probing *behind* the masks,' Rod went on, 'so I suppose it's very good training for all of us. In fact . . . that might not be a bad idea.' He flashed a grin at each of them. 'Start poking around inside minds here and there, kids.'

Instantly, all four faces turned blank, their eyes losing focus.

'No, no! Not *now*! I mean, if they *have* been listening to us, they'll have heard us, and just wiped their minds and started thinking disguise thoughts! You've got to catch them when they're *not* ready, take them by surprise. Listen and probe for them whenever you just happen to think of it, at odd moments.'

'But will they not always be masked to us, Papa?' Cordelia protested.

'Not when they're trying to listen to your thoughts,' Rod explained. 'They can't do both at the same time – mask *and* listen. You've tried it yourselves – *you* know.'

This time, the glance the kids exchanged was startled – and worried. Just how much *did* Daddy know, that they didn't know he knew?

'Try to catch them unaware,' Rod urged.

The children sighed philosophically.

'I know, I know,' Rod growled, 'this unpredictable Daddy! First he tells you *to* do it, then he tells you not to! So balance it – sometimes you do it, and sometimes you don't.' He looked up. 'Gee, that's a nice looking horse, up there. I think I'll steal it.'

The children gasped with shock, and looked – and gave their father a look of disgust. 'Thou cast not steal him, Papa,' Gregory said sternly. 'He is already thine.'

'Makes it more convenient that way, doesn't it?' Under his breath, Rod muttered, 'Nice of you to come ahead to meet us, Old Iron. How about I ride you, on the next leg of the trip?'

'Motion sickness, Rod?'

But it was Gwen and Cordelia who rode, at least as far as the inn, and the innkeeper was very obliging – once Rod caught his attention.

It wasn't easy. Rod left the family at the door and stepped inside, bracing himself for an unpleasant scene. He saw a tall, wiry man with a stained apron tied around his waist, setting a double handful of mugs on a table and collecting coppers from the diners. As he turned away from the table, his gaze fell on Rod. 'Be off with you,' he ordered, but he didn't even stop turning. 'We've no alms to give.' By the time he finished the sentence, he was facing the kitchen again, and had started walking.

'I've got money!' Rod called.

The man kept on walking.

Rod dodged around him and leaped into his path, shoving his purse under the innkeeper's nose and yanking it open. The man stopped, frowning. Slowly, his eyes focused on the purse.

Rod shook a few coins out onto his palm. 'See? Silver. The real thing.'

The innkeeper scowled at the coins as though they were vermin. Then his expression lightened to musing, and he pinched up one of the coins, held it in front of his nose to stare at it as though it were some new variety of bug, then methodically set it between his teeth and bit it.

Rod couldn't resist. 'Hors-d'oeuvres?'

''Tis silver.' The innkeeper seemed puzzled.

'Genuine,' Rod agreed.

The man focused on Rod. 'What of it?'

Rod just stared at him for a second. 'We'd like something to eat.'

'We?' The innkeeper turned his head from side to side, inspecting the walls and corners.

'My wife and children,' Rod explained, 'I didn't think you'd want us inside.'

The innkeeper thought that one over for a while, then nodded, frowning. Rod wondered how the man ever managed to make a profit. Finally, the innkeeper spoke. 'Wise.' He kept nodding. 'Wise.' Then he focused on Rod again. 'And what food dost thou wish?'

'Oh, we're not choosy. A big bowl of stew, a plateful of sausage, a couple of loaves of bread, a pitcher of milk, and a pitcher of ale should do us. Oh, and of course, six empty bowls. And six spoons.'

The innkeeper nodded judiciously. 'Stew, sausage, bread, milk, and ale.' He turned away, still nodding. 'Stew, sausage, bread, milk, and ale.' He headed for the kitchens, repeating the formula again and again.

Rod watched him go, shaking his head. Then he turned away to find Gwen and the kids.

He found them sitting under an old, wide oak tree with a huge spread of leaves. 'Will they have us, husband?' Gwen didn't really sound as though she cared.

'Oh, yeah.' Rod folded a leg under him and sat down beside her, leaning back against the trunk. 'He was very obliging, once he tasted our silver and found out it wasn't pewter.'

'What troubles thee, then?'

'Frankly, my dear, he didn't really give a d— ' Rod glanced at the eager faces around him, and finished, ' . . . darn.'

'Assuredly, Tudor doth lack in gallantry,' said a large man, walking into the inn with a companion.

'Aye; it doth pain me to say it, but our noble Earl hath ever been clutch-fisted,' answered his companion. 'This sorcerer, Alfar, now – all one doth hear of him, doth confirm his generosity.'

They passed on into the inn. Rod sat frozen, staring into space.

Magnus put it into words for him. 'Do they speak against their own *lord*?'

'They do,' Gwen whispered, eyes huge.

'And in *public*!' Rod was flabbergasted. 'I mean, peasants have spoken against their rulers before – but never out in the open, where a spy might overhear them. For all they know, we could be . . . ' He ran out of words.

'Yet the lord would have to be *greatly* wicked, for his own folk to complain of him!' Cordelia cried. 'Could they break faith with him so easily?'

'Not ordinarily,' Rod said grimly. 'But we didn't come up here because things were normal.'

A maid came ambling up to them, bearing a tray of food. Her face was smudged, and her apron was greasy – from the scullery, Rod guessed. He braced himself for the contempt he'd grown used to from the peasants, and reminded himself that everybody had to have somebody they could look down on. Maybe that was what they *really* needed tinkers for.

But the maid only held the tray down where they could reach it, shaking her head and marvelling. 'Tinkers! Why doth the master spare good food for tinkers?'

Rod took a plate warily, and sniffed at it. A delighted grin spread over his face. 'Hey! It *is* good!'

'May I?' Magnus sat still, with his hands in his lap. So did the other children, but their eyes fairly devoured the tray.

'Why . . . certes.' The scullery maid seemed surprised by their politeness.

Magnus seized a bowl. 'May I?' Cordelia cried, and the younger two chorused, 'May I?' after her.

'Certes,' the wench said, blinking, and three little hands snatched at bowls.

Rod handed the plate to Gwen and lifted down a huge bowl of stew, then the pitchers. 'Take your cups, children.' Gwen scooped up the remaining two flagons, and the spoons.

The kitchen wench straightened, letting one edge of the tray fall. A furrow wrinkled between her eyebrows. 'Strange tinkers ye be.'

She was trying to think, Rod realized – and she'd have been trying very hard, if some mental lethargy hadn't prevented her. 'Still wondering why your master is serving us more than kitchen scraps?'

Enlightenment crept over her face. 'Aye. That is what I be thinking.'

'Best of reasons,' Rod assured her. 'We paid in silver.'

She lifted her head slowly, mouth opening into a round. 'Oh. Aye, I see.' And she turned away, still nodding, as she began to amble back to the kitchen.

'Why doth she not ask how mere tinkers came by silver money, Papa?' Magnus watched her go.

'I expect she'll think that one up just as she gets to the kitchen . . . '

'Why is she so slow, Papa?' Cordelia seemed concerned.

Rod shook his head. 'Not just her, honey. That's what the innkeeper was like, too.' He gazed after the scullery maid, frowning.

Two men in brocaded surcoats with greyed temples strolled past them towards the inn door. 'Nay, but our Earl doth seek to rule all our trade,' the one protested. 'Mark my words, ere long he will tell to us which goods we may not sell, for that he doth grant patents on them to those merchants who toady to him.'

'Aye, and will belike tax the half of our profit,' the other agreed, but he spoke without heat, almost without caring.

They passed on into the inn, leaving Rod rigid in their wake. '*That* is the most blatant lie I've heard since I came here! Earl Tudor is so *laissez-faire*-minded, you'd almost think he just doesn't care!'

'Folk will believe any rumour,' Gwen offered.

'Yeah, but businessmen check them out – and those two were merchants. If they stray too far from the facts, they go bankrupt.'

A string of donkeys plodded into the innyard, heads hanging low, weary from their heavy packs. Their drovers bawled the last few orders at them, as the inn's hostlers strolled past the Gallowglass family toward the donkeys, chatting. 'They say the sorcerer Alfar is a fair-minded man.'

'Aye, and generous withal. Those who come under his sway, I hear, need never be anxious for food or drink.'

The first shook his head, sadly. 'Our Earl Tudor doth care little for the poor folk.'

'Are they crazy?' Rod hissed. 'Tudor is practically a welfare state!'

' 'Tis e'en as thou dost say,' the second mused. 'Yet at the least, our Earl doth not tax his peasants into rags and naught for fare but bread and water, as Duke Romanov doth.'

'Oh, come *on*, now!' Rod fumed. 'Nobody ever claimed Romanov was a walking charity – but at least he realizes the peasants can't produce if they're starving.'

But Gregory had a faraway look in his eyes. 'Papa – I mislike the feel of their minds.'

Gwen stopped ladling stew and gazed off into space. She nodded, slowly. 'There is summat there . . . ' Then her eyes widened. 'Husband – it doth press on me, within mine head!'

Instantly, the children all gazed off into space.

'Hey!' Rod barked in alarm. He clapped his hands and snapped, 'Wake up! If there is something messing with people's minds here, it could be dangerous!'

They all stared, blinking, then focused on their father. ' 'Tis as Mama doth say, Papa,' Magnus reported. 'Something doth press upon the minds of all the people here – and at ours, too. Only, with us, it cannot enter.'

'Then it knows all it really needs to know about us, doesn't it?' Rod growled. He frowned, and shrugged. 'On the other hand, it already did. Here, I've got a feel of this.'

It wasn't as easy for him as it was for Gwen and the kids. They'd grown up with extrasensory power, they could read minds as easily as they listened for bird songs. But Rod's dormant powers had just been unlocked three years ago. He had to close his eyes, concentrating on the image of a blank, grey well, letting his thoughts die down, and cease. Then, when other people's thoughts had begun to come into his mind, he could open his eyes again, and see while he mind read.

But he didn't have to look about him this time. He could feel it before he even heard another person's thoughts. When he did, he realized that the thoughts resonated perfectly with the pressure-current. It was a flowing wave, rocking, soothing, lulling; but modulated in that lethargic mental massage was a feeling of vague unease and suspicion – and riding within that modulation, as a sort of harmonic, was the central conviction that the sorcerer Alfar could make all things right.

Rod opened his eyes to find his whole family staring at him – and for the first time on his trip, fear shadowed the children's faces.

Rage hit, hot and strong. Rod's whole nervous system flamed with it, and his hands twitched, aching for the throat of whatever it was that had threatened his children.

'Nay, husband.' Gwen reached out and caught his hand. 'We need thy wisdom now, not thy mayhem.'

He resented her touch; it pushed his anger higher. But he heeded her words, and concentrated on the feel of that beloved hand, whose caresses had brought him so much of comfort and delight. He let it anchor him, remembering how his rage had made him do foolhardy things, how his wrath had played into the hands of the enemy. He took slow, deep breaths, trying to remember that he was really more dangerous when he was calm, trying to regain the harmony of his emotions. He concentrated on his shoulders, relaxing them deliberately, then his back, then his upper arms, then his forearms, then his hands. Anger wouldn't help anybody now; anger would only destroy – everything but the enemy. He shivered as he felt the rage loosen, and drain away; then he swallowed, and closed his eyes, nodding. 'I'm . . . all right now. Thanks, darling. Just . . . be careful about grabbing me when I'm like that, OK?'

'I will, my lord.' She released him, but held his gaze with her own.

'OK.' He took a deep breath, and looked up at the children. 'You know what hypnosis is.'

'Aye, Papa.' They stared at him, round-eyed.

'Well, that's what we're facing.' Rod's lips drew back into a thin, tight line. 'Somebody's sending out a mental broadcast that's putting everybody's conscious minds asleep. This whole town is in the early stages of mass hypnosis.'

The children stared, appalled.

Rod nodded. 'Someone, or something, up there, is a heck of a lot more powerful a projective telepath than we've ever dreamed of.'

'But it hath not the feel of a person's mind, my lord!' Gwen protested. 'Oh, aye, the thoughts themselves do – but that lulling, that pressure that doth soothe into mindlessness – 'tis only power, without a mind to engender it!'

Rod had a brief, lurid memory of the genetically altered chimpanzee he'd had to fight some years ago. Actually, it was its power he'd had to fight; the poor beast had no mind of its own. The futurians, who were continually trying to conquer Gramarye, had just used it as a converter, transforming minute currents of electricity into psionic power blasts that could stun a whole army. When they'd finally found the chimp, it had been one of the ugliest, most obscene things he'd ever seen – and one of the most pitiable. Rod shuddered, and looked into his wife's eyes. 'I don't know what it is – but I don't like the climate. Come on – eat up, and let's go.'

They turned back to their food, with relief. But after a bit, Cordelia looked up. 'Not hungry, Papa.'

'I know the feeling,' Rod growled, 'but you will be. Choke down at least one bowlful, will you?' He turned to Gwen. 'Let's take the bread and sausage along.'

She nodded, and began to wrap the food in his handkerchief.

Rod turned back to his children – and frowned. There was something wrong, some flaw in their disguise . . .

Then he found it. 'Don't forget to bicker a little, children. It's not normal to go through a whole lunch without being naughty.'

They passed the last house at the edge of the village. Rod muttered, 'Not yet, kids. Another hundred yards; then we're safe.'

For a moment, Geoffrey looked as though he were going to

protest. Then he squared his shoulders like his siblings, gritted his teeth, and ploughed on for another three hundred feet. Then Rod stopped. 'OK. *Now.*'

With one voice, the whole family expelled a huge sigh of relief. Cordelia began to tremble. 'Papa – 'tis horrid!'

Gwen reached to catch her up, but Rod beat her to it. He swept the little girl into his arms, stopping her shuddering with a bear hug. 'I know, baby. But be brave – there'll be worse than this before we're done with Alfar.' *Or he's done with us*; the thought fleeted through his mind, but he helped it fleet on out; a father whose children could read minds couldn't afford defeatist thinking. *Talk about thought control* . . . Rod cast an appealing glance over Cordelia's shoulder, at Gwen. 'Don't you think it's time for you folks to go home now?'

Gwen's chin firmed and lifted. Below her, three smaller chins repeated the movement. 'Nay, my lord,' she said firmly. ' 'Tis eerie, and doth make one's flesh to creep – yet for us, there is, as yet, no greater danger than we saw last night, and thou mayest yet have need of our magics.'

'I can't deny that last part,' Rod sighed, 'and I suppose you're right – that village may have been nasty, but it wasn't any more dangerous than it was last night. OK – we go on as a family.'

The boys broke into broad smiles, and Cordelia sat up in Rod's arms and clapped her hands together. Rod set her down, set his fists on his hips, and surveyed his children with a stern eye. 'You do realize what's going on back there, don't you?'

They all nodded, and Magnus said, 'Aye, Papa.' Geoffrey explained, 'Alfar doth prepare the town for conquest.'

Rod nodded, his gaze on his second son. 'How will he take them?'

The boy shrugged. 'In peace. He will march in, and they will acclaim him as their friend and master, and bow to him – and all of this without ever a drop of blood shed.'

There was a definite note of admiration in his voice. Rod shook his head. 'Good analysis – but be careful, son. Don't start thinking that ability implies goodness.'

'Oh, nay, Papa! Ne'er could I think so! He is a worthy enemy – but that's just to say he would not be worthy an he were not able; but he would not be an enemy were he not evil.'

Rod took a deep breath and stilled, with his mouth open,

before he said, 'We-e-e-ll . . . there *are* enemies who might not be really *evil* – they'd just be trying to get the same thing you're trying to get.'

But Geoffrey shook his head firmly. 'Nay, Papa. Such be rivals, not enemies.'

Rod stilled with his mouth open again. Then he shrugged. 'OK – as long as you make the distinction.' He took a deep breath, looking around at his family. 'So, I think we've got a better idea, now, about how Alfar works. First he sends his minions in to intimidate anybody who didn't hypnotize easily.'

'There be such, Papa?' Cordelia asked in surprise.

Rod nodded. 'Oh, yes, dear. That particular kind of magic isn't exactly foolproof; there'll always be a few people who aren't terribly open to letting somebody else take over their minds – I hope.'

'And there be those who will not bow to him from fear, either,' Geoffrey said stoutly.

'Oh, yes. And if any of those happen to be knights, or lords, and march against him with their men-at-arms – by the time they get to Alfar, he'll have most of the soldiers convinced they don't *want* to win.'

'Aye. 'Tis the way of it.' Geoffrey looked up at his father with a glow of pride.

'Thanks, son.' Rod smiled, amused. 'Just adding things up.' Then his smile faded. 'But *what* the *heck* kind of projective telepath does he *have*, that can reach out over a hundred miles to hypnotize a whole village?'

They set up camp, with trenches for beds and pine boughs for mattresses. The kids rolled up in their blankets, and were instantly asleep – at least, as far as Rod could see.

He didn't trust them. 'What child is this who, laid to rest, sleeps?' he asked Gwen.

She gazed off into space for a moment, listening with her mind. He decided to try it himself, so he closed his eyes and blanked his mind, envying the ease with which she did it. After a few seconds he began to hear the children's low, excited, mental conversation. He rolled his eyes up in exasperation amd started to get up – but Gwen caught his arm. 'Nay, my lord. Let them speak with one another, I prithee; 'twill lull them to sleep.'

'Well . . . ' Rod glanced back at her.

'Yet what will lull us?' she murmured.

He stared down at her, drinking in her beauty. Her femininity hit him with physical force, and he dropped back down beside her, one arm spread out in return invitation. 'I'm sure I'll think of something, dear – but it takes some creativity, when the kids are watching.'

She turned her head to the side, watching him out of the corners of her eyes. 'Their lids are closed.'

'But not their minds.' Rod pressed a finger over her lips. 'Hush up, temptress, or I'll put you back in your teapot.'

'And what wilt thou do with me, once thou hast me there?' she purred, nestling up against him.

The contact sent a current coursing through him. His breath hissed in. 'I said a teapot, not a pumpkin shell!' He reached out to caress her gently, and it was her turn to gasp. He breathed into her ear, 'Just wait till they fall asleep . . . '

'Beshrew me! But they have only now waked from several hours' rest!' Gwen gazed up at him forlornly.

'Aye di me!' Gwen sighed, snuggling a little closer. 'E'en so, the comfort of thy presence will aid me greatly, my lord.'

'Fine – now that you've made sure *I* won't sleep!'

'Yet must not a husbandman be ever vigilant?' she murmured.

'Yeah – waiting for my chance!' He rested his cheek against her head. 'Now I know why they call you a witch . . . '


'Papa-a-a-a!'

Rod woke instantly; there'd been tears in that little voice. He opened his eyes and saw Gregory leaning over him clutching his arm, shaking him. 'Papa, Papa!' Tears were running down the little boy's cheeks. Rod reached up an arm to snake around him and pull him down, cradling him against his side. The little boy stayed stiff, resisting comfort. Rod crooned, 'What's the matter, little fella? Bad dreams?'

Gregory gulped, and nodded.

'What was it about?'

'Nasty man,' Gregory sniffled.

'Nasty?' For some reason, Rod was suddenly on his guard. 'What was he doing?'

'He did creep upon us.' Gregory looked up at his father, eyes wide. 'Creeping up, to hurl things at us.'

Rod stared into his eyes for a second, then began to pat his back gently. 'Don't worry about it. Even if the nasty man did sneak up on us, your brothers and sister would gang up on him before he could do much damage.' He smiled, and saw a tentative, quivering lift at the corners of Gregory's mouth. He tousled the boy's hair and turned to look at his wife. He saw a large pair of eyes staring back at him. 'Kind of thought you'd wake up, if one of the kids had a problem.'

'I did hear him,' Gwen said softly. 'I did see his dream. And, my lord . . . '

Rod couldn't help feeling that being on his guard was just the thing for the occasion. 'What's wrong?'

'Gregory's mind would not conjure up so mild a phantasm, nor one so threatening.'

The tension was building inside Rod. Anger began to boil up under it. Rod tried to hold it down, reminding himself that he and Gwen could probably handle any attempt to hurt them. But the mere thought that anyone would dare to attack his children, to plant nightmares in their sleeping minds . . . !

Magnus, Cordelia and Geoffrey suddenly sat bolt-upright. 'Papa,' Cordelia gasped, 'what dost thou?'

'Is it that bad already? I'm trying to *hold* my temper.'

'Thou dost amazingly.' Magnus blinked the sleep out of his eyes and leaned closer, on hands and knees, to peer at his father. 'In truth, thou dost amazingly. I would never guess thy rage, to look at thee. Papa, what . . . '

The night seemed to thicken a few feet away from the children. Something hazy appeared, coalesced, hardened, and shot to earth, slamming into the ground a few feet from Magnus's hand. His head snapped around; he stared at a six-inch rock. Cordelia's gaze was riveted to it, too, in horror; but Geoffrey leaped to his feet. 'Ambush!'

The night thickened again, just over Magnus's head. Something hazy appeared . . .

. . . and began to coalesce . . .

'Heads up!' Rod dived for his son. His shoulder knocked Magnus sprawling, and a foot-thick rock crashed down, grazing Rod's hip. He bellowed with pain – and anger at the monster who dared attack his children. His full rage cut loose.

'Ware!' Magnus cried. The children were already looking up, as their father had bade them, so they saw the rocks materializing – two, three, all plummeting to earth as they became real.

'Dodge ball!' Magnus shouted. Instantly, he and his brothers and sister were bounding and bobbing back and forth, Cordelia weaving an aerial dance that would've given a computer tracker a blown fuse, the boys appearing and disappearing here, there, yonder, like signal lights in a storm. Through their flickering pavane, Magnus called in suppressed rage, 'Art thou hurted, Papa?'

'Nothing that a little murder won't cure!' Rod yelled back. 'Children – seek! Discover and destroy!'

The children seemed to focus more sharply, and stayed visible for longer intervals.

Gwen was on her feet, still, her eyes warily probing the night above them.

Then Geoffrey hopped to his left, just as a small boulder materialized right where his chest had been.

Rod stood rigid with horror. If the boy hadn't happened to jump aside, just at that instant . . . 'Somebody's trying to teleport rocks into the kids' bodies!'

''Twould be instant death.' Gwen's face was pale, but taut with promised mayhem.

Rod stood tree-still, his eyes wide open; but the night blurred around him into a formless void as his mind opened, seeking . . .

Cordelia seized her broomstick and shot up into the sky. For a moment, all three boys disappeared. Then Magnus reappeared, far across the meadow, dimly seen in the moonlight. He disappeared again just as Geoffrey reappeared ten feet away, twenty feet in the air. Air shot outward with a pistol-crack, inward with firecracker-pop. The meadow resounded with reports, like miniature machine gun fire. Geoffrey disappeared with a dull boom, and a treetop near by swayed with a bullwhip-crack as Gregory appeared in the topmost limbs.

And stones kept falling, all over the meadow.

'Husband!' Gwen's voice was taut. 'This enemy will mark us, too, ere long.'

That jolted Rod. 'I suppose so – if he doesn't just pick on little kids. Better split up.'

Gwen seized her broomstick and disappeared into the dark sky.

That left Rod feeling like a sitting duck. He supposed he would be able to float up into the sky himself, if he just thought about it – but he'd never done it, and didn't want to have to pay attention to trying to keep himself up while he was trying to find and annihilate an enemy. Capture, he reminded himself – capture, if you can.

But he hoped he'd find he couldn't.

Magnus appeared ten feet away, shaking his head. 'He doth cloak his thoughts well, Papa. I cannot . . . ' Suddenly, his eyes lost focus. Geoffrey's laugh carolled over the meadow, clear and filled with glee. Magnus disappeared with a pistol-crack. Rod leaped for Fess's back and shot across the meadow, a living missile with a double warhead.

He was just in time to see Geoffrey and Magnus shoot up out of the trees, carrying a young man stretched like a tug-of-war rope between them. He struggled and cursed, kicking and whiplashing about with his legs and torso, but the boys stretched his arms tight, laughing with delight, and pulling with far more strength than their little bodies could account for.

The young man shut his mouth, and glared at Magnus.

Foreboding struck, and Rod sprang from Fess's back in a flying tackle.

He smacked into the young man's legs so hard they bruised his shoulder. Above him, the warlock yowled in pain.

Then it was daytime, suddenly full noon. The glare stung Rod's eyes, and he squinted against it. He could make out fern leaves closely packed above, and a huge lizardlike monstrosity staring at them from five feet away. Then its mouth lolled open in a needle-fanged grin, and it waddled toward them with amazing speed. Panic clawed its way up Rod's throat, and he almost let go to snatch out his knife – but the enemy warlock panicked first.

It was night again, total night. No, that was moonlight, wasn't it? And it showed Rod water, endless waves heaving below him. One reached up to slap at his heels, and its impact travelled on up to hit his stomach with chilling dread. He could just picture himself falling, sinking beneath those undulating fluid hills, rising to thrash about in panic, clawing for land, for wood, for something that floated . . . Instinctively, he tightened his hug on the ankles.

Then sunlight seared his eyes, the sunlight of dawn, and bitter cold stabbed his lungs. Beyond the legs he clung to, the world spread out below him like a map, an immensity of green. Jagged rocks stabbed up, only a few yards below his heels. It had to be a mountain peak, somewhere on the mainland.

Darkness again, blackness – but not quite total, for moonlight filtered through a high, grated window, showing him blocks of granite that dripped with moisture, and nitre webbing the high corners of the cramped chamber. Huge rusty staples held iron chains to the walls. A skeleton lounged in the fetters at the end of a pair of those chains. Another held a thick-bodied man with a bushy black beard. His brocade doublet was torn and crusted with dried blood, and a grimy bandage wrapped his head. He stared at them in total amazement. Then relief flooded his face, and his mouth opened . . .

Limbo. Nothingness. Total void.

There wasn't any light, but there wasn't any darkness, either – just a grey, formless nothingness. Rod felt an instant conviction that he wasn't seeing with his eyes – especially when colours began to twist through the void in writhing streaks, and a hiss of white noise murmured in the distance. They floated, adrift, and the body in Rod's arms suddenly began to writhe and heave again. A nasal voice cursed, 'Thou vile recreants! I will rend thee, I will tear thee! Monstrous, perverse beasts, who— '

Geoffrey cried out, 'Abandon!'

Suddenly Rod was hugging nothing; the legs were gone. He stared blankly at the space where they'd been. Then panic surged up within him, and he flailed about, trying to grasp something solid, anything, the old primate fear of falling skewering his innards.

Then a small hand caught his, and Geoffrey's voice cried, 'Gregory! Art there, lad? Hold thou, and *pull*!'

Gentle breeze kissed Rod's cheek, and the scents of pine and meadow grass filled his head with a sweetness he did not remember them ever having before. Moonlight showed him the meadow where they had camped, and Gwen darting forward, to throw her arms about him – and the two boys who clung to him. 'Oh, my lord! My bairns! Oh, thou naughty lads, to throw thyselves into such danger! Praise Heaven thou'rt home!'

Cordelia was hugging Rod's neck hard enough to gag him, head pressed against his and sobbing, 'Papa! I feared we had lost thee!'

Rod wrapped his arms around her, grateful to have something solid to hold on to. He looked up to see Geoffrey peeking at him over Gwen's shoulder. Rod nodded, 'I don't know how you did it, son – but you did.'

# Chapter Six

' 'Twas not so hard as that.'

The blankets were around their shoulders now, and a small campfire danced in the centre of the family circle. Cordelia turned a spit over the fire from time to time, roasting a slow rabbit for breakfast.

'Not so hard?' Rod frowned at Geoffrey. 'How could it have been anything *but* hard? That young villain had to be one of the best teleporters in the land! I mean, aside from you boys, the only warlock we've got who can teleport anything but himself is old Galen – and nobody ever sees him!'

'Save old Agatha,' Gwen murmured.

'Nobody ever sees *her* either,' Rod retorted.

'Save old Galen,' Cordelia reminded him.

'He's going to need it,' Rod agreed. He turned back to the boys. 'Toby's the best of our young warlocks, and he's just beginning to learn how to teleport other objects. He's almost thirty, too. So Alfar's sidekick has to be better than Toby.'

'Nay, not so excellent as that.' Magnus shook his head. 'And he was a very poor marksman.'

'For which, praise Heaven.' Rod shuddered. 'But he was *too* good at teleporting himself – even over his weight allowance! I didn't begin to recognize most of the places he took us to!'

'Any child could do the same,' Magnus answered, annoyed.

'I keep telling you, son – don't judge others by yourself. Why didn't he just disappear, though?'

'He could not,' Geoffrey grinned. 'We could tell where he would flee to, and fled there but a fraction of a second behind him.'

'How could you tell where he was going?'

'They held his hands,' Gwen reminded. 'Thoughts travel more readily, by touch.'

Magnus nodded. 'We could feel, through his skin, where he meant to go next.'

Rod stared at him for a moment, then sat back, shaking his head. 'Beyond my comprehension. Thoughts can't travel any FESSter just by touching – can they?'

'No,' Fess's voice murmured through the earphone implanted in the bone behind Rod's right ear. 'But there would be less signal-loss than with a radiated waveform.'

Cordelia sighed, striving for patience with her dullard father. ''Tis not that one doth hear faster, Papa – only that one doth hear more. With touch, even tinges of thought speak clearly.'

'I bow to the guest expert.' Rod managed to keep the fond amusement out of his tone, giving the words a sour twist.

Fess ploughed on. 'The neurons in the warlock's hand did, in all probability, induce the signal directly into the neurons in the boys' hands.'

'He couldn't hide his thought-traces from you.' Rod turned back to Geoffrey. 'So you always had just enough clues to follow him. But how did you manage to bring *me* along?'

Gregory shook his head, eyes round. 'That, Papa, we cannot say.'

'We thought thou couldst,' Magnus added.

Rod scowled. 'No . . . can't say that I did. Except that I was bound and determined that I wasn't going to let go of him . . . '

The children stared at one another, then at their mother.

'What's the matter?' Rod demanded. 'What am I – a monster?'

'Nay, Papa,' Cordelia said softly, 'thou'rt only a warlock – yet a most puissant one.'

'You mean it was just my determination that took me wherever he went?'

Magnus nodded. 'Thy magic followed all else that was needful.'

Rod was still, gazing at the fire for a few minutes while he tried to absorb that. It was unnerving to think that he was beginning to be able to work magic the way his wife and children did – just by thinking of it. Now he was going to have to watch his step to make sure he didn't do it accidentally. He could just hear a casual passerby asking. 'How do you think the weather's going to be today, Mr Warlock?' 'Well, to tell you the truth, I think it's going to rain— ' and *sploosh!* They'd be drenched . . .

He shook off the mood, and looked up to find the children's gazes glued to him. They looked worried; he wondered what they'd been up to. 'So. Finally, he took us into a dungeon.'

''Twas the sorcerer Alfar's dungeon,' Geoffrey explained, and Cordelia gasped.

Rod nodded. 'Convenient. If he could just have figured out some way to get rid of us, we'd be right there to hand for the gaolers. But how did he figure he was going to be able to keep you there? How could he prevent you from teleporting out?'

'I do not think he had thought that far,' Magnus said slowly.

Rod was still nodding. 'Makes sense. I wouldn't be too good

at the details, if I was trying to run from the enemy, but he was coming right along.'

'He was not attempting that,' Geoffrey said, with conviction. 'He meant only to take us to a place in which we would be unwilling to stay.'

Rod smiled slowly. 'Clever kid. Chose a nice one, didn't he?'

'Aye.' Magnus shivered. 'I was well relieved to be quit of that place.'

'But how're you so sure?' Rod asked Geoffrey.

'Because we tried to hale him out, and he would not come.'

Rod stared. Then he took a deep breath and said, delicately, 'Little chancy, wasn't it?'

'Nay. We sought to bring him to Mama.'

Gwen's eyes gleamed. Rod glanced at her, and turned back to the boys with a shudder. 'That's what put us into Limbo?'

'Where?' Magnus frowned. 'Oh! Thou dost speak of the Void!'

Rod didn't like the familiarity with which he spoke of it. 'Been there before, have you?'

Magnus caught the look, and realized its significance. 'Nay, not so often . . . 'Tis only that . . . '

'Spells go awry sometimes, Papa,' Geoffrey explained. 'Assuredly thou must needs realize that.'

'That,' Rod said tightly, 'is why you're supposed to wait till Mama can supervise.'

'She did, the first time.'

'*First* . . . time?'

'Peace, husband.' Gwen touched his arm. ''Tis naught so dangerous as that.'

'Aye', Magnus said quickly. 'When thou dost arrive in that place that is not a place, thou hast but to think of where thou dost wish to be, and lo! Thou art there indeed!'

'I'll try to remember that,' Rod said grimly. He noticed that Cordelia was managing to hold her tongue, but she looked chartreuse with envy. He caught her hand, and she squeezed back. 'So,' he said to Geoffrey, 'how did we wind up in Limbo this time?'

'Why, because we wished to bear him to Mama, and he did not wish to go.'

'I don't blame him, when he's in that mood. So you were trying to go, and he was trying to stay, so . . . '

'We went nowhere.' Geoffrey nodded. 'I saw, then, that we could not win, so I sought safety.'

'What was so tough about it?' Rod frowned. 'I thought you only needed to think yourselves home!'

'We did need some aid,' Geoffrey admitted, and he reached out to clap his three-year-old brother on the shoulder. 'This one had followed us with his mind, where e'er we had gone. I had but to call out to him, and he helped pull us, and showed us the road to home.'

'Yes . . . ' Rod's gaze fastened on his youngest. 'He's had some experience doing that.'

Gregory looked totally blank.

'Not that he'd remember it,' Rod explained. 'He was a little young, at the time – eleven months old. But! Here you are, safe at home – praise Heaven!' He gathered them all into his arms, and squeezed. They gave mock yells of dismay, and Rod relaxed, looking down into their faces. 'And now – you can go home.'

They let loose a squall that must've woken villagers for miles around.

'Nay, Papa, not so soon!'

'It was just beginning to be fun!'

'We're not ready, Papa!'

'Boys get to do all the fun stuff,' Cordelia pouted.

Geoffrey looked straight into Rod's eyes. 'There is no danger, Papa.'

'No danger!' Rod exploded. 'You have a maverick warlock raining cannonballs on you, and you tell me there's no danger? You have a monster magus trying to conjure rock chunks into your bodies, and you tell me it's *safe*? You have a felon enchanter, straight from the glass house, throwing stones at you, and you tell me it's *tame*?'

'But we are whole,' Magnus spread his hands. 'Naught save a bruise or two.'

'Chance! Sheer, freakish good fortune! You're just lucky that sorcerer was a lousy shot!'

'Yet we outnumber him, Papa!'

'He outweighs you! And that's just the *human* danger! What's going to happen the next time you get into a tug-of-war with one of those sorcerer interns? You might be stranded out in that void with no way to get home!'

'Surely not, Papa,' Geoffrey protested. ''Tis as I've said – thou hast but to *think* of . . . '

'Yeah, if you've got somebody tuned in to act as your safety line!'

'But Gregory . . . '

'Gregory might be *with* you!' Rod bawled.

'Yet that doth not afright me, Papa,' the three-year-old cried. 'That grey place doth please me! 'Tis comforting, and . . . '

'Makes you feel right at home, does it?' Rod felt a bitter stab of guilt. 'You should; your mind spent enough time searching there, when you were a baby, trying to find out where Mama and I had gone.'

'An thou sayest it. Therefore do I know my way. There is truly no dang— '

'Now I say NO!' Rod roared, slamming his fist into the turf. Pain shot up his forearm, but his rage shoved it aside. 'What the *hell* do you think you're doing, talking back to your father!' He snatched Magnus's collar, and yanked the boy's face up to his. 'Think you're getting big, do you? Let me tell you, you will *never* be old enough to argue with me!' He threw Magnus back, and whirled to catch at Geoffrey. The six-year-old ducked aside, automatically bringing his arm up to block, managing to knock Rod's arm aside.

Rod froze, eyes bulging, staring down at the boy, rigid as a board, white with rage, nostrils pinching in.

Geoffrey flinched away. 'Papa – I did not mean— '

'I *know* what you meant!' Rod strode forward. 'I know damn well what you— '

But he bumped into something, and Gwen's eyes were looking directly into his. Her voice bored through his fury, droning, demanding, 'Come out! I know thee, Rod Gallowglass, born Rodney d'Armand. I know thee for my lover and husband, and know that thou art there, beneath this beastliness that overcomes thee. Come out, Rod Gallowglass! Let not this shell of anger overwhelm and overmaster thee. Ever hast thou been a caring husband, and a gentle father to my children. Thou art of Gramarye, not Tir Chlis! Thou art my treasure, and my children thy gems! Husband, turn! Come out to me, Rod Gallowglass!'

Rod stared at her, fury mounting higher, but held by the truth of her words. An evil spell . . . He shuddered, and his rage fell into slivers, and ebbed. He sagged, his knees giving way for a moment, and stumbled – and Magnus was there beside him, shoulder under his father's arm, staring up at Rod in fright and concern.

Concern for his father's safety – even after Rod had been

so cruel! This son could not only forgive – he could even run
to help! Remorse charged his anguish, and made him harsh. He
recovered his balance and stood, stiffening. 'Thank you.' But he
clasped the boy's shoulder firmly.

Magnus winced, but stood steadfast.

Rod held the boy's shoulders with both hands, but his gaze
held Gwen's. 'That was foolish, you know. Very risky. Likely
to get you slugged.'

Answering anger flared in her eyes – flared, and was smothered.
''Twas worth the risk, my lord.'

He gave her a brief, tight nod. 'Yes. Thank you. Very much.'
He shook his head. 'Don't do it again. It won't work, again. When
it hits me, just . . . go. Anywhere, as fast as you can. Just go.'

'That, also, would be foolish,' she cried, almost in despair.
'If we do flee, thou wilt pursue – and then thou wilt not hear,
no matter what appeal I plead.'

He stared at her, immobile. Finally, he closed his eyes, clenching his fists so tightly that they hurt. He took three slow,
deep, even breaths, then looked up at her and said, 'But you
must. Not when I'm angry – no, you're right, that would be
dangerous.' He forced himself to say it: 'For both of us.' It
left an astringent taste behind. 'But now. Now. It's getting too
wild up here. Alfar and his henchmen aren't playing games.
They're too dangerous. And if I don't hurt the children, he
will.'

She stared at him for a long moment. The children were
very silent.

Then, slowly, Gwen said, 'An thou dost wish it, my lord, we
will go. Yet I prithee, think again – for we are safer if we are with
thee, as thou'lt be. For then can we ward one another's backs. Yet
if we are apart from thee – if we dwell back in Runnymede – then
may thine enemies seek to strike at thee by hurting us – and thou
wilt not be by us, to defend.'

It was an excuse. It was a rationalization. It was specious
and hollow, and Rod knew it.

But he was scared. He was very scared of what might happen
inside him if he started arguing with her. He was afraid for her,
afraid for the children . . .

But he was also afraid for them if Alfar ever realized that none
of his henchmen could handle the Gallowglasses alone. When he
did, he'd probably do the sensible thing – gang up on them, all his

sorcerers together. And the children were powerful espers already, but they were still children.

But he was more afraid of what might happen to them, if he lost his temper again.

Abruptly, he bowed his head. 'All right. Stay.'

The children cheered.

Their raucous clamour bounced off Rod's ears. He stood in the midst of the rain of their sound, swearing under his breath that he would not let his temper turn against them again.

He was still swearing the next day, inside his head, and searching frantically for a way to ensure their safety. Other than sending them home – he wasn't going to argue with them about that, again. Arguments turned into rage.

'Wilt thou not ride now, my lord?' Gwen sat up on Fess's saddle, with Cordelia in front of her.

Rod shook his head, mute, and ploughed on.

The children glanced at their mother, then back at him, and followed him silently.

Around the curve ahead of them, a husky peasant and his equally husky wife came into view, with five children trudging wearily beside them – wearily, even though it was early in the morning. The husband pushed a handcart piled high with sacks and household belongings.

'More refugees,' Rod grated. 'How many is that, 'Delia?'

'Fourteen, Papa.'

Rod nodded. 'Fourteen in how long?'

'An hour and a half, Papa,' Gregory answered, glancing at the sun.

Rod shook his head. 'That's real evil happening up there, children. People don't leave their homes for mild likes and dislikes – not even for hates. They flee because of fear.'

'We do not fear, Papa,' Magnus said stoutly.

'I know,' Rod returned. 'That's what worries me.'

They plodded on toward the peasant family. Then Geoffrey took a chance and said, 'The sorcerer's guards grow careless, Papa.'

'Why?' Rod frowned. 'You mean because they let these people pass?' He shook his head. 'That's not where they're coming from. Here, I'll show you.' He stepped over to the side of the road as the big peasant and his family came up. The man looked up at him, surprised, and scowled. Then weariness overcame him, and he relaxed, humbling himself to talk to someone who was below his station. 'Hail, tinker! Dost thou travel north, then?'

'Aye,' Rod answered. 'Poor folk must seek their living where they can. Why, what moves in the north?'

The peasant shook his head. 'We know only what Rumour speaks. We ourselves have not seen it.'

Rod frowned. 'So fearsome? What doth Rumour say?'

'That an evil sorcerer hath risen,' the peasant answered. 'He hath overcome the Sire of Maladroit, the Baron de Gratecieux, and even the Count Lagorme.'

Rod stared, incredulous. 'Why? Who doth speak so?'

Geoffrey looked unbelieving, too, at the idea that Alfar's men could have let someone slip out to bear word.

The big peasant shrugged wearily. 'Rumour flies, tinker – and well thou shouldst know it, for 'tis thy tradesmen that do carry such tidings, more often than not.'

'Is it that, then?' Rod's eyebrows lifted. 'Only that a cousin told a neighbour, who told a gossip, who told an uncle, who told . . . '

'Aye, belike.' The big peasant shrugged. 'I know only what my god-sib Hugh son of Marl told unto me – and that the whiles he packed a barrow like to this, and set packs to the backs of his wife and sons. "Whither comes this word?" quoth I; and spake he, "From Piers Thatcher . . . "'

Rod interrupted. 'Lives he on the Count's estates?'

The peasant shook his head. 'Nay, nor on Gratecieux's, nor on Maladroit's. Yet he hath a cousin whose god-sib's nephew hath a brother-in-law whose cousin hath a niece who doth live hard by the good Count's manor – and thus the word doth run.'

'Is't so?' Rod glanced back at Geoffrey, then back to the peasant, bobbing his head and tugging a forelock. 'I thank thee, goodman. We will wend our way a little farther north – but we shall ponder well thy words.'

'Do,' the big peasant advised, 'and turn back toward the south.'

'These things are not certain,' Gwen protested.

'Nay,' the peasant's wife agreed. 'Yet we have heard this word again and, aye, again, for all these months of spring. First Rumour spoke of the Sire – but then of the Baron, and now of the Count. If Rumour doth begin to speak of the Duke, belike we'll find we *can* not flee.' She shook her head. 'Nay, an thou lovest thy little ones, chance not the truth of Rumour.'

'Mayhap thou hast the right of it,' Gwen said with a pensive frown. 'I thank thee – and farewell.'

'God be with thee, goodman.' Rod tugged at his forelock again.

'God be,' the man returned, and took up the handles of his cart again.

As the peasant and his family slogged away towards the south, Geoffrey spun towards his father and fairly exploded in a hissing whisper. 'So easily, Papa! Is all the work of so many guards and sentries brought low so easily, by naught but *gossip*?'

'Indeed it is,' Rod answered sourly. 'Remember that when you command. The fence isn't made, that can stop a rumour.'

Geoffrey threw up his hands in exasperation. 'Then why mount a watch at all?'

'Proof.' Rod grimaced. 'If none of the lords have proof, they won't go to the expense of sending an army northward. After all, what did the King himself do when he heard the unconfirmed word? Sent us!'

'All this, to hold back proof?'

Rod nodded. 'Without that, anybody who wants to believe the news is false, can.'

'Until the sorcerer and his minions overrun them,' the boy said darkly.

'Yes,' Rod agreed, with a bleak smile. 'That is the idea, isn't it?'

'Papa,' said Cordelia, 'I begin to fear.'

'Good.' Rod nodded. 'Good.'

Half an hour later, they saw a small coach in the distance, hurtling toward them. As it came closer, they saw that the horses were foaming and weary. But the woman who sat on the coachman's box flogged them on, with fearful glances over her shoulder at the troop of men-at-arms who galloped after her on small, tough northern ponies, and the armoured knight who thundered at their head on a huge, dark warhorse that would have made two of the ponies.

'What churlishness is this,' Gwen cried, 'that armed men pursue a woman shorn of defence?'

'Don't blame 'em too hard,' Rod snapped. 'I don't think they're terribly much aware of what they're doing.'

'Thou must needs aid her, my lord!'

'Yes,' Rod agreed. 'It isn't too hard to tell who the bad guys are, is it? Especially since we've seen their livery before. Ambush stations, kids.'

'Magnus and Gregory, guard the left,' Gwen instructed. 'Cordelia and Geoffrey, do thou ward the right. Flit toward them, as far as thou canst.' She turned to Rod. 'How wouldst thou have them fell their foes, husband?'

'One by one. Unhorse them.' Rod felt a warm glow at her support.

'Delia caught up her broomstick with a shout of glee.

'How shall we fell them, Mama?' Geoffrey grinned. 'Throw rocks at them?'

Gwen nodded. 'Aye – but take thou also thy belts of rope, and discover how thou mayst make use of them.'

They all quickly untied the lengths of hemp that were lashed about their waists. 'Mama,' said Magnus, 'I think that I could make the nails to disappear from the horses' shoes.'

Rod nodded slow approval. 'I pity the poor horses – but they shouldn't be damaged. They will stop, though.'

'Naught of these will avail against the knight,' Gregory pointed out.

Rod gave him a wolfish grin. 'He's mine.'

'Begone from sight now, quickly!' Gwen clapped her hands.

The children dodged off the roadside into the underbrush, and disappeared.

Gwen hopped down from Fess's back, and caught her broomstick from its sling alongside the saddle. 'Wilt thou need thine horse, my lord?'

''Fraid so, dear. Can you manage without him?'

'Why, certes.' She dimpled, and dropped him a quick curtsy. 'Godspeed, husband.' Then she turned away to dive into the underbrush after the children.

Rod sighed, jamming a foot into the stirrup. 'Quite a woman I've got there, Fess.'

'Sometimes I wonder if you truly appreciate her, Rod.'

'Oh, I think I do.' Rod swung up into the saddle and pulled on the reins. 'We'd better imitate them. Off the road, Steel Stallion.'

Fess trotted off the shoulder and down into the underbrush. 'What did you have in mind for the knight, Rod?'

'About 120 volts. Got a spare battery?'

Fess's answer was lost in the racket, as the coach thundered by them.

Rod looked up at the mounted squad. 'A hundred yards and closing. Got some cable?'

'Forward port compartment, Rod.' A small door sprang open under Fess's withers.

Rod reached in and pulled out a length of wire. He drew out his dagger and stripped the insulation off in a few quick strokes. 'Where do I plug it in?'

The horsehead turned back to look at him. 'Simply place it in my mouth, Rod. I will route current to it. But are you certain this is ethical?'

'Is the sword he's carrying?' Rod shrugged. 'A weapon is a weapon, Fess. And this one won't do him any permanent damage – I hope. OK, *now*!'

They darted up out of the roadside as the squad pounded up. Rod swerved in alongside the knight. The helmet visor turned toward him, but the knight raised neither sword nor shield, no doubt flabbergasted at seeing a tinker riding up alongside him on a horse that would've done credit to a lord. Besides, what need was there to defend against a piece of rope?

Rod jabbed the end of the wire at him, and a fat blue spark snapped across the gap; then the wire was in contact with the armour, and the knight threw up his arms, stiffened. Rod lashed out a kick, and the knight crashed off his horse into the dust of the road.

Someone gave a shout of horror, behind him. Rod whirled Fess around, then darted off to the side of the road before the sergeant could get his thoughts together enough to start a try for retribution.

Along the side of the road, three soldiers lay sprawled, one every hundred feet or so. Another four lined the verge on the far side. Some of the horses were grazing, very contentedly, next to their fallen masters. A few of the others, obviously more intelligent, were galloping away into the distance.

As Rod watched, a small figure exploded into existence right in front of one of the remaining riders. Startled, the horseman flinched back, and his mount reared, whinnying. Geoffrey lashed out a kick to the man's shoulder, and the soldier overbalanced, tipped, and fell. The child slapped the horse's rump, and the beast turned to gallop away with a whinny.

On the other side of the road, a length of rope shot flying through the air like a winged serpent, and wrapped itself around another soldier's neck. He grabbed at it with both hands, then suddenly jolted backward, and slammed down onto the road, still struggling with the coil. With a gun-crack, Magnus appeared beside him, stick in hand. He swung downward, and the soldier went limp. The rope uncoiled and flew off to look a new victim. Pocket thunder made a boomlet, and Magnus ippeared.

Rod winced. 'Bloodthirsty brood I've got here.'

'They are only doing as you told them, Rod – and taught them.'

'Maybe I'd better revise the curriculum.'

'Do not be overly hasty,' the robot murmured. 'That soldier still breathes.'

'I hope it's widespread. Well, back to work.' Rod turned the horse back onto the road – and saw all the soldiers lying in the dust, unconscious. Already, Gwen knelt by the nearest, gazing intently at his face. Cordelia arrowed in to land beside her, and the boys began to appear, like serial thunder.

'They work fast, too,' Rod muttered. He trotted up beside the family grouping, and leaned down to touch Magnus on the shoulder. The boy's head snapped up in surprise. He saw his father, and relaxed, with a sigh of relief.

'You did wonderfully.' Rod beamed with pride. 'All of you. But keep an eye of the soldiers, son. A few of them might come to while you're still trying to overhaul their minds.'

Magnus nodded, glowing with his father's praise. 'I will ward them well, Papa.'

'Stout fellow. I should be back before they wake up – but, just in case.' He straightened up, turning Fess southward.

'Wither goest thou, Papa?'

'To tell that lady she can stop panicking.' Rod kicked his heels against Fess's sides. 'Follow that coach.'

The robot-horse sprang into a gallop. 'Drumming your heels against my sides really serves no purpose, Rod.'

'Sure it does – keeping up appearances. You wouldn't want people to know you weren't a real horse, would you?'

'Surely you cannot be concerned about that with your own family. They all know my true nature.'

'Yeah, but I've got to stay in the habit. If I start trying to remember who knows about you and who doesn't, I'll start making little mistakes, and . . . '

'I understand,' the robot sighed. 'The coach approaches, Rod.'

'Might be more accurate to say we approach the coach.'

'I was under the impression that you had become a Gramaryian, not a grammarian.'

Rod winced. 'All right, already! I'll go for the content, and stop worrying about the form.'

'Then you would make a very poor critic . . . '

'Oh, shut up and head off the coach.'

Fess swerved in front of the coach horses, and the animals reared, screaming with fright. The woman hit the brake with frantic strength, then lashed out with the whip at Rod.

'Hey!' He ducked, but too late; the lash cracked against the side of his head. The roadway tilted and circled, blurring; distantly, he heard the whip crack, again and again. Then the world levelled, and he began to see clearly. The familiar rage surged up in him. Appalled, he tried to remember her fear. The woman stood on the box, brandishing the whip for one more try.

Rod held up a palm. 'Whoa! Hold it! I'm on *your* side!' He pointed to his chest. 'No uniform. See?'

The woman hesitated, but anger and fear still held her eyes wide.

Rod was working hard to stifle a huge flood of anger of his own; his head ached abominably. 'You wouldn't hit a poor, wandering tinker, would you?'

'Aye, if he threatened me or mine.' But sanity began to return to the woman's eyes. 'And why would a poor tinker stop a noble Lady, it not to harm her?'

'To tell you, you can stop running!' Rod cried. 'We knocked out your enemies!'

The woman stood frozen, but hope flared in her eyes.

Rod pointed back along the road. 'Take a look, if you doubt me!'

She darted a quick glance back up the road, then glanced again. She turned back to him, joy beginning to flower in her face. Then her knees gave way, and she collapsed onto the box. 'Praise Heaven! But how didst thou . . . '

'I had a little help,' Rod explained.

She was instantly on her guard again. 'From whom?'

'My wife,' Rod explained, 'and my children.'

She stared. Then weariness filled her face. 'I see them; they pick the corpses of the soldiers. Do not lie to me, fellow. How could a tinker and his bairns and wife fare against an armoured knight and a dozen soldiers?' She hefted the whip again.

'Now, hold on!' Rod felt his anger mounting again, too. He took a deep breath, and tried to remember that the poor woman had been chased for most of the night – probably. 'My wife and kids aren't robbing bodies – they're trying to break the enchantments that bind living men. Unconscious, but living – I hope. You see, we're not quite what we seem to be.'

'Indeed,' she hissed between her teeth, and forced herself to her feet again, swinging the whip up. 'So I had thought!'

'Not *that* way! This tinker outfit is just a disguise!' Rod straightened in the saddle, squaring his shoulders. 'I am Rodney Gallowglass, Lord High Warlock of Gramarye – and that woman back there is the Lady Gwendylon.'

She stared. Then her lips parted, and she whispered, 'Give me a sign.'

'A sign?' Exasperated, Rod bit down on his irritation and forced himself to imagine just how paranoid he'd be feeling in her place. He took another deep breath, expelled it. 'Oh, all right!' Rod closed his eyes and let his mind go blank, concentrating. His usual haze of needs and responsibilities seemed to ebb and clear, till he could hear his children's voices, as though they were right next to him. He singled out the one who looked least threatening and thought, Gregory! Come here!

Air popped outward, and Gregory floated next to his shoulder. 'Aye, Papa.'

The woman stared.

Then her knees gave way again, and she sat down, nodding weakly. 'Aye. Thou art the High Warlock.'

'Papa?' Gregory cocked his head to the side, frowning up at his father. 'Why didst thou call?'

'For what you just did, son.'

The child stared. 'What did I?'

'You proved I'm what I said I was.' He turned back to the woman. 'And whom have I the pleasure of addressing?'

Now it was her turn to pull herself together and remember her dignity. 'I am Elyena, Duchess of Romanov.'

# Chapter Seven

Rod steered the tottering horses off the road and into the meadow near Gwen, holding up the Duchess with his left arm. As he pulled them to a halt, she raised her head, looking about, then crowded closer to him. 'The soldiers . . . '

Rod turned, and saw all the soldiers gathered in a knot under a low tree. Most of them held their heads in their hands. Some had lifted their gazes and were looking around, blinking, their faces drawn and uncertain. The knight lay by them with his helmet off. Gwen knelt over him.

'Don't worry,' Rod said, trying to sound reassuring. 'They feel as though they've just awakened from a bad dream. They're on your side again.' He jumped down from the box. 'Just stay here.'

She did, huddling into herself – and not looking at all reassured.

Rod sighed, and thought sharply, Cordelia!

The little girl leaped up halfway across the meadow and looked around. She located her father and jumped on her broomstick, zooming straight over to him. 'Aye, Papa?'

Rod noticed the Duchess staring. Well, at least she was distracted. 'Cordelia, this lady needs . . . '

But Cordelia was staring past him, toward the windows of the coach, and a delighted grin curved on her lips. 'Children!'

Rod turned, surprised.

Two little faces filled one of the windows, looking about with frank curiosity. Cordelia skipped past Rod, hands behind her back. Cordelia stopped right below them and cocked her head to the side. 'I am hight Cordelia.'

They didn't answer; they just stared.

Rod touched her shoulder. 'They've been having some bad scares lately, honey.'

The elder boy looked up in indignation. 'Was *not* scared!'

'Yeah, sure, you were calm as a mill pond. Just go easy, honey.'

'Oh, Papa!' she said, exasperated. 'Can they not see I wish them no harm?' Before he could answer, she whirled away to the Duchess. 'May I play with them?'

The Duchess stared down at her. Then, slowly, she said, 'Why . . . an they wish it . . . certes.'

That they would wish it, Rod did not doubt; he knew his

daughter. Already the two boys were watching her with marked interest.

'Oh, good!' Cordelia spun back to the children. 'I have brothers, too. Thou mayst play with them also, an thou dost wish it.'

The two boys still looked wary, but Cordelia's friendliness was infectious. The younger opened the coach door, and stepped out. 'I,' he said, 'am Gaston.'

Rod turned away, quite certain the Duchess's attention would be fully occupied for a while, and went over to his wife.

As he came up, she sat back on her heels, gazing down at the knight and shaking her head. Instantly, Rod was alert. 'What's the matter? Is the hypnosis too strong?'

Gwen shook her head again. 'I have broke the spell, my lord. Yet I can bring him no closer to life than this.'

Rod turned, staring down at the knight. He saw a lined face and bald head, with a fringe of grey hair. His skin was grey, and covered with a sheen of sweat. Guilt swept through Rod. He knelt beside the knight. 'But it was only 120 volts! Only 15 amperes! And I only hit him with it for a few seconds!'

Gwen shook her head. 'It may have as easily been the fall, my lord. His heart had stopped, and I laboured to make it begin to beat again.'

'Heart attack?' Rod took a closer look at the knight. 'He's middle-aged – and he's let himself sag out of shape.' He shook his head, looking up at Gwen. 'There was no way I could tell that. He had his helmet on, and the visor was down.'

'In truth, thou couldst not,' she agreed, 'and anything thou hadst done to stop him, might have hurt him this badly.' She lifted her eyes, gazing into his. 'Yet, my lord, I misdoubt me an 'twas any action of thine that did strike him down. He had ridden too many miles in harness.'

Rod nodded slowly. 'Whoever sent him out to lead a troop in full armour, at his age, must've seen him only as a thing, not a person. Who . . ? No, cancel that. Of course – who else? Alfar.'

'We will tend him, milady.'

Gwen looked up, and saw the sergeant kneeling across from her.

'Sir Verin is old, but dear to us,' the soldier explained. 'How he came to this pass, we know not. We will tend him.' He lifted his head, showing haunted eyes. 'Lady – what have our bodies done, the whiles our souls slept?'

'Naught that is any fault of thine.' She touched his hand, smiling gently. 'Trouble not thine heart.'

Geoffrey darted up beside her. 'Mama! There are children! May we go and play?'

Gwen looked up, startled. 'Why . . . '

'We've got company,' Rod explained.


A short while later, the parents sat around a hasty camp fire while the children played near by. The Duchess sat, shivering in spite of the sun's midday warmth. Gwen had fetched a blanket from Fess's pack and wrapped it around her, but the poor lady still shivered with reaction. She gazed at the children, who were winding up a raucous game of tag. 'Ah, bless them! Poor mites.' Tears gathered at the corners of her eyes. 'They know not the meaning of what hath happened.'

'Thou hast not told them, then?' Gwen said softly.

The Duchess shook her head. 'They know what they have seen, and no more.' She looked up at Rod, a hard stare. 'And I will not tell them until I *know*.'

Rod stared back, and nodded slowly, maintaining the glare. But she couldn't hold it long, and her head dropped.

Near by, the children collapsed in a panting tangle.

'Nay, but tell!' Cordelia cajoled. 'Didst thou truly see the evil sorcerer?'

'Nay,' said the youngest; and 'We saw naught,' said the eldest. 'Naught save the inside of our keep. Mother penned us there, and would not even let us go so far as the window.'

'Yet thou didst come in a coach,' Magnus reminded. 'Didst thou see naught then?'

The boys shook their heads, and the youngest said, 'We knew only that Mother bade us follow her down to the courtyard, and placed us in the coach. Through the gate house we heard the clash of arms afar off; yet she drew the curtains closely, and bade us open them not.'

The oldest added, 'We could hear the rumble of the wheels echoing about us, and knew that we passed through the gatehouse. Then the portcullis did crash down behind us, and the noises of war began to grow nearer.'

Geoffrey's eyes glinted.

'Then they began to grow fainter, till they were lost behind us,' the eldest went on, 'and we heard naught but the grating of the coach's wheels.'

The youngest nodded. 'When at last we did part the curtains, there was naught to see but summer fields and groves.'

The Duchess pressed her face into her hands, and her shoulders shook with more than shivering. Gwen tucked the blanket more tightly around her, murmuring soothing inanities. She glanced at Rod and nodded toward the children.

Rod took the cue. 'Er, kids – could you maybe change the subject?'

'Eh?' Cordelia looked up and took in the situation at a glance. 'Oh!' She was instantly contrite. 'We are sorry, Papa.' She turned to the other children, catching the hands of the Duchess's sons. 'Come, let us play at tracking.'

The fatuous look they gave her boded well for her teenaged future, and ill for Rod's coming peace of mind. But they darted away, calling to one another, and Magnus hid his face against a large tree, and began to count.

The Duchess lifted her head, turning it from side to side in wonder. 'They so quickly forget such ill!'

'Well, yes – but you haven't really told them the bad parts,' Rod said judiciously. 'For all they know, their father's winning the battle. And can you really say he didn't?'

'Nay,' she said, as though it were forced from her. 'Yet I did not flee till I looked down from the battlements, and saw that the mêlée had begun to go against him – even as we had feared.' Then she buried her face in her hands, and her shoulders heaved with sobbing. Gwen clucked over her, comfortingly, and Rod had the good taste to keep quiet until the Duchess had regained some measure of control over herself. She lifted her head, gazing out over the meadow with unseeing eyes. 'When first the reeves began to bring us tales of villages suborned, we dismissed them with laughter. Who could come to rule a village, whiles its knight stood by to shield it? Yet the first tale was followed by a second, and a second by a third, then a fourth, then a fifth – and ever was it the same: that a sorcerer had made the people bow to him. Then it was a witch who forced the homage, with the sorcerer's power supporting her; then a warlock.'

'How'd they do it?' Rod asked. 'Did the reeves know?'

The Duchess shook her head. 'They had heard only rumours

of dire threats, and of barns bursting into flame, and kine that sickened and fell. Yet for the greater part, there had been only surliness and complaining from the peasants, complaining that swelled louder and louder. Then the witch or warlock stepped amongst them, and they turned with joyful will to bow to him or her, and the sorcerer whose power lay 'neath. My lord did bid one of his knights to ride about his own estates, and visit the villages therein. The knight returned, and spoke of peasant mobs that howled in fury, brandishing scythes and mattocks, and hurling stones. When he charged, they broke and ran; yet when he turned away, eftsoons they gathered all against him once again.' Her mouth hardened. 'Thus were they bid, I doubt not.'

'Sudden, rabid loyalty.' Rod glanced at Gwen. 'Would you say they didn't really seem to be themselves? The peasants, I mean.'

'Nay, assurdly not!' The Duchess shuddered. 'They were as unlike what they had been, as Maytime is from winter. Such reports angered milord, but not greatly. They angered his vassal, the Baron de Gratecieux, far more; for, look you, the greater part of Milord Duke's revenues was yielded to him by his counts, who gained theirs from their barons. Yet the barons gain theirs from their knights.'

Rod nodded. 'So a knight's village resisting payments is a little more serious to the baron than to his duke.'

The Duchess nodded too. 'He did implore Milord Duke for arms and men, which my lord did give him gladly. Then rode the Baron 'gainst the sorcerer.'

She fell silent. Rod waited.

When she didn't go on, Rod asked, 'What happened?'

The Duchess shuddered. 'Eh, such reports as we had were horrible, in truth! The Baron's force did meet with a host of magics – fell creatures that did pounce from the air, fireballs and rocks that appeared among them, hurtling; arrows that sped without bows or archers, and war-axes and maces that struck without a hand to bear them. Then peasant mobs did charge upon them, howling and striking with their sickles. Yet far worst of all was a creeping fear, a sense of horror that overcame the Baron's soldiers, till they broke and ran, screaming hoarsely in their terror.'

Rod met Gwen's eyes, and her words sounded in his ears alone: *I count a witch-moss crafter, and the warlock who doth hurl stones 'mongst us; and there be witches who do make the weapons fly. Yet what's this creeping horror?*

Rod could only shake his head. He looked down at the Duchess again. 'What happened to the Baron?'

The Duchess shuddered. 'He came not home; yet in later battles, he has been seen – leading such soldiers as lived, against the sorcerer's foes.'

Rod caught Gwen's eye again; she nodded. Well, they'd met that compulsive hypnosis already. 'How many of the soldiers survived?'

'They were, mayhap, half a dozen that lived to flee of the threescore that marched to battle.'

Rod whistled softly. 'Six out of sixty? This sorcerer's efficient, isn't he? How many of the defeated ones were following Baron de Gratecieux in the next battle?'

The Duchess shrugged. 'From the report we had – mayhap twoscore.'

'Forty out of sixty, captured and brainwashed?' Rod shuddered. 'But some got away – the six you mentioned.'

'Aye. But a warlock pursued them. One only bore word to us; we know not what happened to the other five.'

'It's a fair guess, though,' Rod frowned. 'So right from the beginning, Alfar's made a point of trying to keep word from leaking out.' Somehow, that didn't smack of the medieval mind. 'You say you learned this afterwards?'

The Duchess nodded. 'It took that lone soldier a week and a day to win home to us.'

'A lot can happen in a week.'

'So it did. The sorcerer and his coven marched against the Castle Gratecieux; most of the household acclaimed Alfar their suzerain. The Baroness and some loyal few objected, and fought to close the gates. They could not prevail, though, and those who did acclaim the sorcerer their lord, did open the gate, lower the drawbridge, and raise the portcullis.'

Rod shrugged. 'Well, if they could make whole villages switch allegiance, why not a castleful?'

'What did the sorcerer to the Baroness?' Gwen asked, eyes wide.

The Duchess squeezed her eyes shut. 'She doth rest in the dungeon, with her children – though the eldest was wounded in the brawling.'

Gwen's face hardened.

'How did you learn this?' Rod tried to sound gentle.

'Servants in Gratecieux's castle have cousins in my kitchens.'

'Servants' network.' Rod nodded. 'So Alfar just took over the castle. Of course, he went on to take over the rest of the manor.'

'Such villages as did not already bow to him, aye. They fell to his sway one by one. At last, the other barons did take alarm, and did band together to declare war upon him.'

'Bad tactics.' Rod shook his head. 'The hell with the declaration; they should've just gone in, and mopped him up.'

The Duchess stared, scandalized.

'Just an idea,' Rod said quickly.

The Duchess shook her head. ''Twould have availed them naught. They fought a sorcerer.'

Rod lifted his head slowly, eyes widening, nostrils flaring. He turned to Gwen. 'So he's got people thinking they can't win, before they even march. They're half defeated before they begin fighting.'

'Mayhap,' the Duchess said, in a dull voice, 'yet with great ease did he defeat the barons. A score of sorcerer's soldiers did grapple with the barons' outriders, on the left flank. The scouts cried for a rescue, and soldiers ran to aid them. The sorcerer's men withdrew; yet no sooner had they vanished into the forest, than another band attacked the vanguard of the right flank. Again soldiers ran to bring aid, and again the sorcerer's men withdrew; and, with greater confidence, the barons' men marched ahead.'

Even hearing the story, Rod felt a chill. 'Too much confidence.'

The Duchess nodded, and bit her lip. 'When they came within sight of Castle Gratecieux, a wave of soldiers broke upon them from the forest. At t'other side of the road, rocks began to appear, with thunder-crashes, and also from that side came a swarm of thrown stones – yet no one was there to throw them. The soldiers recoiled upon themselves, then stood to fight; yet they fell in droves. Three of the five barons fought to the last with their men, and were lost. The other two rallied mayhap a score, and retreated. The sorcerer's army pressed them hard, but well did they defend themselves. Naetheless, a half of the men fell, and one of the barons with them. The other half won through to the High Road, whereupon they could turn and flee, faster than the sorcerer's men could follow. A warlock followed them, and rocks appeared all about them; yet he grew careless and, of a sudden, an archer whirled and let fly. The arrow pierced the warlock, and he tumbled from the sky, screaming. Then away rode the baron and his poor remnant – and thus was the word brought to us. And I assure thee, mine husband did honour that archer.'

'So should we all,' Rod said. 'It always helps, having a demonstration that your enemy can be beaten. Didn't your husband take these rumours of danger seriously before then?'

'Nay, not truly. He could not begin to believe that a band of peasants could be any true danger to armoured knights and soldiers, even though they were witches. Yet when the Baron Marole stood before him and told him the account of his last battle, my lord did rise in wrath. He summoned up his knights and men, and did send his fleetest courier south to bear word of all that happed to Their Royal Majesties.'

Rod frowned. 'He sent a messenger? How long ago?'

The Duchess shrugged. 'Five days agone.'

Rod shook his head. 'He should have been in Runnymede before we left.'

She stared at him for a long moment, her eyes widening, haunted. 'He did not come.'

'No,' Rod answered, 'he didn't.'

The Duchess dropped her gaze. 'Alas, poor wight! Need we guess at what hath happed?'

'No, I think it's pretty obvious.' Rod gazed north along the road. 'In fact, he might even have dressed himself as a peasant, in hopes he'd be overlooked. In any case, he's probably the reason Alfar sent his new army out to cut down refugees.'

'Refugees?' The Duchess looked up, frowning. 'What are these?'

'Poor folk, who flee the ravages of war,' Gwen explained.

Rod nodded. 'Usually because their homes have been destroyed. In this case, though, the only ones who've been heading south are the ones who realized what was coming, and got out while they could.'

'You've seen such folk, then?'

Rod nodded. 'A few. I'd say we've been running into one every mile or so.'

The Duchess shook her head slowly. 'I marvel that they 'scaped the sorcerer's soldiers!'

'They started early enough, I guess – but I'm sure the soldiers caught up with plenty of other bands. And, of course, we did manage, to, ah, interfere, when a squad of men-at-arms was trying to stop a family we bumped into.'

The Duchess studied his face. 'What had this family seen?'

'Not a darn thing – but they'd heard rumours.'

'And were wise enough to heed them.' The Duchess's mouth hardened. 'Yet will Their Royal Majesties send an army north, after naught but rumour?'

Rod shook his head. 'Not a chance.'

She frowned. 'Yet how is it *thou* dost . . . ' Then she broke off, eyes widening in surprise, then hope. 'Yet thou *dost* come, thou!'

Rod answered with a sardonic smile. 'Quick-witted, I see. And yes, the King sent us – to find out the truth of the rumours.'

'And thou dost lead thy wife and bairns into so vile a brew of foulness?' The Duchess cried. She turned on Gwen. 'Oh, lady, nay! If thou dost thy children love, spare them this horror!'

Gwen looked up at Rod, startled.

Like a gentleman, Rod declined the unexpected advantage. He only said, 'Well . . . you'll understand that my wife and children are a bit better equipped to deal with evil witches than most might be – so they're not really in so great a danger.'

It earned him a look of warmth from Gwen, but the Duchess cried, 'Danger enow! Lord Warlock, do not let them go! Thou dost not comprehend the might of this fell sorcerer!'

'We've had a taste of it.'

'Then let that taste make thee lose thine appetite! A fulness of his work will sicken thy soul! 'Tis one thing to see a mere squadron of his victims, such as these poor folk . . . ' She waved toward the soldiers. 'Yet when thou dost see them come against thee by the hundreds, thine heart shall shrink in horror! 'Tis not that his magic is so fell – 'tis the purely evil malice of his soul!'

Rod's eyes gleamed. 'You've seen him yourself, then?'

She dropped her eyes. 'Aye, though only from a distance. 'Twas enow.' She shuddered. 'I could feel his hatred washing o'er me, as though I stood 'neath a cloudburst of dirtied water. Methought that I should ne'er again feel clean!'

'But how could the Duke let you come so near the battle!'

'He fought against it, I assure thee – yet the battle did come nigh to me. For when he had dispatched the courier southwards, and his knights had come up with all their men, he donned his armour and rode forth to meet the sorcerer.'

Rod nodded. 'Sounds right. I never would've accused Duke Romanov of hesitating – or of the slightest bit of uncertainty.'

'Error, though?' The Duchess looked up, with a sardonic smile. 'I know mine husband, Lord Warlock. Dearly though I love him, I cannot help but be aware of his rashness. Yet in this matter, I believe, even full caution would have impelled him to battle – for 'twas fight or flee, look you, and, as Duke, he could not flee – for he was sworn to the protection of his people. 'Twas his duty, then, to fight – and if he must needs fight, 'twas best to fight just then, when the sorcerer and his forces were newly come from battle, and would therefore be weakened with battle losses.'

'But strengthened with the men he'd captured.' Rod frowned. 'Or didn't you realize . . . ' He gazed at her, and let the words gel in his mouth.

'What?' She frowned.

Rod cleared his throat, and shifted from one foot to the other. 'Well, er . . . where he recruited his men from. His army, I mean.'

'Ah.' She smiled bitterly. 'From those he had defeated, dost thou mean? Aye, that word was brought to us with the news of Baron Gratecieux's lost battle. The soldier who came back did tell us of old friends he'd seen who, he knew, had fought in the train of one of Gratecieux's vassal knights.'

'Well, at least it's not a surprise now,' Rod sighed. 'I suppose it would take Alfar a little while to process his new recruits— '

'To bind them under his spell?' The Duchess shook her head. 'I know not. I know only that my lord did march out toward the castle that had been Gratecieux's – and I went up to the highest turret, to see them go.'

Rod lifted his head a little. 'Could you see all the way to Gratecieux's castle?'

'Aye; his towers are taller even than those of Their Royal Majesties. We can see only the battlements – yet we can see that much. Not that I had need to.'

Rod frowned. 'You mean they didn't even get that far?'

The Duchess nodded. 'The sorcerer had marched out to meet him. Even when my lord set out, the sorcerer's forces already stood, drawn up and waiting, by a ravine midway betwixt the two castles. 'Tis as though he knew aforetime of my lord's coming.'

'He did,' Rod growled. 'All witches and warlocks here are mind readers.'

The Duchess looked up, surprised. Then her mouth tightened in exasperation. 'Aye, certes. And I knew it. I had but to think – and I did not.'

'It matters not,' Gwen said quickly.

'Truth. What aid could I provide?' The Duchess spread her hands helplessly. 'I could but watch. Yet though the sorcerer had magics, my lord the Duke had guile.'

'Oh, really? You mean he managed to escape the ambush?'

'Aye, and drew them onto ground of his choosing. For they waited on the road, look you, with a wooded slope to the left, and a bank strewn with boulders on the right.'

Rod nodded. 'Good ambush country. What'd your husband do about the roadblock?'

'He saw it afar off, and marched his force off the road ere the slopes had begun to enfold it. Out into the open plain they went, and away toward Castle Gratecieux.'

'Oh, nice.' Rod grinned. 'Go knock on the door while the army's out waiting for you.' His opinion of Duke Romanov went up a notch. No matter; it had plenty of room.

'The sorcerer did not appreciate his wisdom,' the Duchess assured Rod. 'He marched his men post-haste out into the plain to once again block my lord's path, and more men than had bestrode the road, burst from the trees and rock.'

'Of course. Your husband knows an ambush point when he sees one – and it *is* nice to be proven right now and then, isn't it?'

The Duchess exchanged a wifely glance with Gwen.

Rod hurried. 'I gather they did manage to cut him off.'

'They did indeed; yet my lord's troops were drawn up in battle array, and fresh, whiles the sorcerer's straggled hard from a chase. Then they met, with a fearful clash of arms and a howling of men, that I could hear clearly over the leagues. And, at first, my lord's forces bore back the sorcerer's. Little could I see from my tower; but the coil of men did move away, and therefore did I know that the sorcerer retreated, and my lord did follow.'

'Delightful! But I take it that didn't last?'

'Nay.' She spread her hands. 'I cannot tell why, or what did hap to change the tide of battle. I only know that the coil began to grow again, and swelled far too quickly. Thus I knew that my husband's forces did flee – in truth, that I did witness a rout. I stayed to see no more, but flew down to gather up my boys, and bundle them into the coach. I bade them keep the curtains close, and lie upon the floor; then turned I to old Peter, the groom, and I did cry, 'The coachman hath gone to fight by my lord's side! Up, old Peter, and aid us in our flight!' Yet he did not stir; he only glowered up at me, and spat at my feet. 'Not I,' he growled. 'Ne'er again shall I serve a lordling!'

Rod didn't speak, but flint struck steel in his gaze.

Gwen saw, and nodded. ' 'Twas even so. The sorcerer's spells had reached out to entrap his mind.'

'What did you do?' Rod asked the Duchess.

'I fled,' the Duchess said simply. 'I did not stay to seek another coachman, lest old Peter's surliness turn to malice. I had no wish to have spellbound creatures seek to drag me down. Nay, I sprang up on the box myself, and seized the whip. I attempted to crack it over the horses' heads, but it only whistled past them; yet that was enow, and they trotted forward. Through the gates and over the drawbridge I drove, with my heart in my throat, for fear the team would seize the bits, and run wild away; yet they trotted obediently, and I found that I had moved in barely ample time. For even as my coach's wheels roared onto the drawbridge, the portcullis shot down behind me with a crash, and the bridge beneath me began to tremble. As soon as I was clear, I did look back, and, surely, did see the bridge begin to rise.'

'Yet thou wast free!' Gwen breathed.

The Duchess shook her head. 'Nay, not yet. For as I raced away from the castle, I did see my lord's soldiers charging towards me with the sorcerer's men-at-arms hot on their heels. I knew I must pass near to their flight ere I could win free to the southward road; I prayed that our faithful men, seeing me, would turn to fight, and gain us the last vital moment in which to escape. Yet were my hopes dashed, for as they came nigh me, fire kindled in their eyes, and a dozen of them ran to catch my horses' reins, howling for my blood and my children's heads – they, who but minutes before had fought in our defence!' She buried her face in her hands, sobbing.

Gwen wrapped an arm around her, and murmured, 'They did not know. I have broke this spell from two hands of men now, and thus can tell thee how it is: their minds are put to sleep, and the thoughts that float above that slumber are not theirs. The men themselves, who swore thee faith and served thee well, do keep the faith they swore! If they are waked, and learn what their bodies did while their minds slept, they will be heart-struck, even as these.' She nodded towards the soldiers gathered under the tree.

'Heart-struck, as am I!' the Duchess sobbed. 'For when they are waked from their enchantment, what shall I say to them? "That scar upon thy cheek is my own doing, but I did not truly mean to do it?" For, look thee, as they threw themselves at the horses' bits, I struck out with the whip, and scored them wheresoe'er I might — on their hands, their arms, their chests or, aye, even their faces! And they fell back, then they fell back . . . ' Her voice dissolved into weeping again.

'You had no choice.' Rod's voice was harsh.

'No choice, in truth!' Gwen cried. 'Wouldst thou have let them drag thine horses to a halt, wrench ope thy carriage, and drag out thy bairns, to take to Alfar?'

The Duchess shuddered. ''Tis even as thou dost say.' She caught her breath, swallowed, and nodded. ''Tis even so. I could not let them triumph.'

'But Alfar did?'

'Oh, aye, of that am I certain — and my lord doth lie in the sleep of death! Or, if I am blessed, only battered and bloody, but alive in a dungeon! Ah, how shall I look into his eyes again, if ever he is freed, if ever we do meet again? For which, pray Heaven! Yet what shall I say? For I was not there to hold his castle against his return!'

'He was probably in chains before he came anywhere near home.' Rod carefully didn't mention the alternative. 'If I know Duke Romanov, he probably didn't even start the return trip.'

Gwen nodded. 'All the land doth know that thy husband would sooner die than flee, milady. Belike they dragged him down fighting, and bore him away to prison.'

'Aye.' She took a deep breath, and squared her shoulders. 'Aye, that is most likely. He would not have even known his men had fled. And they would seek to capture him, no matter the cost — would they not? For surely, an imprisoned Duke is a mighty weapon! Yet I did flee.'

'And thus he would have bade thee do!'

Rod nodded. 'Yes, he would have. If he'd thought you might have stayed to fight against an enemy like *that*, he'd have been in panic — and a less effective fighter for it; his fear for you would have shackled his sword arm.' He shook his head. 'No, knowing that you'd do everything you could to get the children to safety, if he lost the battle, was all that gave him a clear enough mind to fight the battle.'

The Duchess sat still, head bowed.

''Tis even as milord doth say,' Gwen murmured, 'and thou dost know it to be true. Thou art thyself the daughter of noblemen.'

Slowly, then, the Duchess nodded, 'Aye, 'tis true. I have done naught but my duty.'

'And your lord will praise you for it,' Rod assured her. 'Bewail his loss – but don't bewail your own conduct. You know you did exactly as you should have.'

The Duchess sighed, straightening and poising her head.

'Indeed, 'tis true – yet I did need to hear one speak it anew. I thank thee, Lady Gallowglass – and thou, Lord Warlock.' But her eyes were on Gwen's when her sudden smile showed.

Rod heaved a sigh of relief. 'I take it you've been driving without a rest.'

'Aye, the poor horses! Though I slowed to a walk as often as I dared – yet are the poor beasts near to foundering.'

'They lasted.' Rod turned to glance at the horses grazing. A couple had already dozed off. 'It's a wonder, though – they must've been going for a whole day and night.'

The Duchess nodded. 'Less a few hours. We began our flight late in the afternoon.'

Gwen caught Rod's eye, with a covert smile. He didn't hear her thoughts, but he didn't have to; they no doubt would've been something along the lines of: *Subtle as a nuclear blast.*

'Papa! PapaPapaPapaPapaPapa!'

Rod looked up, glad of the reprieve.

The children came pelting across the meadow – or at least, the Duchess's two did. Rod's brood behaved more like spears.

'Papa!' Javelin Geoffrey struck into him, and clung. Rod staggered back a step, caught his breath, and said, 'Yes. What's so important that it can't wait a second?'

'Illaren's papa!' Geoffrey crowed. 'We saw him!'

Illaren, the elder of the Duchess's children, nodded eagerly.

His mother sat galvanized.

'You what?' Rod caught his son under the shoulders and held him at arm's length. 'Now, be very careful what you say, son. Remember, you could hurt people's feelings very badly, if you're making a mistake . . . Now. You don't mean to tell me you just saw Duke Romanov *here*, do you?'

'Oh, no, Papa!' Geoffrey cried in disgust; and Magnus exploded. ''Twas last night, Papa – when we chased the warlock!'

'The nasty one, who threw rocks,' Gregory chimed in. 'Art thou mindful, Papa, of when he took thee to the dungeon?'

'Yes, I remember.' Suddenly, vividly, in his mind's eye, Rod saw the prisoner shackled to the wall again. 'You mean . . . the man in chains . . . ?'

'Aye! Wouldst thou not say, Papa, that he was . . . ' He turned to Illaren, nose wrinkling. 'How didst thou picture thy father?'

'A great bear of a man,' Illaren supplied.

'Aye!' Geoffrey whirled back to Rod. 'With hair of so dark a brown 'twas near to black. And richly clad, with gilded armour!'

Rod nodded, faster and faster. 'Yes . . . yes! Yes, on the armour, too – what there was left of it, anyway.'

'But that is Father!' cried the younger boy.

'Art thou certain!' The Duchess came to her feet, staggering.

Geoffrey stilled, staring at her, eyes huge. 'In truth, we are.'

'Dost thou truly mean . . . '

'They're right.' Rod turned a grave face to her. 'I didn't recognize him, at the time – but I should have. It *was* your husband, my lady Duchess. I'm sure of it.'

She stood rigid, staring at him.

Then her eyes rolled up, and she collapsed.

Gwen stepped forward, and caught her in an expert grip. 'Be not affrighted,' she assured the two boys. 'Thy mother doth but swoon – and 'tis from joy, not grief.'

'But Illaren's papa is sorely hurted, Papa!' Magnus reminded Rod.

'Yes.' Rod fixed his eldest with an unwavering stare. 'He was hurt – and imprisoned. Remember that.'

Magnus stared up at him, face unreadable.

'A Duke.' Rod's tone was cold, measured. 'With all his knights, with all his men-at-arms, with all his might, he was sorely wounded, captured, and imprisoned.' He turned his head slowly, surveying his children. 'Against a power that could do *that*, what could four children do? And what would happen to them?'

'But we are *witches*!' Cordelia cried.

'Warlocks!' Geoffrey's chin thrust forward.

'So,' Rod said, 'are they.'

'They have come against us,' Geoffrey cried, 'and we have triumphed!'

'Yes – when there were six of us, and one of them. What's going to happen if we meet all of them together?' He stared into Geoffrey's eyes. 'As the Duke did.'

'We will *not* go back!' Cordelia stamped her foot.

Rod stiffened, his face paling. 'You . . . will . . . do . . as . . . I . . . tell you!'

Magnus's face darkened, and his mouth opened, but Gwen's hand slid around to cover it. 'Children.' Her voice was quiet, but all four stilled at the sound. Gwen looked directly into Rod's eyes. 'I gave thy father my promise.'

'*What* promise?' Cordelia cried.

'That if he did insist, we would go home.' She raised a hand to still the instant tumult. 'Now he doth insist.'

Rod nodded slowly, and let his gaze warm as he looked at her.

'But, Mama . . . '

'Hush,' she commanded, 'for there is this, too – these horrors that the Duchess hath spoke of to me. Nay, children, 'tis even as thy father hath said – there is danger in the north, horrible and rampant. 'Tis no place for children.'

Cordelia whirled on her. 'But *you*, Mama . . . '

'Must come with thee, to see thee safely home,' Gwen said, and her tone was iron. 'Or dost thou truly say that I have but to bid thee "Go", and thou'lt return to Runnymede straightaway? That thou wouldst truly not seek to follow thy father, and myself, unseen?'

Cordelia clenched her fists and stamped her foot, glaring up at her mother with incipient mutiny, but she didn't answer.

Gwen nodded slowly. ''Tis even as I thought.' She lifted her gaze to Rod. 'And there is this, too – I do not believe the Duchess and her sons are safe yet.'

Rod nodded. 'Very true.'

Gwen nodded, too, and turned back to the children. 'We must needs guard them.'

'But the soldiers . . . '

'Did lately chase them,' Gwen reminded. 'Who is to say the sorcerer's power may not reach down from the north to ensnare them again, and turn them 'gainst the Duchess and her boys?'

Illaren exchanged a quick, frightened look with his brother.

'But, Mama . . . ' Geoffrey cried.

'Thou wilt do as thou art bid,' Gwen commanded, 'and thou wilt do it presently. Thou, whose care is ever the ordering of battles – wilt thou truly deny that the course of wisdom is to guard this family, and take them to King Tuan, to bear witness?'

Geoffrey glowered back up at her, then said reluctantly, 'Nay. Thou hast the right of it, Mama.'

'Doesn't she always,' Rod muttered; but nobody seemed to hear him.

'But Papa won't be safe!' Cordelia whirled to throw her arms around his midriff.

Rod hugged her to him, but shook his head. 'I've faced danger without you before, children. There was even a time when I didn't have your mother along to protect me.'

Magnus shook his head, eyes wide with alarm. 'Never such danger as this, Papa. A vile, evil sorcerer, with a whole army of witches behind him!'

'I've gone into the middle of an army before – and I only had a dagger against all their swords, and worse. Much worse.'

'Yet these are witches!'

'Yes – and I've got more than a mental dagger to use against them.' Rod held his son's eyes with a grave stare. 'I think I can match their sorcerer, spell for spell and power for power – and pull a few tricks he hasn't even dreamed of, since he was a child.' He hauled Magnus in against him, too. 'No, don't worry about me this time. Some day, I'll probably meet that enemy who's just a little too much stronger than I am – but Alfar isn't it. For all his powers and all his nastiness, he doesn't really worry me that much.'

'Nor should he.'

Rod looked up to see his youngest son sitting crosslegged, apart from the huddle. 'I think thou hast the right of it, Papa. I think this sorcerer's arm is thickened more with fear than with strength.'

'An that is so,' said Geoffrey, 'thou must needs match him and, aye, e'en o'ermatch him, Papa.'

'Well.' Rod inclined his head gravely. 'Thank you, my sons. Hearing you say it, makes me feel a lot better.' And, illogically, it did – and not just because his children had, when last came to last, become his cheering section. He had a strange respect for his two younger sons. He wondered if that was a good thing.

Apparently, Cordelia and Magnus felt the same way. They pried themselves away from Rod, and the eldest nodded. 'If Gregory doth not foresee thy doom, Papa, it hath yet to run.'

'Yes.' Rod nodded. 'Alfar's not my Nemesis.' He turned back to Gregory. 'What is?'

The child gazed off into space for a minute, his eyes losing focus. Then he looked at his father again, and answered, with total certainty, 'Dreams.'

# Chapter Eight

The Duchess slapped the horses with the reins, and the coach creaked into motion as they plodded forward. They quickened to a trot, and the coach rolled away. Gwen turned back from her seat beside the Duchess, and waved. Four smaller hands sprouted up from the coach roof, and waved frantically too.

Rod returned the wave until they were out of sight, feeling the hollowness grow within him. Slowly, he turned back toward the north, and watched the soldiers moving away, bearing their wounded knight on a horse-litter. They had decided to go back into the sorcerer's army, disguised as loyal automatons. Gwen had told them how to hide their true thoughts with a surface of simulated hypnosis – thinking the standardized thoughts that all Alfar's army shared. She had also made clear their danger: Alfar would not look kindly on traitors. They understood her fully, every single man jack of them; but their guilt feelings ruled them, and they welcomed the danger as expiation. Rod watched them go, hoping he wouldn't meet any of them again until the whole rebellion had been squelched.

Somehow, he was certain that it would be. It was asinine to place faith in the pronouncements of a three-year-old – but his little Gregory was uncanny, and very perceptive. Acting on the basis of his predictions would be idiocy – but he could let himself feel heartened by them. After all, Gregory wasn't your average preschooler.

On the other hand, just because he had a ten-year-old's vocabulary didn't mean he had a general's grasp of the situation. Rod took his opinions the way he took a palm reading – emotionally satisfying, but not much use for helping decide what to do next. He turned to Fess, stuck a foot in the stirrup, and mounted. 'Come on, Alloy Animal! Northward ho!'

Fess moved away after the departing squadron. 'Where are we bound, Rod?'

'To Alfar, of course. But for the immediate future, find a large farmstead, would you?'

'A farmstead? What do you seek there, Rod?'

'The final touch in our disguise.' But Rod wasn't really paying attention. His whole being was focused on the devastating, terrifying sensation of being alone, for the first time in twelve years. Oh, he'd been on his own before during that time – but never for very long, only a day or two, and he'd been too busy to think about it. But he had the time now – and he was appalled to realize how much he'd come to depend on his family's presence. He felt shorn; he felt as though he'd been cut off from his trunk and roots, like a lopped branch. There seemed to be a knot in his chest, and a numbing fear of the world about him. For the first time in twelve years, he faced that world alone, without Gwen's massive support, or the gaiety of his children – not to mention the very considerable aid of their powers.

The prospect was thoroughly daunting.

He tried to shake off the mood, throwing his shoulders back and lifting his chin. 'This is ridiculous, Fess. I'm the lone wolf; I'm the man who penetrated the Prudential Network and overthrew its Foreman! I'm the knife in the dark, the vicious secret agent who brings down empires!'

'If you say so, Rod.'

'I *do* say so, damn it! I'm *me*, Rod Gallowglass – not just a father and a husband! . . . No, damn it, I'm Rodney d'Armand! That "Gallowglass" is just an alias I took when I came here, to help me look like a native! And Rodney d'Armand managed without Gwen and the kids for twenty-nine years!'

'True,' Fess agreed. 'Of course, you lived in your father's house for nineteen of them.'

'All right, so I was only on my own for ten years! But that's almost as long as I've been married, isn't it?'

'Of course.'

'Yes.' Rod frowned. 'On the other hand, it's *only* as long – isn't it?'

'That, too, is true.'

'Yeah.' Rod scowled. 'Habit-forming little creatures, aren't they?'

'There, perhaps, you have touched the nub of it,' the robot agreed. 'Most people live their lives by habit patterns, Rod.'

'Yeah – but they're *just* habits.' Rod squared his shoulders again. 'And you can always change your habits.'

'Do you truly want to, Rod?'

'So when I get home, I'll change them back! But for the time being, I can't have them with me – so I'd better get used to it again. I can manage without them – and I will.'

'Of course you will, Rod.'

Rod caught the undertone in Fess's voice and glared at the back of his metal skull. 'What's the "but" I hear in there, Fess?'

'Merely that you will not be happy about it . . . '

'Rod, no! This is intolerable!

'Oh, shut up and reverse your gears.'

The robot heaved a martyred blast of white noise and stepped back a pace or two. Rod lifted the shafts of the cart and buckled them into the harness he'd strapped onto Fess in place of a saddle.

'This is a severe debasement of a thoroughbred, Rod.'

'Oh, come off it!' Rod climbed up to the single-board seat and picked up the reins. 'You used to pilot a spaceship, Fess. That's the same basic concept as pulling a cart.'

'No – it is analogous to *driving* a cart. And your statement is otherwise as accurate as claiming that a diamond embodies the same concept as a piece of cut plastic.'

'Hair splitting,' Rod said airily, and slapped Fess's back with the reins.

The robot plodded forward, sighing, 'My factory did not manufacture me to be a cart horse.'

'Oh, stuff it! When my ancestors met you, you were piloting a miner's burro-boat in the asteroid belt around Sol! *I've* heard the family legends!'

'I know; I taught them to you myself,' Fess sighed, again. 'This is merely poetic justice. Northward, Rod?'

'Northward,' Rod confirmed, 'on the King's High Way. Hyah!' He slapped the synthetic horsehide with the reins again. It chimed faintly, and Fess broke into a trot. They swerved out of the dirt track onto the High Road in a two-wheeled cart, leaving behind a ragged yeoman gazing happily at the gold in his palm, and shaking his head at the foolishness of tinkers, who no sooner came by a bit of money than they had to find something to spend it on.

As they trotted northward, Fess observed, 'About your discussion with your wife, Rod . . . '

'Grand woman.' Rod shook his head in admiration. 'She always sees the realities of a situation.'

'How are we defining "reality" in this context, Rod?'

'We don't; it defines us. But you mean she was just letting me have my own way, don't you?'

'Not simply that,' Fess mused. 'Not in regard to anything of real importance.'

'Meaning she usually talks me into doing things her way.' Rod sat up straighter, frowning. 'Wait a minute! You don't mean that's what she's done this time, too, do you?'

'No. I merely thought that you achieved her co-operation with remarkable ease.'

'When you start using so many polysyllables, I know you're trying to tell me something unpleasant. You mean it was too easy?'

'I did have something of the sort in mind, yes.'

'Well, don't worry about it.' Rod propped his elbows on his knees. 'It was short, but it wasn't really easy. Not when you consider all the preliminary skirmishes.'

'Perhaps . . . Still, it does not seem her way . . . '

'No . . . If she thinks I'm going to lose my temper, she stands firm anyway – unless she sees good reason to change her mind. And I think having given me a promise is a pretty good reason. But at the bottom of it all, Fess, I don't think I'm the one who convinced her.'

'You mean the Duchess?'

Rod nodded. 'Mother-to-mother communication always carries greater credibility, for a wife and mother.'

'Come, Rod! Certainly you don't believe yourself incapable of convincing your wife of your viewpoint!'

'Meaning I think she won't listen to me?' Rod nodded. 'She won't. Unless, of course, I happen to be right . . . '

It wasn't hard to tell when they reached the border; there was a patrol there to remind him of it.

'Hold!' the sergeant snapped, as two privates brought their pikes down with a crash to bar the road.

Rod pulled in on the reins, doing his best to think like a crochety old farmer – indignant and resentful. 'Aye, aye, calm thysen! I've held, I've held!'

'Well for thee that thou hast,' the sergeant growled. He nodded to the two rankers. 'Search.' They nodded, and went to the back of the cart, to begin probing through the cabbages and bran sacks.

''Ere! 'Ere! What dost thou?' Rod cried, appalled. 'Leave my cabbages be!'

''Tis orders, gaffer.' The sergeant stepped up beside him, arms akimbo. 'Our master, Duke Alfar, demands that we search any man who doth seek to come within the borders of Romanov.'

Rod stared, appalled – and the emotion was real. So Alfar had promoted himself!

'Duke Alfar? What nonsense is this? 'Tis Ivan who is Duke here!'

'Treason!' another private hissed, his pike leaping out level. Rod's fighting instincts impelled him to jump for the young man's throat – but he belayed them sternly, and did what a poor peasant would do: shrank back a little, but manfully held his ground. He stared into the boy's eyes, and saw a look that was intense, but abstracted – as though the kid wasn't quite all there, but wherever he was, he cared about it an awful lot.

Hypnoed into fanaticism.

The sergeant was grinning, and he had the same sort of shallow look behind the eyeballs. 'Where hast thou been, gaffer? Buried in thy fields, with thine head stuck in a clod? Ivan is beaten and gaoled, and Alfar is now Duke of Romanov!'

'Nay, it cannot be!' But Rod eyed the soldiers' uniforms warily.

The sergeant saw the glance, and chuckled in his throat. 'Aye. 'Tis Alfar's livery.' He scowled past Rod. 'Hast thou not done yet? 'Tis a cart, not a caravan!'

Rod turned to look, and stared in horror.

'Aye, we've done.' The troopers straightened up. 'Naught here, Auncient.'

'Nay, not so,' Rod snapped. 'I've still a few turnips left. Hadst thou not purses large enow for all on't?'

'None o' yer lip,' the sergeant growled. 'If thou hast lost a few cabbages, what matter? Thou hast yet much to sell at the market in Korasteshev.'

'Why dost thou come north?' demanded one of the men-at-arms – the one with the quick pike.

Rod turned to him, suddenly aware of the danger. He gazed at the trooper, his eyes glazing, as the world he saw became a little less than real, and his mind opened to receive impressions. What was really going on behind the soldier's face?

He felt a pressure, almost as though someone were pressing a finger against his brain. Mentally, he stilled, becoming totally passive. He sensed the differences in the minds around him; it was like smelling, as though each mind gave off its own aroma.

But four of them were all thinking the same thought: *Stop those who flee, to make Alfar stronger and greater.* However, someone coming into the Duchy was very boring. He was no threat – just more potential, just one more mind that would help magnify Alfar's glory.

But the fifth mind was alive and alert, and teeming with suspicion. A dozen questions jammed up at its outlet, demanding to be asked. Underneath them lay the suspicion that the stranger might be a spy or, worse, an assassin. And at the bottom of the mind writhed a turmoil of unvoiced thoughts, all rising from a brew of emotions: ambition, suspicion, shame, anger, hatred. Rod carefully suppressed a shudder, and bent all his efforts toward thinking like a peasant farmer. He was a rough, unlettered country man, who laboured twelve hours a day on his lord's fields, and four hours a day on his own – the four to raise a cash crop that could all be fitted into one small cart. Of course, he tried hard to get the most money he could for all that work – the small, additional amount that would make the difference between poverty and an adequate living for himself and his family during the winter. What did these arrogant bastards mean by trying to keep him from Duke Romanov's fat market in Korasteshev! And where did they get the idea to act so high and mighty? Just because they were wearing leather armour and carrying pikes! Especially when anyone could see that, under the green and brown uniforms, they were dirty peasants, like himself – probably less. Probably mere serfs, and the sons of serfs.

The soldier shifted impatiently. 'Tell, peasant! Why dost thou seek to come into— '

'Why, t' sell m' bran 'n' cabbages 'n' turnips,' Rod answered. 'Dosta think I'd wast m' horse for a day's pleasure?'

The sentry ignored the question. 'You're Earl Tudor's man,' he growled. 'Why not sell in Caernarvon? Why come north all the way to Korasteshev?'

' 'Tis not all the way,' Rod snorted. 'I live scarce three leagues yon.' He nodded towards the road behind him. 'Korasteshev is closer for me.' He glared at the trooper – but he let his mind dwell hungrily on the thought of the prices he could get in Korasteshev. Everyone knew Duke Romanov's barons were fighting among themselves – and the more fool the Duke, for letting them! And every peasant knew that, when armies fought, crops got trampled. Nay, surely the folk in Korasteshev would be paying far more for cabbages than those in Earl Tudor's peaceful Caernarvon!

The soldier's face relaxed. So, the cranky old codger's greedy! Well and good – greed, we know how to deal with . . .

Rod just barely managed to restrain a surge of indignation. Old?!? Codger, OK – but *old*? He diverted the impulse into suspicious fuming: Who was this bare-cheeked brat to be asking *him* questions? Why, he was scarcely done suckling his mother's milk!

He was gratified to see the young man redden a little – but the boy's suspicion wasn't quite finished yet. He ran a trained eye over Fess. 'How comes a poor dirt farmer to have so fine a horse?'

Panic! Anxiety! The one thing that men might really blame him for. Rod had been caught. And hard on the heels of that emotion came a surge of shame. He glanced at Fess. *Eh, my wife was beautiful, ten years agone! Small wonder that Sir Ewing took notice of her* . . .

He turned back to the young man. 'Sir Ewing gave him to me, saying he was too old to bear an armoured knight still.'

The suspicion was still there in the younger soldier's mind; it just changed direction. The young man was trying to find a flaw in the story. 'Why would a knight give even a cast-off charger to a poor peasant?'

The shame again. Rod let it mount, burning. 'Why, for . . . favours . . . we did him, me and mine.' *Mostly 'mine'.* There was a brief, lurid image of a strapping, tow-headed man in bed with a voluptuous young woman, with chestnut hair – not that you could see much else of her . . . and the vision was gone. But the shame remained, and rage mounted under it. 'For favours.' Rod's face had turned to wood. 'Not that 'tis any affair of thine.'

' "Affair", is it?' The young man let a mocking grin spread. 'Aye, thine "affair" now, is only the selling of thy cabbages, I warrant.' He turned to the sergeant. 'Why do we linger, wasting time on this peasant, A);uncient?'

'Why, for that he hath not set his horse to going,' the sergeant growled. 'Be off with thee, fellow! Get thy cart out from our station! Get thee hence to the market!'

'Aye – and I thank thy worships,' Rod said sourly. He turned away and slapped the reins on Fess's back – but very gently, to avoid the metallic ring. Fess started up again, plodding away.

Rod kept a tight rein on his thoughts. It was such a huge, aching temptation to indulge himself in speculation! But he was certainly still in range of the young telepath, and would be for several miles at least – even if the kid's powers were weak. And if they were strong . . . No, Rod kept a steady mental stream of embarrassment and anger seething. That the young bastard should have subjected him to such personal questions! What a filthy mind he must have! And where did such a low-born serf's son get any right to be questioning *him*, old Owen, about his comings and goings?

Underneath that surface spate, in bursts of pure thought not encoded into words, boiled the host of questions. Interesting, that the ranker had asked the questions, and the sergeant hadn't even seemed to notice that his authority was being usurped. Interesting, that the sorcerer's sentries would pose as underlings; they had, at least, some craftiness in their disguises. That the young warlock was one of those who had volunteered to work for Alfar, completely willingly, Rod had no doubt; the youngster clearly had the inferiority complex and paranoia of the persecuted witchling grown to manhood – and the ambition that stemmed from it. Inwardly, Rod shuddered – if he'd been Alfar, he'd never have been able to sleep easily, knowing that his underlings would very cheerfully have sliced him to bits and taken his place.

On the other hand, the fact that they hadn't indicated that Alfar was either an extremely powerful old esper, or was surrounded by a few henchmen who were genuinely loyal. Or both.

But the chance that telepaths were constantly running surveillance over the duchy, was just too high. Rod couldn't afford to take chances. His concentration might falter at just the moment that one of the sentry-minds happened to be listening to the area he was in. He had to take more thorough mental precautions.

Accordingly, he let the tension from the confrontation at the border begin to ebb away, and began to relax – as 'old' Owen, of course. *What does it matter, what the fuzz-cheeked brat said? I'm in Romanov – and I can sell my crop for that much greater price! But*

*my, it's been a long day!* He'd been up before dawn, Owen had
– as he always was, of course; but travelling was more wearying
than threshing. His eyelids were sagging. How nice it would be
to nap for a bit – just a little bit! Maybe the half of an hour, or
so. In fact, he was beginning to nod. It wasn't safe, driving when
he was so sleepy. Nay, surely he'd better nap.

So he steered the cart off the side of the road, reined the horse
to a stop, lashed the reins to the top bar of the cart, clambered
over the seat into the back, and found himself a small nest among
his baskets. The boards weren't too much harder than his pallet
at home – and at least he could lean back.

He let his head loll, eyes closing, letting the drowsiness claim
him, letting his thoughts darken and grow still . . .

'Rod.'

Rod jolted upright, blinking, hauling his mind out of the
fringes of the web of sleep. 'Huh? Wha? Wha's'a mattuh?'

'Did you intend to doze, Rod?'

'Who, me? Ridiculous!' Rod snorted. 'Just putting on a very
good act. Well . . . OK, maybe I got carried away . . . '

'As you wish, Rod.' Fess was peacefully nibbling at the roadside
grass. Rod made a mental note to dump the robot's wastebasket.
The time being, of course, Fess's act was as necessary as Rod's.

Of course, he did have to keep it an act. He lay back against
a bran sack, closed his eyes, and let drowsiness claim him again,
let the surface of his mind flicker with the images of Owen's
imaginary day.

Underneath, he tried to remember what had happened inside
his head when he had first come to Gramarye, how it had felt.

He remembered the shock when he had found out that someone
was reading his mind. He had been eyeing one of the teenaged
witches with admiration, speculating about her measurements,
when she had gasped, and turned to glare at him. He remembered
how embarrassed he'd been, and the clamouring panic inside as
he realized someone could read his mind. Worse, that any of the
Gramarye 'witches' could – and that there were dozens of them,
at least!

But by the time he'd met Gwen, only a week or so later, she
hadn't been able to read his thoughts. For nine years, that had
been the one mar in an otherwise blissful marriage. There had
been spats, of course, and there had been the constant, underlying tension that always stems from two people trying to make one

life together; but the loving reassurance she'd had every reason to look forward to, the warmth of being able to meld her mind with her husband's, just hadn't been there. That had put a continuing, unspoken strain on the marriage, with Gwen hiding feelings of having been cheated – not by Rod, but by life – and Rod trying less successfully to bury his feelings of inferiority.

Then, when the family had been kidnapped to the land of Tir Chlis in an alternative universe, Rod had encountered his analogue, the alternate High Warlock, Lord Kern – who was very much like Lord Gallowglass, enough so to be Rod's double. But there had been some major differences under the skin – such as Kern's roaring temper. And huge magical powers – one of which was the ability to blend his mind with Rod's, to lend him Kern's powers. That had wakened Rod's own slumbering esper powers – and afflicted him with a hair-trigger temper. Fortunately, it had also roused a mind reading ability he'd never suspected he'd had. And, suddenly, Gwen had been able to read his mind; he'd no longer been telepathically invisible.

So, if he had been open to mind reading when he came to Gramarye, but had been telepathically invisible when he'd met Gwen, his mind had probably closed itself off in that first panic of embarrassment, finding out that somebody could read his thoughts when he most definitely hadn't wanted her to.

Of course, when the girl got done looking indignant, she *had* looked rather pleased . . .

He tried to remember how he had felt at that moment, and caught it – exposed, vulnerable. Being so open was intolerable; he couldn't allow other people to know so much about him, that they might be able to use to hurt him. He couldn't let them have the advantage of knowing what he was going to do, before he did it.

He could feel himself pulling back, withdrawing, pulling inward, politely but firmly closing himself off, locking out the rest of the world. He would smile, he would still interact with them – but they could not, would not, know his inner self . . .

He came out of the reverie with an inward shudder. With an attitude like that, it was amazing his marriage had lasted the first nine years. On second thought, knowing Gwen, it was understandable; he hoped he'd made it up to her, since then.

By turning into a howling demon whenever a few things went wrong all at the same time?

*Be fair*, he told himself, frowning. If she'd rather have him emotionally open, she had to accept everything that implied. Could he help if, underneath the mask, he wasn't really a very nice guy?

Now he was being unfair to himself. Wasn't he? Surely there had to be a way to be open, without going berserk every so often.

There had to be, and he'd get busy searching for it – as soon as the current crisis was out of the way.

He stilled, suddenly remembering that his technique might not have worked. He might not have managed to regain his telepathic invisibility; he might still be exposed to passing telepaths.

So he sat very still, letting his mind open up, eyes still closed in mock slumber. He let his thoughts slumber, too, let them idle into dreams, while his mind opened up to all and any impressions.

He didn't hear a thought.

He would've believed there wasn't a thinking being for a hundred miles – and it wasn't just human thoughts that were missing, either. When he concentrated on mind reading this way he always heard a continuing background murmur of animal minds – simple, vivid emotions: hunger, rage, desire. Even earthworms radiated sharp, intense little spikes of satisfaction as they chewed their way cheerfully through the dirt.

But not now. Either the worms had ploughed into sandy soil, or his mind was closed off from both directions. He couldn't hear anything – not the background murmur, not the defiance of a skylark, nothing. He felt as though a vital part of him had been chopped off, that he was less than he had been. After three years as a telepath, this was a sudden, devastating impoverishment.

But it was necessary. Without it, he'd very quickly be detected and, shortly thereafter, be dead.

He felt a little better, after that realization. No, he decided, mental deafness was definitely preferable to permanent sleep. Besides, the 'deafness' was only temporary.

He hoped.

He shrugged off the thought, and cranked his eyelids open just enough to see through the lashes. The road was clear, as far as he could see. Of course, someone might be coming up behind him, so he kept up the act. He sat up slowly, blinking around him as though he couldn't remember where he was. Then he lifted his head, as though remembering, smiled, yawned, and stretched. He leaned forward, elbows on knees, and blinked at the scenery around him while he waited for his body to come awake. Finally, Owen reached down to untie the reins, sat up, and clucked to his horse, giving his back a light (very light) slap. The horse lifted his head, looked back to see his master awake, then turned front again and leaned into the horsecollar. The wagon creaked, groaned, and clattered back onto the High Road again.

As the wooden wheels rolled away on the paving stones, Rod worked at fighting down a rising fear – that, when this struggle with renegade espers was over, he might not be able to come out of his shell again, might be permanently maimed mentally, and never again able to be fully with his family. 'It's done, Fess. I've closed my mind off. The rest of the world is telepathically invisible to me.'

'And you to it?' Fess sounded surprised. 'Wasn't that a bit drastic, Rod?'

'Yes – but in a land of hostile telepaths, I think it was necessary.'

The robot was silent for a few hoofbeats, then nodded slowly. 'It is a wise course, Rod. Indeed, I would have counselled it, if you had asked me.'

Rod caught the implied reproach. 'I couldn't, though – not while an enemy telepath might have been able to read my mind.' He was silent for a few seconds, then added, 'It's scary, Fess.'

'I can understand that it would be, Rod, after three years as a telepath. But I should think Alfar would be even more frightening.'

'What, him?' Rod shrugged. 'Not really. I mean, if worst comes to worst and I don't come back, Tuan will start marching.'

'A rather gruesome interpretation. What *do* you fear, Rod?'

'Being stuck here, inside myself.' Rod shuddered. 'And not being able to unlock my mind again.'

# Chapter Nine

The sun was low, ahead and to the left, bathing the road, and the dusty leaves that bordered it, in an orange glow that made the whole world seem somewhat better than it really was – and Rod began to relax as he gazed at it. It was a magical road, somehow, twisting away through gilded leaves to some unguessable, wonderful fairy world ahead.

Around the turn, a man cried out in alarm, and a chorus of bellowing shouts answered him. Quarterstaves cracked wood on wood, and clanked on iron.

Rod stared, snapping out of his reverie. Then he barked 'Charge!' and Fess sprang into a gallop. The cart rattled and bumped behind him, melons and cabbages bouncing out into the roadway. Rod swerved into the turn with one wheel off the ground – and saw a grey-haired man whirling a quarterstaff high, low, from side to side, blocking the furious blows of three thicked-bodied, shag-haired thugs with five-day beards. Two of them had iron caps – which was just as well, since they weren't very good with their staves. Even as Rod watched, the grey-head managed to crack his staff down on one of their skulls. The man howled and flinched back, pressing a hand to his head; then, reassured that he wasn't injured, he roared and leaped back into the fight, flailing a huge, windmilling arc of a blow that would have pulverized anything in its way. But the older man's staff snapped out at an angle, blocking the blow – and the thug's stick shot down the smooth wood, straight toward the victim's knuckles. The traveller's staff pushed farther, though, coming around in a half circle, and the thug's stick ploughed into the ground. By that time, the other end of the older man's staff was swinging up to block a short, vicious blow from the thug on the other side.

Anger flared in Rod, the smouldering resentment of injustice. 'Anybody that good has *earned* help!' Rod snapped. 'We can't let him be killed just because he's outnumbered! *Never!*'

Fess's hooves whipped into a blur that no real horse could have managed. Rod swung his whip back, fighting against his own anger to withhold the blow until the right moment.

A handful of soldiers broke through the screen of brush at the roadside, riding into view from a woodland track.

Rod hauled on Fess's reins – not that the horse needed it; but it helped Rod to force down his anger, contain the frustration at not striking out. 'Hold it, Fess! Company's coming. Maybe we'd better leave this goodman to natural processes.'

The sergeant saw the fracas, swung his arm in an overhand circle that ended pointing towards the thugs, and shouted as he kicked his mount into a gallop. His troopers bellowed an answer, and their horses leaped into a charge.

The thugs were making too much noise to hear, until the soldiers were only thirty feet away. Then one of them looked up and shouted. The other two turned, stared for one moment of panic, then whirled and plunged into the underbrush with howls of dismay.

The sergeant reined in just in front of the older man.

'I thank thee, Auncient.' The traveller bowed, leaning on his staff. 'They'd have stripped me bare and left me for wolf-meat!'

'Nay, certes! We could not allow such work, could we, then?' The sergeant grinned to his men for a chorus of agreement, and turned back to the traveller. 'Such goods as wayfarers own, are ours to claim.' He leaned down, shoving an open palm under the traveller's nose. 'Thy purse, gaffer!'

The older man stared at him, appalled. Then he heaved a sigh, and untied his purse from his belt. He set it in the sergeant's hand. 'Take it, then – and surely, I owe thee what I can give, for thy good offices.'

'Dost thou indeed?' The sergeant straightened, opening the purse with a sly grin. But it faded quickly to a scowl of indignation as he looked into the little bag. He glared down at the traveller. 'Here, now! What manner of jest is this?'

'Why, naught!' the traveller said, surprised. 'What few coins I have, are there!'

'Few indeed.' The sergeant upended the purse, and five copper coins clinked into his palm. He growled and tossed them into the dust. 'Come, then! None take to the road without a few shillings at least, to provide for themselves.'

The older man shook his head. 'I had no more – and my daughter's near to term with her first. I must be there; she'll have need of me.'

'She will, indeed,' the sergeant growled, 'and thou'lt be wanting.' He nodded to his men. 'Strip him, and slash his clothes. We'll find shillings, though they be within his flesh.'

The traveller stepped back, horrified, as the soldiers crowded in, chuckling. Then his face firmed with resignation, and his staff lifted.

'Seize him!' the sergeant barked.

'So much for natural processes.' Rod's anger surged up, freed. '*Now*, Fess!'

The great black horse sprang forward.

One of the soldiers chopped down at the traveller with his

pike; but his victim's quarterstaff cracked against the pike-shaft, and it swerved, crashing into the shield of the trooper next to him. 'Here now!' the man barked, and swung his own axe.

'Nay, nay!' the sergeant cried in disgust. 'Is one lone . . . '

A bellow of rage drowned him out, and his eyes bulged as Rod's whip wrapped itself around his throat. Rod yanked back as Fess crashed into a trooper, and the sergeant shot out of his saddle. The trooper screamed as his horse went flying. Fess slammed into another horse, reaching for its rider with steel teeth, as Rod turned to catch up a club he'd hidden among the grain sacks, and whirled it straight-armed down at the steel cap of a third trooper with a bellow of fury. The blow rang like the parish bell on a holy day, and the soldier slumped to the ground, his helmet flying off. Fess tossed his head as he let go of the second trooper's arm, and the man spun flying to slam into a tree. Rod turned just as the fourth trooper hit the ground. The traveller's staff rose and fell with a dull thud. Rod winced, his rage ending as suddenly as it had begun, transmuting into leaden chagrin. He looked about him at the three fallen men. He fought against it. He'd been right, damn it! And none of them were really hurt. Nothing permanent, anyway . . .

Then he turned, and saw the older man looking up, panting, eyes white-rimmed, staff leaping up to guard again.

Rod dropped the reins and held his hands up shoulder-high, palms open. 'Not me, gaffer! I'm just here to help!'

The staff hung poised as the battle tension ebbed from the traveller's muscles. Finally, he lowered his guard, and smiled, 'I give thee thanks, then – though I'm no one's "gaffer".'

'Not yet, maybe – but you will be, soon.' Rod forced a weak smile. 'I couldn't help overhearing.'

'Nay, I think thou didst attempt such hearing – and I thank thee for it.' The traveller grounded the butt of his staff, and held out his hand.

'I am called Simon, and my village is Versclos.'

'I am, errr . . . ' Rod leaned down to shake Simon's hand, groping frantically to remember the name he'd used for his "old farmer" act. 'Call me Owen. Of Armand.'

'Owen of Armand?' Simon lifted an eyebrow. 'I've not heard of that village.'

'It's far from here – to the south.' *Galactic south, anyway.*

'I thank thee for thy good offices, Owen of Armand.' Simon's

handclasp was warm and firm. 'Indeed, had it not been for thee
— ' He broke off suddenly, staring.

Rod frowned.

Simon lifted his head with a jolt and gave it a quick shake.
'Nay, pardon! My mind wanders. Had it not been for thee, these
liveried bandits would have stripped me bare – and sin' that there
were no shillings for them to find . . . '

Rod's mouth thinned and hardened. 'They probably would
have stripped you down to your skin, then used their knives
to look for pockets.'

'I do not doubt it.' Simon turned toward the soldiers. 'Yet
'tis not their doing. They labour under a wicked enchantment.
Come, we must attend to them.' And he turned away to kneel
down by one of the troopers, leaving Rod with a puzzled frown.
That had been rather abrupt – and, polite though he was, Simon
had very obviously been trying to change the subject. What had
he suddenly seen in Rod, that had so offended him? 'Odd victim
we have here,' he muttered.

'Odd indeed,' Fess agreed. 'To judge by his vocabulary and
bearing, one would think him too well-qualified to be a road
wanderer.'

Rod lifted his head slowly. 'Interesting point . . . Well, let's
give him a hand.' He lashed the reins around the top bar of the
cart and swung down to the ground.

Simon was kneeling by the sergeant, one hand on the man's
shoulder, but still holding to his staff with the other. He stared
into the man's face, frowning, head cocked to the side, as though
he were listening. Rod started to ask, then saw the abstracted glaze
in Simon's eyes, and managed to shut his mouth in time to keep the
words in. He'd seen that same look in Gwen's face too many times
to mistake it – especially since he'd seen it in all his children's faces,
too, now and then – especially Gregory's. Exactly what was going
on, Rod didn't know – but it was certainly something psionic.

The sergeant's eyes opened. He blinked, scowling against pain,
then sat up, massaging his throat. 'What hast thou . . . ' Then his
eyes widened in horror. 'Nay, I! What have *I* done to *thee*?'

Rod relaxed, reassured. The sergeant had his conscience back.

The man's eyes lost focus as he took a quick tour back through
memory. 'I have . . . nay, I have oppressed . . . I have murdered!
Eh, poor folk!' He squeezed his eyes shut, face clenched in pain.
'I have seen these hands cut down fleeing peasants, then steal

what few coins they had! I have heard mine own voice curse at villagers, and hale forth their sons to serve in the sorcerer's army! I have—'

'Done naught.' Simon spoke sternly, but without anger, his voice pitched and hardened to pierce the sergeant's remorse. 'Be of good cheer, Auncient – for thou didst labour under enchantment. Whilst thy mind slumbered, ensorcelled, thy body moved at the bidding of another. His commands were laid in thee, and thy body remembered, and governed its actions by his orders. Whatsoe'er thou dost recall thine hands doing, or thy voice crying, 'twas not thine own doing, but Alfar's.'

The sergeant looked up, hope rising in his gaze.

Rod held his face carefully impassive. Interesting, very interesting, that Simon knew the nature of the spell. Even more interesting, that he could break it.

Which meant, of course, that he was a telepath. And which meant that the startled look he had given Rod was because he saw a man before him, but didn't sense a mind to go with it. Rod could understand his amazement; he'd felt the same way a few times, himself . . .

It also raised the interesting question of how Simon had escaped Alfar's drag-net. Or did the sorcerer routinely leave witches and warlocks free to roam about the countryside, even though they hadn't signed up with him? Somehow, Rod doubted it.

The sergeant gave Simon a glance up from the depths of despair. 'What nonsense dost thou speak? When could so vile a spell have been laid upon me?'

'Why, I cannot tell,' the traveller answered, 'for I was not there. Yet, think – 'twas in all likelihood hard after a battle, when thou hadst been taken prisoner.'

The sergeant's eyes widened, and he turned away, but he was not seeing the roadside, nor the trees. 'Aye, the battle . . . Our gallant Duke led us against the sorcerer's vile army, and they fought poorly, advancing on us with pikes lowered, but with their gazes fixed. 'Twas daunting, for their pikes never varied, nor the even tread of their feet; but our Duke cried, "Why, they are puppets! And they can do only what their master wills, when he pulls their strings. Onward, brave hearts – for he cannot govern a thousand separate fights!" And he lowered his lance, charging straight toward the foe. We took heart with a shout and followed, and 'twas even as he said, for we had but to sidestep the pikes.

Though the men behind them sought to follow, we could move faster, and step through to stab and cut. Thus the sorcerer's army began to give ground – not through retreat, but through being forced back bodily.

'But something vile and huge struck at us from the sky with a scream and, of a sudden, the air was filled with flying rocks. Sheets of fire enveloped our army, and we cried out in fear. Daunted, we gave ground, and the sorcerer's troops strode after, to follow.

'Then, of a sudden, the man in front of me turned, with a strange look in his eye – eerie and fey. "Turn, man!" I cried, and stabbed past him with my pike, knocking aside a blow that would have slain him. "Turn, and fight for thy Duke!" "Nay," quoth he, "for what hath the Duke done ever, save to take from us as much, and return as little, as he might? I shall fight for the sorcerer now!" And he raised his pike to strike at me. Yet whatever spell held him, it had slowed him. I stared in horror at what I had heard him say, then saw his pike sweeping down at me. I struck it aside; but all about me, the Duke's soldiers in the front of the army were turning to strike at their comrades behind. In an instant, I was hard put to defend myself – yet 'twas from men of mine own livery! Distant behind them, I saw the Duke on his tall horse, surrounded by pikes; yet those at his back, that jabbed at his armour, were held by his own men! He turned, roaring in rage, and his sword chopped in a half circle, reaping pike-heads like corn; yet a dozen sprang up for every one that fell.

'Then, of a sudden, there was a fellow who floated in midair, above the Duke, who dropped a noose about our lord and cast loops of rope to follow it, binding his arms to his sides. He roared in anger, but the warlock shot away from him, jerking him from his horse. He crashed down below the hedge of pikes, and I cried out in despair, striking out with my own pike, blocking the blades about me; yet a heaviness crept over me. I struggled against it and, praise Heaven, felt anger rise to counter; yet even so, the heaviness grew greater and greater. I scarce seemed to feel the pike in my hands. Then all darkened about me, as though I had fallen asleep.' Slowly, he lifted his head, looking up at Simon. 'I recall no more of the battle.'

Simon nodded. 'Belike thou, in thy turn, didst turn upon thy comrades behind. Yet be of good cheer; for they, belike, fell also under the spell. What else dost thou recall?'

'Why . . . ' The soldier turned away again, his eyes glazing. 'Only brief snatches. I am mindful of marching in the midst of a troop, a thousand strong or more. The sorcerer's livery bounded its rim, with those of us who wore the Duke's colours within; and in our centre rode our Great Duke himself, his helmet gone, a bloody rag tied about his head – and his arms bound behind him!' He squeezed his eyes shut, bowing his head. 'Alas, my noble lord!'

'Buck up!' Rod reached out to clasp the man's shoulder. 'At least he's still alive.'

'Aye, verily! For he did glare about him, cursing!' The sergeant's eyes glittered. 'Ah, gallant Duke! Him the spell could not entrap!'

'He's a strong-willed man,' Rod agreed. 'What else do you remember?'

'Why . . . coming home.' The sergeant's mouth tightened. 'Eh, but what manner of homecoming was this? For I saw an armed band haling milord Duke away to his own dungeons. Then, with wild cheering, all soldiers turned to welcome the sorcerer Alfar as he rode through the gates in a gilded coach – and I, I was one of them!'

'What did he look like?' Rod demanded.

The sergeant shook his head. 'I cannot truly say. 'Twas naught but a brief glimpse 'twixt the curtains of a rolling coach as he went by. A slight man, with a flowing beard and a velvet hat. No more could I tell thee.'

Simon nodded. 'And after that?'

'After? Why – the guardroom. And those of us who wore the Duke's livery had no weapons. Yet we played at dice, and quaffed wine, the whiles they who wore the sorcerer's livery took us, one by one, away, and brought us back wearing Alfar's colours.' His face worked; he spat.

'What happened when you were taken away?' Rod asked gently.

The sergeant shrugged. 'I went willingly; wherefore not? The sorcerer was all-wise and good; assuredly his folk could not harm me!' His mouth tightened, as though he'd tasted bitterness. 'They took me, one soldier on either side, their pikes in their hands, though there was no need for such.'

'And wither did these two take thee?'

'To the chamber of the Captain of the Watch; yet 'twas not he who waited there within. And I would not have known the place, for 'twas darkened, and filled with sweet aromas. A candle burned on a table, and they sat me in a chair beside it, the whiles the door closed behind. 'Twas all dark then, and I could see that one sat across from me; yet I could not tell his face nor colours, for they were lost in shadow. "Sleep," he bade me, "sleep well. Thou hast fought hard; thou hast fought bravely. Thou hast earned thy reward of slumber."

'Thus he spake; and truly, mine eyes did close, and darkness folded about me, and 'twas warm and comforting.' He looked up, blinking. 'The rest, thou hast heard. I have but now waked from that slumber. What I remember, I recall as though 'twere a dream.'

'What was the dream?' Rod frowned, intent. 'What happened after they hyp—, put your mind to sleep?'

The sergeant shrugged. 'Naught. We lazed about the guardroom for a day, mayhap two, and all the talk was of the excellence of the sorcerer, and how well-suited to the duchy would be his rule.

'Then, of a sudden, the captain cried, "To horse!" and we ran for our weapons. "The peasant folk flee," cried he. "They have taken to the roads; southwards they wander to bear treacherous words to Earl Tudor and King Loguire. Out upon them, barracks scum! Out upon them, and haul them back or slay them where they stand!" And out we rushed, to horse and to road, and away to the south we thundered, galloping, seeking poor folk to slaughter.' He squeezed his eyes shut, pressing his hand over his eyes. 'Alas, poor souls! What guilt was theirs? Only that they sought to shield their wives and bairns from war and evil! What fault was theirs, that earned so harsh a reward?' He lifted his gaze to the traveller, and his eyes were wide and haunted. 'For we found them, a single family; and we found a dozen such, one by one; and one by one, we slew them. Our swords whirled, cleaving through blood and bone, flinging wide a spray of crimson. Then, when all the corpses lay pooling all their scarlet gore together in a single pond, we did dismount, slit their purses, and search bodies to carry away what few coins they had hoarded, to bear back to Alfar the sorcerer.' He buried his face in his hands. 'Ay me! How shall I live, with such pictures seared upon my brain?' He turned to Rod. 'But we have plunder – aye, booty rich indeed! For every peasant family had a coin or two – and we have thirty shillings! A pound, and half again! Wealth indeed, to hale home to Alfar!' He threw back his head, and howled, 'A curse upon the man, and all his minions! A curse upon one who could do such evil to his fellow man! And curses, too, upon the witches who do serve him – on all witches, for surely such evil lies in all their hearts.'

'Nay, not so!' Simon spoke sternly. ''Tis only this handful of miserable recreants who do evil to their fellow men! Belike they are unable to gain fellowship of other men and women, and blame their loneliness not on themselves, but on the other folk, who do not befriend them. I doubt me not an they do tell themselves the goodfolk envy them their magic, and therefore spurn all witches. Thus do they reason out some licence for themselves to steal, and lord it over other folk.'

Rod was impressed. He hadn't expected such insight, in an average yeoman.

Neither had the sergeant. He stared up at Simon, wide-eyed. 'How well thou dost know them!'

'As well I should.' Simon's mouth tightened at the corners. 'For I am myself a warlock. But!' He held up a palm, to stop the sergeant's startled oath. 'But like the greater number of my fellows, I have learned the ways of hiding all my powers, and deal with other folk as well as any man. I have had a wife who was not a witch. Together, we reared children who, though they had some Power, learned well to hide it, and have grown up in the liking of their fellows. We do not seek for power; we do not seek for wealth. We have already what we most care for – the good regard of others.'

The sergeant's mouth went crooked. 'An thou hast so deep a regard for we humble common folk, why canst thou not ward us from these evil ones?'

'Why, so they did,' Simon answered, 'those warlocks and witches who had real power. I knew one crone who was a healer – many had she mended in both mind and body; and I have known warlocks, gentle men who did speak with those whose minds were labouring in confusion, or disarranged, and led them out into the light of sanity again. But I myself?' He shrugged. 'My powers were never so great. I have known warlocks who can disappear, and appear again some miles distant, and I have heard of some who can make their thoughts be heard in others' minds – aye, even those who are not witches. But I?' He shook his head, with a sad smile. 'I am none of these. I have power, aye; yet it is weak and feeble – enough to prevent my being a man, like other men, yet not enough to make me a warlock like to other warlocks. Neither fish nor flesh, I know not where to nest. Oh, I can hear what others think if they are near to me – but that is all. I did not know I could do more,' his smile hardened, 'until Alfar did bind with his spell, boys from mine own village – and they did drop their hoes, and turn to march away toward his castle, for his army, I doubt not. I ran after one, and caught him by the arm. "Wither dost thou go?" I cried; but he turned sneering to me, and raised his fist, to strike me away. Yet,' and Simon's lips curved in a small smile, 'I have some skill in arms. I fended off his blow, and struck ere he could draw his fist again, and I did stretch the poor lad senseless upon the road. And whiles he lay thus, unwillingly in slumber, I knelt beside him, frantic in my need, crying out to him, "Wake! Dost'a not see thou art ensorcelled?" For this was my neighbour's son, look you, who had been my children's playfellow. I could not stand aside to let the sorcerer take him while breath yet passed within my lungs. With every grain of my poor, puny witch power, I did seek to reach and wake his slumbering mind, where it lay 'neath Alfar's spell.'

The sergeant stared at him, round-eyed. 'And did he waken?'

Simon nodded, closing his eyes. 'He did. Praise Heaven, for he did. And when his body likewise woke, he sat up bewildered, for he'd no notion how he'd come to be there, lying in the mid-road, half a league from home. I took him back to his father; yet I bethought me that what I could do for one, I might so hap to do for others. Thus, when any boy from our village did gain that far-off gaze and wander toward the High Road in a trance, I followed, struck him down, and woke his mind; and when the spell began to wrap itself around my neighbours' minds also, I waited till night fell, and they slumbered, then passed from house to house, standing against the wall and seeking to wake them from their enchantments. At length I fell ill from exhaustion – but my village held, alone free from the weird.

'And so, at last – two days agone – a warlock came himself, a meagre, pimply-faced lad, but with soldiers at his back. Then I could do naught; the boys all marched away; yet, at the least, their parents saw they were compelled.'

'Yet did the warlock not seek thee out?'

Simon shrugged. 'He did attempt it; for with a whole village yet free-minded, he knew there must needs be a witch or warlock who had prevented it. Yet as I've told thee, my power's weak; I can only hear thoughts. And that I was adept at hiding what little force I had. I was careful not to think of witch powers, or spell breaking; I thought only of suspicion, and how much I did resent Alfar's dominion.' He shook his head slowly. 'He could not find me; for every mind in all that hamlet thought as I did.'

'And this was but two days agone?' the sergeant cried.

'Two days,' Simon confirmed.

'Then 'tis months that thou hast held thy neighbours' minds 'gainst Alfar's spell!'

'It is. Yet in all comely truth, 'tis not till now that Alfar's had soldiers to spare for such an errand.'

'Aye.' The sergeant's face hardened again. 'Yet with the Duke captured, he could spare the men, and the time – for all present threats were laid.'

'I doubt it not. Yet I assure thee, I did tremble with relief when that warlock passed from our village. Then I bethought me that I'd cheated Death quite long enow. Nay, I reasoned that I'd done my part, and had escaped thus far more by luck than skill – and, in comely truth, my daughter doth draw near to her confinement. Accordingly, I sought the better part of valour, and turned my steps southward, hoping I might break from his evil-seized, ensorcelled realm into the free air of Earl Tudor's county.' He turned to Rod. 'And I have come near – so near! 'Tis but a half day's journey now, is't not?'

Rod nodded. 'Guards at the border, though. You'd have trouble getting across.'

Simon smiled, amused. 'Not I.'

'Aye.' The soldier gave him an appraising glance. 'Thou hast something of the look of the wild stag about thee. I doubt not an thou couldst find thy freedom through the forest trails, where no sentry's eye doth watch.'

'Just so. Yet I think I must not go.'

'Nay!' The sergeant leaned forward. 'Go thou must! Make good thine escape whilst thou may!'

'And if I do? Wilt thou?'

The sergeant lowered his gaze. 'I must go back – for I've blood on mine hands, and must atone.'

'Stuff and nonsense!' Simon snorted. 'These deaths were Alfar's doing, and none of thine. Do thou make thine escape to join King Tuan's army, and march back to take thy vengeance 'gainst the sorcerer.'

The sergeant shook his head. 'Nay. 'Twould take too long. And . . . if we journey north again, my men and I, and take our places amidst the sorcerer's force – then there will be peasant lives spared, when next they send out to sweep the roads. And when King Tuan comes, there will be swords to fight for him, within the sorcerer's ranks.'

''Tis worthy,' Simon mused.

'And stupid!' Rod snorted. 'The first warlock who runs a security check on the army, listening for traitorous thoughts, will find you out. All you'll accomplish is an early execution.'

The sergeant glared at him, then turned back to Simon. 'Canst thou not teach us the way of hiding our thoughts?'

'I can tell thee the way of it,' Simon said slowly, 'yet 'tis not quickly learned. It will require constant practice – and never mayest thou relent. Such vigilance is well-nigh impossible, for one who hath but newly learned. Thou mayest quite easily be found out.'

'Then give them choice,' the sergeant said. 'Wake them from their spellbound sleep, and say to them what thou hast said to me. I doubt me not an all of them will choose as I do – to ride back north.'

Simon smiled, and shrugged. 'Can I do less? I, who am practised at such dissimulation? Nay. I shall be a half day's ride behind thee.'

'That,' Rod said, 'is just a form of suicide. The only thing that's uncertain about it, is the date.'

Simon looked up, in mild surprise. 'Yet thou dost journey northward.'

'Well, yes,' Rod admitted, 'but I have duty involved. It's required of me – never mind why.'

'As it is of me – no matter why.' Simon gave him a sardonic smile and rose to his feet, standing a little taller, a little straighter. 'Craven was I, to ever flee. My work remains. I must turn back, and set my face against the north, that I may go to aid more souls who labour in enchanted sleep, the whiles their bodies wake.'

'Nay, thou must not!' The sergeant stepped forward, alarmed. 'In truth, thou hast done all any man should ask of thee!'

''Tis good of thee to speak so.' Simon smiled with gentle warmth. 'Yet I'm beholden to them – for look you, these are my people, and have been all my life. They have aided me in all the daily trials that a poor man undergoes, and tended me and mine in illness, and consoled us in bereavement – as I have done for them. Such bonds are not severed only for reason that I'm the only one able to give aid now. Nay, i' truth I played the craven, when that I did flee.'

'Thou didst not,' the sergeant asserted. 'What will it profit them, for thou to turn back? Thy spell-breaking will but draw the warlock to thee again – and when he hath taken thee, thy folk will rest spellbound once more.'

Simon fairly beamed, but shook his head. 'I may escape his notice, as I've done already. Nay, I'll not again play coward.'

The sergeant hissed. 'Thou was not craven to be afeared; for certes, thou hast much to fear. Therefore, an thou will wake my men from this foul spell, we all shall company thee.'

'And make the danger greater?' Rod stepped forward, frowning. 'How much chance do you think you boys would have against a squad of twenty, Auncient?'

The sergeant hesitated, frowning.

Rod pressed the point. 'One civilian, going north with five armed men? Alfar's witch-sentries would smell a rat, even if they didn't have noses.'

Simon's face lit with a delighted smile. 'Yet think, goodman! They could say I was their prisoner!'

Rod gave the sergeant a jaundiced eye. 'Do you have any orders about taking prisoners?'

'Nay,' the sergeant admitted. 'We were commanded to but slay and rob.'

'You'd stand out like a haystack in a cornfield.' Rod shook his head. 'Pleasant fellow, isn't he, this Alfar? Efficient, though. Nasty, but efficient.'

'Nay; he's most plainly evil,' the sergeant growled.

'Yeah, but you don't fight evil by standing out in front of a full army and declaring war on them. At least, not when you're only a handful.'

Simon gave the sergeant a sad nod. ''Tis even so, Auncient. Thou and thy men were best to fare on southward.'

The sergeant's jaw tightened; he shook his head. 'I will not choose to go – nor, I think, will even one of my men.'

'Well, if you're bound and determined,' Rod sighed, 'let's make your lives as expensive as possible. Even just a handful of men can do an amazing amount of damage.'

'Indeed?' The sergeant turned to him eagerly. 'How dost thou mean?'

'You could be guerrillas,' Rod explained. 'The word means

"little wars", and that's just what you do – make little wars alone like good little Alfarites – but whenever there's a chance, you can turn into raiders.'

The sergeant clamped his lips, turning away in exasperation. 'What use are bandits, 'gainst an army?'

'A lot, if you choose the right targets. For example, if you break into the armoury and steal all the crossbows bolts, or even break all the arrows . . . '

The sergeant lifted his head, eyes lighting. 'Aye – that would hamper an army's fighting, would it not?'

'Some,' Rod agreed, 'though there are still spears, pikes and swords. At this level of technology, commandos have a tougher time hurting the main army. Actually, I was thinking of you getting into the kitchens and pouring a few bucketfuls of salt on the food.'

Slowly, the sergeant grinned.

'It'll work even better if you can link up with the other groups who've had their spells broken,' Rod added.

The sergeant stared. 'There be others?'

'There will be.' Simon's eye glittered.

Rod glanced at him, and tried to suppress a smile. He turned back to the sergeant. 'Yes, er, a southern witch, yesterday – she broke the spell on another squad, like yours, and they opted to go back north, too.'

'Allies!' the sergeant cried, then frowned in doubt. 'But how shall we know them? We cannot ask every soldier in the sorcerer's army, "Art thou of the band whose spell is broke"?'

'Scarcely,' Rod agreed. 'But any bands Simon frees from now on, he can give secret names – ones you can say aloud for everyone to hear, but that only the ones whose spells are broken will recognize. For example, from now on, you'll be, um . . . Balthazar.' He turned to Simon. 'And you can name the auncients of the next two groups you free, "Melchior" and "Casper".'

'What use is this?' the sergeant demanded.

'Well, if another soldier comes up to you and says he has a message from Auncient Melchior, you can exchange information, because you'll know he's a part of the freedom movement. But you shouldn't get together, mind you. The bigger your force, the easier you'll be to find.'

'Then what use this sending of messages?'

'So you can all agree to hit the same target at the same

time. For example, you might want to make a big enough raid to actually take over a castle, or something. And, of course, when King Tuan's army marches north, you can all meet just behind the sorcerer's army, and hit them from the back while he hits 'em from the front.'

'Doth he come, then?' The sergeant fairly pounced on the idea.

'Oh, he'll come,' Rod said, with more certainty than he felt. 'A message went south, yesterday.'

Simon and the sergeant both stared at him.

With a sinking heart, Rod realized he'd made a bad slip. 'I couldn't help overhearing,' he added, lamely.

'Certes, thou couldst not,' Simon murmured. 'Yet I bethink me thou'rt not the humble yeoman farmer that thou dost seem.'

'Aye,' the sergeant agreed. 'Thou'rt a man of arms, by thy knowledge. What rank hast thou? What is thy station?'

'Proxima Centauri Terminal,' Rod answered. 'And as to my rank, just take my word for it – I've got enough to know what I'm talking about. And as to the name, call me, er "Kern".'

Instantly, he knew it was a bad choice. *If people call you Kern*, said his id, from its morass of superstitious fear, *you'll lose track of who you are. You'll start thinking you are Kern, and you'll be absorbed into him*.

*Ridiculous*, his ego responded. *Kern's will can't reach across universes. The name's just a word, not a threat to your identity*.

His superego surveyed the two, came to its own conclusions, and declared it a draw.

Rod swallowed, firmed his jaw, and stuck to his story. 'Kern,' he said again. 'That's all you need to know. Just take it and go with it as far as you can, Auncient.'

'Indeed I will. Yet why ought I not to know who it is who doth command me?'

'Not command,' Rod pointed out. 'I'm just giving you advice. It was your idea to go back north, not mine. If you want a command, I'll tell you to go south.'

'Nay,' the sergeant said quickly. 'Yet I thank thee for thy good, um, "advice".'

'My pleasure, I'm sure. And, of course, if the worst should happen, and they should capture you . . . '

'I will not betray thee,' the sergeant said firmly. 'Let them bring hot irons; let them bring their thumbscrews. I shall breathe no word.'

'You won't have to. All they'll have to do is read your mind. You may be able to keep from saying it aloud, but you can't keep from thinking about it.'

The sergeant looked doubtful.

Rod nodded. 'So the whole idea is to not know anything more than is absolutely necessary. But – just in case we should be able to get something moving, mind you . . . '

'Aye!'

'If someone should come to you and say that Kern says to attack a given place at a given time, you'll know what to do.'

The soldier lifted his head, with a slow grin. 'Aye. I shall indeed now. And I swear to thee, I will execute what thou dost command.'

'Good man.' Rod slapped him on the shoulder. 'Now – let's get to waking up your men.' He turned to Simon. 'If you would, Master Simon? The sooner we can split up and hit the road, the better.'

Simon nodded, with a smile, and turned away to the fallen troopers.

'Well done,' Fess's voice murmured behind Rod's ear. 'You excel as a catalyst, Rod.'

'Oh, I'm great at knocking over the first domino,' Rod muttered back. 'Only trouble is, this time I have to set them up, too.'


# Chapter Ten

The osprey circled above them, its wings dipping as it balanced in the updraught. Rod scowled up at it, wondering if its eyes were green, like Gwen's. 'Simon, how far are we from the coast?'

'Mayhap a day's ride,' Simon followed Rod's gaze. 'Ah, I see. 'Tis a fish-hawk, is't not?'

'Far as I know. But if the ocean's only twenty miles off, it's probably genuine.' Rod turned to his companion. 'Thought you were a dirt farmer. How would you know what a fish-hawk looks like?'

Simon shrugged. 'As I've said, the ocean's not that far.'

Which was true enough, Rod reflected. He didn't really have anything to be suspicious about – but in enemy territory, he couldn't help it. He wasn't that far from suspecting the nearest boulder might be a witch in disguise.

'Then, too,' Simon said, amused, 'I've never claimed to be a farmer.'

Rod looked up, surprised. 'True enough,' he said slowly. 'I did just the same. After all, what other occupations would there be in a small village?'

'''Tis hard by the King's High Way,' Simon explained. 'I keep an inn.'

Rod lifted his head, mouth opening before the words came. 'Oh'. He nodded slowly. 'I see. And quality folk stop in frequently, eh?'

'Mayhap twice in a month. There was ever a constant coming and going with the castle of Milord Duke. I did hearken to their speech, and did mimic it as best I could, the better to please them.'

He'd hearkened to a lot more than their speech, Rod reflected. The aristocrats would no doubt have been aghast, if they'd known a mind reader served them. And, of course, Simon couldn't have had too many illusions left about the lords.

So why was he still loyal?

Probably because the alternative was so much worse. 'I don't suppose they taught you how to read?'

'Nay; my father sent me to the vicar, for lessons. He kept an inn before me, and knew 'twould be useful for an innkeeper to read and write, and cast up sums.'

So. Unwittingly, Rod has stumbled into one of the local community leaders. 'An enlightened man.'

'Indeed he was. And what art thou?'

Every alarm bell in Rod's head broke into clamour. Admittedly, he'd made a pretty big slip; but did Simon have to be so quick on the uptake? 'Why . . . I'm a farmer. Do I look so much like a knight, as to confuse you? Or a Duke, perhaps?' Then his face cleared with a sudden, delighted smile, and he turned to jab a finger at Simon. '*I* know! You thought I was a goldsmith!'

Simon managed to choke the laugh down into a chuckle, and shook his head. 'Nay, goodman. I speak not of thine occupation, but of what thou *art* – that thou art there, but thou'rt not.'

Rod stared, totally taken aback. 'What do you mean, I'm not here?'

'In thy thoughts.' Simon laid a finger against his forehead.

'I have told thee I can hear men's thoughts – yet I cannot hear thine.'

'Oh.' Rod turned back to the road, gazing ahead, musing – while, inside, he virtually collapsed into a shuddering heap of relief. 'Yes . . . I've been told that before . . . ' *Glad it's working. . .*

Simon smiled, but with his brows knit. ''Tis more than simply not hearing any thoughts. When my mind doth "listen" for thee, there is not even a sense of thy presence. How comes this?'

Rod shrugged. 'I can guess, but that's all.'

'And what is thy guess?'

'That I'm more worried about mind readers than your average peasant.'

Simon shook his head. 'That would not explain it. I have known some filled with morbid fear their thoughts would be heard – and I think they had reason, though I sought to avoid them. Still, I could have heard their thoughts, an I had wished to. Certes, I could sense that they were there. Yet with thee, I can do neither. I think, companion, that thou must needs have some trace of witch power of thine own, that thy will doth wrap into a shield.'

'You trying to tell me I'm a witch?' Rod did a fairly good imitation of bristling.

Simon only smiled sadly. 'Even less than I am. Nay, I'd not fear that. Thou canst not hear thoughts, canst thou?'

'No,' Rod said truthfully – at least, for the time being.

Simon smiled. 'Then thou'rt not a witch. Now tell me – why dost thou come north? Thou must needs know that thou dost drive toward danger.'

'I sure must, after you and the auncient finished with me.' Rod hunched his shoulders, pulling into himself. 'As to the danger, I'll chance it. I can get better prices for my produce in Korasteshev that I can in all of Tudor's county! And my family's always hungry.'

'They will hunger more, an thou dost not return.' Simon's voice dropped, full of sincerity. 'I bid thee, friend, turn back.'

'What's the matter? Don't like my company?'

Simon's earnestness collapsed into a smile. 'Nay – thou art a pleasant enough companion . . . '

Personally, Rod thought he was being rather churlish.

But Simon was very tolerant. 'Yet for thine own sake, I bid thee turn toward the south again. The sorcerer's warlocks will not take kindly to one whose mind they cannot sense.'

'Oh, the warlocks won't pay any attention to a mere peasant coming to market.' At least, Rod hoped they wouldn't.

'The prices in Romanov cannot be so much better than they are in Tudor.' Simon held Rod's eyes with a steady gaze. It seemed to burn through his retinas and into his brain. 'What more is there to thine answer?'

Reluctantly, Rod admitted, 'There is more – but that's all you're going to get.'

Simon held his gaze for a minute.

Then he sighed, and turned away. 'Well, it is thy fate, and thou must needs answer for it thyself. Yet be mindful, friend, that thy wife and bairns do depend upon thee.'

Rod was mindful of it, all right. For a sick instant, he had a vision of Gwen and the children waiting weeks, without word of him. Then he thrust the thought sternly aside, and tried to envision the look in his boys' faces if he abandoned his mission and came back to be safe. 'You have obligations to the people of your village, Master Simon. So have I.'

'What – to the folk of thy town?'

'Well, to my people, anyway.' Rod had the whole of Gramarye in mind, not to mention the Decentralized Democratic Tribunal. 'And once you've accepted an obligation of that sort, you can't put it aside just because it becomes dangerous.'

'Aye, that's so,' Simon said, frowning. ''Tis this that I've but now come to see.'

Rod turned to him, frowning too. 'But you've already done your part, taken your risks. No one would call you a coward for going south now!'

'I would,' Simon said simply.

Rod looked directly into his eyes for a moment, then turned away with a sigh. 'What can I say to that, goodman?'

'Naught, save "gee-up" to thine horse.'

'Why?' Rod asked sourly. 'This cart may be pulled by a horse, but it's being driven by a pair of mules.'

Sundown caught them still on the road, with grainfields at either hand. 'Nay,' Simon assured Rod, 'there is no town near.'

'I was afraid of that,' Rod sighed. 'Well, the earth has been my bed before this.' And he drove off the road, pulling Fess to a stop in the weeds between the track and the field. He was cutting vegetables into a small pot before Simon could even volunteer.

The innkeeper eyed him quizzically, then asked, 'Dost ever have a pot with thee?'

'I was a tinker once. Habits stick.'

Simon smiled, shaking his head, and leaned back on an elbow, 'I think such travels are not wholly new to thee.'

'We're even,' Rod snorted. 'I get the feeling spell-breaking isn't all that new to *you*.'

Simon was still for a moment, but his eyes brightened. 'Almost could I believe thou didst read minds.'

'If I did, I'd need to have yours translated. So when did you start spell-breaking?'

Simon sat up, hooking his forearms around his shins, resting his chin on his knees. 'The men of the village came oft to mine inn for drinking of beer, which they took as part-price for the produce they brought. Anon would come one whose heart was heavy, with thoughts in turmoil, to drink and be silent – mayhap in hopes that beer would quiet his unrest.'

Rod nodded. 'Strange how we keep trying that solution. Especially since it never works.'

'Nay; but speaking thy thoughts to a willing ear, can help to calm them; and the troubled ones would talk, for I would hearken, and give what sympathy I could. Yet one there came who seemed like unto a wall in winter – like to spring apart at the first freeze. He could not talk, but huddled over his flagon. Yet the jumble of his thoughts rode upon such pain that they fairly screamed. I could not have shut my mind to them, even had I wished to – and brooding over all was the shadow of a noose.'

Rod looked up sharply. 'The kid was suicidal?'

'Aye. And he was no child, but in his thirties. 'Tis these passages from one state to another that do wreak their havocs within us, and his children all had grown.'

Rod couldn't understand the problem; but he had Gwen for a wife. 'What could you do about it?'

'Fill another flagon, and one for myself, and go to sit by him. Then, 'neath the pretext of conversing – and 'twas very much a pretence, for I alone did speak – I felt through the snarl of his thoughts, found the sources of his pain and shame, then asked aloud the questions that did make him speak them. And 'twas not easy for him thus to speak – yet I encouraged, and he did summon up sufficient resolution. I meant only to have him thus give me a pretext to discuss his secret fears, to tell him they were not so fearsome – yet I found that, once he had spoken them aloud, and heard his own voice saying them, these secrets then lost half their power. Then could I ask a question whose answer would show him the goodness within him that could counter his hidden monsters, and, when we were done, he'd calmed tolerably well.'

'You saved his life,' Rod accused.

Simon smiled, flattered. 'Mayhap I did: I began, then, to give such aid to all such troubled souls that I encountered. Nay, I even sought them out when they did not come into my inn.'

'Could be dangerous, there,' Rod pointed out. 'Just so much of that hauling people back from the edge, before the neighbours decided you had to be a witch to do it. Especially since you were poaching on the parish priest's territory.'

Simon shook his head. 'Who knew of it? Not even those I aided – for I gave no advice nor exhortation. And look you, 'twas a village. We all knew one another, so there was naught of surprise should I encounter any one of them, and chat a while. Yet withal, the folk began to say that troubled souls could find a haven in mine inn.'

'Definitely poaching on the priest's territory,' Rod muttered. 'And that was an awful lot of grief to be taking on yourself.'

Simon shrugged, irritated. 'They were my people, Master Owen. *Are*, I should say. And there were never more than three in a year.'

Rod didn't look convinced.

Simon dropped his gaze to the camp fire. 'Thus, when Tom Shepherd lapsed into sullenness, his brothers brought him to my tap-room. In truth, they half-carried him; he could no longer even walk of his own.' He shook his head. ''Twas an old friend of mine – or should I say, an old neighbour.'

'What was the matter with him?'

Simon turned his head from side to side. 'His face was slack; he could not move of his own, and did but sit, not speaking. I drew a stool up next to his, and gazed into his face, the whiles I asked questions which he did not answer; yet all the while, my mind was open, hearkening at its hardest, for any thought that might slip through his mind.'

'Sounds catatonic.' Rod frowned. 'I shouldn't think there would've been any thoughts.'

'There was one – but only one. And that one did fill him, consuming all his mind and heart with a single graveyard knell.'

'Suicidal, again?'

Simon shook his head. 'Nay. 'Twas not a *wish* to die, look thou, nor even a willingness, but a sureness, a certainty, that he *would* die, was indeed that moment dying, but slowly.'

Rod sat very still.

'I laboured mightily 'gainst that compulsion. Yet I could but ask questions that would recall to mind the things that would make him wish to live – wife, and bairns, and careful neighbours; yet naught availed.' He shook his head. 'One would have thought he had not heard; for still throughout him rang the brazen knell of death.' Simon sighed, turning his head slowly from side to side. 'In the end, I could but bid his brothers take him to the priest, but the good friar fared no better than I.' He shrugged. 'I could not cast into his mind thoughts to counter that fell compulsion. The power was not in me.'

Rod nodded, understanding Simon was only a telepath, not a projective.

Simon picked up a stick, and poked at the fire. 'He died, in the end. He ate not, nor drank, and withered up like a November leaf. And I, heartsick, began to wonder how such a doom came to burden him. For he'd ever been a cheerful fellow, and I could see that one had laid a spell upon him. Aye, I pondered how one could be so evil as to do so fell a deed.

'So I commenced long walks throughout the county will at length I found that same wholehearted, whole consumption of a mind – yet 'twas not one mind, but a score; for I came into a village, and found that half the folk who lived there were bewitched. Oh, aye, they walked and spoke like any normal folk – but all their minds were filled with but one single thought.'

'Death?' Rod felt the eeriness creeping over the back of his skull.

'Nay.' Simon shook his head. ''Twas praise of Alfar.'

'Oh-h-h.' Rod lifted his head slowly. 'The sorcerer's enchantment team had been at work.'

'They had – and, knowing that, I went back to mine own village and, in chatting with my fellow villagers, asked a question here, and another there, and slowly built up a picture of that which had occurred to Tom Shepherd. He'd met a warlock in the fields, who had bade him kneel to Alfar. Tom spat upon the ground, and told that warlock that his Alfar was naught but a villain, who truly owed allegiance to Duke Romanov, even as Tom Shepherd did. The warlock then bade him swear loyalty to Alfar, or die; but Tom laughed in his face, and bade him do his worst.'

'So he did?'

'Aye, he did indeed! Then, knowing this, I went back to the village where half had been of one thought only, and that thought Alfar's. I found only ten of a hundred still free in their thoughts, and those ten walking through a living nightmare of fear; for I spoke with some, and heard within their thoughts that several of them had defied the warlocks, and died as Tom Shepherd had. Even as I stood there, one broke beneath his weight of fear, and swore inside himself that he'd be Alfar's man henceforth, and be done with terror.' Simon shuddered. 'I assure thee, I left that village as quickly as I might.'

He turned to look directly into Rod's eyes, and his gaze seemed to bore into Rod's brain. 'I cannot allow such obscenities of horror to exist, the whiles I sit by and do naught.' He shook his head slowly. 'Craven was I, ever to think I could walk away and leave this evil be.'

'No,' Rod said. 'No, you can't, can you? Not and still be who you are.'

Simon frowned. 'Strangely put – yet, I doubt me not, quite true.'

The campsite was quiet for a few minutes, as both men sat watching the flames, each immersed in his own thoughts. Then Rod lifted his head, to find Simon's gaze on him. 'Now,' said the innkeeper, ''tis thy turn. Is't not?'

'For what?'

'For honesty. Why dost thou go north?'

Rod held his gaze for a few moments, then, slowly, he said, 'Same reason as yours, really – or one pretty much like it. I've seen some of Alfar's work, and it's sickened me. I can't call myself a man if I let that happen without fighting it. At the very least, I've got to help keep it from spreading – or die trying.'

'As indeed thou mayest,' Simon breathed. 'Yet that is not the whole of thine answer, is it?'

'No – but that's all you're going to get.'

They gazed at one another for several heartbeats, the blade of Rod's glare clashing off the velvet wall of Simon's acceptance. Finally, the innkeeper nodded. ''Tis thine affair, of course.' He sounded as though he meant it.

He turned back to the fire. 'Thou art mine ally for this time. I need know no more than that the sorcerer's thine enemy.'

'Well, that – and that the stew's ready.' Rod leaned over to sniff the vapours. 'Not bad, for field rations. Want some?'

When Simon rolled up in his cloak to sleep, Rod went over to curry Fess. The job wasn't really stage dressing at all – Fess's horsehair may have owed more to plastic than to genetics, but it still collected brambles and burrs on occasion.

'So.' Rod ran the currycomb along Fess's withers. 'Alfar started out with nothing but feelings of inferiority, and a grudge against the world.'

'An ordinary paranoid personality,' Fess noted.

'Yeah, except that he was an esper. And somewhere along the line, he all of a sudden became a lot more powerful than your average warlock.' He looked up at Fess. 'Maybe just because he managed to talk some other witches into joining him?'

'Perhaps.' The robot sounded very sceptical. 'I cannot help but think there is more to the matter than that.'

'Probably right, too . . . So. Alfar had a sudden boost in power, and/or got together a gang. Then he started leaning on the local citizenry, like any good gangster.'

'The process seems to begin with intimidation,' Fess noted.

Rod stopped currying for a minute. 'Maybe . . . Even the soldiers were scared when they were marching against him . . . ' He shrugged. 'Hard to say. In any event, he's finally able to mass-hypnotize whole villages – though from the soldier's account, it needs to be redone in depth, on an individual basis.'

'The soldiers' mass hypnosis was done during the heat of battle, Rod, and very quickly. The peasant villages seem to have been done more leisurely, by Simon's statement – over a period of days, perhaps even weeks.'

'True – so it would be more thorough. Though, apparently, some are harder to hypnotize than others.' He looked up at Fess again. 'And espers appear to be immune.'

'So it would seem, to judge by Simon.'

'Yes . . . ' Briefly, Rod wondered about that. Then he shrugged

it off. 'Anyhow. When Alfar'd built enough of a power base, one of
the local knights got worried and tried to knock him down before
he grew too big. But he was already too big.'

'Indeed,' Fess agreed. 'He was already powerful enough to
overcome a knight with his village force.'

Rod nodded. 'And by the time he was big enough to worry
the local baron, he'd absorbed the forces of several knights. So
the baron fell, and the chain reaction began – the baron, then the
count, then finally the duke himself – and it doesn't end there,
does it?'

'Certainly not, Rod. After all, he now has the resources of
a duchy to draw on.'

'Yes. We all know what he's going to do now, don't we?'

'But surely Gwendylon and the children have already borne
word to Tuan and Catharine, Rod – and the Duchess's personal
account must certainly have been very persuasive. I doubt not that
Tuan is already gathering his forces.'

'Gathering them, yes. But it's going to be at least a week
or two before he can march north.'

'Surely Alfar cannot consolidate his newly won forces with
sufficient speed to enable him to carry the attack to Tuan!'

'Oh, I don't think he would, anyway.' Rod looked up into
Fess's imitation eyes. 'All the Duke's horses and all the Duke's
men aren't quite enough to take on the King's army.'

'True,' the robot conceded. 'Therefore, he will attack Earl
Tudor.'

'You really think he'd dare strike that close to Tuan?'

'Perhaps not. Perhaps he will seek to conquer Habsburg first.'

'It's just great, having outgoing neighbours . . . and if he man-
ages to swallow Habsburg, he'll have to digest him before he can
take on Tudor.'

'I doubt that he would try. He might be able to defeat the
Earl quickly, but he must surely need a week or two to complete
the indoctrination of the captured soldiers.'

'And while he's digesting, he's right next to Tuan. No, you're
right. He'd try to march through Tudor, and attack Tuan right
away. Which means *our* job is to keep him from being able to
attack another baron, before Tuan attacks him.'

'What methods do you propose, Rod?'

Rod shrugged. 'The usual – hit and run, practical jokes,
whispering campaigns – nothing sensible. Keep him off-balance.

Which shouldn't be too hard; he's going to be feeling pretty insecure, right about now.'

'He will indeed. And, being paranoid, he will seek to eliminate whatever enemies he does see, before he turns his attention to attack.'

'Maybe. But a paranoid also might decide to attack before the next baron can attack him, and start his own secret police to take care of internal enemies.' Rod clenched a fist in frustration. 'Damn! If only you could predict what a single human being would do!'

'Be glad you cannot.' Fess reminded, 'or VETO and its totalitarians could easily triumph.'

'True,' Rod growled. 'Truer than I like. And speaking of our proletarian pals, do you see any evidence of their meddling in this?'

'Alfar's techniques do resemble theirs,' Fess admitted.

'Resemble? Wish fulfilment, more likely! He's got the kind of power they dream of – long-distance, mass-production brainwashing! What wouldn't any good little dictator give for that?'

'His soul, perhaps?'

'Are you kidding? Totalitarianism works the other way round – everybody *else* gives their souls to the dictator!'

'Unpleasant, but probably accurate. None the less, there is no evidence of futurian activity.'

'Neither totalitarians nor anarchists, huh?'

'Certainly not, Rod.'

'Not even the sudden, huge jump in Alfar's powers?'

'That ability does bother me,' Fess admitted. 'A projective telepath who seems to be able to take on a whole parish at one time . . . Still, there's no reason to believe the totalitarians would be behind it.'

'Oh, yes there is,' Rod countered. 'From everything Simon's told me, and it just backed up what Gwen said – the trance these people seem to walk around in, is thoroughly impersonal.'

'Almost depersonalized, you might say? I had something of the same thought, too, Rod. I recognize the state.'

'Yes – mechanical, isn't it?'

'True. But that is not conclusive evidence of futurian meddling.'

'No – but it does make you wonder.' Rod gave the synthetic horsehair a last swipe with the brush. 'There! As new and shiny as though you'd just come from the factory. Do you mind a long tether, just for appearances?'

'I would mind not having it. It is certainly necessary, Rod.'

'Must keep them up, mustn't we?' Rod reached into the cart, pulled out a length of rope, tied one end to Fess's halter and the other to a convenient tree branch. 'Besides, you can break it easily, if you want.'

'I will not hesitate to do so,' Fess assured him. 'Sleep while you can, Rod. You will need the rest.'

'You're such an optimist.' Rod pulled his cloak out of the cart and went back to the campfire. 'I'm not exactly in a great mood for emptying my mind of the cares of the day.'

'Try,' the robot urged.

'If I try to sleep, I'll stay awake.' Rod lay down and rolled up in his cloak. 'How about trying to stay awake?'

'Not if you *truly* want to sleep. I could play soft music, Rod.'

'Thanks, but I think the nightbirds are doing a pretty good job of that.'

'As you wish. Good night, Rod.'

'I hope so,' Rod returned. 'Same to you, Fess.' He rolled over towards the fire . . .

. . . and found himself staring into Simon's wide-open, calm, and thoughtful eyes.

'Er . . . hi, there.' Rod forced a sickly grin. 'Say, I'll bet you're wondering what I was doing, rambling on like that – aren't you?'

'Not greatly,' Simon answered, 'though I do find thy conversation to be of great interest.'

'Oh, I'm sure.' Rod's stomach sank. 'Does it, er, bother you, to, er, hear me talk to my horse?'

'Not at all.' Simon looked faintly surprised. 'And 'tis certainly not so desperate as talking to thyself.'

'That's a point . . . '

''Tis also scarcely amazing.' Simon favoured him with a rather bleak smile. 'Be mindful, I'm an innkeeper, and many carters have stopped at my inn. Every one I've known, has spoken to his horse.'

'Oh.' Rod hoped his surprise didn't show in his face. 'You mean I'm not exactly unusual?'

'Only in this; thou'rt the first I've heard who, when he spoke to his horse, made sense.'

Rod supposed it was a compliment.

# Chapter Eleven

They were up at first light, and on the road by dawn. With the main issues out of the way, the two of them chatted together easily – Simon the innkeeper, and Owen the farmer. And if, as morning wore on, Owen's tales of his children bore a startling resemblance to the experiences of Rod Gallowglass, it can scarcely be surprising. On the other hand, all the stories had nothing to do with juvenile witch powers; Rod stayed sufficiently on his guard not to make that particular slip.

It wasn't easy. Rod found they had a lot in common – wives, and children. He also found Simon to be surprisingly refreshing. Instead of their usual dire predictions about the horrors of adolescence that lay in store for the unwary father, Simon restricted his anecdotes to childhood disasters – though, when pressed, he admitted that all his children were grown, and the tale of his daughter's impending first birth was quite true. Rod immediately began insisting, all over again, that Simon turn back to the south and his daughter, the more so because Simon had mentioned earlier that his wife had died quite a few years ago; but the innkeeper merely informed Rod that his daughter really lived north of his home village – wherefore, he had been doubly cowardly to flee. There wasn't much Rod could say to that, so he relaxed and enjoyed Simon's company. So, by the time they came to the first village, Rod was feeling in fine form – which was fortunate, because they were greeted by a mob.

The peasants stormed out of the village, howling and throwing stones and waving pitchforks – but not at Simon and Rod. Their target was a small man, who sprinted madly, managing to stay a dozen yards ahead of them.

'Slay the warlock!' they cried. 'Stone him! Stab him! Drain his blood! Burn him! Burn him! Burn Him BURN HIM!'

Simon and Rod stared at each other, startled. Then Simon snapped, 'He could not be of Alfar's brood, or soldiers would even now be cutting down these peasants! Quickly, Owen!'

'You heard him!' Rod cracked the whip over Fess's head, keeping up the act. 'Charge!'

Fess leaped into a gallop. Cartwheels roared behind him.

Rod pulled up hard as they passed the fleeing warlock, and Simon shouted, 'Up behind, man! For thy lifeblood's sake!'

The running man looked up, startled, then jumped into the

cart, as Simon rose to his feet and cried out, in a voice that seared through the crowd's shouting:

'I, too, am a magic worker! *Two* warlocks face thee now! Dost thou still wish wood to kindle?'

The crowd froze, the words of violence dying on their tongues.

Simon stood relaxed, but his face was granite. Slowly, he surveyed the crowd, picking out individual faces here and there. But he didn't say a word.

Finally, a fat little man stepped forward, shaking a club at Simon. 'Step aside, fellow! Withdraw thy cart and horse! Our quarrel's with this foul warlock, not with thee!'

'Nay,' Simon answered. 'To the contrary; every warlock's business is every other's, for there are few of us indeed.'

'*Every* warlock?' the fat man bleated in indignation. 'Is Alfar's business also thine?'

His words set off an ugly murmur that increased in ugliness as it built.

'Alfar's business ours?' Simon's eyes widened. 'Why would it not be?'

The noise cut off as the crowd stared at him, frozen.

Then the people began to mutter to one another, worried, a little fearful. One scrawny warlock by himself was one thing – but two together, with Alfar's backing . . .

Simon's voice cut through their hubbub. ''Twould be better an thou didst now go back unto thine homes.'

'What dost thou speak of!' the fat little man cried. 'Turn to our homes? Nay! For we have one who must be punished! What dost thou think thyself to . . . '

His voice ran down under Simon's stony glare. Behind him, the crowd stared, then began to whisper among themselves again. Rod heard snatches of 'Evil Eye! Evil Eye!' He did the best he could to reinforce the idea, staring at the fat little leader with his eyes narrowed a little, teeth showing in a wolfish grin.

'Thou wilt go,' Simon said, his voice like an icepick.

Rod could scarcely believe the transformation. He could've sworn Simon was at least two inches taller and four inches broader. His eyes glowed; his face was alive and vibrant. He fairly exuded power.

Cowed, the crowd drew in upon itself, muttering darkly. Simon's voice rose above. 'We have shown thee plainly wherein doth lie the true power in this land – but it need not be turned against thee. Go, now – go to thine homes.' Then he smiled, and his aura seemed to mellow – he seemed gentler, somehow, and reassuring. 'Go,' he urged, 'go quickly.'

The crowd was shaken by the transformation. Their emotions had been yanked back and forth; they didn't know whether to resent Simon, or be grateful to him. For a moment, they stood, uncertain. Then one man turned away, slowly. Another saw him, and turned to follow. A third saw them, and turned, then a fourth. Then the whole crowd was moving back toward the village.

The fat little man glanced at them, appalled, then back towards Simon. 'Retribution shall follow,' he cried, but fear hollowed his voice. 'Retribution, and flames for all witches!'

Rod's eyes narrowed to slits, and he gathered himself; but Simon laid a restraining hand on his shoulder, and said mildly, 'Go whilst thou may – or retribution there shall be indeed, and I shall not lift one finger to stay it.'

The little man glanced at Rod in sudden terror, then whirled about, and hurried to follow the villagers back towards the houses.

Rod, Simon and the stranger only watched him, frozen in tableau till he'd disappeared among the buildings. Then, the moment he was out of sight, Simon heaved a long sigh, going limp.

'I should say,' Rod agreed. 'You do that kind of thing often?'

'Nay.' Simon collapsed onto the board seat. 'Never in my life.'

'Then you've got one hell of a talent for it.' Privately, Rod had a strong suspicion that Simon was at least a little bit of a projective, but didn't realize it.

Even with his nerves a-jangle from facing down a mob for the first time, Simon remembered the fugitive. He turned, looking back into the cart. 'Art thou well, countryman?'

'Aye,' the stranger wheezed, 'thanks to thee, goodmen. An thou hadst not come, there had been naught but a bloody lump left of me. E'en now I tremble, to think of them! From the depths of my soul I thank thee. I shall pray down upon thee one blessing, for every star that stands in the sky! I shall . . . '

'You shall live.' Rod couldn't repress the grin. 'And we're glad of it. But if you're a warlock, why didn't you just disappear?' Then a sudden thought hit him, and he turned to Simon. 'Is he a warlock?'

'Aye.' Simon nodded, his eyes on the stranger. 'There is the feeling I've had, twice aforetime, when I've met another warlock and heard his thoughts – that feeling of being in a mind enlarged, in a greater space of soul.'

Rod knew the feeling; he'd met it himself. With a variant form and intensity, it was one of the great benefits of being married to another esper – and one of the curses of being an esper himself, when he was near another telepath whom he didn't like. He'd decided some time ago that it was mental feedback – but controlled feedback. It must've been, or it would've torn both minds apart. The born witch, he thought, must develop a perceptual screen in infancy, a sort of blocking mechanism that would reduce the recycled mental energy to comfortable levels.

'He is a warlock,' Simon said again. 'Why, therefore, didst thou not disappear, goodman?'

'Why, for that I could not.' The stranger smiled apologetically, spreading his hands and cocking his head to the side. 'What can I say to thee? I am a very poor warlock, who can but hear others' thoughts, and that only when they're hard by me. E'en then, I cannot hear them well.'

'I, too,' Simon said, with a sad smile. 'I can but hear one that's within the same house as I.'

'And I, only when they are within a few yards,' the stranger said, nodding. 'But so little as that is enough, I wot, so that, now and again, summat of others' thoughts do come into mine head, unknowing – the thought comes that so-and-so is a-love with such-and-such, or that this one wishes the other dead. And, again and now, I let slip an unguarded word or two, and the one I'm speaking to doth stare at me, in horror, and doth cry, "How couldst thou know of that? None have heard it of me; to none have I spoken of it!"'

'So they figured out what you were.' Rod nodded.

'Aye; and it cost me what few friends I had, from my earliest years; yet it made me no enemies; for I am, as I've said, a most powerless warlock, and all, thankfully, knew that I meant no one harm.'

Rod could believe it. The stranger was short, slump-shouldered and concave-chested, flabby, with a little pot-belly. His hair was dun-coloured. He had large, pale eyes, a snub nose, and a perpetual hangdog look about him. He couldn't have been much over thirty, but already his cheeks were beginning to sag. In a year or five, he'd have jowls. A *schlemiel*, Rod decided, a poor soul who would never intentionally hurt anybody, but would always be clumsy, both physically and socially. 'Nobody really wanted you around, huh? But they didn't mind you, either.'

'Aye,' the stranger said, with a rueful smile.

'I know that way of it,' Simon sighed. 'There was such a lad in my village.'

'There always is,' Rod said. 'It's a necessary social function. Everybody needs somebody whose name they can't quite remember.'

'Well said,' Simon smiled. 'And thou dost touch my conscience. How art thou called, goodman?'

'Flaran,' the stranger answered, with the same smile.

'Flaran,' Simon repeated, thoughtfully. 'Tell me, Flaran – when Alfar the sorcerer began to rise to power, did thy fellows expect thee to hail him?'

Flaran's smile gained warmth. 'They did that. Thou hast endured it thyself, hast thou not?' And, when Simon nodded, he chuckled. 'So I thought; thou hast spoke too much of what I have seen myself. Aye, all my neighbours did think that, solely because I've a touch of the Power, I should cry that Alfar was the greatest hope this duchy hath ever seen. Yet I did not. In truth, I said I did not trust the man.'

Simon nodded. 'Yet they thought thou didst give them the lie.'

'They did,' Flaran agreed. 'Straightaway, then, mine old friends – or neighbours, at least – began to mistrust me; in truth, as Alfar's fame and power have grown, they have doubted me more and more.'

'Still, thou'rt of them.' Simon frowned. 'When last came to last, thou wert of their clan and kind. I would think they would not hound and stone thee.'

'Nor did I – and still I misdoubt me an they would have. But folk began to pass through our village, pushing handcarts and bearing packs upon their backs; and, though we did not have great store of food or ale, "Stay," we urged them. "Nay," they answered, "for the sorcerer's armies do march, and we do flee them. We dare not bide, for they'll swallow up this village also." Then they turned, and marched on toward the south.'

Rod and Simon exchanged a quick glance. Simon nodded in corroboration. Rod understood; Simon had been one of the ones who had come marching through the village, and had not stayed. 'And this small ball of a man with the great mouth?' Simon turned back to Flaran. 'Was he of thy village, or of the strangers?'

'Of the strangers,' Flaran answered, 'and he did come into our
village crying doom upon all who had any powers. None could be
trusted, quoth he, for all witch folk must needs hate all common
men, and must needs fight them; therefore, any witch or warlock
must needs be an agent of Alfar's.'

Simon's eyes burned. 'Indeed? Would I could have done more
than send him back to thy village.'

'Nay, friend. Thou wouldst but have made my neighbours
certain in their hatred. Even as 'twas, he did turn my fellows
against me – though, in all truth, the news from the north had
made them so wary, they needed little turning. I came into the
inn for a pint, but when I stood near to the landlord, I heard
his thoughts, his rage and mistrust, his secret fear that the fat
little stranger might be right, that mayhap all witch folk *should*
be stoned. Nay, I dropped my flagon and fled.'

'And, of course, they all ran after you.' Rod reflected that
the panic instinct must have taken over.

Flaran shuddered. ''Tis even as thou dost say. 'Twas not
even an hour agone. I dodged and hid, then dodged and ran.
At last they found me out, and I could hide no longer. Nay, I
fled off down the road – but I was wearied, and must needs fight
to stay running. Heaven be praised that thou didst come up the
High Road then, or I had been a paste of a person!'

Simon reached out to clap Flaran on the shoulder. 'Courage,
friend – this bloodlust shall fade, as it hath aforetime. Ever and
anon have they come out hunting witches – and ever and anon
hath it passed. This shall, also.'

Flaran braved a small smile, but he didn't look convinced.

Rod wasn't, either – the whole thing had too much of the
deliberate about it. It was preplanned, well-organized whipping-up
of sentiment, and there was only one group organized enough to
do the whipping-up – but why would Alfar be trying to work up
antiesper sentiment?

The answer hit him like a sap, in instant balance to the
question: Alfar would whip up the witch hunt to eliminate his
competition. After all, the only force in the duchy that could
stand against him were the witches who hadn't signed up with
him. Left alone long enough, they just might band together in
self-defence – as Simon and Flaran were doing, even now. If they
organized a large enough band of fugitive witches and warlocks,
they would constitute a power that might actually unseat him. And

what better way to eliminate the independents, than the time-tried old witch hunt?

When you looked at it that way, it made excellent sense – especially since the unaligned espers would tend to be opposed to him; they'd be the most sensitive to his kind of hypnotic tyranny. 'Say, er – did either one of you ever feel one of Alfar's men trying to take over your mind?'

Both men looked up, startled. Then Simon nodded, gravely. 'Aye. It was . . . ' he shuddered, 'most obscene, friend Owen.'

'I could barely feel it,' Flaran added, 'yet it turned my stomach and made my gorge to rise. And it raised such a wave of fear in me, that I thought it like to shake me to pieces. To feel fingers of thought, stroking at thy mind— ' He broke off, looking queasy.

'Try not to think of it,' Rod said, cursing his impulsiveness. 'Sorry I brought it up.' And these two, he reflected, were the gentle kind. What would happen when Alfar's men tried to take on a warlock who had a bit more arrogance? Or even just one who liked to fight? He would have flown into a rage, and gone hunting for Alfar.

And Rod couldn't blame him. The thought of someone meddling with *his* mind started the sullen flow of anger. He recognized it, and tried to relax, let it drain away – but the image of Gwen and the children rose up in his mind, with the instant thought of some overbearing young warlock trying to touch *their* minds – and the rage exploded with a suddenness that left him defenceless against it, shaking his body with its intensity, wild and searing, searching for a target, any target, striving to master Rod, to make him its instrument. He held himself still, fighting to contain it, to keep it inside himself, to keep it from hurting anyone else.

But both warlocks were staring at him. 'My friend,' Simon said, wide-eyed, 'art thou well?'

Such a mild question, and so well-intentioned! But it broke the fragile membrane of Rod's control.

He hurled himself away from the cart, off the road and into the field beside. *Don't hurt them. Let it blow, but don't hurt them*. He needed some way to channel the anger, some way to let it spend itself harmlessly, and running was as good as anything else.

A boulder loomed up ahead of him, a rock outcrop four feet high, with smaller boulders around the base. Rod seized one about a foot across, hefting it up above his head with a grunt of agony. He stood for a moment, poised, glaring at the boulder, then hurled his rock with all his might, shouting, 'Blast you!'

The rock hit the boulder with a crack like a gunshot. Stone chips flew, and the smaller rock split and clattered to the base of the boulder.

'Burn in your own magic!' Rod screamed at it. 'Fall down a rathole, and forget how to teleport! Jump into the sky and don't come back down!' He raged on and on, a five-minute stream of incoherent curses.

Finally, the anger ebbed. Rod sank to one knee, still glaring at the boulder. Then, slowly, he bowed his head, gasping for breath, and waited for the trembling to stop.

When his heartbeat had slowed, he stood up, swaying a little. Then he forced himself to turn back toward the cart, fifty yards away – and saw Flaran staring at him.

But Simon stood near him, leaning on his staff, waiting, watching him with gentle sympathy.

That was what stung – the sympathy. Rod winced at the sight; it magnified his chagrin tenfold. He turned away, muttering, 'Sorry about that. I, er . . . I don't do that too often.' *I hope.*

'Thou didst only as I did feel,' Simon assured him.

'Well . . . thanks.' That didn't really help. 'I just get outraged at the thought of someone trampling on other people, without even thinking about them!'

Simon nodded. 'And when the object of thy wrath is not nigh thee, 'tis harder to forebear. Indeed, thou didst well to seek a thing of stone unfeeling, to wreak thy vengeance on.'

'But the force of it's wasted – is that what you're thinking? Why spend all that energy, without hurting the thing I'm angry at?'

Simon scowled. 'I had not thought that – but aye, now that thou dost say it. 'Tis better husbandry to contain thine anger till thou canst use its force to right the wrong that angers thee.'

'Easy enough to say,' Rod said, with a sardonic smile. 'But how do you contain your anger? I know it sounds simple – but you should try it, sometime! You would . . . ' He broke off, staring at Simon. Slowly, he said, 'You have tried it, haven't you?' Then, nodding, 'Yes. I think you have. The last line had the ring of experience behind it.'

' 'Tis even so,' Simon admitted.

'*You* had a temper? *You* flew into rages? You? Mr Nice Guy himself? Mr Calmness? Mr Phlegmatic? *You?*'

'Indeed,' Simon admitted, and, for the first time, his smile was tinged with irony. ''Tis not so easy, friend Owen, to hide thy knowledge of others' thoughts. 'Tis most tempting, in moments of anger, to use those thoughts against them – to say, "*Me* a coward? When thou didst face the battle with panic clamouring through thy veins, and would have fled, had thy captain not stood behind thee with his sword?" For indeed, he *had* marched forward, and none who saw him would have thought him less forward, and none who saw him would have thought him less than brave. Yet I knew, I – and was fool enough to speak it aloud. Then, to another, "How canst thou call me a lecher, Father, when thou hast thyself lusted after Tom Ploughman's wife?"'

Rod whistled. 'You *don't* take on the clergy!'

'Aye, but in my youthful pride, I thought that I had power o'er all – for I had but newly learned that I could hear others' thoughts and, in my delight and careless strength, did hearken to the thoughts of all about me. No person in that town was free from my thought-hearing. When one did sneer at me, I used my hoarded knowledge of his darkest secrets and proclaimed his shame for all to hear! He did swell up with rage, but durst not strike where all might see, and know the truth of what I'd said. Nay, he could only turn away with snarls – and I would gloat, rejoicing in my newfound power.'

Rod frowned. 'How long did you get away with that?'

'Thrice.' Simon grimaced, shaking his head. 'Three times only. For when the anger passed, the folk I'd wronged began to ponder. They knew they'd never spoken of their secret fears or lusts to any person living. By chance, they spoke to one another . . . '

'By chance, my rabbit's foot! You'd insulted each one publicly; they knew who to compare notes with!'

'Like enough,' Simon sighed. 'And once they all knew that I'd spoken things none of them had ever said aloud, 'twas but a small step to see that I must needs be a warlock, and one who would not hesitate to use that knowledge I gained from others' thoughts to their harm. They spread that word throughout the town, of course . . . '

'"Of course" is right,' Rod murmured, 'especially with the village priest in there. Who'd doubt his word? After all, even if he did covet his neighbour's wife, at least he didn't do anything about it.'

'Which is more than could be said for most of his flock,'

Simon said, with a tart grimace. 'Aye, he too did speak of my "fell power" – and the rumour ran through all the town, to harry all my neighbours out against me.' His face twisted with bitterness. 'I' truth, 'twas no more than my desert; yet I felt betrayed when they came against me as a mob, screaming, "Thought thief! Slanderer!" and "Sorcerer!" – betrayed, for that most of them had gossiped 'gainst me, one time or another – yet I'd forgiven them.'

'Yes – but you had a weapon they couldn't use.'

'Aye – not "wouldn't", but "couldn't".' Simon's grimace turned sardonic. 'And for that reason, they did raise the hue and cry, and harried me from their town.' He shuddered, closing his eyes. 'Ah, praise Heaven that I have no powers other than thought-hearing! For in mine anger, I would have turned and hurled great stones at them, fireballs, sharp knives; I would have raised these folk up high, and slammed them to the earth!' He shuddered again, and his eyes sprang open, staring.

Rod could see the anger rising in him again, and spoke quickly, calmly. 'Easy, easy. It was a long time ago.'

'And the wrong's been righted. Aye.' Simon managed to dredge up his smile again. 'I did learn the error of my ways; I did repent, and did full penance. For when I fled my native village, I wandered, blind with rage, immersed in bitterness, neither knowing nor caring whither my steps progressed. Forty leagues, fifty leagues, an hundred – till at last, worn out with hatred, I sank down in a cave and slept. And in my slumber, a soothing balm did waft to me, to calm my troubled spirit. When I waked, I felt refreshed, made new again. Wondering, I quested with my mind, to seek out the agency that had wrought this miracle. I found a well of holy thought which, in my slumber, I had drawn upon, unwitting. 'Twas a company of holy brothers and, by great good fortune, the cave I'd tumbled into was scarce an hundred yards from their community.' Simon gazed off into the distance. 'My soul did seek their solace, and did lead my steps unto them.'

'Possible,' Rod agreed. 'But I thought there was only one monastery in this land – the Abbey of St Vidicon, down south.'

'Nay; there's another, here in Romanov, though 'tis not over-large.'

Rod nodded, musing. He knew that the main monastery was a conclave of espers, who knew about the outside universe and modern technology, and who were continually experimenting with their psi powers, trying to find new ways to use them. Could this northern monastery be the same type of thing? Maybe not, if they hadn't noticed Simon's troubled spirit so close by.

On the other hand, maybe they had . . . 'So just being near the monks, healed your soul!'

Simon nodded. 'Indeed, their peace pervaded me. I made a broom, and swept the cave; I made a bed of branch and bracken. As the days passed, I made a cosy house there, and let the friars' peace still my rage, and fill my soul.' He smiled, gazing off into the past. 'Their serenity abides within me still, so deeply did it reach.' He turned to Rod. 'After some weeks, I did begin to ponder at their peace and calmness. What was its source? How did they come by it? I hearkened more carefully to their thoughts. And of them all, I found most wondrous were those that dwelt on herbs and their effects. So I commenced to spend much time within the minds of the monks who laboured in the stillroom, distilling liquors and elixirs. I drank up every fact, each notion.

'As the leaves turned toward winter, I built a door to my cave; I tanned furs and made a coat, then sat down by my fire and hearkened all the more closely; for the monks were pent up for the winter. The snows lay deep; they could not venture forth. Then even friends could grate each upon the other's nerves. The brotherhood was ripe for rifting. Quarrels did erupt, and I hung upon their every shout, eager to see if they might still be holy. Yet I was amazed; for, even when their tempers flared, the monks remembered their devotions. They forgave each other, turned away!' Simon sighed, shaking his head. 'How wondrous did it seem!'

'Damn straight!' Rod croaked. 'How'd they do it?'

'By their devotion to their God,' Simon said, with a beatific smile, 'and by being ever mindful that He, and His Way, were more important than themselves, or their pride – or, aye, even their honour.'

'Their honour?' Rod stiffened, staring. 'Hey, now! You can't mean they thought that God wanted them to be humiliated!'

Simon shook his head. 'Nay, quite the contrary! They trusted their God to prevent such!'

Rod felt a certain foreboding creeping over him. He turned his head to the side, watching Simon out of the corners of his eyes. 'How was He supposed to do that?'

'By giving them to know, within themselves, which deeds

were right to do, and which were wrong. Then, even though a man forbore to do some deed that other men did expect of him, he might yet know himself to be worthy, even though his fellows did jeer. Thus might he turn aside in pride, without a trace of shame – for look thou, when all's said and done, humiliation is within thee, not something visited upon thee by thy fellows.'

Rod frowned. 'Are you trying to tell me a man can save face even though everybody else is pointing the finger of scorn at him?'

Simon shook his head. 'There was never need to. For if any man stepped aside from a quarrel, and another ridiculed him for it, the first had but to say, "My God doth not wish it," and the other would comprehend, and only respect him for his forbearance. Indeed, 'twas not even needful for the first man to say aught aloud; 'twas only needful that he say unto himself, in his heart, "My God hath commanded me to love my neighbour," and he would not think less of himself for retreating.' He looked directly into Rod's eyes. 'For this "honour" that thou dost hold dear, this "face" thou speakest of, is most truly but thine own opinion of thyself. We commonly suppose that 'tis what others think of us, but 'tis not so. 'Tis simply that most of us have so little regard for ourselves that we believe others' opinions of us to be more important than our own. Therefore have we the need to save our countenances – our "faces", which terms means only what others see of us. Yet we know that only by what they *say* they think of us – so our "faces", when all is truly said, are others' opinions of us. We feel we must demand others' respect, or we cannot respect ourselves.' He shook his head, smiling. 'But 'tis false, dost thou see.'

'Surprisingly, I think I do.' Rod frowned. 'If any man really has a high opinion of himself, he won't care what others think of him – as long as *he* knows he's good.'

In the cart, Flaran shifted impatiently. He had been following the conversation from a distance and seemed displeased by its direction.

Simon nodded, eyes glowing. ''Tis true, 'tis true! Yet few are capable of that. Few are so sure of themselves, that their own opinion can matter more to them than all the rest of their fellows' regard – and those few who are, be also frequently insufferable in their arrogance.'

'Which means,' Rod pointed out, 'that they really don't have much faith in themselves – or they wouldn't have to make such a show of their supposed superiority.'

' 'Tis true, by all accounts. Nay, most of us, to have any sure sense of worth, must needs rely on some authority that's above us all, that doth assure us we are right. It will suffice, whether it be law, philosophy – or God. Then, should tempers flare, and thou dost draw back thine hand to smite me, and I, in wrath, set mine hand upon my dagger – one of us must needs retreat, or there will be mayhem sure.'

'Yes,' Rod agreed, 'but what happens if neither of us is willing to? We'd lose face, we'd lose honour.'

Simon nodded. 'But if I can say, "I will not strike because my Lord hath commanded me to love mine enemy" – why, then can I sheathe my dagger, step back, withdraw, and think myself no less a man for the doing of it.' His smile gained warmth. 'Thus may my God be "the salvation of my countenance".'

Rod nodded slowly. 'I can see how that would work – but you'd have to be a real believer.'

'Indeed,' Simon sighed, and shook his head. ' 'Tis the work of a saint, friend Owen – and I am certainly none such.'

Well, Rod had his own opinion about that.

'Yet there was sufficient of the monks' peace that did invest me so that, when the seasons turned to spring, and a villager came to beseech me for a cure for his cow, which was a-calving but had taken ill – why, in my lone-ness, I delighted in his company, even for so short a while. I did distil the herbs that he did need, and sent him on his way. Some weeks later, another came – then another, and another. I welcomed their company, and strove to gain their liking – yet I minded me what I had learned of the good brothers – that the folk themselves were of greater import than their actions, or careless words. Thus did I learn to contain mine anger, and never reveal in wrath aught that I might have learned from their thoughts. Eh, but there were times it was not easy; for though their lips spoke courteously, their minds could hold insults grievous about the weird wood-hermit whose aid they sought.' He smiled, amused at the memory of himself, the staunch innkeeper, as a wild-eyed anchorite. 'Yet I was mindful that they were my fellow men, and of infinite worth thereby. Sorely tried I was, from time to time, to utter words that would have blasted pride – the hidden truths about themselves that would have made them shrink within. Yet I forbore, and was ever mindful that they were for cherishing. I served them all, from the poor peasant to the village priest, who first felt me to be a challenge yet finally came to respect me.'

Rod smiled, amused. 'Yes. I suppose if you can deal with those who wear their authority like mantles, you can deal with anything.'

'Aye.' Simon frowned, learning forward. 'And even as I have done, so mayest thou do also.'

Rod stared at him a minute, then turned away. He started back toward the roadway, to avoid having to meet Simon's gaze. 'What – withhold my anger, even against such a sink of corruption as Alfar?' He shook his head. 'I can't understand how you can do that, with someone who's caused so much misery to so many people!'

At the mention of Alfar's name, Flaran climbed out of the cart, and came to join them where they stood.

'Loose anger at the deeds,' Simon murmured, 'but withhold it from the man.'

Rod ground his teeth. 'I hear your words, but I can't comprehend their meaning. How can you separate the man from his actions?'

'By being mindful that any human creature is a precious thing, and can turn aside from his own evil, if he can but recognize it.'

'Can, sure.' Rod's shoulders shook with a heave of inner laughter. 'But, will? What are the odds on that, Master Simon?'

'Any person may be misled.'

Rod shook his head. 'You're assuming that Alfar's basically good – just an ordinary man, who's given in to the temptation for revenge, discovered he can actually gain power, and been corrupted by it.'

'Certes.' Simon peered up at him, frowning. 'Is it not ever thus, with those who wreak wrong?'

'Maybe – but you're forgetting the possibility of evil. Actual, spiritual evil.' Rod looked up, and noted Flaran's presence. He weighed what he was about to say, and decided that he didn't mind Flaran's hearing it. 'Sure, all human souls have the potential for goodness – but in some, that potential is already buried before they're two years old. And it's buried so deeply that it's almost impossible to uncover it. They grow up believing that nobody's really capable of giving. They themselves can't love, or give love

– and they assume everybody who talks about it is just putting on an act.' He took a deep breath, and went on. 'Though it's not really necessary to talk about that. All you really need is the word "corruption". Alfar succumbed to the temptation to do something he knows is wrong, because he loved the idea of being powerful. And now that he's tasted power, he'll do anything rather than give it up. No matter who he has to hurt, how many he has to kill, how much suffering he causes. Anything's better than going back to being what he really is – just an ordinary, humdrum human being, who probably isn't even very well-liked.'

Flaran's eyes were huge; he stood frozen.

'Yet be mindful, he's human,' Simon coaxed. 'Hath that no meaning for thee, friend Owen?'

Rod shook his head. 'Don't let the fact that he's human, make you believe that he thinks *you* are. He can't – he's treating people as though they were bolts for a crossbow – something to use, then forget about. He tramples through other minds without the slightest thought. Doesn't he realize these are real, feeling people, too?' He shook his head. 'He can't, or he wouldn't be doing it. He's got to be totally without a conscience, totally calloused – really, actually, evil.'

'Yet he is a person withal,' Flaran piped up, timidly. 'Even Alfar is not a devil, Master Owen.'

'Not in body, maybe,' Rod grunted. 'I can believe he doesn't have horns, or a barbed tail. His soul, though . . . '

'Yet he doth have a soul,' Flaran pleaded. 'Look you, he may be an evil man – but he's a man none the less.'

Rod drew a deep, shaky breath, then let it out slowly. 'Friend Flaran . . . I beg you, leave off! I've seen Alfar's works, and those of his minions. Let us not speak of his humanity.'

Flaran was silent, but he stared at Rod, huge-eyed.

Rod steeled himself against the look and picked up the reins. He slapped them on Fess's back, and the robot-horse started forward.

When the silence had grown very uncomfortable, Rod asked, 'That fat little loudmouth who was leading that mob – how did he figure out that Flaran was a warlock?'

'Why . . . he heard my neighbours speak of it. I would guess . . . '

'Doesn't seem likely,' Rod said, frowning. 'He was a stranger, after all. How would he find out about the local skeletons, so quickly?'

'I think,' Simon said, 'that Alfar doth have adherents, minor witches and warlocks who can do little but read minds, salted here and there about the duchy – and their prime duty is to espy those of Power.'

'Oh?' Rod held himself still, kept his tone casual. 'How'd you hear about that?'

'I did not; but now and again, I've felt the touch of a mind that quested, but did not seek anything, or anyone, of which it was certain. And, anon, I've caught snatches of thought clearly between warlocks, warning that such-and-such had some trace of Power.'

'How did they not espy thee?' Flaran asked, surprised.

Simon smiled. 'I am, as we've said, rather weak at warlockery. And, too, I've learned to hide what poor weak powers I have, thinking like one who hath none at all, keeping the surface of my thoughts ever calm, and quite ordinary. 'Tis the key to not letting slip the odd comment that doth reveal thee – to think like an ordinary man; then you'll speak and act like one.'

Flaran nodded, gaze locked onto Simon's face. 'I will hearken to that. I will heed thee.'

'Do so; 'twill save thee much grief. Nay, begin to think like John Common even now, for we never know when Alfar's spies may be listening.'

Flaran started, darting a quick glance over each shoulder, then huddled in on himself.

'And, friend Owen, there's naught to fear for thee,' Simon reassured Rod, 'no spy would even know thou'rt there!'

Flaran looked up, astounded. 'Why! How is that!'

'Oh, I'm, er, er – invisible. To a mind reader.' Rod said it as nonchalantly as he could, and tried to throttle down a burst of anger. How dare Simon let slip information about him! *Serves you right*, he told himself, in an attempt at soothing. And it was true; he should've known better than to confide in a stranger. But Simon was so damn likeable . . .

'Ah, if only I could so hide me!' Flaran cried. 'Nay, then, tell! How dost thou do it?'

'Nice question,' Rod grated. 'I really couldn't tell you. But I think it has something to do with my basic dislike of all human beings.'

Flaran stared at him, shocked.

'When you really get down to it,' Rod admitted, 'I guess I just don't really like people very well.'

That rather put a damper on the conversation for a while. They rode on northward, each immersed in his own thoughts.

For his part, Rod couldn't help feeling that both of his companions were trying to become immersed in *his* thoughts, too. Not that they didn't both seem to be good people – but Rod was beginning to be very suspicious. The talk about mental spies had made him nervous, and he found himself remembering that Simon and Flaran *were* both strangers, after all.

A wave of loneliness hit him, and he glanced up at the skies. In spite of the longing, he was relieved to see the air clear, with a singular dearth of winged wildlife. At least his family was safe from getting mixed up in the mess.

Odd, though. He wasn't used to having Gwen listen to him.

# Chapter Twelve

He did notice the squirrel peering at him from the branches, and the doves stopping their preening to watch him from the roof of the inn, as they pulled the cart into an innyard. Rod climbed down and stood, surprised how much his joints ached from the four-hour ride. He tied the reins to a hitching post, and turned back to see Flaran climbing down from the cart also, and Simon stretching his legs carefully.

'Don't worry,' Rod assured him, 'they still work.'

Simon looked up, and smiled. 'The question is, do I wish they wouldn't?'

'Just at a guess, I'd say you're still having fun.' Rod turned into the inn. 'Shall we see what the kitchens hold?'

The question was as much good business as hunger; Rod was able to trade a bushel of produce for three lunches. Flaran insisted on paying Rod the penny he'd been planning to spend on beer, and Simon matched him. Rod protested, but wound up accepting.

Dinner came with a liberal supply of gossip. 'Ye come off the road?' the landlord asked, as he set their plates in front of them. 'Then say – it's true, what they say of Alfar?'

'Er – depends on what you've heard,' Rod said, feeling wary. 'Myself, I've heard a lot about the man.'

'Why, that he has dropped from sight!' A peasant leaned over from another table. 'That none have seen him since he took Castle Romanov.'

'Oh, really?' Rod perked up noticeably. 'Now, that's one I hadn't heard!'

''Tis most strange, if 'tis true,' the peasant said. 'Here's a man who hath appeared from nowhere, conquered most of the duchy – and vanished!'

'Ah, but there's reason, Doln,' an older peasant grinned. 'Some say he was stole away by a demon!'

'Eh, Harl – there's some as says he *is* a demon,' chirped a grandfather.

'Well, that would certainly explain why he appeared out of nowhere,' Rod said, judiciously.

The third peasant caught the note of scepticism, and looked up with a frown. 'Dost'a not believe in demons?'

'Dunno,' Rod said, 'I've never seen one.'

'Such talk of demons is nonsense, Kench,' Doln scoffed. 'Why should demons take him away, when he's doing good demons' work?'

'Some say he's roaming the land, clad as a peasant,' Harl grunted.

'Wherefore should he not?' Kench grinned. 'He is a peasant, is he not?'

'Aye, but he's also a warlock,' Harl reminded, 'and they say he seeks through the land for folk who would aid him well in his governing.'

Doln looked up, with a gleam in his eye. 'That, I could credit more easily.'

'Thou wilt credit aught,' Kench scoffed.

'Belike he doth prowl unseen,' Harl mused. 'Would he not seek out traitors?'

Flaran and Simon stiffened, and Rod could feel little cold prickles running up his spine.

The peasants didn't like the idea, either. They glanced quickly over their shoulders, twisting their fingers into charms against evil. 'How fell it is,' Harl gasped, 'to think that one could spy on thee, and thou wouldst never know it!'

Rod thought of mentioning that spies usually tried very hard to make sure nobody noticed them, but decided not to.

'Take heed of those rumours, and thou dost wish it,' the

landlord chuckled. 'For myself, I note only that the land is well-run.'

The others turned to look at him, lifting their heads slowly.

'That's so,' Doln nodded. 'Dost'a say, then, that Alfar's still in his castle?'

'Belike,' the landlord shrugged. ''Tis that, or his captains govern well in their own rights.'

'That, I doubt.' Rod shook his head. 'I never yet heard of a committee doing any really effective governing. There has to be one man who always has the final say.'

'Well, then.' The landlord turned to Rod with a grin. 'I must needs think Alfar's in his castle.' And he turned away to the kitchen, chuckling and shaking his head. 'Rumour! Only fools listen to it!'

'In which case, most people are fools,' Rod said softly to Simon and Flaran. 'So, if there's a rumour going around that you don't want people to believe, the thing to do is to set up a counter-rumour.'

'Which thou dost think Alfar hath done?' Simon had his small smile on again.

'No doubt of it. Just look at the results – anybody who might have been thinking of a counter-coup while Alfar was gone would be thoroughly scared off. On the other hand, he *might* really be roaming the countryside in disguise.'

'Would that not make witch folk loyal to him?' Flaran grinned. 'For would he not be most likely to choose his own kind to aid him in his governing?'

With his usual unerring social grace, he had spoken a bit too loudly. Harl looked up, and called out, 'All witch folk would be loyal to Alfar. Wherefore ought they not to be?'

Flaran and Simon were instantly on their guard.

Rod tried to pull the sting out of it. He turned to Harl, deliberately casual. 'For that matter, wouldn't every peasant be loyal to him? The rumour's that he's looking for talented *people* for his, er, reign.'

'Why . . . 'tis so.' Harl frowned, suddenly doubtful.

Doln looked up, eyes alight. 'Aye! He could not find witches enough to do all the tasks that are needed in governing, could he?'

'No.' Rod repressed a smile. 'He certainly couldn't.'

Doln grinned, and turned to discuss the possibility with Harl and

Kench. Rod reflected, with some surprise, that even a Gramarye peasant could have ambition. Which, of course, was perfectly natural; he should have foreseen it. He'd have to discuss the issue with Tuan when he went back to Runnymede; if it wasn't planned for, it could become dangerous.

He turned back to Flaran. 'We can't be the only ones who've figured this out. Now, watch – the common people will of a sudden start being *really* loyal to Alfar – because they're going to think they have a chance to rise in the world.'

'Indeed they may.' Flaran grinned. 'Would not the low-born have opportunity under the rule of an upstart?'

Rod frowned; the comment was a little too Marxist for his liking. 'Yeah, if they happen to be the lucky ones out of thousands, the ones he wanted.'

'Yet I should think that he has these by him already,' said Simon. 'He hath chosen his people ere he began this madcap climb. I would not look for him to place any great trust in those new to his banner.'

Flaran frowned; he had definitely not wanted to hear that.

'But the hope of it could make a lot of people like him,' Rod pointed out. 'Just the idea that a lowborn peasant's son has come to rule a duchy, will pull an amazing amount of support to him.'

'Can rumour truly do so much?' Flaran breathed.

'That, and more,' Rod said grimly. 'Which is the best reason of all for thinking Alfar's still in his castle.'

Flaran stared. Then he closed his eyes, shook his head, and opened them again.

'I, too, am puzzled.' Simon frowned. 'How can a rumour mean . . . ' His voice trailed off as his face cleared with understanding.

Rod nodded. 'All he has to do is stay inside the castle and make sure the rumour gets started. Once it's running, it's going to keep building peasant loyalty on the one hand, and make everybody a little more wary about thinking disloyal thoughts, or doing any plotting, on the other – for fear Alfar himself might be listening in.'

Flaran shuddered, and glanced quickly about the room – and, suddenly, Rod had a sinking feeling in his stomach. Alfar could indeed be in that very tap-room, could be one of the peasants, could be the landlord, lying in wait for one of Tuan's agents to

come by – such as Rod himself. He could be about to spring the
trap on Rod, any second . . .

Then chagrin hit, and hard on its heels, anger. This was just
what Alfar wanted Tuan's agents to be thinking. It was called
'demoralization', and it had almost worked. Rod's respect for the
sorcerer went up, as his animosity increased. He was amazed that
a medieval peasant could be so devious.

On the other hand, maybe he had some help . . .

Simon leaned over to Rod and murmured, 'Do not look, or
disguise it if thou must – but yon wench hath kept her eye on
us since we came through the door.'

'That is a little odd,' Rod admitted. 'None of us is exactly
what you'd call a model of masculine pulchritude.'

'True enough,' Simon answered, with a sardonic smile. 'Yet
'tis not with her eyes alone that she's kept watch over us.'

'Oh, really?' All of a sudden Rod's danger sensors were tuned
to maximum – not that they'd done much good so far. He pulled
out a coin, flipped it – and made sure it 'accidentally' flipped her
way. As he turned to pick it up, he managed a quick glance at her,
and decided it wasn't much of a surprise that he hadn't noticed her
sooner. She was average size, no heavier than she ought to be, with
a pretty enough face and dark blonde hair.

Rod picked up the coin and turned back to Simon. 'Not
exactly your stereotyped witch, is she?'

Simon frowned. 'A very ordinary witch, I would say.'

'That's a contradiction in terms. She's also not very experienced
at hiding her interest.'

'Oh, she doth well enough,' Simon demurred. 'Yet I've more
experience at this sort of hiding than most, Master Owen – and,
when one of us doth say that which doth amaze her, her shield
doth slip.'

Rod frowned. 'Then why didn't she head for the door as
soon as we started talking about her?'

'Because thy mind is hid, let alone thy thoughts – and for
myself, I'm thinking one thought and saying another.' He grinned
at Rod's surprise. 'Be not amazed – what women can do, we men
may learn to do. As for Flaran, I speak so softly that he cannot
hear.'

Rod glanced quickly at the klutz; he was looking rather nettled. Rod turned back to Simon. 'Then there's no real danger, is
there?'

'Oh, there is alarm in her.' Simon glanced at the serving-wench, then back at Rod. 'We had best be on our way, Master Owen, and quickly, ere she calls another who doth serve Alfar.'

Rod turned towards the girl, considering risks and coming to a quick decision. 'No, I don't think that's really necessary.' He beckoned to the wench. Fear leaped in her eyes, but she had no reason for it, and did need to keep her cover while she studied them – so she came. Slowly, as though she were being dragged, but she came. 'What may I offer, goodmen? Ale? Or more meat?'

'Neither, just now.' Rod plastered on a friendly smile. 'Tell me – does it bother you that I'm not here, when I really am?'

She stared at him in shocked surprise, and Simon muttered, 'Well done; she is quite disarmed. Certes, Alfar's her master. She holds watch for witches.'

Rod's dagger was out before Simon finished the first sentence, its point touching the wench's midriff. She stared at the naked steel, horrified.

'Sit.' Rod kept the smile, but it had turned vicious.

'Sir,' she gasped, gaze locked on the blade. 'I dare not.'

'Dare not disobey me? No, you don't. Now sit.'

Trembling, she lowered herself to the empty stool. Rod took her hand, gave her a glowing smile. 'Simon, dig around and see what you can find.' He let the smile turn fatuous, clasped both hands around hers, and leaned forward, crooning, 'Now, pretty lass, sit still and try to pay no heed to the fingers you'll feel in your mind – and if their touch disgusts you, be mindful that you would have spoken words with your mind, that would have sent soldiers to slay us.' He lifted her hand to his lips, kissed it, then beamed at her again. 'I know – you feel like nothing so much as leaping up and screaming. But if you do, my knife is close at hand – and do not think that you can snatch it with your mind faster than I can stab – for, in this case, the hand is quicker than the mind.' He saw her glance at the knife, and warned. 'I assure you, I've dealt with witches before.' Which, he reckoned, was his understatement of the year.

Her gaze darted back to his face, terrified. 'But . . . why dost thou kiss mine hand, when thou'rt mine enemy?'

'So that anyone watching . . . there, young Doln is staring at me – no, don't look! – and his gaze is anything but friendly. In fact, I think he favours my heart for the main course. No, don't hope – I assure you, I'm a better fighter than he, far better.' He saw the flicker of fear in her eyes, and decided to press it. 'Sit very still, now. You wouldn't want me to hurt him, would you?'

'Oh, do not!' she cried. Then, realizing she'd given away more than military secrets, she blushed and dropped her eyes.

'Aye, well done,' Simon purred. 'Gaze at the tabletop, there's a good lass, and naught else; think of naught but its grain, and its colour . . . Now!'

The girl stiffened with a gasp, head flung back, eyes shut; then she slumped in her chair.

'Stand away from her!' Doln was on his feet, knife out.

Rod stood slowly, his grin turning wolfish, knifepoint circling. 'Why, it shall be as you say – I shall stand away from her. Shall I stand toward you, then?'

Harl scowled and stood up behind Doln, but the youth's eyes showed doubt. He stood his ground, though – swallowing hard, but he stood.

'Gently, now, gently.' Simon soothed. 'She sleeps, lad – she but sleeps.'

Doln glanced at him, then at the unconscious girl, and the white showed all around his eyes.

'Softly, lad.' Rod followed Simon's lead. 'We're not hurting her.' He darted a quick glance at Simon. 'Nay, unless I mistake, my friend seeks to aid her.'

'What manner of aid is this, that steals away her sense?' Doln cried.

'What manner indeed!' Flaran huddled back in his chair, eyes wide with terror.

Kench's glare would have killed a viper, and Harl gathered himself and stepped up behind Doln. The girl sighed, and her head rolled back.

'Ask her,' Rod said softly. 'She'll be awake in a minute.'

Doln's gaze darted to her. Her eyelids fluttered, then opened. She looked around her, uncomprehending, then suddenly realized where she was, and her eyes widened; she gasped.

'Marianne!' Doln dropped to one knee, clasping her hand. 'What have these fellows done to thee!'

Her gaze darted down to him; she shrank away. Then she recognized him, and relaxed a little. She looked around, and her gaze centred on Rod. Slowly, it turned to Simon, then back at Doln, and her lips quivered with a smile. 'Nay, be not afeared for me, good Doln. I am well – aye, more well than I have been for some weeks.' She turned back to Simon, frowning, then back to Doln. 'These good men have aided me.'

Doln looked from one to another wildly. 'What manner of aid is this, that makes thee to swoon?'

'That, thou dost not need know,' Simon advised. 'Stand away, now, I beg thee, for we must have further converse with thy Marianne.'

'I am not his,' she said, with a touch of asperity, then instantly balanced it with a dazzling smile at Doln. 'I did not know thou hadst concern for me.'

Doln swallowed heavily, and stood, but his eyes were still on her. 'I . . . I do care for thy welfare, Marianne.'

'I know it, now – and I thank thee.' Her colour had come back completely now. She clasped his hand, and looked up at him through long lashes. 'Most deeply do I thank thee. Yet I prithee, do as this goodman doth bid thee, and stand away, good Doln, for truly must I speak with them.'

Reluctantly, Doln backed away from the table – and bumped into Harl, who muttered a curse, and turned away to his stool. Doln did, too, gaze flicking from Simon to Marianne, then to Rod, then back to Marianne again. Then Kench muttered something, and Doln turned to him, frowning, then fell to muttering with Harl and the gaffer, casting frequent glares at Rod and Simon.

He didn't notice Flaran. But then, who ever did?

Marianne turned back to Simon with a happy smile, patting her hair into place. 'I must needs thank thee for more things than one. Nay, ask what thou wilt. I will most gladly answer.'

Rod rubbed a hand over his face to cover a smile, then turned to Simon. 'Mind telling me what went on there?'

'Only what thou hast seen aforetime,' Simon answered. 'She laboured under a spell. I have broken it.'

'A *spell*?' Rod stared at Marianne, appalled. 'A *witch*?'

'Even so.' The girl bowed her head in shame. 'I see now that I must have been.'

Simon reached out and caught her hand. 'There's no shame in it, lass. 'Tis no fault of thine, that thou wert enchanted.'

'But it is!' She looked up at him, wide-eyed. 'For I hid my witch power from the goodfolk, full of guilt and embarrassment – till I began to believe that I was better than they, for I could read minds and make things more by mere thought, whilst they could not. Nay, it did come to seem to me that we witch folk were the true nobility, the new nobility, who could and should rule the world – aye, and better than the lords do!'

'This, thou dost count fault of thine own?' Simon asked, with a smile.

'Is't not?' She blushed, and looked down. 'Alas, that ever I thought so! Yet I did – and no other witch did seem to feel as I did, no honest one; for I listened for their thoughts, and heard them afar. Nay, none thought to lead the witches to their rightful place – not even within the Royal Coven. Thus, when Alfar began to reach out for vassals, declaring he would lead the witch folk on to glory and to rule, I declared him my leader on the instant, and pledged him my fealty. All that he asked, I swore I would do.'

'And the service that he asked of thee?'

'Only this.' She gestured around at the inn in disgust. 'Here is my glory and rule! To work as I had done, and watch, then speak to them of any witch folk I found who, in either deed or thought, did struggle 'gainst Alfar. So I did – and most joyously.' She plunged her face into her hands. 'Eh, what a bitch I have been, what a vile, dastardly traitor! For three witches I have delivered unto them – poor, weak souls, who only sought to flee to safety!' She lifted her tragic eyes to gaze at Simon. 'Yet truthfully did it seem to me that any witch who did not acclaim Alfar, must needs be a traitor to her own kind. Therefore did I summon aid from Alfar's coven, and soldiers came, under the command of a warlock, to take those witches away, and . . . ' She buried her face in her hands again. 'Aiee! What did they do to those poor folk!'

Her shoulders shook with weeping. Simon reached out to touch her, clasping her shoulder. 'Nay, be not so grieved! For thou didst these things not of thine own free will and choice!'

Her gaze leaped up to his, tears still coursing down her cheeks. 'Yet how could it be otherwise?'

'When first thou didst begin to think thyself greater than thy neighbours, the sorcerer's folk had already begun their vile work on thee.' Simon's smile hardened. 'These first thoughts, that witches ought to govern by right of birth, were not truly thine. But they were oh, most gently and skilfully worked in, among thoughts of thine own, that thou mightst think them so.'

'Truly?' she gasped, wide-eyed.

Simon nodded. 'Be sure. I have myself slipped through thy thoughts, witch – I must ask thy pardon – and I know.'

'Oh, the pardon is instantly given!' she cried. 'How can I

thank thee, for breaking this spell?' Then her face lit up, and she clapped her hands. 'I know! I shall wander northward, and myself seek to break spells that bind goodfolk!'

Rod darted a quick glance at Simon, and saw the foreboding in his face. He turned back to Marianne. 'Er – I don't think that would be the best idea.'

Her face fell. 'Would it not? What, then . . . '

'Well, basically the same thing – just do it right here.' Rod managed to smile. 'What Alfar was having to do, but for our side. Keep working as a serving-wench, and spy out witch folk who're going south. But when you find them, *don't* report them to Alfar's henchmen.'

'But that is so small an aid!' she cried, disappointed.

'Those whom thou dost save will not think it so,' Simon assured her.

'But they would be just as much saved if I were not here at all.'

'Not so.' Rod shook his head. 'If you left this post, Alfar's men would find it out quickly enough, and they'd send some other witch here to do the job. The only way you can protect the fugitives is to stay here and cover for them.'

'Assuredly there must be work of greater import I can do!'

An imp pricked Rod with temptation. He grinned, and succumbed. 'There is, now that you mention it. You can find another witch or two, who plan to stay.'

'Others?' She stared, amazed. 'How will that aid?'

'Because each of them can find two other witches,' Rod explained, 'and each of those, two more, and so on and on – and we can build up a network of witches opposed to Alfar, all throughout the duchy of Romanov.'

She frowned, shaking her head. 'What aid will that be?'

'King Tuan will march north, sooner or later. When he does, we'll send word through the net, for the witches to gather where the battle's going to be, to help.'

'Help in a battle?' Her eyes were round. 'How?'

'We'll send word about that, too. Just be ready to do it.'

Slowly, she nodded. 'I do not fully comprehend – yet I do trust in thee. I shall do as thou dost bid.'

'Good lass! And don't worry, you'll understand plenty. It won't be very complicated – just to gather at a certain place, and attack whatever part of the sorcerer's army you're assigned.'

'An thou sayest it.' She still seemed doubtful. 'But how shall I know what to do, or when?'

'Someone will tell you. From now on, your name is, er, "Esmeralda", to anyone else in the anti-Alfar network. So, if someone comes in and says he has word for Esmeralda, from Kern' – again, Rod wished he hadn't chosen that name – 'you'll know it's a message from me.'

'But wherefore ought I not to be called Marianne?'

'So nobody can betray you. This way, if they tell Alfar or his men they've a traitor named "Esmeralda", they won't know who it really is.'

'And "Kern" is thy false name?'

*I sure hope so.* 'It's as good name as any. The whole idea is that we don't know each other's real names, remember. Will you do it – be Esmeralda, and watch for witches to *not* report?'

Slowly, she nodded. 'Aye – if thou dost truly believe this is the greatest aid I can offer.'

'Good lass!' Rod clasped her hand, relieved – she was too young, and really too sweet, to wind up in Alfar's torture chambers. Better to leave her where it was safe. 'Now, er – would you please go reassure your friend Doln, there? I can't help this feeling that he's just dying to shove a knife between my ribs.'

'Certes.' She flushed prettily, and stood. 'I thank thee, goodman.' She turned away, becoming shy and demure as she neared her swain.

'I think she hath forgot thee quite,' Simon said, with his small smile.

'Yes. And that's the way it should be, isn't it?' Rod was watching Doln, whose gaze was riveted to Marianne's face. He caught her hand, and Rod turned back to Simon and Flaran with a sigh. 'Young love! Isn't it wonderful?'

'In truth.' Simon watched the young couple over Rod's shoulder. 'Yet I cannot help but think, friend Owen, that there's some truth to her words – not that her thoughts of overweening greatness were her own, nay, but that, shall we say, Alfar's seeds fell on fertile ground?'

'Oh, well, sure! People can't be hypnotized if they *really* don't want to be – and this particular kind of long-range telepathic hypnosis couldn't have worked so well if she didn't already have a bit of that resentful attitude – it's called "feelings of inferiority".'

'Inferiority?' Flaran stared. 'Yet how can that be? Witch power makes us greater than other folk!'

Rod didn't miss the 'us'. 'Yeah, but they don't *feel* that way. All they know is that they stand out, that they're different, and that if people find out just *how* different, nobody'll like them.' He shrugged. 'If nobody likes you, you must be inferior. I know it doesn't really make sense, but that's how our minds work. And, since nobody can stand to think so little of themselves, pretty soon the warlock starts telling himself that he's not really inferior – it's just that everybody's picking on him, because they're jealous. And, of course, people do pick on witches – they've been doing it, here, for hundreds of years.'

'Aye!' Flaran seized the thought. ''Tis not merely a matter of our telling ourselves others bully us – 'tis true!'

'Oh, yeah, it's so easy to feel persecuted, when you really are. But that must mean you're *worse* than inferior.' He made a backwards arc with his forefinger. 'If people're picking on you, and they're nice people, ones you ordinarily like and, all of a sudden, they're picking on you – then you must be worse than second-rate; you must be evil! But who can stand thinking they're outright evil?'

'Evil folk,' Flaran answered quickly.

'And there you have it.' Rod spread his hands. 'Instead of saying, "I'm second-rate," they're saying, "I'm evil" – they'd rather be first-rate evil than second-rate good.'

Flaran stared, lost.

'Or!' Rod held up a forefinger. 'Or you decide that you're not evil, and you're not second-rate, either – they're just picking on you because they're jealous. So their picking on you proves that you're better than they are. They're just afraid of the competition. They're out to get you because you're a threat to them.'

Flaran's head lifted slowly, and Rod could see his eyes clearing with understanding.

Rod shrugged. 'All the witch folk probably have that attitude to some degree – it's called paranoia. But they keep it under control; they know that even if there're wisps of truth attached to the notion, there's more truth in thinking of their neighbours as being basically good folk – which they are. And if the witch has even a grain of humility, she's as much aware of her faults as she is of her powers – so they manage to keep their feelings of persecution under control. It's a sort of a balance between paranoia and reality. But it does make them ready, even eager, victims, for Alfar's style of brainwashing – er, persuasion.'

Flaran turned away, staring at the table. The colour had drained out of his face, and his hands trembled.

Rod watched him, shaking his head with a sad smile. *The poor kid*, he thought, *the poor innocent*. In some ways, Flaran probably would have preferred to just go along from day to day for the rest of his life, feeling inferior and picked-on. And it must've been very demeaning to find out that his feelings were, if not normal, at least standard for his condition – it was bad enough being born an esper, but it was worse finding out you weren't even exceptional.

He turned away to catch Simon's eye. The old man had a sympathetic look, and Rod smiled back, nodding. They both knew – it was rough, learning the facts of life.

Back on the road, Rod and Simon tried to strike up a cheerful family topic conversation again; but the mood had changed, and it was an uphill fight all the way. When they each realized that the other guy was trying just as hard, they gave it up.

Of course, the ambience wasn't helped much by Flaran riding along on Rod's other side sunk in gloom, glowering at the road. So they rode along in silence, the unease and tension growing, until Rod'd had about as much as he could take.

'Look, Flaran, I know it's hard to accept the idea that Alfar's turning the whole population into puppets – but that is what he's doing. So we have to just admit it, and try to go beyond it, to figure out what we can do about it. See? Feeling lousy won't do anybody any good.'

Flaran looked up at Rod, and his attention came back, as though from a great distance. Slowly, his eyes focused. 'Nay, nay, 'tis not that which hath me so bemused, friend Owen.'

Rod just looked at him for a moment.

Then he said, 'Oh.' And, 'Really?'

He straightened in his seat and tilted his head back, looking down at Flaran a little. 'What *is* bothering you?'

'These thoughts which the serving-wench hath uttered.'

'What – about witches being naturally superior?' Rod shook his head. 'That's nonsense.'

'Nay, 'tis good sense – or, if not good, at least sense.'

Flaran gazed past Rod's shoulder at the sky. 'Truly, witches should rule.'

'Oh, come off it! Next thing I know you'll be telling me how Alfar's really a good guy, and is really freeing the peasants, not conquering them!'

Flaran's eyes widened. 'Why – that is true.' He began to nod, faster and faster. 'In truth, 'tis all true. He doth free the peasants from the rule of the lords.'

Rod turned away, his mouth working, and swallowed heavily. He looked up at Simon. 'Check him, will you? Give him the once-over. He sounds as though the spell's beginning to creep over him.'

'Oh, nay!' Flaran said in scorn, but Simon frowned, gazing off into space for a moment. Then he shook his head. 'I do not read even so much as he doth utter, Master Owen – only thoughts of how goodly seem the fields about us, and the face of the wench who served us.' His eyes focused on Rod's again. 'Still, those are not the thoughts of a spellbound mind.'

'Spellbound? Nay, certes!' Flaran cried. 'Only because I speak truth, Master Owen?'

'Truth?' Rod snorted. 'Somebody must have warped your mind, if you think that's truth!'

'Nay, then – lay it out and look at it!' Flaran spread his hands. 'It doth seem the common people must needs have masters . . . '

'I could dispute that,' Rod growled.

'But not gainsay it! From all that I have seen, 'tis true!' Flaran craned his neck to look over Rod's shoulder at Simon. 'Wouldst thou not say so, Master Simon?'

'Someone must govern,' Simon admitted reluctantly.

'And if one must govern – why, then, one must be master!' Flaran slapped his knee. 'And is it not far better for the peasant folk to have masters who were born as they were, peasants? Who know the pain of poverty, and the grinding toil of the common folk? Is that not far better for them than the rule of those who are born to silver plates and ruby rings, in castles, who have never known a hard day's work, nor a moment's want? Nay, these lords even look down from their high towers, and speak of we poor folk as though we were chattels! Things to be owned! Cattle! Not men and women!'

Rod stared, horrified. 'Where'd you hear that line of rubbish?'

Flaran reddened. 'Can there be truth in rubbish?'

'I don't know who you've been talking to,' Rod said, 'but it sure wasn't a lord. Most of 'em don't say things like that – and where would you have had a chance to hear 'em talking, anyway?'

'Mine ears do be large, Master Owen. I may be foolish in my speaking, but I am wise in my listening. I have spoken with folk who serve the lords, and thus have I learned how they speak of us. And, too, I have hearkened to my neighbours, to their groans and cries of grief under the lord's rule – and I cannot help but think that they do not serve the best of masters.' Flaran shook his head. 'Nay, the words of that serving-wench do make most excellent sense – for who could better know the people's wants than those who can hear their thoughts? And who can better guard them in their labours, than one who knows what it is to labour so?'

'Excuses,' Rod growled. He turned away, and saw, in the distance, a party of peasants coming out of a side road, clad in rough homespun and bowed under the weight of huge packs. 'There!' He stabbed a finger at them. 'That's the kind of sense you've been making! Poor people, wandering the roads, lost and alone, because their homes have been destroyed in battle! Folk bereft, whose villages still stand, but who have packed what they can carry and have fled because they fear the rule of an upstart they don't trust!'

'Yet peasants' homes do ever burn in wars,' Flaran cried, 'ever and aye, when the lords do seek to resolve some private quarrel with their armies! This time, at the least, the war may bring them some benefit, for he who wins will have been born among them!'

'Excuses,' Rod said again, 'rationalizations!' He turned to look squarely at Flaran. 'Let me tell you what that is – a rationalization. It's giving something the appearance of rationality, or reason, when it doesn't have the reality of it. It's finding a way to justify what you want to do, anyway. It's finding an excuse for something you've already done – a way to make it seem to be good, when it really isn't. That's all you're doing here – trying to find a way to make the wrong things you want to do, seem right. All your arguments really boil down to "I want power, so I'm going to take it". And the real reasons are envy and revenge!'

He noticed, out of the corner of his eye, that the peasants had stopped, staring up at them, on both sides of the cart. All the better – let witnesses hear it!

'Yet how canst thou speak so?' Flaran frowned, cocking his head to the side. 'Thou hast thyself an enormous power!'

Rod froze. How had he let his cover slip? 'What . . . power . . . is . . . that?'

'Why, the talent of not being seen by the mind! Our friend

Simon hath said it – to a thought-hearer, thou dost not seem to be here at all!'

'Nay, then!' the younger man cried, 'even I have noticed it, weak though my powers are!'

Rod shrugged; that was explanation enough, for the moment.

'How great a talent that is!' Flaran cried. 'What great advantage must it needs give thee, if one doth seek thee with evil intent! If thou wert of Alfar's band, he would surely create thee Duke of Spies!' He smiled, leaning forward, eyes glittering. 'Would that not be most excellent, Master Owen? Wouldst thou not be delighted to be a duke?'

'I'd say it would be horrible,' Rod grated. 'Do you realize what that would mean? I'd be helping to enforce one of the harshest tyrannies humanity has ever known! Stop and think!' He held up a forefinger. 'Even under the tightest dictatorships Old Terra ever knew, people have still been able to have one thing that was theirs, alone to themselves – their minds. At least their thoughts were free. But Alfar's trying to change all that; he's trying to set up a tyranny so complete that nobody can even call his thoughts his own!'

'How small a thing that is!' Flaran waved away the objection. 'Thoughts are naught, Master Owen – they are gossamer, mere spiders' webs! What are free thoughts against a filled belly, and an ease of grinding toil? What is freedom of thought, against freedom from want? What worth hath the secrecy of the mind, when weighed against the knowledge that the King doth hold every least peasant to be his own equal? But think!' He gazed off into space, eyes glittering. 'Think how sweet this land could be, an witches ruled it! What an earthly paradise we could make here for ourselves, an folk of good heart could labour freely with their minds, to build it!'

Rod stared, astounded by the younger man's enthusiasm. Then he leaned back, letting his mouth twist to show his scepticism. 'All right – tell me.'

'Why! What could they not do, an witches could use their power openly? Never would there be drought or flood, for witches could move the storms about so as to water all the land! Never would murrain slay cattle or other stock, for witches could be open in their curing! Nor, for that matter, would folk need to die from illness, when witch-physicians could be by to aid them! Never would the peasants go hungry, to give their substance unto their lord, that he might deck himself with finery, or gamble through the night!

Never would the people grumble in their misery, unheard, for a warlock would hear their thoughts, and find a means of ending that which troubled them!'

'Yeah, unless those peasants were grumbling because the king-warlock was doing something they didn't like! Then he'd just shut them up, by hypnotism!'

'Oh, such would be so few!' Flaran gave him a look of disgust. 'Why trouble thyself for a mere handful of malcontents? Ever will some few be discontented with their lot!'

'Right – and Alfar's one of them! But it wouldn't be just a few malcontents, if the witch folk ruled – it'd be the vast majority, the normals, who'd be feeling like half-humans, because they didn't have any witch power! And they'd resent the governing ones who did – but they'd know the witches would wipe out anybody who dared utter it! So they'd keep quiet, but live in terror, and their whole lives would be one long torture! Just ordinary people, like these men around us!' He gestured at the peasants, who were pressing close all about them, eyes burning. 'Better move along, boys. I'm having trouble keeping my temper; and when warlocks fight, bystanders may get hit with stray magic.'

'Ah, art thou a warlock, then?' Flaran cried.

Rod ground his teeth in frustration, furious with himself for the slip he'd made; but he made a brave try at covering. 'According to you, I am. Didn't you just say my invisible mind was a great talent?'

'In truth I did – and if thou art a warlock, then art thou also a traitor!' Flaran leaped to his feet, face dark with anger, suddenly seeming bigger – almost a genuine threat.

Rod wasn't exactly feeling pacific himself. 'Watch your tongue! I'm a King's man, and loyal to the bone!'

'Then art thou a traitor to witchhood!' Flaran stormed. 'Naught but a tool for hire, and the King's pay is best! Nay, thus art thou but a tool of the lordlings, a toy in their games – but it is we who are their pawns and moved about the land for their mere amusement! And thou dost abet them! Thou, who, by blood, ought to join with Alfar and oppose them! Nay, thou'rt worse than a traitor – thou'rt a shameless slave!'

'Watch your tongue!' Rod sprang to his feet, and the cart rocked dangerously. But Flaran kept his footing easily and, for some reason, that ignited Rod's anger into a blow-torch. 'Beware who you're calling a slave! You've fallen so far under Alfar's spell that you've become nothing but his puppet!'

'Nay – his votary!' Flaran's eyes burned with sudden zeal. 'Fool thou art, not to see his greatness! For Alfar will triumph, and all witch folk who do oppose him will die in torments of fire! Alfar is the future, and all who obstruct him will be ground into dust! Kneel, fool!' he roared, leaping up onto the cart-seat, finger spearing down at Rod. 'Kneel to Alfar, and swear him thy loyalty, or a traitor's death shalt thou die!'

The thin tissue of Rod's self-control tore, and rage erupted. 'Who the hell do you think you are, to tell me what to swear! You idiot, you dog's-meat gull! He's ground your egg into powder, and there's nothing left of the real you! You don't exist anymore!'

'Nay – *I* exist, but *thou* shalt not!' Flaran yanked a quarterstaff from the peasant next to him and smashed a two-handed blow down at Rod.

Rod ducked inside the swing, coming up next to Flaran with his dagger in his hand, but a dozen hands seized him and yanked him back, the sky reeled above him, framed by peasant faces with burning eyes. He saw a club swinging down at him – and, where the peasants' smocks had come open at the necks, chain mail and a glimpse of green-and-brown livery.

Then pain exploded through Rod's forehead, and night came early.


# Chapter Thirteen

A blowtorch, set on 'low', was burning its way through Rod's brain. But it was a very poor blowtorch; it seemed to go over the same path again and again, in a regular, pulsing rhythm. He forced his eyes open, hoping to catch the bastard who was holding the torch.

Blackness.

Blackness everywhere, except for a trapezoid of flickering orange. He frowned, peering more closely at it, squinting against the raging in his head, and figured out that it was the reflection of a flame on a rock wall. There were stripes up and down – the shadows of bars, no doubt. There were a couple of other stripes, too, zigging and zagging – the trails of water droplets. Then Rod became aware of fragile orange webs, higher up, gossamer nitre, lit by the firelight.

He added it all up, and enlightenment bloomed – he was in a dungeon again. The firelight was a guard's torch, out in the hall, and the trapezoid was the shadow of the little barred grille in the door.

He heaved a sigh and lay back. This kept happening to him, time and again. There'd been the gaol in Pardope, the Dictator's 'guest chamber' in Caerleath, the dungeon under the House of Clovis, and the cell in the Duke's Castle in Tir Chlis, where Father Al had taught him how to use his ESP talents . . . and the list went on. He frowned, trying to remember back to the first one, but it was too much for his poor, scrambled brain.

He put the list away, and very slowly, very carefully, rolled up onto one elbow. The blowtorch shot out a fiery geyser that seemed to consume his whole head, right down his backbone, but only for a few moments; then it subsided, and fell into perspective as a mere headache. A real beaut, Rod had to admit – those soldiers hadn't exactly been deft, but they'd made up for it with enthusiasm. He pressed a hand to his throbbing forehead, remembering the chain mail under the peasant tunics. It was a very little trap he'd walked into – but he couldn't imagine a less appetizing bait than Flaran.

Not that it hadn't worked, though.

He lifted his head slowly, looking around him. Compared to the other dungeons he'd been in, this one was definitely second-rate. But at least he had a couple of roommates, manacled to the wall across him – though one of them had lost quite a bit of weight over the years; he was a pure skeleton. Well, not 'pure' – he did have some mould patches here and there. The other one had some patches, too, but they were purple, shading towards maroon. It was Simon, and his chin was sunk on his chest.

Rod squeezed his eyes shut, trying to block out the headache, trying to think. Why should Simon be here? He wasn't a spy. Rod considered the question thoroughly, till the brainstorm struck; he could ask. So he cleared his throat, and tried. 'Er . . . Simon . . . '

The other man looked up, surprised. Then his face relaxed into a sad smile. 'Ah, thou dost wake, then.'

'Yeah – kind of.' Rod set both palms against the floor and did a very slow push-up. The headache clamoured in indignation, and he fell back against the wall with a gasp – but victorious; he was sitting up. The headache punished him unmercifully, then decided to accept the situation and lapsed into the background. Rod drew in a long, shuddering breath. 'What . . . what happened? You shouldn't be here – just me. What'd Flaran have against you?'

'He knew me for what I was,' Simon sighed. 'When the soldiers had felled thee, young Flaran turned on me, raging. "Who was this 'Owen'? Thou, vile traitor, will speak! Wherefore did this false, unminded man march northward into our domain?"'

'"Our"?' Rod frowned.

Simon shrugged. 'By good chance, I did not know the answers he sought. I said as much, and he whirled toward the soldiers, pointing back at me, screaming, "Torture him! Hale him down now, and break his fingers, joint by joint!" "Nay," I cried, "I have naught to hide," and I abandoned all pretence of cloaking my mind, casting aside all shields and attempts at hiding.'

'What good could that do? As mind readers go, he was barely literate.'

'Oh, nay! He was a veritable scholar!' Simon's mouth tightened. 'Thou, my friend, wert not alone in thy deceptions. I felt naught, but I saw his face grow calm. Then his eyes lit with excitement – but they soon filled with disappointment, and he did turn away to the soldiers in disgust. "There's naught here – naught but an old man, with some talent for spell-breaking. He could have gone free but, more's the fool, he hath come back north to seek to undo our work." Then the auncient said, "he's a traitor, then," and the look that he gave me was venomed – yet there was that strange emptiness behind it.'

Rod nodded. 'Spellbound.'

'Indeed. Then the auncient said further, "Shall we flay him?" and cold nails seemed to skewer my belly. But Flaran gave me a measuring glance, and shook his head. "Nay. He may yet prove useful. Only bind him and bring him." Then he did fix his gaze upon me, and his eyes did seem to swell, glowing, to burn into my brain. "An thou dost seek to break spells on these soldiers," he swore, "I will slay thee."'

'So.' Rod lifted his eyebrows. 'Our young klutz wasn't quite the fool he seemed to be, was he?'

'Nay. In truth, he did command. He bade the soldiers march home, and all did turn to take up the journey. Some hundreds of yards further, we came to tethered horses. The soldiers untied them and mounted – and there were pack mules for myself and for thee, and a great chestnut charger with a saddle adorned with silver for Flaran.'

Rod watched Simon for a moment, then said, 'Not exactly an accident we ran into them, was it?'

Simon smiled, with irony. 'In truth, 'twas quite well-planned.'

'Even to the point of rigging up a peasant mob to be chasing Flaran at just the right time to run into us on the road.' Rod's mouth tightened. 'He knew that was a sure way to make us take him in. And he stayed with us just long enough to make sure we were what he thought we were, before he turned us over to his bully boys.'

'He did give us the opportunity to turn our coats to Alfar's livery,' Simon pointed out.

'Yes. Generous of him, wasn't it?' Rod scowled. 'But how did he catch onto us?'

Simon sighed, and shook his head. 'I can only think that some spy of his must have sighted us, and followed unbeknownst.'

'Yeah – that makes sense.' With a sudden stab of guilt, Rod realized that Alfar had probably had spies watching him from the moment he crossed the border. After all, he'd certainly had Rod in sight before then. Rod just hadn't counted on the sorcerer's being so thorough.

Nothing to do about it now. Rod shook himself – and instantly regretted it; the headache stabbed again. But he thrust it all behind him, and asked, 'How far did they ride?'

'All the rest of the day, and far into the night,' Simon answered.

'But it was only mid-morning.' Rod frowned. 'That must have been . . . let me see . . . ' He pressed a hand against his aching head, and the clank of the wrist-chain seemed to drive right through from ear to ear. But he absorbed the pain and let it disperse through his skull, trying to think. 'Sixteen hours. And I was out cold all that time?'

Simon nodded. 'Whenever thou didst show sign of wakening, Flaran bade his soldiers strike thee again.'

'No *wonder* my head's exploding! How many times did they hit me?'

'More than half a dozen.'

Rod shuddered. 'I'm just lucky I don't have a fracture. On the other hand . . . ' He frowned, and lifted a hand to probe his skull, then thought better of it. 'I guess I'll have to hope. Why didn't he want me awake?'

'He did not say; yet I would conjecture that he did not wish to chance discovery of the range of thy powers.'

Rod felt an icicle-stab. 'Powers? What're you talking about? I just happen to be invisible to any listening witches, that's all.'

'Mayhap; yet in this, I must needs admit that, in Flaran's

place, I would have done as he did. For whether thou dost shield thy mind by chance, or by intention, truly matters not – such shielding bespeaks great witch power. Nay, thou'rt a true warlock, Master Owen, whether thou dost know it or not – and a most puissant one, to be able to hide thy mind so thoroughly.' Simon leaned back against the wall. 'And there is ever, of course, the chance that thou dost know it indeed, and dost hide thy thoughts by deliberation. And if that were the case, and if I were thine enemy, I would not wish to gamble on the extent of thy powers. I, too, would not chance thy waking.'

Rod just gazed at Simon. Then he looked away, with a sigh. 'Well, I can't fault your logic – or his wisdom. But why did he bring you along?'

Simon shrugged. 'Who can say? Yet I doubt not he'll seek to force thee to answer certain questions, whether thou dost know them or not – and if thine own pain is not enough to make thee speak, mayhap he'll think that mine will.'

Rod shivered. 'That boy's a real charmer, isn't he?'

'In truth. He did turn to me, jabbing with a finger. "Do not seek to hide thy thoughts," he cried, "nor to disguise them, or I shall bid them slay thee out of hand." I assured him I would not, the more so since I saw no point in such disguising. For what could he learn from my mind, that's of any import?'

'And that he didn't learn from travelling with the two of us.' Rod was glad that the light was too dim for Simon to see his face burning. 'Or that he couldn't find out by, let us say, more "orthodox" means? For example, if he's keeping tab on your thoughts, he knows I'm awake now.'

'Aye. I doubt me not an we'll see him presently.'

'No doubt at all; I'm sure he's still in charge of our case . . . So he was giving the orders, huh? To the soldiers, I mean.'

'Aye. There was no doubt of that.'

Rod nodded. 'Then he's probably the one who arranged the ambush.'

Simon gazed at him for a moment, then nodded slowly. 'That would be likely.'

'So he's not exactly the simple half-telepath he claimed to be.'

Simon's lips curved with the ghost of his smile. 'Nay, Master Owen. He is certainly not that.'

'He didn't happen to let out any hints about his real self, did he?'

Simon shook his head. 'The surface of his thoughts stayed ever as it had been. For aught that I could hear from him, his name was ever Flaran; yet his thoughts were all extolling Alfar, and how greatly advantaged the land was, since he'd taken power.'

Rod frowned. 'Nothing about the job at hand?'

'Aye; he did think how greatly thy capture would please Alfar.'

'I should think it would.' Rod closed his eyes, leaning his head back against the wall, hoping the cold stone might cool the burning. 'No matter what else we might say about our boy Flaran, we've got to admit he was effective.'

A key grated in the lock. Rod looked up at a slab of dungeon warder with a face that might have been carved out of granite. He didn't say a word, just held the door open and stepped aside to admit a lord, gorgeously clad in brocade doublet and trunk-hose, burgundy tights and shoes, fine lace ruff, and cloth-of-gold mantle, with a golden coronet on his head. His chin was high in arrogance; he wore a look of stern command. Rod had to look twice before he recognized Flaran. 'Clothes do make the man,' he murmured.

Flaran smiled, his lips curving with contempt. 'Clothes, aye – and a knowledge of power.'

The last word echoed in Rod's head. He held his gaze on Flaran. 'So the rumour was true – Alfar was wandering around the country, disguised as a peasant.'

Flaran inclined his head in acknowledgement.

'Well, O Potentate Alfar.' Rod leaned back against the wall. 'I have to admit you did a great job of disguising yourself as a peasant. Could it be you had experience to draw on?'

Alfar's eyes sparked with anger, and Simon seemed to shrink in on himself in horror. The sorcerer snapped, 'Indeed, I was numbered 'mongst the downtrodden till a year agone.'

'But that's all behind you now, of course.'

His voice was a little too innocent. Alfar's gaze hardened. 'Be not mistaken. Think not that I'm a peasant still – for thou dost lie within my power now, and thou wilt find it absolute.'

Rod shrugged. 'So you're a powerful peasant. Or did you honestly think you could be something more?'

'Greatly more,' Alfar grated, 'as thou wilt discover.'

'Oh?' Rod tilted his head to the side. 'What, may I ask?'

'A duke – Duke Alfar of the Northern coast! And thou, slave, shalt address me as such!'

'Oh.' Rod kept his lips pursed from the word. 'I'm a slave now, am I?'

'Why?' Alfar's eyes kindled. 'What else wouldst thou call thyself?'

Rod watched him for a second, then smiled. 'I'm a peasant, too. Aren't I?'

'Assuredly,' Alfar said drily. 'Yet whatsoever thou art, thou art also a most excellent thought-hearer, an thou hast been able to probe 'neath my thoughts to discover who I truly am.'

'Oh, that didn't take mind reading. None at all. I mean, just look at it logically: who, in all the great North Country, would be the most likely one to go wandering around disguised as a *schlemazel* peasant, supporting Alfar's policies with great verve and enthusiasm, and would have authority to command his soldiers?'

'One of my lieutenants, mayhap,' Alfar said, through thinned lips.

Rod shook his head. 'You never said one word about having to refer a decision to someone higher up – at least, not from Simon's reports about what happened while I was out cold. But you did mention "our" domain, which meant that you were either one of the lieutenants, viewing himself as a partner – and from what I'd heard of Alfar, I didn't think he was the type to share power . . . '

'Thou didst think aright,' Flaran growled.

'See? And that left the "or" to the "either" – and the "or" was that the "our" you'd used was the royal "our". And that meant that Flaran was really Alfar.' Rod spread his hands. 'See? Just common sense.'

'Scarcely "common",' Alfar frowned. 'In truth, 'tis a most strange mode of thought.'

'People keep telling me that, here,' Rod sighed. He'd found that chains of reasoning were alien to the medieval mind. 'But that was the royal "our", wasn't it? And you are planning to try for the throne, aren't you?'

Alfar's answer was an acid smile. 'Thou hast come to the truth of it at last – though I greatly doubt thou didst find it in such a manner.'

'Don't worry, I did.' Rod smiled sourly. 'Even right now, with you right next to me, I can't read your mind. Not a whisper.'

'Be done with thy deception!' Alfar blazed. 'Only a warlock of great power could cloak his thoughts so completely that he seems not even to exist!'

Rod shrugged. 'Have it your way. But would that mighty warlock be able to read minds when his own was closed off?'

Alfar stared.

Then he lifted his head, slowly, nodding. 'Well, then.' And, 'Thou wilt, at least, not deny that thou art Tuan's spy.'

'*King* Tuan, to you! But I agree, that much is pretty obvious.'

'Most excellent! Thou canst now tell to Tuan every smallest detail of my dungeon – if ever thou dost set eyes upon him again.'

For all his bravado, a shiver of apprehension shook Rod. He ignored it. 'Tuan already knows all he needs.'

'Indeed?' Alfar's eyes glittered. 'And what is that?'

'That you've taken over the duchy by casting a spell over all the people – and that you'll attack him, if he doesn't obliterate you first.'

'Will he, now! Fascinating! And how much else doth he know?'

Rod shrugged. 'None of your concern – but do let it worry you.'

Alfar stood rigid, the colour draining from his face.

Then he whirled, knife whipping out to prick Simon's throat. 'Again I will demand of thee – what information hath Tuan?'

His gaze looked with Rod's. Simon paled, but his eyes held only calm and understanding, without the slightest trace of fear.

Rod sighed, and capitulated. 'He knows your whole career, from the first peasant you intimidated up to your battle with Duke Bourbon.'

'Ah,' Alfar breathed. 'But he knoweth not the outcome. Doth he?'

'No,' Rod admitted, 'but it was a pretty clear guess.'

''Twas the Duchess, was it not? She did escape my hunters. Indeed, my spies in Tudor's county, and in Runnymede, attacked her, but were repulsed by puissant magics.' His gaze hardened. 'Magics wielded by a woman and four children.'

Inwardly, Rod went limp with relief hearing his family's safety confirmed. But outwardly, he only permitted himself a small smile.

'Yet thou wouldst know of that, wouldst thou not?' Alfar breathed. 'Thou didst dispatch them on that errand, didst thou not?'

Rod looked at the drop of blood rising from the point of the dagger, considered his options, and decided honesty wouldn't hurt. 'It was my idea, yes.'

Alfar's breath hissed out in triumph. 'Then 'twas thy wife and bairns who did accompany the Duchess and her brats, whilst yet they did live!'

Alarm shrilled through Rod. Did the bastard mean his family was dead? And the anger heaved up, rising.

Oblivious, Alfar was still speaking. 'And thou art he who's called Rod Gallowglass, art thou not?'

'Yes. I am the High Warlock.' Rod's eyes narrowed, reddening. Simon stared, poleaxed.

Alfar's lips were parted, his eyes glittering. 'How didst thou do it? Tell me the manner of it! How didst thou cease to be, to the mind, the whiles thou wert apparent to the eye?'

'You should know,' Rod grated. 'Weren't you eavesdropping?'

'Every minute, I assure thee. I held thy traces the whiles thou didst buy a cart and didst drive out to the road. Then, of a sudden, there were no thoughts but a peasant's.'

'Quite a range you've got there.'

'More than thirty leagues. How didst thou cloak thy thoughts?'

'I didn't – not then.' Rod throttled the rage down to a slow burn, keeping his mind in control, floating on top of the emotion. 'I just started thinking like a peasant.'

Alfar stared. Then he frowned. 'Then thou dost counterfeit most excellently.'

'I had some acting lessons.' And they were coming in handy, helping him keep the rage under control. 'I didn't pull the real disappearing act until I was across the border.' Privately, he found it interesting that Alfar could have been so thoroughly deceived. Either he wasn't very good at reading thoughts in depth, or Rod was even better at believing himself to be somebody fictitious than he had thought.

'Ah, 'twas then? Tell me the manner of it.' But his knife hand was trembling.

None the less, Simon was staring at Rod, not Alfar, and with awe, not fear.

And he'd been friendly to Rod, and he was an innocent bystander . . .

Rod shrugged. 'I withdrew, that's all. Pulled back into my shell. Decided nobody was worth my trouble.'

Alfar stared at him. Then he frowned. 'Canst say no more than that?'

Rod shrugged. 'Details. Techniques. Remembering times in my past when I wanted to get away from people, and letting the feeling grow. None of it could teach you how to do it. The first time, it just happens.'

Alfar watched him, eyes narrowed.

Then he straightened, sliding the knife back into its sheath, and Simon almost collapsed with a sigh of relief.

Rod felt a little relief, too, but the anger countered it.

''Tis even as I've thought,' Alfar said, with grim satisfaction. 'From aught I've heard of thee, thy chivalry exceeds thy sense.'

'Would you care to explain that?' Rod's voice was velvet.

'Why, 'tis plainly seen! Would a sensible captain risk his own pain, or mayhap even life, on a perilous mission? Nay! He would send a spy, and let the underling be racked and torn! But thou, who dost pride thyself on thine honour— ' he made the word an obscenity, 'wouldst rather waste thine hours spying out the enemy thyself!'

Now Rod understood the man – and he didn't bother hiding his contempt. 'Just sit back in Runnymede and read through intelligence reports, huh?'

'That would be wise.' Alfar stood, arms akimbo, smirking down at him. 'Or dost thou truly believe thou couldst accomplish more in thine own person?'

Rod studied the sorcerer – cocky stance, chip on the shoulder, the whole arrogant air (and didn't overlook the menace, or the sadistic glitter at the back of the eye) and wondered why he didn't feel more fear. He did know, though, that he'd better not let Alfar know that.

So he stuck his chin out just that little bit farther, and made his tone defiant. 'I only know this: by the time I realized that it was really dangerous, it was too much a hazard to let anyone else go in my place.'

'How gallant.' Alfar's scorn was withering.

'It seems I was right.' Rod held his gaze on Alfar's eyes. 'If you could catch onto me, you could catch onto anybody I might send. How'd you see through my disguise?'

A slow smile spread over Alfar's face. He lifted his head, chest swelling, and stepped towards Rod, almost strutting. 'I did sense danger when my spies sent word that the High Warlock did journey northward. Yet sin' that thou didst come with thy wife and bairns, it might well have been naught but a pleasure jaunt. Naetheless, he did note that thou hadst but lately spoken with Tuan and Catharine.'

Rod shrugged. 'I do that all the time.' But his interest was piqued. 'So your man couldn't eavesdrop on my conversation with Their Majesties, huh?'

Alfar flushed, glowering.

'Well.' Rod leaned back against the wall. 'Nice to know my wife's noise-shield works so well.'

'Is that how thou dost manage it!' Alfar's eyes gleamed. 'In truth, their thoughts are well-nigh impossible to single out from all that buzzing hum of thoughts that doth surround them.' He nodded, with a calculating look. 'Thy wife hath talent.'

Rod quailed at the threat his tone implied – especially since Gwen hadn't held a shield around the royal couple. 'Just be glad I sent her back.'

'Mayhap I had ought to be. Mayhap 'tis fitting that what my lieutenants could not accomplish, mine actions could.'

'Lieutenants?' Rod stared in disbelief, then let a slow smile grow. 'You mean that lousy marksman was one of your *best*?'

Alfar's gaze darkened. ' 'Twas purposely done. I bade him discourage thee, not slay thee or thine.'

'Wise.' Rod nodded. 'If you had, I'd've broken off the spy mission right there, and shot back to Runnymede to tell Tuan to call out the army. But you did a great job of warning us you were there.'

'Aye – and did secure a gauge of the range and strength of thy powers, and thy wife's and bairns'. Wherefore did I send mine other lieutenants to afright thee a second, then a third time, that I might learn thy pattern of attack, and its weaknesses. Nay, if thy wife and bairns had come north farther, I would have known well how to deal with them.'

The chill had settled around Rod's backbone, and wasn't leaving. 'I did have some notion that it was getting a little too thick. So when the Duchess and her boys came along, I took advantage of the excuse to send my family back south to safety.'

Alfar nodded. 'And went on northward thyself. Then thou didst stop by a farmstead, where thou didst buy a horsecart and peasant garb – and my man lost trace of thee, the whiles thou didst don thy smock and buskins.'

*Very* interesting! Rod hadn't gone invisible until he'd crossed the border. 'Let me guess: that's when you decided you'd better get involved on the personal level.'

Alfar nodded. 'Even as thou hadst, I did don peasant garb, and took the southward road, afoot and unguarded.' He smiled, amused, as though to say, Why would Alfar need guards?

Rod resolved to take the first possible opportunity to demonstrate exactly why. Aloud, he said, 'Why didn't you ride to the border first? You could have intercepted me there.'

'Oh, I was certain I would discover thee as I went! Thou hadst, after all, no need to use aught but the High Road – and good reason not to, for thou wouldst then have been most strikingly noticed in byways where only villagers do journey. Yet long ere I encountered thee, I did come upon a troop of guardsmen, and something about them caught my notice. I did look deeply into their auncient's eyes and thoughts and, 'neath the surface, discovered that he was no longer spellbound! That, even though they wore my colours!' His smile was not pleasant. 'I found occasion to journey with them, begging their protection and, as we walked, wove my spell about each one in turn. When only the auncient remained disenchanted, I bade his troopers seize him, so they did. Then did I pose him questions, the whiles I hearkened to the answers that rose within his mind, unspoken.'

Rod decided he'd better find a new interrogation technique; this one was obviously so easy to invent that it boded fair to becoming common.

'From his mind,' Alfar went on, 'I gained the image of the man who'd broke his spell . . . ' He nodded toward Simon. 'And I saw, to my surprise, that he was accompanied by a most ill-favoured, surly peasant.'

Rod straightened in indignation. 'Hey, now!'

Alfar smiled, satisfied that his barb had drawn blood. 'But 'twas easily seen that the spell-breaker must needs be the High Warlock. Why, he had so great a look of dignity!'

Simon looked up, startled.

Alfar's eye glinted. 'And his serving man had so churlish a look!'

But Rod wasn't about to bite on the same bait twice. He shrugged. 'I won't argue. When it comes to churls, you should know what you're talking about.'

Alfar flushed, and dropped a hand to his dagger.

Rod leaned back lazily. 'What did you do with the soldiers?' He was tense, dreading the answer.

Alfar shrugged. 'What ought I to do? I enchanted the auncient too, and sent them on northward to rejoin mine army.'

Rod lifted his head, surprised. 'You didn't punish them? No racks, no thumbscrews? No crash diets?'

Alfar looked equally surprised. 'Dost thou punish an arrow that has fallen to earth, if thine enemy hath picked it up, and set

it to his bowstring? Nay; thou dost catch it when he doth loose it
at thee, and restore it to thy quiver. Oh, I sent them on northward.
I did not wish to chance their beholding thee again – or, more's to
the point, thy spell-breaker. But at the next guardpost, I showed
my badge of authority,' he fingered the medallion on his breast,
'and bade the soldiers disguise themselves as peasants, to wait
in ambush where a country way joined the High Road. Then I
summoned a lesser warlock to abide with them, in readiness to
transmit orders to march, when he should receive a thought-code
– Alfar's greatness, and why all witches ought to join with him.'
He smiled, vindictively.

Rod knew better than to withhold ego-oil when the one with
the inferiority complex held the knife. 'So that's why the sudden
diatribe, eh?'

'Certes.' Alfar's eyes danced. 'There's method in aught I do.
Then I did march southward, my thoughts ranging ahead of
myself, till I heard Simon's. I found a village warlock, then,
and bade him lead his people out to chase me . . . '

'The little fat guy. But of course, you made sure all their
rocks would miss, and they wouldn't catch you.'

'Why, certes.' Alfar grinned, enjoying the account of his own
cleverness. 'And as I had foreknown, thou couldst not forbear to
save a poor weakling, beset by human wolves.'

'Yes.' Rod's mouth twisted with the sour taste of his own
gullibility. 'We fell right into it, didn't we? Just picked you up,
and carried you right along.'

'Thou wast, in truth, most gracious,' Alfar said, with a saccha-
rine smile. ''Twas but a day's work to discover that 'twas Simon
broke the spells, yet that he could do little more – and that thou
must needs be the High Warlock.'

'My natural greatness just shone through those peasant rags, er?'

'Oh, indubitably. Yet 'twas more truthfully thy face.'

'Naturally noble, eh?'

'Nay, only familiar. Mine agents had borne me pictures in their
minds, more faithful than any painter could render. Oh, thou hast
disguised thyself somewhat, with peasant's smock and grime; yet
I know something of deception myself, and can look past surface
features to those that underlie them. Yet I knew thee even ere I'd
set eyes upon thy face; for thou wast there to mine eyes, but not to
my mind, and only a most puissant warlock could shield himself
so thoroughly.'

Rod shrugged. 'I seem to have had that knack before I started doing any of what you call magic . . . But go on.'

'Pay heed!' Alfar held up a forefinger. 'Even then, I offered thee thine opportunity to join with me and mine! And only when thou didst refuse, and that with such force that I knew thou couldst not be persuaded, did I seize thee.' His gaze intensified, locked on Rod's eyes. 'E'en now, an thou dost wish to join with me, I will rejoice, and welcome thee!'

'Providing, of course, that I can prove I mean it.'

'Of course. What use art thou, if I cannot rely on thee to the uttermost?' His eyes glittered, and his mouth quivered with suppressed glee. 'Indeed, I've even now the means to ensure thy loyalty.'

Dread shot through Rod and, hard after it, anger. He throttled it down and growled, 'What means?'

'Thou hast no need to know. Thou dost not, after all, wish to ally thy fortunes with mine.'

The rage surged up, and Rod let it rise. 'I'll grind your head under my heel if I can ever find a forked stick big enough to hold your neck down!'

Alfar went white, and sprang at Rod, his knife slipping out. Fear shot through Rod, like a spark to gunpowder and the anger exploded, shooting through his every vein and nerve, smashing out of him in reaction.

Alfar slammed back against the far wall and slid to the floor, dazed.

Rod's chains jangled as they broke apart and fell.

He thrust himself away from the wall, rising to his feet, borrowed rage-power filling every cell of his body. The headache throbbed through him, darkening all he saw except for an oval of light that contained Alfar, crumpled in a heap. Rod waded towards the fallen man, feeling anger envelop him, pervading him, as though Lord Kern's spirit reached across the void between the universes to take possession of him. His anger rose with the weight of all his man-slayings, pointing out to explode the sorcerer.

Then Alfar's eyes cleared; he saw Rod's face, and his eyes filled with terror. Rod reached out to touch him – but thunder rocked the cell, and the sorcerer was gone.

Rod stood staring at the empty space where the sorcerer had been, finger still pointing, forgotten. 'Teleported,' he choked out. 'Got away.'

He straightened slowly, thrusting outward with his mind,

exploding his mental shield, opening himself to all and every sense impression about him, concentrating on the human thoughts. Nowhere was there a trace of Alfar.

Rod nodded, perversely satisfied; Alfar hadn't just teleported out the cell – he'd whipped himself clean out of the castle, and so far away that he couldn't be 'heard'.

# Chapter Fourteen

Rod sagged back, sitting against the cell wall as the biggest reason for his anger abated. His emotions began to subside, but still within him there was an impulse towards violence, a lust for battle that kept the anger and built it, filling his whole body with quaking rage.

That scared Rod. He tried to force the mindless rage down; and as he did, Simon's voice bored through to him: 'Owen! Owen! Lord Gallowglass! Nay, I'll call thee as I knew thee!' A hand clasped his wrist; fingers dug in. 'Master Owen! Or Rod Gallowglass, whichever thou art! Hast thou lost thyself, then?'

'Yes,' Rod grated, staring at the wall, unseeing. 'Yes. Damn near.'

Simon groaned. 'Is there naught of the High Warlock left in thee?'

'Which one?' Rod growled. 'Which High Warlock?'

Simon answered in a voice filled with wonder. 'Rod Gallowglass, High Warlock of Gramarye! What other High Warlock is there?'

'Lord Kern,' Rod muttered, 'High Warlock of the land of Tir Chlis.' He rose to his feet, and stood stock-still, stood against the humming in his mind, the thrumming in his veins. Then he forced the words out. 'What is he like – this High Warlock?'

'Which one?' Simon cried.

'Yes.' Rod nodded. 'That's the question. But tell me of this Rod Gallowglass.'

'But thou art he!'

'Tell me of him!' Rod commanded.

Simon stared, at a loss. But no matter what he thought of the oddness of Rod's question, or the irrationality of what he did, Simon swallowed it, absorbed it, and gave what was needed.'

'Rod Gallowglass is the Lord High Warlock.'

'That doesn't help any,' Rod growled. 'Tell me something different about him.'

Simon stared for a moment, then began again. 'He is somewhat taller than most, though not overmuch . . . '

'No, no! Not what he *looks* like! That doesn't help at *all*! What's he like *inside*?'

Simon just stared at him, confounded.

'Quickly!' Rod snapped. 'Tell me! *Now!* I need an anchor, something to hold to!'

'Hast thou lost thyself so truly, then?'

'*Yes!*'

Finally, the actuality of the emergency struck home to Simon. He leaned forward and said, earnestly, 'I have not known thee overlong, Rod Gallowglass, and that only in thy guise as old Owen. Yet from what I've seen of thee, thou art . . . well, aye, thou art surly. And taciturn. Yet art thou good-hearted withal. Aye, thou hast ever the good of thy fellows at heart, at nearly every moment.' He frowned. 'I've heard it said of thee, that thou hast a wry humour, and dost commonly speak with wit. Yet I've not seen much of that in old Owen, save some bites of sarcasm – which are as often turned against himself, as against any other.'

'Good.' Rod nodded. 'Very good.'. He could feel the anger lessening, feel himself calming. But underneath it there was still fury, goading him to action, any action. Lord Kern. 'Tell me . . . ' Rod muttered, and swallowed. 'Tell me something about myself, that doesn't apply to Kern – for most of what you've said might be true of him, too. I don't know; I scarcely met the man. It might, though. Tell me something about me that's definitely mine alone, that couldn't be his!'

'Why . . . ' Simon floundered, 'there is thy garb. Would he go about as a peasant?'

'Possible. Try again.'

'There is thy horse . . . '

'Yes!' Rod pounced on it. 'Tell me about him!'

'' Tis a great black beast,' Simon said slowly, 'and most excellent in his lines. Indeed, 'twas the one great flaw in thy guise; for any could see that he was truly a knight's destrier, not a common cart horse.' He frowned, gazing off into space. 'And now I mind me, thou dost call him "Fess".'

'Fess.' Rod smiled. 'Yes. I could never forget Fess, no matter what. And Lord Kern couldn't possibly have one like him. He's been with me as long as I've been alive – no, longer. He's served my family for generations, did you know that?'

'Assuredly, I did not.' Simon watched him, wide-eyed.

'He's not what he seems, you know.'

'Aye, certes, he's not!'

'No, not just that way.' Rod frowned. 'He's, er, magical. But not your kind of magic – mine. He's not really a horse of any kind. He could be anything.'

'A pooka,' Simon murmured, unable to tear his gaze away.

'No, not *that* way! He's cold iron, underneath that horsehair – well, an alloy really. Plus, he's got a mind that's really a thing apart.' Rod remembered how easily he could take the basketball-sized sphere that held Fess's computer-brain out of the horse-body and plug it into his starship, to astrogate and pilot. 'I mean, his brain's *really* a thing apart. But he's always calm – well, almost always. And supremely logical. And *always* has good advice for me.' The core of anger was shrinking; it had almost disappeared, and Rod could feel the last tendrils of rage withdrawing into it. If Lord Kern really had reached across the void between the universes in response to Rod's anger, he had lost his grip. And if it was really just his own bloodlust driving him towards violence, it was under control again now. Rod's mouth quirked into a sardonic smile. 'Thank you, Milord. I appreciate your assistance, and will call upon it frequently, when there is need. But for now, I am myself again, and must trace this foul sorcerer in the ways which I deem best, in this world in which horses may be of metal, with machines for brains.'

Simon cocked his head, trying to hear, but not quite catching Rod's words.

Rod felt Kern's presence – or the bulk of his own anger, whichever it was – ebb. Whether 'Kern' was real, or just a projection of his subconscious, it was not as thoroughly gone as it could be. He heaved a sigh, and turned to Simon. 'Thank you. You pulled me out of it.'

'Gladly,' Simon said, 'though I misdoubt me an I comprehend.'

'It's really very simple. You see, there's another High Warlock, in another kingdom, far, far away – *extremely* far away; there isn't even a way to measure it. It's in another universe, if you can believe that.'

'Believe it, aye. Understanding is another matter.'

'Just try and drink it in,' Rod advised. 'We won't have an

examination in this course. Now, this other High Warlock is my analogue. That means that he corresponds to me in every detail; what he does in his universe, I do in mine. I visited his country for a while, and had occasion to borrow his powers; he channelled them through me, of course. But now it seems that was habit-forming; he keeps trying to reach across to this universe, and take up residence in my body.'

Simon paled. 'Surely he cannot!'

Rod shrugged. 'Maybe not. Maybe it's just my own lust for violence, the temptation to commit mayhem, and I'm labelling it "Lord Kern" to try to separate the actions I believe to be wrong from my conscience.' He glowered off into space. 'That doesn't really work, of course. The responsibility's mine, no matter what illusion I create as an excuse. Even if I *say* Lord Kern did it, it'll really be me who committed the deed. It'll still be me, even if I try to disguise it.' He turned to Simon with a bleak smile. 'But I seem to be able to lie to myself very convincingly. I'm thoroughly capable of persuading myself that I'm somebody else, when I want to.'

'So.' Simon frowned. 'I have convinced thee that thou art thyself again?'

Rod nodded. 'More importantly, you've shown me that I can restore myself to my real personality, instead of the make-believe one, welding my thoughts and my actions back into a whole again. It's a matter of remembering who I am. Fess was the key; Fess was the final thing that did it. Because, you see,' he quirked a smile, 'Fess couldn't exist in Lord Kern's universe.'

Simon frowned. 'I do not understand why not; yet will I accept thine assurance.' Then his eyes sparked, and widened. 'Yet mayhap I do comprehend. Thine horse doth stand for thee, doth he not? For if he could not be, in this Lord Kern's land, then neither couldst thou!'

'Not without being imported, no.' Then Rod stiffened, turning aside from Simon, feeling as though an electric current were passing through him. 'Yes . . . he does stand for me in a lot of ways, doesn't he?' The computer mind in the horsehair body was rather symbolic of technological Rod in Gramarye's medieval culture . . .

But of himself . . . ?

'I think 'tis so,' Simon was saying. 'And even as thine horse is the key to returning thee to control of thine actions, so thine anger is the key to summoning this "Lord Kern" which, thou dost say, thou hast created, to take responsibility for thine own fell deeds, that thou mayest give thyself the lie that 'tis no fault of thine own.'

Rod stood still for a moment, then nodded slowly. 'Yes. And it is a lie.' He dropped down, to sit on his heels. Simon sat by him. 'Ever since I came back from Lord Kern's universe, I've been flying into rages – and it's scary, very scary.'

'So.' Simon's eyes glinted. 'Thou hast been afraid to draw on thine own powers, for fear of summoning him.'

Rod stared at him for a while. Then, slowly, he nodded. 'Yes, that would make sense, wouldn't it? Association. Using magic for the first time resulted in Lord Kern's being a house guest within my skull; so using them again, should bring him back. A certain illogical sort of reason to it, isn't there?'

'It doth sound so, when thou dost say it.'

'Yes – but stating it also makes me able to see that it doesn't make sense.' Rod grinned. 'I *have* to draw on my powers, though. There have been times when they came in almighty handy. Just now, for example – Alfar had his dagger at my throat, so I had nothing to lose.' He shuddered. 'And "Lord Kern" almost took over completely, this time.'

'Aye.' Simon smiled. 'Thou didst fear, didst thou not? To use thy powers, for fear of summoning "Lord Kern".'

Rod nodded, chagrined. 'Even if he's just an illusion I made up. Yeah. I'd still be afraid of it.'

'Yet thou dost wish to use these powers.' Simon raised a forefinger. 'Whether they be Lord Kern's, or but thine own magics, that thine anger doth conjure up, thou dost fear to use them, lest thou shouldst yield to temptation, and let thine hands do what thou dost abhor.'

Rod nodded slowly. 'Nicely said. Separating the thought from the action. Yes. I *have* always been a bit schizoid.'

'Then contain the power thou dost conjure up,' Simon urged. 'Thus thou mayst reunite thy thoughts with thine action by containing thine active part within the pen thy thoughts do make. Contain "Lord Kern", even as thou dost contain thine anger. Assuredly thou hast not forgot our conversation, touching on that point? 'Twas directly after thou . . . '

'After I beat up on that poor, unsuspecting, defenceless rock. Yes.' Rod nodded, lips tight with chagrin. 'Yeah, I remember it. But I still don't understand how you keep the lid on your anger.'

'Nay, I do not!' Simon frowned, shaking a finger at Rod. 'If the anger arises, do not attempt to bury it, nor to pretend that it's not there. Let it be in thine awareness, and do not seek to throttle it – but contain it.'

Rod frowned. 'And how do you manage that?'

'By distancing thyself from the person who doth anger thee,' Simon answered. ''Tis not easily done, I know – for when the folk of the village had come to like me, and their priest had become my friend, I did come from out mine hermitage to live among them. I built myself mine inn – with their aid. And, in good time, I found myself a wife.' His head lifted, gazing off into the past again. 'She bore my bonny bairns, and together we laboured to rear them.'

'That's right – you do have a daughter.'

'Two – and a son. Who, by Heaven's grace, went for a soldier in the last war, and remained in the south to serve Lord Borgia. Beshrew me, but I love him! Yet whilst he grew, he tried me sorely!'

'I wouldn't say I know *all* about that,' Rod growled, 'but I'm sure learning. How did you deal with it?'

'By holding in my mind, and never letting go, the notion that 'twas not me his anger aimed at, but at that which I stood for.'

'Authority,' Rod guessed. 'Limits on his actions.'

'Aye – and the tree from which he needed to separate himself, the shoot, or he'd not be a being in his own right. Yet 'twas more than that – 'twas that he was not angry at me, but at what I'd done or said.'

'That doesn't make much sense.' Rod frowned. 'What you're trying to say is, it was anger, not hatred.'

Simon gazed off into space. 'Mayhap that is the sense of it. Yet whether it be anger or hatred, anger at thee or at what thou hast done, be mindful that, if worst comes to worst, thou hast but to recall that this person, this event, is but a part of thy life, not the whole of it – a part with which thou mayest have to deal but, when the dealing's done, canst look out from thy life.'

'What if you *can't*?' Rod exploded. 'What if you're tied to them? What if you have to deal with them continually, every day? What if you *love* them?'

Simon sat, grave and attentive. He nodded. 'Aye. 'Tis far more easy to hold thy temper with one whom thou dost see but an hour or two each day, for thou canst go to thine home, shut the door behind thee, and forget them.' His face eased into a gentle smile. 'Be mindful that these you love are people, too, and deserving of as much respect and care as those with whom thou dost deal for but an hour or two each day. If thou dost not treat thy family well, pretend they're friends.'

The thought gave Rod an icy chill. 'But they're not! They're inextricable parts of my life – parts of myself!'

'Nay!' Simon's eyes blazed, and his face was the countenance of a stern patriarch. 'Never must thou believe them so! For look you, no one else can be a part of thee; they are themselves withal, and are *apart* from thee!'

Rod just stared, astounded by the intensity of Simon's emotion.

Simon shook his head slowly. 'Never think that, simply because thou dost love a person, or she doth love thee, that she is no longer her self, a separate thing, apart.'

'But . . . but . . . but that's the *goal* of marriage!' Rod sputtered. 'For two to become one!'

' 'Tis a foul lie!' Simon retorted. ' 'Tis but an excuse for one to enslave another, then make her cease to be! Thy wife is, withal, one person, contained within her own skin, and is, and ought to be, one whole, of which all the parts are fused together, a being, separate, independent – one who loves thee, yet who is apart.' Suddenly, he smiled, and his warmth was back. 'For look you, an she were not a separate person, thou wouldst have none to love thee.'

'But . . . but, the word marriage! Isn't that what it means – two people, being welded together into a single unit?'

Simon shook his head impatiently. 'That may be what the word doth mean. Yet be not deceived; two cannot become one. 'Tis not possible. I confess it hath a pretty sound – but doth its beauty suffice to make it right?'

Rod stared at Simon, astounded by the old man's words.

'What of thee?' Simon demanded. 'Would it be right for one to attempt to make thee someone other than thou art?'

'No! I'm me, damn it! If anybody tried to make me somebody else, he'd eliminate me!'

'Then 'tis wrong for thee to attempt to make another become part of thee!' Simon stabbed at him with a forefinger.

Rod frowned, thinking it over.

'An two folk do wed,' Simon said softly, 'they should take pleasure in one another's company – not essay to become one another.' He smiled again, gently. 'For how canst thou become a part of someone else, save by erasing either themselves, or thee?'

Rod lifted his head, then slowly nodded. 'I see your point.

And as it is with my family, so it is with Lord Kern, isn't it? He keeps trying to become Lord Gallowglass – and if he did, Rod Gallowglass would cease to exist.'

'Ah, then!' Simon's eyes lit. 'Dost thou, then, mislike this notion of thyself and Lord Kern merging together, fusing, growing into something larger and greater?'

'I'd kill the man who tried to wipe me out that way!' Rod leaped to his feet in anger. 'That's not making me bigger and better – that's stealing my soul!'

Simon only smiled into Rod's wrath, letting its force pass him by, untouched. 'Yet if the thought so repels thee with this Lord Kern – who, thou hast told me, is thine other self – how can it be right if the "other half" is thy wife?'

Rod stared, poleaxed, his anger evaporated.

'Is it thy wife, or thy bairns – or the fear of ceasing to be?'

Rod dropped down to sit crosslegged again, leaning forward intently. 'Then why do I only get angry when they oppose me? Why don't I get angry when they agree with me?'

'For that, when they oppose thee, there is danger of *thy* self being digested; but when they agree with thee, 'tis they who may be merged into thee.'

Rod mulled that over. 'So it's a threat. I get angry when there's a threat.'

'Certes,' Simon said, surprised. 'What else is anger's purpose?'

'Yes – self-preservation,' Rod said slowly. 'It's the impulse to fight – to get rid of a threat.' His mouth quirked into a sudden smile, and his shoulders shook with a silent, internal laugh. 'My lord! Me threatened, by my three-year-old son?'

'Art thou not?' Simon said softly.

Rod sobered. 'It's ridiculous. He couldn't possibly hurt me.'

'Oh, he can,' Simon breathed, 'in thy heart, in thy soul – most shrewdly.'

Rod studied his face. Then he said, 'But he's so little, so vulnerable!' Then he scowled. 'But, damn it, it *is* hard to remember that when he's coming up with one of those insights that make me feel stupid!'

Simon nodded, commiserating. 'Thou must, therefore, be ever mindful, and tell thyself again: "He doth not lessen me." For that is what we truly fear, is it not? That our selves will be diminished and, if 'tis diminished too much, 'twill cease to exist. Is that not what we resist, what anger guards against?'

'But it's so asinine,' Rod breathed, 'to think that such a small one could hurt big me!'

'Aye – and therefore must thou bring it to mind anew, whenever thou dost feel the slightest ghost of anger.' Simon sat back, smiling. 'And as 'tis with thy bairns, so 'tis with Lord Kern.'

Rod just sat, spellbound, then, slowly, he nodded. 'So that's the key to holding my temper? Just remembering that I'm myself?'

'And that Lord Kern is not Rod Gallowglass. Just so.' Simon closed his eyes and nodded. 'Yet 'tis not so easily done, Lord Warlock. To be mindful of thyself thou must needs accept thyself – and to do that, one must be content with his self. Thou must needs come to believe that Rod Gallowglass is a good thing to be.'

'Well, I think I can do that,' Rod said slowly, 'especially since I've always felt Rod Gallowglass is an even better thing to be, when he's with his wife Gwen.'

'Thy wife?' Simon frowned. 'That hath a ring of great wrongness to it. Nay, Lord Warlock – an thou dost rely on another person for thy sense of worth, thou dost not truly believe that thou hast any. Thou shouldst enjoy her company because she is herself, and is pleasing to thee, is agreeable company – not because she is a part of thee, nor because the two of thee together make thy self a worthwhile thing to be.'

Rod frowned. 'I suppose that makes sense, in its way. If I depend on Gwen for my own sense of worth, then, whenever she finds me less than perfect, or finds anything at all wrong with me, I'll believe I'm not worth anything.'

Simon nodded, his eyes glittering, encouraging.

'And that would feel to me as though she were trying to destroy me, make me less than I am – which'll make me angry, because I'll feel that I need to fight back, for my own survival.'

Simon still nodded. ''Tis even as it happed to me – till I realized why, with my wife and myself, each quarrel was worse than the last – for, of course, she felt even as I did – that she must needs attack me, to survive.' He shook his head, like a cautioning schoolteacher. ''Tis wrong of thee to make her the custodian of thy value. That is thine own burden, and thou must needs accept it.'

Rod nodded. 'Learn to like being inside my own skin, eh?'

'Aye,' Simon smiled, amused. 'And do not seek to so burden thine horse, either.'

'Yeah – Fess.' That jolted Rod back to the issue. 'He was the symbol that pulled me back to my own identity. Does that mean I'm closer to my horse than my wife?'

'I think not.' Simon throttled a chuckle. 'For when all's said and done, a horse is a thing, not a person. It may have a temperament all of its own, and some quirks and snags of mood just as person hath; and each horse may be as unique and separate as each human is from another – yet when all's said and done, it hath not an immortal soul, and cannot therefore challenge thee in any way that will truly make thee feel any less. It cannot lessen thy sense of self, any more than a shoe or a shovel can.'

Rod nodded slowly. That made sense – more than Simon knew; for Fess wasn't a living horse, but a computer in a body full of servo-mechanisms. Sure, the computer projected a personality by its vocodered voice – but that personality was only an illusion, a carefully-crafted artifact, albeit an intangible one. Fess was, really, only a metal machine, and his identity was as much an illusion as his ability to think. 'My horse is like a sword, in a way,' he said, thoughtfully.

Simon laughed softly. 'In truth, he doth seem to be somewhat more than a shoe or a shovel.'

'No, I was thinking of mystique. For a knight, his sword was the symbol of his courage, his prowess – and his honour. Each sword was a separate, unique, individual thing, to the medieval mind, and its owner invested it with a full-fledged persona. He even gave it a name. Sometimes, in the legends, it even had a will of its own. You couldn't think of a famous sword without thinking of the knight who owned it. Excalibur evoked the image of King Arthur, Durandal evoked pictures of Roland, Gram brought to mind Siegfried slaying Fafnir. The sword was the symbol of the knight who bore it.'

'As thine horse is the symbol of thee?'

Rod frowned. 'That doesn't quite feel right, somehow – but it's close. Metaphorically, I suppose Fess is my sword.'

'Then use him.' Simon's eyes glowed. 'Draw thy blade, and go to slay the monster who enslaves us.'

Rod sat still a moment, feeling within him for fear – and, yes, it was there; but so was the courage to answer it. But courage wouldn't do much good, really; in this case, it'd just let him go ahead into a situation that was too dangerous for him to survive. How about confidence, though? Could he summon Lord Kern, let himself fill with anger, and not be mastered by it? He thought of Fess, and all the qualities in himself that Fess represented, and felt a calm certainty rising in response to the mental image. He nodded. 'I'm up to it. But if I start to fall in, pull me out, will you?'

'Gladly,' Simon answered, with a full, warm smile.

'Then, hold on.' Rod stood, grasped Simon's shoulder, and thought of Alfar, of his arrogance, his insolence, and the threat he represented to Rod and his children. Hot anger surged in answer, anger building towards rage. Rod felt Lord Kern's familiar wrath – but he was aware of it, now, as something that was a part of him, truly, not implanted from someone else – and, being of himself, it was as much under his control as his fingers, or his tongue. He opened his mind, concentrating on the world of thought. The world of sight dimmed, and his blood began to pound in his ears. Only the thoughts were real – the darting, scheming thoughts of the warlocks and witches; the dulled, mechanical plodding thoughts of the soldiers and servants – and the ceaseless background drone that had to be the projective telepath who had hypnotized a whole duchy. What else could it be that emitted such a constant paean of praise, such a continual pushing of thought against mind?

Whatever it was, Rod was suddenly certain that it was the key to all the pride and ambition that was Alfar's conquest. He scanned the castle till he found the direction in which it was strongest, then willed himself to it.

# Chapter Fifteen

It was a small room, a round room, a room of grey stone blocks with three tall, skinny windows. But those windows were sealed with some clear substance, and the air of the chamber was unnaturally cool – climate-controlled. Every alarm bell in Rod's head screamed. He glanced at Simon. The older warlock tottered, dazed. Rod held him up, growling, 'Steady. That's what happens when a warlock disappears.'

'I had . . . ne'er had the opportunity aforetime.' Simon gasped. He looked around him, whites showing all around his eyes. Finally, he turned back to Rod, awe-struck. 'Eh, but thou'rt truly the Lord Warlock, thou.'

'The same,' Rod confirmed, 'but none the less your pupil in fathering and husbandry.'

'As I am to thee, in wizardry.' Simon pointed a trembling finger at the metal box in the centre of the room. It sat on a slender pedestal at chest height, and had a grey, iridescent cylinder atop one end. The other sprouted a cable that dropped down to the floor, ran over to the wall and up it, to a window, where it disappeared – probably to a transmitting antenna, Rod decided. 'What,' Simon asked in a voice that shook, 'is that spawn of alchemy?'

'Probably,' Rod agreed. 'It's a machine of some sort, anyway.' He could feel the insistent pounding of the message, extolling Alfar's virtues over and over again. It was much stronger than it had been when he was in the dungeon. It belaboured him, convincing, persuading by sheer repetition. Alfar was master, Alfar was great, Alfar was rightful lord of all that was human . . . 'I think I know what it is, Simon – or, at least, what it does. If I'm right, the last time I saw one of these, it was alive.'

'How?' Simon stared, horrified. 'A living thing cannot be a machine.'

'No more than a machine can be a living thing. But this one sure seems to be. If you didn't know better, wouldn't you swear that that thing's thinking at us?'

'Wh— *this*?' Simon pointed at the contraption, features writhing with revulsion. 'Assuredly it doth not!'

'Assure me again – I could need it.' Under his breath, Rod murmured, 'Fess. Where are you?'

'Here, Rod, in the castle stables,' Fess's voice answered from behind his ear.

'Close your eyes,' Rod growled, 'and don't worry about what's happening.' He closed his eyes, envisioning Fess, and the stable he was in. In excellent repair, probably, since it had been Duke Romanov's just a week ago – but slipping a bit now. The straw surely needed changing, for example, and the manure needed clearing. But he needed Fess, needed him badly, right *here* . . . He made the thought an imperative, an unworded summons, sharp, demanding.

Thunder rocked the little room, and Fess was there, looking about him wildly, Rod saw as he opened his eyes again. The robot's voice came out slurred. 'Whhhadt . . . wherre . . . I have . . . have I . . . telllepo . . . ' Suddenly his head whipped up, then slammed down. All four legs spraddled out, stiff, knees locked. The neck was stiff, too, pointing the head at the floor; then it relaxed, and the head began to swing between the fetlocks.

'Seizure,' Rod explained. 'It always happens when he can't avoid witnessing magic.'

But Simon didn't answer. He was staring at the electronic gizmo, and his eyes had glazed. He took a stumbling step toward it. Of course, Rod thought. This close to the gadget . . . He grabbed Simon by the shoulders, and gave him a shake. 'Simon! Wake up!' He clapped his hands sharply, an inch in front of Simon's nose. Simon started, and his eyes came back into focus. 'What . . . Lord Warlock! For the half of a minute I thought . . . I could believe . . . '

'That the background noise is right, and Alfar's a good guy.' Rod nodded, mouth a thin, straight line. 'Not surprising. Now I'm sure what that weird device is – but let's confirm it.' He turned back to Fess, felt under the pommel of the saddle for an enlarged vertebra, and pushed it. It clicked faintly. After a moment, Fess's head lifted slowly and turned to look at Rod, the great plastic eyes clearing. 'I . . . had a . . . seizure, Rrrod.'

'You did,' Rod confirmed. 'But let me show you something you can cope with.' He took a step toward the pedestal, pointing. 'There's a background thought-message, constantly repeating, Fess. Over and over, it praises Alfar to the skies – and it's much stronger here than anywhere else.'

The robot's head tracked him. Then Fess stepped closer to the metal box. The great horse head lifted, looking at the box from the top, then from the front, then the back. Finally Fess opined, 'There is sufficient data for a meaningful conclusion, Rod.'

'Oh, ducky! What's it add up to?'

'The the futurian totalitarians are supporting Alfar's conquests.'

'Are they really,' Rod said drily. 'Care to confirm my guess as to what it does?'

'Certainly. It's a device that converts electricity into psionic power. I would conjecture that the large, rectangular base contains some sort of animal brain in a nutrient solution, with wires carrying power from an atomic pack into the medulla, and leads from the cerebrum carrying power at human thought frequencies into a modulator. The cylinder at the rear of the machine would seem to perform that function. This modulated message is fed out through the cable, which presumably goes up to an antenna on the roof of this tower.'

'Thanks.' Rod swallowed against a suddenly queasy stomach. 'Nice to have my guess confirmed – I suppose. Their technology has improved since we met the Kobold, hasn't it?'

'The state of the art advances constantly, Rod.'

'Relentlessly, you might almost say.' Rod turned to Simon. 'It projects thoughts. Not a living thought, you understand – a recorded one, made as carefully as people make chairs, or ships, or castles, but just as thoroughly made. Then that thought is set down, as you'd write a message in ink, almost – and sent out from this machine to the whole of the duchy, again and again, drumming itself into people's heads. Warlocks and witches can at least realize they're being bombarded – but the average peasant in the field has no idea it's happening. But warlock or witch, it doesn't seem to matter – it converts them all.'

'Who placed it here?' Simon's voice trembled.

'People from the future.' Rod's face was set, stony. 'People who want the whole universe to be ruled by one single power.' He glared around at the blank stone walls. 'Where're its builders? Hiding somewhere, out of harm's way, while Alfar and his coven do their dirty work for them. But I must admit I'm disappointed – I was hoping to find a few of them here, keeping guard.' He could feel indignation spurring his anger higher; he began to tremble.

'Peace, peace.' Simon grasped his forearm. 'Wherefore would they? Why guard what none know of, and none need tend?'

'Yeah – it's really automatic, isn't it? And just because I expected them to be here, doesn't mean they should feel obligated to show up. But I was at least expecting a human witch or a warlock to be doing the thinking! Maybe hooked up to a psionic amplifier – but none the less one of Alfar's henchmen, taking it in relays! But . . . this is it!' He spread his hands toward the machine. 'This is all there is! Here's the spectacular sorcerer – here's the arch-magus! Here's your rebel warlock, fantastically powerful – until its battery runs down!'

' 'Twill suffice,' Simon said, beside him.

'Damn straight it will!' Rod turned to rummage in Fess's saddlebag. 'Where's that hammer I used to carry?'

'May I suggest that it would be more effective, and more immediate, to turn the machine off, Rod?'

Rod shrugged. 'Why not? I'm not picky – I'll wreck it any way I can!' He turned to the machine, looking it up and down. 'Where's the off switch?'

'I detect a pressure-pad next to the cylinder,' Fess said. 'Would you press it, please, Rod?'

'Sure.' Rod pressed the cross-hatched square. The machine clicked, whirred for a second, then pushed one end of the cylinder toward Rod. He lifted it off, holding it warily at arm's length. 'What is it?'

'From the circuitry, Rod, I would conjecture that the cylinder is the transducer. This disc, therefore, would be the recorded message.'

'Oh, is it, now!' Rod whipped his arm back for a straight pitch, aimed at the wall.

'Might I also suggest,' Fess said quickly, 'that we may find a use for the disc itself?'

Rod scowled. 'Always possible, I suppose – but not very satisfying.' He dropped it into his belt-pouch. 'So we've stopped it from mass-hypnotizing the population. Now, how do we wake them up?'

'Why not try telepathy?' the robot suggested. 'The message is recorded thought, placed in contact with the transducer; presumably it will function just as well, from contact with living thought.'

Rod turned to his friend with a glittering eye. 'Oh, Master Simon . . . '

In spite of himself, the older man took a step backward. But, stoutly, he said, 'Wherein may I aid, Lord Warlock?'

'By thinking at the machine.' Rod tossed his head toward the gadget. 'But you'll have to put your forehead against it.'

Simon's eyes bulged; his face went slack in horror.

'Oh, it won't hurt your mind,' Rod said quickly. 'That much I'm sure of. This end of the machine can only receive thoughts – it can't send out anything.' He turned, bowing, and pressed his forehead against the transducer. 'See? No danger.'

'Indeed,' Simon breathed, awestruck. 'Wherefore dost thou not give it thine own thoughts?'

'Because I don't know how to break Alfar's spell.' Rod stepped back, bowing Simon toward the machine. 'Would you try it, please? Just press your forehead against that round plate, and pretend it's a soldier who's been spellbound.'

Simon stood rigid for a few seconds. Then he took a deep breath, and stepped forward. Rod watched him place his forehead against the transducer, with admiration. The humble country innkeeper had as much real courage as a knight.

Simon closed his eyes. His face tensed as he began his spell-breaking thought sentence.

Rod stiffened as the 'message' hit him, full-strength. It had no words; it was only a feeling, as though someone very sympathetic was listening to him, listening deeply, to everything Rod could tell, down to his very core – then, kindly, gently, but very firmly, contradicting. Rod shook his head and cleared his throat. 'Well! He's certainly getting across, isn't he?' He turned to Fess. 'How'll we know whether it works or not?'

'By Alfar's reaction, Rod. He doubtless detected our disabling his message, but refrained from attacking us, wary of your power.'

Rod's head lifted. 'I . . . hadn't . . . thought of that.'

'I consider it a distinct possibility,' Fess mused. 'Now, however, Alfar must realize that we are destroying the very base of his power – that he must attack us now, or lose all he has conquered.'

Quintuple thunder roared in a long, ripping sequence, and Alfar was there with three witches and a warlock at his back, chopping down at Rod with a scimitar.

Rod leaped back with a whoop of delight. The sword's tip hissed past him, and he and Fess instantly jumped into place between Simon and the sorcerer's band. One of the witches stabbed a hand at them, all five fingers stiff and pointing, and a dozen whirling slivers of steel darted toward them.

Fess took a step to his left, blocking Rod and Simon both. The darts clanged against his horsehide, and he stepped back – just in time to step on the witch's foot. She screamed and careened away, hobbling as Alfar lashed at Rod with the scimitar again. But this time, Rod leaped high and kicked the sword out of his hand as Fess reared, lashing out at the other warlock and witch with his forehooves. Rod sliced a karate chop at Alfar, and the sorcerer leaped back, but not quite quickly enough – Rod's fingertips scored his collar-bone, and Alfar howled in pain. The witch was staring at Fess, wild-eyed, backing away slowly, and Rod could feel a crazy assortment of emotions crashing through him – anger, fear, confusion, love. She was the emotional projective, hitting Fess with everything she had, totally confounded by his complete lack of response.

Which reminded Rod who he was, and that the emotions were illusions. He managed to ignore them as Alfar wound up for a whammy. But he didn't have time; a stone leaped out of the wall, and slammed straight at Rod. He side-stepped, but the block caught him on the shoulder. Pain shot through him, and his temper leaped up in response. He slumped back against the wall, striving frantically to reign in his temper, trying to channel it, knowing that rage would slow his reflexes; they'd get under his guard, and chop him down. Another block shot straight at him and he dropped to a crouch, ducking his head. The block cracked into the wall behind. Another whirled tumbling and slammed into Fess's hindquarters. Rod galvanized with alarm – if that boulder had hit Fess in the midriff, it might have staved in his armoured side, and damaged his computer brain!

That was just distraction enough. He saw the stone coming, and spun away – but not fast enough. Its corner cracked into his hip, and agony screamed through his side, turning his whole leg into flame. His knee folded, and he fell.

And Alfar was above him with his scimitar again, chopping down with a gloating grin.

Rod rolled at the last second. The huge blade smashed into the stone floor, and twisted out of Alfar's hands. One of the fallen stones shot up off the floor, straight at his face. Alfar screamed in shock, and stepped back – and tripped over something, crashing down onto his back.

Rod was up on one knee, trying frantically to force himself to his feet. He stared at the obstacle Alfar had stumbled over, and it stared back for a fraction of a second – Geoffrey! The boy grinned just before he leaped to his feet, his eighteen-inch sword whipping out to stab down at the fallen sorcerer, who just barely managed to twist out of the way in time. His hand flailed about the floor till it found the scimitar's hilt, and wrapped fast around it.

A block of stone smashed at Geoffrey. He dodged, but Rod roared with rage when he saw how closely the block had come. He sprang at the telekinetic – but Alfar jumped into his path, slashing with the scimitar again. Rod leaped back, letting the blow whistle past him, then lunged over it with a chop. Alfar just barely managed to twist aside.

The telekinetic was surrounded by blocks of stone smashing into each other. Her lips were drawn back in a feral snarl, and drops of sweat beaded her forehead. Geoffrey ducked in under the hedge of stone and stabbed upward. The telekinetic screamed and jumped back, stumbled over Gregory, and fell. Magnus's cudgel whacked her at the base of her skull and she went limp.

Cordelia crouched glaring at the other witch – but between them was a storybook witch, complete with cone hat, broomstick, hooked nose, warts, and insane cackle, hands clawing at the child. A ghost materialized beside her, moaning, and something huge, flabby and moist, with yellow, bloodshot eyes, lifted itself up off the floor, extruding pseudopod tentacles toward the little girl. But Cordelia spat, 'Aroint thee, witch! Dost thou think me a babe?' and threw her broomstick at the illusionist. It speared through the storybook witch and arrowed toward the illusionist, who screamed and threw up her hands to ward it off – and the ghost, witch and monster disappeared. But the broomstick whirled and whipped about, belabouring the woman from every side faster than she could block, whacking her about the head and shoulders. She screamed and darted toward the chamber door – and Gwen's full-sized broomstick swung down from the ceiling and cracked into her forehead. Her eyes rolled up, and she crumpled.

Rod twisted aside from Alfar's scimitar and reached out to brace himself against the wall, just as his burning leg tried to give out under him again. He shoved against the stone, shifting his weight onto his good leg, and drew his sword just in time to parry another cut. He riposted and thrust, faster than Alfar could recover. The sorcerer darted back, just an inch farther than Rod's thrust, and saw two of his lieutenants on the floor. He was just in time to see Fess's hoof catch the emotional projective a glancing blow on the temple. She folded at the knees and hit the flagstones, out cold. He shrieked, and Rod leaped, catching the sorcerer's arm with his left hand to steady himself. Alfar whirled, saw Rod's sword chopping down, screamed again – and Rod caught the unspoken image of another place. He closed his eyes and willed himself *not* there, just as Alfar teleported toward it. Dimly, Rod heard a thunder-boom, and knew Alfar had managed to disappear from the tower room. His eyes sprang open – and he found himself still clinging to the sorcerer's arm, in the midst of formless greyness, lit by dim, sourceless light. There was nothing, anywhere – nothing but his enemy.

Alfar looked about him, and screamed, 'We are lost!' Then he squeezed his eyes shut, and Rod caught the impulse toward somewhere he didn't recognize. He countered grimly. Their bodies rocked as though hit by a shock wave, but stayed put. 'You're in the Void,' Rod growled, 'and you're not getting out!'

Alfar screamed, hoarse with terror and rage, and whirled to chop at him with the scimitar. But Rod yanked him close, caught his sword hand, and cracked it against his good knee. Pain shot through him, almost making him go limp – but Alfar was still screaming, in hoarse, panting caws, and the scimitar went whirling away through empty space. Rod slammed an uppercut into the sorcerer's face. He dodged, but the blow caught him alongside the jaw. His head rocked, but he slammed a knee into Rod's groin. Rod doubled over in agony, but clung to Alfar's arm and a shred of sense; his right hand slipped the dagger out of his boot and he shot his last ounce of strength into a sudden stab into Alfar's belly. The blade jabbed up under the ribcage, and Alfar folded over it, arms flailing, eyes bulging in agony. Conscience smote; Rod yanked the dagger out and stabbed again, quickly, mercifully, into the heart. He saw Alfar's eyes glaze; then the body went limp in his hands. Rod held it a second, staring, unbelieving. Then chagrin hit, and he felt his soul quail at the reality of another manslaughter. 'It was him or me,' Rod grated; but no one heard except himself.

He let go, shoving, and the body drifted away from him, turning slowly, trailing an arc of blood. It swung away, revolving, and faded into the mists, a thin red line tracing its departure.

Rod turned away, sickened. For a long, measureless instant, he drifted in space, numbed, absorbing his guilt, accepting the spiritual responsibility, knowing that it had been justified, had been necessary – and was none the less horrible.

Finally, the tide of guilt ebbed, and he opened his mind to other thoughts – Gwen, and the children! Had they all come through that mêlée alive? And what the hell had they been doing there, anyway? Never mind the fact that if they hadn't been, they'd be short one husband and father by now – none the less! What were they doing where it was so dangerous?

Helping him, obviously – and they'd have to help him again, or he'd never find how to get out of here. He wasn't scared of the Void; he'd been here before, between universes.

And, of course, he'd get home the same way now. He closed his eyes, and listened with his mind. There – Gregory's thought, unvoiced, a frightened longing for his father – the same beacon that had brought him home before. Rod sighed and relaxed, letting the boy's thought fill his mind. Then he willed himself back to his three-year-old son.

'Is that all of them?' Rod ground his teeth against a sudden stab of pain from his upper arm.

'Be brave, my lord,' Gwen murmured. She finished binding the compress to his triceps. 'Aye, every one of them has come – every witch and warlock of the Royal Coven. E'en old Agatha and Galen have come from their Dark Tower to flit from hamlet to village, speaking with these poor peasants, who have waked to panic, and the loss of understanding.'

'I don't blame 'em,' Rod grunted. 'If I all of a sudden came to my senses and realized that I'd been loyal to an upstart for the last few weeks while my duke was casually bumped off, I'd be a little disoriented, too. In fact, I'd be frightened as hell.' He winced as Gwen bound his arm to his side. 'Is that really necessary?'

'It must,' she answered, in a tone that brooked no argument. 'Yet 'tis but for a day or two, 'til the healing hath begun.'

'And I didn't even notice I'd been sliced, there.' Rod looked down at the bandage. 'Well, it was only a flesh wound.'

Gwen nodded. 'Praise Heaven it came no closer to the bone!'

'Lord Warlock!'

Rod looked up.

They were in the Great Hall of Duke Romanov's castle. It was a vast stone room, thirty feet high, forty wide, and eighty long – and empty, for the moment, since all the boards and trestles had been piled against the walls at the end of the last meal, for the evening entertainments. The High Table was still up, of course, on its dais, and Rod sat in one of the chairs, with Gwen beside him – though pointedly not in the Duke's and Duchess's places.

An auncient, still wearing Alfar's livery, came striding toward them from the screens passage, eyes alight with excitement.

'Did you look up the traitors?' Rod demanded.

'Aye, milord.' The auncient came to a halt directly in front of Rod. ''Twas that to be said for the sorcerer's having used our bodies for his army, the whiles he lulled our souls into slumber – that when we waked, we knew on the instant which soldiers had been loyal to the usurper of their own wills, e'en though they'd remained wakeful.'

Rod nodded. 'By some strange coincidence, the ones who had been giving the orders.' There had been a few opportunistic knights who had been loyal to Alfar without benefit of hypnotism, too. Rod had had to lock them in a dungeon himself, medieval castle rules being what they were. One of them had resisted; but after the others saw what happened to him, they went quietly. It was just too embarrassing, being defeated by a bunch of children . . . A couple of them, quicker to react, had escaped as soon as peasants started waking up all around them. That was all right; Rod had a few thousand mortified soldiers on his hands, who needed something to do to appease their consciences. A hunt was just fine.

But the common soldiers who had allied with Alfar could be left to the tender mercies of their erstwhile comrades – once Rod had made it clear that he expected them to, at least, survive. 'So you found the deepest, darkest dungeon, and locked them in it?'

'Aye, milord.' The auncient's eyes glowed. 'We loosed its sole tenant.' He turned towards the screens passage with a bow, and in limped the prisoner. His doublet and hose were torn, and crusted with dried blood; his face was smeared with dirt, and his hair matted. There was a great livid gash along the right-hand side of his face, scabbed over, that would leave a horrible scar; but his back was straight, and his chin was high. Two knights were with him, blinking, dazed, as disorientated as any of the soldiers, but straight and proud. Simon followed after, looking perplexed.

Rod shoved himself to his feet, ignoring the searing protest from his wounded hip, and the auncient announced: 'Hail my lord, the Duke of Romanov!'

Rod stepped down from the dais to clasp his one-time enemy by the shoulders. 'Praise Heaven you're alive!'

'And thee, for this fair rescue!' The Duke inclined his head. 'Well met, Lord Warlock! I, and all my line, shall ever be indebted to thee and thine!'

'Well, maybe more the "thine" than the "thee".' Rod glanced behind him at the children who sat, prim and proper, on the dais steps with their mother fairly glowing behind them. 'When push came to shove, they had to haul my bacon out of the fire.'

'Then I thank thee mightily, Lady Gallowglass, and thee, brave children!' The Duke inclined his head again.

Blushing, they leaped to their feet and bowed.

When the Duke straightened, there was anxiety in his face. 'Lord Warlock – my wife and bairns. Did they . . . escape?'

'They did, and my wife and children made sure they reached Runnymede safely.' Rod turned to Gwen. 'Didn't you?'

'Certes, my lord. We would not have turned aside from what we'd promised thee we'd do.'

'Yes – you never did promise to *stay* safe, did you? But Alfar mentioned something about a dire fate in store for you . . . '

•

'Indeed!' Gwen opened her eyes wider. 'Then it was never taken out from storage. I wonder thou wast so merciful in thy dealings with him.'

'Well, I never did like lingering deaths.' But Rod couldn't help feeling better about it all.

'He also implied that the Duchess and her boys didn't stay safe . . . '

'False again,' Gwen said quickly, just as the Duke's anguish was beginning to show anew. 'We saw them to Runnymede, where they bide safely in the care of Their Royal Majesties.'

'Yes . . . what are monarchs for?' But Rod noted the flash of shame that flitted across Romanov's features – no doubt in memory of his rebellion.

'We played with them not three hours agone, Papa,' Geoffrey said.

The Duke heaved a sigh, relaxing. Then the father and host in him both took over. 'Three hours? And thy children have not dined in that time?' He spun to the auncient. 'Good Auncient, seek out the cooks! Rouse them from their dazes and bid them bring meat and wine – and honey-cakes.'

The children perked up most noticeably.

'Three hours agone.' The Duke turned back to the children with a frown. 'Was this in Runnymede?'

The children nodded.

The Duke turned back to Rod. 'How could they come to aid thee, then?'

'Nice question.' Rod turned to Gwen again. 'It *was* rather dangerous here, dear. Just how close were you, while you were waiting for me to need you?'

'The lads were in Runnymede, my lord, even as thou hast but now heard,' Gwen answered. 'They could bide there, sin' that they may travel an hundred leagues in the bat of an eyelash.'

Rod had a notion that their range was farther than that, much farther, but he didn't deem it wise to say so – especially not where they could hear (or mind read).

'At the outset,' Gwen continued, 'Cordelia and I did bide with them, for we could attend to thy thoughts e'en from that distance, and fly to thine aid if thou didst come near to danger. It did greatly trouble me, therefore, when thy thoughts did so abruptly cease.'

Cordelia nodded confirmation, her eyes huge. 'She did weep, Papa.'

'Oh, no, darling!' Rod caught Gwen's hands. 'I didn't mean to . . . '

'Nay, certes.' She smiled. 'Yet thou wilt therefore comprehend my concern.'

Rod nodded slowly. 'I'd say so, yes.'

'I therefore did leave the boys in care of Their Royal Majesties, and Brom O'Berin, and flew northward again. I took on the guise of an osprey . . . '

Rod rolled his eyes up. 'I *knew* when I saw that blasted fish-hawk that far inland, that I was in trouble!' Of course, he knew that Gwen couldn't really shrink down to the size of a bird any more than a butterfly could play midwife to a giraffe. It was just a projective illusion, making people think that they saw a bird instead of a woman. 'If I hadn't shielded my thoughts, I probably would've seen through your spell!'

'An thou hadst not shielded thy thoughts, I would not have had to fly near enough to see thee,' Gwen retorted. 'And though thou hadst disguised thyself, I knew thee, Rod Gallowglass.'

That, at least, was reassuring – in its way.

'Then,' Gwen finished, ''twas but a matter of hearkening to the thoughts of that goodman who did ride beside thee.' Gwen turned to Simon. 'I thank thee, Master Simon.'

The older man still looked confused, but he bowed anyway, smiling. 'I was honoured to be of service, milady – e'en though I knew it not.'

'And when thou wert taken,' Gwen went on, 'I did summon Cordelia to me, to bide in waiting, in a deserted shepherd's croft. Then, when thou didst burst forth from thy shield, I could not help but hear thy thoughts for myself.'

'Not that you were about to try to ignore them,' Rod murmured.

'Nay, certes!' Gwen cried in indignation. 'Then, when thou didst come unto the tower chamber, I knew the moment of battle was nigh, and did summon Cordelia from her croft to fly to the tower; and when the unearthly device did cease to compel, and did commence to disenchant, I knew the time of battle had come. Then did I summon thy sons, that the family might be together once again.'

'Very homey,' Rod grinned. 'And though I was mighty glad to see you all, I don't mind saying I'm even gladder to know the kids were safe, right down until the last moment.'

'Certes, my lord! I would not endanger them.'

Rod gave her the fish-eye. 'What do you call that last little fracas we went through – homework?'

'Oh, nay! 'Twas far too great a delight!' Geoffrey cried.

'Homework's delight,' Gregory lisped.

'Papa!' Cordelia cried indignantly; and Magnus's chin jutted out a quarter-inch further. ' 'Twas scarce more than chores.'

'We'd fought each of them aforetime,' Geoffrey reminded him, 'and knew their powers – save Alfar, and we left him to thee.'

'Nice to know you have confidence in me. But there could've been accidents . . . '

'So there may ever be, with bairns,' Gwen sighed. 'Here, at least, they were under mine eye. Bethink thee, husband, what might chance an I were to leave them in the kitchen, untended.'

Rod shuddered. 'You've made your point; please don't try the experiment.' He turned to the Duke. 'Ever begin to feel redundant?'

'Nay, Papa,' Magnus cried. 'We could only aid thee in the ending of this campaign.'

'Truly,' Gregory said, round-eyed, 'we knew not enough to bring the sorcerer to bay.'

But Rod had caught the sly glance between Magnus and Geoffrey. Under the circumstances, though, he deemed it wiser not to say anything about it.

'Now, mine husband.' Gwen clasped his hands. 'In this last battle, I did hear thy thoughts at all times. Thine anger was there, aye, but thou didst contain it. Hast thou, then, so much ta'en this goodman's advice to thine heart?' She nodded at Simon.

'I have,' Rod confirmed. 'It worked this time, at least.'

'Dost thou mean thou wilt not become angry again, Papa?' Cordelia cried, and the other children looked up in delight.

'I can't promise that,' Rod hedged, 'but I think I'll have better luck controlling it. Why – what were you planning to do?'

Whatever they would have answered was forestalled by the cooks, stumbling in with dinner. They set down the platters on the table, and the children leaped in with joyful cries. Magnus got there first, wrenched off a drumstick, and thrust it at his father. 'Here, Papa! 'Tis thy place of right!'

'Why, thank you,' Rod said, amused. 'Nice to know I have some rank around here.'

'I shall have the other.' Cordelia reached for the other drumstick.

'Nay; thou hast never favoured the legs of the fowl!' Geoffrey's hand darted out, and grabbed the bone before hers.

'Loose that!' Cordelia cried. ''Twas my claim was first!'

'As 'twas my hand!'

'Yet I came to the bird before either of thee!' Magnus laid a hand on the bone of contention. 'My remembrance of our father doth not bar me from this choice!'

'Er, children,' Rod said mildly, 'quiet down, please.'

''Tis mine!'

'Nay! 'Tis mine!'

'I am eldest! My claim is first!'

'Children!' Rod hiked his volume a bit. 'Cut it out!'

Gwen laid a restraining hand on his arm. That did it; his temper leaped.

Cordelia turned on her brothers. 'Now, beshrew me an thou art not the most arrogant, ungentlemanly boys the world hath ever . . . '

Rod stood rigid, trying to contain his soaring anger. Then Simon caught his eye. Rod stared at the older man's calm, level gaze, and felt a measure of strength that he hadn't known he had. He took a deep breath and reminded himself that their bickering might make them look childish (as it should) but not him – if he didn't start shouting with them. The thought checked his anger and held it. He was himself. Rod Gallowglass – and he wasn't any the less himself, nor any less important, nor any less in any way, just because his children didn't need him.

But he did know how to get their attention. He reached out, grasped the last drumstick, and twisted it loose.

The children whirled, appalled. 'Papa! Nay! Thou hast no need! Thou already hast one, Papa!'

''Tis not justice,' little Gregory piped, chin tucked in trucu-lently over folded arms.

'But it does settle the argument,' Rod pointed out. He turned to Gwen, presenting the drumstick with a flourish and a bow. 'My dear, you saved the day. Your glory is as great as mine.'

'But, Papa!' Cordelia jammed her fists on her hips, glowering up at him. 'Thou'rt supposed to be a *nice* daddy now!'

'Why,' Rod murmured, 'wherever did you get an idea like that?'